Thos L. Casey

VII. Coleopterlogical Notices. IV

Thos L. Casey

VII. Coleopterlogical Notices. IV

ISBN/EAN: 9783741193354

Manufactured in Europe, USA, Canada, Australia, Japa

Cover: Foto ©Andreas Hilbeck / pixelio.de

Manufactured and distributed by brebook publishing software
(www.brebook.com)

Thos L. Casey

VII. Coleopterlogical Notices. IV

IV.

BY THOS. L. CASEY.

Read May 9, 1892.

The following pages are principally confined to studies in our Rhynchophora, taken up some time since for the sole purpose of distributing the nondescript material, forming a considerable part of my cabinet, with a measurable degree of scientific order and succession. As usual in such cases, the compass of the work gradu. ally outgrew the limited and personal objects had in view at the beginning, and the investigations in several genera and groups became sufficiently advanced to suggest the propriety of publishing them, with the hope that they might prove useful to others similarly engaged.

There is but little further to state in way of introduction. The studies have been limited for the greater part to those groups which appeared to stand most in need of revision, either by reason of the large number of specific forms recently brought to light, especially by skillful collecting in our western country, or because of apparent misconception regarding generic identity, as in the case of the group Desmorbines of LeConte. This section of the Erirhinini corresponds with the Smicronychina of the European fauna, where it is represented only by the genus Smicronyx, characterized by its connate tarsal ungues and the basal constriction of the rostrum. In our own fauna it is rather more abundant and diversified.

The Barini, or Baridiides, to which the greater part of the present paper is devoted, constitute probably the largest tribe of American Curculionidæ, and, in South America, form the most varied and characteristic element of the family, possibly excepting the Zygopini. It is interesting to note in this connection, that the recent researches of Mr. S. H. Scudder on the fossil beetle fauna of several of our western Tertiary horizons seem to show that the relative importance of the Barini in America dates from somewhat remote geological epochs.

New York, May 9, 1892.

CURCULIONIDÆ.

ERIRHININI.

DORYTOMUS Steph.

The separation of this genus from Erirhinus is largely a matter of convenience, as the femoral teeth, constituting the principal distinguishing feature, are subject to great specific variations in development, sometimes being barely distinguishable even on the anterior femora, where they are generally most distinct. The genus presents also considerable diversity of structure, and a very noticeable lack of uniformity in the degree of sexual disparity, the three species of the first group having extremely marked sexual differences pervading the entire anterior portion of the body. In the second group, also consisting at present of three species, the sexual divergence is still strong, although much less marked and affecting only the beak and antennæ, while in the third and by far the largest section the sexual differences become very feeble.

In Dorytomus the body is oblong or oblong-oval, generally somewhat stout, more or less flattened above and frequently subinflated behind, strongly punctured, especially in the elytral striæ, and with pubescence which is composed usually of short robust decumbent hairs condensed in feebly defined spots, or, rarely, of scales similarly uneven in distribution, generally without, but occasionally with, erect bristling setæ in addition. The colors are usually rufo-testaceous in different degrees of intensity, rarely becoming piceous or black and more frequently paler ochreous or flavate. The tarsal claws are slender, divaricate, very strongly arcuate, swollen internally near the base but never distinctly toothed. Other structural characters will be referred to in the table given below.

The species are rather numerous, generally well characterized structurally but variable in coloration. They belong especially to the arctic fauna, extending southward in North America as far as

Arizona, and probably also throughout the elevated central region of Mexico.

The following tabular statement may possibly facilitate the identification of the greater part of those species at present known to collectors :—

Anterior legs elongated in the male ; beak long, slender, strongly, evenly arcuate at least in the female, the antennæ inserted near the middle in the latter sex ; femoral teeth minute ; species large and homologous with the European *longimanus*..2

Anterior legs not elongated in the male ; beak long and slender, much longer and with the antennæ inserted at or near the middle in the female ; species moderately large 3

Anterior legs not elongated in the male ; beak shorter, stouter and more nearly straight, the antennæ inserted near apical third in the male and but slightly less apical in the female ; species smaller......................................4

2—Elytra with long sparse erect and bristling setæ ; beak in the female much longer than in the male ; basal joint of the anterior tarsi extremely elongate in the latter sex...1 **inæqualis**

Elytra with short and more close-set erect setæ ; beak not much longer in the female ; basal joint of the anterior male tarsi subequal in length to the remainder...2 **brevisetosus**

Elytra devoid of erect setæ ; beak only very slightly longer in the female ; basal joint of the anterior male tarsi a little shorter than the remainder.

3 mucidus

3—Anterior femur of the male with a rather small, very acute tooth.

Body piceous-black, the antennæ rufous ; elytra distinctly and gradually inflated behind..4 **laticollis**

Body much broader, pale ochreous-testaceous throughout, the sterna blackish ; elytra subparallel ....5 **amplus**

Anterior femur of the male with a large rectangular tooth ; beak in that sex shorter and stouter ; body dark rufo-testaceous, variegated with uneven darker spots..6 **parvicollis**

4—Elytra with erect bristling setæ 5

Elytra without erect setæ...6

5—Prothorax distinctly constricted behind the apex.

Body generally dark in color ; prothorax less transverse ; elytral setæ sparse but long and conspicuous...7 **hystricula**

Body pale ochreous-flavate ; prothorax short and strongly transverse ; erect setæ more numerous and much shorter.............................8 **hispidus**

Prothorax not, or but just visibly and broadly constricted near the apex.

Larger species, the prothorax rather large, strongly transverse and finely punctate ; beak longer ; erect setæ short and abundant, somewhat recurved...9 **hirtus**

Small species ; prothorax small, coarsely punctate ; beak very short, barely as long as the prothorax ; erect setæ long, finer and sparser.

10 filiolus

6—Vestiture generally coarse but hair-like, more or less condensed in uneven maculæ on the elytra 7
Vestiture distinctly squamiform, dense, more or less condensed and variegated or marmorate on the elytra..14
7—Beak punctate but not at all sulcate or carinulate...............................8
Beak punctate and with more or less distinct grooves and fine carinæ..........9
8—Body black, densely clothed with gray pubescence...11 **mannerheimi**
Body pale rufo-testaceous, sparsely clothed with long white hairs ; elytra with a triangular black basal cloud and a post-medial piceous spot, the latter divided by the suture ....12 **nubeculinus**
9—Prothorax strongly constricted behind the apex, the latter more or less broadly subtubulate..10
Prothorax not, or but very feebly constricted behind the apex 11
10—Coloration uniform or very nearly so throughout the upper surface.
   Condensed pubescent areas of the elytra large and suffused.
     Color rufo-testaceous.
       Body less robust, darker, testaceous, more inflated behind, the beak longer and more slender, blackish, the eyes large and more approximate above..13 **luridus**
       Body larger, more robust and more parallel, paler and more flavate in color, the beak shorter, decidedly stouter, always pale, the eyes smaller..14 **rufulus**
     Color black ; form narrow ; beak rather long, somewhat more than one-half as long as the elytra in the female.................15 **cuneatulus**
   Condensed pubescent areas very small and remote, each consisting of several longer white hairs ; strial punctures very coarse..........16 **alaskanus**
   Coloration not uniform ; elytra with a more or less distinct and pale sublateral vitta.
     Sutural notch triangular, deep and clearly limited, each elytron being acute and minutely subprominent at apex ; condensations of the elytral vestiture almost obsolete ....17 **marginatus**
     Sutural notch subobsolete, each elytron broadly rounded ; elytral condensations well marked.
       Pronotum with four small condensed spots in a posteriorly arcuate transverse line ; head with a deep frontal fovea..............18 **indifferens**
       Pronotum without trace of the four spots transversely arranged, but with two approximate, sparsely pubescent vittæ along the middle, and a lateral vitta, dilated at the middle and inclosing at this point a small subglabrous spot ; frontal fovea obsolete ....19 **vagenotatus**
11—Prothorax strongly transverse, with the apex much narrower than the base...12
Prothorax small and but slightly transverse, the apex nearly as wide as the base...13
12—Coloration pale.
   Small species, pale ochreous-testaceous throughout, with a broad indefinite and slightly darker subsutural vitta on each elytron, from the base nearly to the apex ; punctuation coarse ; vestiture rather long, coarse.
                                           20 **rufus**

Larger species, broader, more depressed, pale ochreous-testaceous, the head
and beak piceous-black, also with a feeble indefinite subsutural cloud on
each elytron from before the middle nearly to the apex ...21 **fusciceps**
Coloration dark.

Pronotum very coarsely, deeply punctate ; coloration nearly uniform.
22 **brevicollis**

Pronotum finely, densely punctate, paler along the base and apex ; each
elytron with a blackish cloud in the middle toward base and another
toward apex ....23 **subsignatus**

13—Beak pale, blackish toward apex...........................24 **longulus**

14—Pronotum with a broad densely squamose vitta at each side.
25 **squamosus**

Pronotum with four median spots forming a transverse rectangle, the two
anterior continued each feebly to the apex, the two posterior to the base,
also with a small spot at each side between the rectangle and the lateral
margin, the spots composed of long robust hairs ; elytral vestiture squamiform and strongly marmorate ....26 **marmoreus**

There are two other species, apparently belonging to this genus
and recently described by Dietz (Trans. Am. Ent. Soc., XVIII,
pp. 262, 265)[1] under the names *Alycodes dubius* and *Elleschus
angustatus.* I have not studied the types of these species, but
dubius seems to be allied to the normal eastern forms such as
indifferens ; angustatus is almost certainly closely related to *squamosus,* a small narrow species, with the femoral teeth very small,
the anterior alone distinct.

In regard to *Erirhinus lutulentus* and *rutilus* of Boheman, but
little can be stated positively. The description of the latter seems
to apply very well, however, to *Anthonomus nubilus* Lec., while
E. lutulentus may possibly be the same as *Anchodemus angustus*
Lec.

It is more than probable that the true affinities of Elleschus lie
strongly in the direction of Dorytomus, and that the toothed claws
form an exception of no more relative importance than the simple
claws of certain of the Anthonomini. It will in fact be found

---

[1] It should be stated in passing, that the genus Euclyptus of Dietz (l. c. p.
271) seems to be identical with Phyllotrox Sch. This genus is widely distributed throughout North America and at least the northern part of South America,
also in the intervening islands. To the nine species mentioned in the Munich
Catalogue, should be added *nubifer* and *ferrugineus* Lec., and *testaceus* Dietz ;
there are several other species in my cabinet still undescribed. Phyllotrox is
one of the characteristically American genera of true Erirhinini, and is decidedly
out of place in the Anthonomini.

extremely difficult to maintain the Erirhinini, Anthonomini and Tychiini as satisfactory tribes, their limits being not at all well defined under the present scope. It would be more in accordance with natural affinities to unite them, and the resultant tribe might then be readily subdivided into numerous well-marked groups or subtribes.

1 **D. inæqualis** n. sp.—Oblong, slightly subcuneate, feebly convex; integuments black, obsoletely mottled with testaceous, especially laterally; vestiture rather dense but not altogether concealing the shining surface, somewhat fine, moderately long, subrecumbent, finely and confusedly mottled paler and darker, with numerous long erect and bristling setæ. *Head* with a large deep frontal fovea, the eyes large, feebly convex; beak long, equally, evenly and rather strongly arcuate throughout in both sexes, two-thirds longer than the prothorax, deeply punctate and longitudinally sulcate, with the antennæ inserted rather beyond apical two-fifths in the male, slightly more slender, very much longer, fully two-thirds as long as the body, cylindrical, finely but closely seriato-punctate, with the antennæ inserted at the middle in the female. *Prothorax* in the male large, transversely oval, fully as wide as the base of the elytra and more than one-third as long as the latter, in the female much smaller and more transverse, distinctly narrower than the base of the elytra and scarcely more than one-fourth as long as the latter; punctures rather coarse, deep, moderately dense. *Elytra* with the sides straight in basal two-thirds, nearly parallel in the male but feebly divergent from the humeri in the female, obtusely parabolic in apical third; striæ slightly impressed, the punctures coarse, very deep and approximate; intervals nearly flat, finely, not densely punctate. *Abdomen* finely and densely punctate. Length 5.4–6.5 mm.; width 2.3–2.8 mm.

California (Los Angeles).

The sexual differences in this species are more pronounced by far than in any other within our fauna. In the male the basal joint of the antennal funicle is but slightly longer than the next two, the anterior legs slender and very long, the femur and tibia each one-half as long as the entire body, the latter evenly, feebly arcuate and slightly spinulose along the inner margin, and the corresponding tarsi have the basal joint longer than the remainder and but slightly shorter than the prothorax, with the inner edge finely and unevenly serrulato-granulose. In the female the second joint of the funicle is slightly longer but not as long as the next three, and the anterior legs are normal, the tarsi stout, with the basal joint shorter than the remainder. This species has been confounded with *mucidus* heretofore, but differs greatly as may be judged by the description.

2 **D. brevisetosus** n. sp.—Oblong, very feebly convex above; integuments rather shining, piceous-black, confusedly mottled with rufous, especially toward the sides ; vestiture rather dense, moderate in length, subrecumbent, confusedly mottled and with numerous very short erect setæ. *Head* very densely pubescent, especially above the eyes and with a deep frontal fovea ; eyes large, feebly convex ; beak in the male two-thirds longer than the prothorax, feebly arcuate, coarsely, deeply, rugosely punctate and longitudinally sulcate, with the antennæ inserted slightly beyond the middle, the basal joint of the antennal funicle as long as the next three ; in the female the beak is a little more slender, evenly and strongly arcuate, much more than twice as long as the prothorax, smooth, more finely, sparsely punctate, with the antennæ inserted a little behind the middle, the basal joint of the funicle as long as the next four. *Prothorax* not coarsely, deeply, somewhat sparsely punctate, with an impunctate median line ; in the male it is transversely oval, slightly narrower than the elytra and about one-third wider than long, in the female smaller, more transverse, more broadly truncate at apex, much narrower than the elytra and about one-half wider than long. *Elytra* three-fourths longer than wide, the sides straight and parallel in the male or feebly divergent from the base to apical third in the female, the apex obtusely rounded, the sutural notch rather large and distinct ; strial puncture rather large, deep, closely approximate ; intervals finely, somewhat distinctly and closely punctate. *Abdomen* rather strongly, not densely, unevenly punctate. Length 5.7–7.0 mm.; width 2.3–2.9 mm.

Arizona.

This species is closely related to *mucidus*, but may be distinguished by the slightly longer beak with the antennæ a trifle less apical in insertion in both sexes, by the abundant, erect but short setæ, bristling throughout the dorsal surface, and by the relatively more elongate anterior legs of the male, the basal joint of the tarsus in that sex being about equal in length to the remainder ; it is distinctly shorter in *mucidus*.

3 **D. mucidus** Say.—Curc. 14, Ed. Lec., I, p. 277 (Erirhinus) ; Gyll.: Sch. Gen. Curc., III, p. 291 ; Lec. : Proc. Am. Phil. Soc., XV, p. 164.

Oblong, flat above, convex at the sides, somewhat densely clothed with short robust pointed and subrecumbent hairs, which are whitish in color and with barely a trace of sparse and extremely short semi-erect setæ toward apex only ; integuments black and rufo-testaceous confusedly mottled. Beak slender in the male, feebly arcuate, coarsely, densely, rugosely striato-punctate, about one-half longer than the prothorax, with the antennæ inserted at apical two-fifths, in the female more strongly arcuate, cylindrical, smooth, finely, less densely, confusedly punctate, twice as long as the prothorax, with the antennæ inserted at the middle; antennæ slender, with the basal joint of the funicle about as long as the next four together, the second as long as the next two, differing but slightly in the sexes. Prothorax larger and longer in the male than in the female, one-half wider than long and but slightly narrower than the elytra in the former, three-fourths wider than long and much narrower than the elytra in the latter; sides strongly arcuate, rounded and convergent but not at all constricted near the apex; disk strongly but not very coarsely punctate, the punctures distinctly separated. Elytra parallel, ogival toward apex, from two-thirds to three-fourths longer than wide, the strial punctures coarse, deep, moderately close-set, the intervals feebly convex, minutely, feebly, rather sparsely punctulate. Length 5.0–6.5 mm.; width 2.0–3.0 mm.

Canada, Indiana and Nebraska. The sexual differences are slightly less pronounced than in *brevisetosus* and very much less so than in *inæqualis*, and this species is readily distinguishable from both by the absence of erect setæ. In the male the anterior legs are elongated, but the basal joint of the tarsus is shorter than the remainder and about one-half as long as the prothorax.

4 **D. laticollis** Lec.—Proc. Am. Phil. Soc., XV, p. 164.

Piceous-black, variegated with small distant spots of rufo-piceous, polished, the vestiture sparse, consisting of short robust and recumbent hairs, condensed in numerous small paler spots and also toward the sides of the prothorax, without trace of erect setæ. Head strongly, not very densely punctate and with a deep frontal fovea; beak very slender, cylindrical, in the male strongly arcuate, straight toward base, rather finely but deeply, linearly punctate and fully one-half as long as the elytra, very finely, sparsely and inconspicuously setose, the antennæ inserted just behind apical third, the basal joint of the funicle fully equal to the next three. Prothorax small, transverse, three-fourths wider than long, the sides abruptly rounded and strongly convergent anteriorly, the apex very briefly tubulate and broadly arcuate, three-fourths as wide as the base; punctures deep, perforate but not very large, rather sparse, the median impunctate area very feebly defined toward the center only; apical margin rufescent. Elytra at base nearly one-third wider than the prothorax, almost four times as long, slightly wider behind the middle, broadly constricted behind the humeri, the strial punctures coarse, deep and close-set; intervals nearly flat, finely but strongly, rather closely punctate. Abdomen finely, not very densely punctate. Length 4.4 mm.; width 1.9 mm.

The description is drawn from a male taken in Michigan. It also occurs at Lake Superior and in Iowa according to LeConte.

5 **D. amplus** n. sp.—Oblong, feebly convex, robust, strongly shining, pale brownish-flavate throughout; vestiture very sparse, consisting of small robust and recumbent hairs, feebly condensed in subtransverse wavy lines on the elytra behind, also denser at the humeri; erect setæ completely wanting. *Head* finely but deeply and rather densely punctate and setose, the frontal fovea small but deep; beak in the male slender, strongly arcuate, evenly cylindrical, finely but deeply, rather closely lineato-punctate, very slightly more than one-half as long as the elytra, with the antennæ inserted near apical two-fifths, first funicular joint as long as the next three, second equal to the following two combined. *Prothorax* small, transverse, nearly three-fourths wider than long, the sides subparallel and strongly, almost evenly arcuate, not very abruptly rounded near the apex but distinctly constricted, the apex truncate, very broadly tubulate, more than three-fourths as wide as the base; punctures rather fine but deep, quite sparse, the impunctate line narrow and not attaining the apex. *Elytra* at base nearly two-fifths wider than the prothorax, about four times as long as the latter and scarcely noticeably wider behind the middle, the sides gradually ogival in apical third, with the sutural notch rather large; humeri rectangular, rounded, broadly exposed; strial punctures rather small but very deep, perforate and close-set; intervals flat, very minutely feebly sparsely and inconspicuously punctate. *Abdomen* finely, distinctly, subrugosely punctate. Length 5.4 mm.; width 2.3 mm.

Colorado.

A rather large species allied to *laticollis* and *parvicollis*, but differing in its entirely pale reddish-ochreous coloration, and much broader form. The two specimens before me are apparently males.

6 **D. parvicollis** n. sp.—Oblong, moderately stout, feebly convex, shining, rufo-testaceous, irregularly mottled with piceous-black, especially toward the middle; vestiture rather sparse, consisting of short robust and recumbent pale hairs, unevenly and feebly condensed and mottled, without trace of erect setæ. *Head* finely, deeply, very densely punctured and with a deep frontal fovea; beak in the male somewhat stout, feebly but distinctly arcuate, coarsely deeply and closely punctate in longitudinal furrows, strongly and conspicuously setulose and slightly longer than the head and prothorax, distinctly less than one-half as long as the elytra, with the antennæ inserted just beyond apical two-fifths; in the female the beak is very long, slender, less sulcate, strongly, evenly arcuate, fully two-thirds as long as the elytra, with the antennæ inserted just beyond the middle; basal joint of the funicle sub-

equal to the next three in both sexes. *Prothorax* small, transverse, about two-thirds wider than long, nearly similar in the sexes, abruptly, strongly rounded and very strongly narrowed near the apex, the latter broadly and rather strongly tubulate, four-fifths as wide as the base, broadly, feebly arcuate, feebly sinuate in the middle; punctures not very coarse but deep, dense although distinctly separated, the impunctate line completely obsolete. *Elytra* at base from one-third to one-fourth wider than the prothorax, four times as long as the latter, parallel in the male but gradually distinctly wider behind in the female, obtusely ogival at apex; strial punctures moderately large, very deep, perforate, close-set; intervals nearly flat, minutely, feebly, rather sparsely punctate. *Abdomen* finely, evenly, not densely punctate. Length 4.5–5.5 mm.; width 2.0–2.2 mm.

Indiana.

Allied to *laticollis*, but distinguishable by the pale coloration and especially by the shorter, more robust beak of the male and the slightly larger eyes of the same sex; the beak and head are also much more coarsely and densely punctate and setose. The tooth of the anterior femur is larger in the present species than in *laticollis*, and the elytra are parallel in the male and not gradually feebly inflated behind.

7 **D. hystricula** n. sp.—Oblong-oval, convex, feebly shining, piceous-black and more or less rufescent toward the sides, to pale rufo-testaceous throughout; legs always pale; vestiture dense, consisting of short stout pointed and decumbent hairs, cinereous in color and but feebly mottled, the pronotum with two narrow indefinitely nubilate darker vittæ, the elytra bristling also with long erect stiff setæ, not close-set in a single line on each interval. *Head* and beak very densely punctate throughout, the latter not longitudinally carinulate or sulcate, in the male short, about as long as the prothorax, with the antennæ inserted at apical third, in the female just visibly longer, but not longer than the prothorax, with the antennæ inserted at apical two-fifths, in both sexes feebly, evenly arcuate and stout; antennæ stout, the basal joint of the funicle as long as the next three, second much shorter than the next two, outer joints gradually thicker and transversely oval, club thick, oval, pointed. *Prothorax* one-half wider than long, parallel and broadly arcuate at the sides, moderately constricted and broadly sub-tubulate at apex, the punctures not coarse but deep and dense; impunctate line obsolete. *Elytra* at base one-third wider than the prothorax, about three and one-half times as long as the latter, the sides parallel and nearly straight; apical third evenly ogival; sutural notch broad and rather large; striæ un-impressed, the punctures moderately coarse, deep, somewhat close-set; intervals minutely, very feebly and somewhat closely punctate. *Abdomen* closely, rather coarsely, confusedly and subrugosely punctured. Length 2.7–3.3 mm.; width 1.1–1.5 mm.

California (San Francisco to Los Angeles).

One of the most abundant of the Californian species and represented before me by a large series. It varies greatly in color, and closely resembles *mannerheimi* Gemm.; the latter, however, completely lacks the long coarse erect setæ which are so conspicuous in *hystricula*.

8 **D. hispidus** Lec.—Proc. Am. Phil. Soc., XV, p. 167.

Oblong, somewhat stout, convex, feebly shining, pale flavo-testaceous throughout except the sterna of the hind body, which, as in *hirtus*, are blackish; vestiture dense, consisting of robust recumbent hairs, feebly subdenuded in uneven wavy blotches on the elytra behind the middle, and with coarse erect bristles of moderate length. Head very densely punctate and coarsely pubescent, the beak in the female subglabrous toward apex, very feebly, evenly arcuate, rather slender, not quite as long as the head and prothorax, the antennæ inserted at apical two-fifths; between the bases of the antennæ there is a dilated flat polished and impunctate area. Prothorax small, more than one-half wider than long, parallel and rounded on the sides, convergent and sinuate, but not strongly constricted, near the apex, the latter three-fourths as wide as the base; punctures moderate in size, deep, dense, the impunctate line narrow and distinct. Elytra at base fully one-third wider than the prothorax, much more than three times as long, parallel, gradually, evenly parabolic in more than apical third; strial punctures moderately large, very deep and close-set; intervals about three times as wide as the punctures. Abdomen densely, rugosely punctate. Legs short. Length 3.6 mm.; width 1.4 mm.

New Mexico. Cab. LeConte. A distinct species not closely allied to any other; it differs from *hirtus* in its smaller, narrower prothorax, and the shorter and sparser pubescence of the elytra, although the erect setæ are similar to those of that species in length and abundance; also, as remarked by Dr. LeConte, in the absence of the interantennal sulcus.

9 **D. hirtus** Lec.—Proc. Am. Phil. Soc., XV, p. 166.

Oblong, robust, convex, somewhat shining, pale flavo-testaceous, the beak piceous; sterna and their parapleuræ black; vestiture dense, consisting of long robust recumbent hairs, yellowish-white in color, scarcely mottled but subdenuded in a large clouded spot

near the middle of each elytron; elytra and beak toward apex
bristling with stiff suberect setæ.   Beak in the female not very
stout, evenly, feebly arcuate, as long as the head and prothorax,
rather sparsely punctate and subglabrous except above in basal
half, with an elongate indentation between the antennæ, the latter
inserted just behind apical third, the basal joint of the funicle not
quite as long as the next three; club moderate, not darker in color.
Prothorax two-thirds wider than long, parallel and rounded at the
sides, convergent and just visibly constricted anteriorly, the apex
nearly three-fourths as wide as the base; disk rather finely, somewhat closely punctate, without distinct impunctate line.   Elytra at
base barely one-fourth wider than the prothorax, three and one-half
times longer than the latter, subparallel, ogival in apical third, the
striæ feebly impressed, the punctures rather small, not very close-
set; erect setæ forming a single line on each interval.   Length 3.7
mm.; width 1.65 mm.

California (San Diego).   Cab. LeConte.   Represented by the
unique female type.   *Hirtus* is allied to *hystricula*, but is immediately distinguishable by its larger and more transverse prothorax,
stouter bodily form, longer beak, very much finer strial punctuation and many other characters.   The erect setæ of the elytra are
decidedly shorter and more numerous than in *hystricula*.

10 **D. filiolus** n. sp.—Oblong-oval, rather stout, convex, shining, pale
flavate throughout; vestiture rather sparse, consisting of long, somewhat fine,
recumbent and ashy pubescence, not perceptibly variegated, the elytra bristling with long sparse and erect bristles, disposed in a single line on each
interval.   *Head* and beak finely, rather densely, evenly punctate, the frontal
fovea deep but not very large; beak short, stout, just visibly, evenly arcuate,
about as long as the prothorax in the female, not longitudinally furrowed or
carinulate; antennæ inserted beyond apical two-fifths, somewhat stout, short,
the basal joint of the funicle as long as the next three, seventh abruptly wider,
transverse, club short, very robust, oval.   *Prothorax* short and transverse, two-
thirds wider than long, strongly rounded on the sides, convergent and nearly
straight but not in the least constricted toward apex, the latter much narrower
than the base; punctures rather coarse, very deep and dense but not actually
in contact, and with traces of a narrow impunctate line.   *Elytra* at base one-
third wider than the prothorax, three and one-half times as long, subparallel,
the apex conjointly ogival; striæ feebly impressed, coarsely, deeply and closely
punctate, the intervals very minutely, feebly, sparsely and indistinctly punctured.   *Abdomen* shining, finely, not very closely, distinctly punctate, sparsely
and finely pubescent.   Length 2.5 mm.; width 1.15 mm.

Colorado.

The single specimen serving as the type is probably a female. This species is one of the smallest of the genus and is somewhat allied to *hystricula*, but differs greatly in its coarser, sparser punctuation, sparser pubescence and especially in the form of the prothorax, which is shorter, more strongly narrowed anteriorly and not at all constricted behind the apical margin.

11 **D. mannerheimi** Gemm.—Col. Hefte., VIII, p. 122 (Erirhinus); Lec.: Proc. Am. Phil. Soc., XV, p. 166; *vestitus* Mann.: Bull. Mosc., 1853, II, p. 242 (Erirhinus).

Oblong, moderately stout, convex, scarcely shining, densely and almost uniformly clothed throughout with short robust recumbent hairs of a dark cinereous tint, and without long erect setæ; body black, the legs piceous; antennæ paler, piceous. Beak very short, stout, densely punctured and setose but not longitudinally grooved, opaque, feebly arcuate and equal in length to the prothorax; antennæ inserted but slightly beyond apical two-fifths, the basal joint of the funicle robust and but little longer than the next two. Prothorax short, fully one-half wider than long, parallel and rounded on the sides, strongly constricted and broadly subtubulate at apex, extremely densely, not very coarsely punctured, without impunctate line. Elytra at base much wider than the prothorax and about three and one-half times as long, the sides parallel and straight, rounded in apical third, with a small sutural notch: striæ rather coarsely deeply and closely punctate, not strongly impressed; intervals but slightly wider than the strial punctures, densely punctulate. Length 2.7 mm.; width 1.25 mm.

Alaska. Cab. LeConte. Easily distinguishable from the other Alaskan species by its dense and uniform pubescence and shorter, broader, more parallel form. It is doubtful if the name substituted by Gemminger should be retained, as the south African *vestitus* is possibly a true Erirhinus. The anterior femora in *mannerheimi* are distinctly toothed; the others are not in a favorable position for observation in the single specimen which I have studied. The pronotal vittæ, mentioned by Mannerheim, are obliterated in this example, and the small subdenuded spots of the elytra are extremely feebly defined.

12 **D. nubeculinus** n. sp.—Narrowly oblong-oval, convex, shining, sparsely clothed with long white robust and squamuliform hairs, somewhat

unevenly arranged on the elytra and erect and bristling on the head; color pale rufo-testaceous; head and beak blackish, the tip of the latter pale; elytra with a broad triangular basal area and an elongate narrow subsutural spot behind the middle of each blackish; sterna and side-pieces black. *Head* very densely punctate, without distinct frontal fovea; beak short, stout, just visibly bent, rather finely, deeply and moderately densely punctate but not at all sulcate or carinulate, in the male barely longer than the prothorax, with the antennæ inserted at apical third; basal joint of the antennal funicle fully as long as the next three, club moderate, not at all darker in color, with the first joint subglabrous toward base. *Prothorax* short, two-thirds wider than long; sides parallel and nearly straight in middle two-thirds, convergent and rounded near the base, convergent and very feebly sinuate behind the apex, the latter three-fourths as wide as the base; punctures very dense, rather fine, deep; median line very narrowly and feebly carinulate. *Elytra* at base fully one-third wider than the prothorax, nearly four times as long, parallel and straight at the sides, ogival in apical third, the sutural notch subobsolete; striæ barely impressed, coarsely deeply and closely punctate, the intervals not quite twice as wide as the striæ, finely, rather sparsely and confusedly punctate. *Abdomen* rather strongly punctate, blackish toward base and in the median parts of the fifth segment. *Legs* short; femoral teeth rather large and distinct but acute.   Length 3.0 mm.; width 1.2 mm.

Colorado.

A small narrowly convex species of peculiar coloration, with long coarse and sparse but conspicuous vestiture, and short non-sulcate beak.   It is not closely allied to any other form which I have seen.

13 **D. luridus** Mann.—Bull. Mosc., 1853, II, p. 241 (Erirhinus); Lec.: Proc. Am. Phil. Soc., XV, p. 165.

Oblong, subcuneiform, moderately convex, polished, rufo-testaceous, the head piceous; vestiture rather sparse, consisting of short robust recumbent pale hairs, confusedly condensed and mottled on the elytra, longer and more slender on the pronotum; erect setæ entirely wanting.   Head rather coarsely, strongly punctate, the fovea very small; beak not very stout, almost straight, deeply, coarsely punctured in longitudinal furrows, evenly and just visibly arcuate in the female, straight and slightly bent near the apex in the male; in the male it is a little less than one-half as long as the elytra, with the antennæ inserted at apical third, the first funicular joint but little longer than the next two, in the female barely one-half as long as the elytra, the antennæ inserted just behind apical third, with the basal joint of the funicle fully as long as the next three.   Prothorax small in both sexes, nearly one-half wider than long, rather coarsely, closely punctate, with a narrow imperfect impunctate line, constricted at apex, rounded and subparallel on the sides. Elytra at base distinctly wider than the prothorax, a little more than three times as long as the latter, wider behind; strial punctures coarse, deep and close-set; intervals finely but deeply, evenly, not very closely punctate. Abdomen strongly punctate. Length 3.4–4.3 mm.; width 1.4–1.8 mm.

Alaska, Washington State and California (San Francisco and Los Angeles). This is a very abundant, widely distributed and constant species and may be easily recognized by the characters stated in the table. In one immature specimen before me a large region of the elytra toward the suture is piceous-black, confusedly speckled with paler spots.

14 **D. rufulus** Mann.—Bull. Mosc., 1853, II, p. 240 (Erirhinus); Lec.: Proc. Am. Phil. Soc., XV, p. 165.

Oblong, rather convex, rufo-testaceous and feebly shining throughout; sterna and side-pieces picescent; vestiture sparse and scarcely at all condensed in spots, consisting of short prostrate pale hairs. Head deeply punctate, without frontal fovea, the beak in the female moderately stout, feebly arcuate, distinctly longer than the head and prothorax, deeply punctato-sulcate; antennæ inserted rather behind apical third, the basal joint of the funicle subequal to the next three. Prothorax one-half wider than long; sides parallel evenly and rather strongly arcuate; apical constriction small and strong, the apex four-fifths as wide as the base, broadly tubulate; punctures moderate in size, narrowly separated, with a fusiform impunctate space at the middle. Elytra at base nearly two-fifths wider than the prothorax, almost four times as long, scarcely perceptibly wider behind the middle; sides convergent and nearly straight in apical third, the apex narrowly obtuse; sutural notch obsolete; strial punctures not very large but deep, moderately close-set; striæ not impressed; intervals wide, minutely, indistinctly punctate. Abdomen not coarsely, strongly, rather sparsely punctured. Femora not very stout, the tooth small, distinct and very acute. Length 4.3 mm.; width 1.8 mm.

Alaska. Cab. LeConte. The single specimen, from which the above outline is drawn, is a female, the abdomen being evenly convex toward base. It is quite closely allied to *luridus* but is a larger, stouter species, with shorter and thicker beak, always pale in color and with decidedly smaller eyes, so that when the insect is viewed in profile, there is a large part of the head visible above them.

15 **D. cuneatulus** n. sp.—Rather narrowly cuneate, convex, polished, black throughout, the pronotum and elytra occasionally with small feebly-marked paler spots near the humeri; vestiture sparse, consisting of short robust recumbent hairs, whitish in color and confusedly and vaguely condensed in spots and transversely wavy lines behind the middle of the elytra. *Head* strongly but only moderately closely punctate, the fovea almost obsolete; beak somewhat stout, cylindrical, equal in thickness, strongly, longitudinally furrowed and closely, obscurely punctate in both sexes, but differing greatly in length; in the male decidedly short, as long as the head and prothorax, straight, feebly bent near the apex, the antennæ inserted at apical third; in the female rather long, evenly, very feebly arcuate, about two-fifths as long as the body, with the antennæ inserted rather beyond apical two-fifths; antennæ somewhat slender, the first funicular joint not quite as long as the next three in both sexes, the second about as long as the next two in the female, but slightly shorter in the male, rufo-testaceous with the club darker. *Prothorax* nearly two-fifths wider than long, not differing greatly in the sexes, parallel and broadly rounded at the sides, strongly constricted and broadly tubulate at apex, coarsely deeply and moderately closely punctate, without distinctly marked impunctate area. *Elytra* at base distinctly wider than the prothorax, fully three times as long as the latter, broadly feebly inflated behind, obtusely ogival in apical third; striæ feebly impressed, coarsely deeply and closely punctate, the intervals minutely and not very densely so. *Abdomen* rather strongly indistinctly and subrugosely punctured. Length 3.3–3.7 mm.; width 1.3–1.6 mm.

California (Siskiyou Co.).

A small, somewhat narrow and convex species allied to *luridus*, but distinguishable by its black coloration and by the much greater sexual disparity in the length of the beak, the latter being actually a little shorter in the male than in the corresponding sex of *luridus*. The body is narrower and the antennal club larger and relatively longer in *cuneatulus*.

16. **D. alaskanus** n. sp.—Narrow, oblong, subparallel, moderately convex, shining, piceous-black, the elytral suture and flanks pronotum at base and apex, legs and antennæ, except the club, paler; vestiture very sparse, consisting of short robust recumbent hairs, condensed, larger and whiter in very small remote spots on the elytra. *Head* strongly deeply and closely, the beak very densely and opaquely, punctate, the latter longitudinally channeled, in the male rather stout, feebly arcuate toward apex, equal in length to the head and prothorax, the antennæ inserted at apical third, the basal joint of the funicle rather robust, not as long as the next three. *Prothorax* one-half wider than long, subparallel and rounded on the sides, strongly constricted at apex, the latter broadly and briefly tubulate, nearly as wide as the base; disk rather coarsely deeply and somewhat sparsely punctate, with a central feebly-defined, elongate subimpunctate area. *Elytra* at base about one-third wider than the prothorax, rather more than three times as long; sides almost straight and

parallel in basal two-thirds; apex ogival, the sutural notch minute; disk
with just visibly impressed series of coarse, deep, not very close-set punctures,
the intervals minutely, feebly and somewhat sparsely punctate. *Abdomen*
finely, sparsely punctured.   Length 3.0 mm. ; width 1.1 mm.

Alaska.   Cab. LeConte.

A small species allied to *luridus*, but narrower, more sparsely
pubescent, darker in color and with a shorter beak in the male ; the
antennal club is distinctly longer and larger than in *luridus*.   In
form it somewhat resembles *subfasciatus*, but the prothorax is less
strongly rounded on the sides and the punctuation very much
coarser and sparser.

17 **D. marginatus** n. sp.—Oblong, feebly convex, rather dull, rufo-
testaceous ; sterna, abdomen except near the apex, a feeble clouded transverse
area on the pronotum before the middle, head, beak except at tip and a broad
subsutural vitta on each elytron, from the base nearly to the apex, more or less
blackish ; vestiture moderately dense, consisting of short robust recumbent
hairs, feebly condensed in small and paler spots on the elytra, unevenly denser
toward the sides of the pronotum and paler in two small approximate spots
before the middle.   *Head* very densely, deeply punctate, without frontal fovea,
the squamules erect, dense and bristling along the inner margin of the eyes ;
beak as long as the head and prothorax, rather stout, deeply punctato-sulcate,
feebly arcuate ; antennæ inserted near apical third, the basal joint of the
funicle as long as the next three, club moderate, piceous-black.   *Prothorax* one-
third to one-half wider than long, subparallel and rounded on the sides, distinctly constricted behind the apex, rather coarsely, very deeply and densely
punctate, without impunctate line.   *Elytra* at base one-third wider than the
prothorax, from more than three to nearly four times longer than the latter,
parallel and nearly straight on the sides, acutely ogival in apical third ; sutural notch rather large, deep and triangular ; striæ not impressed, the punctures moderately coarse, very deep and close-set ; intervals minutely, indistinctly but rather closely punctate.   *Abdomen* somewhat coarsely, moderately
closely punctate.   *Legs* rather short ; femora stout, moderately but distinctly
dentate.   Length 3.6–4.0 mm. ; width 1.4–1.6 mm.

California.

This is a rather distinct species, allied to *vagenotatus*, but always
easily separable by the well-defined abbreviated subsutural vitta.

18 **D. indifferens** n. sp.—Oblong-oval, rather shining and convex,
dark rufo-testaceous in color, the head, beak, sterna and the elytra indefinitely toward the middle, black or piceous ; elytral suture always narrowly
rufous ; tip of beak pale testaceous ; legs and antennæ rufo-testaceous ; vestiture rather sparse, consisting of short robust pointed and prostrate hairs,
whitish in color, confusedly condensed and subdenuded on the elytra.   *Head*
not coarsely but deeply, very densely punctate, finely sparsely squamulose,

with a round perforate fovea on a line through the posterior margin of the
eyes, beak rather stout, nearly straight, feebly bent toward apex, coarsely,
densely punctato-sulcate, equal in length to the head and prothorax in the
female, slightly shorter in the male, the antennæ inserted at apical third, or
slightly behind this point in the female, the basal joint of the funicle about
as long as the next three, second almost as long as the succeeding two, club
moderate. *Prothorax* fully one-half wider than long, the sides parallel, broadly,
distinctly arcuate, abruptly, deeply constricted behind the apex, the latter
transversely truncate, three-fourths as wide as the base; punctures not coarse,
very deep, dense but not coalescent, with a very fine subcariniform median
line. *Elytra* at base two-fifths wider than the prothorax, not quite four times
as long; sides subparallel, gradually rounded in apical two-fifths, sutural
notch shallow, broadly angulate; striæ feebly impressed, not very coarsely
but deeply and closely punctate; intervals nearly three times as wide as the
punctures, minutely, rather indistinctly punctate. *Abdomen* polished, finely,
distinctly, not densely punctate, two basal segments blackish, the remainder
rufous. *Legs* rather slender; femora with a small acute tooth, rather feebler
on the intermediate as usual. Length 3.0–4.0 mm.; width 1.3–1.7 mm.

New York; Illinois; Iowa; Kansas.

A common Atlantic form, resembling *rufus* and *vagenotatus*, but
distinguishable by the small and deep perforate frontal fovea, which
is completely obsolete in those species, and also by its larger size
and different coloration.

19 **D. vagenotatus** n. sp.—Oblong, feebly convex above, piceous-black;
abdomen toward apex, legs, antennæ except the club, pronotum laterally and
a narrow suffused stripe near the side of each elytron paler and more or less
rufous; integuments confusedly marmorate with small confused condensed
patches of short white pointed hairs, less mottled and almost uniformly pubescent along the lateral paler stripe. *Head* very densely, deeply punctate,
without frontal fovea, the squamules near the eye abundant but short; beak
moderately stout, broadly, feebly arcuate toward apex, distinctly longer than
the head and prothorax, deeply, densely punctato-sulcate, the antennæ in the
male inserted just behind apical third, the first funicular joint about as long
as the next three, second not quite as long as the next two, club rather large,
elongate, conoidal and gradually pointed. *Prothorax* one-half wider than long,
parallel and strongly, evenly arcuate on the sides, strongly constricted behind
the apex, the latter subtubulate; punctures moderately coarse, very deep and
dense; impunctate line subobsolete. *Elytra* at base one-third wider than the
prothorax, three and one-half times as long, parallel and straight at the sides,
obtusely parabolic in apical fourth; sutural notch small, feeble and cuspiform,
not triangular; strial punctures coarse, very deep, rather close-set; intervals
about twice as wide as the punctures, minutely, sparsely punctulate. *Abdomen*
finely, sparsely punctate. *Legs* long; tooth of the anterior femora large, rectangular. Length 3.6 mm.; width 1.5 mm.

Indiana.

The type and unique specimen is a male, the abdomen having a large rounded and deep impression near the base. It is allied to *rufus* but differs in its larger size, coloration, longer beak and more elongate antennal club, longer legs, more distinct femoral teeth, and in the finer, shorter vestiture, more distinctly defined in white marmorate patches on the dark elytra.

20 **D. rufus** Say.—Descr. N. A. Curc., July, 1831; Ed. Lec., I, p. 293 (Erirhinus).

Oblong, feebly convex, pale flavo-testaceous throughout, the elytra feebly clouded with brownish toward the middle; integuments shining, not very densely clothed with robust squamuliform hairs, confusedly condensed in transversely wavy spots and whitish in color. Head very densely punctate, the squamules along the inner margin of the eye erect and bristling; beak rather stout, somewhat longer than the head and prothorax in the female, and with the antennæ inserted beyond apical two-fifths, rather coarsely, densely lineato-sulcate and punctate, very feebly arcuate; antennæ rather slender, the basal joint of the funicle not quite as long as the next three, second but slightly longer than the third; club moderate, slightly darker in color, sparsely pubescent. Prothorax one-half wider than long; sides subparallel and rather strongly arcuate, convergent and just visibly sinuate near the apex; punctures rather coarse, very deep, somewhat dense, without impunctate line. Elytra at base one-third wider than the prothorax, but slightly more than three times as long, parallel, obtusely rounded in not more than apical third; sutural notch small but deep; strial punctures coarse deep and very close-set; intervals flat, twice as wide as the strial punctures, sparsely, very feebly punctulate. Legs short, stout, the femoral teeth minute but distinct on the anterior. Length 3.0–3.2 mm.; width 1.3 mm.

Kansas. The three specimens before me exhibit scarcely any variation. This species may be readily known by its pale ochreous color, feebly clouded along the median parts of the elytra, the small size, coarse, subsquamiform vestiture and by several other distinctive characters.

21 **D. fusciceps** n. sp.—Oblong, rather broad and subdepressed, pale ochreous-flavate, the head and beak piceous-black; sterna piceous, each elytron almost imperceptibly clouded with a darker tint in a broad subsutural

area from basal third to apical fifth ; vestiture very dense but scarcely at all condensed in spots, consisting of very short robust and decumbent hairs, becoming squamulose in a small spot at each side of the pronotal disk. *Head* very densely punctate, with a small frontal fovea; beak stout, very feebly arcuate, as long as the head and prothorax, deeply punctato-sulcate; antennæ moderate, inserted at apical third, the basal joint of the funicle fully as long as the next three. *Prothorax* short and strongly transverse, three-fourths wider than long; sides parallel and almost straight in middle third, convergent toward base and rather abruptly, strongly so and straight in apical fourth ; apex truncate, about three-fifths as wide as the base; punctures rather small, very dense, without impunctate line, a narrow median line infuscate. *Elytra* large and broad, barely two-thirds longer than wide, fully one-third wider than the prothorax and four times as long, subparallel, gradually ogival behind in apical two-fifths ; sutural notch very feeble, cuspiform ; strial punctures moderate ; intervals from two to nearly three times as wide as the striæ, finely, very densely and subrugosely punctate. *Legs* rather short; femoral teeth small, the anterior acute. Length 4.3 mm.; width 1.9 mm.

Iowa.

Represented by a single specimen deprived of abdomen, but probably a male. It is allied to *rufus*, although very much larger and relatively wider, with denser punctuation and shorter much less conspicuous vestiture. In *fusciceps* the subapical constriction of the prothorax is totally obsolete; it is broad and almost obsolete in *rufus* and deep and abrupt in *marginatus*.

22 D. brevicollis Lec.—Proc. Am. Phil. Soc., XV, p. 165.

Oblong, rather convex, not very stout, shining, blackish-piceous, the beak, legs and antennæ rufescent; vestiture consisting of short robust and prostrate hair, whitish in color and more or less condensed in indefinite spots on the elytra, rather dense and conspicuous. Head very deeply, densely punctate, with a deep frontal fovea; beak rather longer than the head and prothorax, deeply punctate, finely sulcate, feebly arcuate, moderately stout; antennæ somewhat slender, the basal joint of the funicle rather long, fully as long as the next three. Prothorax one-half wider than long, subparallel and strongly arcuate at the sides, strongly convergent and just visibly sinuate toward apex, the latter rather narrow, not more than two-thirds as wide as the base; punctures coarse, deep and dense, with a small elongate impunctate spot at the middle. Elytra at base one-third wider than the prothorax, very nearly four times as long, straight and parallel at the sides, rounded in apical third;

sutural notch almost obsolete; strial punctures coarse, deep and close-set. Abdomen rather coarsely and closely punctate. Length 3.7 mm.; width 1.4 mm.

Lake Superior and Minnesota. Resembles *rufulus* somewhat, but differs in its narrower form, more strongly convergent sides of the prothorax toward apex, the latter being very much narrower when compared with the base, in its decidedly coarser punctuation, especially of the pronotum, and in the coarser, denser vestiture. The two specimens before me are apparently males, and the one from Minnesota is pale flavo-testaceous throughout, probably from immaturity, with the frontal fovea practically obsolete, this not being so constant a feature as it apparently is in *indifferens.*

23 D. subsignatus Mann.—Bull. Mosc., 1853, II, p. 241 (Erirhinus).

Rather slender, convex, feebly subcuneate; body piceous-black, the pronotum rufescent toward base and apex, the elytra dark rufo-testaceous, each indefinitely clouded with blackish in the middle toward base and also near the apex; legs and antennæ pale, the club of the latter dark. Head and beak finely deeply and extremely densely punctate, dull, the beak finely, obsoletely carinulate, rather stout, almost straight and scarcely longer than the prothorax, the antennæ inserted at fully apical third in the male, the basal joint of the funicle not longer than the next two, second not as long as the third and fourth combined. Prothorax nearly one-half wider than long, rather wider and very strongly rounded before apical third, the sides thence strongly convergent and scarcely visibly constricted to the apex; disk finely, very densely punctate, with a narrow partial impunctate line. Elytra at base very slightly wider than the disk of the prothorax, nearly four times as long as the latter, just visibly widest behind the middle, gradually rounded in apical two-fifths, the apex narrowly obtuse; striæ rather distinctly impressed, not very coarsely but deeply and closely punctate; intervals minutely, rather densely and subrugosely punctate. Abdomen finely, densely punctate. Femoral teeth all large and prominent. Length 3.2 mm.; width 1.3 mm.

Alaska. Cab. LeConte. This species somewhat resembles *luridus,* but is much narrower and is easily recognizable by the exceptionally fine and dense punctuation, especially of the anterior portion of the body.

24 **D. longulus** Lec.—Proc. Am. Phil. Soc., XV, p. 166.

Elongate-oval, convex, subcuneate, rather shining, rufo-testaceous, often more or less clouded with piceous-black, the head and beak toward apex always darker; vestiture not very dense, consisting of short stout pointed and semi-erect hairs, whitish in color. Beak strongly punctate, very feebly sulcate, moderately stout, almost perfectly straight, as long as the head and prothorax, with the antennæ inserted at apical two-fifths in the female, a little shorter with the antennæ inserted at apical third in the male; antennæ moderate, the basal joint of the funicle as long as the next two; club rather large, densely pubescent and piceous-black. Prothorax small, subcylindrical, with broadly arcuate sides, one-third to two-fifths wider than long, not constricted at apex, convex, finely, rather densely punctate, without distinct impunctate line. Elytra at base fully one-third wider than the prothorax, feebly, gradually inflated posteriorly and widest behind the middle, the apex thence gradually, acutely ogival; sutural notch small but distinct, broadly angulate; strial punctures rather coarse, deep and close-set; intervals feebly convex, about twice as wide as the strial punctures, minutely, sparsely punctate. Under surface deep black and rather dull throughout, finely, confusedly punctate. Length 3.2–3.7 mm.; width 1.25–1.5 mm.

Alaska. A rather isolated species easily recognizable by its narrowly convex and cuneate-oval form, almost perfectly straight beak darker toward tip, rather fine pronotal punctures and several other characters.

25 **D. squamosus** Lec.—Proc. Am. Phil. Soc., XV, p. 166; *tessellatus* ‖ Walsh,: Proc. Ent. Soc. Phila., VI, p. 267 (Anthonomus).

Narrowly oblong-oval, convex, dark rufo-testaceous throughout; sterna often blackish; integuments somewhat shining, rather densely clothed with small elongate and recumbent scales, yellowish-white in color, feebly, sparsely and very indefinitely, coarsely mottled on the elytra toward the suture, and less dense in middle two-thirds of the pronotum. Beak evenly, quite distinctly arcuate, equally, evenly cylindrical throughout and as long as the head and prothorax in both sexes, densely punctate, longitudinally, feebly carinulate laterally, the antennæ inserted at fully apical third in the male and but slightly behind this point in the female; basal joint of the funicle barely as long as the next three; club small, stout, very abrupt, the basal joint in great part subglabrous. Prothorax wider than long, subparallel and broadly rounded at the sides, distinctly constricted and broadly subtubulate at apex, very densely, deeply punctate, without distinct impunctate area. Elytra at base fully one-third wider than the prothorax, parallel and nearly straight at the sides, rounded in apical third, the sutural notch small but deep and angulate; strial punctures moderately coarse, deep, somewhat close-set, each bearing a distinct elongate squamule. Length 2.7–3.3 mm.; width 0.9–1.3 mm.

Illinois and Kansas. Easily distinguishable by the narrow convex form, dark rufo-ferruginous color and the vestiture, which is dense and distinctly squamiform toward the sides of the body, but more hair-like along the median parts of the upper surface. The tooth of the anterior femora is very small but distinct, that of the others nearly obsolete. In one narrow male there is a small denuded spot in the middle of each of the lateral squamose vittæ of the pronotum.

26 **D. marmoreus** n. sp.—Oval, convex, rather dull, black; antennæ, legs and elytra in a very feebly defined sublateral vitta rufescent; vestiture dense, consisting of narrow recumbent lanceolate scales, white in color in two narrow approximate pronotal vittæ and a small median spot at each side, and, on the elytra, along the suture and in very uneven discal spots, elsewhere subdenuded and piceous-black. *Head* and beak extremely densely punctate, dull, squamulose, the latter longitudinally rugose but scarcely carinulate, thick, feebly arcuate, not quite as long as the head and prothorax; antennæ inserted just behind apical third, the basal joint of the funicle as long as the next three, club moderate, densely pubescent throughout. *Prothorax* small, one-third wider than long, subparallel, evenly and moderately arcuate at the sides, becoming more convergent, nearly straight and not visibly constricted anteriorly; apex broadly arcuate, nearly three-fourths as wide as the base; disk rather coarsely, very deeply and extremely densely punctate, without trace of impunctate line. *Elytra* at base nearly one-half wider than the prothorax, more than three times as long as the latter, acutely parabolic in apical two-fifths, the sutural notch very small and feeble, strial punctures moderately coarse, very deep, close-set; intervals minutely, indistinctly punctate. *Abdomen* not coarsely but deeply, very densely punctate. *Legs* short; femora stout, picescent toward apex, the tooth small but distinct on all, the intermediate and posterior with a large polished glabrous area on the posterior side in basal half. Length 3.2 mm.; width 1.4 mm.

New Mexico.

This is an isolated species, comparable only with *squamosus*, but differing greatly in its rather more robust form, stout beak, black color and strongly marked maculation of linear white scales.

SMICRONYX Schönh.

Pachytychius Lec. nec Jekel; *Desmoris* Lec.

The genus Pachytychius of Jekel, as represented by the European *squamosus* Gyll., examples of which have been recently sent me by M. Desbrochers des Loges, has the beak unconstricted at base and similar to that of Tychius, and the tarsal claws small, simple, divergent and distant at base, forming in fact one of the connective bonds between the Erirhinini and Tychiini. Pachytychius does not appear to be represented in the American fauna, and the two species provisionally placed there by LeConte are entirely identical in all structural characters, which can in any way be considered of generic worth, with the form described by that author as *Smicronyx corpulentus* and the other species placed in Smicronyx.

Desmoris of LeConte was founded upon two species of rather larger size than the others, but, if care be taken to examine *D. constrictus*, it will be found a perfect homologue of such species as *Smicronyx sordidus* and *griseus*, in all points of facies and structure.

Smicronyx is a rather large genus, constituting a special group of the Erirhinini, characterized by the strong basal constriction of the beak and the simple tarsal claws which are invariably connate in basal third or fourth. It is somewhat heterogeneous in the external aspect of its species, both here and in Europe, but as far as can be perceived is entirely uniform in the essential generic structures referred to, as well as in abdominal structure, in the coarsely facetted eyes, somewhat approximate beneath, and in the deeply sinuate apical margin of the prosternum. The elytra are, as a rule, distinctly wider at base than the disk of the prothorax, but are not as elongate as in Dorytomus, and are generally acutely rounded behind in apical half, with the tenth stria very short and remote from the ninth, closely approaching the latter behind the humeri. The scutellum is small, the legs rather short and stout, the femora unarmed, the tibial spur distinct, and the third tarsal joint dilated and bilobed, the fourth being somewhat short or moderate in length.

The species are small in size, and include among them some of the most minute curculionides known to us at present. Those of our fauna may be provisionally classified as follows:—

Fifth elytral interval densely clothed nearly throughout with white scales; second joint of the antennal funicle almost as long as the first; body robust, oval, convex, densely but unevenly squamose...1 **lineolatus**

Fifth interval not conspicuously vittate; second funicular joint very variable
in length but always much shorter than the first.............................2
2—Elytral scales almost uniform in size and density throughout the disk,
uniform in coloration or more or less conspicuously mottled.................3
Elytral vestiture very uneven, condensed in subtransversely wavy areas, in
which the scales become larger, denser and generally paler in color......16
3—Elytra inflated and only slightly longer than wide............................4
Elytra not inflated, much longer than wide, parallel at the sides toward base...5
4—Prothorax distinctly narrower than the base of the elytra, the latter with
a large subbasal area of dark brown or blackish scales.
    Elytral striæ coarse and distinctly punctate....................2 **discoideus**
    Elytral striæ fine throughout; form narrower..............3 **corpulentus**
Prothorax scarcely perceptibly narrower than the base of the elytra, and with
two conspicuous white discal vittæ....................................4 **amœnus**
5—Vestiture uniformly bright orange-red in color, dense throughout.
                                            5 **fulvus**
Vestiture vaguely nubilate with whitish, the elytra with a large quadrate
subbasal spot of velvety black..................................6 **quadrifer**
Vestiture varying in its shades of ochreous or cinereous, uniform, confusedly
mottled or otherwise variegated.......................................6
6—Sides of the prothorax parallel and straight in basal two-thirds to three-
fourths...7
Sides of the prothorax evenly and distinctly arcuate in basal two-thirds approximately..8
7—Prothorax narrowed but scarcely at all constricted near the apex; body
large, oblong..7 **profusus**
Prothorax very strongly and abruptly constricted behind the apex; recurved
setæ of the elytra long, coarse, sparse but strongly hispid and conspicuous.
                                    8 **intricatus**
8—Elytra at least very nearly three times as long as the prothorax............9
Elytra distinctly less than three times as long as the prothorax................13
9—Third elytral interval rather wider and more prominent; body clothed
with an extremely dense crust of uniform ochreous scales........9 **pusio**
Third elytral interval not more prominent.................................10
10—Elytral scales extremely dense, widely imbricated.......................11
Elytral scales scarcely contiguous, sometimes sparse........................12
11—Prothorax rather large, somewhat broadly inflated and much wider than
long...10 **corniculatus**
Prothorax small, about as long as wide, subcylindrical; species small.
    Scales of the upper surface very large, broadly oval......11 **imbricatus**
    Scales smaller and narrower, elongate-oval.
        Elytra at base scarcely more than one-third wider than the prothorax;
        body narrow...12 **silaceus**
        Elytra at base about one-half wider than the prothorax; body more
        robust..13 **spurcus**
12—Elytra more or less rufous ....14 **vestitus**
Elytra black ....15 **sparsus**

13—Elytral vestiture uniform in coloration or very feebly and confusedly
  mottled 14
Elytral vestiture broadly white toward the sides, abruptly and broadly brown
  along the suture..16 **pleuralis**
14—Elytral scales moderate in size, rather persistent 15
Elytral scales very large, oval and pointed, easily removable...17 **obtectus**
15—Beak in the female very long and slender, with the antennæ inserted far
  behind the middle.
  Pronotum more shining, the punctuation finer and sparser; size rather
    small ....18 **sordidus**
  Pronotum densely punctate.
    Larger species, the legs usually red; beak in the female squamulose only
      near the base..19 **constrictus**
    Smaller species, the legs piceous; beak of the female more or less squamose
      in basal half..20 **griseus**
Beak in the female much shorter, with the antennæ inserted at the middle;
  elytral vestiture just perceptibly more condensed on the sutural interval.
                                                                 21 **connivens**
16—The elytral vestiture uneven only toward the suture; prothorax about
  as long as wide, slightly constricted behind the apex........22 **seriatus**
The vestiture uneven throughout the elytral disk.....................................17
17—Elytra much longer than wide, not wider near the middle.................18
Elytra but very slightly longer than wide, appreciably wider near the middle
  than at base...22
18—Elytra more or less rufous, at least toward the sides........................19
Elytra black throughout 20
19—Prothorax large, very nearly as long as wide, the punctures coarse,
  rounded and not confluent.
  Smaller species, the pronotal scales narrower sparser and hair-like toward
    the middle..23 **fiducialis**
  Larger, the pronotum evenly but not extremely densely squamose through-
    out ....24 **scapalis**
Prothorax rather large, transverse, strongly rounded at the sides, the punc-
  tures oval and more or less confluent, forming long rugæ; vestiture dense
  but strongly mottled..25 **flavicans**
Prothorax moderately large, convex, strongly constricted near the apex, nearly
  as long as wide, the punctures rounded, dense but not confluent; body
  rufous ....26 **congestus**
Prothorax small or moderately large, always strongly rounded on the sides
  and with the punctures reniform or lunate; elytral vestiture consisting
  of isolated wavy lines or spots of condensed scales, the interspaces almost
  glabrous.
  Pronotal punctures rather sparse, widely isolated on the disk, the inter-
    spaces polished..27 **tychioides**
  Pronotal punctures dense.
    Pronotum with a median impunctate line, which is almost entire and
      finely granulato-reticulate...28 **sagittatus**

Pronotum without trace of median impunctate line; prothorax small.

29 **sculpticollis**

20—Prothorax not or very feebly constricted behind the apex.................21
Prothorax very strongly constricted and subtubulate at apex, the pronotal punctures small, oval, subconcentrically arranged; legs red.

30 **instabilis**

21—Legs black.

Larger species; basal constriction of the beak strong ....31 **cinereus**
Smaller, the constriction feeble; pronotal sculpture coarse and rugose.

32 **apionides**

Legs rufous or rufo-piceous; pronotal punctures oval or sublinear, distinctly separated.

Interspaces of the pronotal punctures polished; elytral scales large and conspicuous but not dense, only moderately uneven in distribution.

33 **perpusillus**

Interspaces strongly and densely punctulate and dull; elytral scales smaller and more elongate..34 **defricans**

22—Prothorax distinctly wider than long, much more than one-half as wide as the elytra at their point of greatest width.

Pronotal punctures very dense, reniform or sublunate; elytra in great part rufous ....35 **gibbirostris**

Pronotal punctures large, rounded, very dense; elytra black throughout.

36 **squalidus**

Prothorax much narrower, never more than slightly exceeding one-half the maximum width of the elytra, nearly as long as wide; body much smaller than in *squalidus* ....37 **ovipennis**

1 S. lineolatus n. sp.—Robust, convex, oblong-oval, black, the tibiæ rufescent; scales of the upper surface white, moderate in size, unevenly distributed, feebly mottled toward the suture, forming a dense conspicuous line at the base of the third and seventh intervals, and, on the fifth, almost throughout its extent; on the under surface white and very dense but sparser on the metasternum than on its episterna. *Head* squamulose, the transverse constriction fine, deep; beak in the male moderately stout, evenly arcuate, punctate, sparsely squamulose, equal in length to the head and prothorax, with the antennæ inserted at apical two-fifths, in the female longer, evenly, strongly arcuate, smooth, much longer than the head and prothorax and three-fifths as long as the elytra, the antennæ inserted at about the middle; antennæ long, slender, the second funicular joint but slightly shorter than the first and longer than the next two, the club rather slender, elongate, fusiform, very densely pubescent. *Prothorax* one-third wider than long, not strongly inflated, usually more strongly arcuate before the middle, strongly and broadly constricted behind the apex, the latter nearly four-fifths as wide as the base; disk strongly, densely punctate, with a broad darker median vitta in which the scales become narrow, sparse and transversely arranged. *Elytra* at base nearly one-half wider than the prothorax, not quite three times as long, the sides rapidly convergent toward the acutely parabolic apex, becoming parallel and nearly straight in basal half; striæ rather coarse, deep, punctured at the bottom. Length 2.3–3.3 mm.; width 1.15–1.55 mm.

Illinois; Texas.

A distinctly marked species, apparently rather abundant. My first specimens were received some years since from Mr. F. M. Webster.

In this species the pronotal scales are not arranged like those of *corpulentus* and *discoideus*, where they radiate from a central point. The punctures toward the middle of the pronotum are also different, being transverse and not rounded.

2 **S. discoideus** Lec.—Proc. Am. Phil. Soc., XV, p. 169 (Pachytychius).

Robust, oval, convex, black, the legs slightly rufo-piceous; scales moderate in size, closely decumbent, widely overlapping, white or yellowish-white, the middle of the pronotum broadly, and a large sutural basal and small lateral median area of the elytra, both uneven, clothed more sparsely with blackish scales; recurved setæ of the elytra in the form of elongate concolorous scales and scarcely visible under low power. Beak in the male thick, punctured, squamulose, dull, evenly, feebly arcuate, but slightly longer than the head and prothorax, with the antennæ inserted at apical third, in the female much longer, a little more slender, smoother, less punctate, evenly, moderately arcuate, two-thirds as long as the elytra, with the antennæ inserted at apical two-fifths; antennæ long, the second funicular joint three-fourths as long as the first and fully as long as the next two. Prothorax two-fifths wider than long, parallel, evenly and strongly rounded on the sides, constricted behind the apex. Elytra at base one-fourth wider than the prothorax, a little more than twice as long; sides arcuate, convergent behind and feebly sinuate in the male; disk convex, the striæ becoming coarse, deep and strongly punctate in the basal darker area. Tarsal claws slender, feebly divergent, connate in basal fourth. Length 3.0–3.2 mm.; width 1.6–1.75 mm.

Illinois. A well-known species of rather large size and obese form. One badly preserved male before me, taken by Mr. Wickham, at Elko, Nevada, cannot be distinguished from the eastern forms except by its slightly shorter beak.

3 **S. corpulentus** Lec.—Proc. Am. Phil. Soc., XV, p. 170.

Robust, convex, rather broadly oval, black, the legs bright rufous; scales of the upper surface elongate-oval, narrowly truncate at apex,

widely overlapping and extremely dense, yellowish in color, a large
suffused sutural spot from the middle of the elytra to the scutellum,
becoming narrower anteriorly, equally densely clothed with brown
scales; median parts of the pronotum rather darker, the scales being
slightly sparser; recurved setæ indistinct.   Head finely but roughly
punctate, squamulose anteriorly, the constriction fine, deep; beak
in the male not very thick, feebly, evenly arcuate, dull, punctate,
sparsely squamose, quite distinctly longer than the head and prothorax, the antennæ inserted at apical third, in the female longer,
smoother, minutely, sparsely punctate except toward base, evenly,
moderately arcuate, three-fifths as long as the elytra, the antennæ
inserted at apical two-fifths; antennæ moderate, second funicular
joint fully as long as the next two but rather longer in the female
than in the male; club somewhat large, elongate-oval.   Prothorax
one-half wider than long, the sides subparallel, strongly, evenly
arcuate, more convergent anteriorly and very broadly, just visibly
constricted.   Elytra at base one-fourth wider than the prothorax,
nearly three times as long; sides nearly straight and scarcely at all
arcuate in basal half; disk just visibly wider behind the middle;
apex acutely, evenly ogival; striæ fine throughout.   Length 2 0–2.8
mm.; width 1.0–1.55 mm.

Texas (Austin and El Paso); Arkansas and Louisiana.   I found
this species some years ago in great abundance on the banks of the
Colorado River, in June.   It is allied to *discoideus* and differs in
its fine elytral striæ toward the middle and base, in the narrower
bodily form and smaller size, red legs, and in the color of the vestiture.   The brown subbasal spot of the elytra is frequently obsoles-
cent.

4 S. amœnus Say.—Curc. 26, Ed. Lec., I, p. 294 (Tychius); Lec.: Proc.
Am. Phil. Soc., XV, p. 168 (Pachytychius).

Broadly oval, convex, black, the legs rufous to piceous; upper
surface clothed densely throughout with rather large, coarsely strigose scales, which are not imbricated on the elytra, confusedly mottled whitish and dark brown, the whitish scales more conspicuous
at the base of the third interval and in two distant vittæ on the disk
of the pronotum, often visible only in basal half; under surface and
lateral edges of the prothorax densely clothed with whitish scales.
Beak thick, feebly arcuate, longer than the head and prothorax,
dull, rugose, densely squamose and with the usual fasciculate tufts
at base; antennæ inserted at apical two-fifths, the second joint of

the funicle two-thirds as long as the first and not quite equal to the next two. Prothorax strongly inflated and rounded on the sides, two-fifths wider than long, strongly narrowed and broadly distinctly constricted toward apex, the latter scarcely more than three-fifths as wide as the disk. Elytra at base only just visibly wider than the disk of the prothorax, a little more than twice as long, just perceptibly longer than wide, broadly rounded at the sides and gradually strongly narrowed behind to the acutely rounded apex; striæ coarse, not entirely concealed by the vestiture. Length 2.0–2.6 mm.; width 1.15–1.4 mm.

Lake Superior and Dakota. The description is taken from the male.

5 S. fulvus Lec.—Proc. Am. Phil. Soc., XV, p. 172.

Oblong-oval, convex, black throughout, the legs sometimes dark piceous; integuments densely, uniformly clothed above with moderately large elongate-oval reddish-orange scales, which become smaller, nearly white and somewhat uneven in distribution beneath; recurved setæ fine and not conspicuous. Beak in the male rather slender, smooth, shining and feebly punctate beyond the antennæ, punctate, opaque and slightly squamulose toward base, feebly arcuate, nearly as long as the head and prothorax, with the antennæ inserted just beyond the middle, in the female much longer but not thinner, cylindrical, almost perfectly straight, smooth, shining, feebly punctate and opaque near the base, three-fifths as long as the elytra, with the antennæ inserted distinctly behind the middle; fulvous corniculate tufts at the base conspicuous; antennæ rather short, the second funicular joint but slightly longer than the third. Prothorax a little wider than long, the sides quite strongly convergent from base to apex, broadly, feebly arcuate, distinctly constricted behind the apex, the latter scarcely three-fifths as wide as the base. Elytra parallel in basal half, two-fifths wider than the prothorax and three times as long, the sides not constricted before the apex; striæ indicated by broad partings in the vestiture. Legs moderate; tarsal claws thick, connate in basal third. Length 2.6–3.0 mm.; width 1.1–1.25.

Missouri, Nebraska, Kansas and New Mexico. A sufficiently abundant and isolated species, without any especially close ally in our fauna.

6 S. quadrifer n. sp.—Oblong-oval, moderately convex, black, the legs more or less rufous; vestiture dense, consisting of oval imbricated scales,

whitish toward the sides and along the middle of the pronotum and broadly
in the middle of the elytra, brown elsewhere, yellowish-white and very dense
beneath, the elytra with a large sutural quadrate spot from basal sixth to
just behind the middle, which is abruptly limited and clothed with piceous-
black scales; recurved setæ not very conspicuous. *Head* squamose, the constriction deep; beak in the male thick, feebly arcuate, slightly longer than
the head and prothorax, densely opaque, conspicuously squamose and hispid
almost throughout, the basal tufts distinct; antennæ inserted near apical
third, the second joint of the funicle but slightly longer than the third. *Prothorax* very slightly wider than long, subparallel and broadly, rather feebly
arcuate at the sides, distinctly constricted behind the apex. *Elytra* at base
two-fifths wider than the prothorax, not quite three times as long, parallel
and nearly straight at the sides in basal half, the striæ indicated laterally
only by the finest partings of the vestiture, more distinct toward the suture.
Tarsal claws rather small, connate in basal third. Length 2.2 mm.; width
1.0 mm.

Arizona.

The large subbasal quadrate spot of velvety black will serve to
render this species easily recognizable. It somewhat resembles
vestitus in outline, but is rather stouter. Two specimens.

7 **S. profusus** n. sp.—Oblong, convex, black, the legs scarcely piceous;
body densely clothed above with large, broadly oval, piceous scales, widely
overlapping, feebly and confusedly intermixed with slightly paler scales on
the elytra and narrowly paler along the middle of the pronotum; scales of
the under surface rather paler and not quite so large; recurved setæ of the
elytra not conspicuous, more evident anteriorly. *Head* squamose; constriction
deep; beak in the male short, rather stout, feebly, evenly arcuate and slightly
tapering from base to apex, densely punctate, hispid throughout with stout
erect setæ, and, in addition, very densely squamose toward base, as long as
the head and prothorax, the antennæ inserted just visibly beyond the middle,
in the female but little longer, more slender, feebly arcuate, smooth, polished,
very minutely, sparsely punctulate and glabrous, but rather suddenly swollen,
hispid and very densely squamose in a little more than basal fourth, slightly
longer than the head and prothorax but not more than two-fifths as long as
the elytra, the antennæ inserted at basal two-fifths; antennæ rather long, the
second funicular joint as long as the next two in the female, shorter in the
male. *Prothorax* nearly one-third wider than long, the sides parallel and
straight in basal two-thirds, then rounded convergent and feebly constricted
to the apex, the latter not more than one-half as wide as the base; punctures
when denuded rather large, round and well separated. *Elytra* at base one-
half wider than the prothorax, about three times as long, parallel in basal
two-thirds, then rapidly, acutely ogival; striæ indicated by narrow partings
of the vestiture. Tarsal claws rather small, subparallel, connate toward base.
Length 2.4–3.7 mm.; width 1.15–1.7 mm.

Arizona (Benson).   Mr. G. W. Dunn.

A widely isolated species, one of the largest of the genus, but varying remarkably in size.   It was taken in abundance.

8 **S. intricatus** n. sp.—Oblong-oval, robust, convex, black throughout; scales of the upper surface large, very dense, dark brown and whitish confusedly intermixed, the recurved setæ very coarse, semi-erect, sparse but very conspicuous: scales of the under surface also large, generally paler but intermixed with a few which are darker. *Head* squamose anteriorly; constriction strong; beak in the male very thick but somewhat long, evenly, distinctly arcuate, feebly tapering, coarsely, very densely punctured, glabrous toward apex, densely hispido-squamose toward base, longer than the head and prothorax and a little more than one-half as long as the elytra; antennæ inserted at apical two-fifths, sparsely clothed with long parallel-sided squamules; second funicular joint one-half longer than the third. *Prothorax* convex, parallel and nearly straight at the sides in basal three-fourths, then rounded and deeply constricted; apex three-fourths as wide as the base; punctures not very large, round, distinct and well separated. *Elytra* at base fully one-half wider than the prothorax, not quite three times as long, barely more than one-third longer than wide, slightly widest behind the middle, the apex broadly ogival; striæ strong and not very fine. Tarsal claws moderate. Length 2.8 mm.; width 1.45 mm.

Texas (El Paso).   Mr. Dunn.

The moderately large size, robust convex form, large scales and generally rough hispid appearance will aid in the identification of this distinct species.   It is represented before me by a single male. A specimen from Arizona is slightly more elongate, with the beak less punctate and squamose, the antennæ being inserted just beyond the middle; it is probably the female.

9 **S. pusio** Lec.—Proc. Am. Phil. Soc., XV, p. 171.

Oblong-oval, convex, moderately stout, black, the legs and beak piceous, extremely densely clothed throughout with rather large overlapping non-strigose scales, uniformly pale ochreous-yellow in color; recurved setæ very sparse, subdecumbent and not at all conspicuous.   Beak in the female rather slender, distinctly, evenly arcuate, about one-half as long as the elytra, smooth and minutely, sparsely punctate in apical half, punctured, dull and densely squamose toward base and feebly bifasciculate just before the very feeble transverse impression; antennæ inserted at the middle, short, strongly squamulose, the second funicular joint slightly longer than the third.   Prothorax slightly wider than long, the sides convergent and very obsoletely constricted near the apex. Elytra at base rather more than one-third wider than the prothorax, nearly three times as long, two-fifths longer than wide, parallel and straight at the sides in basal three-fifths, then narrowly parabolic; striæ indicated only by the finest and feeblest partings of the dense crust of scales; third interval a little more prominent and convex. Length 1.75 mm.; width 0.75 mm.

Lower California (Cape San Lucas). Cab. LeConte. A minute but distinct form, not closely allied to any other and readily recognizable by the dense crust of ochreous-yellow scales, and the rather prominent third interval of the elytra. It is distinctly stouter than the Arizonian *silaceus*.

10 **S. corniculatus** Fahr.—Sch. Gen. Curc., VII, ii, p. 309 (Tychius); *squamulatus* Lec.: Proc. Am. Phil. Soc., XV, p. 173.

Oblong-oval, rather robust, convex, black, the legs paler; vestiture dark gray, feebly and distantly mottled with whitish on the elytra, and generally with a short whitish line at base of the third interval; scales broadly oval, very dense, a tuft of erect squamules above each eye, and with the usual erect recurved squamules on the pronotum and elytra. Beak in the male a little longer than the head and prothorax, rather thick, punctate and squamose, very feebly arcuate, with the antennæ inserted at apical two-fifths, in the female distinctly longer, more slender and tapering, smooth, a little more arcuate and nearly one-half as long as the body, with the antennæ inserted slightly behind the middle, the second joint of the funicle one-half longer than the third. Prothorax small, one-fourth wider than long, narrowed and feebly constricted near the apex. Elytra at base one-half wider than the prothorax, very nearly three times as long, one-half longer than wide, the sides straight and parallel in basal half, then gradually acutely ogival; striæ fine. Length 2.0–2.4 mm.; width 0.9–1.1 mm.

Massachusetts and Pennsylvania (near Philadelphia); Michigan— Cab. LeConte. This is one of our most abundant eastern species, somewhat resembling *flavicans*, but smaller and less mottled. It agrees throughout with the description given by Fahræus, which was founded upon a Pennsylvania example sent to him by Zimmermann.

11 **S. imbricatus** n. sp.—Narrowly oblong, convex, black throughout and very densely clothed above with large broad ogival scales, which widely

overlap in a longitudinal direction, blackish-gray and whitish confusedly intermingled, the latter more prevalent toward the sides ; scales of the under surface smaller and nearly white, extremely dense ; recurved setæ sparse, dark brown and inconspicuous. *Head* densely squamulose, the vestiture decumbent ; transverse sulcus distinct ; beak in both sexes densely clothed almost throughout with short sparse setæ and large recumbent and close-set scales, tufted and erect at base, in the male short, just visibly bent, stout, scarcely longer than the head and prothorax, the antennæ inserted at apical two-fifths, in the female distinctly longer, evenly, distinctly arcuate, scarcely more slender, a little more than one-half as long as the elytra, with the antennæ inserted just beyond the middle ; antennæ moderate, the second funicular joint nearly one-half longer than the third ; basal joint not quite as long as the next three in the female, slightly shorter in the male. *Prothorax* very small and narrow, nearly as long as wide, with subparallel and very feebly arcuate sides, subapical constriction broad and feeble ; apex four-fifths as wide as the base. *Elytra* at base very nearly twice as wide as the prothorax, a little more than three times as long, two-thirds longer than wide ; sides straight and parallel to the middle, then narrowly parabolic, the sides in apical third strongly convergent and nearly straight ; striæ fine, completely concealed by the large scales.   Length 1.7–2.2 mm. ; width 0.7–0.9 mm.

California (Majave) ; Arizona (Riverside).   Mr. H. F. Wickham. This species resembles *seriatus*, but is easily distinguishable by its still smaller subcylindrical prothorax, and very large imbricated scales of the upper surface.   It was taken in considerable abundance and I have before me eight specimens.

12 **S. silaceus** n. sp.—Narrowly oblong-oval, moderately convex, black, the legs dull rufo-piceous, the tarsi blackish ; vestiture consisting of moderately large, elongate-oval scales, extremely dense, widely overlapping, pale ochreous in color, feebly variegated with a slightly darker brown, finer and sparser in two wide approximate pronotal vittæ, which are thereby darker in tint ; on the under surface whitish, broadly rounded and dense ; recurved setæ stout but short and not very conspicuous. *Head* squamulose, the constriction distinct ; beak in the male short, stout, dull, densely punctate, squamulose except beyond the antennæ, very feebly arcuate, subequal in length to the head and prothorax, with the antennæ inserted at apical third, in the female slightly longer, more slender and arcuate, smooth, polished and minutely, sparsely punctate in apical two-fifths, slightly longer than the head and prothorax and just visibly more than one-half as long as the elytra, with the antennæ inserted at apical two-fifths ; basal fasciculate tufts rather distinct ; antennæ short, the second funicular joint but slightly longer than the third. *Prothorax* very nearly as long as wide, the sides broadly, evenly arcuate, feebly convergent and very broadly, feebly sinuate near the apex. *Elytra* at base one-third to two-fifths wider than the prothorax, nearly three times as long, one-half longer than wide, the sides parallel and straight in basal half,

then gradually acutely ogival; striæ indicated by narrow partings of the vestiture.   Length 1.4–1.7 mm.; width 0.6–0.7 mm.

Arizona.

The five specimens in my cabinet display scarcely any variation. This is one of the most minute species of the genus, and will be easily known by the characters given.

13 **S. spurcus** n. sp.—Rather broadly oblong-oval, moderately convex, black, the beak piceous; legs rufous, blackish near the base, the tarsi blackish; vestiture of the upper surface consisting of extremely dense, widely imbricated, pale ochreous-yellow scales, rather small in size, uniformly dense throughout the pronotum, scarcely visibly uneven in coloration on the elytra, nearly similar beneath and equally dense; recurved setæ stout, rather abundant but concolorous and not very conspicuous. *Head* densely squamose, the constriction rather feeble; beak in the female slender, distinctly, evenly arcuate, rather densely squamose in basal half but nude, polished, minutely, sparsely punctate thence to the apex, about three-fifths as long as the elytra; antennæ inserted at apical two-fifths, the second funicular joint but slightly longer than the third. *Prothorax* very nearly as long as wide, the sides broadly, feebly arcuate and gradually convergent, nearly straight and not perceptibly constricted anteriorly to the apex, the latter three-fourths as wide as the base; sculpture entirely concealed by the dense even crust of scales. *Elytra* at base fully one-half wider than the prothorax, three times as long, one-half longer than wide, the sides straight and parallel in basal half, then angulato-parabolic; striæ indicated only by narrow and rather ill-defined partings of the vestiture.   Length 1.9 mm.; width 0.85 mm.

Texas.

The single female before me represents a species somewhat allied to *silaceus*, but decidedly different in its shorter, broader form, wider elytra, longer beak in the female and uniformly, densely covered pronotum.

14 **S. vestitus** Lec.—Proc. Am. Phil. Soc., XV, p. 172.

Rather narrowly oblong-oval, convex, blackish, the beak, antennæ, legs and elytra rufo-testaceous, the latter with the suture and base clouded with piceous; vestiture consisting of rather small elongate-oval yellowish scales, moderately dense, sometimes quite sparse, not mottled, intermixed with distinct recurved setæ.   Beak in the male short, stout, feebly arcuate, tapering, smooth and nude toward apex, scarcely longer than the head and prothorax, with the antennæ inserted at apical two-fifths, in the female much longer, smooth, cylindrical, subglabrous and subimpunctate, slightly squamose toward base, evenly, moderately arcuate, rather more than one-half as long as the elytra, with the antennæ inserted distinctly behind the middle; antennæ slender, the second funicular joint fully as long as the next two in the female, slightly shorter in the male. Prothorax nearly as long as wide, evenly rounded at the sides, feebly narrowed but scarcely at all constricted toward apex. Elytra at base one-half wider than the prothorax, a little more than three times as long, parallel in basal half, the sides broadly, feebly but distinctly constricted before the apex. Length 1.7–2.2 mm.; width 0.7–1.0 mm.

Kansas, Colorado and Montana. The tarsal claws in this distinct and easily recognizable species are unusually long and divergent but connate at base.

15 **S. sparsus** n. sp.—Oblong-oval, convex, deep black throughout, the vestiture of the upper surface consisting of small elongate-oval whitish scales, uniform throughout and very sparsely scattered over the elytra, the striæ indicated by partings which are wider than the grooves, rather denser, and wider beneath on the sterna and their side-pieces. *Head* subglabrous, alutaceous, finely but strongly reticulate; transverse constriction well marked, fine; beak in the male rather long, evenly cylindrical and somewhat thick throughout, feebly, evenly arcuate, sparsely but strongly punctate and subglabrous in apical half, finely and sparsely squamulose and more opaque toward base with the two fasciculate basal tufts small, distinctly longer than the head and prothorax and one-half as long as the elytra; antennæ inserted at the middle, the second funicular joint subequal to the next two. *Prothorax* slightly wider than long, the sides feebly convergent, broadly, evenly arcuate nearly to the apex, the subapical constriction not large but distinct; apex three-fourths as wide as the base; disk not very coarsely but deeply, closely and evenly punctate, the punctures not much obscured by the vestiture. *Elytra* at base one-half wider than the prothorax, three times as long, fully one-half longer than wide, parallel and nearly straight at the sides in basal half, then gradually ogival, not constricted before the apex; striæ fine, deep, consisting of narrow approximate linear punctures near the sides. Tarsal claws rather long, stout, pointed, distinctly divergent but completely connate at base. Length 2.5 mm.; width 1.1 mm.

Colorado.

The single specimen represents a species allied to *sordidus* and *griseus*, but differs in the small, widely-scattered scales and black legs. From the male of *sordidus* it differs in its much longer, non-tapering, sparsely squamulose beak, with the antennæ inserted at the middle. The male of *griseus* I have not at hand, but the female differs from the type of *sparsus* in its very much larger and more elongate prothorax.

16 **S. pleuralis** n. sp.—Robust, oblong-oval, convex, black, the legs red
with the tarsi darker, extremely densely clothed above with large scales, abruptly white in lateral sixth of the pronotum and more than lateral fourth of
the elytra, elsewhere above dark red-brown, smaller, whitish, very dense
beneath ; brown scales above easily denuded, the white more persistent. *Head*
finely granulate, obscurely areolate ; transverse impression feeble ; beak rather
slender, distinctly arcuate, strongly punctured throughout, opaque toward
base, squamulose, the scales suberect laterally toward base, equal in length
to the head and prothorax ; antennæ inserted a little beyond the middle, the
basal joint of the funicle about as long as the next two, second rather more
than one-half longer than the third. *Prothorax* very nearly as long as wide ;
sides parallel, broadly, evenly arcuate, convergent and distinctly constricted
very near the apex, the latter two-thirds as wide as the base ; disk where
denuded strongly, rather closely, evenly perforato-punctate, the interspaces
narrow but smooth and polished. *Elytra* at base one-third wider than the
prothorax, two and one-half times as long, not more than one-third longer
than wide, nearly straight and parallel at the sides in basal half, then narrowly parabolic, with the convergent sides nearly straight ; striæ fine, deep
toward the middle when denuded. Length 2.0 mm. ; width 1.0 mm.

Arizona.

A single specimen which is probably a female ; the second ventral
segment is minutely but quite distinctly angulated posteriorly at the
sides.

17 **S. obtectus** Lec.—Proc. Am. Phil. Soc., XV, p. 171.

Oblong-oval, convex, deep black throughout, polished when denuded, the pronotum then strongly, closely, evenly punctured ;
integuments densely clothed with rather large, deeply and coarsely
strigose, elongate-oval scales, widely overlapping longitudinally on
the elytra, dark brown in color, very feebly and indefinitely mottled
with cinereous toward the sides ; recurved setæ as usual. Beak in
the male rather thick, feebly arcuate, densely squamose, opaque,
scarcely longer than the prothorax, the antennæ inserted near apical
two-fifths, in the female slightly thinner, nearly straight, as long
as the head and prothorax, otherwise similar to that of the male,
the antennæ inserted just visibly beyond the middle ; basal squamulose tufts very prominent ; antennæ moderate, the basal joint of
the funicle subequal to the next three, second one-half longer than
the third. Prothorax large and long, fully as long as wide, the
sides parallel and broadly arcuate, becoming convergent and strongly
constricted toward apex, the latter three-fourths as wide as the base.
Elytra at base not more than one-third wider than the prothorax,

scarcely more than twice as long; sides parallel and straight in basal half, then narrowly parabolic; striæ fine, deep, strongly punctured laterally.   Length 1.8–2.8 mm.; width 0.75–1.2 mm.

California (Los Angeles and San Diego).   A very distinct species, easily identifiable by its large elongate prothorax.   The vestiture is very easily abraded, and, out of a large series which I took at San Diego, there is scarcely a specimen having more than a few scattered scales on the upper surface.   One specimen in my cabinet is labeled "Arizona."

18 S. sordidus Lec.—Proc. Am. Phil. Soc., XV, p. 173.

Oblong-oval, convex, black, the legs dull rufous; integuments densely clothed with moderately large, broadly oval scales, uniform in coloration, ochreous to cinereous on the upper surface, whiter beneath; recurved setæ small and distant.   Beak in the male short, thick, nearly straight, feebly tapering from base to apex, coarsely, densely squamose except near the apex, coarsely punctate, scarcely longer than the head and prothorax, with the antennæ inserted a little beyond the middle, in the female long, very slender, equally, evenly cylindrical and feebly arcuate throughout, smooth, finely, sparsely punctate, squamose only very near the base, one-half longer than the head and prothorax and scarcely visibly shorter than the elytra, with the antennæ inserted somewhat behind basal two-fifths; antennæ slender, the second funicular joint slightly shorter than the next two.   Prothorax distinctly narrowed from base to apex, broadly, rather strongly rounded at the sides, deeply constricted behind the apex, the latter three-fourths as wide as the base; disk convex, slightly wider than long.   Elytra at base one-fourth to one-third wider than the prothorax, two and one-half times as long.   Length 2.1–2.4 mm.; width 0.8–1.05 mm.

Texas.   A rather small species, allied completely in the structure of the beak, both in the male and female, to *constrictus* (Desmoris). The original description is greatly in error in stating that the tarsal claws are not connate; they are rather long and completely connate in basal fourth.   The head behind the transverse groove is abruptly and completely glabrous, highly polished, sometimes with merely a very feeble transversely wavy strigilation, while in *griseus* it is dull and strongly, coarsely reticulate.

19 S. constrictus Say.—Journ. Ac. Nat. Sci., Phila., III, p. 313; Ed. Lec. II, p. 176 (Rhynchænus); Lec.: Proc. Am. Phil. Soc., XV, p. 168 (Desmoris).

Oblong-oval, black, densely and uniformly clothed with elongate-oval appressed scales, cinereous to ochreous in color, each interval of the elytra with a single series of short robust recurved squamules.

This species is either one of the most variable of curculionides in structural peculiarities affecting parts of the body referred to by LeConte for generic characters, or the large series before me is made up of closely allied species which can only be differentiated by the collection of abundant material from carefully recorded localities. I will at present simply describe certain modifications noticed in three female types taken in Iowa, New Mexico and northern California respectively:

1—Beak fully one-half as long as the body, extremely slender; basal joint of the funicle barely as long as the next two, the second fully three-fourths as long as the first; legs, tarsi and antennæ pale rufous; beak rufescent.

2—Beak very long, nearly two-thirds as long as the body, thicker; basal joint of the funicle fully as long as the next three; second one-half as long as the first; legs, antennæ and beak throughout black.

3—Beak much shorter, stouter, two-fifths as long as the body; basal joint of funicle longer than the next two; legs rufous, the tarsi darker; beak and antennæ blackish, the club paler.

In the male the beak is very much shorter and thicker, densely punctate, squamose, with the antennæ inserted just beyond the middle. Length 2.2–4.0 mm.; width 1.0–1.8 mm.

Iowa to Arizona, northern California. A very abundant species; the smallest and largest in my series of thirty or more specimens are both females.

20 **S. griseus** Lec.—Proc. Am. Phil. Soc., XV, p. 171.

Narrowly oblong-oval, convex, black, the legs dark rufo-piceous; scales moderate in size, broadly oval, dark brownish and paler, dense but not overlapping on the upper surface, white and very dense beneath. Beak in the female very slender, cylindrical, just visibly bent, much longer than the head and prothorax and nearly two-thirds as long as the elytra, punctured, opaque and squamulose toward base, smooth and with small subelongate erosions toward apex; antennæ inserted slightly behind the middle, short, the scape not quite attaining the eye; second funicular joint but slightly longer than the third. Prothorax large, fully as long as wide, sub-parallel and broadly, evenly and strongly arcuate at the sides, rather strongly but gradually narrowed and broadly, feebly constricted toward the apex, the latter three-fourths as wide as the base; disk convex, rather coarsely, deeply, densely punctate, widest behind the middle. Elytra at base scarcely more than one-fourth wider than the prothorax, just visibly more than twice as long, one-half longer than wide, parallel in basal half, then regularly, acutely ogival, not constricted before the apex; striæ deep but not very coarse. Tarsal claws rather small, nearly parallel, connate toward base. Length 2.3 mm.; width 0.9 mm.

Texas. Resembles *scapalis*, except in the color and disposition of the scales and in its very much smaller size.

21 **S. connivens** n. sp.—Oblong-oval, moderately stout and convex, piceous-black, the beak, antennæ and legs throughout rufous; vestiture very dense and uniform, consisting of moderately large, coarsely strigose, grayish-white scales, with intermixed recurved setæ, concolorous, dense and but slightly smaller on the under surface. *Head* not very densely squamulose, the constriction feeble; beak in the female very slender, gradually, just visibly thicker from the antennæ to the base, feebly, evenly arcuate, polished and impunctate in apical half, thence gradually more punctured, opaque and sparsely, finely squamulose to the base, much longer than the head and prothorax and about three-fifths as long as the elytra, the basal tufts composed of long slender squamules; antennæ inserted at the middle, the second funicular joint three-fourths as long as the first and about equal to the next two. *Prothorax* very nearly as long as wide, the sides broadly arcuate, gradually convergent, broadly and just visibly sinuate to the apex, the latter scarcely more than two-thirds as wide as the base; disk strongly, densely punctate and subrugose, the punctures tending strongly to coalesce. *Elytra* at base two-fifths wider than the prothorax, not quite three times as long, slightly less than one-half longer than wide, the sides straight and parallel in basal three-fifths, the apex evenly ogival; striæ indicated by coarse partings of the vestiture. *Legs* rather long and decidedly slender; tarsal claws as usual. Length 2.3 mm.; width 1.0 mm.

Missouri (St. Louis). Mr. Hugo Soltau.

A moderately small species, without any striking features, but evidently different from any other here brought to notice. It appears to combine certain of the characteristics of *sordidus* and *flavicans*, but differs from the former in its much shorter beak and medial antennæ in the female, and from the latter in the disposition of the vestiture. It is represented by a single female specimen.

22 **S. seriatus** Lec.—Proc. Am. Phil. Soc., XV, p. 172.

Oblong, rather convex, piceous, clothed densely with elongate-oval scales, yellowish and confusedly, feebly nubilate with white above, especially at the base of the third interval, uneven in distribution near the suture, very dense and white throughout beneath; upper surface with the usual stout recurved setæ not especially prominent. Beak in the female rather long, punctate, decidedly squamulose except beyond the antennæ, very feebly, evenly arcuate and about three-fifths as long as the elytra; antennæ inserted at the middle, rather short, the second funicular joint but very slightly longer than the third. Prothorax small, as long as wide, the sides rounded, feebly convergent and quite distinctly constricted anteriorly, densely and confusedly squamose and setose. Elytra at base nearly one-half wider than the prothorax, about three times as long, one-half longer than wide; sides parallel and straight to the middle, then gradually narrowly parabolic; striæ fine, with large elongate punctures toward the sides; vestiture generally more denuded toward the middle. Length 1.75–2.5 mm.; width 0.7–1.0 mm.

California (Mariposa)—Cab. LeConte; Arizona and Texas. A small species, distinguishable by its small elongate prothorax and rather long beak, which is punctured and more or less squamulose almost throughout, even in the female. In the male it is short, very densely squamose and hispid, as long as the head and prothorax and with the antennæ inserted near apical third. It was taken in great abundance by Mr. Dunn at Benson, Arizona.

The Texan form identified by LeConte as *corniculatus*, belongs to this species.

23 **S. fiducialis** n. sp.—Oblong-oval, convex, rather shining when denuded, black, the legs rufous, blackish at base; elytra broadly pale and rufescent toward the sides; vestiture of the pronotum dense and squamiform at the sides, becoming sparser and fine toward the middle, that of the elytra dense and nearly uniform, consisting of elongate-oval, pointed, yellowish scales, more condensed and coarser in wavy subtransverse areas; on the under surface yellowish-white, the scales smaller and more rounded, dense. *Head* finely squamulose, the constriction deep, the two corniculate tufts long and conspicuous; beak in the male moderately thick, even throughout, not tapering, dull, punctate, deeply furrowed and feebly arcuate toward apex, a little longer than the head and prothorax, nearly one-half as long as the elytra; antennæ inserted at apical third, the second funicular joint but slightly longer than the third. *Prothorax* very nearly as long as wide, the sides broadly, evenly, not very strongly arcuate, moderately convergent, broadly and feebly sinuate toward apex; disk convex, rather coarsely, deeply, evenly and densely punctate, the punctures rounded and all distinct. *Elytra* at base scarcely two-fifths wider than the prothorax, two and one-half times as long, more than one-half longer than wide, evenly elongate-ogival throughout, the sides not

becoming quite parallel toward base; striæ fine, deep and abrupt toward the suture. Length 2.5 mm.; width 1.1 mm.

Iowa.

The only species with which this can be compared are *flavicans* and *scapalis*, but it differs greatly from the former in its longer prothorax, with even circular and distinct punctures and slender sparse squamules toward the middle; in *flavicans* the pronotum is coarsely, densely squamose throughout, and the sculpture consists of more or less pronounced oblique furrows, caused by the coalescence of the punctures. *Scapalis* is a much larger, stouter species, with different color and structure of the vestiture.

24 **S. scapalis** Lec.—Proc. Am. Phil. Soc., XV, p. 168 (Desmoris).

Oval, convex, black; legs dull-rufous, blackish toward base; vestiture consisting of ochreous-yellow scales, moderately dense and forming subtransversely wavy condensed areas on the elytra. In the male the beak is densely punctured, moderately slender, rather longer than the head and prothorax, the antennæ inserted slightly beyond the middle, the basal joint of the funicle equal to the next two; in the female it is slightly longer but scarcely more slender, smoother, almost straight, the antennæ inserted scarcely at all behind the middle, the basal joint of the funicle distinctly longer than the next two, the club longer and narrower. Prothorax very nearly as long as wide, widest behind the middle; sides broadly arcuate, convergent and sinuate toward apex; disk rather coarsely, deeply, densely punctate. Elytra at base about one-third wider than the prothorax, scarcely more than twice as long, the sides straight and parallel in basal third, then gradually ogival; striæ narrow, deep, abrupt, obscurely punctate at the bottom. Length 3.7–4.2 mm.; width 1.7–2.0 mm.

Illinois. One of the largest species of the genus, greatly resembling *flavicans* in the color and disposition of the elytral vestiture, but very different in its more elongate prothorax. It differs radically from *constrictus*, with which it has been associated, in the less pronounced sexual differences in the beak, and in the peculiar arrangement of the elytral scales.

25 **S. flavicans** Lec.—Proc. Am. Phil. Soc., XV, p. 171.

Oblong-oval, rather stout, convex, blackish, with the legs paler, densely clothed with oval scales, ochreous to white in color, strongly mottled on the elytra and generally with a short whitish line at the base of the third interval. Beak in the male one-half as long as the elytra, very feebly arcuate, punctured and squamose, the antennæ inserted a little beyond the middle, the second joint of the funicle slightly longer than the third; in the female but very slightly longer, more slender, smooth, squamulose toward base, very feebly arcuate, the antennæ inserted slightly behind the middle, the second funicular joint as long as the next two. Prothorax slightly wider than long, the sides convergent but not noticeably constricted toward apex, the latter two-thirds as wide as the base. Elytra at base two-fifths wider than the prothorax, between two and three times as long, one-half longer than wide, the sides nearly straight and parallel in basal half; striæ fine. Length 2.3–3.0 mm.; width 1.0–1.5 mm.

Texas, Dakota and Indiana. A rather common species, above the average in point of size, and easily recognizable by the peculiar condensations of larger and paler scales on the elytra, the vestiture of which is, however, very dense throughout. In one male specimen the beak is not longer than the head and prothorax, and very much less than one-half as long as the elytra.

26 **S. congestus** n. sp.—Oval, convex, pale rufo-testaceous throughout, the elytral suture narrowly picescent; vestiture sparse and uneven, yellowish-white, consisting of fine slender sparse squamules, which become larger and squamiform in the condensed spots, of which there are several on the pronotum; elytra with large subtransverse wavy condensed areas; metasternum and abdomen sparsely clothed with very fine elongate squamules, the metepisterna densely squamose. *Head* with a few fine squamules anteriorly; constriction evident; beak in the male moderately thick, not tapering, feebly bent toward apex, opaque, sparsely squamulose, the basal tufts not well developed, longer than the head and prothorax and more than one-half as long as the elytra; antennæ inserted rather beyond apical third, slender, the second funicular joint scarcely longer than the third, both elongate and one-half longer than the fourth. *Prothorax* but slightly wider than long, sub-parallel and strongly, evenly arcuate at the sides, feebly narrowed and finely distinctly constricted near the apex; disk convex, rather coarsely, deeply and closely punctate, the punctures circular. *Elytra* at base one-third wider than the disk of the pronotum, two and one-half times as long, two-fifths longer than wide, ogival, the sides gradually becoming almost parallel and feebly arcuate toward base; striæ distinct. Length 2.0–2.2 mm.; width 1.0–1.15 mm.

Colorado; District of Columbia.

There is no species with which this can be regarded as closely allied. It somewhat suggests *tychioides*, but the pronotal sculpture is of an entirely different order, and it differs from any other form known to me in the elongate third joint of the antennæ. The specimen from the District of Columbia exactly resembles the Colorado type, but has the beak still longer, two-thirds as long as the elytra, smoother, more evenly arcuate, with the antennæ inserted at apical two-fifths; it is without doubt the female.

27 S. tychioides Lec.—Proc. Am. Phil. Soc., XV, p. 171.

Oval, convex, shining, black, the elytra with a very feeble sublateral rufescent vitta; legs red, black near the coxæ; tarsi blackish; vestiture of the upper surface sparse and uneven, very fine and sparse on the pronotum, yellowish and condensed in uneven subtransverse spots of coarse scales on the elytra, the interspaces thinly sprinkled with fine short squamules; under surface very densely clothed throughout with small rounded yellowish-white scales. Beak thick and gibbous toward base, strongly tapering, thin and smooth toward apex, evenly, rather feebly arcuate, slightly longer than the head and prothorax; antennæ inserted slightly beyond the middle, the second funicular joint nearly as long as the next two. Prothorax rather large, strongly convex, slightly wider than long, strongly rounded at the sides, the latter moderately convergent, broadly and just visibly sinuate near the apex; punctures reniform or lunate, small, rather sparse, becoming larger and rugose laterally, without trace of median line; interspaces polished, not reticulate. Elytra at base one-fourth wider than the prothorax, a little more than twice as long, one-third longer than wide, elongate-ogival, becoming almost parallel near the base. Length 2.2 mm.; width 1.1 mm.

Kansas. I am not certain of the sex of the single example before me, but the thick, strongly tapering beak would appear to indicate the male.

28 S. sagittatus n. sp.—Oblong-oval, convex, feebly shining, black, the antennæ piceous with the club paler; legs and tarsi pale rufous, coxæ darker; elytra black, with a broad pale rufous and oblique vitta on each from the humeri to the apex; vestiture almost entirely denuded in the type, but apparently sparse and uneven as in *tychioides*. *Head* dull, the constriction moderately strong; beak thick, dull, equal in diameter and extremely feebly evenly arcuate throughout, a little longer than the head and prothorax; antennæ inserted at apical third, the second funicular joint but slightly longer than the third. *Prothorax* moderate in size, convex, quite distinctly wider than long, the sides evenly, rather strongly rounded, convergent but scarcely constricted anteriorly; disk dull, the sculpture fine, not very deep, extremely dense and peculiar, consisting of long oblique uneven eroded channels, which are evidently formed by the coalescence of reniform punctures of the *tychioides* type, but also with an even median line, entirely impunctate and finely granulato-reticulate. *Elytra* at base one-third wider than the prothorax, fully two and one-half times as long, one-half longer than wide, ogival in apical half, the sides thence straight and parallel to the base ; humeri right, prominent but narrowly rounded ; striæ deep, punctate toward the sides. Length 2.0 mm. ; width 0.85 mm.

Rhode Island.

This species, while allied to *tychioides* and *sculpticollis*, is distinct from both in the narrow granulose clearly limited impunctate median line of the pronotum ; the latter is larger than in *sculpticollis*, but smaller than in *tychioides*. It is represented by a single male example.

29 **S. sculpticollis** n. sp.—Narrowly oval, convex, feebly shining, black, the antennæ piceous, the legs red, darker near the coxæ, the tarsi piceous ; elytra bright rufous, the suture broadly, suffusedly blackish ; vestiture sparse and uneven, fine and sparse at the sides of the prothorax, confusedly mottled with condensed areas of larger yellowish-white scales and small sparse slender squamules on the elytra ; under surface clothed sparsely with small elongate squamules, very dense on the met-episterna. *Head* dull, subglabrous ; constriction very deep ; beak in the male thick, dull, punctate, sparsely squamulose, evenly cylindrical, not tapering, evenly, feebly arcuate, distinctly longer than the head and prothorax, with the antennæ inserted just behind apical third, in the female slightly longer and smoother, evenly cylindrical, evenly, moderately arcuate, nearly three-fifths as long as the elytra, with the antennæ inserted at apical two-fifths ; antennæ moderate, the second funicular joint much shorter than the next two. *Prothorax* small, slightly wider than long, convex, strongly, evenly rounded at the sides, feebly narrowed but scarcely at all constricted near the apex, very deeply, densely sculptured, the sculpture consisting of moderately small reniform punctures, close-set and often coalescent, with the narrow interspaces more or less punctulate, without trace of median line. *Elytra* at base one-half wider than the prothorax, fully two and one-half times as long, elongate-ogival, the sides becoming parallel and nearly straight in basal half ; striæ distinct, obsoletely punctate. Length 2.1–2.25 mm. ; width 0.9–1.0 mm.

Virginia ; Indiana ; Texas.

A common species, allied to *tychioides*, but abundantly distinct in its much smaller, more coarsely and densely sculptured prothorax and very different beak, also in the shorter second funicular joint, and sparser and narrow scales of the metasternum.

30 **S. instabilis** n. sp.—Oblong-oval, stout, convex, intense black, polished when denuded, the pronotum feebly alutaceous, with the punctures

rather small, not very deep and slightly oval, the interspaces finely punctulate; scales whitish, narrowly oval, dense; legs bright rufous, the tarsi darker. *Head* minutely punctate; constriction strong; beak rather thick, feebly arcuate, densely punctate in basal half, the apical regions sparsely so and shining, equal in length to the head and prothorax; antennæ inserted slightly beyond the middle, the basal joint of the funicle not quite as long as the next three, second one-half longer than the third. *Prothorax* large, not quite as long as wide, the sides rounded before the middle, thence feebly convergent and nearly straight to the base, very deeply constricted at some distance behind the apex, the latter tubulate and barely three-fourths as wide as the base; disk widest before the middle. *Elytra* at base two-fifths wider than the prothorax, two and one-half times as long, not quite one-half longer than wide, the sides straight and parallel in basal half, then narrowly parabolic; striæ fine, deep, scarcely at all impressed and with elongate narrow punctures laterally. Length 2.0 mm.; width 0.9 mm.

California (Napa Co.).

The single specimen, which I took at Suscol Station, is almost entirely denuded above, with only a small spot of white scales near the middle of each elytron and others yellowish in color scattered thence to the apex; the two spots are unsymmetrical and therefore simply remnants of the vestiture; the specimen is probably a female. The beak is sparsely and rather finely setulose, with a small abrupt tuft of white squamules above each eye. This species is easily separable from *obtectus* by its shorter, more obese form and red legs, from *cinereus* by its large prothorax, and from both by the different sculpture of the pronotum.

31 S. cinereus Mots.—Bull. Mosc., 1845, II, p. 376; Lec.: Proc. Am. Phil. Soc., XV, p. 173.

Oblong-oval, convex, black throughout, the legs rarely with a feeble piceous tinge; integuments densely clothed with elongate-oval dark brown and cinereous scales, confusedly and not conspicuously mottled on the elytra, the surface polished black when denuded, the pronotum rather finely but very deeply and closely punctate, the punctures not in actual contact, perforate. Beak differing scarcely at all in the sexes, short, thick, strongly, densely punctate, sparsely squamulose, with two erect tufts at base, very feebly arcuate and but very slightly longer than the head and prothorax; antennæ inserted near apical third in the male and two-fifths in the female, the basal joint of the funicle fully as long as the next three, second barely longer than the third. Prothorax but slightly wider than long, the sides broadly arcuate, broadly, feebly constricted behind the apex, the latter scarcely three-fourths as wide as the base. Elytra at base one-half wider than the prothorax, very nearly three times as long, one-half to three-fifths longer than wide, straight and parallel at the sides in basal half to three-fifths; striæ fine, deep, distinctly punctured toward the sides. Length 2.1–2.7 mm.; width 0.9–1.2 mm.

California (San Francisco), abundant. The commonest species of the middle coast regions of California, and easily known by the characters given. I cannot perceive that the elytra are notably elongate in this species, as remarked by LeConte, but the very feeble sexual difference in the beak is a distinguishing character.

32 **S. apionides** n. sp.—Narrowly oblong-oval, convex, deep black throughout the body, legs and antennæ; vestiture sparse, consisting of small remote setiform squamules on the elytra, with small sparse condensed spots of wider white scales, the latter also more abundant on the pronotum toward the sides; under surface sparsely and unevenly squamose. *Head* finely granulato-reticulate, the transverse impression feeble but distinct; beak in the male short, thick, feebly arcuate, dull and granulose, punctate, sparsely setulose, not fasciculate at base, very slightly longer than the head and prothorax, with the antennæ inserted just beyond the middle, in the female nearly similar, slightly longer, scarcely thinner or more arcuate, smoother and more shining throughout, distinctly longer than the head and prothorax and fully one-half as long as the elytra, with the antennæ inserted at the middle; antennæ moderate, the second funicular joint but very slightly longer than the third. *Prothorax* slightly wider than long, convex, the sides broadly, evenly arcuate, becoming more convergent and nearly straight near the apex, the latter three-fourths as wide as the base; constriction almost completely obsolete; punctures coarse, very deep, coalescent in threes or fours forming oblique sinuous lines. *Elytra* at base three-fifths wider than the prothorax, three times as long, three-fifths longer than wide, the sides nearly straight and parallel in basal half, the posterior half subacutely ogival; striæ rather fine, deep toward the suture but becoming simply series of coarse elongate punctures laterally. Length 1.6–1.75 mm.; width 0.65–0.7 mm.

North Carolina (Asheville).

A very distinct minute species, represented in my cabinet by a single pair. It may be recognized by the sparse and uneven vestiture, and the coarse deep and peculiar sculpture of the pronotum.

33 **S. perpusillus** n. sp.—Oblong-oval, convex, blackish-piceous; legs rufous with the tarsi darker; vestiture consisting of oval white scales, moderately large and generally not quite contiguous, and, on the pronotum, decidedly separated and varying in width; recurved setæ of the elytra fine distant and not conspicuous; scales of the under surface small, rounded, white, very nar-

rowly separated. *Head* scarcely shining, the frontal constriction very broad and feeble; beak slender, cylindrical, smooth and extremely minutely, feebly punctulate in apical half, punctate and sparsely squamose toward base, distinctly longer than the head and prothorax and nearly three-fifths as long as the elytra, evenly and distinctly arcuate; antennæ inserted at the middle, rather short, the second funicular joint but slightly shorter than the next two. *Prothorax* very nearly as long as wide, the sides broadly, evenly arcuate toward base, becoming slightly more convergent and nearly straight anteriorly, the constriction very feeble; punctures small, shallow and not dense; interspaces shining. *Elytra* at base one-half wider than the prothorax, two and two-thirds times as long, one-half longer than wide; sides nearly straight, and parallel in basal half, then convergent, the apex acutely rounded; striæ fine but deep. Length 1.6 mm.; width 0.6 mm.

Florida.

The unique type is a female and the species is not closely allied to any other known to me, being easily determinable by its small size and white scales, the latter close-set but generally not quite contiguous.

34 **S. defricans** n. sp.—Narrowly oblong-oval, convex, black, the legs dark rufous, the tarsi piceous; upper surface clothed unevenly with moderately large oval whitish scales, generally denser, or at least more persistent, in a broad line from the humeri to the middle of each elytron; stout recurved bristles short. *Head* dull, densely granulose; transverse impression rather feeble; beak opaque, shining and finely, deeply sulcate in apical half, sparsely setulose toward base, densely so above the eyes, very feebly arcuate, stout, tapering, as long as the head and prothorax; antennæ inserted at apical two-fifths, the basal joint of the funicle rather robust, as long as the next three, second nearly one-half longer than the third. *Prothorax* very nearly as long as wide; sides subparallel and broadly arcuate, convergent and very feebly constricted near the apex, the latter three-fourths as wide as the base; disk subopaque, finely, rather feebly and moderately densely punctate, the interspaces minutely, very densely, deeply punctulate. *Elytra* at base not quite one-half wider than the prothorax, scarcely three times as long; sides straight and parallel in basal three-fifths, then parabolically rounded; striæ fine but deep, the surface polished when denuded. *Legs* moderate, the tarsal claws very small, connate in basal half. Length 1.4–1.8 mm.; width 0.6–0.7 mm.

California (Lake and Monterey Cos.).

The three specimens in my cabinet exhibit but slight variability and are of uncertain sex; it is probable that the sexual differences in the beak are, however, very slight. This species is not closely allied to any other, and is easily distinguishable, among the Californian forms, by its minute stature.

35 **S. gibbirostris** n. sp.—Stout and convex, oval, black, the legs except near the base rufous ; elytra pale rufous, narrowly blackish along the suture ; upper surface sparsely and unevenly clothed with yellowish scales and fine slender squamules, the former dense at the sides of the pronotum toward base and narrowly along the middle, and on the elytra in subtransverse uneven spots and fasciæ; under surface moderately densely squamose. *Head* polished, the constriction evident ; beak in the male moderately thick, very feebly, evenly arcuate, dull, densely punctate, strongly gibbous before the constriction, a little longer than the head and prothorax and about one-half as long as the elytra ; antennæ inserted at apical two-fifths, the second funicular joint but slightly longer than the third. *Prothorax* moderately large, quite distinctly wider than long, the sides subparallel, broadly, rather strongly arcuate, convergent and broadly sinuate toward the apex, the latter three-fourths as wide as the base; disk convex, dull, very densely punctate, the punctures small, deep, lunate, the interspaces densely punctulate. *Elytra* at base not more than one-third wider than the prothorax, two and one-half times as long, about one-fourth longer than wide, just visibly wider behind the middle than at base, the sides straight, broadly parabolic in apical two-fifths, the striæ deep and distinct. Length 1.9 mm.; width 1.0 mm.

Delaware.

The single male represents a species allied somewhat to *sculpticollis*, but differing in its larger, more densely sculptured pronotum, much shorter elytra, gibbous beak and different vestiture, the sides of the pronotum being simply sparsely, finely squamulose, and the third elytral interval conspicuously squamose at base in *sculpticollis*.

36 **S. squalidus** n. sp.—Stout, strongly convex, oval, black, the legs dark rufo-piceous ; vestiture of the upper surface dense, consisting of rather large imbricated scales, confusedly mottled whitish and piceous, the former generally predominating ; scales of the under surface very small, rounded, yellowish-white and extremely dense ; recurved setæ sparse and slender. *Head* feebly squamulose anteriorly, the constriction moderate ; beak in the male thick, very feebly arcuate, rough, densely punctate, sparsely hispid and dull almost throughout, much longer than the head and prothorax and one-half as long as the elytra, with the antennæ inserted at apical third, in the female longer, more slender and arcuate, finely, rather densely punctate but shining and nearly glabrous in apical half, nearly three-fourths as long as the elytra, with the antennæ inserted at the middle; basal tufts not well developed ; antennæ rather slender, the second funicular joint three-fourths as long as the first and equal to the next two in the female, very little shorter in the male. *Prothorax* rather large and inflated, the sides strongly arcuate, convergent and rather strongly constricted near the apex, the latter not more than three-fifths as wide as the middle ; disk convex, rather coarsely, deeply, extremely densely punctured, one-fourth wider than long. *Elytra* at base not more than one-third wider than the prothorax, two and two-thirds times as

long, one-fourth longer than wide, distinctly wider at the middle than at base, parabolic in apical half.   Length 2.3–2.7 mm.; width 1.2–1.4 mm.

Pennsylvania; District of Columbia; Indiana.

A common eastern form resembling *ovipennis* but much larger, with a relatively larger, more inflated prothorax, more elongate beak and longer second funicular joint.   I found it labeled "*amœnus*" in my cabinet, a mistake which may possibly be common; *amœnus* is a widely different species, with the prothorax scarcely perceptibly narrower than the base of the elytra.   One specimen before me is labeled "Arizona," but perhaps erroneously.

37 **S. ovipennis** Lec.—Proc. Am. Phil. Soc., XV, p. 170.

Oval, strongly convex, stout, black, the legs rufescent; scales of the upper surface moderately large, very dense, confusedly mottled with whitish and different shades of brown or piceous, the white scales usually more numerous and forming a distinct line at the base of the third interval.   Beak in the male rather stout, densely squamose, a little longer than the head and prothorax; antennæ inserted at apical two-fifths, the second funicular joint but slightly longer than the third.   Prothorax small, slightly but quite distinctly wider than long, the sides evenly, rather strongly arcuate, convergent and very feebly constricted anteriorly, the apex fully three-fourths as wide as the base; disk densely, strongly punctate.   Elytra at base nearly one-half wider than the prothorax, almost three times as long, barely one-fourth longer than wide, distinctly wider in the middle than at base, gradually, acutely ogival in apical half; striæ indicated by coarse and uneven partings of the vestiture.   Length 1.8–2.0 mm.; width 0.8–1.1 mm.

Texas to Montana.   The measurement given in the original description is slightly too great.

PROMECOTARSUS n. gen.

I have separated under this name three species closely allied to Smicronyx, but differing in the longer, more glabrous tarsi, having a smaller third joint, with the fourth joint very long and subequal in length to the entire remainder.   In general appearance the species are more cylindrical than in Smicronyx, and more nearly resemble Endalus.   The principal characters may be expressed as follows:—

Body cylindrically convex, the elytra but very slightly wider than the prothorax, the vestiture dense, consisting of small, imbricated, almost completely

non-strigose scales, with a series of recurved, subrecumbent setæ on each strial
interval. Beak constricted at base, the head nearly spherical, eyes as in
Smicronyx. Prothorax constricted at apex, the ocular lobes more or less distinct. Scutellum very small. Prosternum deeply sinuate at apex. Metasternum æs long as the first ventral segment. Abdomen flat, sutures two to four
equally and feebly recurved at the sides, the second segment barely as long
as the next two and not quite as long as the fifth. Legs, excepting tarsal
structure, nearly as in Smicronyx.

In this genus, which constitutes one of the intermediate forms
connecting Smicronyx with the Hydronomi, the claws are long and
generally widely divergent, but in one species become subparallel;
they may be described as connate very near the base, with the
suture distinct. Promecotarsus is clearly, therefore, a transitional
form but must be classed with Smicronyx, these two genera constituting the group Smicronychi.

The species may be easily known as follows:—

Ungues widely divergent; prothorax very nearly as long as wide; ocular
   lobes not prominent.
   Prothorax abruptly, deeply constricted near the apex, the latter but slightly
      narrower than the base...1 **maritimus**
   Prothorax gradually more strongly narrowed and broadly, feebly constricted
      toward apex, the latter scarcely more than two-thirds as wide as the base.
                                                          2 **densus**
Ungues subparallel; prothorax much wider than long, with the ocular lobes
   prominent...3 **fumatus**

1 **P. maritimus** n. sp.—Subcylindrical, convex, piceous, the legs feebly
rufescent with the tarsi black; vestiture very dense, pale, the broad recurved
squamules very short and subrecumbent. *Head* shining, glabrous, the transverse groove deep; beak in the male moderately thick, densely, rugosely
punctate, sparsely squamulose, abruptly, strongly bent at the antennæ, thence
more shining and feebly tapering to the apex, fully as long as the head and
prothorax; antennæ inserted at apical third, the funicle long, the basal joint
as long as the next two, second almost as long as the third and fourth, outer
joints a little longer than wide, not noticeably thicker, club very slender, fusiform, the basal joint almost glabrous. *Prothorax* nearly one-fourth wider than
long, parallel and broadly, evenly, rather strongly arcuate at the sides, deeply
constricted behind the apex, the latter transversely truncate and but slightly
narrower than the base; disk feebly convex, very densely, not coarsely, subrugosely punctate. *Elytra* at base but slightly wider than the prothorax,
rather more than twice as long, fully two-fifths longer than wide, the sides
subparallel and nearly straight in basal three-fifths, the apex narrowly parabolic; striæ deeply impressed. *Legs* moderate, the tarsi as long as the tibiæ.
Length 2.0–2.2 mm.; width 0.8–0.95 mm.

California (San Diego). Mr. Chas. Fuchs.

The three specimens in my cabinet are males, and the beak is probably much longer and more evenly arcuate in the female. This species somewhat resembles *densus*, but is smaller, narrower and differs greatly in the form of the prothorax, as well as in the somewhat longer second joint of the antennal funicle.

2 **P. densus** n. sp.—Robust, subcylindrical, convex, black, extremely densely clothed with rather small, broadly oval, yellowish-white and uniform scales, which are widely overlapping, granulose in texture and not strigose, similar in structure and density on the under surface ; recurved setæ distinct. *Head* glabrous, finely, strongly reticulate ; constriction fine, deep ; beak in the female slender, polished, exceedingly finely, remotely punctate, but thicker, dull and rugosely punctate near the base, nearly evenly and quite strongly arcuate, almost three-fifths as long as the elytra ; antennæ inserted scarcely beyond basal third, rather long and slender, the second funicular joint about as long as the next two ; club moderately robust, very sparsely pubescent and shining toward base. *Prothorax* but slightly wider than long, the sides parallel and very feebly arcuate in basal two-thirds, then moderately convergent and broadly constricted to the apex, the latter rather more than two-thirds as wide as the base ; disk moderately convex, evenly, densely squamose, finely, very densely punctate throughout. *Elytra* at base but slightly more than one-fourth wider than the prothorax, not quite two and one-half times as long, one-half longer than wide, the sides parallel in basal three-fifths, then narrowly angulato-parabolic ; striæ indicated by fine but sharply defined partings of the dense crust of scales. *Legs* somewhat stout, the tarsi long and slender, the third joint only moderately dilated, the last joint long ; claws long, divergent, connate at base. Length 2.5 mm. ; width 1.05 mm.

Nebraska.

Easily distinguishable by the dense and uniform crust of non-strigose imbricated scales and the subcylindrical form, as well as by the characters given in the table.

3 **P. fumatus** n. sp.—Moderately robust, convex, subcylindrical, black throughout, extremely densely clothed with a crust of widely overlapping, dark, yellowish-gray scales, uniform in color, very broad and excessively minutely, indistinctly strigilate ; recurved setæ fine but distinct. *Head* glabrous, minutely, feebly reticulate and rather strongly shining, the constriction fine but moderately deep ; beak in the male thick, evenly cylindrical, distinctly arcuate, moderately densely punctate, not quite as long as the head and prothorax, with the antennæ inserted just beyond the middle, in the female a little more slender, evenly, distinctly arcuate, smooth and remotely punctulate except near the base, scarcely visibly longer than the head and prothorax, barely one-half as long as the elytra, with the antennæ inserted at basal two-fifths ; antennæ moderately slender, the second funicular joint as long as the

next two; club slender, gradually, acutely pointed, rather densely pubescent. *Prothorax* transverse, one-third to two-fifths wider than long, the sides parallel, broadly, evenly arcuate in basal two-thirds, then strongly convergent and deeply, abruptly constricted, the apex transverse between the very prominent ocular lobes; disk very densely squamose, the sculpture dense and subrugose when denuded. *Elytra* at base between one-third and one-fourth wider than the prothorax, fully three times as long, one-half longer than wide, the sides parallel and nearly straight in basal three-fifths; striæ indicated by clearly defined narrow partings of the vestiture. Length 2.2–2.3 mm.; width 0.95 mm.

Montana (Helena). Mr. H. F. Wickham.

Closely allied to *densus*, but differing in its much shorter prothorax, shorter beak in the female, with the antennæ distinctly less basal, in its gray and not ochreous vestiture and in many other minor characters. It was taken in abundance, and the six specimens before me are very uniform in size.

TYCHIINI.

TYCHIUS Schönh.

In subdividing the comparatively few American representatives of this genus, I have made use of some characters which do not exist among the European species, or at least, which have apparently not been mentioned in systematic works. Our species may be readily divided into four subgeneric groups as follows:—

Antennal funicle 7-jointed.
 Body more or less robust and oval, the elytral intervals entirely devoid of
  recurved setæ ....**I**
 Body narrower, oblong; elytral intervals with recurved semi-erect setæ...**II**
Antennal funicle 6-jointed.
 Body elongate-oval, with robust recurved setæ, the entire facies almost as
  in group II; eyes large, very nearly circular ....**III**
 Body much smaller, the species generally minute, with or without erect
  setæ; eyes more or less transversely fusiform ....**IV**

None of these divisions seems to correspond exactly with the European Miccotrogus, although I am not certain of the habitus of that subgenus, specimens sent to me by M. Desbrochers under the name *M. picirostris* having the antennal funicle certainly 7-jointed. It can be confidently affirmed, however, that the structure of the funicle is without full generic significance in our species, for the reason that groups II and III agree so satisfactorily in all other structural features. At the same time, there is sufficient heterogeneity to warrant a division into subgenera on the lines above suggested. There is nothing to indicate that Miccotrogus possesses greater systematic value than any one of these American groups.

The species may be easily recognized by the following characters :—

Subgenus I.

Elytral vestiture narrowly vittate, often alternating fulvous and cinereous on the intervals, the striæ broadly visible; anterior tibiæ of the male strongly, acutely toothed internally near the middle................ ......1 **lineellus**
Elytral vestiture nearly uniform in color, the striæ indicated by fine and indistinct partings; anterior tibiæ not dentate in the male.
　Beak thick, only feebly diminishing in diameter from base to apex.
　　Body broadly oval, the scales very narrow and hair-like.....2 **sordidus**
　　Body more narrowly oval, the scales broader and more densely crowded.

3 tectus

　Beak thick at base, rapidly and finely attenuate toward apex; elytral vestiture mingled with a very few widely scattered rounded scales toward apex...4 **arator**

Subgenus II.

Abdomen with sparse semi-erect setæ, in addition to the dense squamosity.
　Setæ borne by the strial punctures of the elytra long semi-erect white and conspicuous.
　　Prothorax less transverse, with a broad median vitta which is entirely clothed with large white imbricated scales; setæ throughout the body robust..5 **soltaui**
　　Prothorax strongly transverse, with a very fine white median line which contains no large non-strigose scales, except in the broader portion near the base; setæ throughout longer and fine....................6 **hirtellus**
　Setæ borne by the strial punctures short, thicker, recumbent and inconspicuous...7 **aratus**
Abdomen densely squamose but without trace of setæ; scales of the elytra smaller and more densely imbricated along the suture than elsewhere.
　Beak very feebly narrowed toward apex; prothorax a little less transverse, wider at the middle than at base; elytra with many more setæ than scales on the disk ....8 **semisqamosus**
　Beak rapidly and finely acuminate, thicker toward base; body stouter; sides of the prothorax parallel behind; elytra with many more large whitish oval scales than setæ ....9 **lamellosus**

Subgenus III.

Beak short, feebly tapering from base to apex; elytra with large imbricated scales and very robust recurved fulvous setæ.....................10 **prolixus**

Subgenus IV.

Elytra without long erect bristles, although sometimes with abundant short strongly recurved setæ, which are not very conspicuous.

Vestiture finely and feebly variegated in color, and with a large sutural
spot of white imbricated scales behind the scutellum...11 **variegatus**
Vestiture nearly uniform in color, the scales of the upper surface all narrow
and elongate, the squamules borne by the strial punctures similar to
the others or very nearly as wide.
Elytral intervals each with a single nearly even series of narrow scales,
fulvous to white in color ....12 **simplex**
Elytral intervals confusedly clothed with scales throughout their width.
Elytral scales evenly but not very densely distributed, narrow and
slender, ochreous-yellow in color, the middle scales of each interval
semi-erect, especially toward apex......................13 **sibinioides**
Elytral scales broader and more closely recumbent, denser along the
suture, more broadly so behind the middle......................14 **mica**
Elytra with stiff straight and strongly hispid erect or inclined setæ.
Elytra with large rounded or oval whitish scales, unevenly distributed.
Elytral setæ long and rather slender ....15 **setosus**
Elytral setæ short, broad and scale-like..................16 **subfasciatus**
Elytra with long slender white and fulvous decumbent squamules, entirely
without rounded scales ; erect setæ rather fine and much more numerous.
17 hispidus

The species of groups I and IV are generally taken in abundance
when discovered, while those of II and III are apparently much
less plentiful in individuals, or possibly less gregarious; they are
also a little more closely allied among themselves, forming a more
difficult study.

I

1 **T. lineellus** Lec.—Proc. Am. Phil. Soc., XV, p. 217.

Broadly oval, strongly convex, rather densely clothed above with
long, slender, coarsely strigose scales, which are variable in color,
and, to some extent also, in distribution ; in the best marked specimens they are subcupreous in two broad pronotal vittæ, and on the
alternate intervals of the elytra, elsewhere cinereous, but often
cinereous throughout; on the under surface they are whitish,
broader, non-strigose and feathery in structure. The male has the
beak short, abruptly tapering beyond the antennæ, and the anterior tibiæ strongly, acutely toothed internally just beyond the
middle; in the female the beak is longer, nearly straight, slender
but abruptly thicker very near the base. Length 3.7–4.7 mm.;
width 1.7–2.2 mm.

California (Siskiyou to San Diego). This is a common species
throughout the State.

2 T. sordidus Lec.—Proc. Am. Phil. Soc., XV, p. 217.

Robust, oval, convex, rather densely and uniformly clothed throughout with small slender scales, silvery gray to yellowish in color, and generally a little more condensed along the elytral suture; erect setæ completely wanting. Beak rather short, slender, straight, cylindrical, feebly tapering and slightly bent near the apex, barely as long as the prothorax, finely, densely punctate, squamulose and more or less carinulate; antennæ inserted at apical third, rather slender, the second funicular joint but slightly shorter than the first, slender, outer joints barely perceptibly wider, the club rather elongate, obliquely pointed at apex, rounded at base, almost equally trisected by two straight sutures. Prothorax slightly wider than long, the sides rapidly convergent from base to apex, broadly and evenly arcuate, constricted behind the apex, the latter scarcely more than one-third as wide as the base, the punctures circular, deep and dense. Elytra parallel, broadly rounded behind, one-fourth longer than wide, much wider than the prothorax and more than twice as long. Posterior femora feebly toothed. Length 4.0–4.7 mm.; width 2.1–2.4 mm.

Iowa and Illinois. Our largest species, sufficiently common and very readily recognizable by the characters given. The three specimens before me are probably males; in the female, the antennæ are undoubtedly less apical.

3 T. tectus Lec.—Proc. Am. Phil. Soc., XV, p. 217.

Oblong-oval, convex, black, the antennæ rufescent; body covered densely throughout with yellowish-white scales, whitish along the suture and middle of the pronotum and also toward the sides of the body; scales rather wide but parallel and subelongate, strigose. Beak evenly, moderately arcuate, subcylindrical, feebly tapering only very near the apex, finely, densely punctured throughout, densely squamulose but nude beyond the antennæ, in the male much shorter than the prothorax, with the antennæ inserted near apical third, in the female much longer, as long as the prothorax, with the antennæ inserted at the middle; antennæ slender, the basal joint of the funicle as long as the next three, second slightly longer than the third. Prothorax in the male two-fifths wider than long, with the sides inflated before the middle and the apex less than one-half as wide as the base, in the female longer, one-fourth wider than long, with the sides parallel and nearly straight, the apex more than one-half as wide as the base. Elytra three-fifths longer than wide, scarcely wider than the disk of the prothorax in the male but distinctly wider in the female, the sides subparallel in basal three-fifths; intervals without median line of squamules, the hairs of the strial punctures white and quite evident. Length 2.6–3.7 mm.; width 1.15–1.7 mm.

Colorado and Montana. Numerous specimens. In one female, not otherwise differing, the beak is deformed, the apical parts being swollen polished and impunctate, separated from the post-antennal portion by a broad depression. The same deformity exists to a less marked degree in a male specimen, and the species seems to be peculiarly liable to this kind of rostal malformation. An extremely feeble transverse impression at the antennæ is however apparently normal in some species, such as *aratus* Say.

4 **T. arator** Gyll.—Sch. Curc., III, p. 414; Lec.: Proc. Am. Phil. Soc , XV, p. 216.

Oblong-oval; rather stout, convex, black, the legs piceous; antennæ and apical parts of the beak rufo-testaceous; body very densely clothed throughout with elongate dark ochreous scales, which are coarsely strigose, but intermixed with a few larger ones, toward the apex of the elytra, which are non-strigose in structure and rather paler in color; intervals of the elytra without setæ, the strial squamules distinct. Beak thick, tumid, densely punctured and squamulose behind, but very thin, glabrous, shining and sparsely punctured before, the point of antennal insertion, feebly arcuate, the thin apical portion straight, rather shorter than the prothorax in both sexes but a little longer in the female than in the male, the antennæ inserted at the middle in the former and at apical two-fifths in the latter, with the basal joint of the funicle as long as the next two, the second two-thirds as long as the first. Prothorax two-fifths wider than long, the apex much less than one-half as wide as the base. Elytra distinctly wider than the prothorax in both sexes, one-half longer than wide. Length 3.0–3.6 mm.; width 1.4–1.7 mm.

Texas (Dallas)—Mr. Wickham; Illinois—Cab. LeConte. This species is very isolated in all of its characters, and cannot be compared with any other known to me. The hind femora are feebly toothed beneath.

II. .

5 **T. soltaui** n. sp.—Narrowly oblong-oval, moderately convex, black, the antennæ and tip of beak rufous; vestiture complex, consisting, on the beak, of slender semi-erect hispid squamules, recumbent behind an abrupt transverse line at the posterior margin of the eyes; on the pronotum, of slender dark fulvous squamules, partly erect and hispid, mingled, in a narrow line near the sides, with large whitish scales and with a broad median vitta, entirely composed of broad white scales; on the elytra of large dense imbricated scales and semi-erect robust recurved setæ, the latter disposed in single lines, the strial setæ also distinct; on the under surface of large oval white scales, generally concave along the middle, mingled with stout sparse setæ on the abdomen. *Head* densely clothed with recumbent fulvous scales behind the transverse hispid line; beak in the male stout, rapidly, finely acuminate, nude beyond the antennæ, nearly straight and scarcely as long as the prothorax; antennæ inserted near apical third, the basal joint of the funicle not quite as long as the next three, seventh much wider than the sixth. *Prothorax* one-fourth wider than long, very slightly wider before the middle than at base, the sides rounded convergent and distinctly constricted anteriorly, the apex nearly three-fifths as wide as the base; punctures very dense, entirely concealed. *Elytra* barely one-fourth wider and two and one-half times longer than the prothorax, the sides becoming straight and parallel toward base, obtusely rounded at apex. Posterior femora rather slender, obtusely and feebly toothed. Length 2.6 mm.; width 1.1 mm.

Wyoming (Laramie).

A rather narrow species, allied to *hirtellus* and differing in the broad vitta of white scales along the middle of the pronotum, the more elongate prothorax, shorter, much coarser semi-erect setæ above and on the abdomen, and in the generally narrower form of the body. The single male was taken by Mr. Hugo Soltau.

6 **T. hirtellus** Lec.—Proc. Am. Phil. Soc., XV, p. 218.

Oblong-oval, moderately convex, piceous, the antennæ and tip of beak rufous; vestiture complex, consisting of dark brownish-fulvous narrow strigose squamules on the pronotum, largely replaced toward the sides by oval pointed non-strigose scales, strongly imbricated and not quite recumbent, again darker along the middle of the flanks beneath, narrowly white along the median line, more broadly toward base; on the elytra the vestiture consists of moderately large oval pointed pale brownish scales, strongly imbricated throughout, rather smaller, still denser and more ochreous on the sutural interval, the striæ indicated by fine partings in the dense crust, with the white hairs borne by the strial punctures distinct;

intervals each with a single series of long stiff erect but rather fine setæ; on the under surface the scales are whitish and very dense throughout, intermixed with long setæ on the abdomen. Beak in the male short, thick, densely hispido-squamulose, nude and polished near the apex, subequal in length to the prothorax, the antennæ inserted near apical third. Prothorax nearly one-half wider than long, the sides strongly evenly arcuate, convergent and strongly constricted near the apex, the latter about one-half as wide as the base. Elytra one-fourth wider than the prothorax and very nearly three times as long, broadly angulato-emarginate at base. Posterior femora obsoletely dentate. Length 2.9 mm.; width 1.25 mm.

Texas. Readily known by its complex vestiture, transverse prothorax, and fine long and semi-erect setæ. The fifth ventral segment is deeply and rather widely impressed or excavated in the male.

7 T. aratus Say.—Curc., p. 26; Ed. Lec. I, p. 294.

Oblong-elongate, convex, black, the legs, antennæ and tip of beak rufescent; body densely clothed throughout with scales of various forms and colors; those of the beak robust and hair-like, usually more or less bristling near the point of antennal insertion; those of the pronotum slender, strongly strigose, converging obliquely backward, fulvous, but whitish along the middle and laterally near the base; those of the elytra very large, broad, widely imbricated, granulose and not at all strigose in structure, and of various shades of gray and blackish, confusedly intermingled; intervals of the elytra each with a single series of long coarse bristling recurved setæ. Beak scarcely longer than the prothorax, just visibly arcuate, very feebly tapering from base to apex, slightly constricted at the antennæ, the apical portion nude and shining; antennæ with the first funicular joint as long as the next two. Prothorax one-half wider than long, the apex rather abruptly narrowed and constricted, less than one-half as wide as the base. Elytra at base one-fourth wider than the prothorax, two and two-thirds times as long, three-fifths longer than wide, the sides subparallel and straight in basal three-fifths, evenly, obtusely rounded behind. Posterior femora rather slender, strongly, obtusely prominent beneath at apical fourth, and with the usual subapical emargination. Length 3.3 mm.; width 1.4 mm.

Montana. The type specimen, which appears to be a male, agrees so thoroughly with the description of Say, that there can be little doubt of its representing the true *aratus*. It is unfortunate, however, that there should be two names in the same genus and within the same faunal limits which are mutually so similar. The term "olivaceous," applied by Say to the color of *aratus*, might have wide limits of meaning.

8 **T. semisquamosus** Lec.—Proc. Am. Phil. Soc., XV, p. 217.

Narrowly oblong-oval, rather convex, piceous, the legs, antennæ and tip of beak rufescent; vestiture complex, consisting of narrow elongate fulvous squamules on the pronotum, which become broad white scales in the middle and at each side but only near the base, anteriorly there are also some widely scattered large brown scales; on the elytra the intervals are clothed throughout with stout recurved and subrecumbent brown setæ, among which there are very sparsely strewn large dark gray-brown scales, the latter dense imbricated and reddish along the sutural interval; on the under surface the scales are whitish, elongate-oval and dense throughout. Beak in the male short, thick, not as long as the prothorax, feebly tapering from base to apex, densely squamulose except near the tip, the antennæ inserted at apical two-fifths, the basal joint of the funicle very stout, not as long as the next three, second but slightly longer than the third, narrow at base, three to seven subequal, moniliform; club abrupt, oblong-oval. Prothorax very nearly as long as wide, the apex three-fifths as wide as the base, finely and feebly constricted. Elytra at base scarcely one-third wider than the prothorax, three times as long, the sides straight and parallel in basal two-thirds; striæ fine, impressed, with the white squamules distinct. Length 2.5 mm.; width 1.0 mm.

California. This species can be easily identified by the narrow form, sparse scales of the elytra except along the suture, and absence of erect ventral hairs. The large scales of the upper surface are, as usual, granulose in structure and not strigate.

9 **T. lamellosus** n. sp.—Rather broadly oblong-oval, convex, piceous, the tibiæ, antennæ and tip of beak rufescent; vestiture dense and varied, consisting on the pronotum of long narrow fulvous strigose squamules, gradually intermixed toward the sides and almost replaced by large whitish scales, also narrowly along the middle, more broadly toward base; on the elytra the non-strigose scales are very large, broad, ogival, pearly white in color, dense

along the middle and lateral edge of each elytron, also dense and more yellowish along the sutural interval; recurved fulvous setæ rather abundant; on
the under surface the scales are elongate-oval, whitish and dense. *Head* and
beak very densely, finely squamulose, the latter short, very stout, strongly
tapering from base to apex, with the portion beyond the antennæ very thin,
nude and shining, feebly arcuate, in the male not more than three-fourths as
long as the prothorax, with the antennæ inserted just behind apical third, the
first joint of the funicle very stout, pedunculate at base, not as long as the
next three, second one-half longer than the third, seventh a little larger than
the sixth. *Prothorax* very nearly as long as wide, the sides parallel and nearly
straight in basal two-thirds, then broadly rounded, convergent but scarcely at
all constricted to the apex, the latter about one-half as wide as the base; disk
densely, not coarsely punctate. *Elytra* at base rather more than one-fourth
wider than the prothorax, not quite three times as long, the sides parallel and
nearly straight in basal three-fifths; striæ very fine. *Legs* moderate, the hind
femora feebly dentate, emarginate near the apex. Length 2.8 mm.; width
1.3 mm.

Utah.

The single male before me represents a species allied to *semisquamosus*, but differing in its more robust form, much more abundant and whiter scale-like plates of the elytra, relatively narrower
apex of the prothorax, more rapidly and finely acuminate beak, and
in several other characters. The fifth ventral segment has in the
center a small deep punctiform fovea, which is not visible in the
male of *semisquamosus*.

<h2 style="text-align:center">III.</h2>

10 **T. prolixus** n. sp.—Oblong-elongate, convex, blackish, the antennæ
and tip of beak paler; vestiture very dense throughout, consisting, on the
pronotum, of long slender subrecumbent and strigose squamules, pale fulvous
in color but whitish along the middle and near the sides toward base, not
intermixed with more slender and erect setæ but with a few broad non-strigose
scales in the whitish areas, though only near the base; on the elytra the
scales are very large, dense, rounded, finely granulose in texture, widely imbricated and dark reddish-gray in color, each interval with a single uneven
series of very coarse strongly recurved reddish pointed setæ; the under surface is densely clothed with elongate-oval concave and whitish scales. *Head*
squamose; eyes rather large, almost perfectly circular: beak in the male thick,
densely hispido-squamose and with a prominent tuft above each eye, almost
straight but bent at base, rather rapidly narrowed, glabrous and shining beyond the antennæ, barely equal in length to the prothorax; antennæ inserted
at apical two-fifths, the first funicular joint rather longer than the second and
third, which are subequal and each distinctly longer than wide. *Prothorax*
one-fourth wider than long, the sides just visibly convergent and broadly,
feebly arcuate from the base nearly to the apex, then rather abruptly, deeply

constricted, the apex rather more than one-half as wide as the base. *Elytra* one-third wider than the prothorax and not quite three times as long, the sides parallel and straight in basal two-thirds; apex obtuse, with a small sutural notch. *Legs* long and rather slender, the hind femora feebly, obtusely prominent beneath at apical fourth. Length 3.3 mm.; width 1.35 mm.

Nevada.

The six-jointed antennal funicle isolates this species from all others which it most resembles in external aspect. The single type specimen is a male, and has the fifth abdominal segment scarcely impressed but longer than the two preceding together, the second suture flexed strongly backward at the sides extending a little beyond the anterior margin of the fourth segment, the third and fourth sutures scarcely at all bent at the sides.

IV.

11 **T. variegatus** n. sp.—Robust, oblong, rather convex, blackish, the antennæ and beak slightly paler; vestiture above not very dense, on the pronotum not altogether concealing the punctures and consisting of short very coarse pointed fulvous and white setæ, replaced by large white scales in the middle near the base and toward the sides; on the elytra, of very short stout subrecumbent setæ, fulvous and whitish in color, white and denser on the subapical umbones, and replaced by large imbricated white scales in a small elongate spot behind the scutellum, also more narrowly and indistinctly, in a small sutural line at the apex; under surface and legs clothed throughout very densely with white scales, sometimes feebly variegated with pale brown. *Head* and beak extremely densely squamose, the scales above usually dark ochreous-red, but whiter along the sides, the impressed line behind the eyes distinct, the eyes wider than long; beak extremely thick but rapidly tapering and subglabrous toward the tip, feebly arcuate, about as long as the prothorax in the male, with the antennæ inserted at apical third, scarcely longer in the female but with the antennæ inserted just beyond the middle; antennæ moderate, the first funicular joint fully as long as the next two, second a little longer than the third, both elongate, fourth shorter, club rather small. *Prothorax* one-third wider than long, the sides broadly, evenly arcuate, becoming parallel toward base, convergent and deeply constricted near the apex, the latter nearly two-thirds as wide as the base; punctures very coarse, deep, moderately dense. *Elytra* fully one-third wider than the prothorax, scarcely more than twice as long, one-fourth longer than wide, subparallel, obtuse at apex, with a small cuspiform sutural notch; striæ very coarse, crossed transversely at the bottom by rather distant ridges. Hind femora not at all prominent beneath. Length 2.0–2.4 mm.; width 0.9–1.2 mm.

Arizona (Benson); Texas (El Paso). Mr. G. W. Dunn.

The large series before me indicates but slight variability, and the characters given above will readily serve to identify this species,

which is the largest and one of the most isolated of the small forms
peculiar to the desert regions of Arizona.

12 **T. simplex** n. sp.—Oblong-oval, rather convex, piceous, the elytra
more or less rufescent; beak rufous except near the base; vestiture moderately
dense, on the head and basal parts of the beak consisting of oval dense closely
recumbent and very small scales, on the pronotum of rather sparse slender
cinereous or more or less fulvous squamules, generally with sparsely scattered
oval scales toward the sides, on the elytra of slender cinereous or cinereous
and fulvous squamules, posteriorly recurved and subrecumbent in a single
series on each interval, with scattered rounded scales toward the sides, the
squamules of the strial punctures coarse and distinct, the upper surface otherwise glabrous; under surface densely clothed with small broadly oval whitish
scales. *Head* moderate in convexity, the transverse line at the posterior limit
of the eyes distinct, the eyes small transversely fusiform; beak moderately
thick, feebly tapering, tumid above near the base, glabrous and shining beyond the antennæ, feebly arcuate toward base, nearly as long as the head and
prothorax, with the antennæ inserted at apical two-fifths in the male, slightly
longer and thinner in the female, with the antennæ inserted at the middle;
antennæ slender, the basal joint of the funicle long, moderately thick, feebly
obconical, fully as long as the next three, second a little longer than the third,
the latter slightly elongate, outer joints gradually thicker. *Prothorax* one-
fourth wider than long, the sides nearly straight and parallel in basal two-
thirds, then rounded and rather strongly constricted to the apex, the latter
transverse and three-fifths as wide as the base; punctures coarse, deep, not
quite contiguous; base lobed in the middle. *Elytra* one-third longer than
wide, fully one-third wider than the prothorax, obtusely rounded behind;
striæ coarse, punctured. *Legs* slender, the posterior femora not toothed.
Length 1.4–1.7 mm.; width 0.7–0.9 mm.

Texas (El Paso); Arizona (Benson and Tuçson).

Of this distinct species I have a large series, the principal variation being in the color of the squamules of the pronotum and median
series of the elytral intervals.

13 **T. sibinioides** n. sp.—Robust, oblong-oval, convex, piceous, the legs,
antennæ and beak rufous; vestiture of the upper surface nearly uniform,
consisting of long slender ochreous-yellow strigose squamules, without trace
of intermingled scales, rather dense, those of the strial punctures similar to
the others and equally wide, those along the middle of the intervals semi-erect;
under surface more densely clothed with broader whitish scales. *Head* densely
squamulose; transverse line not distinct; beak thick but very strongly tapering from base to apex, evenly, rather strongly arcuate, very slender and nude
beyond the antennæ, elsewhere strongly punctured, subcarinulate and densely
squamulose, in the male a little longer than the prothorax, with the antennæ
inserted at apical two-fifths, in the female but slightly longer, but with the
glabrous apical portion much longer and almost evenly cylindrical, the

antennæ inserted a little behind the middle ; antennæ slender, the basal joint of the funicle about as long as the next two, second and third both slightly elongate, club moderate. *Prothorax* small, one-third wider than long, the sides rounded, convergent and scarcely perceptibly constricted anteriorly, becoming parallel in basal half; apex transversely truncate, two-thirds as wide as the base. *Elytra* fully one-third wider than the prothorax, scarcely three times as long, barely one-fourth longer than wide ; sides parallel in basal half or slightly more. Posterior femora rather slender, not at all toothed. Length 1.6–1.75 mm. ; width 0.8–0.9 mm.

Arizona (Santa Rita Mts.).   Mr. H. F. Wickham.

The elytra have a very small sutural notch, but are not individually broadly rounded as they are in Sibinia.   This peculiar type is well represented in Brazil.   Four specimens.

14 **T. mica** n. sp.—Oblong-oval, rather convex, rufo-piceous throughout ; vestiture moderately dense, generally whitish, pale brown on the disk of the pronotum, consisting throughout, on the upper surface, of parallel but rather broad strigose recumbent scales, rather dense on the pronotum, becoming broader and whiter on the flanks but not different in structure and without trace of intermixed setæ or broad rounded scales ; on the elytra similar, recumbent and uniform in structure throughout, but somewhat denser toward the suture ; on the under surface larger, elongate-oval, denser. *Head* squamose, the transverse line fine ; eyes wider than long ; beak in the male stout, densely squamulose except at the tip, feebly arcuate, gradually and not very rapidly tapering, scarcely longer than the prothorax, with the antennæ inserted at apical third ; antennæ rather short, the first funicular joint very robust, strongly narrowed at base, as long as the next two, second one-half longer than the third, the latter barely longer than wide. *Prothorax* small, nearly one-third wider than long, the sides subparallel and almost straight in basal half, then rounded, convergent and deeply constricted to the apex, the latter broadly arcuate, two-thirds as wide as the base ; punctures dense. *Elytra* one-third wider than the prothorax, two and one-half times as long, one-fourth longer than wide, obtuse at apex, becoming parallel in about basal half; striæ somewhat coarse. *Legs* rather slender, the posterior femora not prominent beneath. Length 1.5 mm. ; width 0.7 mm.

Arizona.

This species is not closely allied to any other, but is represented by a singe rather imperfect male example.   It is easily distinguishable by the uniform structure of the parallel strigose scales of the upper surface, and by the absence of erect bristles.

15 **T. setosus** Lec.—Proc. Am. Phil. Soc., XV, p. 218.

Oblong-oval, moderately convex, more or less pale piceo-rufous ; vestiture uneven, consisting of small subrecumbent robust setæ, sparsely scattered throughout the upper surface, intermixed with large rounded non-strigose scales of a whitish tint, especially noticeable on the prothorax except in a large, more or less distinct spot toward base on each side of the median line, and on the elytra in a large rounded or subannular sutural spot before the middle, along the sutural interval and near the humeri and subapical umbones; the alternate strial intervals with a single series of long stiff erect and widely spaced setæ; under surface densely clothed with large whitish scales. Beak rather long and slender, squamose but only just visibly thicker toward base, distinctly longer than the head and prothorax; antennæ inserted just beyond the middle, the first funicular joint not as long as the next three, second and third subequal, both longer than wide. Prothorax small, one-third wider than long, constricted behind the apex. Elytra two-fifths wider than the prothorax and a little less than three times as long, one-third longer than wide. Posterior femora unarmed, rather slender. Length 1.35–1.8 mm.; width 0.65–0.8 mm.

California (Yuma); Arizona (Benson and Tuçson). A rather abundant species, easily recognizable by the mixture of large rounded unevenly distributed scales and long stiff erect setæ, bristling on the elytra. Although the ample series before me shows great variation in size, I am unable to detect any sexual differences in the structure of the beak.

16 **T. subfasciatus** n. sp.—Oblong-oval, moderately convex, dark red-brown; tip of beak pale rufous; antennal club black; vestiture complex, uneven in distribution, consisting of short subrecumbent and very robust setæ and larger rounded whiter scales, the latter especially evident on the elytra along the entire sutural interval and in a wide feebly defined vitta from the humeri to the subapical umbones, also in a conspicuous transverse area, wider and subannulate toward the suture, situated scarcely before the middle of the length; the alternate strial intervals with a single series of short, erect, very stout and widely spaced setæ; under surface densely clothed with large rounded concave and whitish scales. *Head* covered with large umbilicate scales, the beak moderately stout, feebly, evenly arcuate, very feebly tapering from the base, a little longer than the head and prothorax, densely squamose except beyond the antennæ, the latter inserted at apical two-fifths, short, the first funicular joint not quite as long as the next three. *Prothorax* two-fifths wider than long, the sides convergent from base to apex and feebly arcuate, the subapical constriction feeble; apex nearly three-fourths as wide as the base. *Elytra* one-third wider than the prothorax and fully three times as long, two-fifths longer than wide, parallel at the sides in more than basal half, obtusely rounded behind; striæ coarse, punc-

tured, the strial setæ white, slender, but distinct. *Legs* rather short but slender, the femora not dentate. Length 1.6–1.7 mm.; width 0.75 mm.

Texas (Big Springs). Mr. H. F. Wickham.

Allied to *setosus*, but easily distinguishable by the somewhat smaller scales of the upper surface, shorter and stouter erect setæ, and by the shorter, rather thicker beak and longer elytra. In both of these species the erect bristles are confined to the alternate intervals, except toward apex. Sexual differences are not evident, even in the length or structure of the beak. The third and fourth ventral sutures are almost obliterated by the dense crust of scales, but appear to be sinuate near the sides, although not flexed backward to any noticeable extent. Four specimens.

17 **T. hispidus** n. sp.—Oblong-oval, rather convex, piceous, elytra, except on the suture, more broadly toward base, legs, beak and antennæ, rufous ; vestiture moderately dense, not very uneven, consisting, on the upper surface, of long slender squamules, subrecumbent, whitish and pale fulvous confusedly intermingled, evenly distributed over the pronotum and entire width of the elytral intervals, and without trace of large rounded scales ; all the elytral intervals throughout their length with single series of long erect bristling setæ, whitish in color and rather widely spaced ; squamules of the strial punctures distinct, white ; under surface rather densely clothed with large oval whitish scales. *Head* finely squamulose, the transverse impression subobsolete ; eyes transversely fusiform ; beak in the male rather stout, very feebly tapering and slightly arcuate throughout, squamulose except near the apex, about as long as the head and prothorax, with the antennæ inserted just behind apical third ; in the female very slightly longer, thick, squamulose and subinflated in basal half, very thin, glabrous and cylindrical in apical half, the antennæ inserted at the middle ; antennæ rather short, the basal joint of the funicle subequal to the next three, second one-half longer than the third. *Prothorax* one-fourth wider than long, the sides very feebly arcuate, slightly constricted behind the apex, the latter two-thirds as wide as the base. *Elytra* two-fifths wider than the prothorax and very nearly three times as long, about one-half longer than wide, suboval, the sides parallel and just visibly arcuate, gradually convergent and more rounded toward apex, the latter less obtuse than usual. Posterior femora unarmed. Length 1.4–1.8 mm.; width 0.65–0.8 mm.

Arizona (Santa Rita Mts.). Mr. H. F. Wickham.

This inconspicuous species is somewhat allied to *setosus* and *subfasciatus*, but only in possessing erect bristling setæ, otherwise it differs greatly in the entire absence of large rounded scales on the upper surface, and in the strongly marked sexual characters of the beak, the latter, somewhat unusually, being more rapidly and strongly inflated toward base in the female than in the male, nearly as in *Centrinus hospes*, which inhabits the same region. My series consists of seven specimens.

THYSANOCNEMIS Lec.

In this genus the sexual divergencies in the structure of the beak are extremely pronounced and far more noticeable than in Tylopterus, with which it is closely allied; the present forms may be distinguished from Tylopterus, however, by the much coarser, less dense and non-sericeous vestiture. The fringe of hairs of the front tibiæ in the male is not a character of generic importance, and often disappears completely. The five species in my cabinet may be mutually distinguished by the following table:—

Elytral intervals subequal in width and prominence.
   Body pale rufo-testaceous, the elytra with a broad, darker and generally
      less densely squamulose band, narrowed toward the suture, often indis-
      tinct; sometimes also with a short angulate sutural band of paler scales
      near apical third...**fraxini** Lec.
   Body piceous-black, the beak and legs rufous, the tibiæ with a narrow sub-
      median band blackish, the femora dark except toward base; vestiture
      strongly mottled with black and whitish, fulvous near the base of the
      elytra especially near the humeri, and on the pronotum except toward
      the sides and in the middle toward base; on the elytra a whitish band at
      basal fourth and a narrower angulate band at apical third are especially
      noticeable. Head squamose; eyes separated by barely one-half of their
      own width; beak in the male short but rather thin, feebly arcuate, as
      long as the prothorax, with the antennæ inserted at apical third; in the
      female very thin, smooth, cylindrical, evenly, distinctly arcuate, as long
      as the head and prothorax, with the antennæ inserted at about the middle;
      antennæ long, the funicle slender, with the basal joint more than one-half
      as long as the remainder, club robust, blackish, not as long as the pre-
      ceding six joints. Prothorax one-half wider than long, narrowed in apical
      third, the sides thence parallel and almost straight to the base. Elytra
      nearly one-half wider than the prothorax, three times as long, parallel,
      broadly rounded at apex, with the subapical umbones rather distinct.
      Length 3.0–3.3 mm.; width 1.3–1.6 mm. Arizona (Winslow). Mr. H.
      F. Wickham...**graphica** n. sp.
Body uniformly pale ochreous-testaceous throughout.
   Vestiture dense, pale yellowish, consisting of elongate subrecumbent
      scales, intermixed with narrower hairs on the pronotum, each elytral
      interval with a single series of very broad semi-erect distant scales.
      Head convex; eyes separated by rather more than one-half of their
      own width; beak in the male rather thick, cylindrical, feebly arcuate,
      finely, sublinearly punctate, barely as long as the head and prothorax;

antennæ inserted rather beyond apical third, the first funicular joint scarcely as long as the next three, club not as long as the preceding six joints combined. Prothorax nearly four-fifths wider than long, rounded and narrowed in apical half, the apex transversely truncate and about three-fifths as wide as the base. *Elytra* at base two-fifths wider than the prothorax, more than three times as long, broadly, feebly sinuate at base, the sides straight and parallel in basal three-fifths. Length 2.8 mm.; width 1.4 mm. Arizona..........**squamiger** n. sp.
Vestiture dense, consisting, on the pronotum, of long slender pointed subrecumbent squamules, on the elytra of similar squamules and with a single series of long robust lanceolate and suberect scales on each interval; the latter scales very coarsely and deeply strigose, ochreous and piceous-black in color. Head densely hispido-squamose between the eyes, the latter separated by much less than one-half of their own width; beak in the male very short, thick, feebly bent, equal in length to the prothorax; antennæ inserted at apical third, the basal joint of the funicle but slightly longer than the next two, club very long, fusiform, deeply annulated, longer than the preceding six joints combined. Prothorax scarcely more than one-half wider than long, the sides strongly convergent and nearly straight in apical half, the apex one-half as wide as the base; punctures rather coarse, very dense; vestiture uniform. Elytra nearly one-half wider than the prothorax, more than three times as long, the sides parallel and nearly straight in basal three-fifths. Length 3.5 mm.; width 1.75 mm. Southern California.
                 horridula n. sp.
Elytral intervals distinctly alternating in width, the wider rather more convex and more densely clothed; body uniformly pale ochreous-testaceous throughout ....:...**helvola** Lec.

In *graphica*, which is a very isolated species, intermediate in habitus between Thysanocnemis and Tylopterus, the pronotal vestiture is fulvous except narrowly along the median line and at the sides toward base, where it becomes white, the white lateral area curved inward just behind the middle of the disk, giving the appearance of a transverse interrupted band.

Otidocephalini.

OTIDOCEPHALUS Chev.

Since the last revision of this genus by Dr. Horn (Proc. Am. Phil. Soc., XIII, p. 448), several remarkable forms have been discovered in Florida and our extreme southwestern territories. In the memoir referred to, seven species were recorded as occurring within the United States, and one other was subsequently added by LeConte. Besides *O. perforatus*, for which a separate genus is proposed below, fifteen species are now brought to notice; probably many more still remain unknown. Mexico appears to be the principal focal centre of Otidocephalus, and, although well represented in Brazil, the genus would seem to be relatively less abundant there, being largely replaced by Erodiscus.

The species are readily subdivided into well-marked groups based upon femoral, rostral and ungual structure, size of the eyes and nature of the vestiture as follows:—

Beak without dorsal excavation ; femora dentate 2

Beak with a large and very deep excavation near the middle ; femora unarmed...9

2—Tarsal claws with a large, acutely angulate, internal lobe ; body with erect setæ 3

Tarsal claws broadly swollen within toward base, but not at all angulate; body entirely without erect setæ 8

3—Elytra with more or less dense recumbent vestiture in addition to the erect setæ, the pubescence tufted in structure 4

Elytra with sparser recumbent or subrecumbent and paler hairs, simple in structure and always confusedly distributed over the surface..............5

Elytra with stiff erect white setæ, intermingled with longer, more slender, blackish hairs, all forming single series on the intervals 6

Elytra with simple erect setæ, either black or whitish in color, forming single series on the intervals 7

4—Elytra each with four glabrous or subglabrous vittæ.

  Vittæ narrow and sharply defined, with a few scattered tufts only near the apex...1 **vittatus**

  Vittæ much wider, always with unevenly scattered pubescent tufts throughout the length, punctured and indefinitely limited ; body smaller and relatively stouter...2 **nivosus**

Elytra without four subglabrous vittæ.

  Pubescence moderately dense, paler along the elytral suture and median line of the pronotum ....3 **ulkei**

  Pubescence uniform in color throughout the upper surface, pale brownish-cinereous, broadly dense on the elytral intervals, but denuded in a narrow space on each side of the series of punctures, producing a multi-vittate appearance ; dorsal setæ very short ....4 **insignis**

5—Elytra without well-defined series of punctures, confusedly and unevenly punctate throughout ....5 **estriatus**

Elytra with impressed even series of coarse deep punctures.

  Body very robust, the subrecumbent setæ coarse, abundant, pure white and very conspicuous ; pronotum sparsely, unevenly and not coarsely punctate ....6 **egregius**

  Body narrow, the subrecumbent shorter hairs sparse, somewhat dark in color and not very conspicuous ; pronotum coarsely and very densely punctate ....7 **scrobicollis**

6—Elytral series feebly impressed, coarsely, deeply and rather remotely
  punctured..8 **floridanus**
7—Eyes separated by much less than one-half of their own width.
  Elytral punctures fine, the series not impressed on the disk, the setæ confined in great measure to the alternate intervals, except toward apex ;
  body rather stout ....9 **lævicollis**
  Elytral punctures coarser, the series just visibly impressed, the setæ more
  abundant and conspicuous, widely spaced along all of the intervals ; body
  smaller and narrower ....10 **speculator**
Eyes widely separated.
  Elytra strongly inflated behind, the setæ very sparse, rather short, whitish
  in color and only distinct toward apex...................11 **myrmecodes**
  Elytra but slightly wider behind the middle than at base ; setæ numerous,
    long, blackish in color ; strial punctures coarser.
  Body stouter, the antennæ rufous.............................12 **ruficornis**
  Body slender, the antennæ black .. ..13 **myrmex**
8—Ferruginous, the elytra blackish in apical half or more ; body with short,
  white, slender, sparsely scattered and recumbent squamules ; femoral
  teeth very minute...14 **dichrous**
9—Polished, black, the legs, beak and antennæ piceous ; pronotum and elytra
  glabrous, without erect setæ, except a few borne from a series of punctures
  along the apical margin of the former on the flanks, and, on the latter,
  several toward apex, and one much longer and isolated on each side of
  the scutellum...15 **cavirostris**

The division of the genus by the form of the prothorax is im-
practicable, as, in several species, this part is more or less cylindrical
in the male and obovate in the female, notably so in *speculator*.

1 **O. vittatus** Horn.—Proc. Am. Phil. Soc., XIII, 1873, p. 448.

Elongate-oval, strongly convex, black, polished, densely clothed
with white pubescence formed of recumbent tufted hairs ; each
elytron with four narrow, feebly convex, abruptly defined, glabrous
vittæ and a much narrower uneven line very near the suture, the
glabrous vittæ narrow, but slightly more than one-half as wide as
the pubescent stripes, and each with a series of small widely and
unevenly spaced punctures bearing short piceous setæ. Beak short,
thick, three-fifths to three-fourths as long as the prothorax, deeply,
unevenly punctate at the sides, the antennæ inserted at apical two-
fifths in the female and but just visibly beyond in the male. Prothorax coarsely, unevenly punctate, with a polished fusiform tumid
and almost entire median impunctate line. Elytra but slightly
wider behind the middle than at base, almost twice as long as wide.

Legs rather stout, pubescent, the femora somewhat strongly toothed. Length 7.0–8.3 mm.; width 2.5–3.0 mm.

Southern California. My series of five specimens indicates but slight variability, and the species, which is one of the largest of the genus, may be readily known by the narrow, abruptly glabrous, polished vittæ of the elytra.

2 O. nivosus n. sp.—Oval, feebly subcuneate, black, polished, densely clothed with white recumbent pubescence formed of tufted hairs, intermingled with short stiff sparse piceous setæ, the elytra each with five subglabrous vittæ, the first adjoining the suture; those of the disk fully two-thirds as wide as the pubescent stripes, all more or less confusedly punctate toward their lateral limits, and always unevenly and sparsely covered with tufted pubescence. *Head* sparsely pubescent, densely so between the eyes which are separated by but slightly.less than their own width; beak short, thick, straight, coarsely, rugosely punctate, rather densely pubescent in tufts throughout, three-fifths to three-fourths as long as the prothorax, the antennæ inserted at apical third in the male, the second joint of the funicle almost as long as the first. *Prothorax* but slightly longer than wide, strongly inflated at about the middle, the base and apex subequal in the male, but the former relatively narrower in the female, coarsely, closely and unevenly punctate, with a subentire tumid impunctate line. Scutellum densely tomentose. *Elytra* at base one-half to two-thirds wider than the base of the prothorax, slightly wider behind the middle than at base, three-fourths longer than wide. *Legs* moderate; femoral teeth small, acute; anterior tibiæ obtusely strongly swollen or subdentate within at the middle. Length 6.0–6.5 mm.; width 2.4–2.6 mm.

Arizona (Peach Springs); Texas (El Paso).

This species is closely allied to *vittatus*, but differs constantly in a number of structural features. The prothorax and elytra are both less elongate, and the subglabrous stripes of the latter are wider, indistinctly limited and always more or less pubescent; the antennæ are rather more apical in insertion, the femoral teeth smaller, and the anterior tibiæ more strongly and angularly swollen within at the middle. The size is noticeably smaller than in *vittatus*. Three specimens.

3 O. ulkei Horn.—Proc. Am. Phil. Soc., XIII, p. 449.

This species is described as being moderately densely clothed with pubescence, which is recumbent and composed of tufted hairs as in *vittatus* and *insignis*, the vestiture paler along the middle of the pronotum and elytra. The femora are minutely toothed. Length (exclusive of the head) 6.5 mm.

Lower California. A single specimen in the cabinet of Mr. Henry Ulke of Washington.

4 O. insignis n. sp.—Rather robust, subcuneate, very strongly convex, polished, black throughout, densely clothed with tufts of pale brownish-cinereous pubescence, rather denser and whiter beneath, especially on the sternal parapleuræ, semi-erect on the pronotum, where they are mixed with sparse, anteriorly directed and erect black setæ, becoming white on the flanks and toward base, recumbent on the elytra and mingled with posteriorly-inclined, short sparse and whitish setæ, mixed with blackish near the apex, the elytral intervals becoming abruptly glabrous near the series of punctures, producing a narrowly multi-vittate appearance, the median line of the pronotum and the elytral suture not at all paler. *Head* densely clothed with recumbent whitish tufts between the eyes, concealing the sculpture, more sparsely so behind; eyes separated by fully their own width, feebly convex; beak thick, one-half as long as the prothorax, straight, not carinate above, coarsely punctured and longitudinally, indefinitely sulcate and rugose toward the sides, sparsely punctate on the disk toward apex, sparsely clothed with erect hispid setæ; antennæ inserted at apical two-fifths, the funicle densely hispido-setose, the second joint nearly twice as long as wide, three-fourths as long as the first and one-half longer than the third, club rather large, oval, extremely densely clothed with short brownish pubescence. *Prothorax* one-fourth longer than wide, the base a little wider than the apex, the sides strongly rounded and inflated at basal third, thence sinuate to the base; disk coarsely, deeply, unevenly punctate, the punctures denser above, sparser on the flanks, with a smooth impunctate median line in apical half. *Scutellum* rather large, triangular, extremely densely clothed with white pubescence forming a tumid mass. *Elytra* at base two-thirds wider than the base of the prothorax, but only one-fourth wider than the disk, nearly two and one-half times as long, not quite twice as long as wide, perceptibly wider behind the middle than at base; disk with unimpressed series of fine, unevenly and moderately spaced punctures, the series but just visibly impressed near the lateral margin. *Legs* long; femora strongly toothed; tibiæ arcuate toward base. Length 8.5 mm.; width 3.3 mm.

Texas (El Paso). Mr. G. W. Dunn.

The largest species which I have seen, and allied to *ulkei* in the development of the remarkable tufts of setæ, densely covering the integuments; each of these tufts is composed of three or four long slender hairs, which are united and attached at base by a short stout common foot-stalk. It differs from *ulkei* in the sculpture of the beak, in the denser vittæ of the elytra, uniform in color and not paler at the suture, and in its larger size.

5 O. estriatus n. sp.—Robust, extremely convex, shining, black, the beak antennæ and entire elytra more or less rufo-piceous but dark; pubescence simple, very sparse, recumbent, whitish, intermingled on the pronotum and elytra, especially toward apex, with extremely few remote blackish setæ; under surface rather sparsely clothed with long flexible whitish hairs, very dense on the sternal parapleuræ. *Head* coarsely, deeply, very densely punctate, flat and longitudinally rugose between the eyes, sparsely clothed with short whitish hairs; eyes large, rather convex, separated by four-fifths of their own width; beak thick, scarcely arcuate, not quite as long as the prothorax, gradually, distinctly dilated toward apex, with two approximate eroded and unevenly punctate grooves in basal half, separated by a smooth impunctate line, laterally very coarsely, deeply, densely punctate and rugose but not sulcate, above toward apex strongly punctate and with two widely distant longitudinal impressions; antennæ inserted at apical third, the second funicular joint obconical, three-fourths as long as the first, club elongate-oval, densely pubescent, darker in color. *Prothorax* very slightly longer than wide, the apex broadly arcuate, a little wider than the base; sides subparallel and nearly straight in apical two-thirds, then gradually rounded, convergent and sinuate to the base; disk coarsely, deeply, unevenly and closely punctate, the punctures becoming finer near the apex, sparse on the flanks toward base and with a narrow subentire tumid impunctate line along the middle. Scutellum small, densely covered with yellowish-white tomentum. *Elytra* at base two-thirds wider than the base of the prothorax, two and one-half times as long, three-fourths longer than wide, only slightly wider behind the middle than at base; humeri obtusely angulate, scarcely rounded, subprominent; disk without series but with moderately fine, deeply impressed punctures unevenly distributed in longitudinal vittæ, separated by subimpunctate narrower lines, which have exceedingly remote larger punctures bearing the stiff erect setæ. *Legs* moderate in length, sparsely pubescent, the femora distinctly, acutely toothed beneath. Length 5.5 mm.; width 2.2 mm.

New Mexico (Las Vegas). Mr. Meeske.

The uneven sculpture and sparse recumbent vestiture distinguish this species from any other within our fauna; it may perhaps be allied to the Mexican *flavipennis* Chev.

6 **O. egregius** n. sp.—Oblong-ovoidal, strongly convex, rather robust, black and polished throughout, the upper surface clothed sparsely but conspicuously with short robust recurved white setæ, unevenly scattered on all the interval of the elytra and mingled with longer finer erect and more widely dispersed piceous setæ; legs and under surface rather sparsely but distinctly clothed with short and more recumbent white hairs, dense and tufted on the sternal side-pieces and mesosternum between the coxæ, also with sparser tufted hairs on the prosternum and toward the anterior margin of the metasternum. *Head* coarsely but not very densely or deeply punctate; eyes large although not very prominent, separated by one-third of their own width; beak thick, just noticeably wider at apex, feebly bent, three-fourths as long as the prothorax in the male, smooth and impunctate broadly along the middle, with a feeble impressed line between the antennæ, coarsely, closely punctate and longitudinally sulcate laterally, hispid with erect setæ; antennæ inserted at apical third, long, slender, the first funicular joint a little longer than the next two, club rather small, elongate, pointed, asymmetrically fusiform. *Prothorax*

distinctly longer than wide, the base and apex subequal in the male, the former relatively narrower in the female ; sides feebly arcuate, convergent and straight toward base ; punctures rather small, feeble, remote and unevenly distributed. Scutellum densely pubescent. *Elytra* oblong, at base almost twice as wide as the prothorax, nearly two and one-half times longer, three-fifths longer than wide, not distinctly wider behind the middle than at base, the sides subparallel ; striæ broadly, rather strongly impressed, coarsely, deeply and not very closely punctate ; intervals convex, minutely, sparsely and unevenly punctate. *Legs* rather short and stout, the femora strongly toothed ; tibiæ bent toward base. Length 5.0 mm. ; width 1.9 mm.

Arizona.

The two specimens before me represent one of the most distinct species of the genus, recognizable at once by the numerous coarse recurved white setæ of the upper surface, the subparallel elytra, relatively narrow prothorax, large eyes and large femoral teeth. It does not appear to be at all closely allied to any of the Mexican species.

7 **O. scrobicollis** Boh—Sch. Gen. Curc., VII, ii, p. 205 ; Horn : Proc. Am. Phil. Soc., XIII, p. 450.

Black, polished, narrowly, feebly subcuneate, bristling with long coarse erect and blackish setæ, with a few short paler subrecumbent hairs interspersed. Head and beak coarsely closely and unevenly punctate ; eyes separated by three-fourths of their own width ; beak rather slender, not quite as long as the prothorax, confusedly, longitudinally sulcate and rugose, with an elongate feeble impression in the middle between the antennæ, the latter long, the second funicular joint barely one-half as long as the first ; basal joint of the club long and evenly obconical, with the sides straight. Prothorax but slightly longer than wide, the sides sinuate behind the apex and more broadly before the base, the apex broadly arcuate and scarcely wider than the base ; disk very coarsely, densely punctate. Scutellum small, pubescent. Elytra at base three-fifths wider than the base of the prothorax, two and one-half times longer, not quite twice as long as wide, slightly wider behind the middle than at base, the humeri narrowly rounded ; disk with feebly impressed series of coarse, rather close-set punctures. Legs slender, the femora very long, the tooth small. Length 4.2 mm. ; width 1.6 mm.

Pennsylvania to Texas. A well-marked species which cannot fail of recognition by reason of the sparse dual vestiture, coarse sculpture and long slender feebly toothed femora. It does not appear to be abundant.

8 **O. floridanus** n. sp.—Slender, feebly cylindro-cuneate, polished, black throughout, the upper surface bristling with long sparse erect setæ, white and piceous indiscriminately intermingled, the piceous setæ longer and much thinner than the white, the latter rather robust; under surface very remotely, feebly albido-pilose, the scutellum, sternal parapleuræ and mesosternum between the narrowly separated coxæ densely clothed with recumbent white tufted pubescence. *Head* sparsely, unevenly, distinctly punctate, without frontal fovea, the eyes separated by scarcely more than two-thirds of their own width; beak moderately thick, very short, nearly straight, scarcely two-thirds as long as the prothorax, narrowly polished and tumid along the middle between two punctured erosions, coarsely, closely punctato-rugose at the sides, sparsely hispido-setose; antennæ moderate. *Prothorax* almost evenly truncato-fusiform, much longer than wide, the base and apex about equal in width, the latter only very feebly arcuate; sides evenly, feebly arcuate, scarcely at all sinuate near the base; disk rather finely, sparsely, unevenly punctate, widest at the middle. *Elytra* distinctly more than twice as long as the prothorax, and, behind the middle, twice as wide as the disk of the latter, gradually slightly narrower thence to the base; humeri rather broadly exposed but obliquely truncate: disk with very feebly impressed series of rather coarse, deep, somewhat distant punctures, the punctures of the interstitial series minute and very remote. *Legs* rather short and thick, the femoral teeth large and prominent; tibiæ bent toward base. Length 4.0 mm.; width 1.3 mm.

Florida.

A slender species, somewhat resembling *myrmex* in form, but abundantly distinct in the mixture of long white and blackish setæ of the upper surface, the longer elytra, and in the subcylindrical and not obovate prothorax.

9 **O. lævicollis** Horn.—Proc. Am. Phil. Soc., XIII, p. 451.

Rather robust, feebly cuneate, strongly convex, polished, black throughout, the tarsi piceous; upper surface very sparsely covered with moderately long erect setæ, white in color but becoming blackish on the disk of the pronotum anteriorly, and shorter and denser near the base, very remote in single series on the elytra, where they are confined for the most part to the alternate intervals; under surface and legs covered with sparse semi-erect white setæ, the scutellum and sternal parapleuræ densely pubescent. Head almost completely impunctate, narrow, slightly depressed, opaque, sparsely punctate and sparsely setose between the eyes, the latter large, prominent and separated by less than one-third of their own width; beak moderate, coarsely punctate and rugose at the sides, with a feebly impressed longitudinal line in the middle between the antennæ. Prothorax extremely minutely and remotely punctate, strongly narrowed toward base, the latter scarcely three-fourths as wide as the apex in the female; disk but slightly longer than wide. Elytra scarcely more than one-half longer than wide, twice as long as the prothorax, and, behind the middle, twice as wide; striæ unimpressed, except feebly near the sides, composed of fine, not very close-set punctures. Legs rather long; femoral teeth only moderately developed, acute; tibiæ feebly bent toward base. Length 3.3–4.3 mm.; width 1.3–1.8 mm.

New York to Texas. Easily distinguishable by the large prominent approximate eyes, and fine punctures of the unimpressed elytral series. The specimen described is a female.

10 **O. speculator** n. sp.—Subcuneate, strongly convex, black and highly polished throughout, the upper surface bristling with very sparse long erect setæ, white in color but blackish on the disk of the pronotum toward apex, and forming an even single series on each of the elytral intervals, very sparse, shorter, finer and less erect on the under surface, the scutellum and sternal parapleuræ densely albido-pubescent. *Head* smooth, scarcely at all punctate, the interocular surface setose, not depressed, slightly dull and remotely punctate; eyes large, prominent, separated by scarcely more than one-third of their own width; beak in the male short, thick, straight, two-thirds as long as the prothorax, smooth and impunctate above, coarsely punctato-rugose at the sides, and above, in apical two-fifths, having two wide, depressed, dull and reticulate, parallel and rather approximate areas, the narrow interval being impressed along the middle; in the female smoother above at apex; antennæ moderate, the first funicular joint robust, as long as the next two, second a little longer than the third, both elongate, the club elongate, pointed, asymmetrically fusiform. *Prothorax* distinctly longer than wide, with the apex broadly arcuate; base nearly as wide as the apex in the male but scarcely three-fourths as wide in the female; disk almost impunctate, but with a few rather coarse punctures at the sides near the apex. *Elytra* one-half longer than wide, twice as long as the prothorax, and, behind the middle, distinctly more than twice as wide as the latter in both sexes; humeri very broadly exposed, obtusely rounded; disk with very feebly impressed series of rather coarse distant punctures, the sutural series more strongly impressed as usual. *Legs* moderate, the femoral teeth rather small, acute. Length 3.5–3.7 mm.; width 1.4–1.5 mm.

Texas.

This species, which is represented in my cabinet by three specimens, is closely allied to *lævicollis*, but differs in its smaller size, less robust form, more abundant and conspicuous white setæ of the elytra distributed along all of the intervals, and in the coarser punctures of the elytral series. The sparse setæ of the pronotum seem to be inclined to serial arrangement in basal half.

11 O. myrmecodes Chev.—Ann. Ent. Soc. Fr., 1832, p. 445; *chevrolati* Horn : Proc. Am. Phil. Soc., XIII, p. 450.

Cuneate, strongly convex, polished, black throughout, almost glabrous above, the head and basal parts of the beak with short sparse erect white setæ, also a few of the latter longer and widely spaced along the intervals of the elytra becoming white toward apex; prothorax feebly piceo-setose; under surface and legs very sparsely clothed with short white hairs, the scutellum and sternal parapleuræ as usual densely albido-pubescent. Head finely, remotely punctate, with a large deep elongate fovea between the eyes, the latter separated by a little less than their own width; beak short, polished, strongly punctured on the sides; antennæ black. Prothorax almost one-third longer than wide, strongly convex longitudinally in apical two-thirds, gradually feebly inflated anteriorly, strongly, rather unevenly punctate, especially in apical half and near the base. Elytra less than twice as long as wide, convex longitudinally, strongly inflated behind, where they are more than twice as wide as the disk of the prothorax; striæ unimpressed except near the sides and composed of fine but deep, rather close-set punctures. Legs long, the femora slender, rather minutely toothed; tibiæ almost straight. Length 3.7–5.0 mm.; width 1.4–2.0 mm.

Rhode Island, District of Columbia, North Carolina and Indiana; numerous specimens. This is a distinct species, easily known by its strongly, posteriorly inflated elytra, feebly developed dorsal setæ, slender, straight, finely toothed femora and deep frontal fovea. I do not know the law or precedent under which the name given by Chevrolat was changed by Dr. Horn; If *myrmecodes* Say is a synonym of *myrmex* Hbst., as seems to be undoubtedly the case, Chevrolat's name cannot be preoccupied.

12 O. ruficornis n. sp.—Rather stout, convex, very feebly subcuneate, black throughout and highly polished; antennæ and tarsi brownish-rufous; upper surface with numerous but very sparse, long, erect, blackish setæ, becoming whiter near the elytral apex laterally and also on the under surface, where they are much shorter and subrecumbent; scutellum and sternal parapleuræ densely albido-pubescent. *Head* and beak rather sparsely but evidently and unevenly punctate; eyes separated by slightly less than their own width, the interocular surface broadly, feebly impressed between two feeble and distant carinæ; beak short, rather thick, nearly straight, not dilated

toward apex, subglabrous, three-fourths as long as the prothorax, with two
parallel uneven grooves on the disk, rather distant and obsolete at the middle,
and, on each side at the declivity, a longitudinal groove, entire, but becoming
feebler toward the apex, also coarsely punctate at the sides toward base, the
punctures of the upper surface near the apex almost obsolete; antennæ moderate, the first funicular joint rather slender, obconical, second slightly longer
than the third, club rather small, evenly elliptical, less than one-half longer
than wide. *Prothorax* strongly convex, one-fourth longer than wide, the apex
broadly arcuate, much wider than the base; sides feebly divergent from the
apex to the middle, then more strongly convergent and nearly straight to the
base; disk finely, remotely and unevenly punctate, the punctures impressed
and distinct. *Elytra* at base two-thirds wider than the base of the prothorax,
slightly but distinctly wider behind the middle, three-fourths longer than
wide, the series scarcely at all impressed and composed of rather small, moderately close-set punctures. *Legs* rather stout, the femoral teeth large; tibiæ
only just visibly bent toward base. Length 4.7–5.0 mm.; width 1.7–1.8 mm.

Arizona.

Allied closely to *myrmex*, but larger and stouter, with the elytral
series finer and less impressed. I should have referred the two
specimens in my cabinet to *mexicanus* Chev., as they agree tolerably well with the description of Rosenskoeld, but the elytra are
evidently much shorter, their length being given as almost three
times that of the prothorax in that species, while in *ruficornis* they
are only twice as long.

13 **O. myrmex** Hbst.—Käfer, VII, p. 56; Horn: Proc. Am. Phil. Soc.,
XIII, p. 450; *myrmecodes* Say: Curc. p. 15; Ed. Lec., I, p. 278; *americanus*
Chev.: Ann. Ent. Soc. Fr., I, 1832, p. 105; Gyll. et Rosen.: Sch. Curc. III, p.
366; VII, p. 205.

Narrowly and very feebly subcuneate, very strongly convex,
polished, black throughout, the upper surface with numerous long
erect blackish hairs, on the elytra disposed in a single widely-spaced
series on each interval, on the under surface and legs generally
whiter, the sternal side-pieces densely clothed with white pubescence,
recumbent, and tufted in structures as usual. Beak short; antennæ
slender, the funicular joints two to four subequal, each slightly
elongate; eyes moderate, separated by a little less than their own
width. Prothorax strongly convex before the middle, sparsely,
rather strongly and unevenly punctate, one-fifth longer than wide,
the apex broadly arcuate and but slightly wider than the base.
Scutellum densely pubescent. Elytra very nearly twice as long as
wide, rather distinctly wider behind; punctures coarse, the series

feebly impressed. Legs rather slender; femoral teeth large; tibiæ bent toward base. Length 3.6–4.4 mm.; width 1.2–1.6 mm.

This is a common species, easily recognizable by its narrow form, the long blackish and somewhat abundant setæ of the upper surface, and the strong strial punctures. My specimens are from New Jersey, Pennsylvania and Indiana.

14 **O. dichrous** Lec.—Proc. Am. Phil. Soc., XV, p. 191.

Rather narrowly and feebly cuneate, less convex above than usual, polished and ferruginous throughout, the elytra piceous black in apical half to two-thirds; erect setæ completely wanting, the body throughout with extremely sparse recumbent squamules, very slender in form and white in color; scutellum densely tomentose; sternal side-pieces not densely pubescent, the met-episternum with a narrow uneven line of squamules. Head finely, sparsely but distinctly punctate, with a deep elongate-oval interocular fovea; eyes moderately large, strongly convex, coarsely faceted, separated by fully one-half of their own width; beak very short, thick, cylindrical, feebly sculptured even toward the sides; antennæ nearly normal, but with the club very indistinctly annulated, the scrobes passing beneath at a great distance from the eyes. Prothorax distinctly elongate, subcylindrical, feebly and gradually inflated to slightly behind the middle, sparsely, distinctly but unevenly punctate. Elytra behind the middle twice as wide as the prothorax and much wider than at base, almost twice as long as wide; humeri broadly exposed; striæ feebly impressed, composed of coarse, deep, close-set punctures. Legs long, with short sparse recumbent squamules, not setose; femoral teeth very minute, the posterior femora long and sublinear; third tarsal joint very widely bilobed; claws divaricate, thick, strongly arcuate, gradually swollen internally toward base but not in the least angulate. Length 4.1–4.7 mm.; width 1.4–1.75 mm.

Georgia and Florida. The large series in my cabinet seems to indicate but little variability, except in the extent of the blackish area of the elytra. This remarkable species is aberrant in its vesti-ture and in the structure of the tarsal claws.

15 **O. cavirostris** n. sp.—Narrowly subcuneate, highly polished, strongly convex, black, the legs, beak and antennæ piceo-rufous; body almost completely glabrous, a few erect setæ near the anterior margin of the prothorax, a long seta near the scutellum and a few toward the elytral apex being all that are visible

in the type ; scutellum, mesosternal side-pieces and met-episterna posteriorly, densely clothed with recumbent white pubescence. *Head* sparsely but distinctly punctate toward base and between the eyes, elsewhere entirely impunctate ; eyes rather large, moderately prominent, separated by a little less than their own width ; beak very short and robust, barely more than one-half as long as the prothorax, parallel, rather wider than thick, with a large and extremely deep excavation just behind the middle, occupying the entire width, rounded and bounded by an acute densely ciliate edge on the sides and behind, the anterior edge obtuse and transverse ; bottom of the cavity ascending anteriorly and feebly bicarinate ; rostral surface between the cavity and apex and also at the sides throughout, strongly though not very densely punctate ; antennæ short, the basal joint of the funicle robust, second slightly elongate, third not quite as long as wide, outer joints thicker, club nearly as long as the preceding six joints, strongly annulated. *Prothorax* distinctly longer than wide, widest at two-fifths from the base, the sides thence almost straight and very feebly convergent to the broadly arcuate apex, and strongly convergent and constricted to the base, the latter barely three-fifths as wide as the apex ; disk finely but strongly, almost evenly and somewhat closely punctate. Scutellum distinct. *Elytra* scarcely more than one-half longer than the prothorax, and, at base nearly twice as wide as the base of the latter but not wider than the disk, gradually rather strongly inflated posteriorly, and, behind the middle, two-fifths wider than the disk of the prothorax, three-fourths longer than wide, very strongly, evenly convex longitudinally ; humeri rather prominent, narrowly rounded, the exposed basal portion oblique ; striæ feebly impressed except toward apex, the punctures small, moderately close-set and distinct. *Legs* rather long, very slender, the femora linear, scarcely at all sinuate toward apex and completely unarmed ; tarsal claws normal. Length 1.9 mm. ; width 0.6 mm.

Florida.

The single specimen of this extremely interesting species was taken in the southern part of the State by Mr. F. Kinzel, and very kindly presented to me by Mr. Wilhelm Jülich. It is related to the Cuban *poeyi* Chev. in the extraordinary rostral excavation and unarmed femora, but differs in coloration and, probably also, in its smaller size and more sparsely punctate head. It is by far the most minute of our species, and, together with *poeyi*, might well be separated as a distinct genus.

OOPTERINUS n. gen.

This genus is founded upon a remarkable species described by Dr. Horn under the name *Otidocephalus perforatus*. It differs from Otidocephalus in having the elytra ovate, rounded on the sides, widest a little before the middle, gradually attenuate and acutely rounded behind, and with the humeri entirely obsolete, in the complete absence of scutellum, and in its small eyes. The elytra are probably subconnate. In its short deeply sinuate prosternum, short beak, and toothed claws, Oopterinus resembles Otidocephalus.

O. perforatus Horn.—Proc. Am. Phil. Soc., XIII, p. 451.

Oval, piceous, the elytra and legs still paler, the upper surface with a few rather short, semi-erect, widely scattered whitish setæ. Head sparsely but strongly punctate, the interocular surface impunctate but with a small rounded median fovæ ; eyes remarkably small, coarsely granulated, separated by fully their own width ; beak rather thick, feebly arcuate, almost as long as the prothorax, strongly punctured at the sides and with a short longitudinally impressed line between the antennæ, the latter slender, the second funicular joint obconical, one-half longer than the third ; club oval, rather sparsely pubescent. Prothorax longer than wide, strongly narrowed and feebly constricted toward base, very coarsely, deeply, slightly unevenly but rather closely punctate. Elytra ovate, two-thirds longer than wide, widest before the middle, the sides evenly rounded ; humeri obsolete ; punctures very fine, disposed in even series which are entirely unimpressed except near the base. Legs very slender, the femora broadly emarginate near the apex but not toothed. Length 3.3 mm.; width 1.3 mm.

The single specimen in the LeConte cabinet has no indication of locality, but the original type, in the cabinet of Mr. Ulke, is from Maryland.

CRYPTORHYNCHINI.

CONOTRACHELUS Schönh.

The following rather isolated species may be referred at present to the groups outlined by Dr. LeConte.

C. compositus n. sp.—Oblong-oval, moderately convex, not at all shining, black, the legs and antennæ rufo-piceous ; elytra clothed densely with short recumbent hairs, piceous in color, fulvous along the ridges and yellowish in three elongate spots at the base of each, the two outer coalescent, the pronotum more sparsely pubescent, with a few whitish hairs scattered in an oblique line at each side ; upper surface throughout bristling with short stiff erect setæ. *Head* and beak densely hispid with short bristles and more recumbent hairs ; front foveate ; beak separated from the head by a deep transverse impression, very short and thick, distinctly and evenly arcuate, four-fifths as long as the prothorax, very deeply coarsely and densely punctato-subsulcate and dull; antennæ inserted at apical third, the second funicular joint scarcely as long as the first but rather longer than the next two. *Prothorax* not quite as long as wide, the sides in basal three-fourths parallel, straight but convergent near the base, rather prominent at apical fourth, thence convergent and constricted to the apex; disk evenly convex but exceedingly coarsely, roughly punctato-foveate, the foveæ closely crowded and irregular, with a fine strong carina in apical half, rendered more prominent by a depression in the surface at each side of it. *Elytra* at base three-fifths wider than the prothorax, two and three-fourths times as long, one-third longer than wide, the sides parallel toward base, sinuate near the apex; humeri broadly exposed, prominent and obtusely carinate; disk with unimpressed series of large deep rather close-set punctures; intervals flat, the third obtusely tumid at the base, before the middle and through apical third, the fifth more especially from basal third to the subapical impression, the seventh at the humeri and to a greater or less degree along its entire extent. *Abdomen* with not very dense large and small punctures. Femora with two acute spiniform teeth; tarsal claws divergent, strongly toothed. Length 5.4 mm.; width 2.5 mm.

Arizona.

May be associated with *affinis* for the present, but widely distinct from any other described species known to me.

C. carinifer n. sp.—Oblong-oval, feebly convex above, not shining, piceous-black, the elytra, legs and antennæ more or less rufescent; elytra clothed densely with short recumbent hairs, fulvous, mottled unevenly with whitish, the latter more evident in a transversely lunate area at apical third, also with a few widely scattered extremely short recurved and semi-erect setæ; pronotum glabrous although sparsely setose. *Head* finely, closely punctate, fulvido-pubescent, the beak long, slender, arcuate, two-fifths as long as the body in the male, finely but strongly punctato-sulcate, separated from the eyes at the sides by a deep vertical groove; antennæ inserted just behind the extreme apex, very slender, the second funicular joint longer than the first. *Prothorax* one-fifth wider than long, the sides parallel, broadly, feebly, evenly arcuate nearly to the apex, then rounded convergent and constricted; apex broadly arcuate and nearly three-fourths as wide as the base; disk with extremely large deep and closely crowded foveæ, each bearing a short anteriorly directed seta; surface evenly convex but finely, very strongly carinate along the middle. *Elytra* one-half wider than the prothorax, two and one-half times as long, one-third longer than wide, ovoidal, the sides becoming parallel toward base; humeri widely exposed, rounded; disk with unimpressed series of coarse deep close-set punctures; intervals flat, the alternate broadly, feebly carinate, the carinæ entire. *Abdomen* coarsely, closely punctate. *Legs* moderate, the femora uni-dentate. Length 4.3 mm.; width 2.2 mm.

Texas (Austin).

This is an interesting species, allied to *naso*, but having the antennæ of the male still more apical in insertion, and the pronotal sculpture nearly as in *fissunguis*.   A single specimen.

C. integer n. sp.—Oblong-oval, moderately convex above, dull, black, the elytra and legs with a feeble piceous tinge; pubescence of the elytra not very dense, consisting of short recumbent hairs, ochreous or fulvous in color, nearly evenly distributed and scarcely at all mottled, mixed with short sparse setæ, not paler or denser behind the middle, the pronotum sparsely setose. *Head* densely and rather finely punctate, the yellowish pubescence not extending beyond the front; beak long, slender, arcuate, about one-half as long as the elytra in the male, strongly sulcate, the antennæ inserted beyond apical third. *Prothorax* very nearly as long as wide, the sides broadly rounded anteriorly, becoming parallel and nearly straight in basal three-fifths, finely, moderately constricted just behind the apex; the latter not more than one-half as wide as the base; disk coarsely, extremely densely, unevenly and subconfluently punctate, evenly convex and with a fine entire median carina. *Elytra* one-half wider than the prothorax and not quite three times as long, two-fifths longer than wide, the sides becoming subparallel in basal half; humeri right, widely exposed but rounded; disk with series of moderately large deep close-set punctures, the alternate intervals with fine strongly-marked entire carinæ. *Abdomen* coarsely, very deeply and densely punctate. *Legs* long; femora moderately robust, subfusiform, obtusely and very feebly uni-dentate, the toothed appearance caused principally by the abrupt and deep subapical emargination; tarsal claws divergent, strongly toothed.   Length 6.0 mm.; width 2.9 mm.

Arizona (Tuçson).

The single male represents a species allied to *naso*, but with the pubescence of the elytra much sparser and not at all condensed or whiter behind the middle, and the pronotal sculpture more than twice as coarse, being fully as coarse as in *geminatus*.   Both this species and *carinifer* have the peculiar oblong-oval form and general rostral structure of *naso*, and should evidently be associated with it.

C. duplex n. sp.—Robust, suboval, strongly convex, blackish-piceous, the elytra rufous; vestiture of the anterior parts very sparse, in the form of long stiff anteriorly directed setæ, on the elytra of moderately dense, somewhat uneven prostrate hairs, coarser denser and paler yellowish toward the humeri and transversely behind the middle, also with long stiff erect setæ. *Head* densely punctate and with sparse subrecumbent yellow hairs, the front with a deep median fovea; eyes moderate, remotely separated; beak moderately thick, feebly, evenly arcuate, fully as long as the head and prothorax, very deeply, longitudinally punctato-sulcate, strongly carinate along the middle; antennæ inserted at apical third, the second funicular joint very long, about

as long as the first and twice as long as the third. *Prothorax* very nearly as
long as wide, the sides subparallel and just visibly arcuate in basal two-thirds,
then convergent and rather strongly constricted, the apex somewhat strongly
arcuate, three-fourths as wide as the base; disk very coarsely, deeply punctate, the punctures even but closely crowded and polygonal, without trace of
any kind of median line. *Elytra* three-fifths wider than the prothorax, two
and two-fifths times longer, only slightly longer than wide, the sides becoming
straight and nearly parallel in basal half; humeri right, narrowly rounded,
broadly exposed at base; disk with series of rather coarse punctures; intervals three, five, seven, eight and nine more or less strongly and uninter-
ruptedly carinate. *Abdomen* coarsely deeply and densely punctate. *Legs* not
very robust, the femora with a single fine tooth; claws feebly divergent acutely
toothed internally near the base. Length 4.3 mm.; width 2.3 mm.

California. Mr. Harford.

Somewhat resembles *fissunguis* in form, but differs in the alternately broadly carinate elytral intervals and the long bristling erect
setæ, as well as in the structure of the claws. The precise locality
is unknown, but is in all probability southern, as Conotrachelus does
not appear to enter the true Pacific coast fauna.

C. rotundus n. sp.—Robust, oval, convex, black, the legs rufescent;
vestiture of the pronotum sparse, of the elytra rather dense and consisting of
very short robust subrecumbent squamules, smaller even and ochreous on the
alternate intervals, whiter broader and submaculate on the others, the upper
surface throughout with stout erect clavate bristles, rather sparsely but evenly
distributed and moderate in length. *Head* finely, very densely punctate; eyes
remote; front and basal parts of the beak densely squamulose; beak rather
thick, evenly arcuate, fully as long as the head and prothorax, deeply, longitudinally sulcate; antennæ inserted near apical third, rather stout, the second
funicular joint scarcely as long as the first. *Prothorax* small, two-fifths wider
than long, the sides feebly convergent from the base and rather strongly
arcuate, more strongly convergent near the apex but not distinctly constricted; apex broadly arcuate and about three-fourths as wide as the base;
disk with extremely coarse uneven and densely crowded foveæ, the surface
rough but evenly convex and without median line. *Elytra* abruptly four-
fifths wider than the prothorax, not quite three times as long, not longer than
wide, the sides parallel and nearly straight to the middle, then convergent
and rounded feebly sinuate before the apex; disk with broadly, deeply impressed series of moderately large deep punctures, the intervals nearly equal
throughout and broadly, evenly convex, not in the least carinate at any point.
Abdomen rather coarsely, densely punctate. *Legs* not very stout, the femora
each with a single rather small but distinct tooth; tarsal claws rather divergent, bent downward near the base and with a long straight internal tooth
near the base, widely diverging from the claw and almost equalling it in
length. Length 3.0 mm.; width 1.9 mm.

Texas (near Austin).

A distinct species, easily distinguishable by its rather small size, obese form and peculiar thick clavate bristles. Together with *duplex*, it should be placed at the end of LeConte's group "I b," but there are no described species with which either of them can be compared.

The genera allied to Ryssematus, which have thus far occurred within the United States, may be readily distinguished as follows:—

Intermediate coxæ narrowly separated; second ventral segment not as long
    as the next two combined.
    Tarsal claws unequally cleft, approximate but not counate at base.
Ryssematus

    Tarsal claws simple, stout, subparallel, subconnate at base, the suture dis-
        tinct..**Chalcodernius**
Intermediate coxæ widely separated, the mesosternum between them depressed
    and flat; second ventral segment longer than the next two; tarsal claws
    small, slender, approximate at base but free...............**Chaleponotus**

RYSSEMATUS Chev.

R. pruinosus Sch. is somewhat aberrant in its more elongate-oval form and in the longer flatter abdominal segments, also in its very slender beak, joined at the lower part of the head at an obtuse angle.

R. ovalis n. sp.—Evenly oval, strongly convex, shining, glabrous, dark rufo-testaceous throughout. *Head* strongly convex, finely, densely punctate, with a small interocular fovea; eyes moderate, unusually distant, separated by rather less than their own width above; beak rather slender, evenly, moderately arcuate, shining, finely, sparsely lineato-punctate, a little longer than the head and prothorax; antennæ inserted just behind the middle, the scrobes horizontal, nearly attaining the lower portion of the eye; funicle long, slender, all the joints longer than wide, the first almost as long as the next three, second but slightly longer than the third, the club moderate, scarcely longer than the three preceding joints, oval, abrupt. *Prothorax* not quite twice as wide as long, the apex strongly constricted and tubulate, less than one-half as wide as the base; sides evenly convergent and arcuate from the base, the latter transverse, broadly, feebly bisinuate and with the usual narrow declivous margin; disk finely, deeply strigilato-punctate, the strigæ externally oblique anteriorly, the median line very fine and not distinctly cariniform. *Elytra* slightly wider than the prothorax and nearly three times as long, oval, the sides becoming parallel near the base, the humeri obliquely, feebly rounded externally to the prothorax and not exposed at base; disk with

strongly impressed striæ of moderately coarse deep elongate punctures, the
intervals equally convex, becoming somewhat acute toward apex, finely and
unevenly punctate along the sides of the grooves. *Abdomen* finely, rather
sparsely punctate. *Legs* short, the femora very robust, the denticle strong;
tibiæ stout, bent toward base, enlarged toward, and externally prominent at,
the apex. Length 3.8 mm.; width 2.0 mm.

Texas.

A rather small, evenly convex and isolated species, having the
eyes much more widely separated than in any other form which I
have seen. The structural characters are, however, all of this
genus. The ocular lobes are moderately well developed as usual in
this group.

Chalcodermus includes but three species within our faunal limits,
—*æneus, inæquicollis,* and *collaris.* The species identified by
LeConte as *spinifer* Boh., belongs to a widely different tribe of
Curculionidæ.

CHALEPONOTUS n. gen.

This genus is allied to Chalcodermus, but differs in the following
characters:—

Antennal scrobes feebly descending to the lower angle of the eyes, the basal
joint of the funicle not as long as the second. Second abdominal segment
much longer than the next two combined, the suture broadly, evenly angulate throughout its width. Middle coxæ widely separated. Tarsal claws
small, slender, approximate at base but not at all connate.

It also differs in many other features, the body, for example, being
more finely sculptured, and the elytral intervals elevated as in many
species of Ryssematus. The mandibles are very thick, strongly,
evenly arcuate in external outline, the apex prolonged and acute.

C. elusus n. sp.—Oval, convex, shining, black, glabrous, each puncture
bearing a very minute seta. *Head* finely, not very densely punctate; eyes
rather distant, separated by nearly their own width on the front; beak rather
slender, cylindrical, evenly, feebly arcuate, as long as the head and prothorax,
finely, sparsely punctate, shining, the antennæ inserted a little beyond the
middle, the second funicular joint elongate, fully as long as the next two,
outer joints thicker, the seventh scarcely as long as wide, club scarcely longer
than the three preceding joints, oval, pointed, not very abrupt. *Prothorax*
scarcely more than one-fourth wider than long, subconical, the sides evenly
convergent and broadly arcuate from the base to the distinct but not strong
subapical constriction, the apex arcuate, a little more than one-half as wide
as the base; disk finely, deeply and evenly punctate, the punctures separated

by nearly their own widths, with a narrow impunctate spot at the middle.
Scutellum small, tumid. *Elytra* one-third wider than the prothorax, two and
one-half times as long, ogival, the sides becoming scarcely parallel at base,
the humeri oblique to the base of the prothorax; disk with fine impressed
striæ, having moderately small deep elongate and remote punctures, wider
than the striæ, the intervals equal, strongly, angularly convex, with a feeble
series of small punctures at each side of the summit. *Abdomen* finely, sparsely
punctate. *Legs* moderate; femora not very stout, the denticle strong, inclined;
tibiæ rather slender. Length 4.0 mm.; width 2.0 mm.

Indiana.

Easily distinguishable by the fine even separated punctures of the
prothorax, the latter being unusually elongate. A single specimen.

ACAMPTUS Lec.

This is a conspicuously distinct and aberrant genus with the met-
epimera invisible, the episterna distinct, the anterior coxæ large,
prominent, contiguous but excavated internally to receive the very
short thick beak, the eyes concealed in repose, antennal club solid,
and third and fourth abdominal segments short. The tibiæ termi-
nate in an unusually large internal spur and the tarsi are slender
and cylindrical, with the third joint undilated; the claws are slender, free and divergent. The body is narrow and elongate, bristling with thick erect clavate setæ. The two species may be thus
distinguished:—

Elytra shorter, scarcely more than one-half longer than wide and not twice as
    long as, the prothorax, the latter broadly and feebly constricted behind
    the apex; dorsal bristles short and sparse throughout, the elytral ridges
    moderate...**rigidus** Lec.
Elytra much longer, fully three-fourths longer than wide and more than twice
    as long as the prothorax, the latter broadly and deeply constricted behind
    the apex; dorsal bristles twice as long and very close-set, extremely
    robust and squamiform; elytral ridges strong. Body elongate, parallel,
    subcylindrical. Head and beak densely squamose, the latter bristling
    with erect scales especially toward base, not more than two-thirds as long
    as the prothorax, the antennæ inserted near the middle, the funicle gla-
    brous, the basal joint about as long as the next two, outer joints gradu-
    ally thicker, coarctate, club rather small. Prothorax fully as long as wide,
    the apex broadly arcuate and slightly narrower than the base, coarsely,
    indistinctly punctate. Scutellum small, distinct. Elytra one-third wider
    than the prothorax, the sides straight and nearly parallel in basal three-
    fourths, each with four ridges bearing long erect close-set scales, the in-
    tervals alutaceous, biseriately punctate. Length 4.3 mm.; width 1.65
    mm. New York...**echinus** n. sp.

The vestiture is pale yellowish in color throughout, the integuments in *echinus* being dark red-brown. In both of the species the prothorax is very obliquely truncate at the sides, so that the head and beak are invisible from above; the ocular lobes are small. The antennal funicle is 7-jointed and not 6-jointed as indicated in the original description.

MICROMASTUS Lec.

The principal sternal characters of this genus appear to have been in great part misconceived by the author. The beak is moderately thick and perfectly free, the prosternum broadly, feebly impressed, the impression punctate, setose and much wider than the beak, the anterior coxæ large, conoidal, prominent and subcontiguous. The intermediate coxæ are somewhat widely separated, the mesosternum between them transversely tumid, densely punctate and setose. The metasternum is only moderately short and is longer than in Acalles; epimera and episterna both invisible, the third and fourth abdominal segments short. Micromastus is an isolated genus intermediate between Conotrachelus and Acalles.

ACALLES Schönh.

The following is a large species belonging in the neighborhood of *nobilis* :—

A. profusus n. sp.—Oval, convex, black rather sparsely clothed with large recumbent scales, without erect setæ, the scales dark brown in color but in great part white and denser on the head and basal parts of the beak, in several small isolated spots on the prothorax, on the elytra especially near the sides in basal fourth and in a transverse band near apical fourth, on the femora toward apex and throughout the tibiæ. *Head* and beak rather coarsely, densely punctate, the latter finely carinate along the middle, rather longer than the prothorax ; antennæ inserted at the middle. *Prothorax* very nearly as long as wide, the sides broadly arcuate, somewhat more convergent toward apex, the subapical constriction fine ; apex broadly arcuate and a little more than three-fourths as wide as the base ; disk coarsely, very densely punctate, the median impunctate carina strong but not entire. *Elytra* oval, more than twice as long as the prothorax, and, in the middle, nearly one-half wider ; foveæ very large, deep and close-set, each with a rather small subquadrate scale. *Abdomen* coarsely, rather closely punctate. Length 7.5 mm. ; width 3.7 mm.

Texas.

Differs from *porosus* and *basalis* in its larger size and strongly carinate pronotum, and from *nobilis* in its less inflated elytra and the dense white scales covering the basal third of the beak.

CANISTES n. gen.

This genus is founded upon a remarkable species somewhat resembling an unusually robust Calandrinus. It is however allied to Acalles, as may be seen from the following diagnosis:—

Body oblong-oval, strongly convex. Beak moderate in length received in a very deep and abruptly limited sternal sulcus, extending almost to the metasternum. Eyes not very large, almost completely concealed in repose, the ocular lobes moderate. Antennæ inserted just behind the middle of the beak, the funicle 7-jointed, slender, the basal joint not quite as long as the second, the latter nearly as long as the next three combined ; outer joints but slightly thicker ; club abrupt, rather large, elongated, cylindric-oval, fully as long as the preceding five joints, very densely pubescent, solid but with a distinct apical segment. Metasternum very short, the episterna distinct, parallel, the epimera not visible. Abdomen with the first suture distinct, broadly, strongly arcuate, the second segment much longer than the next two together. Legs thick and robust ; femora unarmed ; tibiæ aberrant, the intermediate and posterior gradually and rapidly increasing in width to the middle, then abruptly narrowed, the apical half parallel and not wider than the base, the inner side straight throughout ; tarsi short, slender, the third joint dilated and bilobed ; claws small, simple, very slender, free and divergent. Scutellum completely obsolete.

Canistes differs greatly from Acalles in abdominal structure, but resembles *A. nuchalis* not only in this feature, but in the broadly visible met-episterna. The new genus which must be formed for *A. nuchalis* will however differ from Canistes in its distinctly annulated antennal club and normal tibiæ. In general facies Canistes departs widely from any other type of North American cryptorhynchs.

C. schusteri n. sp.—Subparallel, black, the antennæ rufous with the club still paler and subsericeous ; body sparsely and very unevenly squamose, the head extremely densely clothed with small fulvous recumbent scales, the pronotum with some similar but more elongate scales toward the sides and also bristling with short erect and sparse setæ, especially toward apex, the elytra smooth, alutaceous almost glabrous, with a few widely scattered scales of various shapes, some recumbent, others erect, especially visible toward base, in a transverse line at apical third, and thence narrowly along the suture to the apex, the abdomen with a few elongate and widely dispersed scales ; legs densely and conspicuously clothed throughout with small recumbent brown scales, erect and bristling externally along the tibiæ. *Head* densely punctate; beak feebly arcuate, not quite as long as the prothorax, smooth, shining and finely, sparsely punctate except in less than basal half, where it is punctate and squamose. *Prothorax* slightly wider than long, wider at the middle than at base, the sides in basal half nearly straight, strongly convergent and deeply sinuate anteriorly, the constriction very large, deep, extending entirely across the dorsal surface; disk coarsely perforato-cribrate, the punctures separated by much less than their own diameters, the interspaces flat and polished, without modified median line. *Elytra* scarcely wider than the prothorax, two-thirds longer, narrowed and broadly constricted behind, the apex narrowly obtuse; disk with very fine sparse punctures, not striate, the punctures however becoming coarse and seriate very near the base. *Abdomen* finely, sparsely punctate, smooth and polished toward base. Length 3.3 mm.; width 1.6 mm.

Missouri (St. Louis).

The single specimen was discovered by Mr. Moritz Schuster of St. Louis, to whom it gives me pleasure to dedicate a most interesting addition to our Cryptorhynchini.

TYLODERMA Say.

This genus is widely differentiated from Cryptorhynchus by the short thick beak, consequently received in a much more shallow emargination of the tumid mesosternum, by the small eyes, almost completely concealed in repose by the ocular lobes, and by the six-jointed antennal funicle; in addition, it should be stated that the femora are unarmed and are only moderately stout. The third tarsal joint is dilated and bilobed, and the tarsal claws are small slender free and simple. The species usually vary greatly in the size of the body and in intensity and coarseness of sculpture, especially that of the elytra.

In a perfectly natural succession of the North American forms we can readily recognize four typical groups, represented respectively by *foveolata*,[1] *fragariæ*, *variegata* and *ærea*, the species in each group being rather closely allied among themselves. The

---

[1] It is desirable to make the rules of nomenclature as uniform as possible, and independent of linguistic exceptions. This can be accomplished in one direction by adopting a constant gender for each particular ending of the generic symbol, taking as a guide the general Latin rule in each case. In this instance, it is the general rule that words ending in " a " are feminine, consequently all generic symbols ending in "a," of whatever derivation, should require a feminine termination in the specific word. It would be a decided advance if a table of genders could be drawn up and agreed to, for every possible ending of the generic symbol.

second of those mentioned is monotypic and is perhaps the most aberrant in general form and habitus. The species occur throughout the United States, and are also well represented in Brazil; those which I have been able to study may be characterized as follows:—

Body more or less dull, very coarsely, deeply sculptured, the prothorax with large uneven foveæ.
 Elytra with a squamulose spot at each side of the scutellum.
  Elytral series becoming subobsolete and feebly punctate near the apex.
   Pronotal foveæ much larger than the scutellum; vestiture composed of brownish-white squamules..............................1 **foveolata**
   Pronotal foveæ sensibly smaller and more distant, not much larger than the scutellum at any point; squamules broader in form and white.
   2 morbillosa
  Elytral series distinct throughout, the punctures of the two series nearest the suture on each deep and large to the apex; body much narrower and more cylindrical, the prothorax from above not constricted at the sides toward apex ....3 **angustula**
 Elytra without trace of a squamulose spot near the scutellum; elytral series broadly, deeply impressed to the apex; prothorax not sensibly sinuate at the sides anteriorly; humeri much less broadly exposed, not at all truncate at base but broadly rounded to the base of the prothorax.
 4 contusa
Body smoother and more shining, glabrous or very sparsely and unevenly pubescent, less distinctly polished in *fragariæ*, the pronotum punctate rather than foveate.
 Elytra oval, widest near basal third; pronotum very coarsely deeply and densely punctate; integuments in great part rufo-piceous...5 **fragariæ**
 Elytra becoming parallel and straight at the sides toward base.
  Integuments more or less pale; pronotal punctures coarse uneven and impressed.
   Prothorax rather longer than wide, densely and confusedly punctured toward apex; elytra black, sparsely mottled with rufous.
   6 variegata
   Prothorax not as long as wide, much more broadly inflated toward base, remotely and unevenly punctate throughout; elytra rufous, occasionally very distantly and just perceptibly mottled with blackish: beak shorter ....7 **rufescens**
  Integuments black or piceous-black, often æneous, rather shining; pronotum more or less minutely punctate.
   Elytral humeri very narrowly exposed at base ....8 **baridia**
   Elytral humeri broadly exposed.
    Upper surface with very sparse whitish recumbent hairs.
    9 subpubescens
   Upper surface glabrous.
    Punctures of the pronotum strong though sparse throughout; body rather robust ....10 **nigra**

> Punctures of the pronotal disk very fine or subobsolete; body narrower.
>
> Punctures of the pronotal flanks strong and unevenly distributed over the entire surface..11 **aerea**
>
> Punctures of the flanks entirely obsolete, except in the subapical constriction ....12 **punctata**

T. longa Lec. (Proc. Am. Phil. Soc., XV, p. 248) belongs to Cryptorhynchus as at present organized, and has the eyes large and approximate, as usual in that genus. I have before me one or two species from Brazil, which are similarly elongate-cylindrical in form and otherwise closely allied to *longa*. In these forms the antennal funicle is short and 7-jointed, the outer joints very short, gradually slightly thicker and coarctate; they should perhaps form a distinct genus.

1 **T. foveolata** Say.—Curc., p. 19; Ed. Lec., I, p. 284; Germ.: Sch. Curc., IV, p. 140 (Cryptorhynchus); Horn: Proc. Am. Phil. Soc., XIII, p. 468 (Analcis).

Oblong-oval, strongly convex, black and dull throughout, glabrous but with small patches of small slender dense recumbent and whitish scales, of which a small spot at the middle of the vertex and another larger and more elongate between the eyes, a short line at the apex of the pronotum and an obliquely arcuate series from before the middle to near the sides of the base, numerous irregular spots on the elytra and a broad uneven band at apical fourth, are especially noticeable. Head and beak not very coarsely but rather closely and distinctly punctate, with a feeble frontal puncture. Prothorax scarcely as long as wide, strongly rounded at the sides, the latter convergent and broadly sinuate toward the broadly arcuate apex; disk with extremely coarse, deep, uneven but rather close-set foveæ. Elytra between one-third and one-fourth wider than the disk of the prothorax, the sides subparallel and nearly straight in basal two-thirds, the humeri right but narrowly and obliquely subtruncate; disk with unimpressed series of extremely large deep uneven foveæ, which become almost obliterated toward apex. Length 3.7–5.8 mm.; width 1.5–2.7 mm.

The large series before me is from New Jersey, Pennsylvania and Iowa; it is also said to occur in Georgia. In well preserved specimens each of the large foveæ of the pronotum bears a short stiff subclavate seta. The only remarkable variation is in the size of the body.

2 **T. morbillosa** Lec.—Pacif. R. R. Rep., App. 1, p. 58; Horn : Proc. Am. Phil. Soc., XIII, p. 467 (Analcis).

Closely allied to *foveolata*, but a little less robust, the elytra more elongate and with the small spots and posterior interrupted band composed of squamules which are whiter and slightly broader, the scales of the small spots on the head and flanks of the prothorax still broader. The prothorax is shorter, with the apex relatively wider, broadly arcuate, the sides in basal three-fifths nearly parallel and much less arcuate, thence feebly convergent and just visibly sinuate to the apex; foveæ smaller, rather sparser and very unevenly distributed. Elytra one-fourth wider than the prothorax and rather more than twice as long, the sides parallel and nearly straight in basal two-thirds, the apex narrowly parabolic; humeri right, slightly blunt; foveæ very large, uneven in outline, forming vague series and almost contiguous toward base, the series fine, slightly impressed and very feebly punctate toward apex, the two lateral more distinctly punctate and feebly carinate externally in apical half. Length 5.0 mm.; width 2.0 mm.

California (San Francisco). The unique type in the LeConte cabinet is the only specimen which I have seen. This species may possibly prove to be a geographical variation of *foveolata*, but it is impossible to pronounce any definite opinion until more specimens are discovered.

3 **T. angustula** n. sp.—Subelongate, strongly convex, black, the legs dark piceo-rufous; integuments dull, the elytra more shining, subglabrous but with a small condensed spot of recumbent squamules on the front, a few scattered squamules near the centre of the occiput, some very sparse indefinite spots on the prothorax and anterior parts of the elytra especially near the scutellum, an oblique spot near apical fourth and another between this and the apex of each elytron, the squamules whitish in color. *Head* and beak very unevenly but distinctly punctate, the former more sparsely and with an indistinct frontal fovea; beak very short, barely one-half longer than wide; antennæ rufous, the basal joint of the funicle very robust, not quite as long as the second which is slender and obconical; club densely clothed with short coarse pearly pubescence. *Prothorax* not quite as long as wide, the sides broadly, distinctly arcuate in basal three-fifths, becoming more convergent near the base, strongly convergent and nearly straight in apical two-fifths, the apex strongly arcuate and much narrower than the base; disk with extremely large deep uneven and partially confluent foveæ, without smooth median line. *Elytra* elongate, one-fifth wider than the prothorax and almost two and one-half times as long, subparallel, the apical portion ogival, with the extreme apex subtruncate; humeri broadly exposed, obliquely subtrun-

cate ; disk with even series of very large deep rounded punctiform foveæ, the series impressed toward apex, especially the two nearest the suture, in which the punctures are but slightly smaller at the apex ; punctures of the lateral series becoming very small at about posterior third but again larger toward the apex ; intervals between the series each with an even series of very small remote punctures. Length 3.7 mm. ; width 1.3 mm.

Texas (Austin).

The single specimen, which I took at the indicated locality, represents an interesting species somewhat allied to *foveolata*, but much narrower and differently sculptured toward the apex of the elytra.

4 T. contusa n. sp.—Rather narrowly oblong-oval, strongly convex, black throughout, the upper surface rather shining but with a distinct alutaceous lustre, almost glabrous, the squamules slender, recumbent, aggregated in two small spots on the head, one in the middle near the apex and two arranged transversely on the flanks of the pronotum, one or two very feeble spots on the disk of each elytron near basal third and in the usual transverse interrupted band at apical fourth, the squamules pale brownish in color. *Head* and beak finely, sparsely punctate, each puncture with a small seta, the front with a short longitudinal canaliculation connecting the two squamose spots. *Prothorax* nearly as long as wide, widest at the middle, the sides thence strongly convergent and straight to the apex, and feebly convergent and nearly straight to the base, the apex much narrower than the base and strongly arcuate ; foveæ of the surface extremely large, deep, uneven, a wide median line smooth and very narrowly and feebly tumid. *Elytra* barely one-fourth wider than the prothorax, twice as long, parallel and straight at the sides in basal two-thirds, the apex parabolic ; humeri rounded to the base of the prothorax ; disk toward base with extremely large uneven semi-confluent foveæ, arranged in series, becoming smaller and distant but distinct toward apex, the series there being broadly deeply and conspicuously impressed. Length 3.3 mm. ; width 1.3 mm.

Arkansas (Little Rock).   Mr. H. F. Wickham.

A small species, allied rather closely to *foveolata*, but with a more shining and subglabrous surface, much larger denser and more conspicuous elytral foveæ, narrower bodily form, less widely exposed humeri and non-sinuate sides of the prothorax toward apex. In *foveolata* the elytral series are almost unimpressed near the apex.

5 T. fragariæ Riley—Third Ann. Rept. Ins. Mo., 1871, p. 42; Horn: Proc. Am. Phil. Soc., XIII, p. 469 (Analcis).

Ovate, subcuneate, strongly convex, rather robust, piceous, the elytra and legs rufous, the former each with a transverse blackish clouded spot at the middle nearer the side than the suture, and another smaller and rounded at apical fourth; surface feebly shining, the vestiture very sparse, consisting of short robust recumbent hairs, yellowish in color and especially evident on the elytra near the base, in an oblique band just before the middle, and another at apical third not attaining the suture. Head and beak closely and deeply punctate, the former with a small depressed cluster of hairs at the middle of the vertex, separated from the beak by a broad transverse impression which is obsoletely foveate at the middle. Prothorax very nearly as long as wide, broadly rounded at the sides, narrowed and with the sides broadly, just visibly sinuate toward apex, the latter strongly arcuate; disk very coarsely deeply evenly and densely punctured throughout. Elytra at base not wider than the disk of the prothorax, three-fourths longer, widest at basal third where they are two-fifths wider than the prothorax, minutely punctulate throughout, more obsoletely in the black spots, and with obsoletely impressed series of very distant punctures, becoming coarse toward base and minute toward apex. Length 4.0–4.2 mm.; width 1.8–1.9 mm.

Illinois and Missouri. One of the most distinct species of our fauna, perhaps most closely allied to *variegata*, but radically different in its shorter oval and confusedly punctulate elytra, with the humeri scarcely at all exposed at base, and in its very dense cribrate punctures of the prothorax.

6 **T. variegata** Horn—Proc. Am. Phil. Soc., XIII, p. 468 (Analcis).

Oval, strongly convex, rather shining, in great part glabrous, black, the pronotum feebly rufescent near the apex and the elytra with small widely scattered rufous patches, of which a narrow oblique subsutural spot just before the middle and a wide, broadly and posteriorly arcuate band at apical third or fourth, are particularly noticeable, the rufous areas clothed rather sparsely with fine recumbent yellowish-white squamules, the black portions glabrous. Head and beak very densely, rather finely punctate and dull throughout, with a small impressed frontal fovea; beak in the female nearly twice as long as wide. Prothorax slightly longer than wide, the apex narrower than the base and strongly, evenly arcuate; punctures large, deep, unevenly distributed but rather close, fine toward apex. Elytra at base one-third wider than the prothorax, fully twice as long, the sides parallel and nearly straight in basal three-fifths; punctures very large, uneven, impressed and rather distant, becoming smaller and with the series impressed toward apex. Length 3.0–4.2 mm.; width 1.3–1.75 mm.

The specimens in my cabinet are from Florida.

7 T. rufescens n. sp.—Oval, convex, shining, subglabrous, dark rufo-testaceous throughout, the elytra almost imperceptibly clouded with small, very remote and blackish spots, unevenly disposed ; pronotum and elytra with a few widely scattered recumbent whitish squamules, rather long and very slender in form, and slightly more numerous in an oblique area on each elytron near apical fourth, very easily denuded. *Head* rather finely, sparsely punctate, with an impressed median fovea ; beak in the female very short, scarcely one-half longer than wide ; antennæ stout, the basal joint of the funicle very robust, rapidly narrowed to the base and not quite as long as the second, the latter much longer than the next two, slender, evenly obconical, outer joint gradually wider, the club robust, as long as the four preceding joints combined. *Prothorax* scarcely as long as wide, inflated and widest behind the middle, the apex much narrower than the base and strongly rounded ; punctures coarse, impressed, very uneven, sparse and scarcely becoming finer toward apex, the median line narrowly and feebly tumid. *Elytra* at base one-fourth wider than the disk of the prothorax, distinctly more than twice as long, the sides parallel and nearly straight in basal half, then gradually rounded, the apex ogival ; humeri right, narrowly rounded ; striæ generally feebly impressed throughout the length, the punctures moderately large, impressed, uneven and remote, becoming very small feeble and elongate toward apex. *Legs* short, robust, rufo-testaceous, piceous near the coxæ. Length 3.2–4.3 mm. ; width 1.3–1.8 mm.

Indiana.

This species is allied rather closely to *variegata*, but is easily distinguished by its slightly stouter form, pale coloration, wider and more inflated prothorax, much sparser punctuation throughout, the punctures rather larger on the prothorax but smaller and more even on the elytra, and by the shorter beak in the female.

8 T. baridia Lec.—Proc. Am. Phil. Soc., XV, p. 249.

Oval, gradually pointed behind, strongly convex, black throughout, smooth, shining although feebly alutaceous, glabrous, each puncture bearing an extremely small seta. Head and beak finely but strongly, not very densely and unevenly punctate, with a small and somewhat variable frontal puncture. Prothorax one-fourth wider than long, the sides broadly subangulate at the middle, feebly convergent thence to the base, strongly so and nearly straight to the apex, which is strongly arcuate and not more than one-half as

wide as the base; disk smooth, finely but deeply, remotely and
evenly punctate. Elytra at base very slightly wider than the prothorax, fully two and three-fourths times as long, evenly gradually
and acutely ogival, the sides becoming straight and parallel in somewhat less than basal half; humeri feebly, obliquely rounded externally, very narrowly exposed at base; disk with almost unimpressed series of small remote punctures, becoming nearly obsolete
toward apex; intervals with a single uneven series of extremely
minute feeble punctures. Length 3.8–4.2 mm.; width 1.65–1.8 mm.

Texas and Florida. Easily distinguishable by the oval, posteriorly pointed form and feebly exposed humeri.

9 **T. subpubescens** n. sp.—Narrowly elongate-oval, strongly convex,
nearly smooth, slightly alutaceous in lustre, piceous-black with a feeble bronzy
lustre, the upper surface with extremely sparse slender recumbent white hairs,
only distinct on the pronotum laterally and along the lateral parts of the basal
margin; on the elytra they are just perceptibly more numerous in an oblique
area on each at basal third. *Head* convex, dull, minutely, sparsely but distinctly punctate, with a small vertical and larger frontal fovea; beak slightly
rugulose. *Prothorax* about as long as wide, parallel and broadly arcuate at
the sides to slightly beyond the middle, then gradually convergent, broadly
and very feebly sinuate to the apex, the latter strongly arcuate and not more
than three-fifths as wide as the base; disk very finely, feebly, rather evenly
and not very sparsely punctate throughout, the punctures becoming larger
but not denser on the flanks. *Elytra* at base barely one-fourth wider than
the prothorax, but little more than twice as long, very gradually ogival, the
sides becoming nearly parallel toward base; humeri rounded to the base of
the prothorax; disk with very feebly impressed series of small, moderately
distant punctures, which are rather deep and distinct toward base; the punctures disappear completely toward apex but the striæ remain feebly impressed.
Legs rufous. Length 2.9 mm.; width 1.2 mm.

Texas (Austin).

The single specimen represents a distinct species, somewhat intermediate between the *fragariæ* and *ærea* groups; it very closely
resembles *ærea*, but is relatively narrower and may be readily distinguished by the long sparse hairs of the elytra.

10 **T. nigra** Casey.—Cont. Desc. Syst. Col. N. A., I, p. 56.

Broadly oval and robust, black with strong bronzy metallic lustre,
polished. Head and beak dull, the former sparsely, finely punctate,
with an elongate impression at the middle of the vertex; beak very
densely punctate. Prothorax slightly wider than long, the sides
in basal half subparallel and nearly straight, strongly convergent

thence to the apex and rather abruptly, subangularly sinuate at apical third; apex strongly arcuate, fully three-fourths as wide as the base; disk with rather small but deep, sparse and perforate punctures, becoming slightly larger but scarcely denser and unevenly distributed on the flanks. Elytra at base scarcely one-third wider than the prothorax, quite distinctly more than twice as long, gradually ogival to the apex, the sides becoming scarcely parallel toward base; humeri obtusely rounded and rather prominent, obliquely truncate at base; disk with unimpressed series of somewhat large, extremely remote and very feeble punctures in basal half only. Length 3.0–3.7 mm.; width 1.3–1.7 mm.

Indiana and Illinois. The series before me consists of eleven specimens; there is also a large series in the cabinet of Mr. Jülich. This species is allied to *ærea*, but differs in its larger size and more robust form, in the much coarser punctures of the disk of the pronotum, and in the elongate impressed line of the vertex.

11 **T. ærea** Say.—Curc., p. 29; Ed. Lec., I, p. 297; Rosensk.: Sch. Curc., IV, p. 279; Horn.: Proc. Am. Phil. Soc., XIII, p. 469 (Analcis); Lec.: l. c., XV, p. 248.

Narrowly oval, convex, highly polished, bright æneous in lustre, glabrous, each puncture with a minute seta; head, beak and legs dull, finely, strongly granulato-reticulate. Head and beak not coarsely but closely and conspicuously punctate, without distinct frontal fovea. Prothorax slightly wider than long, rather abruptly, moderately inflated at the middle, thence slightly narrower to the base; sides convergent and rather broadly, deeply sinuate to the apex, which is strongly arcuate and about three-fourths as wide as the base; disk with minute feeble sparse and evenly distributed punctures which become larger, deep and rather close-set on the flanks, but rather uneven in distribution and almost wanting toward base. Elytra at base two-fifths wider than the prothorax, two and one-half times as long, the apical half evenly gradually and acutely ogival, the sides becoming parallel and nearly straight thence to the base; disk with unimpressed series of rather small, remote but distinct punctures in basal third only, the series feebly impressed near the sides; remainder of the surface with scarcely a trace of punctuation. Length 2.2–2.8 mm.; width 0.9–1.25 mm.

New Jersey, Iowa and Texas. The measurements given are the extremes of a very large series. The sutural series of punctures is generally visible to a little beyond the middle.

12 **T. punctata** Casey.—Cont. Desc. Syst. Col. N. A., I, p. 57.

Elongate-oval, very strongly convex, polished, black with a strong bronzy lustre, glabrous. Head rather dull, finely, sparsely punctate, with a small vertical fovea, the impression between the head and beak deep but broadly rounded. Prothorax about as long as wide, the sides almost straight and evenly convergent from base to apex, but arcuate for a short distance in the middle; apex fully three-fourths as wide as the base, strongly arcuate; disk almost impunctate, the upper portion toward base with excessively minute and subobsolete sparse punctures; a transverse area just behind the apex is also more distinctly and confusedly punctate, the punctures becoming large and deep in a still narrower and more apical line on the flanks; remainder of the sides without distinct punctures. Elytra at base nearly one-third wider than the prothorax, two and one-half times as long, gradually ogival behind, the sides becoming subparallel in basal half; disk with unimpressed series of coarse, deep, very remote punctures, not extending behind the middle. Length 2.5–3.9 mm.; width 0.95–1.7 mm.

New York (Long Island) and Florida. A polished species resembling *ærea*, but larger, relatively somewhat narrower, with more elongate and more gradually narrowed elytra; it may always be easily recognized by the peculiar punctuation of the prothorax. The elytral punctures, as in *ærea*, vary greatly in size and depth, and, in one very small depauperate specimen from Florida, become nearly obsolete.

PHYRDENUS Lec.

In this genus the anterior coxæ are only moderately separated, the excavation in the mesosternum being much wider, surrounded by a strongly elevated acute edge and not extending beyond the middle of the intermediate coxæ; the beak is strongly compressed toward base and dilated and flattened toward apex, as might be inferred from the relationship of the anterior coxal distance and width of the mesosternal sulcus. The two species in my cabinet may be thus distinguished:—

Second abdominal segment nearly as long as the next two; basal segment
    abruptly much more coarsely and almost uniformly punctate; median
    sulcus of the pronotum equal in width throughout, deep but not very
    wide, the pronotal sculpture coarse ....**undatus** Lec.

Second abdominal segment but slightly longer than the third, the basal segment not more coarsely punctate but having in addition to the finer punctures others much larger and widely scattered. Head and beak roughly
and densely squamose, the former strongly, transversely impressed; beak
not quite as long as the prothorax, feebly bent, roughly and densely sculptured; antennæ inserted just beyond apical third, the second funicular
joint but slightly shorter than the first, equal to the next two together,
outer joints but slightly wider, club long, distinctly annulated. Prothorax very nearly as long as wide, angulate at the sides before the middle,
the disk very uneven, the median impression broad and feeble; punctures
very dense but even and rather fine. Elytra about twice as wide as the
prothorax, not longer than wide; intervals alternately strongly ridged
and flat; punctures coarse and rather uneven. Length 5.4 mm.; width
3.0 mm. Arizona...**bullatus** n. sp.

Bullatus is larger and relatively broader than *undatus*. The
vestiture in the single specimen before me is somewhat imperfect,
but appears to be of the same general character as in *undatus;* the
latter is moderately abundant from New York to Texas.

ZYGOPINI.

PSOMUS n. gen.

A distinct genus is rendered necessary for one of the most minute
zygopides which I have seen. Its principal characters are the following :—

Body small, oval, convex, somewhat resembling Orchestes. Eyes large,
finely faceted, narrowly separated on the front. Beak somewhat slender,
received in repose in a moderately deep prosternal sulcus, thence passing
over, but scarcely upon, the mesosternum. Antennæ very slender, the funicle
long, filiform, the basal joint rather longer than the next two; second longer
than the third; outer joints but slightly thicker; club very small, moderately
thick, oval, not noticeably annulate. Mesosternum depressed, flat, very widely
separating the coxæ. Met-episterna rather narrow, parallel, interposed between the posterior coxæ and the elytra. Abdomen nearly flat, the sutures
straight, transverse, all deep and strong, the segments subequal in length.
Pygidium completely covered. Legs moderate, the tibiæ and tarsi very short;
tarsal claws small, divergent, bent downward near the base and obtusely
toothed or lobed within.

The systematic position of Psomus is evidently near Acoptus,
with which it agrees in sternal structure; the facies is however
completely different, and structurally it differs in its very slender
antennæ with small non-annulate club, short tarsi with the claws

somewhat appendiculate and not simple, in its still more equal ventral segments and relatively larger eyes. The femora are broadly sinuate beneath toward apex, but not in the least dentate.

P. politus n. sp.—Oval, strongly convex, highly polished, black, the tip of beak, antennæ, tibiæ and tarsi very pale luteo-flavate; femora black; body almost glabrous, the upper surface with a few remote inconspicuous setiform squamules, especially evident and somewhat bristling between the eyes, on the prosternum and flanks of the prothorax. *Head* finely punctate; beak a little more than one-third as long as the body, smooth, shining, rather coarsely but not densely, sublinearly punctate, the antennæ inserted rather behind basal third. *Prothorax* small, conical, three-fifths wider than long, the sides almost straight, subapical constriction very feeble; apex broadly arcuate, about two-thirds as wide as the base; disk finely but strongly, not closely punctate. Scutellum small, tumid, albido-setose. *Elytra* at base abruptly two-fifths wider than the prothorax, between three and four times as long; sides rounded, convergent and feebly sinuate toward apex, becoming parallel near the base; humeri rather tumid, obtuse; disk with very fine but distinct striæ, feebly, remotely crenato-punctate; intervals wide, broadly convex, each with a single series of extremely minute distant and feebly setiferous punctures. *Abdomen* rather closely, subrugosely punctate. Length 1.5–1.8 mm.; width 0.7–0.9 mm.

Indiana.

This is an interesting addition to the Zygopini of the United States and constitutes a widely isolated generic type. Two specimens.

ZYGOPS Schönh.

I have before me two species of this genus which may be thus characterized:—

Lateral vittæ and median pale spots of the pronotum abruptly defined; postmedial whitish spots of the elytra arranged transversely; upper portion of the pygidium black, except narrowly near the edges and along the subcarinate median line; abdomen with a denuded spot near each side of the fifth segment..**seminiveus** Lec.
Lateral pronotal vittæ rather well defined, the median spots not at all defined, replaced by large indefinitely nubilate areas; post-medial spots of the elytra oblique; pygidium with mixed pale and dark scales; fifth ventral segment almost uniformly clothed throughout with white scales. Body otherwise nearly resembling *seminiveus*, the beak more coarsely and rugosely punctate and much less strongly carinate in the middle toward base. Length 7.7–9.0 mm.; width 3.9–4.8 mm. Texas (southwestern). Mr. G. W. Dunn ....**suffusus** n. sp.

Besides the characters mentioned, it should be added that the elytral pale spots in *suffusus* are composed of white and pale brown scales, the larger white areas being narrowly margined with the brown tint, while in *seminiveus* all the scales are whitish.

BARINI.

This immense tribe forms an important subdivision of Lacordaire's second section of those apostasimerous phanerognathic Curculionidæ, which have the antennal club articulate or divided by distinct sutures, and the third tarsal joint bilobed. There are, however, several important exceptions to these characters even in the tribe under consideration, and it may prove almost as natural to consider the Barini as forming one of the tribes in the second of two great primary divisions of the Curculionidæ—as limited by LeConte—based upon the form of the mesosternal epimera; the first having the epimera undeveloped laterally and the second having this part produced and angulate upward or ascending at the sides of the body, obliquely truncating the elytra at the humeri and often visible from above. At all events the latter is the principal structural character separating the Barini from other curculionides, and is the most constant and significant feature of the tribe.[1]

Among the few tribes possessing this peculiarity, the Barini may be known at once by the distinct scutellum, generally free beak with obliquely descending or inferior antennal scrobes and by the unemarginate prosternum, but it must be admitted that there seems to be quite as strong a bond of affinity between the Barini and Cryptorhynchini, as between the former and the Ceutorhynchini, with which they are to be associated by reason of mes-epimeral structure. Lacordaire distinguishes the Barini from the Ceutorhynchini principally by the presence of a distinct scutellum in the former; so, as in many other large and complicated divisions of the Coleoptera, we are forced to rely for tribal characters mainly upon habitus, supported by one or two tolerably constant special peculiarities. As thus defined by the conformation of the mes-epimera, the Barini include an extremely large proportion of all the special modifications of structure found elsewhere in the Curculionidæ.

[1] In the Zygopini it sometimes occurs it is true, but here it is always sporadic and of but little if any systematic value.

The beak may be excessively short and stout or correspondingly long and slender, arcuate or nearly straight or variously bent at different parts of its extent, divided from the head by a transverse constriction or not, and with the antennæ inserted at every conceivable point, from near the extreme apex as in the male of *Conoproctus 4-pustulatus*, to near the base as in Simocopis of Pascoe or our own Plocamus. The scrobes obliquely and rapidly descending or nearly horizontal, sometimes completely inferior, coalescent beneath toward base or remaining widely separated.

The antennæ are comparatively constant in structure, especially the funicle, which is invariably seven-jointed, with the basal joint, and more rarely also the second, elongate to a greater or less degree, the first sometimes as long as the entire remainder as in Barinus; the second joint is, however, almost always at least somewhat longer than the third. The club is modified to a very noticeable extent, but it is seldom that these variations of structure can be employed in differentiating the genera; it may be very small or conspicuously longer than the entire funicle as in Orthoris, and its basal joint may constitute from two-thirds of the whole to very much less; in *Centrinus acuminatus*, for example, the two basal joints together compose less than one-half of the mass, with the first much shorter than the second; the basal joint is frequently subglabrous, at least toward base, and especially in Baris with its immediate allies and in some of the subgenera of Limnobaris; in one of the subgenera of Centrinus (Odontocorynus) it becomes conspicuously modified in the male.

The mandibles vary greatly in structure, from stout, thick, arcuate and broadly decussate to the long, straight, prominent and perfectly non-decussate, without trace of internal denticulation, the latter type being nearly similar in shape, but not in plane of motion, to those of Balaninus, showing that Centrinus and Balaninus may have a certain obscure relationship apart from their general similarity of form. In Eunyssobia and Plocamus they move in a nearly vertical plane, precisely as in Balaninus, but in spite of all these resemblances I am of the opinion that Balaninus is more closely allied to the Anthonomini, and that it should constitute a simple tribe in that vicinity.

I have found the various modifications of the mandibles of positive value in delimiting the genera allied to Centrinus. It was the opinion of Lacordaire that the forms assumed by the mandibles were so erratic in this and allied tribes, as to be of very little use

in classification, and, assuming the definition and scope of certain
genera as known to this author, such as the Schönherrian Baridius
and Centrinus, there can be no doubt that he was entirely justified
in coming to the conclusion expressed in the foot-note on page 3,
vol. VII, of the "Genera." Whatever opinion may be held, however, concerning the usefulness of mandibular modifications for the
purposes to which they are here applied, it can only be said that I
have found the generic groups defined by them to be quite homogeneous within themselves in external appearance and distinctly
separated from each other in general habitus, and these facts admit-
tedly constitute one of the best tests of generic validity. In addition we are enabled in this way to really define and fix some tangible
limits to the genus Centrinus, which has never been accomplished
by any other means. The fact that the prosternal sulcus and degree of separation of the anterior coxæ prove to be of uncertain
value for generic definition in Centrinus and its immediate allies,
because of the marked sexual divergencies in the conformation of
these parts in many species, taken in connection with the intro-
generic homogeneity of facies of the groups defined by mandibular
structure, prompts me to believe that we have here, at least, a prac-
tical solution of one of the most perplexing problems of the Curculionidæ.

The prosternum is subject to almost every possible modification;
it may be either perfectly flat or variously foveate or longitudinally
sulcate to a greater or less degree. The sulcus when present does not
generally receive the beak in repose, but there are at least three
genera—Coleomerus, Diorymerus and Aulobaris—in which the beak
can be placed in the groove just as in any normal cryptorhynch, and,
in Coleomerus, the groove often extends posteriorly far into the metasternum; in the other two genera, however, it does not pass beyond
the prosternum. The apical margin is usually entire, but frequently
sinuate in the middle, and, at a short distance behind the apex, there
is a more or less distinct transverse constriction. The degenerative
remnants and modifications of the transverse constriction and longitudinal sulcus or of a combination of the two, frequently give rise
to subapical foveæ of various forms, sometimes continued posteriorly by folds of the surface.[1] The anterior coxæ are of every

---

[1] In some genera the two subapical foveæ serve as receptacles for the robust
basal joint of the antennal funicle, when the beak is placed closely against
the body, these portions of the sulcus or constriction being therefore preserved
for a useful purpose.

possible degree of separation, from complete contiguity as in an undetermined Brazilian genus which I have before me, to extreme separation as in some of the madaride genera; in our own genera they are always more or less separated.

The pygidium plays an important part in the classification of the Barini, but the weight attached to it was somewhat over-estimated by LeConte, for the degree of exposure of this part, as well as its relative departure from the vertical, often depends to a considerable extent upon the sex of the individual. In Baris, for example, the species as a rule have not only the pygidium, but in addition nearly the entire propygidium uncovered in the male, the female having merely the pygidium exposed. This sexual character is still more pronounced in some of the centrinide genera, in which there are many species having the pygidium exposed at apex in the male, but entirely covered in the female, and, in two of the species, forming the genus Centrinogyna, it is completely exposed, vertical and unusually large in the male, but oblique and practically entirely covered in the female. It is impossible, therefore, to divide the tribe into two perfectly natural groups based upon pygidial structure, but the latter is nevertheless very useful in characterizing the genera.

There are but few other points to which attention need be directed at the present time, in view of what has been already published. The eyes do not vary sufficiently to call for special remark; they are nearly always widely separated above and beneath, well developed and finely faceted; in Coleomerus, however, they are narrowly separated above.[1] The body is of nearly all possible shapes, from extremely slender and cylindrical as in Barilepton and the Madopterides through the oval and elliptical, convex and flattened forms, to the extremely robust and strongly rhomboidal outline of Eurypages, Diorymerus, Pachybaris and some other centrinides. The prothorax is frequently tubulate at apex. The scutellum is very variable in structure and vestiture. The met-episterna are narrow or broad, the legs short or long, with the femora dentate beneath as in many tropical types and, less distinctly, in our own Madarellus and Pseudobaris, or completely unarmed as in the majority of genera; the tibiæ straight, or abnormal in structure as in Eisonyx, and almost

---

[1] In the Australian *Platyphœus lyterioides* the eyes are said by Pascoe to be very coarsely faceted and contiguous beneath.

invariably with a short acute internal spur at the apex. The tarsi
may be shorter or longer than the tibiæ, generally with the third
joint dilated and bilobed, but occasionally also with the second as
widely dilated as the third as in Barinus; in Calandrinus, Zaglyptus,
Eunyssobia and Plocamus the tarsi are very slender, with the third
joint not or scarcely wider than the second, while in *Barinus bivittatus* they are extremely broad. The tarsal claws may be connate
or divergent, rarely single; in *Centrinus senilis* Gyll., they become
robust, and excavated along the under surface; they are never
toothed, cleft or appendiculate, this being as singularly constant a
peculiarity of the Barini, as the seven-jointed antennal funicle.[1]
The structure of the abdomen is comparatively constant and of no
value in classification as far as can be observed; the last three sutures
are always posteriorly reflexed at the sides.

The secondary sexual characters of the male are numerous, varied
and often of a decidedly radical nature. In many species of the
genus Centrinus, for example, the male has a long corniform process
before each anterior coxa and a deep prosternal fossa, while the
female is devoid of the processes, and may not only have the prosternum flat or with a very feeble sulcus, but the coxæ also more
widely separated. In some species of Centrinus, as before remarked,
the basal joint of the antennal club is the only part subject to secondary sexual modification in the male. In conformity with a general
rule in the Curculionidæ, the antennæ are usually inserted relatively
nearer the tip of the beak in the male than in the female, the beak
being nearly always smoother, somewhat longer,[2] less punctate, more
slender and sometimes more strongly arcuate in the latter sex.
The abdomen generally has, near the base, a small, moderately deep
impression, as in many tribes not only of this but of other families.
Finally, among the more special and singular secondary male characters, mention should be made of the dentate anterior trochanters
of *Centrinus acuminatus* and *globifer*, and of a very remarkable
structure which I have noticed in an undetermined Brazilian species,
the sides of the prothorax behind the apex having a large impres-

[1] As a most notable exception, it should be stated that in the genus Enops
of Pascoe, the claws are described as bifid; but the author appears to be in
some doubt as to the true affinities of Enops, and it is quite possible that it
will have to be referred to another tribe.

[2] In Conoproctus there is an extraordinary reversion of this rule, the beak
in some species being much longer in the male than in the female.

sion, in the middle of which there is an erect transverse row of long acute spiniform teeth, the surface being perfectly smooth and normal in the female; there are doubtless many other special sexual characters of equal singularity among the tropical species; one of these will be noted under the genus Madarellus.

The thirty-nine genera which seem to be necessary for our species may be recognized as follows:—

Pygidium more or less completely exposed in both male and female, and generally almost vertical...2

Pygidium oblique and entirely concealed in the female, sometimes with the mere apex exposed especially in the male, except in Centrinogyna, where it is vertical and completely exposed in the male.................................17

2—Antennal club shorter, more robust, ovoidal or conoidal and more or less pointed, never fully as long as the preceding six joints combined; pygidium nearly vertical, except in the male of Madarellus; tibiæ usually longitudinally and feebly fluted and externally subcarinate.................3

Antennal club elongate, densely pubescent, longer than the preceding six joints combined; pygidium rather oblique; anterior coxæ narrowly separated; prosternum more or less impressed along the middle, but never abruptly sulcate; tibiæ nearly smooth; claws free, divergent............16

3—Tarsal claws free and more or less divergent...4

Tarsal claws connate at base, nearly parallel or feebly and gradually everted toward apex 13

4—Second funicular joint short or moderate in length, never as much as twice as long as wide 5

Second funicular joint elongate, more than twice as long as wide and fully as long as the next two combined 12

5—Anterior coxæ more or less approximate, never separated by a distance equalling their own width...6

Anterior coxæ remote, the prosternum generally broad and flat between and before them..11

6—Prosternum never deeply and abruptly sulcate, although frequently feebly impressed along the middle 7

Prosternum narrowly, abruptly and deeply sulcate..................................10

7—Beak separated from the head by a shallow impression which is often broadly angulate when viewed in profile...8

Beak separated from the head by a fine deep and abrupt groove; basal joint of the antennal club forming about one-half of the mass, more or less sparsely pubescent and shining 9

8—Antennal club polished and subglabrous toward base...............**Baris**

Antennal club finely and densely pubescent throughout; species generally minute and with scattered white scales, especially dense on the meso- and metasternal side-pieces and at the sides of the last three ventral segments...**Plesiobaris**

9—Body stout and convex, the prothorax broadly constricted near the apex but not tubulate; vestiture generally distinctly squamiform and uniformly distributed ....**Pycnobaris**

Body oblong-elongate, depressed, the prothorax strongly tubulate at apex; vestiture in the form of long robust setæ; sculpture of the pronotum extremely coarsely and deeply cribrate ....**Stictobaris**

10—Anterior coxæ separated by not quite their own width; beak moderately slender, subgibbous at base...**Trepobaris**

11—Prosternum extending but slightly over the mesosternum and broadly, evenly arcuate, the surface transversely bituberculate just behind the coxæ; mandibles prominent, acute, non-decussate, with the internal emarginations very feeble; antennal club rather small; body deeply, rugosely sculptured and partially squamose; femora completely unarmed.

Glyptobaris

Prosternum extending far over the mesosternum, transversely truncate or broadly sinuate and always more or less angulate at the sides of the process, the surface frequently transversely tumid just behind the coxæ; antennal club larger; pygidium more or less oblique in the male; mandibles generally prominent and not or only feebly decussate, but becoming arcuate and strongly decussate in some species of Onychobaris, always deeply notched within.

Anterior coxæ moderately remote; femora unarmed; body always deeply sculptured throughout and finely setulose ....**Onychobaris**

Anterior coxæ very remote; femora minutely toothed, the anterior generally strongly and distinctly so; body deeply sculptured beneath but very feebly so above, subglabrous...**Madarellus**

12—Prosternal sulcus wide, deep, moderately abrupt, receiving the beak in repose...**Aulobaris**

13—Anterior coxæ widely separated...14

Anterior coxæ narrowly separated, the prosternum broadly, feebly impressed along the middle but never sulcate; femora slender and completely unarmed; tibiæ nearly smooth, not fluted; tarsal claws frequently slightly unequal in length 15

14—Prosternum with a wide, deep and abrupt excavation near the anterior margin, which rapidly becomes shallower posteriorly, disappearing before the coxæ; body smooth, polished and very feebly sculptured; femora unarmed ....**Ampeloglypter**

Prosternum deeply and abruptly sulcate along the middle, the sulcus very narrow and never receiving the beak, the latter moderately short and stout.

Pygidium small, flat, not at all prominent and partially covered by the elytra; elytral striæ deeply crenato-punctate, the intervals narrow and convex; femora unarmed...**Desmoglyptus**

Pygidium large, convex and prominent, not inflexed beneath and not at all covered by the elytra; striæ not crenate, the intervals flat but sometimes angularly prominent on the posterior declivity; the femora frequently armed beneath, near apical third, with a very minute subobsolete spiculiform tooth ....**Pseudobaris**

15—Antennal club large, oval, very densely pubescent and nearly as long as the six preceding joints combined, a form suggestive of Rhoptobaris; pygidium convex, inflexed beneath, sinuating the fifth segment when viewed vertically...**Hesperobaris**

Antennal club much smaller.

Beak slender, longer than the prothorax, separated from the head by a very feeble impression; integuments subglabrous; species minute.

Microbaris

Beak robust, shorter, separated from the head by a deep angular impression; integuments more or less densely squamulose; species large.

Trichobaris

16—Prosternum not distinctly tumid before the coxæ, very broadly and scarcely visibly impressed; beak a little more robust, separated from the head by a very broad feeble and indefinite impression; scutellum flat, triangular, sculptured like the surrounding surface; prothorax larger; body more elongate ....**Rhoptobaris**

Prosternum strongly tumid before each coxa; beak slender, separated from the head by a distinctly marked transverse impression; scutellum subquadrate, slightly transverse; prothorax small, subconical....**Orthoris**

17—Mandibles normal in action, their plane of motion horizontal or nearly so; body without erect setæ except in Zaglyptus........................18

Mandibles with their plane of motion almost vertical, the upper part of the condyles nearly in mutual contact within a small emargination of the epistomal lobe, the lower condylic fissures very near the buccal opening; surface of the body bristling with sparse erect spines or spiniform setæ; tarsi narrow, the third joint not sensibly dilated; antennæ inserted on the under surface of the beak...31

18—Tarsi with two free and more or less divergent claws........................19

Tarsi with the claws connate or single 28

19—Mandibles prominent, not decussate when closed or at most very feebly so...20

Mandibles not at all prominent, thick, arcuate, strongly decussate when closed and deeply notched at apex 23

20—Mandibles with the inner edge always completely devoid of denticles or emarginations, generally straight but sometimes feebly arcuate and dehiscent toward apex, in which cases the mandibles cannot be placed in mutual contact throughout their length........................**Centrinus**

Mandibles with the inner edge straight, but more or less finely denticulate or crenulate.

Antennæ inserted far behind the middle of the beak..........................21

Antennæ inserted at or beyond the middle of the beak; body oval or narrower and subparallel...22

21—Anterior coxæ narrowly separated; species small and densely squamose.

Centrinopus

Anterior coxæ widely separated.

Beak separated from the head by a very deep transverse constriction; scutellum large, quadrate or trapezoidal; integuments with dense abruptly defined squamose vittæ; body broadly rhomboidal..........**Linonotus**

Beak separated from the head by an extremely feeble transverse impression,
which is foveate in the middle; scutellum small, rounded, emarginating
the thoracic lobe; body subglabrous and broadly oval.....**Pachybaris**

22—Anterior coxæ narrowly separated; mandibles with the outer edge evenly
and feebly arcuate, not denticulate.

Prothorax not tubulate at apex.

Metasternum very short, the intermediate and posterior coxæ separated
by a distance which is much less than the length of the post-coxal portion of the first ventral segment ....**Microcholus**

Metasternum much longer; body narrower, convex, oblong-oval, densely
squamose, the scutellum conspicuously so ....**Nicentrus**

Prothorax strongly constricted behind the apex, the latter tubulate; metasternum long ....**Centrinites**

Anterior coxæ widely separated; mandibles more or less dentate externally,
particularly near the base.

Pygidium oblique, completely concealed in both sexes, or with the mere
apex exposed...**Calandrinus**

Pygidium fully exposed, unusually large, vertical, convex and very conspicuous in the male, but oblique and practically entirely concealed in
the female...**Centrinogyna**

23—Elytral striæ normal, always distinct, not foveate at base...............24

Elytral striæ almost completely obsolete, each terminating at base in a deep,
posteriorly attenuate fovea 27

24—Third tarsal joint dilated and bilobed; body without erect bristles.....25

Third tarsal joint slender, obconical, not in the least dilated; body with erect
bristles...26

25—Metasternum long, much more than one-half as long as the met-episterna;
prosternum with or without corniform processes in the male, widely or
narrowly separating the coxæ, generally flat, but sometimes deeply excavated in the male, or otherwise modified ....**Limnobaris**

Metasternum shorter, about one-half as long as the met-episterna; body more
broadly oval and convex; prosternum never armed in the male.

Antennal club small or moderate; prosternum flat or broadly impressed,
sometimes more deeply excavated anteriorly; vestiture very sparse but
distinct.

Prothorax broadly constricted anteriorly but not tubulate; prosternum
flat, not impressed, not excavated anteriorly but with a fine deep and
even transverse constriction...**Oligolochus**

Prothorax tubulate; prosternum broadly impressed, deeply excavated
anteriorly ....**Idiostethus**

Antennal club very large, elongate; prosternum narrowly and deeply sulcate along the middle; body almost completely glabrous, polished, the
setæ extremely minute throughout.............................**Stethobaris**

26—Body minute, the bristles very long and conspicuous........**Zaglyptus**

27—Body oval, very convex, subglabrous, the prothorax very strongly tubulate ....**Oomorphidius**

28—Elytral striæ obsolete, represented at the base by small and not very
conspicuous foveæ; body subglabrous; tarsal claws single.....**Eisonyx**
Elytral striæ normal, distinct, not foveate at base.
  Tarsal claws two in number, completely connate in basal third to half....29
  Tarsal claws single...30
29—Beak long, slender, the antennæ inserted behind the middle; elytral striæ
    very fine but broadly, feebly impressed and very coarsely punctate; body
    subglabrous and with remotely scattered white scales........**Zygobaris**
Beak short and stout; body squamose.
  Basal joint of the antennal funicle moderate in length; elytra with large re-
    motely scattered white scales in addition to the denser squamules; species
    very small ....**Catapastus**
  Basal joint of the antennal funicle very long, sometimes as long as the entire
    remainder; elytral vestiture often vittate or with denuded spots, but
    without widely dispersed coarser scales; species moderately large, more
    or less elongate-oval, or narrower and parallel, convex ....**Barinus**
30—Body cylindrical and very slender; basal joint of the antennal funicle
    long ....**Barilepton**
31—Beak long, very slender but strongly inflated behind the point of antennal
    insertion, separated from the head beneath by a deep transverse constric-
    tion; erect setæ spiniform and conspicuous ....**Eunyssobia**
Beak shorter, without basal constriction, the erect bristles much shorter.
                                                          Plocamus

BARIS.

Germar.—Ins. Spec. Nov. 1824, p. 197.
Baridius Schönh. (pars).

This is a large genus of almost universal distribution, but much
more developed in North and South America than in Eurasia.
Assuming the definition of the genus given in the preceding table,
the species occurring within the territory embraced by the present
monograph are of an oval or oblong-oval convex form of body, with
semi-glabrous and usually strongly shining integuments. As compared with most of the other genera of the tribe the sculpture is
rather coarse and only moderately dense. The vestiture consists
of small semi-erect or recurved setæ, which are always sparse and
never broadly squamiform.

The rostrum is invariably short, often excessively so, never quite
equalling the prothorax in length, and, in many cases, not more
than one-half as long. On comparing this form of beak with that
of Centrinus, Limnobaris or even Onychobaris, it can reasonably
be inferred that the habits of the species are notably, if not essentially, different from those of the latter genera.

The legs are very short, the tibiæ strongly mucronate within at apex, and more or less strongly carinate and grooved along the sides, the tarsi moderate in development, with the third joint more or less broadly bilobed or emarginate; the ungues are somewhat variable in length, but never very long.

Our species can be readily divided into two groups, which might be considered of subgeneric value, were it not for the fact that *B. callida* constitutes a connective bond in the important character relating to the form of the scutellum. The first of these groups is characterized by a robust form of body, a greater development of the sparse setæ, broadly sinuate external outline of the tibiæ, feebly marked transverse impression at the base of the beak, and a transverse broadly impressed scutellum, the other by a variable but nearly always more slender form of body, less developed setæ, straight tibiæ, strongly marked basal impression of the beak, and a smaller subquadrate or rounded and unimpressed scutellum. In the first, the anterior coxæ are always very narrowly separated, while in the second they are generally much more widely so, although never very remote when compared for example with Onychobaris, their distance asunder being always less than their own width. I find no appreciable difference between the groups in the nature of the impression of the prosternum, the latter being very variable in degree ; it is sometimes quite marked, but cannot well be made use of in a tabular arrangement of the species. It occasionally disappears completely.

The buccal opening is deep, and has, at the bottom, a long slender truncate process, serving as a pedestal for the mentum, the latter being small and obconical. In the species of the first group the sides of the buccal opening are more or less prolonged downward, forming lateral plates for the protection of the oral organs, especially developed in *strenua*. In the second group, however, the sides of the fissure are horizontal and perfectly continuous with the flat under surface of the beak. The mandibles are small, stout, arcuate and distinctly overlap when closed.

The sexual characters are more marked than in most of the other genera with exposed pygidium, the male being nearly always easily recognizable by the distinct impression at the middle of the abdomen toward base. It is somewhat singular that this impression, in the present case, is always more sparsely and finely punctured than the neighboring surface of the abdomen, while in Blapstinus, of the

Tenebrionidæ, possessing an entirely analogous abdominal impression, which might at first sight be supposed to have been developed from the same causes and for identical purposes, the impression is almost always notably more densely punctured than the surrounding surface. The beak is not subject to great sexual modification, although there are a few exceptions to this rule, as for instance *sparsa*, in which it is distinctly shorter in the male than in the female.

The following table probably includes a large proportion of the forms inhabiting the United States:—

Tibiæ sinuate externally and prominent at apex ; anterior coxæ narrowly separated ; impression between the head and beak feeble ; setæ more developed, generally bristling also from the under surface of the beak ; scutellum usually short, transverse and broadly, deeply impressed, nearly as in Trichobaris ; body never with æneous surface lustre 2

Tibiæ straight, occasionally with a small external dentiform process at apex but never broadly sinuate ; anterior coxæ more widely separated ; impression between the head and beak strong but always broadly angulate when viewed in profile ; scutellum small, subquadrate or rounded, not broadly impressed ; setæ generally inconspicuous ; surface lustre frequently æneous 9

2—Scutellum transverse and impressed 3

Scutellum small, rounded, not transverse 8

3—Elytra at least twice as long as the prothorax, generally distinctly more...4

Elytra very distinctly less than twice as long as the prothorax....................7

4—Elytral intervals strongly elevated, narrow and never more than slightly wider than the grooves, the second and third generally not at all wider than the others 5

Elytral intervals broader, flat and feebly elevated, the grooves unusually shallow ; second and third intervals much wider...................................6

5—Elytral callus prominent, the elytra being abruptly and distinctly wider than the prothorax and with the sides parallel in basal two-thirds.

   Abdomen clothed with rather long white subrecumbent hairs ....1 **ingens**

   Abdomen with short sparse setæ ....2 **striata**

Elytral callus not prominent ; body oval, the prothorax strongly narrowed from the base..3 **umbilicata**

6—Body extremely densely punctured throughout...............4 **arizonica**

7—Small species, dark red-brown in color, the elytra still paler ; elytral setæ almost scale-like, recurved..5 **hispidula**

Much larger species, black throughout ; elytral setæ slender and bristle-like.

   Body very robust, oblong ; elytral intervals all much wider than the grooves, the punctures broadly confused but forming nearly even single lines on the first, fifth and seventh, smaller than in *strenua* and not so coalescent...6 **gravida**

Body less robust and more oval; elytral intervals all narrow and with single anastomosing series, except the second and third, which are wider and with the punctures confused..7 **strenua**

8—Pronotal punctures very coarse, somewhat irregular and nearly as large as the scutellum; second and third elytral intervals much wider than the others; interstitial punctures small ....8 **callida**

9—Prothorax large, always distinctly more than one-half as long as the elytra, the median line—viewed in profile—more strongly declivous toward apex; beak generally extremely short...............................10

Prothorax shorter, not more than one-half as long as the elytra, the median line in profile evenly, feebly arcuate and not more strongly declivous toward apex; beak variable in length but generally longer................17

10—Pronotal punctures sparse, sometimes very remote.........................11

Pronotal punctures close-set and even, never separated by more than their own diameters at any part of the disk; interstitial punctures generally large and more or less approximate 14

11—Interstitial punctures of the elytra fine...12

Interstitial punctures coarse, rounded; pronotal punctures often smaller and closer anteriorly but always sparse toward base; prosternum distinctly impressed 13

12—Legs black or piceous-black.

Integuments dull but smooth; large species, intense black, the body almost evenly oval, strongly convex...............................9 **subovalis**

Integuments highly polished and with a more or less pronounced æneous lustre; species moderate in size.

Beak in the female two-thirds as long as the prothorax ......10 **lubrica**

Beak in the female not more than one-half as long as the prothorax.

11 **tumescens**

Legs red, the tarsi black; pronotal punctures extremely sparse, large and rather feebly impressed ....12 **nitida**

13—Black, the prothorax shorter, strongly transverse in the female; prosternum deeply impressed ....13 **soluta**

Piceous; body more narrowly oval, the prothorax longer and more rounded at apex; elytral setæ longer, semi-erect and conspicuous; beak in the male not more than one-half as long as the prothorax..........14 **floridensis**

14—Interstitial punctures generally broadly confused at least on the alternate intervals, although often forming even series on some of the intervals 15

Interstitial punctures generally forming single series, although sometimes confused on the third and frequently, also, on others very near the base...16

15—Prothorax about as long as wide; all the elytral intervals coarsely, confusedly and somewhat rugosely punctured....................15 **subænea**

Prothorax wider than long.

Color dark piceous-brown throughout; smaller species, the surface polished, the elytral setæ robust and subsquamiform, arranged without order and very conspicuous though not dense ....16 **vespertina**

Color black; lustre more or less dull; elytral setæ more hair-like, less broadly scattered over the intervals and less conspicuous.

Legs black or piceous-black.

Smaller and narrower species, the integuments dull and opaque, the punctures smaller..17 **oblongula**

Larger species, robust and oblong, subparallel; lustre very feebly alutaceous, the elytra quite polished; interstitial punctures coarser and more transverse..18 **transversa**

Legs bright red; larger species, strongly convex, coarsely punctate, the pronotum usually distinctly alutaceous.......................19 **dilatata**

16—Elytra strongly narrowed behind the humeri; small species, the integuments polished and with a distinct piceous tinge......20 **cuneipennis**

Elytra subparallel or very feebly narrowed behind the humeri.

Interstitial punctures broadly confused on the third, and sometimes also on the second, interval, these being then wider than the others; rather small species, dark piceous-brown throughout.....................21 **aprica**

Interstitial punctures forming an approximately even single series on all of the intervals.

Smaller species, piceous to piceous-black in color, the prothorax more strongly rounded on the sides anteriorly; legs somewhat finely punctate..22 **dolosa**

Larger and more elongate-oval, intense black, highly polished, the prothorax shorter and more conical, the pronotum not so declivous anteriorly; legs coarsely punctate......................................23 **zuniana**

17—Dull, finely and extremely densely punctate; interstitial punctures broadly confused at least on the alternate intervals; elytral striæ not very deep, distinctly punctate at the bottom...............................18

Strongly shining; sculpture variable 19

18—Body less stout, the beak rather slender and fully three-fourths as long as the prothorax in the female. California....................24 **opacula**

Body and beak moderately robust, the latter not more than two-thirds as long as the prothorax in the female; punctures slightly larger; elytral lustre less densely opaque. Nebraska............................25 **porosicollis**

19—Abdomen extremely densely and rugosely punctured throughout the width; pronotal punctures coarse and sparse, the interstitial punctures of the elytra moderate; beak rather long.............26 **punctiventris**

Abdomen not so densely or rugosely punctate, at least toward the middle...20

20—Interstitial punctures of the elytra larger, always exceeding in diameter one-third of the width of the narrower intervals, at least toward base...21

Interstitial punctures small, never exceeding in diameter one-third the width of the narrower intervals; æneous metallic lustre predominant..........24

21—Legs red or distinctly rufo-piceous throughout. California..............22

Legs black, or at most with a slight piceous tinge.......................23

22—Pronotal punctures somewhat coarse, deep and very dense, with a rather conspicuous impunctate line; interstitial punctures large, deep and approximate; body black, the elytra more or less rufo-piceous in color; beak unusually long, nearly as long as the prothorax in the female.

27 **rubripes**

Pronotal punctures decidedly coarse, deep and sparser, the impunctate line
almost obsolete; punctures of the intervals coarse but extremely feeble
and rather remote; body piceous in color, the elytra pale rufo-castaneous.
28 **sparsa**

Pronotal punctures very fine, without trace of median impunctate line; large
species..29 **brunneipes**

23—Sides of the prothorax strongly convergent from the base and with a
broad sinuation in more than basal half; beak unusually long and
strongly arcuate..30 **deformis**

Sides of the prothorax subparallel or very feebly convergent, without distinct
sinuation.

Pronotum usually densely punctate, the punctures deep and often almost in
mutual contact throughout, without trace of impunctate line except in
futilis, where it is very variable and sometimes conspicuous.

Legs intense black throughout and rather strongly and closely punctured;
body somewhat robust...31 **futilis**

Legs piceous-black, the knees feebly rufescent; body decidedly slender,
the beak rather slender, strongly arcuate and about four-fifths as long
as the prothorax in the female...............................32 **inconspicua**

Pronotum less densely punctate and with a narrow, moderately definite impunctate line, which, however, occasionally becomes obliterated; sides
of the prothorax almost evenly rounded from base to apex.

Integuments with strong æneous metallic lustre.

Smaller species, about 3 mm. in length..........................33 **confinis**

Larger species, 4 mm. in length, more robust; beak a little shorter and
stouter..34 **subsimilis**

Integuments intense black, without trace of æneous lustre; prothorax
more elongate, the pronotal punctures usually sparser....35 **socialis**

24—Pronotum generally densely punctate..25

Pronotum more sparsely punctate..26

25—Elytral striæ coarse, at least nearly one-half as wide as the intervals.

Body narrowly oval; sides of the prothorax convergent from the base and
strongly, almost evenly arcuate ....36 **aperta**

Body broad, oblong, the prothorax much more transverse; sides abruptly
rounded and convergent anteriorly; lustre strongly æneous.
37 **abrupta**

Elytral striæ very fine, much less than one-half as wide as the intervals.

Striæ finely but remotely crenulate, the intervals often feebly alutaceous in
lustre; large species, the body moderately stout, parallel.
38 **tenuestriata**

Striæ totally impunctate and without trace of crenulation; body small and
slender ....39 **macra**

26—Form narrow, the prothorax but slightly wider than long.
40 **discipula**

Form more broadly ovate, the prothorax more or less strongly transverse.

Lustre strongly æneous.

Beak very short, scarcely two-thirds as long as the prothorax...41 **ærea**

Beak longer.

Base of the prothorax distinctly less than three times as wide as the head ; minute species, with very fine elytral striæ...42 **scintillans**

Base of the prothorax three times as wide as the head or nearly so ; much larger species, the elytral striæ coarse.

Prothorax short and transverse, subequal in width to the elytra, the sides subparallel and strongly arcuate..........43 **æneomicans**

Prothorax longer, the sides convergent and nearly straight from the base.

Pronotal punctures moderately coarse, separated by about their own diameters ; body black throughout, but with strong æneous lustre..44 **hyperion**

Pronotal punctures much coarser and separated by about twice their own diameters ; elytra rufo-piceous ....45 **vitreola**

Lustre highly polished but not æneous.

Legs black ; body elongate-oval, black, with a feeble bluish metallic lustre ....46 **ancilla**

Legs piceous or rufo-piceous.

Larger species, the interstitial punctures of elytra exceedingly minute.

47 **splendens**

Very small species, the interstitial punctures small but deep and distinct ; apex of the prothorax rounded almost evenly and continuously with the sides ....48 **exigua**

The sculpture in Baris varies to an extreme degree, and I have before me specimens of *transversa* with the interstitial punctures varying between wide limits, confused on all the intervals or forming even series. I have been forced, however, to refer extensively to sculpture in separating and describing the species, since this is one of those enormously difficult genera containing a large number of undoubtedly distinct species—as shown by extended series,—which can only be distinguished by bodily facies, and which are devoid of prominent structural differences, but the language employed should not be interpreted too rigidly, as it applies in general only to the typical forms of a species. For example, the pronotal punctuation in *futilis* and *inconspicua* · is said in the table to be dense, but there are specimens of both these species before me, in which the punctures become separated by fully their own width, or what might be termed sparse. In the case of isolated specimens, therefore, a search for the proper identification in the table must be more or less tentative, and it is quite possible that the table itself may be misleading in those cases where I have had to take the characters from single specimens. It has been my constant care to avoid synonymical repetitions, and, except in obvious cases, I have

only accepted those species which could be demonstrated by large
series. The fact that nearly four hundred specimens have been
studied in composing the table, increases my belief that the number
of species at least has not been materially overestimated.

Baris as here considered also occurs abundantly in Brazil, and
the species taken on the banks of the Amazon and La Plata cannot
be distinguished in type from our own representatives. The genus,
even in its restricted sense, is therefore a very large one. The
European species have a distinctly different facies and should be re-
vised from the generic point of view; the species are surely too
heterogeneous to be included in a single genus.

1 **Baris ingens** n. sp.—Oval, rather strongly convex, intense black
throughout, the integuments strongly shining. *Head* finely, sparsely punctate, with a deep frontal fovea, the impression very feeble; beak stout, evenly
and distinctly arcuate, coarsely strongly but not very densely punctate, three-
fourths as long as the prothorax, the setæ long and bristling beneath; antennæ
rather long, the funicular joints less coarctate than usual, broad but obconical
near the club, the latter large, robust, the basal joint distinctly less than one-
half of the mass, transverse. *Prothorax* small, very nearly as long as wide,
the sides in basal two-thirds rather strongly convergent and nearly straight,
then broadly rounded, thence more convergent and slightly constricted to the
apex, which is scarcely two-fifths as wide as the base, the latter transverse,
the median lobe broad and strong; disk with a very uneven and ill-defined
median line, the punctures very coarse and deep, abruptly perforate, one-half
as wide as the scutellum and generally separated by less than one-half of their
own diameters, each bearing a conspicuous fine cinereous seta. Scutellum
moderate, transverse, not strongly impressed. *Elytra* large, one-third longer
than wide, nearly two and one-half times as long as the prothorax, and, at
the large and longitudinally but not laterally prominent humeri, rather
abruptly almost one-third wider than the base of the latter; sides parallel
and nearly straight in basal two-thirds, then gradually rounded to the apex,
which is somewhat parabolic; disk with coarse, deep, strongly and not very
remotely punctured grooves; intervals flat, one-half wider than the grooves,
each with a single uneven series of moderately large, deep, close-set punctures,
the setæ moderate in length, slender, conspicuous. *Abdomen* rather sparsely
punctate, each puncture bearing a long cinereous and conspicuous setiform
hair, giving a strongly pruinose appearance by unaided vision. Anterior
coxæ approximate, separated by scarcely one-fifth of their own width; prosternum not impressed. Length 7.3 mm.; width 3 5 mm.

Arizona.

A conspicuously distinct species, easily recognizable by its large
size, small prothorax, ample elytra and unusually evident but slender setæ, especially pronounced on the abdomen. The type is a

male and has a large although moderately deep, oval impression, occupying the basal half of the abdomen. The transverse groove immediately before each posterior coxa is very wide, extremely deep, cavernous and abruptly limited anteriorly the metasternum thence to the middle coxæ decidedly tumid.

Ingens is more closely related to *striata* than to any other of our species, the differences being expressed in the table.

2 **Baris striata** Say.—Curc. 17, Ed. Lec., I, p. 281 (Baridius).

This is a rather common species of extended distribution, occurring throughout the Mississippi and Missouri valleys, but not, to my knowledge, extending to the Atlantic coast regions. The beak is robust, strongly arcuate and quite distinctly shorter than the prothorax, the latter relatively smaller than usual, fully one-third wider than long, with the sides feebly convergent to apical fourth, then strongly rounded and convergent to the apex, behind which there is generally a feeble constriction; the punctures are very coarse and generally separated by scarcely one-half of their own widths. Scutellum transverse and broadly impressed. Elytra large, a little more than twice as long as the prothorax and abruptly nearly one-fourth wider than that part, the humeral tuberosities small but very distinct; the striæ are very coarse, deep and punctate and the intervals are but slightly wider than the grooves, each with a single uneven series of moderately coarse, very deep, close-set punctures, the setæ moderate in length, erect and distinct but not as conspicuous as in *strenua*.

The prosternum is not impressed in front of the coxæ, and the latter are. somewhat closer than in any other species which I have observed, being separated by rather less than one-fifth of their width. Length 4.8–5.5 mm.; width 2.25–2.7 mm.

The series before me is from Arkansas, Wisconsin and Montana.

3 **Baris umbilicata** Lec.—Proc. Ac. Nat. Sci., Phila., 1868, p. 363 (Baridius); Proc. Am. Phil. Soc., XV, p. 291.

Of this well-marked species I have before me a series of between twenty and thirty specimens, showing great variation in size, and also in certain other more unexpected directions. The body is deep polished black throughout, robust and very strongly convex. The beak is rather long and but feebly arcuate, three-fourths as long as the prothorax in the male, and but very slightly shorter than the latter in the female. Prothorax subconical, more strongly narrowed near the apex, convex, coarsely but not very densely punctate, the punctures circular, about one-half as wide as the transverse scutellum, and separated by their own diameters in some specimens, to scarcely one-half that distance in others. Elytra large, fully twice as long as the prothorax and nearly one-fourth wider than the latter, the grooves exceedingly wide and deep, distinctly and remotely punctate at the bottom, the intervals not at all wider than the grooves, each with a single series of rather coarse very deep and distant punctures, the second and third not wider, the setæ very small, visible, but not in the least conspicuous. Abdomen coarsely deeply and closely punctured.

The male has the abdomen narrowly and deeply impressed nearly through the length of the two basal segments, but in a small specimen from Florida this impression is very small, feeble and situated near the base. Length 3.2–4.8 mm ; width 1.5–2.4 mm.

New York (Long Island), Pennsylvania, District of Columbia, Florida, Texas, Iowa and Colorado (Denver).

4 Baris arizonica n. sp.—Oblong, rather robust, moderately convex, piceous-black, the legs and elytra slightly paler ; lustre somewhat dull from the density of punctuation, the interspaces polished. *Head* very minutely punctured, separated from the beak by an impression which is unusually feeble ; beak long, not very stout, feebly arcuate, nearly as long as the prothorax, finely but strongly, sparsely punctured, very densely so laterally toward base ; antennæ moderate, the club very large, stout, ovoidal, with its basal joint in great part pubescent and only feebly shining toward base, basal joint of the funicle shorter than the next three. *Prothorax* rather short, nearly two-fifths wider than long, the sides parallel and broadly arcuate in basal three-fourths, then rather abruptly but not angularly rounded, thence strongly convergent and distinctly sinuate to the apex ; base not quite three times as wide as the head, broadly and evenly bisinuate ; disk with a very short narrow median impunctate spot, the punctures rather coarse, very deep and extremely dense, two-fifths as wide as the scutellum and almost in mutual contact even toward the middle. Scutellum short, unusually transverse, broadly, deeply impressed in the middle. *Elytra* one-fourth longer than wide, slightly more than twice as long as the prothorax, and, at the feebly tumid humeri, about one-fifth wider than the latter, very broadly, obtusely rounded behind ; disk with coarse but rather shallow, distinctly and transversely punctate grooves, the intervals wide, flat, the second and third much wider than the others, and all densely, confusedly, strongly but not very coarsely punctured ; setæ very short, not conspicuous. *Abdomen* rather finely but strongly, not very densely punctured. *Legs* short, finely, rather feebly, not densely punctate, the outer line of the tibiæ sinuous, the apex prominent ; tarsi pale rufous, the claws rather long. Length 4.0 mm. ; width 1.95 mm.

Arizona.

This species, although much smaller, is related to *striata*. It will be readily known by its very dense punctuation, short prothorax and unusually long beak; it is represented by a single female specimen.

5 **Baris hispidula** n. sp.—Oval, strongly convex, shining, castaneous-brown, the elytra paler red-brown. *Head* with a small frontal fovea, finely but deeply punctured anteriorly, becoming minutely and sparsely so posteriorly, the transverse impression separating it from the beak unusually feeble; beak feebly arcuate toward base, straight in apical two-thirds, four-fifths as long as the prothorax, coarsely, deeply, moderately closely punctate ; antennæ moderate, club rather short and stout, acutely conoidal, its basal joint constituting rather more than one-half the mass and pubescent in apical half. *Prothorax* elongate, just visibly wider than long, the sides almost evenly arcuate throughout, gradually becoming parallel near the base; apex broadly, feebly arcuate, one-half as wide as the base, the latter not quite three times as wide as the head, transverse, the median lobe unusually wide but feeble ; disk with a moderately wide but not entire impunctate line, the punctures moderately coarse, deep, somewhat elongated, separated by about their own widths but tending to form longitudinal rugæ toward base. Scutellum moderate, transverse, broadly impressed. *Elytra* scarcely more than one-fifth longer than wide, two-thirds longer than the prothorax, and, at the moderately tumid humeri, abruptly nearly one-fourth wider than the latter ; sides parallel in basal two-thirds, then gradually convergent, the apex semi-circularly rounded ; disk with coarse, deep, abrupt, rather strongly but not closely punctured grooves, the intervals but very slightly wider than the grooves, each with a single series of coarse, very deep, rather close-set punctures ; setæ semi-erect, rather long, broad, subsquamiform, conspicuous. *Abdomen* rather sparsely but strongly punctate, each puncture bearing a short but robust, pale, subsquamiform seta. Anterior coxæ large, globose, rather approximate, separated by one-fourth of their own width. Length 3.9 mm.; width 1.8 mm.

Colorado. Mr. Jülich.

The type is a male, and has the abdomen rather narrowly and distinctly impressed in the middle toward base. The peculiar pale coloration may, in part at least, be due to immaturity, but the species is remarkably distinct in the coarse and squamiform nature of the short and normally sparse setæ, these, as usual in the present group, also bristling conspicuously from the lower surface of the rostrum.

6 **Baris gravida** n. sp.—Oblong, strongly convex, robust, black, polished, the setæ rather small, semi-erect and moderately conspicuous on the elytra. *Head* obsoletely punctate, the transverse impression distinct, broadly

angulate viewed in profile, and with a large elongate median fovea; beak very short and robust, coarsely, deeply punctate, feebly arcuate, scarcely three-fifths as long as the prothorax; antennæ moderate, the club but slightly longer than wide. *Prothorax* large, one-fifth wider than long, the sides slightly convergent and nearly straight to apical fifth, then very abruptly rounded, thence extremely convergent and straight to the apex, which is much less than one-half as wide as the base, the latter transverse, the median lobe nearly one-third of the total width, rounded; disk with a narrow prominent median line, the punctures moderately coarse, deep and decidedly dense, one-third as wide as the scutellum and almost in mutual contact, uneven in shape. Scutellum transverse, broadly, deeply impressed. *Elytra* a little wider than the prothorax and about two-thirds longer, but very little longer than wide, parallel, very obtusely rounded behind; humeral callus small and feeble; disk with very coarse deep grooves, finely punctate at the bottom, the intervals alternating in width, all much wider than the grooves, the punctures coarse, close-set, broadly confused on all except the first, fifth and seventh, where they form tolerably even single lines. *Abdomen* strongly punctate and setose. Prosternum perfectly flat, separating the coxæ by barely one-fourth of their own width, the punctures dense and only moderately coarse. Length 6.0 mm.; width 3.1 mm.

Texas (Big Springs). Mr. H. F. Wickham.

The single representative is a female and the species is allied to *strenua*, differing however in many strongly marked features, among which should be mentioned the much more obese form, smaller, denser punctures, broadly confused on most of the elytral intervals, the more prominent and subcariniform median line of the pronotum and the relatively shorter beak.

7 **Baris strenua** Lec.—Proc. Ac. Nat. Sci., Phila., 1868, p. 363 (Baridius); Proc. Am. Phil. Soc., XV, p. 291.

The general form of this species, which is one of the largest of the genus, is oblong-oval, robust and strongly convex, the surface polished, black and deeply sculptured. The beak is short, moderately stout and arcuate, and is scarcely two-thirds as long as the prothorax in the female. The prothorax is but slightly wider than long, with the sides distinctly convergent and almost straight nearly to apical fifth, then strongly rounded, thence very strongly convergent to the apex which is somewhat tubulate, the disk has a more or less ill-defined abbreviated impunctate line, the punctures being rather large, deep and separated by slightly less than their own diameters. Scutellum strongly transverse, broadly, deeply impressed, prominent posteriorly at the sides. Elytra abruptly about one-fifth wider than the prothorax, one-fifth longer than wide and

a little less than twice as long as the prothorax, the grooves very
wide and deep, the intervals but slightly wider than the grooves,
very coarsely deeply and approximately punctate, the punctures
contiguous and generally more or less confused toward base. Setæ
cinereous, long, erect and very conspicuous but not squamiform.
Length 4.5–5.8 mm.; width 2.1–2.8 mm.

Arizona, Texas, Kansas and Montana. The series before me
consists of fourteen specimens. In one the thoracic punctures are
larger than usual and somewhat longitudinally subcoalescent. The
prosternum is generally perfectly flat, but in two or three examples
not otherwise materially differing, it becomes more or less distinctly
impressed along the middle.

8 **Baris callida** n. sp.—Oblong-oval, strongly convex, deep black
throughout, polished. *Head* minutely, sparsely, the beak strongly punctured, the latter densely rugulose at the sides, feebly arcuate, moderately
stout, scarcely two-thirds as long as the prothorax; antennæ moderate, the
club rather small, with the basal joint much less than one-half of its total
length, highly polished. *Prothorax* nearly two-fifths wider than long; sides
feebly convergent in basal two-thirds, then rather strongly rounded, thence
moderately strongly convergent and nearly straight to the apex; base about
three times as wide as the head, subtransverse, the median lobe moderate in
size and prominence; disk with an ill-defined central impunctate spot, the
punctures very large, deep, uneven in shape and distribution but rather
dense, nearly as large as the scutellum and as a rule separated by scarcely
one-half of their own dimensions. Scutellum rather small. *Elytra* one-fourth
longer than wide, about twice as long as the prothorax, and, at the large
though moderately tumid humeri, fully one-fourth wider than the latter;
sides subparallel, the apex almost semi-circularly rounded; disk with coarse
deep finely and remotely punctate grooves, the intervals flat or very feebly
convex, but slightly wider than the grooves, each with a single series of small
but deep, moderately distant punctures, the second and third wider and with
the punctures broadly confused, the third nearly twice as wide as the grooves;
setæ very minute and inconspicuous. *Abdomen* very sparsely punctate, the
punctures fine but becoming coarse toward the sides. *Legs* rather short and
robust, polished, sparsely but somewhat strongly punctured. Length 4.0
mm.; width 2.0 mm.

Georgia.

The unique type is a male, and has the abdomen broadly and
feebly impressed in the middle toward base. It somewhat resembles *umbilicata*, but has the pronotal punctures denser and more
uneven, the second and third elytral intervals wide with the punctures broadly confused, and the punctuation of the abdomen fine
and very sparse; it also differs in its decidedly shorter beak and

form of the scutellum.　The prosternum is not distinctly impressed, and the coxæ are separated by slightly more than one-fourth of their own width.

9 **Baris subovalis** Lec.—Proc. Ac. Nat. Sci., Phila., 1868, p. 363 (Baridius); Proc. Am. Phil. Soc., XV, p. 291.

A large and remarkably isolated species, represented by the original type, which is apparently still unique.　The form is almost evenly oval, very convex, intense black throughout, the integuments very dull but smooth and minutely, strongly granulato-reticulate.　The beak in the female is thick, distinctly and evenly arcuate, strongly punctured and about three-fourths as long as the prothorax, the latter large, one-third wider than long, the sides distinctly convergent and nearly straight to apical fourth, then rounded and more convergent to the apex, the base straight and unusually oblique from the middle, the lobe very small, the disk with an ill-defined median impunctate line which does not attain the apex, the punctures not very coarse but deep and separated by rather more than their own widths.　Elytra coarsely and deeply grooved, the intervals flat, about one-half wider than the grooves, each with a somewhat uneven series of small but deep, moderately close-set punctures, broadly confused on the third and fifth, the setæ very minute and inconspicuous.　Prosternum narrowly and feebly impressed, the coxæ separated by distinctly less than one-half of their own width, the sides of the process strongly convergent. Length 5.8 mm.; width 2.9 mm.

Wisconsin.　Cab. LeConte.　There is no other species known to me which at all approaches *subovalis* in general habitus.

10 **Baris lubrica** n. sp.—Oblong-oval, strongly convex, black throughout, highly polished, the lustre quite distinctly æneous. *Head* obsoletely punctured, the beak finely, strongly, sparsely so, feebly arcuate, robust, two-thirds as long as the prothorax, the basal transverse impression unusually feeble; antennæ moderate, the club rather small. *Prothorax* large, scarcely one-third wider than long; sides feebly convergent and very slightly arcuate to apical fourth, then strongly rounded, thence strongly convergent and nearly straight for a short distance to the apex, which is transversely truncate; base three and one-half times as wide as the head, straight and feebly oblique from the rather wide broadly and feebly rounded median lobe to the sides; disk with a wide but very ill-defined elongate impunctate spot, the punctures moderately coarse, sparse, somewhat deep, impressed, minutely umbilicate, about one-third as wide as the scutellum and separated by nearly three times their own diameters.　Scutellum somewhat large, subquadrate, slightly trans-

verse. *Elytra* scarcely more than one-fourth longer than wide, a little less than twice as long as the prothorax, and, at the small and feebly tumid humeri, but slightly wider than the latter; sides behind the humeri very feebly convergent, the apex broadly, almost semi-circularly rounded; disk with moderately coarse, very deep, abrupt, finely remotely and very feebly crenulate grooves, the intervals at least twice as wide as the grooves, flat, each with a series of small, moderately distant, somewhat transversely rugulose punctures, which are more or less confused on the second, third and fifth; setæ small but distinct, silvery. *Abdomen* finely, feebly, sparsely punctured, the setæ of the under surface quite robust, pale and distinct. *Legs* very short, robust, black, finely and sparsely punctured; claws moderate. Length 3.7–4.5 mm.; width 1.9–2.3 mm.

Florida. National Museum.

The type is a female judging by the entirely unimpressed abdomen, but in several of the species allied to this in general habitus, the male sexual characters become very feeble, so that it is occasionally difficult to determine the sex of isolated individuals. The present species is widely distinct although somewhat allied to *nitida;* it may be known, however, by its black legs, finer pronotal punctures, less rhomboidal form of the body, larger scutellum, closer and more transversely rugulose interstitial punctures, and more evident setæ. The anterior coxæ are separated by one-half of their own width.

11 **Baris tumesceus** Lec.—Proc. Ac. Nat. Sci., Phila., 1868, p. 362 (Baridius); Proc. Am. Phil. Soc., XV, p. 292.

Oblong, robust, convex, black throughout, the legs somewhat piceous, polished and feebly æneous, the beak very short, not at all over one-half as long as the prothorax in the female, the prothorax large, one-fourth wider than long, subparallel, strongly rounded and extremely convergent near the apex, the base fully three and one-half times as wide as the head, the disk without median line, the punctures rather coarse and impressed, separated by twice their own diameters. The elytra are but slightly longer than wide and two-thirds longer than the prothorax, coarsely, deeply striate, the grooves distinctly crenulate, becoming deeply and conspicuously so toward base; intervals flat or feebly convex, scarcely one-half wider than the grooves, each with a single series of rather small but deep, moderately distant punctures, the third very much wider than any of the others and with the punctures sparse but confused. Length 4.3 mm.; width 2.2 mm.

Middle States—LeConte; Nebraska.

12 Baris nitida Lec.—Proc. Am. Phil. Soc., XV, p. 292.

A species of medium size and distinct facies, of rather robust, very convex and subrhomboidal form and polished, feebly æneous lustre. Prothorax not quite as elongate as in some of the allied forms, from one-third to two-fifths wider than long, the sides feebly convergent to apical fourth, then strongly convergent and straight or feebly sinuous to the apex, coarsely, very sparsely punctate, the punctures not very deep, impressed and umbilicate. Scutellum very small, nearly circular. The humeri are unusually prominent, and the elytra rather strongly convergent behind them, the striæ moderate in width, deep, the intervals about twice as wide as the striæ, each with a single series of small but rather deep, remote punctures, not confused on the second or third, the setæ very small and not at all conspicuous. The legs are red and the tarsi piceous. Length 3.9–4.4 mm.; width 2.1–2.3 mm.

Florida (Biscayne Bay). I have seen but two specimens; one, the original type, in the cabinet of LeConte, and the other, entirely similar, kindly given me by Mr. W. Jülich of New York.

13 Baris soluta n. sp.—Oblong, robust, convex, black and highly polished throughout; setæ very minute and inconspicuous. *Head* minutely and very remotely punctulate, the transverse impression strong and angulate; beak exceedingly short and thick, finely, not densely punctate, arcuate, gradually flattened toward apex, barely three-fifths as long as the prothorax; antennæ moderate, the club small, compressed, on the narrow side scarcely at all wider than the seventh funicular joint. *Prothorax* transverse, fully one-half wider than long, the sides rounded and feebly convergent to apical fourth, then strongly rounded to the apex; base oblique and straight from the very small and feeble median lobe to the obtuse basal angles; disk coarsely and sparsely punctate, the punctures one-half as wide as the scutellum and separated by nearly twice their own diameters, finer and closer toward apex; impunctate line feebly evident. Scutellum moderate, subquadrate. *Elytra* not wider and fully four-fifths longer than the prothorax, the sides feebly convergent, the apex obtusely rounded; humeri rather prominent; striæ very coarse and deep, not distinctly crenulate toward base; intervals but slightly wider than the grooves, each with a single series of moderately large deep and somewhat close-set punctures, the second and third a little wider, the latter with the series slightly uneven. *Abdomen* coarsely, strongly but not very densely punctate. Prosternum very deeply impressed, almost sulcate, along the middle, separating the coxæ by two-thirds of their own width. Length 4.0–4.3 mm.; width 2.0–2.2 mm.

Louisiana; Arkansas; Colorado.

The type is a female; this sex seems to be invariably much

broader than the male and with a relatively more transverse prothorax.

14 Baris floridensis n. sp.—Oblong-oval, convex, polished throughout,
dark piceous-brown, the pronotum blackish. *Head* and beak sparsely punctured, the latter extremely short, thick, moderately arcuate, one-half as long
as the prothorax ; antennæ normal, the club robust, with its basal joint
polished. *Prothorax* large, scarcely more than one-fifth wider than long ; sides
subparallel in about basal half, then broadly, evenly rounded to the apex,
which is narrowly transverse and truncate ; base three times as wide as the
head, straight and very feebly oblique from the moderately wide and rounded
median lobe to the sides ; disk strongly convex anteriorly and laterally, without trace of median line, the punctures rather coarse, deep, well separated,
subperforate with the edges slightly obtuse, two-thirds as wide as the scutellum and separated by nearly their own widths, becoming slightly smaller and
closer toward apex. Scutellum well developed, not impressed, slightly transverse. *Elytra* scarcely more than one-fourth longer than wide, three-fourths
longer than the prothorax, and, at the rather small and moderately tumid
humeri, slightly wider than the latter ; sides behind the humeri distinctly
convergent and nearly straight, broadly rounded at apex ; disk with moderately coarse, very deep, abrupt, finely, remotely but distinctly punctate
grooves ; intervals scarcely twice as wide as the grooves, flat, each with a
single series of large shallow moderately close-set punctures, the second
distinctly wider and with the punctures smaller closer and broadly confused ;
setæ very small but forming quite visible series by anteriorly oblique illumination. *Abdomen* rather coarsely but sparsely and shallowly punctured. *Legs*
moderate, sparsely but rather strongly punctate. Length 4.0 mm.; width
1.8 mm.

Florida.

The single male serving as the type represents a species quite
closely allied to *soluta*, but differing in its slightly narrower form,
shorter beak, less coarse pronotal punctures and several other characters. The abdomen is rather narrowly and very feebly impressed
in the middle toward base ; the prosternum nearly flat, very widely
separating the coxæ. *Floridensis* may be distinguished from *transversa* by its much sparser punctuation, narrower form, piceous elytra
and longer elytral setæ.

15 Baris subænea Lec.—Proc. Ac. Nat. Sci., Phila., 1868, p. 361 (Baridius); Proc. Am. Phil. Soc., XV, p. 292.

A moderately large but somewhat narrow, strongly convex species, with coarse deep rugulose sculpture and somewhat piceous
color. The beak in the male is moderately robust, feebly arcuate
and about three-fifths as long as the prothorax, the latter rather

more elongate than in any of our other species, scarcely perceptibly wider than long, with the sides distinctly convergent and nearly straight from the base to between apical third and fourth, then strongly rounded, then somewhat strongly convergent and nearly straight to the apex; base about three times as wide as the head, the median lobe pronounced; disk with a narrow ill-defined median line, the punctures coarse, very deep and rather dense, somewhat uneven in size. Elytra not very coarsely but deeply and abruptly grooved, the intervals about twice as wide as the grooves, and all coarsely, closely, confusedly punctured throughout their extent, and coarsely rugose but polished, the second and third less coarsely, more sparsely punctured and smoother. Length 4.5 mm.; width 2.0 mm.

Middle States.

16 **Baris vespertina** n. sp.—Oblong-oval, convex, polished and dark piceous-brown throughout, the setæ long, stout, acuminate, strigose, sparse but conspicuous, semi-erect and arranged without order on the elytra. *Head* minutely but distinctly, not very remotely punctured, the beak not coarsely but deeply, densely so, rugose at the sides, robust, moderately arcuate and about three-fourths as long as the prothorax; antennæ inserted distinctly behind the middle, the scape very short, club moderate, its basal joint polished, pubescent toward apex. *Prothorax* one-half wider than long, the sides just visibly convergent, evenly and distinctly arcuate to near the apex, then gradually more strongly arcuate, convergent and feebly sinuate to the apex, which is broadly arcuate and fully one-half as wide as the base, the latter but slightly oblique, the median lobe small but prominent; disk coarsely deeply and very densely punctate, the punctures two-thirds as wide as the scutellum and almost in mutual contact; median impunctate line narrow, not attaining the apex. Scutellum moderate, quadrate, not impressed but somewhat rugose. *Elytra* slightly wider and nearly four-fifths longer than the prothorax; sides behind the feebly prominent humeri slightly convergent, the apex abruptly and obtusely rounded; striæ moderately deep, not very coarse, the intervals flat, nearly twice as wide as the grooves, the punctures moderately coarse, not very dense but rugose and confused on all the intervals, the second and third a little wider. *Abdomen* strongly, rather coarsely, somewhat closely punctured. Prosternum broadly and just visibly impressed, separating the coxæ by one-half of their own width. Length 3.3–3.5 mm.; width 1.6–1.7 mm.

Arizona.

The form of the prothorax, with the pronotum more declivous anteriorly, shows that this very distinct species should be associated with *transversa* and its allies. In the male the abdomen is broadly and feebly but distinctly impressed near the base.

17 Baris oblongula n. sp.—Dull and strongly alutaceous in lustre, oblong-oval, convex, deep black throughout, the legs slightly piceous. *Head* sparsely, minutely punctate, the beak more coarsely and closely so, densely rugose at the sides, short, thick, arcuate, but slightly more than one-half as long as the prothorax; antennæ moderately slender, the club rather small, not one-half as long as the funicle, the first joint of the latter shorter than the next three. *Prothorax* scarcely one-fourth wider than long; sides broadly, evenly arcuate, becoming nearly parallel toward base, the arcuation only slightly stronger near the apex; base three and one-half times as wide as the head, the median lobe rather narrow, distinct; disk somewhat coarsely, deeply and very densely punctate, the punctures one-half as wide as the scutellum and separated by rather less than one-half their own diameters, with a narrow and distinct impunctate median line extending from the base nearly to the apex. Scutellum moderate, transverse. *Elytra* scarcely more than one-fourth longer than wide, three-fourths longer than the prothorax, at the feebly tumid humeri scarcely at all wider than the latter; sides feebly convergent and just visibly arcuate from the humeri, the apex abruptly, broadly rounded; disk with rather fine but deep and abrupt striæ, which are finely, very feebly punctate, the intervals each with a single row of rather large deep moderately distant punctures, somewhat confused on the second, third and fifth. *Abdomen* strongly, rather closely punctured. *Legs* somewhat sparsely and feebly punctate; tibiæ straight externally, the tarsal claws moderate. Length 3.8 mm.; width 1.8 mm.

Colorado.

The description is drawn from the male, the two basal segments of the abdomen being strongly impressed in the middle. The prosternum is feebly impressed and the coxæ separated by rather more than one-half of their own width. This species may be distinguished by the long, evenly rounded, strongly, densely punctate prothorax, which is subequal in width to the elytra, and by the very dull lustre of the entire upper surface. The pronotal punctures are denser, and, especially, smaller than in *transversa*, which *oblongula* somewhat resembles in form and size.

18 Baris transversa Say.—Curc. 18, Ed. Lec., I, p. 282 (Baridius); *interstitialis* Say: Journ. Acad. Nat. Sci., Phila., III, p. 314 (Rhynchœnus); Curc. 18, Ed. Lec. I, p. 282 (Baridius); *quadrata* Lec.: Proc. Ac. Nat. Sci., Phila., 1868, p. 361 (Baridius); *carinulata* Lec.: Proc. Ac. Nat. Sci., Phila., 1858, p. 79 (Baridius); Proc. Am. Phil. Soc., XV, p. 292 (Baris).

Oblong, rather stout, parallel, convex, black, generally distinctly alutaceous in lustre, never in the least æneous; setæ sparse but quite distinct. Beak very thick, arcuate, punctate, scarcely one-half as long as the prothorax, nearly cylindrical. Prothorax large, rather more than one-third wider than long, the sides very feebly

convergent from the base to apical third, then abruptly rounded and
rather prominent, thence very strongly convergent to the apex, the
latter much less than one-half as wide as the base; disk very convex, coarsely, deeply punctate, the edges of the punctures obtuse;
median impunctate line often obsolete but frequently distinct.
Elytra about equal in width to the prothorax, the humeri slightly
prominent; sides subparallel, the apex broadly obtuse; striæ very
coarse, deep; intervals alternately wide and rather narrow, the
punctures coarse, close, subrugose, confused on the wider intervals.
Prosternum broadly impressed along the middle, separating the
coxæ by a little more than one-half of their own width. Length
3.5–4.8 mm.; width 1.8–2.3 mm.

New York, Indiana, Iowa, Missouri, Colorado and Texas. A
widely distributed, common and easily recognizable species. I think
that there is but little doubt that Say described *transversa* from
one of the numerous sculptural modifications of *interstitialis*, but
as the species is more commonly known under the name *transversa*
and since the name "*interstitialis*" refers to a form which has never
been accurately defined, and has always given rise to confusion and
uncertainty, even on the part of Say himself, the course here pur-
sued would appear to be for the best interests of science. *Carinulata* is not tenable as a species, the smooth median line of the
pronotum being a most variable feature, as is also the interstitial
punctuation.

19 **Baris dilatata** n. sp.—Oval to oblong-oval, robust, strongly convex,
black, the beak rufescent toward apex, the legs bright rufous; integuments
rather shining, without trace of æneous lustre. *Head* obsoletely, the beak
moderately densely, deeply punctate, the latter short, robust, strongly arcuate
toward base, less than one-half (♂) to nearly two-thirds (♀) as long as the
prothorax; antennæ moderate. *Prothorax* large, convex, scarcely one-fourth
wider than long; sides feebly convergent and just visibly arcuate to apical
fourth, then rather strongly rounded but not very prominent, thence strongly
convergent and straight or just visibly sinuate to the apex; base three and
one-half times as wide as the head, transverse, straight, the median lobe
rather wide and strongly developed, rounded; disk with narrow, more or less
imperfect median line, the punctures deep, rather coarse, a little more than
one-half as wide as the scutellum and generally separated by about their own
widths. Scutellum moderate, often moderately impressed in the middle toward
the posterior margin. *Elytra* one-fourth to one-third longer than wide, about
two-thirds longer than the prothorax, and, at the moderately tumid humeri,
quite distinctly wider than the latter; sides subparallel or very feebly convergent; apex broadly, rather abruptly rounded; disk with somewhat fine

but deep, abrupt, obsoletely punctured grooves, the intervals two to three times as wide as the grooves, flat, moderately coarsely, deeply, rather closely punctate, the punctures more or less broadly confused on all, sometimes throughout but often only toward base; setæ very small, distinct but not conspicuous. *Abdomen* sparsely, somewhat finely punctate. *Legs* short, polished, very finely feebly and sparsely punctate; tibiæ straight, minutely prominent at apex. Prosternum scarcely at all impressed, the anterior coxæ distant, separated by but slightly less than their own width. Length 3.8–4.8 mm.; width 1.8–2.4 mm.

California (Lake and San Bernardino Cos.).

A moderately large, distinct and easily recognizable species, not at all closely allied to any other Californian representative of the genus, although having several near eastern relatives. It can always be distinguished from any of the latter by its bright rufous legs and short rufescent beak.

20 **Baris cuneipennis** n. sp.—Oblong-oval, convex, polished throughout, blackish-piceous, the pronotum rather darker than the elytra. *Head* almost impunctate, the beak moderately coarsely and closely so, robust, strongly arcuate, three-fourths as long as the prothorax; antennæ normal, the club rather small and not very abrupt, its basal joint glabrous and highly polished, the last joint of the funicle with a widely spaced crown of unusually long coarse bristles. *Prothorax* one-third wider than long; sides subparallel and almost straight in rather more than basal three-fourths, then strongly rounded, thence strongly convergent but not at all constricted to the apex, which is broadly, very feebly arcuate; base about two and two-thirds times as wide as the head, straight and feebly oblique from the small median lobe to the sides; disk with a narrow imperfect impunctate line, which in one example is finely striate toward the middle; punctures moderate in size, not very dense, somewhat uneven, from one-third to one-half as wide as the scutellum and separated by nearly their own diameters. Scutellum moderate, slightly transverse. *Elytra* about one-third longer than wide, relatively small, two-thirds longer than the prothorax, and, at the distinctly swollen humeri, slightly wider than the latter; sides behind the humeri quite distinctly convergent, the apex rounded; disk with moderately coarse and deep, abrupt, obsoletely punctate grooves, the intervals flat or feebly convex, not very wide, each with a single series of coarse approximate punctures, the third interval noticeably wider than the others and with the punctures smaller and somewhat confused; setæ very minute, scarcely at all observable. *Abdomen* sparsely, moderately coarsely punctured. *Legs* moderate, finely, sparsely punctate; tibiæ straight; third tarsal joint not wider than long; claws moderate. Length 2.8–3.3 mm.; width 1.4–1.6 mm.

Texas (Austin).

The two specimens before me are apparently females. The prosternum is scarcely impressed and the coxæ separated by fully three-fourths of their width, the process being unusually wide. The species is especially notable by reason of its coarsish punctuation, long prothorax and rather short subconical elytra.

21 **Baris aprica** n. sp.—Oblong-oval, strongly convex, polished and dark piceous-brown throughout, the setæ small, distinct but not conspicuous. *Head* excessively minutely and sparsely punctulate, the transverse impression strong and angulate; beak very short, thick, moderately arcuate, feebly flattened toward apex, densely but not coarsely punctate and about two-thirds as long as the prothorax; antennal scape very short, the club rather robust, oval, with the basal joint polished but sparsely pubescent and constituting a little less than one-half the mass. *Prothorax* one-third wider than long, the sides broadly rounded and strongly convergent anteriorly, becoming almost parallel and straight in basal two-thirds; base straight and feebly oblique at the sides, the lobe equalling nearly one-third of the width, rather prominent; disk coarsely deeply and densely punctate, the punctures very narrowly separated, a narrow impunctate line distinct but not attaining the apex. Scutellum moderate, subquadrate, rugose. *Elytra* but slightly wider and three-fourths longer than the prothorax, the sides behind the scarcely prominent humeri just visibly convergent; apex abruptly and obtusely rounded, the sutural notch broad and deep; striæ rather coarse, deep, the intervals but slightly wider than the grooves, each with a single series of large, very deep, even and almost contiguous punctures, the third much wider than the others and with the punctures broadly confused and smaller. *Abdomen* strongly but not coarsely, moderately closely punctured. Prosternum flat, densely punctate, separating the coxæ by rather more than one-half of their own width. Length 3.4–3.6 mm.; width 1.65–1.7 mm.

Arizona; Colorado.

The coarse deep rounded and close-set punctures, forming a single series on each of the elytral intervals, is a type of sculpture which forcibly reminds us of several species of Onychobaris, such as *stictica*, but otherwise there is no resemblance. *Aprica* belongs in the group containing *transversa*, but is not very closely related to any other species. The abdomen in the male has a rather small but distinct subbasal impression.

22 **Baris dolosa** n. sp.—Oblong-oval, strongly convex, piceous-black throughout, polished, the elytra frequently feebly piceous. *Head* obsoletely, the beak finely, sparsely punctured, the latter quite coarsely and closely so at the sides, thick and arcuate toward base, straight and somewhat tapering in apical half, two-thirds (♂) to three-fourths (♀) as long as the prothorax; antennæ moderate, normal. *Prothorax* nearly two-fifths wider than long, the sides nearly parallel and very feebly arcuate to apical fourth, then strongly but moderately narrowly rounded, thence very strongly convergent and nearly straight to the apex; base three times as wide as the head, subtransverse and

straight, the median lobe moderate in width but prominent, narrowly subtruncate at apex ; disk with scarcely a trace of median line, coarsely, very deeply and closely punctate, the punctures one-half as wide as the scutellum or rather more, and separated by about their own diameters. Scutellum moderate, transverse. *Elytra* one-fifth longer than wide, two-thirds to three-fourths longer than the prothorax, and, at the moderately prominent humeri, but very slightly wider than the latter ; sides subparallel, the apex broadly and abruptly rounded ; disk with rather coarse, deep, obsoletely punctured grooves, the intervals scarcely one-half wider than the grooves, flat, each with a single series of coarse strong and very close-set punctures, sometimes slightly confused on the third ; setæ small, semi-erect, cinereous and rather conspicuous. *Abdomen* finely, sparsely punctured. *Legs* moderate, finely, very sparsely punctate. Length 3.2–3.6 mm. ; width 1.5–1.75 mm.

New York (Long Island) ; Pennsylvania ; Indiana ; Iowa.

A comparatively small, convex, strongly and deeply sculptured species bearing a general resemblance to *transversa*, but distinguishable by its much smaller size and the other characters given in the table. The anterior coxæ are widely separated and the prosternum feebly impressed. In the male the abdomen is narrowly and strongly impressed toward base. In the female the pronotal punctures are generally much closer, sometimes very dense, and the prothorax is frequently subprominent at apical fourth ; the above described type is a male from Iowa.

23 **Baris zuniana** n. sp.—Oval, convex, highly polished and black throughout. *Head* minutely, sparsely punctate, the beak finely, deeply and sparsely so and not very densely at the sides, robust, short, arcuate, about three-fourths as long as the prothorax in both sexes ; antennæ moderate, normal. *Prothorax* nearly two-fifths wider than long ; sides convergent and broadly, almost evenly arcuate from base to apex, sometimes feebly sinuate for a short distance near the latter ; base three times as wide as the head, straight and slightly oblique from the small and feeble median lobe to the sides ; disk with or without a narrow, feebly defined impunctate line, the punctures rather coarse, deep, not very dense, two-thirds as wide as the scutellum and separated by nearly one-half their widths, somewhat uneven and noticeably smaller near the apex. Scutellum small, rather transverse. *Elytra* two-fifths longer than wide, about twice as long as the prothorax, and, at the feebly tumid humeri, slightly wider than the latter ; sides thence very feebly convergent, the apex broadly arcuate ; disk with rather wide, very deep, obsoletely punctate grooves, the intervals flat, generally a little less than twice as wide as the grooves, each with a single series of very coarse, somewhat uneven, close-set punctures, those of the fourth and fifth intervals leaving but a narrow margin from their sides to the edge of the grooves ; setæ small but robust and quite distinct. *Abdomen* somewhat strongly but sparsely

punctured. *Legs* rather coarsely, deeply, moderately closely punctate; tarsal claws moderate. Length 3.8–4.0 mm.; width 1.8 mm.

Arizona.

A single pair. In the male the abdomen is strongly impressed in the middle toward base, the impressed area being more finely and sparsely punctured. The prosternum is narrowly but distinctly impressed, coarsely but sparsely punctured, separating the coxæ by rather more than one-half of their width.

24 **Baris opacula** n. sp.—Elongate-oval, narrow, convex, deep black throughout, the legs with a feeble piceous tinge; lustre dull. *Head* finely, sparsely, the beak rather finely but deeply, somewhat closely punctate, the latter arcuate, not very robust, three-fourths as long as the prothorax; antennæ moderate, normal, first joint of the funicle as long as the next three, club rather robust, ovoidal, pointed, not as long as the scape, the first joint partially pubescent, feebly shining. *Prothorax* scarcely one-fourth wider than long, the apex subtruncate, nearly one-half as wide as the base; median lobe of the latter broad and feeble; sides broadly, evenly arcuate throughout, becoming subparallel in basal third; disk rather finely but very deeply and densely punctate, without median impunctate area, the punctures not quite one-half as wide as the scutellum and generally separated by less than one-half their width; interspaces shining. Scutellum small, transverse. *Elytra* one-half longer than wide, distinctly more than twice as long as the prothorax, at the feebly tumid humeri a little wider than the base of the latter, together rather gradually and strongly rounded behind; striæ rather fine, deep, abrupt, finely, remotely punctate, not crenulate except feebly toward base; intervals wide, flat, minutely, strongly granulate, dull, each with a single series of fine, moderately distinct punctures, confused on the second and third intervals; setæ very minute, not at all conspicuous. *Abdomen* polished, convex, rather sparsely punctate, the last segment densely so. *Legs* moderate, finely, sparsely punctate; tibiæ straight externally. Length 4.0–4.7 mm.; width 1.65–2.1 mm.

California.

The prosternum is coarsely, somewhat closely punctate and very feebly impressed, and the coxæ are separated by one-half their width.

This is one of the most isolated species of the genus, easily identifiable by the opaque elytra, fine deep striæ and dense pronotal punctures.

25 **Baris porosicollis** n. sp.—Not very robust, convex, oval, deep black throughout, not strongly shining. *Head* finely, sparsely punctate, separated from the beak by a wide but distinct, obtusely angulate depression; beak rather arcuate, two-thirds as long as the prothorax, finely, closely punctate, more closely and very densely so at the sides; antennæ moderate, the

funicle rather slender except the basal joint, which is somewhat robust and scarcely as long as the next three, club rather small, robust, the first joint almost glabrous, polished. *Prothorax* scarcely more than one-fifth wider than long; sides feebly convergent and almost straight in basal three-fourths, then strongly rounded and convergent to the apex but not constricted; base three times as wide as the head, the median lobe rather narrow, rounded and distinct; disk rather finely, deeply, very densely punctate, the punctures somewhat uneven, one-half as wide as the scutellum and generally separated by one-third their width, a narrow imperfect median impunctate line evident in the type. Scutellum transverse, punctate. *Elytra* scarcely one-third longer than wide, twice as long as the prothorax, and, at the moderately tumid humeri, quite distinctly wider than the latter, broadly, obtusely rounded behind; disk not very coarsely but deeply, abruptly striate, the striæ with remote feeble punctures; intervals moderate in width, the fifth twice as wide as the striæ, flat, each with a single row of moderately large, strong, approximate punctures, confused on the second, third and fifth; setæ rather robust, short but distinct. *Abdomen* rather coarsely and densely punctured toward base. *Legs* finely, moderately closely punctate, the setæ short and silvery; tibiæ straight externally; tarsal claws rather small. Length 4.0 mm.; width 1.8 mm. (♀).

Nebraska.

Easily known by its rather long and narrow, densely punctate prothorax, very close-set punctures of the elytral intervals and somewhat dull lustre. The prosternum is rather deeply impressed, coarsely, moderately densely punctate, the coxæ separated by a little less than one-half their width.

I place with the type three specimens collected by Mr. Wickham at Greeley, Colorado, which differ only in having a single series on the fifth interval in both male and female, but which are otherwise similar throughout.

26 **Baris punctiventris** n. sp.—Oblong-oval, moderately convex, somewhat robust, polished throughout, black, the legs piceous. *Head* obsoletely punctate, the beak rather coarsely but not very densely so at the sides, rather stout but equal throughout, strongly arcuate and almost as long as the prothorax; antennæ normal. *Prothorax* rather short, nearly one-half wider than long; sides subparallel and very feebly arcuate in basal two-thirds, then strongly rounded, thence strongly convergent and nearly straight to the apex, which is transverse; base scarcely two and one-half times as wide as the head, subtransverse and straight, the median lobe small and feebly developed; disk without median line, the punctures coarse deep and perforate, three-fourths as wide as the scutellum, rather unevenly distributed but generally separated by distinctly less than their own diameters, in apical fifth becoming abruptly very minute. Scutellum rather small. *Elytra* about two-fifths longer than wide, a little more than twice as long as the prothorax, and, at the very small

basal and feebly tumid humeri, slightly wider than the latter ; sides behind
the humeri just visibly convergent and very feebly arcuate, the apex evenly
rounded, the sutural notch normal ; disk with deep abrupt obsoletely punctate grooves, moderate in width toward base, becoming much narrower toward
apex ; intervals rather wide, flat, each with a single series of small feeble
punctures, which become larger and close-set toward base but very minute and
widely distant toward apex ; setæ scarcely at all visible. *Abdomen* throughout
coarsely deeply and very densely punctured. *Legs* moderate, the hind tibiæ
scarcely more than two-thirds as long as the femora, straight ; tarsi slender,
the basal joint but slightly longer than the second ; claws small. Length
2.8–3.2 mm. ; width 1.3–1.6 mm.

Louisiana ; Missouri ; Indiana.

This small species can easily be identified by the peculiar punctuation of the pronotum and abdomen as detailed in the description.
The prosternum is very feebly impressed and widely separates the
coxæ. The three specimens before me are apparently females, but
as they differ greatly in relative stoutness of form, it is possible that
the more slender specimen from Louisiana, assumed as the type,
may be a male, and that in that sex the abdominal impression is
obsolete.

27 **Baris rubripes** n. sp.—Oblong, moderately convex, highly polished,
piceous-black, the legs rufous. *Head* minutely, rather sparsely punctured,
with a small punctiform fovea in the transverse impression, the beak strongly,
moderately densely punctate, arcuate, about three-fourths (♂) to four-fifths
(♀) as long as the prothorax ; antennæ somewhat less robust than usual, the
funicle long, with the second joint a little longer than wide, the third feebly
transverse, club short but robust. *Prothorax* two-fifths wider than long, the
sides almost evenly and rather strongly arcuate from base to apex sometimes a
little more abruptly convergent near the latter ; base distinctly less than three
times as wide as the head, transverse, the median lobe narrow but pronounced ;
disk widest slightly before the base, with a rather wide distinct impunctate
area which is subentire ; punctures somewhat coarse, deep and dense, about
three-fourths as wide as the scutellum and separated by less than one-half
their diameters. Scutellum unusually small, subquadrate, slightly tumid.
Elytra two-fifths longer than wide, fully twice as long as the prothorax and
not distinctly wider than the disk of the latter, the humeri feebly tumid ; sides
subparallel, the apex broadly but not very abruptly rounded ; disk with deep,
abrupt and rather wide grooves, which are not distinctly punctate, the intervals about twice as wide as the grooves, flat, each with a single series of coarse
but not very deep, close-set punctures ; setæ very short but moderately distinct. *Abdomen* rather finely, decidedly sparsely punctured. *Legs* moderate,
somewhat strongly punctate ; tarsal claws rather long. Length 3.2–4.8 mm. ;
width 1.3–2.1 mm.

California (Sonoma, Mendocino, Lake and Santa Cruz Cos.).

This species somewhat resembles *tenuestriata* in outward form, but is distinguishable at once by the coarse grooves and large interstitial punctures of the elytra. The abdomen in the male is feebly impressed in the middle toward base, the prosternum narrowly and distinctly impressed, and the anterior coxæ separated by rather more than one-half their width. The usual fine transverse groove bordering the anterior margin of the prosternum is quite distinct. The legs are sometimes darker and rufo-piceous in color. The large series of examples before me displays an unusual diversity in size but is otherwise quite homogeneous.

28 Baris sparsa Lec.—Proc. Ac. Nat. Sci., Phila., 1868, p. 364 (Baridius); Proc. Am. Phil. Soc., XV, p. 293.

This is a small narrow species, dark rufo-piceous in color, polished, with a feeble æneous tinge and with dark rufo-testaceous legs. The beak is rather slender, densely punctured, rather strongly arcuate, subequal in length to the prothorax in the female, but only three-fifths as long as the latter in the male. Prothorax rather elongate, from one-fourth to one-third wider than long, subparallel and broadly arcuate in basal two-thirds, then gradually convergent and straight to the apex, the basal lobe rather prominent; disk with a narrow but rather distinct subentire median line, the punctures deep strong and somewhat coarse, moderately close in the original male type and separated by nearly twice their widths, but rather closer in a single female taken by me in northern California. Elytra with fine but deep abrupt and impunctate striæ, the intervals nearly three times as wide as the grooves, perfectly flat, each with a single even series of coarse but very feeble widely spaced punctures, the setæ minute and almost invisible. The prosternum is broadly, feebly impressed and the anterior coxæ separated by barely one-half of their own width. Length 2.8 mm.; width 1.2 mm.

The above is an outline of the typical *sparsa* from Oregon and northern California, and care must be taken not to confound it with *rubripes* from the vicinity of San Francisco, which is a larger species, with narrower and much more densely and strongly punctate elytral intervals and denser pronotal punctures.

Oregon—Cab. LeConte; California (Hoopa Val., Humboldt Co.).

29 Baris brunneipes n. sp.—Oblong-oval, subparallel, convex, rather stout, black throughout, the legs brownish-testaceous, the femora in great part piceous; lustre throughout strongly shining. *Head* minutely, moderately closely punctate, the beak more strongly, densely so, rugulose at the sides, very stout, arcuate, two-thirds as long as the prothorax; antennæ moderate, the club large, robust, ovoidal, its basal joint polished and sparsely setose. *Prothorax* large, scarcely one-fourth wider than long; sides broadly, evenly arcuate and convergent anteriorly, becoming nearly parallel in more than basal half; base three and one-half times as wide as the head, oblique and nearly straight from the scutellum to the basal angles, the median lobe very small and feebly developed; disk rather feebly convex, finely, densely, deeply punctate, without trace of median impunctate line, the punctures rather less than one-third as wide as the scutellum and separated by scarcely their own diameters. Scutellum very feebly impressed, subquadrate, but slightly wider than long. *Elytra* scarcely more than one-third longer than wide, quite distinctly less than twice as long as the prothorax, and, at the moderately tumid humeri, a little wider than the latter; sides subparallel; apex broadly, rather abruptly rounded; disk with rather narrow but very deep grooves, which are not distinctly punctate or crenulate, the edges slightly obtuse; intervals polished, nearly flat, each with a single series of coarse strong moderately approximate and somewhat uneven punctures, rather smaller and more or less confused on the second, third and fifth; setæ very small and scarcely observable. *Abdomen* rather finely but strongly, moderately closely punctate. *Legs* moderate, feebly, sparsely punctate, the tibiæ straight along the external edge; tarsal claws rather small. Length 4.8 mm.; width 2.3 mm.

California.

The single specimen is a male, and has the abdomen somewhat narrowly and feebly impressed in the middle near the base. The prosternum is very feebly impressed, and the coxæ separated by slightly less than one-half of their own width. The punctures of the prothorax are relatively finer than in any other form known to me, and the species is quite distinct in facies.

30 **Baris deformis** n. sp.—Oblong-oval, somewhat depressed above, black throughout, polished, without æneous lustre. *Head* obsoletely, the beak finely, rather strongly but not densely punctate, the latter rather robust, strongly arcuate, quite distinctly shorter than the prothorax; antennæ moderate. *Prothorax* short and strongly transverse, one-half wider than long, the sides rather strongly convergent and broadly distinctly sinuate in basal two-thirds, then rather broadly rounded, thence more convergent and nearly straight to the apex; base transverse and straight, the median lobe pronounced; disk without trace of median line, rather finely, very deeply and extremely densely punctate throughout. Scutellum moderate, subquadrate, strongly impressed along the middle. *Elytra* long, fully one-third longer than wide and very distinctly more than twice as long as the prothorax, at the small and moderately tumid humeri very slightly wider than the latter; sides nearly straight and distinctly convergent behind the humeri, the apex almost. semi-circularly rounded, with the usual broad sutural notch; disk rather

finely but deeply and abruptly striate; intervals flat, fully twice as wide as the grooves, each with a regular series of somewhat small but deep, rather widely spaced punctures, the second and third a little wider but with the series simply uneven; setæ minute and not conspicuous. *Abdomen* finely but deeply punctured, the punctures distinctly separated toward the middle but becoming coarse and very dense toward the sides. Anterior coxæ widely separated. Length 3.0–3.5 mm.; width 1.5–1.7 mm.

North Carolina; Indiana; Missouri.

The peculiar form of the prothorax will always render this species easily identifiable. The type is a female from North Carolina. I have before me a single specimen from each of the above localities, the interstitial punctures being smaller in the Indiana female than in either of the other two.

31 **Baris futilis** n. sp.—Oblong-oval, convex, highly polished, black and with a strong æneous-metallic lustre. *Head* finely but distinctly, not very sparsely punctured, the beak moderately coarsely and closely so, densely at the sides, moderately robust and arcuate, short, about two-thirds as long as the prothorax; antennæ moderate, the club rather small. *Prothorax* two-fifths wider than long, the sides just visibly convergent and feebly arcuate in basal three-fourths, then strongly rounded, thence strongly convergent and feebly sinuate, faintly constricted to the apex, which is transversely truncate; base three times as wide as the head, straight, subtransverse, the median lobe rather large and prominent, rounded; disk with a more or less distinct impunctate median line; punctures rather coarse, very deep and moderately dense; sometimes crowded almost throughout, two-thirds as wide as the scutellum. Scutellum small, subquadrate. *Elytra* ample, two-fifths longer than wide, quite distinctly more than twice as long as the prothorax, and, at the small tumid humeri, slightly wider than the latter; sides behind the humeri subparallel; apex very broadly, evenly rounded; disk with moderately coarse, very deep, abrupt and finely but distinctly punctured grooves; intervals flat, about twice as wide as the grooves, each with a single somewhat uneven line of coarse, very approximate and slightly rugulose punctures, rather confused on the third, those of the fourth and fifth fully two-thirds as wide as the corresponding intervals; setæ small, suberect and forming quite distinct rows by longitudinal oblique illumination. *Abdomen* rather coarsely deeply and closely punctured toward the sides, more sparsely so in the middle of the first segment. *Legs* short, distinctly but not very densely punctured; tibiæ not prominent externally; claws moderate. Length 2.8–3.6 mm; width 1.25–1.65 mm.

California (Sta. Barbara, Riverside and San Diego).

The prosternum in the type is scarcely at all impressed, the coxæ widely separated, the process being but slightly narrower than their acetabula.

Mr. H. C. Fall informs me that he has beaten this species from willows.

32 **Baris inconspicua** n. sp.—Oblong-oval, not very robust, the upper surface rather feebly convex, black and polished throughout, the legs somewhat piceous. *Head* very minutely, obsoletely punctured, the beak deeply and closely so, strongly arcuate, four-fifths as long as the prothorax ; antennæ rather long, the club large, abrupt, compressed, with the basal joint sparsely setose and polished. *Prothorax* two-fifths wider than long ; sides very feebly convergent and slightly arcuate from the base to apical sixth or seventh, then strongly convergent and feebly sinuate for the very short distance to the apex, which is transversely truncate and unusually wide ; base but slightly more than twice as wide as the head, oblique and straight from the median lobe, which is small but distinct, rounded ; disk not very coarsely but deeply and densely punctate, without impunctate line, the punctures nearly one-half as wide as the scutellum and separated by one-half to two-thirds their own diameters. Scutellum subquadrate, not distinctly impressed. *Elytra* nearly one-half longer than wide, slightly more than twice as long as the prothorax, and, at the small and moderately prominent humeri, slightly wider than the latter ; sides parallel, nearly straight ; apex broadly but evenly rounded ; disk with rather narrow but deep, abrupt, finely, obsoletely punctured grooves, the intervals flat, about twice as wide as the grooves, each with a single even series of small feeble and not very close-set punctures ; setæ very small and inconspicuous. *Abdomen* finely, rather feebly and sparsely punctate. *Legs* rather slender, feebly, sparsely punctate, the tibiæ straight ; tarsal claws moderate. Length 3.2 mm. ; width 1.3 mm. (♀).

Colorado.

In some respects this small species resembles *aperta ;* it differs in its radically different shape of the prothorax, slightly smaller and denser pronotal punctuation, and less minute and distant interstitial punctures of the elytra ; also in its more depressed form and rather shorter beak.

The prosternum is feebly but distinctly impressed and separates the coxæ by fully one-half of their own width.

33 **Baris confinis** Lec.—Proc. Ac. Nat. Sci., Phil. 1868, p. 362 (Baridius) ; Proc. Amer. Phil. Soc., XV, p. 293.

A small and very abundant species, easily distinguishable by the rather short, strongly, moderately coarsely and somewhat sparsely punctured pronotum, the rather wide, flat, somewhat finely distinctly and decidedly remotely punctured elytral intervals, with the punctures forming an even single series on each, and by the finely, sparsely punctured abdomen. I have before me ample series from Indiana and Florida (Key West), which agree very well, the difference being slight, apparently racial in nature and not easily expressible in language. Length 2.8–3.4 mm. ; width 1.3–1.6 mm.

Pennsylvania, North Carolina, Georgia, Florida, Mississippi, Texas and Iowa. I have before me about fifty specimens, one of which, from Iowa, has the prothorax slightly more elongate than any of the others.

34 Baris subsimilis n. sp.—Oval, rather robust and but moderately convex, black throughout, highly polished and with a somewhat strong æneous metallic lustre. *Head* minutely, the beak rather strongly but not very densely punctate, the latter robust, evenly, moderately arcuate, short, about three-fourths as long as the prothorax; antennæ normal. *Prothorax* somewhat transverse, fully two-fifths wider than long; sides just visibly convergent and very feebly arcuate to apical fourth, then strongly but not prominently rounded, thence strongly convergent and straight to the apex, which is transversely truncate; base straight and very feebly oblique from the small and feeble median lobe to the sides; disk with narrow, feebly defined, almost entire median line, the punctures moderate in size and depth, not very dense, about two-fifths as wide as the scutellum and generally separated by nearly their own diameters. Scutellum small, very feebly impressed. *Elytra* ample, one-third longer than wide, a little more than twice as long as the prothorax, and, at the moderately tumid humeri, slightly wider than the latter; sides behind the humeri just visibly convergent, the apex rather gradually, semi-circularly rounded; disk with deep, moderately coarse, minutely, feebly punctate grooves, the intervals flat, about twice as wide as the grooves, each with a single series of fine but rather deep and distinct, moderately close-set punctures, which are confused on the third interval but not at all on the second, and also confused on the fifth toward base; setæ very small, not conspicuous. *Abdomen* rather coarsely, strongly and quite densely punctured. *Legs* coarsely but feebly, sparsely punctate; tibiæ straight; tarsal claws small. Length 3.4–4.0 mm.; width 1.5–1.9 mm.

Pennsylvania; Indiana; Missouri.

This species somewhat resembles a large *confinis*, but has the interstitial punctures more close-set, the abdomen more densely and rugosely punctured, and the beak decidedly shorter and thicker. The prosternum is very feebly impressed and separates the coxæ by about one-half of their own width.

35 Baris socialis n. sp.—Oblong-oval, rather slender, moderately convex, polished, black throughout. *Head* and beak finely, sparsely punctate, the latter not very densely so at the sides, feebly, evenly arcuate throughout, three-fourths as long as the prothorax; antennæ normal. *Prothorax* two-fifths wider than long, the sides slightly but distinctly convergent and feebly arcuate to apical fourth, then more strongly rounded, thence moderately convergent and straight or just visibly sinuate to the apex, which is broadly, feebly arcuate; base subtransverse, a little less than three times as wide as the head, the median lobe small but distinct; disk rather feebly convex, not more strongly so anteriorly, with a rather wide but ill-defined subentire median line, the punctures moderate, deep, somewhat sparsely and unevenly distributed, less than one-half as wide as the scutellum and separated by between once and twice their own diameters. Scutellum moderate, tumid, nearly as long as wide. *Elytra* two-fifths longer than wide, fully twice as long as the prothorax, and, at the rather prominent humeri, distinctly wider than the latter; sides behind the humeri quite distinctly convergent, the apex rather gradually and semi-circularly rounded; disk with somewhat coarse, very deep, finely, remotely punctured grooves, the intervals flat, generally one-half wider than the grooves, each with a single series of somewhat deep, moderately large punctures, the second and third intervals much wider than the others, the former with the punctures slightly uneven, the latter rather broadly confused; punctures generally close-set; setæ very minute and in-conspicuous. *Abdomen* rather coarsely, deeply, moderately closely punctured. *Legs* strongly but sparsely punctured. Length 3.6 mm.; width 1.7 mm.

Missouri; Texas.

Described from the female. This species does not seem to be very closely allied to any other in general facies, but it is difficult to make this clear from description only. It is distinguishable by its sparsely, moderately coarsely punctate and somewhat depressed pronotum from several of those to which it is more closely related. From *confinis*, it differs in its more elongate form and black color, never being in the least æneous.

36 **Baris aperta** n. sp.—Oblong-subcylindrical, dark rufo-piceous, the pronotum blackish; integuments highly polished. *Head* very minutely sparsely and obsoletely punctate, the beak rather sparsely but strongly so, especially at the sides, somewhat slender, strongly arcuate, three-fourths as long as the prothorax; antennæ rather long, moderately robust, normal in structure. *Prothorax* rather more than one-third wider than long, the sides very evenly and rather strongly arcuate from base to apex; base two and two-thirds times as wide as the head, transverse, straight, the median lobe small but distinct; disk convex, without distinct median line, the punctures slightly coarse, deep and dense, about two-thirds as wide as the scutellum and separated by scarcely one-half their own diameters. Scutellum small, slightly tumid. *Elytra* nearly one-half longer than wide, twice as long as the prothorax and not distinctly wider than the latter, rather gradually and semi-circularly rounded at apex, the humeri feebly tumid; disk with abrupt, very deep, moderately coarse grooves which are very obsoletely punctate at the bottom; intervals flat, about twice as wide as the grooves, each with a single line of very fine but distinct, widely-spaced punctures; setæ minute and inconspicuous. *Abdomen* finely, rather feebly and very sparsely punctured throughout, but, as usual, densely so on the fifth segment and pygidium. *Legs* sparsely, feebly punctate; tibiæ not sinuate externally, the tarsal claws moderate. Length 3.0 mm.; width 1.3 mm.

Dakota.

The small size, rounded sides and densely, strongly punctured surface of the prothorax, coarse grooves, and very fine distant interstitial punctures of the elytra, will probably serve to identify this species, which is of unusually cylindrical form. The prosternum is rather narrowly but quite distinctly impressed, and separates the coxæ by a little less than one-half of their own width. The unique specimen is a female.

37 **Baris abrupta** n. sp.—Oblong-oval, convex, rather stout, black throughout, highly polished and with a pronounced æneous lustre; setæ minute and inconspicuous. *Head* minutely, very remotely punctate, the beak strongly but not densely or coarsely so, stout, strongly arcuate, scarcely more than three-fourths as long as the prothorax, the antennæ inserted a little behind the middle. *Prothorax* short and transverse, fully three-fourths wider than long, the sides feebly convergent and almost straight to apical third, then abruptly, strongly rounded and prominent, thence very strongly convergent and feebly constricted to the apex, which is feebly arcuate and scarcely one-half as wide as the base, the latter straight and slightly oblique at each side of the small, broadly rounded median lobe; disk without impunctate line, the punctures strong and rather dense, about two-fifths as wide as the scutellum and separated generally by about one-half of their own diameters. Scutellum moderate, feebly transverse, scarcely impressed. *Elytra* large, very slightly wider than the prothorax and fully twice as long, a little longer than wide, hemi-elliptical in outline, the humeri but very slightly prominent; striæ deep, abrupt, even, not very coarse, the intervals flat, fully twice as wide as the grooves, each with a single series of very small, not closeset punctures, the second and third wider and with the punctures more or less confused. *Abdomen* distinctly but rather sparsely punctured. Prosternum broadly, strongly impressed along the middle, separating the coxæ by fully three-fifths of their own width. Length 3.4 mm.; width 1.65 mm.

Pennsylvania.

The unique type is a male, having a large, rather strong impression toward the base of the abdomen. This species resembles *deformis*, but differs decidedly in its strong æneous lustre, prominent and strongly rounded sides of the prothorax at apical third, and finer interstitial punctures.

38 **Baris tenuestriata** n. sp.—Oblong-oval, convex, black throughout, polished, the elytra finely reticulato-granulose and more or less feebly alutaceous. *Head* minutely and not very sparsely punctate, beak three-fourths as long as the prothorax, stout, feebly arcuate, somewhat coarsely, deeply and closely punctate; antennæ robust, funicular joints three to seven transverse, gradually wider, the club moderately robust and almost perfectly continuous in outline with the outer joints of the funicle, first joint of the latter scarcely

as long as the next three. *Prothorax* one-third wider than long; sides feebly convergent and nearly straight to apical fourth, then strongly rounded, thence convergent and nearly straight to the apex; base three times as wide as the head, on each side straight and feebly oblique, the median lobe small and very feeble; disk with a narrow, more or less imperfect median impunctate line which is sometimes obsolete; punctures rather coarse, about two-thirds as wide as the scutellum, deep, dense, generally separated by much less than one-half their widths, often almost contiguous. Scutellum rather small, longitudinally, narrowly impressed in the middle, but slightly wider than long, subquadrate. *Elytra* nearly one-half longer than wide, twice as long as the prothorax, and, at the moderately tumid humeri but slightly wider than the latter; sides parallel; apex semi-circularly, not abruptly rounded; disk with fine but deep, abruptly limited grooves, which are finely and distantly crenulate along their edges; intervals flat, three times as wide as the striæ, each with a single series of very small feeble rather distant punctures; setæ extremely small, scarcely observable. *Abdomen* rather strongly but not very densely punctate. *Legs* feebly, sparsely punctate; tibiæ straight externally; tarsal claws moderate. Length 4.2–5.0 mm.; width 1.8–2.2 mm.

California (near San Francisco).

Among the six specimens before me a considerable amount of variation is observable, especially in a rather large male which is relatively stouter, with the prothorax as wide as any part of the elytra, and having the sides parallel in basal three-fourths. The peculiarity of the other discrepant form, which is an unusually large female, lies in the fact that the elytral intervals are slightly convex, the pronotal punctures being densely crowded and contiguous, and without vestige of impunctate median line. I have but little doubt, however, that they belong to this species.

The description is taken from a male, the abdominal impression being unusually wide and extending only slightly upon the second segment. The sexual differences in the beak are hardly noticeable.

39 **Baris macra** Lec.—Pac. R. R. Exp'l and Surv., Ins., p, 58 (Baridius); Proc. Ac. Nat. Sci., Phila., 1868, p. 362; Proc. Am. Phil. Soc., XV, p. 294.

The form of this small and distinct species is unusually narrow, rather more so in fact than any other true Baris which I have seen. The beak in the male is moderately stout, deeply, closely punctate at the sides, distinctly arcuate and about three-fourths as long as the prothorax, the latter scarcely over one-fourth wider than long, with the sides feebly convergent and slightly arcuate from base to apex; the apex is fully two-thirds as wide as the base and broadly, evenly arcuate; disk rather finely, deeply and closely punctate, with a narrow, feebly defined, abbreviated median line. Elytra twice as long as the prothorax, very finely but deeply and abruptly striate, the intervals flat, fully three times as wide as the grooves and each with a single series of extremely minute, very remote and subobsolete punctures, the setæ not obvious.

Macra somewhat resembles *sparsa* in outward habitus, but differs in its still more slender form, finer, closer pronotal punctuation and much more minute interstitial punctures.   Length 2.9 mm.; width 1.1 mm.

California.   Cab. LeConte.

40 **Baris discipula** n. sp.—Oblong, slender, rather convex, black throughout, the legs piceous; integuments highly polished and with a pronounced æneous lustre.   *Head* obsoletely punctate, the beak moderately coarsely and closely so, distinctly arcuate and fully four-fifths as long as the prothorax in the male, nearly straight and fully as long as that part in the female; antennæ normal.   *Prothorax* rather long, scarcely one-third wider than long, the sides subparallel in basal three-fourths, then rather abruptly and strongly rounded, thence strongly convergent and more or less sinuate to the apex; base two and one-half times as wide as the head, subtransverse and straight, the median lobe rather large and distinct; disk with scarcely a trace of median impunctate line, the punctures moderately coarse, deep and somewhat close, about two-thirds as wide as the scutellum, rather uneven in distribution but generally separated by less than their own diameters.   Scutellum very small, slightly tumid, nearly circular.   *Elytra* scarcely more than one-fourth longer than wide, not quite twice as long as the prothorax, at the feebly tumid humeri but slightly wider than the latter; disk with rather fine but abrupt, deep, obsoletely punctate grooves, the intervals wide, flat, each with a single series of minute feeble and remote punctures, not confused on the subsutural intervals.   *Abdomen* finely, sparsely punctate.   Length 2.5 mm.; width 1.0–1.15 mm.

Indiana.

A single pair.   In the male the abdomen has a small and moderately deep impression very near the base.   The sexual disparity in the form and length of the beak is rather unusual in Baris, although common in those genera having a greater longitudinal development of this part of the body; it is also very noticeable in *sparsa*.   This species differs from *ærea*, which it resembles in size, lustre and elytral sculpture, in its narrower, more parallel form, longer, rather more coarsely and decidedly more densely punctured pronotum, and longer beak.

41 Baris ærea Boh.— Sch. Curc., VIII, i. p. 141 (Baridius).

This species is one of the smallest of the genus, of moderately stout convex form, and is always highly polished and quite strongly æneous in lustre. The beak is short, robust, feebly arcuate and about two-thirds as long as the prothorax, the latter rather transverse, from one-third to two-fifths wider than long, and with the punctures very sparse, somewhat fine, moderately deep and separated by from two to three times their own diameters, without median impunctate line. The scutellum is small, flat and almost circular. The elytra are not quite twice as long as the prothorax, rather distinctly narrowed behind the humeri, with fine but deep and abrupt, minutely punctulate grooves, the intervals wide, flat, and each with a single series of very minute, remote punctures, not confused on the second or third. Length 2.3–2.9 mm.; width 1.1–1.4 mm.

This series of fifteen or more specimens before me is from Louisiana and Texas.

42 Baris scintillans n. sp.—Oval, moderately convex, black, the legs slightly piceous ; integuments very smooth, brightly polished and with a strong æneous metallic lustre. *Head* obsoletely, the beak finely and very sparsely punctured, the latter rather robust, evenly and moderately arcuate, not distinctly shorter than the prothorax ; antennæ normal. *Prothorax* rather short and transverse, two-fifths wider than long ; sides subparallel and just visibly arcuate to apical third, then strongly rounded, thence strongly convergent and distinctly sinuate to the apex, the latter very feebly arcuate, one-half as wide as the base, the latter about two and one-third times as wide as the head, transverse, the median lobe rather wide and distinct, rounded ; disk without median line, the punctures fine but deep, sparse, about one-half as wide as the scutellum and separated by two to three times their own diameters, almost completely obsolete in apical fifth. *Scutellum* very small, nearly circular. *Elytra* scarcely more than one-fourth longer than wide, a little more than twice as long as the prothorax, and, at basal third, very distinctly wider than the latter ; sides parallel and feebly arcuate, the humeri feebly tumid, not at all prominent laterally ; apex broadly, almost semi-circularly rounded ; disk very finely but deeply and abruptly striate, the striæ not visibly punctate ; intervals wide, flat, three to four times as wide as the striæ, each with a single series of excessively minute, feeble, remote punctures, which are only observable under special conditions of amplification and illumination ; setæ not observable under moderate power. *Abdomen* finely, sparsely punctate, the metasternum quite coarsely, deeply and densely so. Anterior coxæ rather widely separated. Length 2.2 mm. ; width 1.0 mm.

Florida (southern). Mr. Jülich.

The sex of the unique type is not evident, but the abdomen appears

to be very feebly impressed near the base. This is the smallest
species known to me, and is quite distinct, differing from the
form assumed to represent *ærea*, in its smaller size, longer beak,
larger head, still stronger æneous lustre, and more constricted prothorax. The base of the pronotum is nearly three times as wide as
the head in *ærea*, and the grooves of the elytra are much coarser,
the interstitial punctures being more evident; in *scintillans* the
latter are as nearly as possible completely obsolete.

43 Baris æneomicans n. sp.—Oblong-oval, somewhat depressed,
highly polished, black throughout and with a strong æneous metallic lustre.
Head not distinctly punctate; beak finely but deeply punctate, the punctures
sparse even at the sides, thick, strongly arcuate, very nearly as long as the
prothorax; antennæ somewhat slender, the club not very large. *Prothorax*
widest before the base, transverse, fully one-half wider than long, somewhat
inflated, the sides subparallel in basal three-fourths and strongly arcuate,
then moderately convergent and feebly sinuate for a short distance to the apex,
which is transversely truncate; base a little less than three times as wide as
the head, straight and feebly oblique from the small and feeble median lobe
to the basal angles; disk with a narrow and feebly defined but subentire
median line, the punctures coarse and rather sparse, deep and perforate,
about one-half as wide as the scutellum and separated by nearly their own
diameters. Scutellum moderate, subquadrate, not longitudinally impressed.
Elytra two-fifths longer than wide, quite distinctly more than twice as long as
the prothorax, and, at the rather large and tumid humeri, very slightly wider
than the disk of the latter; sides feebly convergent from behind the humeri,
the apex almost evenly and semi-circularly rounded; disk with rather narrow
but abrupt and very deep, finely, remotely punctate grooves, the intervals
flat, rather more than twice as wide as the grooves, each with a single even
series of small but distinct, widely distant punctures, which are not at all
confused on the second or third; setæ very minute and almost completely
invisible. *Abdomen* not very finely but feebly and very sparsely punctured.
Legs rather coarsely and deeply but sparsely punctate; tibiæ straight; tarsal
claws small. Length 3.5 mm.; width 1.65 mm.

Massachusetts.

A decidedly distinct species, distinguishable by the bright æneous
lustre, sparse punctuation, short, laterally arcuate prothorax and
somewhat depressed form. The prosternum is feebly impressed
and widely separates the coxæ. The single specimen is apparently
a female.

44 Baris hyperion n. sp.—Feebly rhomboid-oval, convex, highly
polished and with a strong bronzy-æneous lustre; legs black; setæ very
minute, sparse and inconspicuous. *Head* extremely minutely, sparsely punctate, the beak more strongly but not closely so, very robust, arcuate, flattened

near the apex, four-fifths as long as the prothorax; antennæ moderately stout, the basal joint of the club highly polished. *Prothorax* rather transverse, nearly one-half wider than long, the sides feebly convergent to apical third, then more strongly rounded and convergent but scarcely at all constricted to the apex, which is about one-half as wide as the base, the latter straight and feebly anteriorly oblique from the small but distinct median lobe to the basal angles; disk not coarsely but deeply, conspicuously and somewhat closely punctured, without trace of impunctate line, the punctures nearly one-half as wide as the scutellum and generally separated by about their own diameters. Scutellum small, quadrate, scarcely at all impressed. *Elytra* but little wider than the prothorax, about twice as long as the latter; humeri rather prominent; sides distinctly convergent; apex obtuse; striæ moderately fine, deep, abrupt, the intervals nearly flat, fully twice as wide as the grooves, each with a single series of fine, rather distant punctures, the second, and especially the third, much wider, the latter with the punctures confused. *Abdomen* finely, sparsely punctate. Prosternum strongly impressed along the middle, separating the coxæ by two-thirds of their own width. Length 3.5–4.0 mm.; width 1.65–2.0 mm.

Florida.

Somewhat related to *æneomicans*, but easily distinguishable by its more elongate, more finely punctate prothorax, with the sides much less rounded, and by its relatively shorter beak.

45 **Baris vitreola** n. sp.—Oblong-oval, rather robust, moderately convex, highly polished throughout, black with a strong æneous lustre, the elytra and legs rufo-piceous; setæ extremely minute and scarcely visible. *Head* just visibly and very remotely punctulate, the transverse impression moderate; beak very stout, cylindrical, flattened toward apex, finely but strongly, rather densely punctate, strongly, evenly arcuate and almost as long as the prothorax; antennæ moderate, the club small, oval, with the basal joint polished. *Prothorax* rather small and transverse, fully three-fifths wider than long, the sides quite evidently convergent and nearly straight from the base to apical fourth, then strongly rounded to the apex, the constriction obsolete; base not quite three times as wide as the head, straight and rather strongly oblique from the small and moderately prominent median lobe to the basal angles; disk strongly and sparsely punctate, without trace of impunctate line, the punctures about two-fifths as wide as the scutellum and generally separated by rather more than twice their own diameters. Scutellum subquadrate, scarcely at all impressed. *Elytra* slightly wider than the prothorax and fully twice as long, oblong, the sides behind the feebly prominent humeri just visibly convergent and slightly arcuate; apex broadly obtuse; striæ rather strong, deep, abrupt, finely punctured, the intervals flat, fully twice as wide as the grooves, each with a single series of very fine remote punctures, the third scarcely wider than the others. *Abdomen* sparsely punctate toward the middle, rather closely so laterally, the punctures becoming large but shallow. Prosternum strongly impressed along the middle, separating the coxæ by three-fifths of their own width. Length 3.4 mm.; width 1.75 mm.

Florida.

The unique type is a male, the abdomen being broadly and rather strongly impressed in the middle toward base. There is no species very closely allied to *vitreola*, but *punctiventris* appears to approach it more closely than any other.

46 Baris ancilla n. sp.—Oval, not very stout, convex, strongly shining, the elytra with a scarcely perceptible alutaceous lustre; body black throughout, with a feeble bluish metallic lustre; setæ minute, extremely sparse and inconspicuous. *Head* excessively minutely, sparsely punctate, the beak more strongly but not very densely so, very stout, arcuate, gradually and feebly flattened toward apex, distinctly shorter than the prothorax; antennæ inserted a little behind the middle, the club moderate, with the basal joint polished and constituting rather less than one-half of the mass. *Prothorax* one-third wider than long, the sides evenly rounded and convergent in apical third, becoming nearly straight and parallel thence to the base, the latter twice as wide as the apex, feebly oblique at each side of the small but distinct, rounded median lobe; disk without impunctate space, the punctures strong but not coarse, about one-half as wide as the scutellum and generally separated by rather more than their own diameters. Scutellum small, quadrate, unimpressed. *Elytra* slightly wider than the prothorax and nearly twice as long, the humeri but feebly prominent; sides feebly convergent, gradually parabolic in apical third, the sutural notch strong, broadly angulate; striæ moderate, deep, even; intervals flat, a little more than twice as wide as the grooves, each with a single series of fine feeble and remote punctures, the second and third wider but similarly punctate. Under surface and abdomen æneous in lustre, the latter sparsely punctate. Prosternum sulcate, rather widely separating the anterior coxæ. Length 3.3 mm.; width 1.6 mm.

Florida.

This species is slightly larger than *confinis* and differs in its much sparser punctuation; from *ærea* it differs in its more elongate form, much larger size, wider elytral intervals and finer striæ, and from *exigua*, to which it appears to be more closely allied, it may readily be known by its much finer and more remote interstitial punctures, longer and less rounded prothorax, with less oblique base, larger size and several other characters.

47 Baris splendens n. sp.—*B. interstitialis* Lec. nec Say: Proc. Am. Phil. Soc., XV, p. 293; Boh.: Sch. Curc. III, p. 684 (Baridius)?—Oblong-suboval, moderately convex, black and without æneous lustre but highly polished. *Head* obsoletely punctulate, with an evanescent frontal puncture; beak very robust, evenly, moderately arcuate, two-thirds to three-fourths as long as the prothorax; antennæ normal, the club rather small. *Prothorax* rather transverse, two-fifths wider than long; sides broadly, evenly rounded and convergent anteriorly, becoming subparallel toward base, sometimes feebly prominent at apical fourth ; base not quite three times as wide as the head, straight and distinctly oblique from the very small and feeble median lobe to the sides ; disk finely but distinctly, sparsely and somewhat unevenly punctate, with a narrow, feebly defined median line, the punctures less than one-half as wide as the scutellum and separated by two or three times their own diameters. Scutellum small, almost circular. *Elytra* two-fifths longer than wide, not quite twice as long as the prothorax, and, at the feebly tumid humeri, slightly wider than the latter ; apex broadly, rather abruptly rounded ; disk with somewhat coarse, deep, obsoletely punctate grooves, the intervals flat, generally but slightly wider than the grooves, each with a single series of minute but quite visible, remote punctures, the third interval much wider and with the punctures broadly diffused ; setæ extremely minute, inconspicuous. *Abdomen* finely but rather strongly, sparsely punctate. *Legs* dark rufo-piceous in color, feebly and sparsely punctate. Length 3.3–4.1 mm.; width 1.5–1.9 mm.

Florida (Fernandina). Mr. Schwarz.

The prosternum is rather narrowly and quite strongly subsulcate, and separates the coxæ by scarcely one-third of their own width.

This is a distinct and easily recognizable species, but as it differs so radically from Say's description of *interstitialis* in the nature of the elytral punctuation, I do not think that it can be placed near that species ; the latter is here regarded as being identical with *transversa*. In regard to Boheman's *interstitialis*, there must always be more or less doubt until the type can be compared, as there are several of these peculiar sparsely punctured Florida species, which will equally satisfy his description.

48 **Baris exigua** n. sp.—Oblong-oval, moderately convex, shining and piceous-black throughout. *Head* very minutely and obsoletely punctate, the beak rather coarsely and somewhat densely so, short, arcuate, three-fourths as long as the prothorax ; antennæ moderate, normal, the first joint of the club polished and sparsely setose. *Prothorax* nearly one-half wider than long, widest before the base, the sides evenly, rather strongly arcuate, the apex broadly arcuate and continuous with the sides, the apical angles entirely obsolete ; base nearly three times as wide as the head, straight and slightly oblique from the feeble median lobe to the sides ; disk without trace of median impunctate area, the punctures fine but deep, not very dense, about one-half as wide as the scutellum and separated by distinctly more than their own diameters. Scutellum very small. *Elytra* two-fifths longer than wide, twice as long as the prothorax, and, at the feebly tumid humeri, very slightly wider than the disk of the latter ; sides behind the humeri just visibly convergent, the apex broadly rounded, the sutural notch large and quite deep ; disk with fine but deep, abrupt, finely, remotely punctured grooves, which are feebly crenulate near the base ; intervals flat, nearly three times as wide as the grooves, each with a single series of fine but distinct, widely spaced punctures. *Abdomen* finely, sparsely punctate. *Legs* rather distinctly, moderately

closely punctured; tibiæ straight; third tarsal joint not wider than long, the emargination extending slightly beyond basal third; claws small. Length 2.6 mm.; width 1.2 mm. (♀).

Texas (near Austin).

The singular form of the prothorax, evenly rounded from the sides throughout the apex, the fine pronotal punctures, rather depressed form and small size, will readily distinguish this species. The prosternum is narrowly, feebly impressed, and separates the coxæ by much more than one-half of their own width. The elytral setæ are very minute and almost invisible under moderate power.

PLESIOBARIS n. gen.

The species of this genus are for the most part small, generally quite minute, and for this reason will possibly prove to be somewhat numerous, especially as they are essentially characteristic of our comparatively unexplored extreme southern fauna. One or two species are known to occur in the more northern parts of the United States, but the majority will probably be found to inhabit subtropical Florida extending perhaps to Cuba.

The various representatives were regarded by LeConte as forming part of the genus Pseudobaris, but certainly cannot be appropriately placed there, because of their non-sulcate prosternum, moderately separated coxæ and small but perfectly free claws. They agree well together in the general nature of the vestiture, this being densely squamiform at the base of the third elytral interval, on the meso- and metasternal side-pieces, and at the sides of the last three ventral segments; elsewhere on the dorsal surface the large scales are sparse, and variously distributed according to the species.

The few forms here brought to notice already fall into two groups of almost subgeneric value, which however I will simply indicate in the following table:—

Basal joint of the antennal club large, composing at least one-half of the mass; body cylindrical, the elytral humeri not exposed; elytra each with a large sparsely squamose area behind the middle.

Black, the base of the prothorax rather strongly bisinuate; legs rufo-piceous; rostrum shorter than the prothorax.....................1 **T-signum**

Piceous-black; legs rufous, with the knees black; base of the prothorax transverse, just visibly and broadly bisinuate; very small species.

2 signatipes

Rufo-testaceous, the elytral suture clouded with black; base of the prothorax very broadly and feebly bisinuate; larger species......3 **albilatus**

Basal joint of the club short, composing one-third of the mass or even less ;
    elytra not continuous with the prothorax at the sides, the humeri more
    or less exposed and oblique ; body and legs intense black throughout.
Pronotum with a regular but sparsely squamose design, the scales sparsely
    scattered over the elytra toward the sides, and also more or less distinctly
    clustered in several small spots on the third and fifth intervals.

4 æmula

Pronotum without regular squamose design, the elytral vestiture consisting
    entirely of minute inconspicuous setæ which become slightly more robust,
    but scarcely squamiform, toward the sides, and with a squamose spot at
    the base of the third interval ....5 **disjuncta**

1 **Plesiobaris T-signum** Boh.—Sch. Gen. Curc., VIII, p. 154
(Baridius).

Pennsylvania—Boheman. There are but few statements concerning this species, which can be made with any degree of certainty. It however undoubtedly belongs to the present genus, and
is probably also a member of the *albilatus* division, having the elytra
cylindrical and continuous in outline with the prothorax at the sides.

The omission of exact measurements of length and width is a
serious defect in the great work of Schönherr.

2 **Plesiobaris signatipes** n. sp.—Subcylindrical, convex, polished,
piceous-black, the legs slightly paler, more rufous with the knees black, vestiture extremely minute and inconspicuous with the exception of a few large,
widely scattered, white scales toward the middle and sides of the pronotum,
a denser lineolate spot of the same at the base of the third elytral interval,
and, behind the middle, a short even row of widely spaced scales on the second,
third and fourth intervals, also a few widely distant scales on the fifth interval ; on the under surface the meso- and metasternal side-pieces are densely
clothed throughout with large white scales and also the last three abdominal
segments laterally. *Head* and beak sparsely, feebly punctured, the latter
moderately robust, feebly flattened toward apex, strongly, evenly arcuate and
fully as long as the prothorax, the antennæ moderate, the joints of the funicle
slightly convex at the sides, the second and third subequal and about as long
as wide, the club small, briefly ovoidal, the basal joint composing fully one-
half of the mass. *Prothorax* one-fifth wider than long, the apex feebly arcuate
and two-thirds as wide as the base, the latter transverse, the median lobe
broad and exceedingly feeble ; sides parallel and straight to apical fourth,
then rounded, thence straight and not at all constricted to the apex ; disk
with a rather wide but ill-defined impunctate line, the punctures rather large,
one-half as wide as the scutellum but very feeble and sparse, separated by
more than their own widths, becoming minute and still more feeble toward
the apex, and also near the base except in the middle. *Scutellum* very small,
subogival. *Elytra* barely twice as long as the prothorax and exactly equal
to the latter in width, the sides straight and continuous, broadly but not

abruptly rounded behind ; humeral tuberosities very small and feeble, not at all evident laterally ; disk with very fine, moderately deep striæ, the intervals flat, four or five times as wide as the striæ, the second and third sensibly wider, each with a series of minute, feeble, distant and indistinct punctures. *Abdomen* very minutely, obsoletely and sparsely punctured toward the middle. Prosternum flat, not sensibly impressed, separating the somewhat small coxæ by about two-thirds of their own width.   Length 1.75 mm. ; width 0.6 mm.

Florida (Tampa).   Mr. Schwarz.

The antennal differences between this species and *disjuncta* are very radical in the structure of the club, but I can perceive no other divergencies of a generic nature, and parallel inconstancy of this kind is well known in Onychobaris. *Signatipes* approaches more closely to the published characters of *T-signum*, than other species which I have seen, but differs in its piceous color, apparently sparser pronotal punctures and in several other characters, among the more important of which is the form of the basal line of the prothorax, said to be rather profoundly bisinuate in *T-signum*.

3 Plesiobaris albilatus Lec.—Proc. Am. Phil. Soc., XV, p. 298 (Pseudobaris).

Oblong-cylindrical, convex, polished, rufo-testaceous in color, the beak, under surface, knees and elytral suture piceous-black ; punctures of the upper surface bearing very minute and inconspicuous setæ, with a few large scattered whitish scales toward the middle and sides of the pronotum, and a denser spot of the same at the base of the third elytral interval, the remainder of the elytra with a few large widely dispersed scales arranged subtransversely, and of which a loose spot on the second and third intervals is more distinct ; meso- and metasternal side-pieces and lateral portions of the last three ventral segments abruptly very densely squamose.   The beak is robust, strongly arcuate and fully as long as the prothorax, the antennæ slender, the funicle long, with joints two to four a little longer than wide and decreasing very slightly in length, the club small, with the basal joint composing distinctly more than one-half of the mass.   Prothorax one-third wider than long, the sides parallel and nearly straight to apical fourth, then convergent and constricted, the base broadly and very feebly bisinuate, the disk with a wide but uneven impunctate line, the punctures rather coarse, deep and somewhat dense.   The elytra are as in *signatipes*, but with the intervals equal and about four times as wide as the grooves.   The prosternum is broadly, scarcely perceptibly impressed anteriorly, and separates the coxæ by about two-thirds of their own width.   Claws small, entirely free.   Length 2.2–3.1 mm.; width 0.9–1.3 mm.

Florida (Tampa, Baldwin and Enterprise).   The disposition of the scanty vestiture is somewhat remarkable; for example, on the fifth interval each puncture bears a minute and simple seta, but every third or fourth puncture bears instead, a very large fan-shaped scale placed in a transverse position.   In spite of the great difference in size the present species and *signatipes* are closely allied.

In the species of this group the scattered scales seem to be easily removable, while in *æmula* they are exceedingly persistent.

4 Plesiobaris æmula n. sp.—Subcylindrical, strongly convex, shining, deep black throughout, the vestiture consisting of short broad white scales which are large in the dense spots, but elsewhere small; the scales are only present on the pronotum in an anteriorly dilated lateral vitta, which is prolonged inwardly along the basal margin almost to the middle, then abruptly flexed anteriorly and outwardly as a narrow line terminating at lateral third and middle of the length; on the elytra the scales are condensed in four small almost equidistant spots on the third interval, of which the basal is the largest, and thence to the side margins are widely but almost evenly scattered, but sometimes forming three spots on the fifth interval; on the under surface they are very dense on the meso- and metasternal side-pieces, and at the sides of the last three ventral segments. *Head* and beak not very strongly punctured, the latter short, very thick, strongly arcuate and subequal in length to the prothorax, the antennæ inserted a little beyond the middle, the basal joint of the funicle short, not twice as long as wide, the second and third very short, subequal, the club about as long as the preceding six, with its basal joint composing one-third of the mass. *Prothorax* one-third wider than long, the sides parallel and straight in basal three-fourths, then broadly subangulate, thence convergent, nearly straight and not at all constricted to the apex, the latter truncate and two-thirds as wide as the base, the latter transverse almost straight, the median lobe subobsolete; disk without median line, the punctures deep, moderate in size, very dense but not crowded. Scutellum very small, rounded. *Elytra* more than twice as long as the prothorax and a very little wider, parallel, parabolic in apical third, very finely but deeply striate, the intervals flat, moderately wide the third and fifth much broader than the others, each with a series of small feeble rather distant punctures; humeral tuberosities very feeble. Prosternum flat, separating the coxæ by rather more than their own width. Length 1.6–1.7 mm.; width 0.65–0.7 mm.

Florida.   Mr. E. A. Schwarz.

This species was confounded by Dr. LeConte with the Zimmermann specimen from South Carolina, identified by him as *T-signum* Boh., and referred to below under *disjuncta*.   It is a much smaller species, and is not at all allied to the form mentioned. It was apparently taken in great abundance.

Among the specimens before me there is one which is singularly deformed, the pronotum having, near the base and at lateral fourth, a prominent polished wart-like tubercle. For a considerable distance around the tubercle, the small normal squamules are entirely absent but replaced by large scale-like plates, concave or umbilicate in the centre, each of which completely fills a puncture.

5 **Plesiobaris disjuncta** n. sp.—Subcylindrical, very slender, convex, black throughout, strongly shining, sparsely clothed with very small setæ, especially evident but not at all conspicuous toward the sides of the pronotum, very minute and sparse throughout on the elytra, the latter with a small elongate spot of white squamules at the base of the third interval, the meso- and metasternal side-pieces and sides of the last three ventral segments also densely squamulose, the remainder of the under surface subglabrous. *Head* very feebly, sparsely punctate, the impression rounded, feeble ; beak shining, finely, deeply, moderately densely punctate, rather stout, cylindrical somewhat strongly, evenly arcuate, a little longer than the prothorax ; antennæ moderate, the club rather large, as long as the preceding six joints combined, the latter short and coarctate. *Prothorax* about one-fourth wider than long, the sides feebly divergent and nearly straight from the base almost to the apex, then rounded for a short distance, the subapical constriction very small and feeble ; apex truncate, nearly as wide as the base, the latter broadly, very feebly bisinuate ; disk with moderately coarse, deep, perforate punctures which are almost contiguous, the impunctate line narrow and feebly defined, only visible toward the centre. Scutellum small. *Elytra* at the base abruptly quite distinctly wider than the prothorax, rather more than twice as long as the latter, the sides parallel and almost straight, somewhat abruptly, acutely ogival in apical third ; humeri obliquely rounded, the callus not conspicuous ; disk with fine striæ, becoming coarse near the base, the intervals two to three times as wide as the striæ, each with a single series of fine remote punctures, becoming closer and more distinct toward base. *Abdomen* rather strongly, coarsely and closely punctured, especially toward base. Prosternum broadly, feebly impressed, separating the coxæ by quite distinctly less than their own width. Length 1.7–2.1 mm. ; width 0.6–0.8 mm.

Michigan ; Missouri ; Indiana ; South Carolina.

This species was considered by LeConte as possibly representing Boheman's *Baridius T-signum*, but it is evidently a widely different species. The original description of *T-signum* includes the phrase "elytris antice thoracis basi non latiora," and also states that the rostrum is shorter than the prothorax, the elytra having a small sparsely squamose maculation behind the middle, and the legs rufopiceous. One of the most conspicuous characters of *disjuncta* relates

to the form of the humeri, the elytra being abruptly much wider
than the base of the prothorax, and in the type there is no trace of
a squamose maculation behind the middle of the elytra, nor any
indication of such a spot, as all the punctures are occupied by small
slender setæ.

PYCNOBARIS n. gen.

In many respects this genus is allied to Baris, but its species have
a distinctly different habitus due to the scaly vestiture.　In its
structural characters, it is similar to Baris in the form of the antennal club with its basal joint polished and composing fully one-half
of the mass, also in its short robust beak and free tarsal claws.　The
flat prosternum separates the coxæ rather more widely than in any
species of Baris, and in this peculiarity it approaches Onychobaris ;
the fine and abrupt frontal groove differentiates it, however, from
both of these genera and allies it with Stictobaris, from which again
it differs in its robust convex body and non-tubulate prothorax.　The
prothorax is more distinctly constricted near the apex than in Baris,
but is never tubulate.

The beak is always shorter than the prothorax, the epistomal lobe
short, truncate and limited at each side by a small oblique fissure
as in Baris.　Mandibles well developed, arcuate, overlapping in
repose and deeply notched at apex.　The buccal opening is rather
smaller than in Baris, and its plane is more oblique to the under
surface of the beak behind it.　The scutellum is quite different from
that of the last-named genus being distinctly bisinuate at apex.
Tarsal claws rather long, widely divergent.

Our two species may be defined as follows :—

Vestiture rather sparse, the whitish scales very narrow, producing merely a
　　decided pruinose appearance...1 **pruinosa**
Vestiture dense, the scales broad, almost entirely concealing the surface.
　　　　　　　　　　　　　　　　　　　　　　　　2 **squamotecta**

1 **Pycnobaris pruinosa** Lec.—Proc. Am. Phil. Soc., XV, p. 294
(Baris).

Robust, oblong-oval and strongly convex, black throughout, the
integuments polished but clothed uniformly, although not very
densely, with long narrow subrecumbent scales. The beak is robust
and feebly arcuate, scarcely more than three-fourths as long as the
prothorax, the antennæ rather short and robust, with the second

and third funicular joints short and equal, the outer joints very wide
and subcontinuous with the club in outline, the latter moderate, the
basal joint polished and sparsely setose, constituting about one-half
the mass, the remaining rings short and each abruptly and conspicuously less in transverse diameter than the preceding. Prothorax one-third wider than long, the sides feebly convergent and
broadly arcuate very nearly to the apex, then more convergent and
broadly but distinctly constricted; basal lobe rather narrow but
very prominent, the disk with an extremely narrow impunctate line,
the punctures rather small, about one-fourth as wide as the scutellum and distinctly separated. Scutellum slightly transverse, the
posterior margin with two narrow deep notches. The elytra are
but slightly more than one-half longer than the prothorax, the striæ
very fine but deep, the intervals broad, flat, slightly uneven in width,
finely closely and confusedly punctate throughout, and from five to
six or seven times as wide as the striæ. Prosternum flat, separating
the coxæ by a little less than their own width, nearly as in Onychobaris, but apparently not at all foveate anteriorly. Length 3.2–4.2
mm.; width 1.6–2.2 mm.

Texas and Colorado. Moderately abundant.

2 **Pycnobaris squamotecta** n. sp.—Robust, ovoidal, strongly convex, the integuments black and polished throughout but covered densely with
long wide truncate and recumbent scales of a yellowish tint. *Head* minutely,
sparsely punctate and glabrous, the transverse groove very deep and abrupt,
the beak robust, densely punctate and squamose but narrowly impunctate and
subcarinate in the middle toward base, moderately, evenly arcuate and about
three-fourths as long as the prothorax; antennæ stout, densely squamose,
nearly as in *pruinosa*, the large basal joint of the club highly polished and
having widely scattered stiff setæ. *Prothorax* fully one-third wider than long,
the sides rather strongly convergent and feebly arcuate from the base to apical
fifth, then broadly rounded but not prominent and broadly strongly constricted
to the apex, the latter not at all tubulate, broadly arcuate and two-fifths as
wide as the base; basal lobe small but prominent; disk with a narrow impunctate line, indistinct before the middle, the punctures small, not much
more than one-fourth as wide as the scutellum and separated by nearly one-
half of their own diameter. Scutellum trapezoidal, nearly twice as wide
posteriorly as at base, the posterior margin broadly, feebly bisinuate and the
surface behind broadly impressed, the angles acute. *Elytra*, at the large but
very feebly prominent humeri, only slightly wider than the prothorax, nearly
two-thirds longer than the latter, the apex broadly obtuse; disk with fine
rather shallow striæ, the intervals five or six times as wide as the striæ, finely
but deeply, confusedly and rather sparsely punctate throughout, the scales

of the strial punctures being exactly equal in size and form to those of the intervals. *Abdomen* finely, not densely punctate, the scales large and dense. Prosternum flat, separating the rather large coxæ by not quite their own width. Length 4.7 mm. ; width 2.4 mm.

Texas.

Easily distinguishable from *pruinosa* by the dense vestiture of broad recumbent scales. A single specimen.

STICTOBARIS n. gen.

The few components of this genus are distinguished by a rather depressed body, extremely coarse and deeply perforate sculpture of the pronotum, and a rather short prothorax which is strongly tubulate at apex. The anterior coxæ are large and somewhat narrowly separated. Although the prosternum is feebly impressed, a certain decided relationship with Onychobaris is rendered evident by the two deep foveæ situated near the apex. It resembles Baris in the large basal joint of the antennal club, though this is not a character of decisive generic import, but differs from both the genera referred to in the deep and abrupt transverse frontal groove or constriction.

The beak is rather short and stout, with the epistomal lobe short and broadly sinuate at apex and the mandibles somewhat well developed, arcuate, notched at apex and partially decussate when closed. The vestiture consists simply of rather long sparse stout semi-erect and whitish or yellowish-white setæ or setiform squamules, which are sometimes denser on the second to fifth elytral intervals behind the middle, a character heretofore noticed in one of the groups of Plesiobaris, and also occurring in several species of Centrinus.

The three known species may be thus distinguished :—

Setæ moderate in length, yellowish, condensed at the base of the third interval and also on intervals two to five in a rather large area behind the middle; body oblong; legs rufous...1 **cribrata**
Setæ longer, more robust and whiter, not in the least condensed at the points mentioned under the preceding species.
  Body rather robust, oblong, obtusely rounded at apex ; beak densely punctate ; legs black...2 **pimalis**
  Body narrow, rather narrowly rounded behind ; size much smaller; beak more sparsely punctate ; legs rufous.......................3 **subacuta**

1 **Stictobaris cribrata** Lec.—Proc. Am. Phil. Soc., XV, p. 296 (Onychobaris).

Oblong-oval, somewhat depressed, shining, blackish-castaneous, the legs ferruginous; setæ somewhat robust, moderate in length, yellowish-white, more especially evident toward the sides of the prothorax, in a dense humeral spot and another one more elongate at the base of the third interval, also more or less distinctly denser on intervals two to five in a limited area behind the middle. The beak is robust, strongly arcuate and quite distinctly shorter than the prothorax, the antennæ moderate, the funicle thick, the club rather robust but not large, the basal joint composing fully one-half of the mass, with the pubescence moderately dense. The prothorax is two-fifths wider than long, with the apex strongly constricted and tubulate, the median line narrow and ill-defined, and the punctures perforate, deep, fully three-fourths as wide as the scutellum, uneven in distribution but generally separated by nearly one-half their own diameters. Elytra distinctly more than twice as long as the prothorax, the intervals subequal, about one-half wider than the grooves, the third a little wider. The prosternum is not distinctly impressed and separates the rather large coxæ by scarcely more than one-half their own width. Length 3.3–4.0 mm.; width 1.4–1.7 mm.

Texas (Waco). Cab. LeConte. Easily recognizable by the peculiar arrangement of the elytral setæ.

2 **Stictobaris pimalis** n. sp.—Oblong, subdepressed, shining, intense black throughout and sparsely, evenly clothed with rather long, robust, perfectly white setæ, without trace of condensation, except feebly on the anterior declivity of the humeral callosities. *Head* finely, very sparsely punctate, glabrous, the groove narrow and deep; beak robust, densely and deeply punctate throughout, densely setose, without trace of impunctate line, feebly arcuate, almost as long as the prothorax in the female, but quite distinctly shorter in the male; antennæ moderate, the scape rather long, the second funicular joint but very little longer than the third, outer joints gradually very thick and subcontinuous in outline with the club, the latter moderately robust, with the basal joint constituting rather more than one-half the mass. *Prothorax* two-fifths wider than long, the sides subparallel or very feebly convergent and nearly straight to apical fourth, then abruptly, strongly rounded and almost transversely convergent to the constriction, which is very strong, the apex strongly tubulate, truncate and three-fifths as wide as the base, the latter subtransverse, the median lobe moderate, rounded and distinct; disk with extremely narrow and imperfect impunctate line, the punctures very coarse, deep and dense, three-fourths as wide as the scutellum and more or less polygonally crowded. *Scutellum* moderate, slightly wider than long,

impressed along the middle. *Elytra* slightly wider than the prothorax and distinctly more than twice as long, the humeri not prominent laterally ; sides subparallel, generally feebly arcuate, the apex somewhat obtusely rounded; disk with moderate striæ, becoming coarse near the base, the intervals flat, slightly unequal, two to three times as wide as the striæ, rather finely, not densely, somewhat rugulosely and confusedly punctured throughout. *Abdomen* finely, sparsely punctate. Prosternum broadly and very feebly impressed, with two deep subapical foveæ as in Onychobaris, but less distant ; coxæ large, separated by scarcely more than one-half of their own width. Length 3.5–4.3 mm. ; width 1.45–1.8 mm.

Arizona.

The four specimens in my cabinet form a perfectly homogeneous series, and represent a species differing greatly from *cribrata* in the white pubescence, uniformly distributed and without trace of condensation behind the middle or at the base of the third interval, also in its larger size, denser pronotal punctures and completely black body and legs.

3 **Stictobaris subacuta** n. sp.—Elongate-elliptical, convex, shining, piceous-black, the legs rufous ; setæ long, very robust, uniformly distributed and without trace of condensation at the base of the third interval or behind the middle. *Head* very finely, sparsely and feebly punctate, minutely reticulate and alutaceous, the groove rather shallow but distinct ; beak somewhat coarsely but sparsely punctate, moderately strongly arcuate and subequal in length to the prothorax ; antennæ moderate, the club somewhat robust, normal, the second funicular joint short and but slightly longer than the third. *Prothorax* scarcely one-third wider than long, feebly convergent and nearly straight at the sides to apical fourth, then abruptly, strongly narrowed and tubulate, the apex truncate and fully two-thirds as wide as the base, the latter transverse, the median lobe small and rather feeble, rounded ; disk with a very narrow, incomplete and subobsolete impunctate line, the punctures nearly as in *cribrata*, but rather closer. *Elytra* one-fourth wider than the prothorax and nearly two and one-half times as long, the humeri feebly tumid, not prominent laterally ; sides parallel and feebly arcuate ; apex gradually, rather narrowly parabolic ; disk with somewhat narrow, moderately deep striæ, becoming coarser and somewhat crenulate near the base, the intervals flat, from one-half wider than, to nearly twice as wide as, the grooves, the punctures arranged in nearly even single series, fine and remote but becoming very coarse and rather close-set toward base, more or less confused on the third. Length 3.2 mm. ; width 1.25 mm.

New Mexico (Las Vegas).

Closely allied to *cribrata*, but well distinguished by its much narrower and more convex form, less truncate elytra, more elongate prothorax, and especially by the much longer, still more robust and whiter setæ, without trace of condensed spots. In *cribrata* the third interval is not only more densely setulose, but appears also to be feebly elevated toward base.

TREPOBARIS n. gen.

The single species representing this genus is narrow, elongate-oval and subcylindrical in form, resembling somewhat a very elongate Aulobaris, and perhaps really allied more closely to that genus than to any other. The prothorax is more elongate and parallel than in Aulobaris, and is briefly tubulate at apex, and in antennal structure it differs from the genus in question by its normally short second funicular joint and longer club, and in tarsal structure by the much smaller third joint, not wider than long though distinctly wider than the preceding.

As in Pseudobaris, the prosternum is very deeply and abruptly sulcate, the sulcus being much too narrow to receive the beak, and this is another important feature distinguishing it from Aulobaris. The sulcus is of somewhat peculiar form, being moderately and gradually dilated anteriorly and narrowest at a point just before the coxæ, a contour which suggests a line of development parallel with that of *Aulobaris naso.*

1 **Trepobaris elongata** n. sp.—Elongate, subcylindrical, convex, highly polished and deep black throughout, the setæ of the upper surface excessively minute, the third elytral interval without trace of squamules at base; setæ of the under surface very small, erect. *Head* convex, finely, sparsely punctured, the transverse impression strong, obtusely angulate in profile; beak rather stout, sparsely punctate, rather strongly arcuate at the base, but feebly so thence to the apex, equal in length to the head and prothorax in the male; antennæ moderately slender, the basal joint of the funicle long, the second not twice as long as wide, scarcely one-half as long as the first and much shorter than the next two, the club rather large, oval, densely pubescent, as long as the five preceding joints together and with its basal joint constituting but little more than one-third of the mass. *Prothorax* very nearly as long as wide, the sides just visibly convergent and nearly straight to apical fourth, then broadly rounded and feebly convergent to the fine apical constriction, the apex very briefly tubulate, truncate and fully three-fifths as wide as the base, the latter transverse, the median lobe almost completely obsolete; disk not very coarsely punctate, without impunctate line, the punctures scarcely one-third as wide as the scutellum and separated by fully their own diameters toward the middle, close but not rugulose at the sides. *Scutellum* moderate, transverse, broadly angulate behind. *Elytra* at base equal in width to the prothorax, fully twice as long as the latter, three-fourths longer than

wide, the humeri very small, rectangular, feebly tumid, not prominent laterally ; sides very feebly convergent and just visibly arcuate from the base nearly
to the apex, then rather suddenly and semi-circularly rounded ; disk with
somewhat fine but deep grooves, the intervals flat, nearly three times as wide
as the striæ, equal, each with a single series of minute but deep distinct
rounded and very remote punctures. *Abdomen* rather sparsely punctured.
Prosternum separating the moderately small coxæ by fully their own width.
Length 3.1–4.2 mm. ; width 1.15–1.5 mm.

Texas.

The type described above is a male and has a narrow elongate
and distinct, but not very deep, impression near the base of the
abdomen. The fifth ventral segment is broadly sinuato-truncate
and one-half longer than the fourth.

GLYPTOBARIS n. gen.

The single species forming the type of Glyptobaris possesses
many of the generic characters of Onychobaris, but differs in sculpture and vestiture to a marked degree and inhabits a different geographical region. It resembles Onychobaris in the structure of the
beak and antennæ and especially in the remote anterior coxæ and
broad flat prosternum, but differs distinctly in the form and extent
of the post-coxal parts of the prosternum, and also, somewhat, in
the structure of the mandibles. The latter are acute at apex and
come together along a crenulate line, but do not at all overlap in
repose; they are straight in external outline, not at all arcuate, and
when closed form an isosceles triangle.

The broad prosternum has, anteriorly, two small deep foveæ,
widely distant, arranged transversely, and connected by a very
narrow deep and abrupt groove; from each there extends posteriorly for a considerable distance a fine deep inwardly arcuate
groove, the two being strongly convergent, the triangular space so
inclosed being flat and impunctate. Just behind the coxæ, before
the posterior margin of the broad prosternal process, there are two
distant strongly elevated transverse tubercles, of which no trace can
be seen in any species of Onychobaris, but which evince an unmis-
takable relationship with Madarellus as shown under that genus.

The pygidium is vertical and partially covered above by the over-
hanging tips of the elytra, somewhat as in Desmoglyptus.

1 **Glyptobaris rugicollis** Lec.—Proc. Am. Phil. Soc., XV, p. 297
(Onychobaris).

Oval in form, strongly convex, rufo-piceous and polished. The

head is not punctate but minutely granulato-reticulate and dull, the
beak rather robust, very strongly arcuate and a little longer than
the prothorax, densely, coarsely punctured at the sides.   The prothorax is nearly one-third wider than long, with the sides evenly
and broadly rounded, becoming parallel near the base, the apex not
constricted but sometimes with a short prominent carina on the
sides at the apical margin, the base transverse and with a very
small but prominent median lobe, the disk coarsely, deeply, very
densely sculptured in longitudinal irregularly vermiculate rugæ,
which are in some spots broken up into coarse punctures, and
having a fine, more or less prominent, subentire median carina.
Scutellum very small, ogival and not transverse.   The elytra are
strongly narrowed from base to apex, three-fourths longer and but
slightly wider than the prothorax, the apex narrowly subtruncate,
the disk with rather fine but deep and abrupt, remotely crenulate
striæ, the intervals flat, wide, finely sparsely and unevenly punctate, the yellowish elongate scales forming a large quadrate spot in
basal three-fifths, the most prominent feature in the pattern being
two transverse bands, each consisting of two uneven lunules; elsewhere the vestiture is very sparse and inconspicuous.   Length
3.6–4.3 mm. ; width 1.7–2.0 mm.

Somewhat abundant throughout the eastern and southern Atlantic
States.   The specimens before me are from Indiana, Pennsylvania,
District of Columbia and North Carolina.

ONYCHOBARIS.
LeConte—Proc. Am. Phil. Soc., XV, p. 294.

The species of this genus are characterized in general by their
excessively densely punctured, rather dull integuments, although
there are numerous exceptions having the sculpture as sparse as in
Baris.   Onychobaris is a widely distinct and somewhat extensive
genus, almost exclusively restricted to the desert regions of the
southwest, where it replaces Baris in great measure; at least one
species extends as far to the eastward as the Mississippi River and
another is known from the true Pacific fauna, but the focal centre
of the genus undoubtedly lies in the dry regions of Arizona and
New Mexico.

The vestiture consists of short robust semi-erect setæ as in Baris,
but is often so abundant, from the density of punctuation, as to
give to the surface a grayish-pruinose appearance.   The generic
characters are stated at sufficient length in the table, and there are

but few special peculiarities to which it is necessary to call attention at present; one of these is, however, possibly of considerable
significance from an etiological point of view, and relates to the
modified impression of the prosternum. The prosternum is greatly
developed, rather remotely separating the coxæ, and almost perfectly
flat, but, in the middle, at some distance behind the anterior margin, there are two deep punctiform foveæ, moderately separated and
arranged transversely. These foveæ are generally connected by a
groove, and sometimes form the anterior limit of a more or less
visible but feeble short parallel-sided impression. A still more
advanced development of this peculiar modification of the remnant
of the rostral sulcus, has been described under the genus Glyptobaris.

In Onychobaris the beak is decidedly longer than in Baris, being
generally a little longer than the prothorax, and is always strongly
arcuate and more or less slender; it is separated from the head
by a transverse impression, which is always feeble and invariably
abruptly impunctate and polished. The tarsi vary considerably in
structure, the last joint being frequently as long as the first three
together but generally shorter. The scutellum is transverse, never
impressed, and usually more or less broadly rounded behind. The
male sexual characters are feeble, the abdominal impression being
invariably slight and often scarcely distinguishable.

It is to be regretted that the majority of the species are still
represented by unique examples, and there is consequently reason
to believe that the following table contains only a small proportion
of the forms inhabiting the inhospitable and comparatively unexplored regions which have developed this interesting special type.

Pronotum extremely densely punctured, only rarely with trace of median im-
    punctate line, which is then much abbreviated.................................2
Pronotum less densely punctured, generally with a distinct impunctate line,
    entire or abbreviated, but at least occupying one-half of the total
    length..10
2—Elytral punctures more or less broadly confused on all the intervals; body
    generally broader and more oblong or subrhomboidal.........................3
Elytral punctures forming nearly even single series on all the intervals; body
    more narrowly oval and convex...6
3—Legs, and sometimes also the beak, more or less rufescent...................4
Legs and beak intense black throughout.......................................5
4—Body not strongly depressed, the setæ moderately dense but not very long
    or robust.
  Pronotal punctures coarse, usually with a distinct but very narrow and
    incomplete impunctate line...1 **densa**

Pronotal punctures much smaller, the median line totally obsolete.

2 **corrosa**

Body strongly depressed, roughly sculptured, the elytral setæ long, very robust, dense and conspicuous...3 **depressa**

5—Prosternum feebly impressed along the middle, the anterior coxæ separated by but slightly more than their own width ; large species, with very large prothorax, the latter nearly as long as wide, the elytra relatively short, the beak stout ....4 **millepora**

Prosternum flat, the anterior coxæ smaller and more remote.

Punctures of the elytral intervals broadly confused throughout.

Elytral setæ coarse, long and conspicuous but not very dense.

5 **austera**

Elytral setæ very small, slender and only noticeable because of their greater abundance..6 **insidiosa**

Punctures of the elytral intervals moderate in size, broadly confused only toward base, forming single series toward apex ....7 **subtonsa**

6—Elytral punctures larger, distinct and generally close-set ; intervals narrow ; body less slender 7

Elytral punctures very minute and remote, the intervals wide, flat..............9

7—Body, legs and beak intense black throughout; small species...8 **arguta**

Legs and beak rufous, the entire body also frequently more or less rufo-piceous 8

8—Body rufo-ferruginous, the elytra black, smoother, with alutaceous lustre, the interstitial punctures rather less coarse and separated by about their own diameters ....9 **audax**

Body unicolorous throughout, black or more or less rufo-piceous ; interstitial punctures always coarse, deep and occupying the entire width of the intervals or very nearly.

Larger species, the prothorax nearly as long as wide and the elytra relatively shorter.

Surface strongly shining, black ....10 **stictica**

Surface opaque from the extreme density of the sculpture ; body dark blackish-piceous in color..11 **mystica**

Small species, the prothorax distinctly transverse.

Elytral setæ very small and inconspicuous ; legs and beak pale rufous.

12 **egena**

Elytral setæ longer, conspicuous ; legs and beak darker, piceo-rufous, the former a little shorter.

Sides of the prothorax parallel ; elytral setæ erect, bristling, those of the strial punctures almost as long as the others ......13 **ambigua**

Sides of the prothorax feebly divergent from the base ; elytral setæ shorter, more inclined, more distant and less conspicuous ; those of the strial punctures very small and scarcely at all visible.

14 **pauperella**

9—Body narrow, parallel ; very small species ....15 **seriata**

10—Elytral intervals wider than the striæ...11

Elytral intervals not wider than the grooves.......................................14

11—Intervals remotely punctured 12
Intervals more approximately punctured 13
12—Intervals but slightly wider than the grooves, the punctures coarse and
    more noticeably remote on the alternate intervals; pronotal punctures
    coarse and separated by rather less than their own widths, the surface
    feebly alutaceous ....16 **remota**
Intervals rather more than twice as wide as the striæ, the punctures small
    and remote on all; pronotum dull and strongly granulato-reticulate, the
    impunctate area wide, the punctures smaller and separated by much
    more than their own diameters ....17 **distans**
13—Larger species, the elytral humeri very distinctly tumid and prominent.
    Form moderately broad, the elytra distinctly longer than wide; legs rufous.
    Punctures of the elytral intervals large, rounded, very deep and close-set,
    forming single series; prothorax sometimes slightly inflated.
18 molesta
    Punctures of the elytral intervals smaller, more distant, uneven in size
    and shape, forming single series on some and finer and broadly, sparsely
    confused on others ....19 **illex**
Form very broad, the elytra not longer than wide and strongly narrowed
    from base to apex; legs black, with a feeble piceous tinge.
20 pectorosa
Rather small species, less than 3 mm. in length, the elytral humeri feebly
    and obsoletely tumid, not at all prominent............................21 **diluta**
14—Elytral grooves extremely coarse, the interstitial punctures very coarse
    and semi-coalescent; form broad; antennæ aberrant........22 **porcata**

1 **Onychobaris densa** Lec.—Proc. Acad. Nat. Sci. Phila., 1859, p.
79; ibid., 1868, p. 362 (Baridius); Proc. Am. Phil. Soc., XV, p. 295.

The form in this species is oblong-oval and convex, the integuments densely and deeply sculptured and but feebly shining, and
the setæ silvery and somewhat conspicuous. The beak is rather
slender, strongly arcuate toward base but becoming straight in
apical half, and is slightly longer than the prothorax; the second
joint of the antennal funicle is one-half longer than the third. The
prothorax is scarcely two-fifths wider than long, the sides feebly
convergent and nearly straight to apical fourth, then strongly
rounded, the apex briefly tubulate; punctures somewhat coarse
and very deep, one-half as wide as the scutellum, very densely and
polygonally crowded. The elytra are but slightly longer than wide
and about two-thirds longer than the prothorax, the striæ rather
coarse and deep, the intervals flat, alternately wide and narrow,
somewhat coarsely, deeply, extremely densely and confusedly punctate and rugulose but strongly shining. The abdomen is coarsely,

deeply and rather closely punctured toward base. Length 3.2–3.7 mm.; width 1.4–1.75 mm.

The series before me was collected by Mr. G. W. Dunn, at San Diego, California, from which locality it was originally described.

Mr. H. C. Fall of Pomona, Cal., writes me that this species is found at Coronado, immediately opposite San Diego on the line of the seabeach, where it " frequents the flowers of a low fleshy-leaved plant just above the beach." Mr. Fall states further that he has " taken it in the flowers in July and in the sand beneath the plants in February," and also remarks that in every specimen taken by him " the legs, and beak to some extent, incline to paleness." It may be concluded from these statements that *densa* is confined in distribution to the immediate seashore of Southern California.

2 **Onychobaris corrosa** n. sp.—Oblong-oval, convex, black, the head, beak and legs piceous ; integuments opaque from extreme density of sculpture. *Head* finely but strongly, densely punctured for a short distance behind the transverse polished and impunctate interocular impression, which is normally feeble ; beak thick, not sensibly tapering, rather strongly, evenly arcuate, very densely punctate, the fine median impunctate line obliterated toward base, equal in length to the prothorax ; antennæ moderate, the second funicular joint fully one-half longer than the third. *Prothorax* about one-third wider than long, the sides straight and parallel in basal two-thirds, then broadly rounded and convergent to the apex, which is only feebly constricted ; base broadly bisinuate, the median lobe more prominent than the sides, rather narrowly rounded at apex and broadly cuspiform ; disk without distinct trace of median line, the punctures moderately small, fully one-third as wide as the scutellum, deep and throughout extremely dense and polygonally crowded. Scutellum rather small, transverse. *Elytra* slightly longer than wide, nearly three-fourths longer than the prothorax, and, at the feebly prominent humeri, slightly wider than the latter ; outline behind the humeri evenly hemi-elliptical ; disk with rather coarse deep grooves, the intervals nearly flat, subequal, about one-half wider than the grooves and rather coarsely, deeply, extremely densely and confusedly punctate throughout, somewhat coarsely rugulose, the setæ distinct but sparse, short, subrecumbent and rather robust, those at the bottom of the grooves as large and distinct as the others. *Abdomen* finely, rather closely punctured. Length 3.9 mm.; width 1.8 mm.

Colorado.

The unique type is apparently a female, and the species is quite distinct from any other here noted.

3 **Onychobaris depressa** n. sp.—Oblong-oval, depressed, black, the legs rufo-piceous ; setæ rather short but erect and hispid, broad and sub-squamiform, abundant, cinereous and conspicuous. *Head* coarsely, very

densely punctured and hispid, divided from the beak by a feeble, shining
and impunctate impression, the beak rather slender, strongly, evenly arcuate,
not quite as long as the prothorax, densely and coarsely, rugosely sculptured ;
antennæ nearly normal but with the basal joint of the club composing fully
one-half of the mass, the second funicular joint one-half longer than the third,
the setæ robust. *Prothorax* one-third wider than long, the sides subparallel
and nearly straight in basal three-fourths, then strongly rounded and convergent to the apex which is slightly constricted ; base transverse, the median
lobe rather small but prominent ; disk without trace of impunctate line, but
very narrowly and vaguely subcarinate along the middle, the sculpture uneven and excessively dense, consisting of closely crowded, rather coarse, very
deep punctures, about one-half as wide as the scutellum, the latter small,
moderately transverse, opaque. *Elytra* a little longer than wide, nearly four-
fifths longer than the prothorax, and, at the base, rather abruptly and quite
distinctly wider than the latter, the humeri but feebly tumid ; outline thence
around the apex hemi-elliptical ; disk with moderately fine, not very deep but
abrupt striæ, the intervals wide, flat, alternating from two to three times as
wide as the striæ, finely and feebly, not very densely but unevenly and confusedly punctate and strongly shining. *Abdomen* densely punctured toward
the sides and base, but sparsely so toward the middle of segments two to four.
Prosternum perfectly flat behind the transverse apical constriction, and very
widely separating the coxæ. Length 3.3 mm.; width 1.6 mm.

California (Santa Monica). Mr. Jülich.

A remarkably distinct species, to be known at once by the
coarsely, extremely densely sculptured and subopaque pronotum,
head and beak, and rather shining, finely but unevenly punctured
elytra, also by the strongly depressed body and coarse erect and
robust setæ. The antennal club resembles that of Baris in form
but is densely pubescent throughout. The unique type is a male.

4 Onychobaris millepora n. sp.—Oblong, feebly rhomboidal, convex, rather dull in lustre and grayish-black throughout, the setæ small but
abundant and very distinct. *Head* rather strongly punctured but only near
the anterior margin, separated from the beak by an extremely feeble transversely impunctate and polished impression ; beak rather robust, tapering
from base to apex, strongly, evenly arcuate and not quite as long as the prothorax ; antennæ moderate, the second funicular joint unusually long, not
quite twice as long as wide but subequal to the next two ; club normal, with
its second joint three-fourths as long as the first. *Prothorax* very large, just
visibly wider than long ; sides feebly convergent and nearly straight to apical
fourth, then strongly arcuate and convergent to the apex, the latter not distinctly constricted ; base transverse, the median lobe large and well developed,
rounded ; disk with very narrow, short and ill-defined impunctate line near
the centre ; punctures very small but deep, rounded and in rather close contact throughout, about one-fourth as wide as the scutellum. *Elytra* but just

visibly longer than wide, about one-third longer than the prothorax, and, at
the small and slightly prominent humeri, but little wider than the latter;
sides distinctly convergent, the apex parabolic; disk very finely striate, the
striæ deep, abrupt, impunctate, the intervals flat, alternating slightly in
width, four or five times as wide as the striæ, finely, deeply, closely and confusedly punctured throughout but not rugose. *Abdomen* finely, rather densely
punctate. Prosternum widely separating the coxæ, the latter not quite as
small as usual. Length 4.7 mm.; width 2.25 mm.

New Mexico; Colorado.

The type is probably a male, the middle of the abdomen near the
base being very feebly impressed, and abruptly more coarsely and
very sparsely punctured.

This exceedingly isolated species may be known at once by its
very finely and densely punctured integuments, rather large size,
feebly rhomboidal form, large prothorax and short conical elytra.
As is frequently the case in this genus, the prothorax in some
specimens becomes feebly inflated, especially toward apex, a form
which is however constant and distinctive in some species.

5 **Onychobaris austera** n. sp.—Moderately robust, rhomboid-oval
not very convex, black throughout, very densely sculptured, the setæ cinereous, robust and conspicuous but not dense. *Head* rather finely, deeply, very
densely punctate, the transverse impression feeble, indicated by a narrow
polished and abruptly impunctate line; beak densely, rugosely punctate,
setulose, rather stout and broadly, evenly arcuate in basal half, becoming
straight and slightly tapering thence to the apex, very nearly as long as the
head and prothorax; antennæ inserted at the middle, moderately slender, the
basal joint of the funicle fully as long as the next three, second obconical, but
slightly longer than wide, three to seven transverse, club oval, pubescent,
with the basal joint large. *Prothorax* two-fifths wider than long, the sides
feebly but distinctly convergent and straight from the base to apical third,
then gradually, evenly rounded and convergent to the small but evident subapical constriction, the apex transversely truncate and much less than one-
half as wide as the base, the latter transverse, the lobe constituting a little
more than one-third of the entire width, rounded and prominent; disk very
deeply and densely punctate, without trace of impunctate line, the punctures
somewhat coarse. Scutellum moderate. *Elytra* at the small but prominent
humeral callus much wider than the prothorax, three-fourths longer than the
latter, a little longer than wide, broadly hemi-elliptical in outline; disk with
distinct but not very deep striæ, the intervals flat, slightly unequal, about
twice as wide as the grooves, coarsely, confusedly, closely and rugosely punctured throughout but shining. *Abdomen* rather coarsely and deeply punctate,
the punctures well separated. Prosternum fla·, the coxæ very remote.
Length 3.3 mm.; width 1.7 mm.

California (San Diego). Mr. Ch Fuchs.

Allied to *densa* but differing radically in its black legs, much
smaller and still more dense pronotal punctures, without trace of
the median impunctate line usually quite distinct in that species,
and with much coarser and more conspicuous setæ. It also resembles *depressa*, but is much less depressed, as can be readily seen in
profile, and has the body more rhomboidal; the subsquamiform setæ
are not so coarse and are less dense.

6 **Onychobaris insidiosa** n. sp.—Oblong-oval, moderately convex,
subopaque, grayish-black throughout, the setæ very short. *Head* finely,
closely punctate anteriorly, limited by a transverse impunctate line; beak
very densely, finely but strongly punctate, with a fine dorsal impunctate line,
strongly arcuate, distinctly tapering from base to apex, very slightly longer
than the prothorax ; antennæ slender, the second funicular joint longer than
wide and nearly one-half longer than the third. *Prothorax* about two-fifths
wider than long, nearly as in *densa* but with the punctures much smaller, fine,
deep, nearly in mutual contact but not polygonally compressed, rather more
than one third as wide as the scutellum. Scutellum small, transverse, not distinctly impressed. *Elytra* nearly one-fourth longer than wide, quite distinctly
less than twice as long as the prothorax, and, at the moderately prominent
humeri, slightly wider than the latter ; sides feebly convergent, the apex
semi-circular ; disk with moderately coarse, deep, abrupt, irregularly punctate striæ, the intervals flat, alternating somewhat in width, the wider about
twice as wide as the grooves, all finely, densely, unevenly and subrugulosely
punctured. *Abdomen* shining, finely, not very strongly or densely punctured.
Prosternum flat, the coxæ rather small, separated by one-half more than their
own width. Length 2.3–3.3 mm.; width 1.1–1.6 mm.

Western Texas (Big Springs)—Mr. H. F. Wickham ; Southern
California.

A rather small, extremely densely and somewhat finely sculptured, subopaque species, allied to *densa*, but differing in the much
finer punctures of the pronotum, smaller size and somewhat broader
form. Thirteen specimens.

7 **Onychobaris subtonsa** Lec.—Proc. Am. Phil. Soc., XV, p. 295.

Oval, rather strongly convex and shining, black throughout, the
setæ distinct. The beak in the female is strongly and almost evenly
arcuate, not distinctly tapering from base to apex and is slightly
longer than the prothorax, the second funicular joint one-half longer
than the third. The prothorax is barely one-fourth wider than
long, the sides very feebly convergent and almost straight nearly
to the apex, then strongly rounded and distinctly constricted, the

punctures small, deep, circular, scarcely one-third as wide as the scutellum and not quite in actual contact, although very dense. The elytra are quite distinctly longer than wide, fully two-thirds longer than the prothorax, and the sides behind the humeri are decidedly convergent, the apex being somewhat narrowly semicircular; the striæ are not very coarse or deep but abrupt, the intervals flat, subequal in width, each rather more than twice as wide as the grooves and not very coarsely punctured, the punctures forming almost even single rows, but broadly confused on the fifth throughout and on all toward base. The anterior coxæ are remote and the abdomen rather sparsely punctured. Length 2.6–3.8 mm.; width 1.2–1.6 mm.

Texas, Kansas and Colorado. Easily distinguishable from the species allied to *densa*, by the subserial arrangement of the interstitial punctures and the more elongate form.

8 **Onychobaris arguta** n. sp.—Oblong-oval, rather strongly convex, shining, black throughout, the setæ very small, slender and inconspicuous. *Head* finely, rather sparsely punctate, the impression feeble, polished; beak rather stout, evenly cylindrical and arcuate throughout, densely, deeply, not coarsely but rugosely punctate and quite distinctly shorter than the prothorax; antennæ rather slender, inserted just behind the middle, the first funicular joint fully as long as the next three, the second obconical, one-half longer than wide, three to seven feebly transverse, the former nearly as long as wide. *Prothorax* one-third wider than long, the sides parallel and nearly straight to apical fourth, then rather abruptly, strongly rounded, thence convergent and feebly sinuate to the apex; base transverse, broadly bisinuate; disk rather convex, evenly, closely, not finely punctate, the punctures rounded, deep, about two-fifths as wide as the scutellum and generally separated by about one-half of their own diameters; impunctate line obsolete. Scutellum rather small. *Elytra* slightly wider than the prothorax and from one-half to three-fifths longer, distinctly longer than wide, hemi-elliptical, the humeri moderately prominent; striæ not very coarse, somewhat shallow but abrupt, the intervals slightly unequal, generally nearly twice as wide as the grooves, flat, smooth, each with a single series of deep punctures which are moderately large and rather distant, but becoming coarse and close-set toward base. *Abdomen* rather finely but strongly punctate. Prosternum flat, the anterior coxæ rather large, separated by one-fourth more than their own width. Length 2.65–2.8 mm.; width 1.2–1.3 mm.

California (foot-hills of the southern sierras). Mr. H. C. Fall.

This species is not closely related to any other but should be associated with *audax;* it differs from *ambigua* and *egena* in its black legs and in several other characters as stated in the table. In general form it somewhat resembles *pauperella*.

9 **Onychobaris audax** n. sp.—Oblong, strongly convex, shining, the elytra feebly alutaceous, brownish rufous throughout, the elytra blackish, setæ very small, distant and forming even single lines on the elytra. *Head* toward apex and beak finely but densely punctate, the latter moderately slender, evenly, somewhat strongly arcuate and rather longer than the prothorax; antennæ slender, second funicular joint but little longer than the third. *Prothorax* about one-fourth wider than long, the sides straight and somewhat divergent from the base to apical fourth, then strongly rounded and subprominent, thence very strongly convergent to the apex which is minutely and visibly constricted; base transverse, the median lobe rather narrow but prominent, rounded, constituting less than one-third of the width; disk with but the feeblest traces of a short median line, the punctures very deep, moderately small, one-third as wide as the scutellum, very dense, almost in mutual contact but circular and not polygonally crowded. Scutellum moderate, transverse. *Elytra* about one-fifth longer than wide, two-thirds longer than the prothorax, and, at the small feebly tumid humeri, but just visibly wider than the disk of the latter; sides for a short distance behind the humeri parallel, then elliptically rounded through the apex; disk with rather narrow, deep and finely, remotely but distinctly punctate grooves, the intervals flat, subequal, about twice as wide as the goooves, each with a single series of somewhat small, feeble, rather remote and subtransverse punctures, slightly confused toward base especially on the fifth. *Abdomen* rather finely, not densely punctured. Length 3.0 mm.; width 1.4 mm.

California (southern).

A small and easily recognizable species, having the prothorax rather wider at apical fourth than at base, and with the sides straight. It is also somewhat aberrant in coloration.

10 **Onychobaris stictica** n. sp.—Oblong, not very robust, strongly convex, black, the head and beak feebly rufescent, the legs paler, rufous; integuments polished, moderately densely sculptured. *Head* finely, sparsely punctured, the punctuation obsolete toward base, the feeble transverse impression broadly impunctate and polished; beak moderately stout, rather feebly, evenly arcuate, fully as long as the prothorax, strongly, densely punctate, with a narrow impunctate and subcarinate median line; antennæ normal, the second funicular joint slightly longer than the third. *Prothorax* rather elongate, scarcely one-fourth wider than long, the sides parallel and nearly straight to apical fourth, then broadly, evenly rounded and strongly convergent to the apex, which is quite distinctly constricted; base transverse, the median lobe very broad, distinct; disk without distinct trace of median line; punctures rather small, circular, deep, dense but not quite in actual contact and scarcely one-fourth as wide as the scutellum. Scutellum well developed, transverse. *Elytra* one-fifth longer than wide, one-half longer than the prothorax, at the feebly tumid humeri but just visibly wider than the latter, the sides thence feebly convergent and nearly straight to the apex, the latter semicircularly rounded; disk with rather coarse abrupt and moderately deep

grooves; the intervals flat, subequal, not quite one-half wider than the grooves, each with a single series of large deep rounded and close-set punctures which occupies nearly its entire width; setæ rather long, conspicuous. *Abdomen* polished, rather coarsely strongly and moderately closely punctured. *Legs* moderate; basal joint of the tarsi as long as the next two, the third small, but slightly wider than the second, the fourth much shorter than the three preceding together; claws small. Prosternum very widely separating the coxæ. Length 3.3 mm.; width 1.6 mm.

Arizona (Benson). Mr. G. W. Dunn.

Somewhat similar to *subtonsa* in general outline, but in scarcely any other character. The setæ of the elytra in *subtonsa* are very small, subrecumbent and not conspicuous, while in *stictica* they are unusually long, erect and form even bristling single series on each interval; the indistinct punctures of the grooves also bear smaller setæ which are, however, visible under moderate power. The punctures of the pronotum are a little less dense along the middle.

11 **Onychobaris mystica** n. sp.—Oblong-oval, convex, extremely densely sculptured, opaque, piceous-black, the head, beak and legs rufous, the setæ short but erect, rather stout, distinct and somewhat dense. *Head* strongly, densely punctate toward apex, the transverse groove distinctly impressed and very highly polished, abruptly impunctate, the beak moderately densely punctate, very densely so at the sides, the median impunctate line distinct and entire, strongly, evenly arcuate, equal in length to the prothorax in the male, quite distinctly longer in the female; antennæ moderate, the second funicular joint rather long, scarcely twice as long as wide but subequal to the next two. *Prothorax* rather long, scarcely one-fourth wider than long, the sides subparallel in basal three-fourths, then strongly rounded and convergent to the apex which is broad, truncate and distinctly constricted at the sides; base subtransverse, the median lobe large, rather more than one-third the total width, prominent, broadly rounded; disk without trace of median line, the punctures moderately coarse, nearly two-fifths as wide as the scutellum, deep, excessively dense and polygonally crowded throughout. *Scutellum* rather small. *Elytra* a little longer than wide, barely one-half longer than the prothorax, and, at the small but distinctly prominent humeri, quite noticeably wider than the latter; outline behind the humeri broadly hemi-elliptical; disk with abrupt deep coarse and confusedly punctured grooves, the intervals flat, narrow, subequal, exactly equal in width to the grooves and each with a single series of large, very deep, circular, perforate and very close-set punctures, which are almost as wide as the intervals. *Abdomen* rather coarsely, densely punctured. Length 3.3–4.1 mm.; width 1.4–1.9 mm.

Arizona (Benson and Pinal Mts.)—Dunn and Wickham; Texas (El Paso), Mr. Dunn.

Very easily separated from either *pauperella* or *ambigua*, which

it somewhat resembles in general outline, by its coarser and still
more closely crowded and opaque sculpture, coarser, deeper, more
perforate and much more even interstitial punctures, coarser grooves
and narrower intervals, and by its decidedly larger size. It is
represented by a series of nine specimens, exhibiting scarcely any
variation.

12 **Onychobaris egena** n. sp.—Oblong-oval, convex, very densely
sculptured but rather strongly shining, black, the prothorax beneath with a
piceous tinge ; head, beak and legs bright red ; setæ small, sparse and inconspicuous ; those arising from the punctures of the elytral striæ about as long
as those of the intervals. *Head* shining, rather finely, deeply punctured, the
punctures separated by about their own widths ; impression rather strong ;
beak somewhat stout, evenly, moderately arcuate, feebly tapering toward
apex, shining, rather coarsely, deeply but not very densely punctate, about
as long as the head and prothorax ; antennæ inserted at the middle, the basal
joint of the funicle scarcely as long as the next three, second fully three-fourths
longer than wide, third to seventh increasing in width, the former nearly as
long as wide, the latter strongly transverse, club rather small and narrow, not
abrupt. *Prothorax* one-fourth wider than long, the sides straight and just
visibly divergent from the base to apical third, then broadly rounded to the
small but distinct constriction ; apex very briefly tubulate, truncate and distinctly more than one-half as wide as 'the base, the latter rather deeply bisinuate ; disk without trace of impunctate line, deeply, rather coarsely and
extremely densely punctate, the punctures three-fifths as wide as the scutellum, rounded but in mutual contact. Scutellum slightly transverse. *Elytra*
short, scarcely visibly wider than the prothorax and about one-half longer,
but slightly longer than wide, parabolic in outline, the humeri very slightly
prominent ; disk coarsely, deeply striate, the intervals subequal, narrow, not
distinctly wider than the grooves, each with a single even series of very coarse
deep rounded and close-set punctures. *Abdomen* deeply, rather coarsely,
moderately closely punctured. Prosternum narrowly and just visibly impressed in the middle, the coxæ moderate, remote, separated by much more
than their own width. Length 2.7 mm. ; width 1.2 mm.

Arizona (Pinal Mts.). Mr. H. F. Wickham.

A small species belonging to a group in which the species become
rather closely allied. It perhaps approaches *pauperella* more nearly
than any other form here noted, but differs in its shorter elytra,
with smaller and less conspicuous setæ and much coarser more
close-set interstitial punctures, and also in the coarser punctures of
the head and pronotum. From *ambigua* it differs in its smaller
size, narrower form, much shorter, less visible setæ and narrower,
more coarsely, closely and evenly punctured intervals.

13 Onychobaris ambigua n. sp.—Oblong, convex, piceous-black and rather dull throughout, the head, beak and legs obscurely rufescent; sculpture very dense; setæ rather long, erect, forming conspicuous bristling series on the elytra. *Head* near the apex and beak finely but strongly, very densely punctured, the transverse impression feeble and only narrowly and imperfectly impunctate; beak rather slender, evenly, strongly arcuate, scarcely at all tapering, equal in length to the prothorax, the median subcariniform line almost obsolete; antennæ moderate, the second funicular joint fully one-half longer than the third. *Prothorax* scarcely more than one-fourth wider than long, the sides parallel and straight nearly to apical fourth, then evenly, strongly rounded but not prominent, thence strongly convergent and nearly straight to the apex which is not distinctly constricted; base transverse, straight, the median lobe rather small but rounded and prominent; disk with barely a trace of an impunctate line, rather finely, deeply, extremely densely punctate throughout, the punctures scarcely one-third as wide as the scutellum, circular and not polygonally distorted. Scutellum moderate. *Elytra* not longer than wide, barely two-fifths longer than the prothorax, and, at base, rather abruptly a little wider than the latter; outline thence hemi-elliptical; disk with not very coarse, moderately deep striæ, the intervals flat, subequal, nearly twice as wide as the striæ, not very coarsely but deeply, closely punctate, the punctures forming somewhat uneven single series on each. *Abdomen* moderately closely punctured. Length 2.8–3.0 mm.; width 1.35–1.6 mm.

Arizona.

A somewhat small species, closely allied to *pauperella*, but easily distinguishable by its larger size and more robust form, also by its shorter elytra, not only actually but relatively to the prothorax; the sides of the latter are parallel in basal three-fourths in this species, but feebly convergent toward base in basal two-thirds in *pauperella*, the widest part of the disk in the latter being at apical third. The prothorax is longer in *ambigua*, and the elytral intervals wider. It is represented by four specimens, one of which is contained in the collection of the National Museum, and was probably collected by Mr. Morrison.

14 Onychobaris pauperella n. sp.—Oblong, suboval, convex, feebly shining, black, the head, beak and legs dark rufo-piceous; setæ moderately long, distinct and forming rather conspicuous single series on the elytra. *Head* finely, rather sparsely punctate toward apex, the beak densely punctured at the sides, rather thick, equal in length to the prothorax, feebly tapering from base to apex, evenly and strongly arcuate; antennæ moderate, the second funicular joint but slightly longer than the third. *Prothorax* nearly one-third wider than long, the sides feebly divergent and nearly straight to apical third, then gradually broadly rounded and convergent to the apex, which is minutely and scarcely visibly constricted; base transverse and straight, the median lobe small but prominent, broadly rounded; disk slightly wider at apical third than at base, evenly, strongly convex, without trace of median line, the punctures rather small but deep, one-third as wide as the scutellum, very dense and even throughout but circular and not in actual contact. Scutellum moderate. *Elytra* about one-fifth longer than wide, one-half longer than the prothorax, and, at the rather small but somewhat prominent humeri, quite distinctly wider than the latter; outline behind the humeri hemi-elliptical, the sides distinctly convergent: disk coarsely, deeply striate, the intervals sometimes feebly alternating in width, slightly, to fully one-half, wider than the grooves, each with a single somewhat uneven series of coarse, deep, close-set and subrugulose punctures. *Abdomen* moderately closely punctured. Prosternum separating the rather large coxæ by one-fourth more than their own width. Length 2.3–2.8 mm.; width 1.0–1.2 mm.

Arizona.

This is one of the smallest species of the genus, somewhat resembling *audax* in outline, but with narrower, much more coarsely closely and roughly punctured elytral intervals, and differing also in its entirely black body and more broadly rounded sides of the prothòrax anteriorly. Four specimens.

15 **Onychobaris seriata** Lec.—Pac. R. R. Expl. and Surv., Ins., p. 58; Proc. Ac. Nat. Sci., Phila., 1868, p. 363 (Baridius); Proc. Am. Phil. Soc., XV, p. 296.

The smallest species of the genus and very distinct from any other which I have observed. It is unusually narrow and parallel, moderately convex, black and polished, the beak rather robust, moderately and evenly arcuate and slightly longer than the prothorax, the antennæ normal in structure, the basal joint of the funicle not as long as the next four and the second but very slightly longer than the third. The prothorax is nearly as long as wide, parallel on the sides to apical fourth, then broadly rounded and convergent to the apex, which does not appear to be at all constricted; there is but feeble trace of a short median line and the punctures are deep, about one-third as wide as the scutellum and separated by nearly their own widths toward base, but nearly contiguous toward apex. The elytra are much longer than wide and about two-thirds longer than the prothorax, finely but deeply and abruptly striate, the intervals flat, subequal, about three times as wide as the grooves and each with a single series of very minute distant punctures, each bearing a scarcely distinguishable seta; the striæ become quite coarsely crenulate very near the base. Length 2.3 mm.; width 0.8 mm.

This is the only Onychobaris which has been discovered in the true Pacific fauna. It is represented by the unique type in the LeConte cabinet, said to have been taken near San Francisco.

16 **Onychobaris remota** n. sp.—Oval, strongly convex, not very robust, black with a piceous tinge, the integuments smooth and alutaceous, minutely and densely granulato-reticulate, setæ very minute and short. *Head* finely but strongly punctate anteriorly, the transverse impunctate line marking the feeble impression foveate in the middle; beak finely but deeply, densely punctate throughout, with a fine median impunctate line, rather stout, strongly, evenly arcuate, not more than four-fifths as long as the prothorax; antennæ normal, the second funicular joint fully one-third longer than the third, the club rather large, evenly ovoideo-fusiform, pointed, moderately abrupt. *Prothorax* rather long, scarcely one third wider than long, the sides subparallel or extremely feebly convergent to apical fourth, then strongly rounded and convergent to the apex which is subtubulately constricted ; base transverse, the median lobe broad, strongly, evenly rounded and prominent; disk with a narrow but well marked and subentire median line, the punctures abrupt, perforate, rather deep, not *very* dense, separated by distinctly less than their own widths and about one-third as wide as the scutellum, slightly smaller near the median line. Scutellum moderate, transverse. *Elytra* parabolic behind the humeri, quite distinctly longer than wide, one-half longer than the prothorax, and, at the small and feebly prominent humeri, but slightly wider than the latter ; disk not very coarsely but deeply and abruptly striate, the intervals subequal, flat, about one-half wider than the grooves, each with a single series of rather coarse, subtransverse and distant punctures. *Abdomen* not very densely punctured. Length 3.7 mm.; width 1.7 mm.

Texas (El Paso).

The type appears to be a male, the abdomen being very feebly flattened and more sparsely punctured in the middle near the base, while the type of *distans* is apparently a female ; but the two forms differ so greatly in bodily form and otherwise, that I regret to believe there is but little doubt of their mutual distinctness.

Remota differs from *distans*, irrespective of the shorter beak which may possibly be a sexual character, in its more elongate-oval form, in its much less transverse, more coarsely and pronouncedly more densely punctured prothorax, with narrower median line, and in its longer and more coarsely striate elytra.

17 **Onychobaris distans** Lec.—Proc. Ac. Nat. Sci., Phila., 1868, p. 363 (Baridius) ; Proc. Am. Phil. Soc., XV, p. 296.

A distinct species, moderate in size, somewhat robust and convex, oblong-oval, black, with the integuments feebly shining, alutaceous

and very minutely granulato-reticulate. The beak is somewhat
stout, strongly but not very densely punctate, except at the sides
toward base where it becomes somewhat rugulose, strongly, evenly
arcuate, barely as long as the prothorax, the antennæ normal, with
the second funicular joint but slightly longer than the third, the
club rather large, elongate, ovoidal, pointed and moderately abrupt.
Prothorax two-fifths wider than long, the sides parallel and feebly
arcuate to apical fourth, then strongly rounded and convergent and
feebly sinuate to the apex, the base broadly bisinuate, the disk with a
broad fusiform impunctate line, the punctures rather small, scarcely
more than one-fourth as wide as the scutellum laterally, abrupt and
perforate, rather sparse and separated by much more than their own
widths, becoming a little smaller, more feeble and still sparser toward
the median line. Elytra parabolic, but slightly longer than wide,
one-half longer and just visibly wider than the prothorax, not very
coarsely but deeply and abruptly striate, the intervals flat, subequal,
more than twice as wide as the striæ, each with a single series of
somewhat small but distinct, subtransverse and very remote punctures, each bearing an extremely short but rather robust seta not
projecting beyond its limits. The prosternum very widely separates
the small anterior coxæ, and has, near the apex, a small feeble parallel-sided impression, ending anteriorly in two small punctiform
foveæ. Length 3.4 mm.; width 1.6 mm.

New Mexico. The type in the cabinet of LeConte is, as far as
known, still unique.

18 **Onychobaris molesta** n. sp.—Oval, strongly convex, shining,
black with a piceous tinge, the head, beak and legs rufous; setæ very minute
and inconspicuous. *Head* obsoletely and sparsely punctured even anteriorly,
the feeble impunctate impression with a small deep median fovea; beak
strongly, evenly arcuate, moderately stout, fully as long as the prothorax,
minutely, rather sparsely punctured, the punctures larger and rather close
at the sides; antennæ normal, moderate in length. *Prothorax* moderate in size,
not at all inflated, scarcely more than one-fourth wider than long; sides feebly
convergent and slightly arcuate from the base, more convergent near the apex,
the latter constricted and broadly but briefly subtubulate; base broadly bisinuate, the median lobe rounded and more prominent than the sides; disk
somewhat convex. Scutellum transverse. *Elytra* one-fifth longer than wide,
about two-thirds longer than the prothorax, and, at the small but distinctly
prominent humeri, a little wider than the latter; sides convergent, the apex
parabolic; disk with coarse deep and abrupt grooves, the intervals flat, equal,
scarcely one-half wider than the grooves, each with a single series of very

large deep rounded, rather close-set punctures which are but slightly irregular on the third. *Abdomen* sparsely punctured, but, as usual, densely so at the sides. Length 4.0–4.5 mm.; width 1.8–2.1 mm.

Arizona.

In one specimen the prothorax is inflated and apparently a little wider than the elytra. Two specimens.   ·

19 **Onychobaris illex** n. sp.—Rather narrowly oval, strongly convex, polished, the pronotum feebly alutaceous, black, the head, beak and legs rufous; setæ very minute, sparse and inconspicuous. *Head* minutely, sparsely punctate, the punctures slightly less remote anteriorly; impression feeble, marked by a very narrow polished and impunctate band; beak somewhat stout, nearly evenly, moderately arcuate, deeply, densely punctate, longitudinally rugulose at the sides, almost evenly cylindrical, scarcely longer than the prothorax; antennæ inserted quite distinctly behind the middle, the basal joint of the funicle about as long as the next three, second slightly longer than wide, obconical, remaining joints gradually, moderately transverse and closely coarctate, the club somewhat abrupt, oval, moderate in size. *Prothorax* scarcely one-third wider than long, the sides broadly arcuate and convergent anteriorly, becoming gradually almost parallel from apical third to the base; subapical constriction obsolete, the apex fully one-half as wide as the base, the latter straight and transverse, the median lobe one-third of the total width, rounded and prominent; disk rather finely, somewhat closely punctate, with a narrow impunctate line not attaining the apex, the punctures about one-fourth as wide as the scutellum and separated by about one-half of their own diameters, becoming sparser in the middle, especially toward base. *Scutellum* transversely lunate. *Elytra* slightly wider than the prothorax and barely two-thirds longer, hemi-elliptical, distinctly longer than wide, the humeri small but decidedly prominent; disk with rather fine, moderately deep, abrupt striæ, the intervals flat, from two to three times as wide as the grooves, sparsely but very unevenly punctate, the punctures rather fine and feeble, more or less transverse, arranged in nearly even single lines on some intervals and more or less confused on others. *Abdomen* finely, not densely punctate, the last three sutures very deeply excavated except at the sides. Prosternum flat, with a small transverse groove and two short parallel longitudinal folds anteriorly, the coxæ small and very remote. Length 3.4 mm.; width 1.6 mm.

Colorado.

The single specimen before me represents a species rather closely allied to *molesta*, differing in its more slender form and in the much finer, sparser and transverse punctuation of the elytra, also very noticeably in its much larger pygidium, the types of both of these species being females.

20 **Onychobaris pectorosa** Lec.—Proc. Am. Phil. Soc., XV, p. 295.

Broadly ovate, black and polished throughout, sparsely sculptured, the setæ very minute and only just observable. The beak is strongly arcuate and thickened toward base, but nearly straight in apical half, equal in length to the prothorax and sparsely punctured. The prothorax is nearly one-half wider than long, the sides parallel and straight in basal half, then broadly, evenly rounded and convergent to the apex which is extremely feebly constricted at the sides; base transverse, the lobe equal to one-third the total width, rounded and prominent; disk rather finely, sparsely punctate, with a narrow subentire median line, the punctures scarcely one-fourth as wide as the scutellum, separated by nearly their own widths toward the middle, very dense at the sides but somewhat uneven in distribution throughout. The elytra are but slightly longer than wide, one-half longer and very little wider than the prothorax, the sides nearly straight and unusually strongly convergent, the apex rather narrowly rounded; disk with somewhat coarse, very deep grooves, the intervals alternating slightly in width, from two to three times as wide as the grooves, with rather small but deep, not very close-set punctures, somewhat confused on the wider, but larger and in single series on the narrower, intervals. The antennæ and prosternum are normal in structure. Length 3.8 mm.; width 1.95 mm.

Represented by the unique type in the cabinet of LeConte, taken by Belfrage in Texas, probably at Waco. It is not at all closely allied to any other described species.[1]

21 **Onychobaris diluta** n. sp.—Oval, moderately convex, black and strongly shining throughout, the antennæ piceo-rufous; sculpture not very dense. *Head* minutely, sparsely punctate toward apex, the transverse polished impression rather pronounced; beak slender, strongly arcuate toward base, very feebly so toward apex, distinctly longer than the prothorax and sparsely punctate; antennæ moderate, basal joint of the funicle nearly as long as the next four, second but slightly longer than the third, outer joints rapidly shorter, becoming strongly transverse and coarctate, club normal but rather large. *Prothorax* somewhat more than one-third wider than long, the sides parallel in basal two-thirds, then broadly rounded and convergent to the apex which is distinctly subtubulate; base straight and feebly, posteriorly oblique from the rather small but strongly rounded median lobe to the sides; disk with narrow median impunctate line in basal half, the punctures deep, rounded, rather small, not quite one-third as wide as the scutellum, very dense and contiguous toward the sides but becoming narrowly separated near

---

[1] Specimens possibly of this species are just received from St. Louis, Mo.

the middle. Scutellum moderate. *Elytra* slightly longer than wide, two-thirds longer than the prothorax, and, at the very feebly evident humeral tuberosities, barely perceptibly wider than the latter; outline behind the humeri hemi-elliptical; disk with rather coarse, very deep, abruptly defined grooves, the intervals flat and subequal, about twice as wide as the grooves, and each with a single series of small, rounded, not very close-set punctures which are about one-half as wide as the intervals; setæ very minute and scarcely observable. *Abdomen* densely punctured, especially toward the sides. Length 2.6 mm.; width 1.2 mm.

Texas.

This small species is not closely allied to any other which I have been able to study. The type is apparently a female and is unique.

22 **Onychobaris porcata** n. sp.—Oblong-suboval, rather convex, black throughout; integuments polished but deeply and closely sculptured; setæ very short and inconspicuous. *Head* finely, rather sparsely punctured throughout, separated from the beak by a transverse impunctate line, the impression almost obsolete; beak densely, strongly punctured, evenly, rather strongly arcuate, but very slightly longer than the prothorax, gradually but feebly tapering from base to apex; antennæ rather short, the second funicular joint but slightly longer than the third, the outer joints rapidly wider, the seventh as broad as the base of the club, the latter short, oval, not at all abrupt, densely pubescent, with the basal joint but slightly less than one-half the mass, and with a transverse polished fovea at base on the anterior side. *Prothorax* rather short, nearly one-half wider than long, the sides subparallel and feebly arcuate in basal three-fourths, then strongly rounded, thence strongly convergent and feebly sinuate to the apex; base transverse, the lobe one-third the total width, strong, rounded; disk extremely deeply, rather coarsely punctate, the punctures not quite in actual contact but very dense, about one-half as wide as the scutellum, rather uneven in distribution; median impunctate line narrow but distinct, not attaining the apex. Scutellum rather small, transverse. *Elytra* scarcely one-fifth longer than wide, about three-fourths longer than the prothorax, and, at the rather prominent humeri, very distinctly wider than the latter; sides distinctly convergent, the apex broadly parabolic; disk with abrupt, coarse but not deep grooves, roughly sculptured at the bottom, the intervals flat, alternately slightly wider than, and equal to, the grooves, the punctures coarse, deep, approximate or semi-confluent, forming single series taking up nearly the entire width of the narrow intervals, more confused on the broader ones. *Abdomen* rather sparsely punctured toward the middle, polished throughout. Anterior coxæ widely separated. *Legs* deeply punctured; last tarsal joint finely and rather densely pubescent throughout. Length 4.1 mm.; width 2.0 mm.

Arizona.

A single specimen which is apparently a female. This very distinct species is quite aberrant in antennal structure.

MADARELLUS n. gen.

A series of *Conoproctus quadripustulatus* Fab. (*quadriplagiatus*
Lac.), taken by Mr. H. H. Smith on the Amazon near Santarem,
shows clearly that Lacordaire's type of Conoproctus is the male.
In the female the form, sculpture and coloration throughout are
similar, but the beak is not so long, more arcuate and tapering, with
the antennæ shorter and inserted near the middle, the pygidium
being broadly rounded, oblique and perfectly normal.   These sexual
differences are extraordinary, but are evinced in an unmistakably
parallel and, as far as the beak is concerned, almost equally striking
manner in another Brazilian species, from the same collection and
not yet identified, but which, from its general habitus and simple
male pygidium, must be assigned to Madarus.   Finally, in *Madarus
biplagiatus*, which I also have before me, the same sexual differences
are observable but to a very slight degree, the antennæ being inserted near apical third in the male and just beyond the middle in
the somewhat shorter beak of the female; *quadripustulatus* is however the only species in which the pygidium is affected sexually.

It is quite evident, therefore, that *biplagiatus* and *quadripustulatus* must be placed in the same genus, and I would suggest that
these species be included under the name Conoproctus Lac., and
that the name Madarus Sch. be reserved for those species mentioned
by Lacordaire (Gen. Col., VII, p. 257), as forming a second section
of Madarus, and having as types *vorticosus* and *migrator*.   Both
Conoproctus and Madarus, as thus limited, have the femora unarmed, and I have here proposed the genus Madarellus, to include
those species having the prothorax short, broad, very abruptly
and strongly constricted at apex, and the femora armed beneath
with a minute spiculiform denticle.   It differs further from Conoproctus in having the posterior lobe of the prosternum broadly
emarginate or subtransverse, with the lateral angles acute and not
broadly rounded as in that genus, in having a post-apical prosternal
fovea with short parallel folds of the surface, and a small triangular
scutellum, truncate at base and not large, short and broadly lunate
as in Conoproctus.   The anterior coxæ, it should be added, are
much more remote and rather smaller than in the latter genus.

In Madarellus the beak is about one-half as long as the body in
the female, evenly, distinctly arcuate, slender, the impression separating it from the head being almost completely obsolete and the

epistomal lobe not at all advanced, very broad with the lateral fissures extremely small, the mandibles well developed, each with two deep notches at apex, feebly arcuate and not overlapping when closed but forming a small triangle. Antennæ normal, the first funicular joint as long as the next four, the second but slightly longer than the third, the club moderate, pubescent, scarcely longer than the four preceding joints combined and with the basal joint constituting less than one-half the mass.

The prosternum is very large, flat, thrown up in a transverse tumid ridge just behind the coxæ, in the position of the two transverse tubercles of Glyptobaris,[1] the ridge strongly declivous behind and produced over the mesosternum, terminating on a line drawn through the middle of the intermediate coxæ, the process very wide, acutely angulate at the sides and broadly sinuate between the angles. At a short distance behind the anterior margin there are two deep angulate more or less coalescent foveæ, each continued posteriorly for a short distance by a fine but distinct fold of the surface. Anterior coxæ small, very remote, separated by fully twice their own width. Legs moderate, the tarsi normal, with the third joint broad, bilobed; claws moderate, perfectly free, somewhat divergent. Scutellum small, triangular or ogival, not in the least emarginate at base.

That two genera, mutually so dissimilar in appearance as Madarellus and Glyptobaris, should in reality be so closely allied, is one of these interesting surprises continually offering themselves in these little-studied groups. I am quite unable to agree with LeConte in his statement that Ampeloglypter makes a gradual transition from Baris to Madarellus, for the latter is much more closely allied to Baris through Onychobaris than is Ampeloglypter, this genus forming one of the pseudobaride series; but, at the same time, the position assigned to Madarus by Lacordaire seems to be equally unnatural.

1 **Madarellus undulatus** Say—Journ. Ac. Nat. Sci., Phila., III, p. 315; Ed. Leo., II, p. 177 (Rhynchænus); *sanguinicollis* Dej. Cat. 3ed, p. 311.

This species is so well known, that a detailed description is needless at the present time. The form is subcuneate, rather wider at the middle of the prothorax than at any other part, the thoracic punctures extremely minute, feeble and sparse, but becoming rather closer, stronger and feebly rugulose or subasperate anteriorly, rugu-

[1] Compare also the South American genus Scambus Sch.

lose at the sides, and with an even series of small but deep punctures just before the basal margin not quite extending to the scutellum. The elytral striæ are in the form of narrow but deep abrupt grooves, minutely and distantly punctate at the bottom, the intervals flat, wide, each with a single series of excessively minute distant punctures, except the lateral three, where the punctures become distinct but feeble, not very dense, confused and transversely rugulose or subasperate. The lustre throughout is highly polished, and the color black, the prothorax being often entirely red, but I do not notice that this character is at all geographical in origin as stated by LeConte (Proc. Am. Phil. Soc., XV, p. 301), a good series before me from Indiana being composed of both color modifications in equal numbers. It varies greatly in size. Length 2.7–4.7 mm ; width 1.3–2.2 mm.

Entire Atlantic region, extending westward to Kansas and Texas. The anterior femora are armed beneath with a small tooth, which is rendered more prominent by reason of a deep and abrupt subapical emargination immediately beyond it. The intermediate and posterior femora are not distinctly denticulate in *undulatus*, but in an entirely similar, but shorter and broader species before me, from Santarem, Brazil, all the femora are distinctly spiculate beneath.

The pygidium in this genus is distinctly oblique in the male but vertical in the female, which corresponds somewhat with the pygidial differences of the male and female in *Conoproctus quadripustulatus.*

AULOBARIS.

LeConte—Proc. Am. Phil. Soc., XV, p. 288.

This genus is one of the most distinct of the tribe, and is remarkably homogeneous in the general aspect of its species, which are unusually convex, polished and, with the exception of *dux*, almost evenly ellipsoidal in form.

Aulobaris differs from all of our other genera of pygidiate Barini, in having the second funicular joint elongate and fully as long as the next two combined. In its free and divergent tarsal claws it resembles Baris, but in spite of this there is a certain assemblage of characters which suggests a rather closer relationship with Pseudobaris. In fact *Aulobaris pusilla* was originally described as a Pseudobaris, and *Pseudobaris anthracina* (Lec. nec Boh.) as an Aulobaris, showing how closely they approach each other in external

facies. But in addition to this they are allied in the deep sulcus
of the prosternum common to both; it is however rather less abruptly defined at the edges in the present genus, and besides differs
radically in serving as a partial shelter for the beak in repose.

In *A. naso* the sulcus is broadly sinuate at the sides, the latter
projecting inward just before the coxæ, touching the middle of the
beak when the latter is folded in against the body. These projec-
tions of the sides before the coxæ, although not very prominent,
are extremely interesting as being the nearest approach to similar
modifications of the sides of the rostral sulcus observable in many
cryptorhynchs. Aulobaris in fact possesses several suggestive
cryptorhynchine characteristics. It is interesting in this connection to call attention to the close general similarity of certain
barides, as Eisonyx and Aulobaris, to such cryptorhynchs as Bar-
opsis and Tyloderma.

The remaining characters of Aulobaris are not of especially decisive value, but it should be mentioned that the third tarsal joint is
unusually wide and deeply bilobed, and that the prosternum is prolonged behind slightly over the mesosternum, the process being wide
flat and broadly arcuate at apex. In Madarellus it is still further
prolonged upon the mesosternum and is broadly sinuate or subtruncate throughout its width. In all of our species there is a small
cluster of squamules at the base of the third elytral interval, as in
many species of Pseudobaris.

In *A. scolopax* the sexual characters are very pronounced, the
abdomen in the female being strongly conical and upwardly ascending toward apex, with the pygidium small. In the male it is nearly
horizontal, with the pygidium much larger. These pygidial differences are of the same general order as in Baris. In the female of
scolopax the prothorax is much shorter than in the male, as in
Centrinus scutellum-album.

The species are not numerous and may be separated as follows :—

Prothorax feebly transverse and much narrower than the elytra, moderately
    convex, with the basal lobe rather prominent.
  Prosternal sulcus sinuate at the sides and produced inwardly near the
    coxæ ; elytral punctures coarse, deep and rounded...................1 **naso**
  Prosternal sulcus straight at the sides, without the ante-coxal projection ;
    elytral punctures small, feebly impressed and slightly transverse.
    Piceous-black to pale rufo-piceous in color.
      Smaller and darker species...2 **pusilla**
      Larger species, paler in color...............................3 **scolopax**

Intense black, highly polished, the legs black or rufescent; body rather
more robust, the prothorax more strongly constricted at the apex.

4 ibis

Prothorax strongly transverse and rather wider than the elytra, very strongly
convex toward base, the basal lobe small and feeble; elytral punctures
coarse...5 **dux**

1 **Aulobaris naso** Lec.—Proc. Am. Phil. Soc., XV, p. 299.

Ellipsoidal, strongly convex, polished and piceous-black throughout, the setæ very minute on the upper surface, with a few squamules at the base of the third interval, each puncture of the under
surface bearing an elongate recumbent strigose scale. Head finely
but distinctly punctate, the transverse impression feeble and finely
subfoveolate in the middle; beak rather slender, strongly, evenly
arcuate and as long as the head and prothorax, the antnueæ slender,
first funicular joint long, the second more than twice as long as wide,
two-thirds as long as the first and equal to the next two, third a
little longer than wide, outer joints but slightly wider, club oval,
densely pubescent, equal in length to the preceding five joiuts combined, the basal joint constituting much less than one-half the mass.
Prothorax conical, strongly convex, one-third wider than long, with
the sides broadly and evenly arcuate and only very feebly constricted
near the apex, which is transversely truncate and not quite one-half
as wide as the base; punctures small but deep and distinctly separated. Scutellum moderate, transverse. The elytra are slightly
longer than wide, two-thirds longer and scarcely perceptibly wider
than the prothorax, hemi-elliptical in outline, the humeral tuberosities very feeble, the striæ rather coarse and deep, with the intervals
about twice as wide as the grooves, and each with a single series
of large deep rounded and somewhat close-set punctures. Length
2.8–3.3 mm.; width 1.3–1.6 mm.

The four specimens in my cabinet are from Kansas and Iowa, and
the reference of certain Californian specimens to this species by Dr.
LeConte is apparently incorrect, these being identical with *pusilla*.

The reference to *nasutus* (l. c. ante) is somewhat confusing. Le-
Conte refers to Say's Curc., Ed. Lec., I, p 295, but this reference
was probably intended to be Proc. Ac. Nat. Sci., Phila., 1868, p.
364, where the author has described this species under that name,
forgetting that he had already described a *Centrinus nasutus*. As
Centrinus and Aulobaris are widely different genera, there was no
necessity for the change of name, but since they are both proposed

by the same author, and as *naso* is the name adopted in the most extensive monograph of our Rhynchophora, it is preferable to continue it.

The prosternal groove is very large deep and abrupt, serving as a partial shelter for the beak, which, in repose, is placed in the groove with its apex extending far beyond it and resting on the flat surface of the mesosternum. The strong arcuation of the beak prevents it from touching the bottom of the groove however, and, at the sides, it is in contact only just before the coxæ, where there is an internal horizontal projection, not distinctly observable in any other species.

2 Aulobaris pusilla Lec.—Proc. Ac. Nat. Sci., Phila., 1868, p. 363 (Baridius); Proc. Am. Phil. Soc., XV, p. 298 (Pseudobaris).

Almost exactly similar throughout to *naso*, but rather shorter, relatively stouter, and with the interstitial punctures smaller, much feebler, close-set and subtransverse. The second funicular joint is fully three-fourths as long as the first and as long as the next two, the club small and not longer than the four preceding joints together. The prosternal sulcus is as wide and deep as in *naso*, but the sides are straight and not broadly sinuate, there being no visible trace of the internal projection just before the coxæ referred to under that species. Length 2.5–3.0 mm.; width 1.1–1.4 mm.

I have seen specimens from New York, District of Columbia, North Carolina and one labeled "California." Dr. LeConte evidently limited his attention to the prosternal sulcus only, in placing this species in Pseudobaris.

3 Aulobaris scolopax Say—Curc. 26, Ed. Lec., I, p. 295 (Baridius).

Similar in form, and in antennal and prosternal structure to *pusilla*, but distinctly larger, pale red-brown in color, the elytral striæ finer, the intervals wider, the punctures broadly confused on the second and third but forming single lines on the others, small, feeble, moderately close-set and slightly transverse. The punctuation of the pronotum varies greatly, being sometimes decidedly coarse and at others quite fine; the punctures also vary in density, although usually distinctly separated, and there is a narrow incomplete impunctate line, which occasionally entirely disappears, as remarked by LeConte. This latter fact is however characteristic of the entire tribe, when the impunctate line is not especially broad and decided or cariniform. Length 3.3–3.7 mm.; width 1.65–1.8 mm.

Indiana, Kentucky and Wisconsin. Moderately abundant.

4 **Aulobaris ibis** Lec.—Proc. Ac. Nat. Sci., Phila., 1868, p. 365 (Baridius).

Nearly similar to the preceding species in form but more robust, polished and intense black with the legs black or rufescent and with the sculpture rather sparser. The antennæ are slender, the second funicular joint much more than twice as long as wide, three-fourths as long as the first and rather longer than the next two, the latter equal and quadrate; club very small, oval, abrupt, subequal in length to the three preceding joints combined. Prothorax two-fifths wider than long, the punctures variable in size as in *scolopax*. Elytral intervals each with a single uneven series of small very feeble moderately distant and subtransverse punctures. Prosternal sulcus wide, very deep, straight and moderately abrupt. Length 3.0–3.6 mm.; width 1.5–1.8 mm.

Georgia—LeConte; Florida (Enterprise) in abundance — Mr. Schwarz. One specimen is labeled "Massachusetts" but this is possibly an error.

5 **Aulobaris dux** n. sp.—Rather robust and subcuneiform, very strongly convex, polished throughout, black with a piceous tinge, the legs dark rufous; setæ small, slender, sparse and inconspicuous above, but robust, squamiform, yellowish-white, abundant and distinct beneath, the elytra with small squamulose spots at the base of the alternate intervals, more noticeable on the third. *Head* minutely, sparsely punctured, the impression broad and feeble in profile; beak rather slender, finely, strongly but not very densely punctate, evenly and rather feebly arcuate, thickened toward base, a little longer than the head and prothorax; antennæ slender, the second funicular joint fully three-fourths as long as the first and as long as the next two, the latter both slightly longer than wide, seventh rather transverse, club not much longer than the three preceding joints combined. *Prothorax* large, nearly one-half wider than long, strongly rounded at the sides near the base, then rapidly narrowed to the apex, the sides strongly convergent and feebly arcuate in apical two-thirds, subapical constriction very feeble, apex about one-half as wide as the base, the latter transverse, the lobe very feeble; disk strongly convex, almost tumid toward base viewed laterally, finely but deeply punctate, the punctures sparse, separated by nearly twice their own widths, with a narrow impunctate area near the centre. Scutellum quite large, transverse, broadly rounded behind, rugosely punctured. *Elytra* not quite as wide as the prothorax and three-fourths longer than the latter, the sides nearly straight and rather strongly convergent from the base, the apex not very broadly rounded; humeri feebly tumid, not at all prominent; disk deeply, strongly striate, the intervals about twice as wide as the grooves, each with a series of coarse, deep, transversely oval, moderately close-set punctures, which are more or less uneven or confused on the third and fifth, especially in the female. *Abdomen* strongly

rather closely punctured. Prosternum with a very deep parallel-sided sulcus, as wide as the beak, the coxæ separated by about their own width. Length 3.9–4.2 mm. ; width 1.8–2.0 mm.

Nebraska.

This is the largest species of the genus which I have seen, and differs greatly from the others in its distinctly subcuneate form, with the prothorax wider toward base and much more swollen throughout the width.

AMPELOGLYPTER.
LeConte—Proc. Am. Phil. Soc., XV, p. 299.

A distinct genus, evidently composite in its characters and forming one of the transitions from Madarellus to Pseudobaris, but, in spite of the polished glabrous integuments and finely striate, impressed and subimpunctate elytra, which give it an external resemblance to the former, it is in realty much more closely allied to the latter of these genera.

The prosternal modification is peculiar to this genus, although feebly suggested in some other forms such as Glyptobaris.   In *sesostris* it is widely and rather feebly impressed, the impression becoming flat and obsolete between the coxæ, subimpunctate throughout, widening slightly anteriorly, and ending near the apical margin, at the transverse prothoracic constriction. At its anterior limit it is deepest, and is bounded by an abrupt declivous wall which is transverse and nearly straight; the sides of the excavation are also abrupt for a short distance behind the apex. In *longipennis* it is rather wider and more feeble, but deep and abruptly limited at each apical angle. It is easy to perceive here an extreme development of the two deep foveæ and connecting groove mentioned under Onychobaris and its allies, only here the two angles of the impression, which represent the foveæ, are relatively much more widely separated.

The anterior coxæ are small, rather distant and separated by more than their own width. The beak and antennæ present no noticeable peculiarities, being nearly as in Pseudobaris. The claws are moderately long, closely connate in basal third, subparallel and gradually, feebly everted toward tip as in the pseudobarides generally, and differing radically from the normally free and divergent form seen in Madarellus.

Our three species may be readily distinguished as follows :—

Prothorax parallel at the sides in basal two-thirds, the beak shorter, strongly
arcuate ; second funicular joint quadrate ; elytra not more than twice as
long as the prothorax ; color intense black throughout, the antennæ and
tarsi rufous ....1 **ater**
Prothorax convergent at the sides from the basal angles ; beak longer and
less stout ; antennæ more slender, the second funicular joint distinctly
longer than wide.
  Intense black throughout the body and antennæ, the tarsi rufous ; prothorax short, the apex not much more than one-half as wide as the base ;
  elytra nearly two and one-half times as long as the prothorax.

2 longipennis

  Pale rufo-testaceous throughout ; prothorax less transverse, the apex much
  more than one-half as wide as the base ; elytra about twice as long as the
  prothorax ; size somewhat smaller ....3 **sesostris**

   1 **Ampeloglypter ater** Lec.—Proc. Am. Phil. Soc., XV, p. 300;
ampelopsis (Madarus), Walsh and Riley, i. litt.

Oblong, moderately convex, highly polished and black throughout, the antennæ and tarsi rufous. Head minutely, sparsely punctate, convex, separated from the beak by a distinct transverse
impression ; beak rugulose, very robust, strongly, evenly arcuate,
slightly longer than the prothorax in the male; antennæ stout, first
funicular joint robust, fully as long as the next three, second exactly
quadrate, three to seven much shorter and all strongly transverse,
increasing gradually in width, club robust, densely pubescent, the
basal joint constituting much less than one-half the mass. Prothorax two-fifths wider than long, the sides straight and subparallel in
basal two-thirds, then very abruptly and strongly rounded, almost
rectangular, thence subtransversely convergent for a considerable
distance to the apical tubulation, which is strong, constituting one-
fourth of the total length ; disk with a rather wide and subentire
impunctate line, the punctures very distinct, deep, sparse, with large
impunctate areas laterally, rugulose at the sides. The elytra are
about one-fourth longer than wide, twice as long as the prothorax
and a little wider than the latter at the somewhat prominent humeri ;
striæ very fine but deep and abrupt ; intervals flat, very wide and
almost impunctate, the punctures of the single series being remote,
very feeble and scarcely visible. Abdomen extremely densely punctate toward the sides. Length 2.8 mm.; width 1.3 mm.
   Easily distinguishable by the rather broad form, with short parallel-sided prothorax and somewhat thicker beak. Eastern States.

2 **Ampeloglypter longipennis** n. sp.—Sub-oval, moderately convex, very highly polished; body and antennæ throughout intense black; tarsi rufous; setæ very minute. *Head* opaque; beak shining, rugulosely punctate at the sides, rather slender, moderately arcuate and fully one-half longer than the prothorax in the female, distinctly shorter, more arcuate and a little stouter in the male; antennæ nearly as in *sesostris*. *Prothorax* short, nearly two-thirds wider than long, the sides strongly convergent and nearly straight to apical third, then broadly rounded and more convergent to the broad and subtubulate apex, the latter not more than one-half as wide as the base; disk with scarcely a trace of impunctate line, the punctures very fine, sparse and irregularly distributed, forming longitudinal rugæ at the sides. Scutellum very small, rounded. *Elytra* two-fifths longer than wide, nearly two and one-half times as long as the prothorax, and, at base, a little wider than the latter; humeri longitudinally tumid and somewhat prominent; sides behind them feebly convergent and nearly straight, the apex abruptly rounded; disk with extremely fine but deep abrupt grooves and wide flat subimpunctate intervals as in *ater*, the grooves finely, remotely punctate at the bottom. Under surface and abdomen toward the sides very densely punctate but not very dull in lustre. Length 3.0–3.3 mm.; width 1.3–1.6 mm.

Pennsylvania; Maryland; Nebraska.

This species is allied to *sesostris*, having an entirely similar structure of the prothorax, beak and antennæ, but is larger, still more highly polished especially toward the sides of the upper surface, intense black in color and with relatively longer elytra, the prothorax, also, is shorter and broader, with the sides more rapidly convergent from the base, and the tubulate apical portion is shorter, less abrupt and much narrower when compared with the basal width. The pronotum is more finely punctate and devoid of impunctate line, but occasionally has a small impressed fovea at the centre of the disk. The two specimens from Maryland have the elytra dark castaneous but do not otherwise differ. Sixteen examples. *Longipennis* is generally confounded in cabinets with *ater*.

3 **Ampeloglypter sesostris** Lec.—Proc. Ac. Nat. Sci., Phila., 1868, p. 364 (Baridius); *vitis* Riley: 1st Missouri Report, p. 131 (Madarus).

Rather narrowly oval, moderately convex, polished, pale redbrown throughout, the setæ extremely minute. Head dull, obsoletely punctulate; beak shining, rather slender and one-half longer than the prothorax in the female, feebly arcuate, abruptly more strongly so at base, the transverse impression rather strong; antennæ inserted just behind the middle, the funicle rather slender, the second joint much longer than wide and fully one-half longer than the third, three to seven equal in length, gradually wider, the

club oval, pointed, densely pubescent and as long as the preceding
five joints, with its basal joint constituting two-fifths of the mass.
The prothorax is feebly narrowed and straight at the sides to apical
third, then broadly rounded, more convergent and deeply sinuate to
the apex, the latter subtubulate and three-fifths as wide as the base;
disk finely but rather sparsely, distinctly and unevenly punctate,
with a subentire impunctate line. Elytra one-fourth longer than
wide, a little wider than the prothorax and not distinctly more than
twice as long as the latter, striate and subimpunctate as in *ater*.
Under surface, except along the middle of the abdomen, and also
the legs throughout deeply, densely punctate and opaque. Length
2.7 mm.; width 1.2 mm.

The two specimens in my cabinet are from Illinois, and are not
as large as the type measured by LeConte (3.0 mm.).

DESMOGLYPTUS n. gen.

This genus is closely allied to Pseudobaris and has the prosternum
deeply and abruptly sulcate throughout its length, the anterior coxæ
being somewhat remote and separated by fully their own width.
The beak, antennæ, tarsal claws and scutellum are also nearly as
in Pseudobaris, but the other characters are so different that the
unique species cannot be appropriately associated with the members of that genus.

The general appearance and elytral sculpture are essentially unlike anything else in the present tribe which I have been able to
study, but it is possible that the *Baridius cribratus* of Boheman
may be somewhat similar, or perhaps even congeneric. The form
of the body reminds us strongly of Copturus, and the opaque surface, deep impressed and strongly crenulate striæ, with narrow and
convex intervals, together with the unusually prominent subapical
umbones, are a combination of characters apparently isolating the
genus widely from its allies. It should be stated, however, that
the peculiar outline is feebly suggested in *Pseudobaris angusta.*

Desmoglyptus differs from Pseudobaris radically, also, in the formation of the pygidium and elytral apices, the latter being deeply
and vertically truncate or deflexed, covering a large part of the
pygidium, which is small, vertical and flat. In Pseudobaris the
pygidium is large, convex and prominent, the elytra being normal
at apex and leaving it completely exposed. In Desmoglyptus the
third tarsal joint is abruptly very large, but not quite as wide as

long, the emargination being unusually deep; the basal node of the fourth joint is distinct and a little longer than wide.

The single species is described below; it has comparatively little affinity with Ampeloglypter, where it was provisionally placed by LeConte.

1 **Desmoglyptus crenatus** Lec.—Proc. Am. Phil. Soc., XV, p. 300 (Ampeloglypter).

Very narrow, subcylindrical, pale red-brown throughout and densely opaque, the setæ not distinct. Head rather convex, minutely, obsoletely punctate, the beak equal in length to the prothorax in the male, robust, strongly, evenly arcuate, feebly flattened toward apex, obsoletely punctate, the antennæ inserted well beyond the middle, normal in structure, the first funicular joint as long as the next three, two to seven equal in length, the outer gradually slightly wider, the club oval, about as long as the preceding five joints together, pubescent, with the basal joint constituting much less than one-half the mass. Prothorax nearly as long as wide, the apex broadly subtubulate, the sides parallel and straight in basal two-thirds; apical margin feebly arcuate and three-fourths as wide as the base; disk without impunctate line, the punctures rather coarse, deep and dense. Scutellum small, rounded. Elytra three-fourths longer than wide, a little wider than the prothorax and about twice as long as the latter, the humeri slightly prominent; sides parallel in basal three-fifths, broadly sinuate behind the humeri, the apex narrowly subtruncate; disk of each strongly umbonate or callous in the middle near apical fourth, the striæ coarse deep and impressed, remotely but strongly crenate, the intervals narrow, convex, each with a single series of remote minute and excessively feeble punctures, which are scarcely at all observable under moderate power. Abdomen not densely punctate, with a very large broad and deep basal impression in the male; in this sex the thickened posterior edge of the fifth segment is deeply, transversely excavated opposite the apex of the pygidium, and from the bottom of this excavation there projects a small, short and transverse polished tubercle. Length 2.7–3.0 mm.; width 1.0 mm.

The two specimens before me are males and one of them is labeled "Arizona." LeConte gives Virginia and Maryland as the habitat of his types.

PSEUDOBARIS.

LeConte—Proc. Am. Phil. Soc., XV, p. 297.

In geographical distribution this distinct genus coincides with Baris and is well represented in Brazil. The species within our territories are much less numerous than those of Baris, and are usually of a narrower and more cylindrically convex form. Some, however, are robust, but are then more oval and ellipsoidal and less oblong than in the genus referred to. The generic characters have been given in the table and need not be repeated at the present time.

One of the most striking peculiarities of the genus is the deep, abrupt, parallel-sided and subimpunctate prosternal sulcus. The fact that the sulcus should be so well developed and abruptly defined at the sides in most of the species, when it can fulfill no function as a shelter for the beak, because of the robust form and much greater lateral dimensions of the latter, might be regarded as a proof that the Barini are simply cryptorhynchs which have become modified through changed habits or some other altered environment, and, that under their influence, the beak and mesosternal epimera have become modified with comparative rapidity. The prosternal sulcus, being a long established and extremely permanent structure, would survive in an essentially unaltered state for a long period after all need of it had disappeared.

The species known to me may be distinguished by the following characters:—

Elytral vestiture uniform, generally short and sparse.
  Elytra with a small condensed pubescent spot at the base of the third interval.
    Pronotal punctures sparse, the impunctate line obsolete.
      Large species, robust, piceo-testaceous in color ....1 **farcta**
      Moderate in size, rather robust, black throughout, polished, without trace of æneous lustre, the pronotal punctures and elytral striæ coarse and deep; intervals not carinate toward apex...2 **luctuosa**
    Pronotal punctures much closer.
      Body elongate-oval, rather alutaceous in lustre, median impunctate line of the pronotum narrow and distinct but not quite entire.

3 discreta

      Body broadly oblong-oval, highly polished, the median line obsolete.

4 fausta

  Elytra without basal condensed spot on the third interval.
    Form more broadly oval; interstitial punctures large, deep, rounded and conspicuous, especially toward base.

Larger species, very broadly oval and subdepressed, dull in lustre ;
elytral grooves coarse, the setæ very minute...........5 **pectoralis**
Smaller, more elongate-oval, highly polished, the elytral striæ much
less coarse, the setæ longer, semi-erect and quite conspicuous.
6 **lugubris**
Form slender, cylindrical, the interstitial punctures small, feeble, remote
and transversely subrugulose................................7 **angusta**
Elytral vestiture consisting of very small inconspicuous setæ and long white
widely dispersed squamules.
Larger species, with the pronotal punctures moderate in size, very dense
and with a more or less distinct and abruptly defined median impunctate
line ....8 **nigrina**
Small species, with the pronotal punctures coarse and slightly separated,
without trace of median impunctate line ....9 **cælata**

The Mexican *acutipennis* of Say also belongs to this genus, and
has the elytral intervals prominent and subcarinate on the posterior
declivity, as in several other species of the Central American regions.

1 **Pseudobaris farcta** Lec.—Proc. Ac. Nat. Sci. Phila., 1868, p. 362
(Baridius) ; Proc. Am. Phil. Soc., XV, p. 297.

A conspicuous species, the largest of the genus, of a broadly
evenly oval, very convex form, dark piceo-rufous color and polished
integuments. The beak is evenly but rather feebly arcuate, robust,
becoming rapidly thin and flattened near the apex, slightly shorter
in the male than in the female, and, in both sexes, distinctly shorter
than the prothorax ; the antennæ are normal, with the second funicular joint one-half longer than the third. The prothorax is nearly
one-half wider than long, the sides convergent and broadly arcuate
from base to apex, broadly and distinctly constricted near the latter,
the constriction being evident and more densely, rugosely punctate
almost entirely across the dorsal surface ; base transverse, the median
lobe small but very prominent ; the disk is coarsely but not very
densely punctate, without impunctate line. Elytra quite distinctly
wider, and fully three-fourths longer than the prothorax, hemi-
elliptical, the disk with rather coarse deep and abrupt grooves, the
intervals flat, scarcely twice as wide as the grooves, the second and
third much wider, the punctures rather large, moderately deep, not
very close-set and distinctly transverse, forming single series on
each, but sparsely confused on the second and third. The anterior
coxæ are separated by their own width, the prosternum before them
narrowly deeply and abruptly sulcate. Length 4.7–5.0 mm.; width
2.4–2.6 mm.

Texas, three specimens; Kansas and Colorado—LeConte.

2 **Pseudobaris luctuosa** n. sp.—Rather broadly, almost evenly oval, strongly convex, intense black and highly polished throughout. *Head* minutely, sparsely punctate, the transverse impression rather strong; beak densely punctate only on the sides behind the antennæ, somewhat tumid above at base, strongly, evenly arcuate, slender and nearly one-third longer than the prothorax in the female, rather thicker and but very slightly longer than the latter in the male; antennæ moderate, the second funicular joint unusually long and subequal to the next two together. *Prothorax* short, nearly one-half wider than long, the sides broadly arcuate and convergent anteriorly, gradually becoming parallel toward base, the apex broad, truncate, tubularly but very briefly produced; base transverse and straight laterally, the median lobe one-third the total width, rounded and decidedly prominent; disk strongly convex, coarsely, very deeply and rather sparsely punctate, the punctures fully one-half as wide as the scutellum and separated by their own widths or more. Scutellum small, transverse, impressed. *Elytra* twice as long as the prothorax, and, at the feebly tumid humeri, scarcely perceptibly wider than the latter; outline hemi-elliptical; disk with coarse, very deep, not distinctly punctate grooves, the intervals subequal, about one-third wider than the grooves, each with a single series of shallow, rather remote and transversely subrugulose punctures; setæ not at all visible except a small spot of white squamules at the base of the third interval. Under surface somewhat sparsely punctured. Length 3.5–3.7 mm.; width 1.7–1.8 mm.

Florida (Cedar Keys).

This species is named *anthracina* Boh. in many cabinets, and was placed in Aulobaris by LeConte (Proc. Am. Phil. Soc., XV, p. 289), but is evidently not the species described under that name in the work of Schönherr. The phrases "thorax postice longitudine fere latior," for a strongly transverse prothorax, and "[thorax] supra fere planus . . . evidenter crebre . . . punctatus," for a strongly convex, coarsely and sparsely punctate modification of this part, and "elytra . . . thoracis . . . dimidio longiora," for fully twice as long, will not at all answer for this insect. As no allusion to a pygidium is made in the original description, it is possible that *Baridius anthracinus* Boh. may be a species of the genus Limnobaris, but we shall probably never know definitely until the type can be consulted.

3 **Pseudobaris discreta** n. sp.—Elongate-oval, strongly convex, black throughout and rather shining, the prothorax duller and alutaceous; setæ small, subrecumbent sparse but quite visible, not intermixed with longer squamules but larger and coarser and forming a more or less distinct spot at the base of the third and fifth intervals. *Head* and base of the beak opaque and densely granulato-reticulate, the former minutely and obsoletely punctate,

the latter abruptly coarsely, densely so near the base and at the sides, elsewhere shining and almost impunctate, the transverse impression feeble and not at all shining; beak slender, rather feebly but evenly arcuate, somewhat abruptly thicker very near the base in the densely punctured part, distinctly longer than the prothorax; antennæ slender, the second funicular joint nearly twice as long as wide and one-half longer than the third, the latter a little longer than wide. *Prothorax* barely one-fifth wider than long, the sides subparallel in basal two-thirds, then strongly rounded and convergent to the apex, the later strongly constricted and subtubulate; base transverse, the median lobe very small but prominent, scarcely rounded and rather cuspiform; disk with narrow ill-defined non-entire impunctate line, the punctures deep, one-third as wide as the scutellum, dense but narrowly separated. *Elytra* two-fifths longer than wide, fully twice as long as the prothorax and a little wider than the latter, the humeri slightly prominent, the sides very feebly convergent; apex somewhat abruptly and obtusely rounded; disk with moderately fine deep striæ, the intervals subequal, flat, about twice as wide as the grooves, each with a more or less uneven single series of moderately large but shallow, subtransverse, somewhat close-set punctures. *Abdomen* rather closely punctured. Prosternum abruptly, deeply sulcate, the sulcus extending deeply nearly to the posterior limits of the coxæ, the latter separated by about their own width. Length 4.0 mm.; width 1.7 mm.

Texas.

A distinct species somewhat resembling *angusta* in form. The tarsal claws are unusually long. A single specimen.

4 Pseudobaris fausta n. sp.—Oblong-oval, convex, black and highly polished throughout, the setæ small, very sparse, not conspicuous, the elytra without dispersed squamules but with a small feebly condensed spot at the base of the third interval. *Head* minutely, sparsely but rather deeply punctulate, the impression feeble; beak rather stout, evenly, moderately arcuate, feebly tapering, deeply, densely punctate and about as long as the prothorax; antennæ inserted at the middle, the basal joint of the funicle not quite as long as the next three, the second obconical, one-half longer than wide, club rather large, abrupt, densely pubescent, with the basal joint constituting one-third of the mass. *Prothorax* nearly one-half wider than long, the sides nearly straight and parallel to slightly beyond the middle, then broadly rounded and convergent, the subapical constriction very broad and feeble; base transverse, the median lobe moderate in width, very prominent and rounded; disk rather coarsely, very deeply, moderately closely punctate, without impunctate line, the punctures rather uneven in distribution, fully one-third as wide as the scutellum and generally separated by about one-half of their own diameters. Scutellum strongly transverse, lunate. *Elytra* distinctly wider than the prothorax and not quite twice as long, the humeri moderately prominent; sides distinctly convergent, nearly straight, the apex broadly rounded; disk deeply, not very coarsely striate, the intervals twice as wide as the grooves, each with a single series of very coarse, transversely oval, moderately distant punctures, the second and third wider and with the punctures smaller, very sparse but more confused. *Abdomen* deeply but not densely or coarsely punctate. Prosternum with a wide, rather shallow, unusually feebly defined sulcus, the bottom of which is coarsely, closely punctate, the coxæ moderate in size and separated by much more than their own width. Length 3.65 mm.; width 1.75 mm.

Arizona.

Lugubris is the only species with which the present can be compared, but there are many radical points of difference. In *fausta* the form of the body is much broader, and the punctuation throughout very much coarser, with but the feeblest trace of a narrow and partial impunctate line on the pronotum. The prosternal groove is rather narrow, much deeper and more sharply defined in *lugubris*, and, in the latter, there is no condensed spot at the base of the third interval.

5 **Pseudobaris pectoralis** Lec.—Proc. Am. Phil. Soc., XV, p. 420.

Rather broadly oval and quite distinctly depressed, black throughout, dull and strongly alutaceous, the setæ not distinctly visible under moderate power. The beak is slender, moderately and evenly arcuate, fully as long as the prothorax in the male, and a little longer in the female, not rapidly flattened toward apex and separated from the head by a rather deep but broad impression; antennæ moderate, the second funicular joint quadrate and but very slightly longer than the third. Prothorax rather short, nearly one-half wider than long, the sides strongly convergent from base to apex and broadly, distinctly arcuate, sometimes feebly prominent near apical third and feebly constricted subapically, the disk with a narrow ill-defined impunctate line, the punctures coarse, deep, not very dense and unevenly distributed. Elytra a little wider than the prothorax, fully twice as long, a little longer than wide and hemi-elliptical behind the humeri, the disk coarsely, deeply grooved, the intervals flat, subequal throughout and about one-half wider than the grooves, the punctures somewhat coarse, deep, close and more or less confused, larger and generally forming a more even single series on the fourth and occasionally, also, on the second and sixth intervals. The prosternum is deeply and abruptly sulcate, the sulcus becoming shallow and coarsely punctate between the coxæ which are separated by about their own width. Length 4.3 mm.; width 2.1–2.2 mm.

Florida. A distinct and rather large species. I have before me a single pair, agreeing in every detail with the original type.

6 **Pseudobaris lugubris** n. sp.—Oval, moderately robust, strongly convex, black throughout and polished, the setæ short, sparse but distinct, not condensed at the base of the third interval and without longer scattered squamules. *Head* finely, distinctly, the beak rather coarsely, punctured, more densely in the male, strongly arcuate and quite distinctly longer than the prothorax in both sexes, the antennæ moderate, with the second funicular joint distinctly longer than the third. *Prothorax* nearly one-third wider than long, the sides subparallel or very feebly convergent and nearly straight to apical third, then strongly rounded and convergent to the apex, the latter broad, truncate, three-fifths as wide as the base and briefly tubulate; base transverse, the median lobe small but prominent, broadly rounded at apex; disk with a narrow ill-defined impunctate line which does not attain the apex, the punctures rather fine, scarcely one-fourth as wide as the scutellum and dense, somewhat unevenly distributed and very narrowly separated. *Elytra* hemi-elliptical, distinctly longer than wide, not quite twice as long as the prothorax and a little wider than the latter; disk with moderately fine but very deep abrupt grooves, the intervals flat, subequal, about twice as wide as the grooves, each with a single series of somewhat small, shallow, moderately remote punctures. Prosternum deeply, abruptly sulcate, the coxæ rather small and separated by a little more than their own width. Length 3.0–3.3 mm.; width 1.3–1.6 mm.

New Mexico (Albuquerque).

A rather small species, resembling *nigrina* in outline, but with smaller, feebler interstitial punctures and devoid of scattered squamules; from *angusta* it is at once distinguishable by its much more broadly oval form. The smallest and narrowest specimen before me is a female, the largest a male. Four specimens.

I have united with this species a still smaller specimen from Texas, which differs in its slightly coarser and very dense pronotal punctures and scarcely larger but much deeper interstitial punctures; it possibly represents a distinct species.

7 **Pseudobaris angusta** Lec.—Proc. Ac. Nat. Sci., Phila., 1868, p. 363 (Baridius); Proc. Am. Phil. Soc., XV, p. 298; *P. angustula* Lec., ibid. p. 420.

Oval, subcylindrically convex, rather polished, deep black throughout. The beak is slender, evenly, rather strongly arcuate and equal in thickness from base to apex, just visibly longer than the prothorax in the male, but nearly one-third longer than that part in the female, the antennæ normal, with the second funicular joint about one-half longer than the third. Prothorax very nearly as long as wide, broadly constricted near the apex, the sides nearly parallel in basal two-thirds, the disk rather coarsely, densely punctate, the punctures two-fifths as wide as the scutellum and separated by less than one-half of their own diameters, the median impunctate line obsolete. Scutellum small, transverse, impressed in the middle. Elytra quite distinctly wider than the prothorax and about twice as long, cylindrical and parallel in basal two-thirds, then semi-circularly rounded behind; disk with rather fine, very deep grooves, the intervals flat, equal, twice as wide as the grooves, each with a single series of small, feeble, distant and transverse punctures. The impression of the abdomen in the male is rather narrow and excessively feeble. Length 2.6–3.3 mm.; width 1.0–1.3 mm.

Iowa and Kansas, five specimens. The setæ of the elytra are small, sparse, inconspicuous and unmixed with long dispersed squamules, and by this means, as well as its more slender form, *angusta* can be separated at once from *nigrina*.

The change of name proposed by Dr. LeConte is unnecessary, as Pseudobaris is a genus so widely separated from Baris, that there cannot be a plausible possibility of its suppression.

8 **Pseudobaris nigrina** Say—Curc., p. 31; Ed. Lec., I, p. 295 (Baridius).

A very common and widely distributed species, occurring over the entire extent of the United States. It is moderately robust, oval, strongly convex, black and polished throughout, the beak strongly, evenly arcuate, slender and about one-third longer than the prothorax in the female, but stouter and only equal to the latter in the male. The prothorax is fully two-fifths wider than long, the sides broadly arcuate and convergent anteriorly, gradually becoming parallel in basal half, the apex feebly constricted at the sides; base transverse, with a very small but prominent median lobe, the disk very deeply and densely punctured, with a narrow, more or less incomplete impunctate line, the punctures rather coarse, about one-half as wide as the scutellum and almost in mutual contact. Elytra fully twice as long as the prothorax, the striæ deep but not very coarse, the intervals flat, equal, about one-half wider than the grooves, each with a single series of coarse, rather deep, rounded and not very close-set punctures, the ordinary setæ scarcely observable, the widely dispersed white squamules distinct, and condensed at the base of the third interval. Prosternum normally and abruptly sulcate. Length 2.5–3.5 mm.; width 1.0–1.6 mm.

I have before me a series of over seventy specimens, from all parts of the country, from New York and Florida (Key West), to

California (Lake Co.). The interstitial punctures sometimes become very coarse, deep and approximate, but I can perceive no such departures of structure as might call for a division into distinctly defined subspecies.

9 **Pseudobaris cælata** n. sp.—Rather broadly oval, moderately convex, polished, intense black throughout. *Head* finely, distinctly punctate toward apex, the beak coarsely, deeply, subrugosely so at the sides, evenly but not very strongly arcuate, robust, gradually flattened through apical half, short, in the female barely equal in length to the prothorax, and in the male distinctly shorter; antennæ moderate, the second funicular joint about one-half longer than the third. *Prothorax* rather short, nearly one-half wider than long, the sides subparallel and nearly straight in basal three-fourths, then strongly rounded and convergent to the apex, which is broad, truncate and very briefly subtubulate; base broadly, deeply bisinuate; disk without trace of median line, coarsely, rather densely, very deeply punctate, the punctures regular, abrupt and perforate, circular, three-fourths as wide as the scutellum and separated by much less than one-half of their own diameters. Scutellum small, transversely oval, rough, not distinctly impressed. *Elytra* about one-fourth longer than wide, nearly twice as long as the prothorax, and, at the distinctly tumid humeri, a little wider than the latter; sides distinctly convergent behind the humeri, the outline hemi-elliptical; disk not very coarsely but deeply grooved, the intervals flat, equal, about twice as wide as the striæ. each with a single series of moderately distant, coarse, transversely rugose but not very deep punctures; setæ very minute and not distinct, but mingled with long white widely dispersed squamules, distinctly condensed at the base of the third interval. *Abdomen* rather sparsely punctate, the setæ of the under surface sparse but distinct, white. Prosternum broadly, abruptly but moderately deeply sulcate, the coxæ small and separated by much more than their own width. Length 2.6–2.8 mm.; width 1.2–1.3 mm.

New Mexico (Albuquerque). Mr. Wickham.

A very distinct species, not at all closely allied to any other but assignable to the *nigrina* group, which is distinguished by the widely dispersed white squamules of the elytra. The male has the abdomen narrowly and distinctly impressed toward base. Four specimens.

HESPEROBARIS n. gen.

A single small species thus far alone represents this genus, which is allied rather closely to Pseudobaris. It agrees with Pseudobaris in general habitus, but differs in several important structural modifications of the under surface, relating especially to the form of the prosternal impression and intercoxal process, also in the structure of the antennæ. The antennæ are of the same general type as the peculiar form distinguishing Rhoptobaris and Orthoris. The pygidium beneath emarginates the fifth segment in a rather deeply sinuous arc. In Pseudobaris the fifth segment is much less sinuate, the pygidium being but slightly visible from beneath, but in Microbaris, the latter is gradually, transversely tumid inferiorly and largely visible behind the fifth segment when viewed from beneath.

1 **Hesperobaris suavis** n. sp.—Oval, very convex, shining, black throughout, the legs rufo-piceous; setæ extremely short, visible but not conspicuous, not intermixed with dispersed squamules; sculpture rather dense. *Head* rather deeply and somewhat closely punctate, strongly convex, the transverse impression broad but strong, impunctate; beak moderately arcuate, slender, densely punctate at the sides, a little longer than the prothorax; antennæ moderate, the first joint of the funicle longer than the next three, the second exactly equal to the third, and both slightly transverse, joints two to seven cylindrically coarctate and gradually wider, club elongate-oval as long as the six preceding joints together, densely pubescent throughout, the basal joint one-third the mass and not quite as long as the second. *Prothorax* but very slightly wider than long, the apex nearly three-fourths as wide as the base; sides feebly convergent from base to apex and feebly arcuate, the apex very obsoletely constricted; base transverse, the median lobe small and extremely feeble, almost obsolete; disk with a very narrow ill-defined impunctate line, the punctures somewhat coarse, very dense, deep, one-half as wide as the scutellum and very narrowly separated. Scutellum small, transversely oval. *Elytra* one-fourth longer than wide, twice as long as the prothorax and one-fourth wider than the latter; sides almost straight and parallel in basal three-fifths, then convergent, the apex narrowly subtruncate; humeral tuberosities almost obsolete; disk with not very coarse, abrupt but shallow, opaque grooves, the intervals flat, subequal, scarcely twice as wide as the grooves and each with a single series of rounded close-set punctures, which become coarse and deep toward base but gradually very fine toward the apex. *Abdomen* coarsely, deeply punctate toward base, more finely so behind, the punctures moderately dense. Length 2.4 mm.; width 1.05 mm.

Texas (Austin); Missouri.

The type of this interesting species is a female. The specimen from Missouri is a male, and has the prothorax a little shorter and the elytral sculpture decidedly stronger.

MICROBARIS n. gen.

Another genus allied to Pseudobaris, necessitated by a minute species which I took some years since at Galveston, Texas. In general facies it is quite distinct from either Pseudobaris or Hesperobaris, but the small claws, connate at base, declare its relationship with these genera.

The antennæ are somewhat peculiar. They are slender, the joints of the funicle becoming but slightly wider toward apex, and with the club very small, of imperfect development and probably possessing less than the ordinary degree of sensitiveness; the several joints are not defined by distinctly traceable sutures, and the vestiture is coarse and somewhat sparse, although tolerably uniform throughout.

1 **Microbaris galvestonica** n. sp.—Subcylindrical, strongly-convex, polished, black throughout. *Head* minutely, the beak rather coarsely and densely punctate, the latter subimpunctate toward apex and broadly along the middle, slender, evenly, strongly arcuate and about two-fifths longer than the prothorax; antennæ slender, scape short, inserted behind the middle, funicle slender, the joints coarctate and but slightly transverse toward apex, the first not as long as the next three, the second and third subequal and each distinctly longer than wide, the fourth not at all wider than long, club small, elongate-oval, compressed, sparsely pubescent and rather shining, as long as the preceding four joints together, its structure not distinct. *Prothorax* fully two-fifths wider than long, the sides broadly, strongly arcuate in basal half, becoming strongly convergent and straight but not in the least constricted toward apex, the latter one-half as wide as the base, feebly arcuate; base transverse, the median lobe broad and very feeble; disk wider at basal third than at base, with a very narrow ill-defined impunctate line, the punctures moderately large, about one-half as wide as the scutellum and dense but not polygonally distorted. Scutellum very small, rounded. *Elytra* one-half longer than wide, a little more than twice as long as the prothorax and very slightly wider than the disk of the latter, cylindrical in basal two-thirds, then gradually, parabolically rounded, the humeral tuberosities obsolete; disk with extremely fine but deep and abrupt impunctate striæ, the intervals flat, subequal, four or five times as wide as the striæ, each with a singe series of very minute remote and feeble punctures, each bearing a small but distinct subrecumbent silvery seta. *Abdomen* not very finely, strongly but rather sparsely punctured. *Legs* short, moderately slender. Length 1.6 mm.; width 0.65 mm.

Texas (Galveston).

A single specimen, the sex of which is somewhat doubtful.

TRICHOBARIS.
LeConte—Proc. Am. Phil. Soc., XV, p. 287.

The genus defined under this name by LeConte is one of the most highly specialized of the present group of Barini. It is not at all closely allied to Pseudobaris, although assigned at the present time to the section containing that genus because of the similarity in structure of the tarsal claws; these differ somewhat, however, in being occasionally slightly unequal in length. It has no special affinity with Rhoptobaris. The squamose vestiture so highly developed in the Centrini is also one of the most characteristic features of Trichobaris, giving it a peculiar and easily recognized aspect among the semi-glabrous genera with which it must be associated, for it is easily distinguishable from Pycnobaris by its oblong form. The elongate parallel outline of the body is however not peculiar to this genus, being exhibited equally well in Stictobaris.

In Trichobaris the prosternum is broadly and feebly impressed along the middle and narrowly separates the coxæ, the formation of these parts being nearly as in Baris. The scutellum is large, strongly transverse, broadly, deeply impressed and with the sides acutely angulate, occasionally being prominent and more or less reflexed toward apex or corniform, a development especially characteristic of the present genus, although suggested rather strongly in the first section of Baris.

The vestiture consists of broad scales, sometimes both above and beneath, but often replaced by long slender squamules on the upper surface; they are always recumbent and often subdenuded in various limited areas, especially in two small spots at the base of the pronotum, in two large subconfluent areas at the sides of the prothorax beneath, and, in *mucorea*, also in three small spots at the base of the beak; these spots are not really denuded, but are clothed with smaller and more slender piceous-black squamules. On the abdomen there is always a large subquadrate area more or less completely glabrous, occupying the median portions of the two or three last segments; this is independent of the sex of the individual.

The antennal club varies in structure nearly as in Plesiobaris, enabling us to group the species as follows:—

> Antennal club moderately large, much longer than wide, with the basal joint constituting less than one-half of the mass; vestiture variable but with the squamules always oblique at the sides of the elytral intervals; body generally subdepressed above, the prothorax always more or less quasi-denuded beneath at the sides.
>
> > Vestiture of the upper surface consisting of slender squamules, which do not completely conceal the sculpture.
> >
> > > Pronotum simply punctate, without impunctate and subcarinate median line; antennal club robust and abrupt.....................................1 **trinotata**
> > >
> > > Pronotum densely and confluently punctate, sometimes longitudinally rugose, the sides more or less feebly sinuate just behind apical third; antennal club more slender and elongate, less abrupt, the outer funicular joints more transverse; pronotum with a narrow impunctate median carina; size larger, the vestiture denser.....................2 **mucorea**

Vestiture consisting of large, broad, moderately dense scales ; punctures of the pronotum large, deep, circular and distinct, with a narrow carinate impunctate line ; basal denuded spots not distinct.............3 **insolita**

Antennal club more robust and conoidal, shorter and with the basal joint constituting one-half of the mass ; vestiture consisting of more or less broad scales, more densely placed, not conspicuously oblique at the sides of the elytral intervals ; body more convex, the prothorax never with sub-denuded spots at the sides beneath.

Abdominal impression of the male normally clothed with long recumbent scales ; body very robust ; basal denuded spots of the pronotum large and distinct...4 **compacta**

Abdominal impression of the male bristling with erect robust and pointed hairs ; body narrow and subcylindrical ; basal subdenuded spots of the pronotum almost completely obsolete.

Antennal club robust, much wider than the outer joints of the funicle ; anterior coxæ separated by about one-third of their own width ; elytral striæ indicated by narrow partings of the vestiture...........5 **texana**

Antennal club exceedingly small, scarcely wider than the outer joints of the funicle ; anterior coxæ separated by one-half of their own width ; elytral striæ totally obliterated by the vestiture, the latter excessively dense and composed of much broader scales ; body still narrower.

6 **cylindrica**

1 **Trichobaris trinotata** Say—Curc., p. 17 ; Ed. Lec., I, p. 280 ; *vestita* Boh., Sch. Gen. Curc., III, p. 718 et Klug, i. litt. ; *tripunctata*, Chev. i. litt. (Baridius) ; *cinerea* Dej. i. litt. (Baris) ; *pennsylvanica* Knoch, i. litt. (Curculio) ; *plumbea* Lec., Proc. Acad. Nat. Sci., Phila., 1868, p. 364 (Baridius).

Oblong, parallel, moderately narrow, black throughout, rather dull in lustre and uniformly clothed with long fine hair-like recumbent squamules, pure white in color, but rather sparse and producing merely a grayish pruinose appearance, the scales at the sides of the elytral intervals strongly evenly and posteriorly oblique. Beak densely punctate, fully as long as the prothorax in the male, a little longer and rather slender in the female, the antennal club robust, oval, densely pubescent, as long as the five preceding joints in the former sex, but a little shorter in the latter, the basal joint but slightly more than one-third the total length, the second funicular joint one-half longer than the third. The male is generally larger than the female, and, in both sexes, the median parts of the third and fourth ventral segments are abruptly denuded. The prosternum is rather narrowly but distinctly impressed along the middle, the anterior coxæ being separated by about one-fourth of their own width. Length 3.0–4.4 mm. ; width 1.2–1.75 mm.

Pennsylvania to Florida (Key West), Illinois, extending southward to Texas.　There is considerable doubt in my mind as to the real identity of the Mexican species described by Boheman as *vestita* with the true *trinotata* of Say, the species are mutually so similar that they are liable to be confounded unless carefully compared. *Plumbea* Lec. seems to be identical with this species.

2 **Trichobaris mucorea** Lec.—Proc. Ac. Nat. Sci., Phila., 1858, p. 79 (Baridius).

Much larger and broader than *trinotata*, the vestiture rather more robust and much closer but not extremely dense, white, the squamules long and slender, directed transversely on the pronotum and oblique and interlacing along the sides of the elytral intervals, becoming large and reddish-yellow along the anterior margin of the pronotum, broad and overlapping beneath and replaced by very slender dark piceous squamules in a large spot involving almost the entire flanks of the prothorax beneath, and in three small spots at the sides and on the upper surface of the beak near the base, these areas appearing as if denuded; abdomen abruptly denuded at the middle of the third and fourth segments.　Head glabrous; beak densely squamulose, the antennæ stout, with the second funicular joint longer than wide and one-half longer than the third, club rather large, elongate, conoidal, extremely densely clothed with fine short piceous hairs, the basal joint constituting one-third of the mass.　Anterior coxæ separated by one-third of their own width. Male with the abdomen broadly, feebly impressed in basal half, the vestiture of the impression unmodified, consisting of large closely recumbent scales; fifth segment with a short broadly rounded apical lobe at the middle.　Length 5.0–6.0 mm.; width 2.3–2.6 mm.

Southern and Lower California and Arizona.　Differs very widely from *trinotata*, but perhaps identical with Boheman's *vestita*.　It is recognizable at once by its rather depressed upper surface, large size and the subdenuded area at the sides of the prothorax beneath.

Two of the specimens before me are smaller, with the vestiture decidedly sparser, and with the pronotum strongly, longitudinally rugose, and another much larger, with coarse and distinct pronotal rugæ, but with the vestiture denser than usual; this is therefore an exceptionally variable species, or else I have confounded several very closely allied forms, which cannot be advantageously studied with such small series of specimens.

3 **Trichobaris insolita** n. sp.—Oblong-oval, somewhat robust and distinctly depressed, black throughout, the integuments polished when denuded but densely clothed with large broad recumbent whitish scales. *Head* polished, glabrous, minutely, sparsely and obsoletely punctate, the transverse impression strong and normal; beak only moderately robust, evenly, rather strongly arcuate, abruptly very strongly bent at base at the junction with the head, deeply punctate, squamose especially at the sides, fully as long as the prothorax in the female; antennæ rather slender, the scape but slightly shorter than the funicle, the second joint of the latter much longer than wide and one-half longer than the third which is quadrate, fourth a little wider than long, outer joints but slightly thicker, the club small but longer than wide and rather abrupt, conoidal, densely clothed with robust recumbent cinereous squamules, the basal joint constituting a little less than one-half the mass. *Prothorax* short, about one-half wider than long, the sides subparallel or very feebly convergent and nearly straight to apical third, then broadly rounded and moderately convergent but scarcely at all constricted to the apex, which is fully one-half as wide as the base, transversely truncate; base broadly bisinuate; disk with a narrow entire cariniform impunctate line, the punctures round, deep, perforate moderately large and mutually quite distinctly separated. Scutellum well developed, transverse, broadly impressed, the sides acute, prominent, slightly flexed posteriorly and corniform. *Elytra* two-fifths longer than wide, one-fourth wider than the prothorax and nearly two and one-half times as long as the latter; sides subparallel and straight, the humeri scarcely prominent, the apex broadly rounded and subtruncate, each elytron strongly callous in the middle at apical fourth; striæ rather fine but deep and abrupt, the intervals flat, three times as wide as the grooves, rather finely confusedly and moderately closely punctate when denuded. Prosternum feebly impressed, the coxæ separated by nearly one-half their width. *Legs* moderate; tarsal claws short, connate for one-half their length, parallel, slightly everted toward apex and quite distinctly unequal in length. Length 4.2 mm.; width 1.8 mm.

Florida.

A single female example collected in the extreme southern part of the State by Mr. Francis Kinzel, and kindly given to me by Mr. Jülich. It is somewhat intermediate between the *texana* and *trinotata* groups of the genus, but is widely distinct from any other species. The scales are shorter broader and larger than in any other form known to me, not even excepting *cylindrica*, some of those on the under surface of the prosternum being only slightly longer than wide. The median parts of the third and fourth ventral segments are abruptly glabrous, the normal scales being replaced toward the apex of each by very minute slender squamules sparsely distributed.

4 Trichobaris compacta n. sp.—Oblong, strongly convex, robust, black, densely clothed throughout with long white moderately wide recumbent scales, which are not distinctly oblique at the sides of the elytral intervals, the scales not quite in mutual contact on the upper surface but very nearly so, broad, denser and conspicuous throughout the under surface, excepting the usual abruptly glabrous spot at the middle of the third and fourth ventral segments. *Head* glabrous, minutely, sparsely punctate; beak robust, short moderately arcuate, very densely and evenly squamose throughout, distinctly shorter than the prothorax in both sexes ; antennæ stout but long, the second funicular joint longer than wide, obconical one-half longer than the third, outer joints transverse, the club robust, conoidal, pointed, as long as the four preceding joints combined, slightly pale in color, very densely clothed throughout with small robust subrecumbent squamules, which are white on the basal half, fulvous thence to the tip, the basal joint constituting about one-half the mass, the annulations not very distinct. *Prothorax* two-fifths wider than long, the sides feebly convergent and often broadly sinuate to apical third, then strongly rounded and subprominent, thence strongly convergent and broadly constricted to the apex ; disk with the two basal subdenuded spots large and distinct, the scales directed transversely. Scutellum short, very transverse, broadly impressed, glabrous, corniform at the sides. *Elytra* rather shorter and broader than usual, scarcely more than one-fourth longer than wide, abruptly one-fourth wider than the prothorax and a little more than twice as long as the latter ; sides parallel and straight ; apex abruptly, broadly rounded ; striæ simply indicated by fine partings of the vestiture. Prosternum feebly impressed, separating the coxæ by one-third of their own width. Length 4.5–5.3 mm. ; width 2.0–2.6 mm.

Southern California; Arizona.

Of this distinct species I have before me a series of about fifty specimens. It may perhaps be confounded at first sight with *mucorea*, but is shorter and stouter, the upper surface more convex and the sides of the prothorax less acutely prominent. The scales are broader and denser and are not replaced by piceous squamules at the sides of the prothorax beneath, and are not oblique, or only feebly and accidentally so, at the sides of the elytral intervals. The male has a broad feeble and normally squamose impression in basal half, and the fifth segment is as long as the two preceding combined, with a small shallow emargination at the apex, from the bottom of which there projects a short dentiform lobe, analogous to that of *Desmoglyptus crenatus.*

5 Trichobaris texana Lec.—Proc. Am. Phil. Soc., XV, p. 288.

Parallel, somewhat similar in outline to *trinotata*, but much more densely clothed with yellowish-cinereous scales, which are broader, with the basal denuded spots of the pronotum almost completely obsolete. The beak in the male is quite distinctly shorter than the prothorax, the antennæ stout, the second and third funicular joints equal and slightly wider than long, the outer joints becoming extremely wide and subcontinuous in outline with the club, the latter small but thick, only slightly longer than wide, conoidal, densely pubescent, the basal joint constituting rather more than one-half the mass. Prothorax scarcely one-third wider than long, with the sides straight and parallel to apical third, then broadly rounded and convergent and somewhat constricted to the apex; disk deeply, very densely punctate, without impunctate line. Elytra a little wider than the prothorax and about two and one-third times as long, parallel, abruptly and broadly rounded at apex, the sculpture and striation concealed by the vestiture, the striæ feebly indicated by fine partings of the scales, which are not oblique along the sides of the intervals. Prosternum distinctly impressed, separating the coxæ by about one-third of their own width. Length 4.3–5.1 mm.; width 1.75–2.0 mm.

Texas and Colorado. The third and fourth ventral segments are denuded toward base in the middle, and, in the male, there is a large elongate flattened or very feebly impressed area in basal half, extending substantially to the base, in which the normally recumbent scales become longer, more slender, stiff and semi-erect setæ; there is also a small spot in the middle of the fifth segment in which the vestiture is similarly modified.

6 **Trichobaris cylindrica** n. sp.—Parallel, subcylindrical, convex, very narrow and elongate, black; integuments concealed above by an excessively dense covering of large wide strigose scales, the denuded pronotal spots feebly indicated on the basal margin only, the scutellum glabrous. *Head* glabrous, opaque, almost impunctate, the transverse constriction very strong but not grooved and caused, as usual, by the pronounced gibbosity at the base of the beak, the latter strongly, evenly arcuate, moderately robust, densely squamose, scarcely as long as the prothorax in the male, the antennæ nearly as in *texana* but less stout. *Prothorax* one-fourth wider than long in the male, but still longer in the female, constricted near the apex, the sides broadly rounded, gradually becoming parallel and nearly straight in basal half; base transverse, broadly bisinuate; disk evenly, extremely densely punctate, without trace of median line, the surface completely concealed by the large transversely directed scales, which are in mutual contact. Scutellum moderate, transverse, broadly, deeply impressed but not so acute and prominent at the sides as in *texana*. *Elytra* a little wider than the prothorax and nearly two and one-half times as long, parallel, abruptly and broadly rounded at apex, the pygidium feebly oblique and visible behind, the humeri slightly

prominent; disk completely concealed by a covering of large contiguous scales, which are not even finely parted along the striæ. *Abdomen* densely squamose, middle parts of the third and fourth segments glabrous toward base only. Prosternum not distinctly impressed, separating the small coxæ by fully one-half of their own width. Length 3.5–4.7 mm.; width 1.3–1.7 mm.

Arizona.

Somewhat allied to *texana*, but quite different in its still narrower, cylindrical form and denser vestiture, larger suboval scales which are in close contact throughout, in the smaller and more distant anterior coxæ and less impressed prosternum.

In the male there is, at basal third of the abdomen, a small elongate-oval flattened area in which the scales become bristling semi-erect and acutely pointed setæ.

Several specimens before me are almost completely denuded, and the pronotal punctures are readily observed to be fine deep and frequently subcoalescent in a longitudinal direction, but not forming rugæ like those occasionally seen in *mucorea*, in which species also the sculpture of this part is much coarser. Anteriorly the constriction which is really strong, although not very distinct when normally squamose, is traceable entirely across the dorsal surface, the sculpture in the constriction consisting of strong, longitudinal and coarser rugiform ridges.

RHOPTOBARIS.

LeConte—Proc. Am. Phil. Soc., XV, p. 287.

The single species constituting this genus has nearly all the generic characters of Orthoris, but seems to differ sufficiently in the form and structure of the beak, prosternum and scutellum to fully warrant its generic isolation.

The beak is rather robust, moderately and evenly arcuate, differs considerably in the two sexes, and is separated from the head by an extremely broad and feeble transverse impression. Epistomal lobe short, limited at each side by a very small oblique fissure, and narrowly and deeply sinuate at the apex. Antennæ somewhat slender, the club elongate-ovoidal, densely pubescent and indistinctly annulate, the basal joint composing about one-third of the mass. The mandibles are well developed, arcuate, decussate when closed and deeply notched at apex.

The prosternum is flat, not distinctly tumid before the coxæ and separates the latter by one-third of their own width. Prothorax at base quite perceptibly narrower than the elytra. Scutellum triangular, flat, nearly as long as wide, deeply and densely sculptured like the surrounding surface of the elytra and not impressed. The legs are moderately long, the tarsi slender, the ungues well developed and unusually thick, as in Orthoris.

The oblique pygidium of Rhoptobaris and Orthoris appears to indicate a certain affinity with the Centrini, and, although this character occurs also in the Barini proper, it would seem more natural to place these genera as near the Centrini as possible. The elongate antennal club, also, is more of a centrinide than a baride character, it being highly developed for example in Cylindrocerus.

1 **Rhoptobaris canescens** Lec.—Proc. Am. Phil. Soc., XV, p. 287.

Elongate-oval, black throughout and strongly convex, subopaque, the elytra less densely sculptured and a little more shining, the vestiture consisting of very short, moderately dense setæ, giving a gray pruinose appearance to the surface. The beak is rather stout, distinctly arcuate, one-third longer than the prothorax in the male, but nearly one one-half longer than the latter in the female and distinctly more slender; antennæ inserted slightly beyond the middle, the funicular joints small and subequal, the club elongate, fusiform, abrupt, very densely pubescent, not distinctly annulate, a little shorter than the funicle in the male, but fully as long as the latter in the female. Prothorax in the male two-fifths wider than long with the sides strongly convergent from base to apex and evenly moderately arcuate throughout, not in the least constricted, in the female scarcely perceptibly wider than long, the sides being very feebly convergent from base to apex; disk without impunctate line, finely and very densely punctate throughout. Elytra in both sexes abruptly and quite distinctly wider than the prothorax, and, in the male, nearly three times as long as the latter, in the female not quite two and one-half times longer, the striæ deep and abrupt, not very coarse, the intervals about three times as wide as the striæ, finely, confusedly and very densely punctate throughout. The male is much larger and more robust than the female, and has, at the apex of the fifth segment, a short obtusely rounded dentiform lobe. Length 3.4–4.0 mm.; width 1.3–1.6 mm.

Colorado. Of the habits of this interesting species I believe nothing has been recorded.

ORTHORIS.

LeConte—Proc. Am. Phil. Soc., XV, p. 286.

The external appearance of the species composing this genus certainly conveys but little idea of their true affinities, for, as remarked by Dr. LeConte, they quite closely resemble Orchestes. Rhoptobaris constitutes, however, an excellent connective bond in every way with the more usual habitus of the tribe.

There are several inaccuracies in the original diagnosis of the genus, which is drawn from the female alone. The beak is stated to be "not curved," and the prosternum "broadly though not deeply sulcate in front." The beak, even in the very long slender form occurring in the female of *crotchi*, is feebly, though very sensibly, curved, and in the male of *crotchi* and female of *cylindrifer*, it becomes quite conspicuously so. The modification of the prosternum is peculiar, this part being rather narrowly and deeply impressed along the middle, but not at all abruptly sulcate; the peculiarity consists in the fact that the canaliculation is not a depression below the general surface of the prosternum as in other genera, but is caused by a tumid elevation before each coxa, the impression being an intervening valley between the two prominences.

The beak in Orthoris is slender and separated from the head by a transverse impression, which is narrower and much stronger than in Rhoptobaris; but in the structure of the prostomial lobe and mandibles the two genera are nearly similar. The antennæ are of the same aberrant type as in Rhoptobaris, the club being sometimes greatly elongate, a form feebly suggested in the genus Hesperobaris. The front coxæ are very narrowly but distinctly separated.

Our two species may be easily recognized as follows:—

Lustre alutaceous; setæ longer, confusedly dispersed on the elytral intervals; pronotal punctures finer and dense; beak in the female very long and slender, the antennal club in that sex not quite as long as the funicle.

1 crotchi

Lustre polished; setæ shorter, much sparser and more rigid, arranged in a single line on each interval; pronotal punctures rather coarse and not so dense; beak in the female much shorter and more arcuate, the antennal club distinctly longer than the entire funicle ....2 **cylindrifer**

1 **Orthoris crotchi** LeConte—Proc. Am. Phil. Soc., XV, p. 286.

Moderately short and stout, convex, black throughout and somewhat dull in lustre, the setæ rather long, subrecumbent, flexible, moderately sparse but very conspicuous, confusedly arranged on the elytral intervals. Beak differing greatly in the sexes, very slender, just visibly but evenly arcuate and three-fifths longer than the prothorax in the female, stouter, much shorter and distinctly arcuate near the base and apex in the male, the antennal club in the female scarcely perceptibly shorter than the entire funicle, but not much longer than the preceding six joints in the male. The prothorax is small, conical, truncate at apex and very feebly constricted anteriorly, the punctures scarcely more than one-fourth as wide as the scutellum and separated by barely one-half of their own widths. Elytra abruptly fully two-fifths wider than the prothorax, two and one-half times as long as the latter, one-third longer than wide; sides parallel and straight, the apex broadly and abruptly rounded, the striæ deep; intervals three to four times as wide as the striæ, finely and feebly, not very densely, confusedly and subasperately punctate. Fifth ventral segment longer than the preceding two combined, acutely rounded in the female, a little more obtuse in the male. Anterior coxæ separated by nearly one-fourth of their own width. Length 2.8–3.8 mm.; width 1.1–1.65 mm.

California; Texas; Nebraska (Pine Ridge). In the extensive series before me the largest and smallest specimens are both females.

2 Orthoris cylindrifer n. sp.—General form as in *crotchi*, but polished and more sparsely setose, the setæ moderately long, stiff, erect and bristling on the beak and pronotum, but recurved on the elytra, forming a nearly even single line on each interval. *Head* coarsely punctured, setose, the transverse impression narrow, strong and impunctate, the beak moderately densely punctate, rather slender, strongly arcuate at base and near the apex, somewhat short, scarcely more than one-third longer than the prothorax in the female; antennæ long, the first funicular joint robust and as long as the next three, two to seven small, subequal, club very long, fully three times as long as wide, one-half as long as the prothorax and fully one-third longer than the entire funicle, abruptly wider than the seventh funicular joint, the sides straight and subparallel or very feebly divergent thence to apical third, then gradually pointed, indistinctly annulate, the basal joint longer than wide. *Prothorax* small, nearly one-half wider than long, the sides convergent from the base, feebly but distinctly arcuate, very obsoletely constricted near the broadly truncate apex; base with a small but distinct median lobe; disk rather coarsely and not densely punctate, the punctures almost one-third as wide as the scutellum and very deep. *Scutellum* moderate, transversely subquadrate. *Elytra* abruptly one-half wider than the prothorax, nearly as in *crotchi*, except that the intervals are polished, quite distinctly convex and each with a single uneven series of small subrugulose feeble and rather distant punctures. *Abdomen* sparsely punctate, strongly convex. Prosternum separating the coxæ by barely one-fourth of their width. Length 3.0–3.3 mm.; width 1.2–1.5 mm.

Arizona.

The description is drawn from the female, the only sex which I have seen. The extraordinary development of the antennal club and shorter beak will at once distinguish the present species from *crotchi*. Two specimens.

CENTRINUS.
Schönherr—Curcul. Disp. Meth., p. 308.

Within the wide limits permitted by the short and somewhat ambiguous definition of Schönherr, I here regard as Centrinus, those species of Barini which have the pygidium concealed in both sexes, or never with more than the mere tip exposed, the femora unarmed, the mandibles elongate, prominent, not in the least decussate when closed, with the inner edge entirely free from notches and denticulation, and the tarsal claws free and divergent. In addition, it should be stated that the species are, with very few exceptions, rhomboidal or rhomboid-oval to a greater or less degree, and are all more or less squamose. This definition, also, will at least not exclude those species defined as Centrinus by Pascoe (Ann. Mag. Nat. Hist., Oct. 1889, p. 322) viz: "Claws free; canal nearly obsolete or absent; anterior coxæ separated; prosternum lower than the coxæ; elytra broader than the prothorax."

With these characters are associated others, even in our own somewhat limited fauna, of considerable variety. The beak may be very slender, comparatively robust, or slender and inflated near the base, strongly and evenly or feebly and unevenly arcuate and variously compressed and flattened, the antennæ inserted beyond or behind the middle and the prothorax tubulate or not. The anterior coxæ may be narrowly or quite widely separated, the prosternum flat or variously impressed, foveate or sulcate, often very differently modified in these respects in the sexes of the same species. Finally, the secondary sexual modification of the male may be radically different in kind, consisting either of short or long ante-coxal corneous processes of the prosternum, or of a dentiform extension of the anterior trochanters, or of a short erect tooth-like process projecting from the inner side of the basal joint of the antennal club, never, however, by a combination of any of these three modifications; in some cases, the male appears to be entirely devoid of secondary sexual characters.

In fact within the limits of the genus as thus defined by mandibular structure, many characters which are of generic importance elsewhere, such as the degree of separation of the coxæ, nature of the prosternal impression and conformation of the prothoracic apex, lose all significance of this kind and are merely useful in defining groups. In all probability some of these sexual groups are worthy of a separate designation, but with my present lack of sufficiently exact knowledge concerning the numerous tropical forms, it would be manifestly inappropriate to do more than simply indicate those which exist within our own fauna; this has been attempted in the following table :—

Male with an erect or oblique process of greater or less length before each anterior coxa ; antennal scape not attaining the eye; tarsal claws slender, not excavated beneath.

Anterior coxæ narrowly separated ; body robust.

Beak thick, the antennæ inserted beyond the middle, at least in the male ; prothorax strongly tubulate at apex ....**I**

Beak very slender, the antennæ inserted far behind the middle in both sexes, with the scape very short, coming far from attaining the eyes ; much smaller species...**II**

Anterior coxæ widely separated, the beak moderately slender, often more or less inflated toward base in the female, the antennæ inserted at a greater or less distance behind the middle...**III**

Male with two short arcuate prosternal processes; anterior coxæ rather widely separated, the prosternum flat, with a small subapical excavation ; mandibles aberrant, small, widely separated, the inner edge outwardly oblique and broadly arcuate toward apex, deeply notched externally beneath ; tarsal claws aberrant, long, stout, widely divergent, excavated beneath throughout their length ; elytra with quasi-denuded transverse interrupted bands ....**IV**

Male without trace of prosternal or antennal modification, but with the anterior trochanters dentate; anterior coxæ moderately separated, the prosternum flat ; beak somewhat stout, the antennæ inserted a little behind the middle, the club of peculiar structure, the two basal joints together comprising but slightly more than one-half the mass, the first often much shorter than the second ....**V**

Male entirely devoid of secondary sexual modification of the antennæ, prosternum or trochanters.

Anterior coxæ rather widely separated.

Prothorax subtubulate at apex ; elytral vestiture quasi-denuded in small spots ; beak slender, rather feebly arcuate, the antennæ inserted behind the middle in both sexes, the scape rather long and almost attaining the eye ; tarsal claws long, normal in structure ....**VI**

Prothorax completely non-tubulate; elytral and pronotal vestiture disposed in dense sharply-defined longitudinal lines; beak slender, excessively arcuate, the antennæ inserted behind the middle, the scape very short and extending only two-thirds the distance thence to the eyes...**VII**
Anterior coxæ narrowly separated.
Beak slender, with the antennæ inserted behind the middle, dissimilar in the sexes, shorter, almost evenly arcuate and cylindrical in the male, longer, nearly straight but abruptly bent near the base and broadly, gradually flattened toward apex in the female; prosternum not impressed, but with a small subdenuded point, from which the scales radiate in all directions; scutellum very small, rounded, glabrous; vestiture more or less uneven ....**VIII**
Beak rather stout and cylindrical, the antennæ inserted beyond the middle, the scape extending almost to the eye.................................**IX**
Male without secondary sexual modification of the prosternum or trochanters, but having the outer joints of the antennal funicle obliquely truncate and often prominent internally, and the basal joint of the club with a large glabrous area on the inner side, at the middle of which there is a tumid or dentiform process; pygidium with the apical portion exposed in both sexes; anterior coxæ narrowly separated, the prosternum generally with a deep transversely oval pit behind the apical margin; basal impression of the beak almost obsolete; scutellum rather large and always densely albido-pubescent ....**X**

The species are numerous and are equally abundant in South America; they are generally small and most of the large Brazilian forms will have to be assigned to other diverse genera. Those of the United States may be thus distinguished:—

Subgenus I.

Elytral intervals alternately more densely punctured and pubescent.
Pronotal punctures rather coarse, deep, rounded, not at all coalescent; beak in the male barely as long as the head and prothorax and very thick, especially toward base............................1 **punctirostris**
Pronotal punctures finer, subcoalescent longitudinally; beak in the male much smoother in apical half, more slender, less distinctly robust toward base and fully as long as the head and prothorax.........2 **lævirostris**
Elytral intervals narrower, all coarsely, sparsely and rugosely punctate; body shorter and more broadly oval; upper surface sprinkled with large, widely distant, white scales.
Prosternal processes of the male moderately long; scattered scales of the elytra long and narrow; pronotum with oblique, interrupted rugæ and coarse punctures..3 **striatirostris**
Prosternal processes in the form of very feeble cusp-like elevations of the anterior margin of the coxal cavity; scattered scales of the elytra broad and oval.

Pronotum coarsely, sparsely punctate, the punctures feebly tending to
coalesce obliquely; body obese ....4 **modestus**
Pronotum completely impunctate, but with long deep and oblique rugæ
throughout; body much narrower............................5 **tortuosus**

Subgenus II.

Body robust, rather less densely clothed above with elongate slender squamules, which are generally ochreous-yellow in color, occasionally a little
wider and nearly white; basal joint of the antennal funicle almost as
long as the next four together in the female..................6 **picumnus**
Body smaller and narrower, rather more densely clothed above with broader,
oval, white scales; basal joint of the funicle shorter, about as long as the
next three in the female; beak a little shorter.............7 **albotectus**

Subgenus III.

Beak long, slender, thicker toward base, especially in the female and generally about one-half as long as the body.
  Vestiture of the upper surface consisting of paler and darker squamules,
  confusedly intermingled, with two small subapical quasi-denuded spots.
    Paler scales ochreous-yellow in color; slightly smaller and stouter species, the prosternum perfectly flat in the female ....8 **neglectus**
    Paler scales whitish; prosternum broadly, feebly impressed in both sexes;
    beak in the female much more strongly, but not very abruptly, inflated
    toward base..9 **grisescens**
  Vestiture of the upper surface dense and uniform throughout; subapical
  dark spots totally obsolete.
    Integuments black, densely clothed with white or yellowish-white squamules.
      Scutellum minute.
        Scutellum flat, sparsely squamose; beak in the female but very
        feebly and gradually thicker toward base; vestiture cinereous-white ....10 **perscillus**
        Scutellum polished, with a broad deep glabrous impression along
        the middle, the apex emarginate; beak in the female very much
        thicker and more arcuate toward base, but gradually so; prothorax
        much shorter than in *perscillus;* vestiture uniform ochreous-yellow
        or whitish...11 **finitimus**
      Scutellum much larger, flat, densely squamose; vestiture white; beak in
      the female abruptly and strongly inflated behind the point of antennal
      insertion, extremely slender thence to the apex.............12 **hospes**
    Integuments pale testaceous, the vestiture ochreous-yellow; legs still
    paler, rufous ....13 **clarescens**
Beak decidedly short and thick in both sexes, cylindrical and nearly equal in
diameter from base to apex, barely as long as the head and prothorax;
integuments rufous or rufo-piceous; antennæ with the funicular joints
two to seven much shorter.

Smaller species, the pronotal punctures very dense and polygonally crowded; squamules of the elytra and median parts of the pronotum fine, with widely dispersed, larger and paler scales......................14 **perscitus**

Larger and much broader species, the pronotal punctures smaller, less closely crowded, the elytral squamules longer, denser, paler and without distinct widely dispersed scales.................................15 **exulans**

Subgenus IV.

GERÆUS Pasc.

Narrowly rhomboidal, the elytra with two transverse dark bands interrupted at the suture; scutellum moderately densely squamose; setæ borne by the strial punctures long, white and almost as large as those of the intervals...16 **senilis**

Subgenus V.

Beak in the male fully as long as the head and prothorax; antennæ long and very slender, the club narrow, elongate and densely pubescent.

17 **acuminatus**

Beak in the male scarcely longer than the prothorax; antennæ shorter and much stouter, the club very large, broadly oval, subglobose and sparsely pubescent...18 **globifer**

Subgenus VI.

Narrowly rhomboidal, densely clothed with narrow ochreous scales, the elytra with several more or less unstable dark spots in apical two-thirds, which are clothed with piceous-black squamules.................19 **penicellus**

Subgenus VII.

Rather broadly oval, the humeri not prominent; pronotum with three broad yellow vittæ, the elytra lineate with yellow and black; scutellum small, glabrous, polished; prosternum not impressed, but with a small discal point from which the scales radiate as in the following group.

20 **lineellus**

Subgenus VIII.

Elytral squamules very fine, white, disposed in two somewhat even lines on each interval; legs blackish to dark rufo-piceous.

Elytral squamules uniform throughout, slightly broader only near the scutellum; form narrowly rhomboidal.......................21 **capillatus**

Elytral squamules much coarser on intervals two to four, for a short distance behind the middle, forming a cloud-like spot; form more broadly rhomboid-oval...22 **nubecula**

Elytral squamules coarser, uneven in size, yellowish; legs bright rufous.

23 **clientulus**

Subgenus IX.

Form rather narrowly oval, scarcely at all rhomboidal, the humeral callus small and but slightly prominent; prothorax rather short and transverse,

abruptly narrowed near the apex, the punctures fine, extremely dense
and longitudinally subconfluent; vestiture uniform, ochreous, the squam-
ules slender...24 **falsus**

Subgenus X.

Odontocorynus Schönh.

Group I.

Beak nearly similar in form in the male and female.

Antennæ inserted beyond apical third in the male and at apical two-fifths in
the female ; body rhomboid-oval, sparsely squamose, more or less rufescent in the female, the male black...............25 **scutellum-album**

Group 2.

*Beak compressed, strongly punctate and abruptly bent near the base in the male, but
cylindrical, polished, almost impunctate and more evenly arcuate in the female.*

Squamules borne by the strial punctures of the elytra inconspicuous.
  Pronotal punctures larger, distinct, close but not densely crowded.
    Larger species, the antennal club robust ; punctures of the elytral inter-
      vals coarse and rounded, distinctly defined, each deeply enclosing a
      small white scale.. 26 **denticornis**
    Smaller species, less robust and more parallel, the antennal club smaller ;
      interstitial punctures closer and confused................27 **salebrosus**
  Pronotal punctures small, extremely densely crowded ; antennæ rufescent,
    the club large and robust ; body broadly oblong........ 28 **pinguescens**
Squamules borne by the strial punctures broad and distinct.

29 **pulverulentus**

The identity of subgenus "X" with Odontocorynus Sch., is inferred from the description given by Lacordaire. We have no
species in which the antennal joints four to seven are internally
spinose, but several in which the two or three outer joints of the
funicle are slightly prolonged and acuminate within. The Mexican
Centrinus larvatus and *tonsilis* of Boheman, also belong to this
subgenus without doubt.

I.

1 **Centrinus punctirostris** Lec.—Proc. Am. Phil. Soc., XV, p. 309.

Very robust, oval, convex, piceous-black, the elytra, beak, antennæ
and legs more or less rufescent; vestiture consisting of large whitish
scales, denser toward the sides of the pronotum and also, to some
extent, on the wider of the elytral intervals, giving a subvittate
appearance; under surface densely squamose. Beak decidedly thick,
moderately arcuate, about as long as the head and prothorax, rather
coarsely, deeply punctured, but densely and rugulosely so only at

the sides toward base; antennæ inserted at the middle, the second
funicular joint three-fifths as long as the first; club abrupt, rather
large, very robust, densely pubescent, with the basal joint composing fully one-half of the mass. Prothorax fully one-third wider
than long, the apex tubulate and two-fifths as wide as the base;
punctures rather large, deep, circular, close but not in actual contact, the smooth impunctate line distinct. Elytra large, quite distinctly wider than the prothorax and about twice as long, the sides
just visibly convergent from the humeri to apical third, then gradually and broadly rounded and strongly convergent, the apex acutely
ogival; disk with moderately coarse, abrupt striæ, the intervals flat,
alternating wide and narrower, the wide intervals, beginning with
the first, rather finely, extremely densely punctate, the narrower
more coarsely and not so closely so, the punctures all distinct. Prosternum in the male with an oval and excessively deep pit between
the corneous processes, the latter very robust, somewhat long,
gradually arcuate and inclined forward from the base, obtusely
acuminate at apex and not quite as long as in *lævirostris;* anterior
coxæ separated by about one-third of their own width. Length
5.6 mm.; width 2.7 mm.

Colorado. Cab. LeConte. This interesting species is represented
by the unique male type only.

2 **Centrinus lævirostris** Lec.—Proc. Am. Phil. Soc., XV, p. 309.

Robust, oval, convex, piceous, the integuments moderately shining, somewhat densely clothed with elongate-oval whitish scales on
the pronotum in the middle through basal half and toward the sides,
but elsewhere sparsely covered with fine and darker squamules; on
the elytra the white scales are dense on the alternate intervals beginning with the first, least conspicuously so on the third, the other
intervals more sparsely clothed with slender and darker scales;
under surface densely clothed with large white scales. Beak in the
male moderately slender, smooth, only deeply and rugulosely punctured at the sides toward base, moderately and evenly arcuate and
fully as long as the head and prothorax, the antennæ inserted just
behind the middle, the second funicular joint nearly three-fourths
as long as the first and fully as long as the next two combined;
club small, oval, abrupt, densely pubescent, as long as the preceding
four joints and with its basal joint nearly one-half of the whole.

Prothorax but slightly wider than long, tubulate at apex, the punctures small, deep, close, tending to coalesce longitudinally, the median polished line distinct. Elytral intervals wide and flat. Prosternum with an elongate-oval, excessively deep excavation, with its edges rounded, the coxæ separated by but slightly more than one-fourth of their own width, the large corneous process before each arising vertically for a short distance, then flexed abruptly and obliquely forward, becoming finely acuminate. Length 5.8 mm.; width 2.8 mm.

Missouri. Cab. LeConte. Represented by the unique type. The narrowly vittate elytra will readily serve to identify this distinct species.

3 **Centrinus striatirostris** Lec.—Proc. Am. Phil. Soc., XV, p. 309.

Robust, oval, convex, piceous and shining, the vestiture sparse, whitish, consisting of very elongate narrow scales and finer hair-like squamules indiscriminately mingled on the elytra, the finer squamules not noticeably darker in color; on the under surface they are broader and denser, and on the pronotum are also coarser toward apex and at base near the sides and in the middle, also in a large conspicuous spot at each side of the scutellum. The beak is rather stout and feebly arcuate, but slightly longer than the head and prothorax, deeply punctate and longitudinally rugose at the sides, the antennæ inserted just beyond the middle, the second funicular joint less than one-half as long as the first and about one-half longer than the third, the club rather large, oval, fully as long as the preceding five joints together, densely pubescent, the basal joint two-fifths of the whole. Prothorax strongly tubulate at apex, the disk with coarse rugose sculpture and a narrow impunctate line. Elytra a little wider than the prothorax and about twice as long, the striæ rather coarse, deep, the intervals flat, two to three times as wide as the grooves, coarsely and sparsely punctato-rugulose. Prosternum in the male with a large elongate-oval extremely deep excavation, extending to the coxæ, the latter separated by two-fifths of their own width in both sexes; in the female the prosternum is flat, with a small abrupt oval and extremely deep excavation near the anterior margin. Length 4.4–4.5 mm.; width 2.25–2.4 mm.

Texas. The ante-coxal corneous process of the male is erect, short, stout, acuminate and about as long as the antennal club in the specimen which I have under observation.

4 Centrinus modestus Boh.—Sch. Curc., III, p. 772.

A well-known species of robust, oval, strongly convex form and piceous color, sparsely sprinkled with coarse white scales and narrower brownish squamules above, and more densely covered with whitish scales beneath. The beak is about one-half as long as the body, evenly but not very strongly arcuate, moderately stout, slightly gibbous at base, so that it is separated from the head by an unusually deep and sharply marked transverse impression; antennæ normal, inserted a little beyond the middle, the scape short, extending about two-thirds the distance to the eyes, the second funicular joint scarcely more than one-half as long as the first. Prothorax strongly constricted and almost tubulate at apex. Prosternum with a deep oval abruptly glabrous subapical spot, which is very deeply and transversely excavated at the bottom, and continued posteriorly by a feebly defined canaliculate and squamose impression, which becomes narrower and gradually evanescent before the coxæ, the latter large and separated by scarcely more than one-fourth of their own width, with the middle of the anterior margin of the acetabula elevated in a feeble cusp-like prominence, or short corneous process in the male. Length 4.0–4.5 mm.; width 2.3–2.5 mm.

The four specimens in my cabinet are from Pennsylvania and Florida. In well preserved specimens a small spot of dense scales is evident at each side of the scutellum, and another just before each humeral callus, the former not being as large or conspicuous, however, as in *striatirostris.*

5 Centrinus tortuosus n. sp.—Rather robust, feebly rhomboid-oval, convex, shining, coarsely sculptured, piceous-black, the antennæ paler; vestiture very sparse above, consisting of large white scales and small narrow brown squamules indiscriminately mingled on the elytra, dense beneath, and with the scales white, short, broad and truncate. *Head* almost completely impunctate, the transverse constriction abrupt, almost in the form of a groove; beak rather stout, feebly arcuate, very coarsely, deeply, longitudinally punctate and rugulose at the sides, a little longer than the head and prothorax in the male, the antennæ inserted distinctly beyond the middle, the scape short, second funicular joint one-half as long as the first and nearly as long as the next two, club well developed, oval, abrupt, densely pubescent, about as long as the preceding five joints together and with its basal joint composing about one-half of the mass. *Prothorax* three-fifths wider than long, the sides distinctly convergent and almost straight from the base to apical third, then broadly rounded and convergent to the deep apical constriction, the apex strongly tubulate, truncate, not quite one-half as wide as the base, the latter transverse and perfectly straight, the median lobe less than one-third of the total width, abrupt, prominent and rounded ; disk with coarse oblique parallel wavy rugæ, and with a narrow subcarinate impunctate line in basal two-thirds. Scutellum glabrous, small, subquadrate, broadly emarginate at apex and deeply impressed along the middle. *Elytra* at the large and somewhat prominent humeri, conspicuously wider than the prothorax, distinctly more than twice as long as the latter, the sides rapidly convergent from base to apex and feebly arcuate, the apex narrowly rounded ; disk with moderately coarse, deep, abrupt, finely and remotely punctured striæ, the intervals flat, three times as wide as the grooves, coarsely, not densely punctato-rugulose. Length 3.8 mm.; width 2.0 mm.

Texas.

The single specimen is a male and agrees nearly in prosternal structure with *modestus*, the surface being very broadly and feebly impressed, except just behind the apical margin, where there is a large and transversely oval, extremely deep excavation.   The coxæ are much more widely separated than in *modestus*, the interval being equal to fully one-half of their own width, and the form of the body is more narrowly oval ; it also differs greatly in pronotal sculpture, the latter being finer and in the form of long oblique rugæ.   In the male the middle of the anterior margin of the ante-rior acetabula has a small feeble cusp-like elevation as in *modestus*.

II.

6 **Centrinus picumnus** Herbst—Käfer, VII, p. 30 (Curculio); *oliva-ceus* Gyll.: Sch. Curc., III, p. 763; *sutor* Harris : Trans. Hart. Nat. Hist. Soc., I, p. 81 (Centrinus).

Somewhat broadly oval, convex, black throughout, densely and uniformly clothed above with long more or less narrow lineate squamules, pale ochreous-yellow to whitish in color, a little paler, denser and much wider beneath.   Beak similar in the two sexes, a little longer in the female, very strongly arcuate, fully one-half as long as the body ; antennæ inserted well behind the middle, the second funicular joint but slightly elongate, not one-half as long as the first and one-half longer than the third ; club abrupt, moderate, oval, densely pubescent, nearly as long as the four preceding together and with its basal joint composing nearly one-half of the mass. Prothorax fully one-half wider than long, conical, with the sides feebly arcuate, feebly constricted near the apex, the squamules denser and broader on the small but prominent basal lobe.   Elytra a little wider than the prothorax and nearly twice as long.   Pro-sternum in the male narrowly, extremely deeply excavated along

the middle, with a long erect anteriorly bent horn before each coxa,
the coxæ separated by scarcely more than one-third of their width;
in the female with a small but extremely deep excavation near the
anterior margin, bordered on each side by a longitudinal ridge, ex-
terior to which there is also a deep excavation, devoid of corneous
processes and with the coxæ separated by fully two-thirds of their
own width.   In the male there is a rounded very feebly impressed
spot near the base of the abdomen, which is abruptly nearly glabrous, and in which the ordinary scales become semi-erect and each
deeply split into two or three hair-like processes.   Length 2.1–2.7
mm.; width 1.0–1.6 mm.

New York, Florida, Nebraska, Arkansas and Arizona.   The
sexual modifications in this small group of species are remarkable,
especially in the divergence of prosternal impression, and in degree
of separation of the anterior coxæ.

7 **Centrinus albotectus** n. sp.—Rather broadly oval, convex, black,
densely and uniformly clothed with rather wide white scales, which are but
slightly broader and denser beneath.   *Head* and base of the beak squamose,
the beak strongly, evenly arcuate and slender in both sexes, but scarcely
longer than the head and prothorax in the male, and fully one-half as long
as the body in the female; antennæ in the male with the basal joint of the
funicle as long as the next three, the second small, but slightly longer than
the third, three to five each a little longer than wide, the club small abrupt,
short, oval, scarcely longer than the preceding three joints together; in the
female the club is less abrupt, larger and more elongate, with the basal joint
of the funicle barely longer than the next three.   *Prothorax* fully one-half wider
than long, the sides distinctly convergent from the base and broadly arcuate,
rather strongly constricted behind the apex, the latter sometimes almost tubulate; base transverse and straight, the median lobe small but very prominent;
disk uniformly and very densely punctate and squamose.   Scutellum very
small, almost concealed by the vestiture.   *Elytra* hemi-elliptical, a little
wider than the prothorax and twice as long in the male, but relatively distinctly shorter in the female; humeri moderately prominent; striæ rather
fine, very deep, the intervals flat, three or four times as wide as the striæ,
densely punctato-rugulose.   Prosternum in the male with an elongate-oval,
extremely deep excavation, the coxæ separated by one-half of their own
width; in the female, with a small rounded very deep pit just behind the
apical margin, also somewhat impressed laterally as in *picumnus*, and with the
coxæ separated by two-thirds of their own width.   Length 1.75–2.5 mm.;
width 0.7–1.3 mm.

Florida, Texas (Columbus).

In the male there is a long very slender finely acuminate horn
before each coxa, the process being inclined forward and very feebly

arcuate; in the same sex there is a small semi-glabrous flattened spot near the base of the abdomen, in which the ordinary scales become very sparse small and narrow, but recumbent and not modified in structure. This species may be readily distinguished from *picumnus* by its broader white scales, shorter beak with more pronounced sexual differences, by its smaller size and more slender form. Twelve specimens.

III.

8 **Centrinus neglectus** Lec.—Proc. Am. Phil. Soc., XV, p. 310.

Similar in form and structural characters to *perscillus*, but clothed densely throughout with ochreous-yellow scales, broad beneath, narrow and slender above, where they are unevenly mixed with darker brown scales of the same kind, the brown scales forming also two distant subapical spots. Beak slender, very strongly arcuate, not quite one-half as long as the body in the female, the antennæ inserted a little behind the middle, the scape rather abruptly clavate, extending barely three-fourths of the distance to the eyes; second funicular joint slender but short, scarcely one-half as long as the first and a little longer than the third, the outer joints larger, the club as in *perscillus* Prosternum flat, abruptly declivous anteriorly to the transverse constriction, the coxæ moderate, remote, separated by distinctly more than their own width. Length 3.6–4.0 mm.; width 1.7–1.8 mm.

Texas, Louisiana and Kansas. The specimens before me are females, but the male is said to have a short corneous process before each coxa. The statement in the original description that the second funicular joint is "nearly as long as the first," is a conspicuous error. This species is closely allied to *perscillus*.

9 **Centrinus grisescens** n. sp.—Feebly rhomboideo-elliptical, convex, rather dull, black throughout, densely clothed throughout beneath with large wide yellowish-white scales, and, on the upper surface, with squamules which are narrower, and luteous-white and dark brown intermingled, the latter more evident in two distant spots near the apex as in *neglectus*. *Beak* strongly arcuate, relatively not longer and but slightly more slender in the female than in the male, but notably more arcuate in the former sex, not quite one-half as long as the body; antennæ inserted as in *neglectus*, the second funicular joint much more slender than the first and not quite one-half as long, much shorter than the next two together; club about as long as the preceding four joints combined, not very abrupt, densely pubescent, with the basal joint composing but slightly less than one-half of the mass. *Prothorax* one-third

wider than long, the sides feebly convergent and nearly straight in basal two-thirds, then broadly rounded and gradually convergent to the apex, which is truncate and one-half as wide as the base, the latter straight and transverse, with the median lobe small but abrupt and prominent, rounded ; apical constriction broad and feeble ; disk somewhat coarsely deeply and very densely punctate, with a narrow, more or less incomplete impunctate line. Scutellum moderate in size, quadrate. *Elytra* slightly wider than the prothorax and twice as long, the humeri rather prominent, the sides thence strongly convergent and very feebly arcuate to the narrowly rounded apex ; striæ fine but deep, the intervals flat, three or four times as wide as the striæ, confusedly, rather coarsely punctato-rugulose. Prosternum broadly, distinctly impressed in the middle in both sexes, but much more deeply so in the male the latter having a short erect acuminate horn before each coxa ; anterior coxæ rather large, separated by barely their own width. Length 3.5–4.1 mm.; width 1.65–1.9 mm.

North Carolina (Asheville); Ohio; Illinois; Missouri.

Very closely allied to *neglectus*, but differing in its whitish and not dark yellow vestiture, by the broad distinct impression of the prosternum in both sexes, and quite distinctly less widely separated anterior coxæ. Numerous specimens.

10 **Centrinus perscillus** Gyll.—Sch. Curc., III, p. 762.

Elliptical, moderately robust, the upper surface feebly flattened, black, densely clothed throughout above and beneath with grayish-white elongate scales. Beak slender, very strongly, evenly arcuate, one-half as long as the body, with a narrow smooth impunctate line ; sides toward base densely punctate ; antennæ inserted a little behind the middle, the scape extending thence three-fourths of the distance to the eyes, second funicular joint slender but unusually short, not quite one-half as long as the first and but very slightly longer than the third ; club moderate, oval, densely pubescent, a little longer than the preceding four joints together, and with the basal joint constituting somewhat less than one-half the mass. Prosternum flat, rather abruptly declivous anteriorly to the transverse constriction, separating the coxæ by quite distinctly more than their own width. Length 3.7 mm.; width 1.85 mm.

The two specimens before me are apparently females, and are from Kansas and Minnesota. I think that this is without doubt the species described by Gyllenhal, and the species so identified by LeConte (Proc. Am. Phil. Soc., XV, p. 310), having the second funicular joint as long as the first and the prosternum deeply excavated, is probably some other species which remains unknown to me.

The species described by Gyllenhal is said to be covered densely
with narrow scales, agreeing with the present form, but in *perscillus*
Lec. the scales are especially noted as being "not linear but oval."

11 Centrinus finitimus n. sp.—Rhomboid-oval, convex, slightly
shining, black, the tibiæ feebly rufescent; vestiture yellowish, pale, consisting, on the upper surface, of long, slender but rather large squamules, which
are rather dense and uniformly distributed, and, beneath, of larger and very
dense scales. *Head* dull but smooth, minutely, sparsely punctate, the impression almost obsolete, with a small median fovea; beak long, polished, slender,
evenly, rather strongly arcuate and fully one-half as long as the body, but
very feebly thickened toward base, strongly flattened toward apex, where it
is distinctly dilated, scarcely noticeably enlarged at the point of antennal
insertion, rather coarsely, rugosely and densely punctate, the punctures forming
series and grooves; antennæ inserted at the middle, black, somewhat slender,
and with the basal joint of the funicle barely as long as the second, the latter
as long as the next two combined. *Prothorax* about three-fifths wider than
long, the sides broadly, evenly and strongly arcuate, becoming parallel toward
base and broadly sinuate near the apex, the latter much less than one-half as
wide as the base; disk coarsely, deeply, very densely punctate, the punctures
tending to coalesce longitudinally; impunctate line narrow but almost entire.
Scutellum small, quadrate, enlarged and broadly emarginate at apex, impressed
along the middle, setose at the sides. *Elytra* but slightly wider and three-
fourths longer than the prothorax, the sides strongly convergent, evenly, feebly
arcuate, the apex narrowly, evenly rounded, not very coarsely but deeply
striate, the intervals flat, moderate in width, rather sparsely, confusedly and
rugulosely punctured, polished. *Abdomen* broadly, rather strongly impressed
and more sparsely squamose in the middle toward base. Prosternum with a
very large and deep impression, and two rather short, erect and stout processes
before the coxæ, the latter separated by fully three-fourths of their own width.
Length 2.9–3.3 mm.; width 1.4–1.7 mm.

Texas (Dallas)—Mr. Wickham; Missouri.

This species differs from *perscillus* in its smaller size, broader
form, more transverse prothorax, structure and vestiture of the
scutellum, and generally silaceous squamules of the upper surface.
Seven specimens.

12 Centrinus hospes n. sp.—Rhomboidal, convex, black, the antennæ
piceous, the club pale; vestiture white, consisting of long, slender, rather
dense and uniformly distributed squamules on the upper surface, and large,
broad, very dense scales beneath. *Head* finely, strongly, somewhat sparsely
punctate, with a few squamules toward the eyes, the transverse impression
distinct and somewhat angular; beak in the female one-half as long as the
body, evenly, rather strongly arcuate, the portion beyond the antennæ very
slender, smooth, nude and almost completely impunctate, the portion behind

the antennæ abruptly very strongly inflated, thick, densely punctured and squamose, with a smooth median line; antennæ inserted at basal third, the scape very short, but slightly longer than the basal joint of the funicle, the latter nearly as long as the next three, the second slightly longer than the third, both elongate, joints three to six longer than wide, club oval, abrupt, densely pubescent, almost equally trilobed by the distinct sutures and one-half as long as funicular joints two to seven. *Prothorax* rather short, three-fourths wider than long, the sides broadly, strongly arcuate anteriorly, becoming nearly parallel in basal half and rather strongly sinuate behind the apex, which is truncate and one-half as wide as the base, the latter transverse, the median lobe prominent and equalling one-third of the total width ; disk somewhat coarsely, deeply and very densely punctured, without distinct impunctate line, the vestiture covering the entire surface. Scutellum densely squamose. *Elytra* quite distinctly wider than the prothorax and a little more than twice as long ; sides strongly convergent and feebly arcuate throughout, the apex narrowly rounded; humeral callus strong and prominent; mesepimera not visible from above; striæ rather fine, deep, the intervals wide, rather coarsely, deeply, confusedly, very densely and rugosely punctured. *Abdomen* strongly convex toward base, strongly inclined upward toward apex. Prosternum nearly flat, very densely squamose, the coxæ separated by three-fourths of their own width.   Length 3.5 mm. ; width 1.7 mm.

Arizona (Tucson).   Mr. Wickham.

I have only seen the female, and the remarkable form of the beak, reminding us strongly of Eunyssobia (Euchætes Lec.), is probably peculiar to that sex, as it may be observed to a less degree in several other species of this subgenus, and notably *grisescens ;* at any rate, the peculiar basal enlargement is much more developed in the female than in the male of that species.

13 **Centrinus clarescens** n. sp.—Rather narrowly ovoidal, convex, pale rufo-testaceous throughout, the scutellum, head and beak rather darker and piceous ; vestiture consisting of rather large, moderately elongate, ochreous-yellow scales, rather dense and uniformly distributed above, very dense and broader beneath. *Head* alutaceous, completely glabrous, exceedingly minutely and sparsely punctate ; impression completely obsolete, with an elongate median fovea ; beak in the male slender, strongly, evenly arcuate, gradually and but slightly thicker toward base, distinctly punctured and sparsely squamose at the sides behind the antennæ, shining, polished and almost impunctate elsewhere, dilated at apex and at the point of antennal insertion, and very nearly one-half as long as the body ; antennæ slender, inserted just behind the middle, the first two joints of the funicle equal in length, the second much the more slender and fully as long as the next two, seventh slightly longer than wide and a little thicker than the preceding, club oval, abrupt, but slightly longer than the three preceding joints combined. *Prothorax* about one-half wider than long, the sides broadly, evenly

arcuate, becoming parallel behind the middle and broadly sinuate near the apex, which is truncate and quite distinctly less than one-half as wide as the base, the latter transverse, the lobe less than one-third the width, rounded and rather prominent ; mes-epimera strongly exposed from above in the basal reëntrant angle ; disk somewhat coarsely, very densely, rather rugosely punctured, the impunctate line only narrowly and indefinitely traceable toward the middle. Scutellum small, quadrate, glabrous, impressed along the middle. *Elytra* slightly wider than the prothorax and twice as long, the sides strongly convergent, feebly and evenly arcuate throughout, the apex narrowly, evenly rounded, the humeral callus not distinctly prominent ; disk deeply, not very coarsely striate, the intervals from two to three times as wide as the grooves, densely, confusedly and rugosely punctured. *Abdomen* broadly, feebly impressed and more sparsely squamose in the middle toward base. Prosternum with a large, moderately deep impression, subglabrous at the bottom, and with a short stout erect process before each coxa, the coxæ rather large and separated by four-fifths of their own width. Length 2.9 mm.; width 1.35 mm.

District of Columbia.

The typical representative above described is a male. The species is altogether distinct from any other here noted, and may be known at once by the pale coloration of the integuments and the ochreous scales.

14 **Centrinus perscitus** Herbst—Käfer, VII, p. 28 (Curculio).

Oval, convex, piceous-brown, the elytra rufous; vestiture not very dense, ochreous-yellow, consisting of closer and broader scales beneath, and on the upper surface of narrow squamules which are abruptly much denser along the sides of the pronotum, the elytra also with a few larger whiter and very widely dispersed scales. Beak rather short and thick, evenly, strongly arcuate, as long as the head and prothorax in the female, similar but a little shorter and thicker in the male, the antennæ rather short, inserted at or just behind the middle, the first funicular joint robust, fully as long as the next three, second not twice as long as wide; club rather large, oval, as long as the five preceding joints combined, densely pubescent and indistinctly annulated. Prothorax fully two-thirds wider than long, the sides feebly convergent and very slightly arcuate to apical third, then broadly rounded convergent and broadly sinuate to the apex; disk very densely, not coarsely punctate. Elytra conoidal, narrowly rounded at apex, a little wider than the prothorax and sensibly more than twice as long, the striæ fine but deep, the intervals densely, confusedly punctato-rugulose, flat, three to four times as wide as the grooves. Prosternum in the male narrowly,

deeply excavated and having a very stout acuminate erect process
before each coxa; in the female flat, without trace of impression;
anterior coxæ separated by three-fourths of their own width.
Length 2.5–2.7 mm.; width 1.3 mm.

The two specimens before me are from New Jersey and Indiana.
It is somewhat singular that Dr. LeConte should have failed to see
the corneous prosternal processes in the male of this species; they
are quite conspicuous and must have been concealed by the anterior
femora in the specimens which he examined.

15 **Centrinus exulans** n. sp.—Rather broadly rhomboid-oval, convex,
piceo-rufous throughout and densely clothed with scales, which are narrower
and yellowish in the middle three-fifths of the pronotum, whiter and denser
at the sides and also on the elytra near and especially behind the scutellum.
Head rather coarsely, densely punctate, dull and squamulose, the impression
almost completely obsolete; beak somewhat stout, short, evenly cylindrical,
smooth toward apex but densely punctate, rugose and squamose toward base,
evenly, rather strongly arcuate and not quite as long as the head and prothorax; antennæ inserted distinctly behind the middle, the scape as long as
the next four joints, first funicular joint fully as long as the next three, second
about equal to the succeeding two, club moderate, ovo-conoidal. *Prothorax*
short and transverse, four-fifths wider than long, the sides evenly, strongly
arcuate and convergent from base to apex, becoming parallel near the former
and feebly sinuate near the apex, which is transversely truncate and distinctly less than one-half as wide as the base, the latter straight and transverse, the median lobe one-third of the total width, rounded and prominent;
disk not very coarsely, deeply, densely punctate, the impunctate line feebly
traceable and extremely fine. Scutellum moderate, squamose, slightly transverse. *Elytra* slightly wider than the prothorax and fully twice as long, the
outline almost evenly ogival from base to apex, the latter acutely rounded;
humeral callus quite distinctly prominent; disk rather finely, deeply striate,
the intervals wide, flat, densely and confusedly punctate. *Abdomen* very
densely punctured and squamose throughout. Prosternum nearly flat, separating the coxæ by appreciably less than their own width. Length 3.3 mm.;
width 1.6 mm.

New Mexico (Gallup). Mr. Wickham.

The single specimen is a female, but the species is very distinct
and allied only to *perscitus*. It differs from *perscitus* in its much
larger size and stouter form, in the decidedly shorter relative length
of the intermediate and posterior tibiæ, and in the pronotal punctures which are here very close but circular in outline and not in
actual contact, while in *perscitus* they are coarser and polygonally
crowded. These two species belong to a peculiar type, distinguished
from the other allies of *perscillus* by the very much shorter, stouter
and evenly cylindrical beak.

IV.

16 Centrinus senilis Gyll.—Sch. Curc , III, p. 759 ; Boh., l. c., VIII, p. 215.

Narrowly rhomboid-oval, convex, black, the tibiæ and antennæ rufo-piceous; vestiture white, consisting of long, very slender, not very densely but uniformly distributed squamules on the upper surface, which are replaced, however, by black squamules in two broad transverse elytral bands, interrupted at the suture, one at the middle and the other near the apex; on the under surface the scales are elongate, but broader and denser. Head alutaceous, finely but strongly, sparsely punctured, glabrous, with the exception of a line of very minute squamules along the edge of the eyes; impression very broad and almost obsolete, with a small feeble median fovea; beak abruptly polished, slender, feebly but almost evenly arcuate, gradually slightly thicker and more arcuate at the base, sparsely punctured and squamulose at the sides near the base but elsewhere very minutely, sparsely punctate and glabrous, not at all dilated at the antennæ but gradually wider and flatter toward apex, about two-thirds as long as the body; antennæ inserted just beyond basal third, slender, the scape extending almost to the eye, the first funicular joint slender, clavate, as long as the next two, second slender and as long as the third and fourth, outer joints slightly thicker and nearly as wide as long, club rather small and narrow, oval, pointed. Prothorax barely one-third wider than long, the sides evenly, broadly arcuate, convergent anteriorly, becoming broadly sinuate behind the apex and almost parallel near the base, the latter transverse, the lobe less than one-third the width but strongly rounded and very prominent; apex truncate and distinctly more than one-half as wide as the base; disk dull, not very coarsely, extremely closely and polygonally punctate, the impunctate line not distinct. Scutellum well developed, quadrate, slightly wider and transverse behind, the angles acute; surface flat, moderately densely squamulose. Elytra distinctly wider and three-fourths longer than the prothorax, the sides very strongly convergent, broadly, feebly arcuate, the apex narrowly rounded; humeral callus very prominent; disk rather finely striate, the intervals wide, somewhat dull, finely, rather sparsely, confusedly and slightly rugosely punctate throughout. Prosternum flat and separating the coxæ by fully three-fourths of their own width, but strongly constricted laterally behind the apex, and with a trans-

versely oval, deep, polished and glabrous subapical pit, separated
from the lateral constriction by obtuse elevations.   Length 3.5 mm.;
width 1.65 mm.

Arizona (Santa Rita Mts.).   Mr. Wickham.   The single representative before me is a female; I have not seen the male.   The
remarkable form of the mandibles and the robust excavated tarsal
claws, may ultimately necessitate the generic separation of this
species, for which Mr. Pascoe has already suggested a name.

The spots of the elytra appear to be denuded, but, as in all similar
cases in this genus, these areas are not really denuded but quite as
densely clothed with blackish and sometimes more slender squamules.

V.

17 **Centrinus acuminatus** n. sp.—Narrowly rhomboidal, black,
the antennæ rufo-piceous with the club paler and brown; lustre dull, the
sculpture dense but not very deep; vestiture pure white, consisting of broad,
extremely dense scales beneath and of longer, sparser, evenly distributed
squamules above, not entirely concealing the surface; those of the pronotum
directed transversely, those of the elytral intervals not arranged in lines.
Head finely, sparsely punctate, with a squamose area above each eye, the
transverse impression well marked; beak in the male distinctly robust toward
base, strongly tapering thence to the apex and scarcely longer than the head
and prothorax, in the female distinctly longer and much more slender, strongly
arcuate, densely, deeply sculptured, squamose, the antennæ inserted just
behind the middle, the scape moderate, rather abruptly clavate, the funicle
very long, slender, bristling with an irregular fringe of long flexible white
setæ along its internal side, the second joint very slender, scarcely more than
one-half as long as the first and barely one-half longer than the third, two to
four decreasing in length, outer joints not at all transverse, the club aberrant,
slender, more than twice as long as wide, about as long as the preceding four
joints combined, abrupt, densely pubescent, with the annulations very distinct, almost articulate, and with the two basal joints together occupying
scarcely more than one-half of the length. *Prothorax* one-half wider than
long, the sides broadly, feebly arcuate, gradually convergent and sinuate
anteriorly, becoming nearly parallel toward base; apex distinctly less than
one-half as wide as the base, the latter transverse, with the median lobe small
but distinct; disk rather coarsely but not very deeply punctate, without
median line, the punctures extremely densely, polygonally crowded, forming
almost even hexagons at some points.   Scutellum moderate, very densely
squamose, subquadrate.   *Elytra* about one third longer than wide, nearly
twice as long as the prothorax, and at base, rather abruptly, distinctly wider
than the latter, the humeri small but prominent, the sides rapidly convergent
thence to the apex and feebly arcuate, the apex very narrowly rounded; disk
deeply but not coarsely striate, the intervals three or four times as wide as

the grooves, broadly convex, coarsely densely and deeply punctato-rugulose.
Prosternum very obsoletely impressed along the middle, separating the coxæ
by a little more than one-third of their own width and rather narrowly emarginate behind.　Length 3.2–3.8 mm.; width 1.6–1.75 mm.

Texas; Arizona (Tuçson).

In form and size this very distinct species is nearly similar to
penicellus, but the beak is shorter and the antennæ of singular
structure.　The male differs from the female in having the anterior
trochanters obtusely toothed.　The hind tibiæ are bent outward
slightly and feebly dilated at apex, the internal spur not visible and
the apical margin transversely truncate, a peculiarity of structure
which is very highly developed in Eisonyx.　Three specimens.

18 Centrinus globifer n. sp.—Form, color, sculpture and vestiture
throughout almost exactly as in *acuminatus*, the lustre a little more shining
and the rugose punctures of the elytral intervals not quite so dense.　*Beak*
in the male thick toward base, arcuate, not quite as long as the head and
prothorax, the scape short, gradually clavate, inserted at basal two-fifths, the
funicle robust, cylindrical, bristling with long flexible setæ, especially along
the anterior or internal side, the second joint but slightly more than twice as
long as wide, three-fifths as long as the first and distinctly longer than the
third, two to four decreasing in length, five to seven subquadrate, moniliform, the seventh a little wider than long, the club extremely abrupt, robust,
elliptical, as long as the preceding four joints together, scarcely one-half longer
than wide, the sutures fine but deep, the basal joint narrower and shorter
than the second, the first two together composing only one-half of the mass,
the surface throughout polished and very sparsely pubescent, the first in great
part, and the second near the base, completely glabrous.　The prosternum is
flat, with two deep approximate denuded subapical foveæ, and separates the
coxæ by one-half of their own width.　Length 3.7 mm.; width 1.8 mm.

Texas (El Paso).

The extreme resemblance which this species bears to *acuminatus*
in every external feature is very remarkable, in view of the equally
striking difference in antennal structure, and in the more widely
separated anterior coxæ.　The single male before me has the anterior trochanters obtusely dentate, the tooth lamelliform.　The posterior tibiæ are nearly as in *acuminatus*, although a little shorter, the
posterior femora are also a little shorter thicker and with more
arcuate external outline.

VI.

19 Centrinus penicellus Herbst—Käfer, VII, p. 29 (Curculio);
holosericeus Gyll.: Sch. Curc., III, p. 760 (Centrinus); *pubescens* Uhler: Proc.
Acad. Nat. Sci., Phila., VII, p. 417 (Baridius).

This species is so well known, and so easily recognizable by the
characters given in the table, that but little further need be said of
it.   The antennæ are slender, rather long, the second funicular joint
very slender, fully two-thirds as long as the first and scarcely as
long as the next two together, the latter equal and each distinctly
elongate, the club small, rather abrupt, elongate-oval, pointed and
but slightly longer than the three preceding joints combined, densely
pubescent and with its basal joint constituting scarcely two-fifths of
the mass; the scape is slender, rather abruptly clavate and inserted
just beyond basal third.   The prosternum is flat, extremely densely
squamose, feebly bitumorose at the apex, and with a transverse excavated groove at a sensible distance behind the apical margin, the
coxæ rather large, somewhat prominent and separated by barely
two-thirds of their own width.   Anterior trochanters small and
simple in both sexes.   Length 3.5–3.8 mm.; width 1.7–1.9 mm.

The series before me is from Iowa and Indiana.   I have seen no
specimen in which the apical subsutural denuded spots were completely wanting, but the others are frequently obliterated.   It is
probable that the Cuban *tomentosus* Klug, i. litt., is a different
species from this.

VII.

20 **Centrinus lineellus** Lec.—Proc. Ac. Nat. Sci., Phila., 1859, p. 79.

A finely ornamented small species of rather robust, oval, convex
form, black throughout, the antennal scape rufous; under surface
clothed densely with large yellowish-white scales, the same forming
three distinctly limited broad vittæ on the pronotum, and covering
the second elytral interval throughout, the third in apical two-thirds,
the fourth in basal fourth, the sixth more or less throughout, and
the seventh and eighth except toward the humeri; remainder of the
upper surface clothed with large piceous-black scales.   Beak in the
female slender, evenly and extremely arcuate, a little more than
one-half as long as the body, the antennæ inserted just behind the
middle, the scape short, extending thence only two-thirds the distance to the eyes, the second funicular joint slender, a little more
than one-half as long as the first and distinctly shorter than the
next two, the latter subequal and each a little longer than wide,
outer joints gradually and distinctly transverse, the club small,
narrowly oval, not very abrupt, densely pubescent, as long as the
preceding four joints combined, and with the basal joint composing

nearly one-half the mass. Prosternum flat, with a small denuded but unimpressed spot behind the apex, the apical margin with a close series of long broad porrect scales, extending over the basal parts of the head, the anterior coxæ rather small, separated by fully three-fourths of their own width. Posterior tibiæ normal, slender, finely, acutely dentate externally at apex, with the internal spur distinct. Length 2.8 mm.; width 1.4 mm.

California—Cab. LeConte. Represented by the unique female type.

VIII.

21 **Centrinus capillatus** Lec.—Proc. Am. Phil. Soc., XV, p. 311.

Rather narrowly rhomboid-oval, convex, shining, black, the legs and antennæ paler, rather sparsely clothed above with long slender white hair-like squamules, which are uniform in size and distribution on the elytra, except a little wider just behind the scutellum, very sparse and slender on the pronotum, becoming a little broader toward base in the middle and at lateral fourth, broad and rather dense on the under surface. Beak in the male slender, strongly arcuate, nearly one-half as long as the body, the antennæ inserted well behind the middle, the first funicular joint about as long as the next three, the second more slender, rather more than one-half as long as the first and about equal to the next two, the club small, robust, abrupt, but slightly longer than wide, pale, densely pubescent, with the basal joint constituting distinctly less than one-half the mass. Prothorax rather short, truncate, conical, the sides broadly rounded, the constriction feeble; disk rather coarsely but not very deeply, moderately closely punctate, with a distinct impunctate line. Elytra a little longer than wide, slightly wider than the prothorax and not quite twice as long, conical, narrowly rounded at apex; disk with deep striæ, the intervals nearly three times as wide as the grooves, confusedly but not very densely punctato-rugulose. Prosternum flat, not impressed and without trace of apical constriction, but with a small denuded spot at some distance behind the apex, from which the scales radiate in all directions; coxæ separated by one-half their own width. Length 2.75–3.0 mm.; width 1.3–1.5 mm.

Texas. In the female the beak is more abruptly bent near the base. The prosternum in both sexes is perfectly simple before the coxæ, and without trace of the "slender cusp" mentioned by LeConte.

22 **Centrinus nubecula** n. sp.—Oval, rather robust, moderately convex, black and shining throughout, the anterior tibiæ rufous and longer than the others ; vestiture white, rather sparse, consisting on the upper surface of very slender hair-like squamules, disposed in nearly even approximate lines on the elytra, and becoming coarse and denser scales about the scutellum and in a subsutural area on each just behind the middle; on the pronotum they are coarser and denser near the base before the scutellum and at lateral fourth ; on the under surface they become moderately wide and close, except on the apical half of the prosternum, where they are very fine and sparse but radiating from the peculiar antero-central point mentioned in the other species of this subgenus. *Head* prominently convex, finely, sparsely punctate, the beak strongly arcuate in basal third, thence feebly arcuate and very thin viewed laterally, but broad and flattened viewed anteriorly to the apex, punctured at the sides toward base, nearly one-half as long as the body, the antennæ inserted well behind the middle, nearly as in *capillatus*, the first funicular joint as long as the next three, the second a little more than one-half as long as the first and about as long as the next two. *Prothorax* two-thirds wider than long, the apex truncate, not quite one-half as wide as the base; sides evenly, feebly arcuate and convergent from the base, the constriction broad and feeble ; base transverse and straight, the median lobe small but prominent; disk rather coarsely, strongly, evenly and closely punctate, without evident impunctate line. *Scutellum* small, quadrate, impressed lunately behind. *Elytra* a little wider than the prothorax and not quite twice as long, evenly conoideo-elliptical in outline, the humeri basal, moderately prominent; disk not coarsely but very deeply, abruptly striate, the intervals flat, fully three times as wide as the grooves, rather finely but strongly, not densely and subtransversely punctato-rugulose. *Prosternum* feebly, transversely and indefinitely impressed anteriorly, separating the coxæ by one-half of their own width, without trace of corneous processes. Posterior tibiæ slender, strongly sinuate externally at apical fourth. Length 3.2 mm.; width 1.65 mm.

Texas.

From analogy in the case of *capillatus*, if we regard as the female the form having the beak more abruptly bent near the base and more widely flattened, the unique type of *nubecula* is of that sex, for the beak is even more noticeably flattened than in the species referred to. In the male, the beak is but slightly shorter, and is much more evenly and, on the whole, more strongly arcuate than in the female, and is cylindrical, although feebly flattened very near the apex. For the reasons stated, the male beak appears thicker from a lateral point of view than that of the female, but from an anterior point it is a little thinner.

23 **Centrinus clientulus** n. sp.—Rather narrowly rhomboid-oval, convex, polished, black throughout, except the legs which are bright rufous ;

vestiture consisting of yellowish-white scales, broad and dense beneath, but sparse and generally slender toward the sides of the prothorax: on the upper surface they are rather broadly oval on the elytra behind the middle and near the scutellum, but elsewhere slightly narrower; on the pronotum narrow toward the sides and before the scutellum, but elsewhere very sparse, finer and hairlike. *Head* dull, very minutely, sparsely punctured, the beak in the female about one-half as long as the body, strongly and abruptly arcuate at the base, perceptibly flattened toward apex, deeply punctate at the sides toward base, the antennæ inserted well behind the middle, the basal joint of the funicle elongate, nearly as long as the next four together, second rather slender, not one-half as long as the first, not quite as long as the next two, the club small and especially very short, not more than one-third longer than wide and but slightly longer than the preceding three joints together, very abrupt, densely pubescent, with the basal joint constituting not quite one-half the mass. *Prothorax* rather short, two-thirds wider than long, the sides convergent and broadly arcuate from the base to the distinctly constricted apex, the latter almost tubulate and fully one-half as wide as the base, the latter straight and transverse, the median lobe small and prominent; disk rather coarsely punctate, the punctures shallow, close but not contiguous, with a narrow, more or less distinctly defined impunctate line. Scutellum truncate, not as long as wide. *Elytra* a little more than twice as long as the prothorax, and, at the small, rather prominent humeri, perceptibly wider than the latter; sides thence strongly convergent to the narrowly rounded apex and feebly arcuate; disk rather finely but deeply striate, the intervals between two and three times as wide as the grooves, flat, not very coarsely, moderately closely, strongly punctato rugulose. Prosternum broadly, scarcely visibly impressed, the anterior coxæ separated by about one-half of their own width. Length 2.6–3.0 mm.; width 1.2–1.5 mm.

Texas (Columbus). Mr. Schwarz.

This species is allied to *capillatus*, but differs in the much broader and more uneven scales of the elytra, and in its very pale bright rufous legs.

IX.

24 Centrinus falsus Lec.—Proc. Am. Phil. Soc., XV, p. 315.

Oval, convex, black, the legs more or less rufo-piceous, moderately shining; vestiture whitish, consisting of very slender lineate squamules, sparse on the pronotum, closer and a little broader on the elytra, where they tend to aggregate in a broad line along the middle of the intervals; beneath they are denser wider and squamiform. Beak rather robust, moderately arcuate, a little longer than the head and prothorax, the antennæ inserted distinctly beyond the middle, the second funicular joint cylindrical, about one-half as long as the first and as long as the next two, the club well developed, robust, oval, abrupt, nearly as long as the five preceding joints together, densely pubescent and with the basal joint constituting about two-fifths of the mass. Prothorax much wider than long, with the sides almost parallel and feebly arcuate in basal two-thirds, then strongly rounded, the apical constriction extremely feeble, the punctures fine and very dense, tending to longitudinal coalescence; median impunctate line distinct. Scutellum very densely squamose. Elytra a little wider than the prothorax and more than twice as long, rather less strongly narrowed to the apex than usual, the striæ somewhat fine but deep. Prosternum with a transverse subapical constriction, and a rather narrow moderately deep parallel sulcus along the middle, the sides of the sulcus somewhat abruptly defined; anterior coxæ separated by scarcely more than one-fourth of their own width. Length 3.6–4.0 mm.; width 1.6–1.8 mm.

Alabama and Iowa. In some respects this species forms a satisfactory passage from the species with armed male prosternum, to those of the *scutellum-album* group. I have been unable to note any prominent secondary sexual modification of the male.

X.

25 Centrinus scutellum-album Say—Curc., p. 21, Ed. Lec., I, p. 287 (*Baridius scut.* Germ. : Sch. Curc., III, p. 730).

Subrhomboidal, convex, rather robust, the vestiture consisting of small, more or less narrow sparse white scales, which become large broad and dense on the under surface. Beak nearly straight, a little more than one-half as long as the body, abruptly and strongly bent at base, the flanks flattened and deeply longitudinally punctato-rugulose throughout, more strongly arcuate along the under outline behind the antennæ, the latter inserted near apical third in the male, the basal joint of the funicle moderate in length, the second rather long, fully three-fourths as long as the first and subequal to the next three, joints three to seven small; club large, elongate, oval, densely pubescent, fully two-thirds as long as the funicle, the sutures feeble, arcuate on the inner side, the basal joint constituting a little more than one-third of the whole, nearly as long as wide, with a large tumid glabrous and polished area on the inner side, at the middle of which there is an erect acute spiniform process. Prothorax wider than long, scarcely at all constricted, the punctures rather coarse, deep, rounded, almost in mutual contact. Elytra distinctly wider and about three-fourths longer than the prothorax, coarsely, deeply striate, the intervals very coarsely, confusedly punctate. Prosternum scarcely impressed, but with a large transverse abrupt and very deep excavation just behind the apex, the coxæ separated by scarcely one-third of their own width. Length 3.2–4.5 mm.; width 1.7–2.3 mm.

The description above given is taken from the male and in this sex the pygidium is considerably exposed between the elytral apices, .and very oblique; in the female it appears to be somewhat less exposed. The body is more broadly rhomboidal than in the *salebrosus* group, and the sexual differences in the structure of the beak are not at all evident. The male is black, but the female is almost invariably more or less rufescent and has the prothorax shorter, the pronotal punctures larger and sparser, and the antennal club simple.

This species is represented in my cabinet from New York, Indiana, Missouri and Florida; it also occurs in Brazil.

26 **Centrinus denticornis** n. sp.—Robust, oblong-subrhomboidal, convex, moderately shining, black throughout, the vestiture of the pronotum consisting of very small sparse and slender squamules, evenly distributed but denser toward the sides behind the apical margin, also along the base near the sides and on the median lobe; on the elytra the scales are generally small, moderately wide, evenly and sparsely distributed over the intervals, each lying entirely within a very deep rounded puncture; scales of the under surface large, broad and very dense, the color whitish throughout. *Head* dull and alutaceous, finely but strongly punctured, the transverse impression feeble, the beak abruptly highly polished, in the male rather stout, flattened toward apex, as long as the head and prothorax, deeply, coarsely punctato-rugulose at the sides, the median impunctate line entire, the antennæ inserted near apical third, the scape bent and clavate toward apex, the second funicular joint twice as long as wide, three-fourths as long as the first and one-half longer than the third, the club rather large, oval, densely pubescent, as long as the five preceding joints combined, the sutures fine but straight and distinct, the basal joint one-third of the whole, much wider than long, with a large glabrous polished area on the inner side, not extending beyond apical fourth of its length, which is more or less obtusely dentate. *Prothorax* large convex, the sides broadly rounded, strongly convergent anteriorly, becoming almost parallel in basal half, not constricted near the apex, the latter scarcely two-fifths as wide as the base, which is transverse and straight, with the lobe abrupt, prominent, and the basal angles obtusely rounded; disk with an evanescent partial impunctate line, the punctures not very large but deep, circular, almost in mutual contact but not polygonal. Scutellum subtransverse, densely squamose. *Elytra* distinctly wider than the prothorax but not much more than two-thirds longer than the latter, the humeri large, promi-

nent; sides strongly convergent, the apex rather narrowly rounded in the male, more broadly in the female, the striæ very abrupt, deep, punctate, not very coarse, the intervals flat, two to three times as wide as the grooves, moderately coarsely, evenly, confusedly and very deeply punctured throughout. Prosternum in the male broadly, distinctly impressed along the middle, with a small transversely impressed fovea behind the apex, the coxæ separated by scarcely two-fifths of their own width, almost similar in the female. Length 5.3–6.0 mm.; width 2.8–3.2 mm.

North Carolina; Kansas.

The beak in the male is feebly arcuate and much more strongly so toward base; in the female it is scarcely at all longer but more slender, cylindrical, smooth and minutely, sparsely punctured, except just before the eyes, where the punctures become coarse and close, but not rugose, the antennæ inserted just beyond the middle; in the female the antennæ are more slender and with a smaller simple club. This is probably our largest centrinide.

27 Centrinus salebrosus n. sp.—Oblong-oval, the upper surface moderately convex, black and dull, the legs and antennæ more or less piceous; vestiture whitish, consisting of large broad and very dense scales beneath, finer but extremely variable on the upper surface. *Head* rather strongly and closely punctured, the transverse impression almost obsolete, with a small deep median fovea, the beak in the male moderate in length and thickness, as long as the head and prothorax, distinctly, evenly arcuate but more abruptly bent at base, flattened toward apex and slightly compressed at the sides, densely punctato-rugulose and deeply furrowed on the flanks, the antennæ inserted at apical two-fifths, rather slender, the club rather small, oval, gradually pointed, densely pubescent, the basal joint composing rather more than one-third of the mass, with a small smooth glabrous area on the inner side toward base, at the centre of which there is a more or less distinct dentiform process. *Prothorax* about two-fifths wider than long; sides broadly arcuate, convergent anteriorly, becoming almost parallel in basal two-thirds, the constriction obsolete; apex very nearly one-half as wide as the base, the latter straight and transverse, the median lobe abrupt and densely, coarsely squamose; disk devoid of impunctate line, the punctures not very small, deep and rather dense throughout. Scutellum densely squamose. *Elytra* distinctly wider, and from three-fourths to four-fifths longer than the prothorax, the humeri rather large and abruptly, obtusely prominent; sides behind them unusually feebly convergent, the apex not narrowly rounded; disk with deep, abrupt, not very coarse grooves, the intervals two to three times as wide as the grooves, densely, confusedly punctate, the punctures coarse but indistinct and polygonally distorted. Prosternum not distinctly impressed, separating the coxæ by barely one-half of their own width, and with a deep transverse groove behind the apical margin. Length 2.9–4.7 mm.; width 1.3–2.2 mm.

New York; Indiana; Kentucky; Dakota; Colorado; Texas.

The description is drawn from the male; in the female the beak is quite distinctly longer and rather more slender, evenly, somewhat strongly arcuate throughout, cylindrical, smooth, shining and minutely, sparsely punctate except at base, the antennæ inserted distinctly beyond the middle, and with the club unmodified.

This species is the most protean in its variations of any baride which I have seen; more especially in the vestiture of the upper surface, which may consist of very slender sparse squamules, or robust oval dense and very conspicuous scales, with every intergrade between these limits. The series before me consists of nearly sixty specimens.

28 **Centrinus pinguescens** n. sp.—Oblong-oval, stout, moderately convex, dull black, the antennæ and the tibiæ at least toward apex, rufescent; vestiture on the upper surface consisting of yellowish scales, elongate-oval and dense on the elytral intervals, minute, slender and inconspicuous on the pronotum, but larger and denser at base near the sides and toward the middle and also in the subapical constriction, large, yellowish-white and very dense beneath *Head* somewhat finely, deeply, rather densely and conspicuously punctured, the impression broad and very feeble, with an elongate median fovea; beak in the male rather stout, deeply, coarsely and rugosely punctate, nearly evenly, distinctly arcuate and somewhat abruptly very strongly so near the base, a little longer than the head and prothorax; antennæ inserted well beyond the middle, the basal joint of the funicle rather short, stout, the second fully three-fourths as long as the first and equal to the next two together, sixth and seventh internally prominent, club very robust and abrupt, as long as the five preceding joints combined, extremely densely clothed with short recumbent setiform squamules, the basal joint constituting one-third of the mass, with a glabrous internal area, not extending much beyond the middle, at the centre of which there is a very minute but acute and prominent spicule. *Prothorax* two-thirds wider than long, the sides broadly, evenly rounded in apical half, becoming parallel and straight thence to the base, the subapical constriction feeble but distinct; apex distinctly less than one-half as wide as the base; disk very finely, extremely densely punctured and dull, with barely a trace of a very narrow partial impunctate line. Scutellum very densely and conspicuously squamose. *Elytra* slightly wider and two-thirds longer than the prothorax, but slightly longer than wide, the sides strongly convergent; apex rather abruptly, obtusely but not very broadly rounded; striæ rather coarse, deep, with the setæ minute; intervals flat, more than twice as wide as the grooves, coarsely, deeply, very densely and rugosely punctured throughout. *Abdomen* with the scales slightly smaller and sparser in the middle toward base in the male. Prosternum with a transverse subapical excavation, the coxæ separated by nearly one-half of their own width Length 4.1 mm.; width 2.0 mm.

Arkansas (Little Rock). Mr. Wickham.

This species belongs near *salebrosus*, but differs in its more obese form, finer and still denser pronotal punctuation, shorter second joint of the funicle and very much more robust club. A single male.

29 Centrinus pulverulentus n. sp.—Oval, subrhomboidal, convex, black, the antennal funicle gradually rufous toward apex, the club black; vestiture white, that of the upper surface consisting of small evenly and sparsely placed truncate scales on the pronotum, generally larger and closer along the apical margin; on the elytra the scales are larger, rather sparsely but evenly distributed, elongate-oval and each lying completely within a large oval puncture, the squamules borne by the punctures at the bottom of the striæ rather broad, scale-like and distinct; scales of the under surface large, nearly as wide as long and extremely dense. *Head* finely, deeply, not very sparsely punctate, the usual small frontal fovea distinct; beak rather slender, almost straight but abruptly and strongly arcuate at base, nearly as long as the elytra in the female, and smooth polished, very minutely, sparsely punctate, but rather abruptly, coarsely and closely so at the sides near the base, the antennæ inserted at or just beyond the middle, the first funicular joint not as long as the next three, the second about two-thirds as long as the first and not quite as long as the next two, club well developed, robust, densely pubescent, with the basal joint not longer than the second and constituting less than one-third of the mass. *Prothorax* one-half wider than long, the sides convergent and broadly, nearly evenly arcuate from base to apex, the constriction extremely feeble; base, basal lobe and scutellum as in *salebrosus;* disk with an ill-defined fusiform impunctate spot in the middle, the punctures rather large, deep, dense but scarcely polygonal. *Elytra* distinctly wider than the prothorax and about twice as long, the sides strongly convergent, the apex rather abruptly rounded and about one-half as wide as the basal regions, the humeri prominent; disk coarsely striate, the intervals flat, coarsely punctate, the punctures elongate-oval, nearly in mutual contact. *Prosternum* broadly, feebly impressed, with an abrupt and extremely deep, transversely oval pit, just behind the apical margin, the coxæ separated by about one-half of their own width. Length 4.5–5.0 mm.; width 2.2–2.4 mm.

North Carolina; Texas (Austin); Colorado.

Described from the female. In the male the beak is deeply, coarsely, longitudinally punctato-rugulose, with the antennæ inserted far beyond the middle, the prosternum more deeply impressed along the middle, and the anterior coxæ still more narrowly separated, but the very deep transverse subapical pit is almost similar to that of the female. In antennal structure the male differs from the female in having the second funicular joint shorter, the outer joints more transverse and obliquely truncate at apex, and the basal joint of the club with a short acute erect tooth on the inner side.   This is a very distinct and interesting species.

The female from Colorado is very densely squamose above, and the species probably varies in vestiture to as great a degree as *salebrosus.*

CENTRINOPUS n. gen.

In this genus the beak is long, very slender and strongly arcuate, with the antennæ inserted near basal third, the scape short and extending almost to the eyes, the basal joint of the funicle long, the second short and the club rather small, with its basal joint unusually large.

The mandibles are well developed, quite distinctly notched within near the apex, but with the external outline nearly straight; when closed they are scarcely at all decussate and form together an anteriorly prominent ogive.   The prosternum is deeply canaliculate along the middle in the female, and with a still deeper elongate-oval excavation in the male, being armed in the latter sex before each coxa with a well-developed, abruptly bent, corneous process. The anterior coxæ are somewhat prominent and narrowly separated, being appreciably more approximate in the male than in the female. The mes-epimera are exposed from above and the scutellum is very small and densely squamose.   The pygidium is completely covered in both sexes, and the met-episterna moderately wide and generally more densely squamose than the adjoining surfaces.

The form of the body is somewhat oblong-oval, the humeral callus feebly developed, and the general habitus reminds us considerably of *Limnobaris grisea.*   In the male the abdomen is broadly impressed in the middle toward base, the impressed area clothed with more slender, sparser but recumbent squamules.   Our two species may be identified by the following characters:—

Prothorax feebly transverse; pronotum not conspicuously trivittate, the scales uniform in coloration but not in size and density ; elytra abruptly much wider than the prothorax, the alternate intervals simply more broadly squamose...1 **helvinus**
Prothorax more transverse ; pronotum with three distinct vittæ, the squamules of the intermediate regions not only finer and sparser but darker in color ; elytra but slightly wider than the prothorax, with the alternate intervals much more broadly, densely and conspicuously clothed with paler scales...2 **alternatus**

1 **Centrinopus helvinus** n. sp.—Oval, convex, dark piceous in color, the beak, antennæ and legs more or less rufescent; vestiture pale ochreous-yellow, squamiform, the scales dense beneath especially on the met-episterna; on the pronotum they are fine on the flanks beneath, then coarser and closer in a sublateral vitta, then sparse and fine to the median line where they are again coarser and denser, especially toward base; on the elytra they are more broadly oval, more whitish and densely, unevenly distributed throughout all the intervals, especially on the rather broader third, fifth and seventh. *Head* densely punctured and squamose toward apex, the basal portions of the beak also densely squamose but with the scales erect and bristling, the beak slender, evenly, rather strongly arcuate, a little longer than the head and prothorax, deeply, rather coarsely punctured and longitudinally furrowed but shining, the two punctate grooves lying along the sides of the median impunctate line especially evident; antennæ with the basal joint of the funicle rather longer than the next three, the second but slightly longer than the third, the club moderate, robust, abrupt, oval, pointed, as long as the preceding four joints combined, densely pubescent, with the basal joint composing fully one-half of the mass, the annulations strong, the successive rings decreasing rather abruptly in transverse diameter. *Prothorax* one-third wider than long, the sides very feebly convergent and nearly straight to slightly beyond apical third, then broadly rounded, strongly convergent and feebly sinuate to the apex, which is truncate and not quite one-half as wide as the base, the latter transverse, broadly sinuate toward the median lobe which is very small but abrupt and prominent; disk densely, not coarsely punctured. *Elytra* abruptly one-fourth wider than the prothorax, rather more than twice as long as the latter, the outline hemi-elliptical, the humeri very small and scarcely at all prominent; disk deeply but not coarsely striate, the intervals flat and from two to three times as wide as the grooves. Prosternum with an extremely deep elongate-oval excavation, and with a corneous process before each coxa, the process very thick and erect at base, but then abruptly and angularly bent obliquely forward becoming rapidly finely acuminate, the coxæ rather prominent, separated by about one-fourth of their own width. Length 1.9–2.7 mm.; width 0.8–1.2 mm.

Indiana; Illinois.

The description is taken from the male, the female being similar in form and structure of the beak and antennæ, but having the prosternum simply longitudinally and deeply channeled, the channel squamose and limited at the sides by an obtusely elevated ridge; the coxæ are a little less approximate, being separated by nearly one-half of their own width. The measurements given above are taken from the extremes of a series of over one hundred specimens.

2 **Centrinopus alternatus** n. sp.—Oblong-oval, rather robust, convex, piceous-black; elytra toward the sides rufescent, the antennæ and legs dark rufo-piceous; vestiture yellowish, consisting of fine, not dense squam-

ules beneath ; on the upper surface the scales are pale and dark brown, the former forming three vittæ on the pronotum and densely clothing intervals three, five and seven, the line of the third and seventh uniting near the apex and continuing thence as a single short line to the apical angle ; other intervals having very narrow inconspicuous lines composed of more slender, whitish and brown squamules. *Head* densely punctate and squamulose anteriorly, the base of the beak bristling with erect scales, the beak slender, smooth, polished, rather coarsely but not densely lineato-punctate, strongly, evenly arcuate and a little longer than the head and prothorax, the basal joint of the funicle as long as the next three, the club small but robust, oval, densely pubescent, scarcely as long as the preceding four joints combined, with the basal joint composing nearly three-fifths of the mass, the remaining rings short but very distinct. *Prothorax* two fifths wider than long, the sides subparallel and feebly arcuate in basal two-thirds, then rounded, strongly convergent and broadly constricted to the apex, which is about one-half as wide as the base, the latter transverse and perfectly straight, the median lobe small but abrupt, prominent : disk very densely but not coarsely punctate. *Elytra* but slightly wider than the prothorax and fully twice as long, hemi elliptical, the humeri scarcely at all prominent ; disk deeply, not very coarsely striate, the intervals flat, from two to three times as wide as the grooves, moderately densely, deeply but not coarsely punctate. Under surface extremely densely punctate throughout. Prosternum deeply, longitudinally impressed, squamose, separating the coxæ by not quite one-half of their own width. Length 3.0 mm. ; width 1.35 mm.

Maryland.

A single female. I have, however, seen another specimen in the cabinet of Mr. Jülich. This is a very distinct form, easily distinguishable from *helvinus* by its larger size, more transverse and tri-vittate prothorax, and by the alternately conspicuously squamose elytral intervals. It closely resembles a small *Limnobaris grisea.*

LINONOTUS n. gen.

This genus is founded upon a male representative in the LeConte cabinet, which cannot be distinguished in any way from Boheman's *Centrinus distinctus,* as described from Brazil ; it will include also the Brazilian *C. westwoodi, parallelus* and other allied species.

The body is stout, rhomboidal and convex, the beak long, more or less slender, arcuate and slightly gibbous above at base, the constriction separating it from the head being in the form of a deep transverse and extremely pronounced furrow. The mandibles are large, prominent, non-decussate and strongly dentellate along their inner edge. Antennæ inserted behind the middle, slender, the basal joint of the funicle long and equal to the next three together, the

club small, narrowly oval, pointed and with its basal joint constituting nearly one-half of the mass.

The prothorax is subtubulate at apex, the anterior coxæ large,
prominent and separated by not quite their own width, the prosternum in the male having a large, oval, extremely deep median
excavation and two ante-coxal processes of great length, extending
far in advance of the head, and upwardly everted at apex. The scutellum is large, slightly trapezoidal, smooth, polished, flat, entirely
unimpressed and feebly, sparsely punctulate toward base only.[1]

1 **Linonotus distinctus** Boh.—Sch. Curc., VIII, i, p. 187 (Centrinus).

Black, polished, the pronotum with two broad lateral vittæ of
orange-red scales, the vittæ abruptly flexed beneath anteriorly, extending to the prosternal excavation. Elytra each with a single
broad vitta of the same color, occupying the entire width of intervals three and four, and extending from the base to apical fourth.
Met-episterna and sides of the last three ventral segments similarly
clothed. Length 5.8 mm.; width 3.1 mm.

The male referred to above is labeled "Texas," and, if this is
correct, indicates a distribution similar to that of *Hemirhipus fas-
cicularis.*

PYCHYBARIS.
LeConte—Proc. Am. Phil. Soc., XV, p. 302.

The original type is still the only known species assignable to
this distinct and somewhat isolated genus. The body is short and
very robust, feebly setose, polished and, although normally centri-
niform in pygidial structure, possesses many of the characteristics
of Onychobaris, as remarked by its author.

The beak is rather long, strongly arcuate, with the punctures not
very dense and arranged in subimpressed series, more confused at
the sides toward base, the mandibles not in the least decussate when
closed, but coming together on the axial line as in Centrinus. The
antennæ are inserted far behind the middle of the beak, with the
scrobes moderately oblique, attaining the eyes, the scape short, the
funicle gradually thick toward apex, almost continuous in outline

---

[1] Since this was written I have received specimens of the true *distinctus*,
taken near Rio de Janeiro, and find that they are identical with the Texan
representative.

with the finely and densely pubescent club, the latter moderate in size, oval, with the basal joint rather large.

The prosternum is flat, broad between the coxæ, the latter separated by their own width, the external sides of the cavities prolonged anteriorly for a short distance by deep and conspicuous closed fissures, as noticeable in some other genera of the present tribe; anteriorly, the apical constriction is totally obsolete, but in its place there are the two deep and somewhat approximate foveæ, with connecting groove, as in Onychobaris, each fovea being prolonged posteriorly for a short distance.

The scutellum is moderate in size, flat and almost circular. Legs moderately robust, the tibiæ rather roughly sculptured and feebly fluted externally; but this character is apparently not very important from a systematic point of view, as it recurs in several other genera, not especially related, such as Limnobaris. Tarsi robust, with the third joint very large and deeply bilobed, the claws small, rather slender, free and divergent.

1 **Pachybaris porosa** Lec.—Proc. Am. Phil. Soc., XV, p. 302.

Robust, convex, polished, black, the beak, legs and antennæ more or less rufo-piceous; vestiture very sparse, consisting of minute scarcely distinguishable setæ on the prothorax, and longer posteriorly recumbent and robust setæ on the elytra, where they are piceous in color and inconspicuous, very small but whitish on the under surface. Beak slender, strongly arcuate, striato-punctate, fully as long as the head and prothorax in the female and quite distinctly shorter in the male, the antennæ moderate, the scape short, first joint of the funicle as long as the next four, second a little longer than wide and slightly longer than the third. Prothorax short, two-thirds wider than long, the sides broadly rounded and strongly convergent anteriorly, feebly constricted but not tubulate at apex, becoming nearly parallel toward base, the latter transverse, the median lobe small, prominent and truncate, the truncation feebly emarginate to receive the scutellum; disk rather coarsely, deeply but not closely punctate, without impunctate line. Elytra scarcely perceptibly wider than the prothorax and three-fourths longer than the latter, not quite as long as wide; outline parabolic; disk with very coarse deep obsoletely crenulate grooves, the intervals about one-half wider than the grooves, each with a single series of very coarse deep rounded and close-set punctures. Length 3.8–4.0 mm.; width 2.3 mm.

Florida (New Smyrna and Biscayne Bay). Apparently not uncommon and belonging to the subtropical fauna of the peninsula. The allusion in the original description to whitish hairs on the elytra is inexact.

MICROCHOLUS.
LeConte—Proc. Am. Phil. Soc., XV, p. 303.

This isolated genus is characterized by a broad, moderately convex body, with normally striate elytra, an unimpressed prosternum, non-tubulate prothorax and small tarsal claws, and differs greatly from Oomorphidius, under which name I have separated two of the species assigned to it by its author, in several important characters as given in the table.

The mandibles are rather long, prominent, feebly arcuate in external outline, scarcely at all or feebly decussate when closed, and much more angulate anteriorly in this state than in Oomorphidius and Eisonyx. In fact in this and several other ways, Microcholus forms a tolerably satisfactory intermediate between the genera mentioned and Centrinus.

The two species at present known should be separated subgenerically as follows:—

Subgenus I.

Beak compressed toward base, minutely, feebly punctate even at the sides, the apex flattened and subdilated; scutellum rather large, elongate-oval and tumid; elytral striæ much coarser, impunctate; tarsal claws very stout; integuments nearly glabrous above........................1 **striatus**

Subgenus II.

Beak cylindrical, neither compressed toward base nor flattened at apex; scutellum very minute, triangular; elytral striæ fine, remotely punctate; tarsal claws very small but slender; integuments rather densely but unevenly squamose..................................2 **puncticollis**

In general outline of the body *M. puncticollis* almost perfectly resembles *Simocopis umbrina* Pasc.; the beak is however quite different.

I.

1 **Microcholus striatus** Lec.—Proc. Am. Phil. Soc., XV, p. 304.

Broadly oblong-oval, moderately convex, black, the legs rufopiceous; pronotum polished, the elytra slightly alutaceous; integuments almost glabrous above, with a cluster of large white scales at the base of the pronotum at each side and a few before the scutellum, also several widely dispersed on the elytra and a small group at the base of the third interval; under surface sparsely, the legs, meso- and met-episterna and sides of the last three ventral segments more or less densely, clothed with large white scales. Head separated from the beak by a very feeble impression, the beak fully as long as the prothorax, flattened near the apex and strongly compressed toward base, strongly, evenly arcuate, sparsely, very minutely punctate throughout and moderately stout; antennæ slender, the basal joint of the funicle slender, fully as long as the next four, the second slender and as long as the next two, club small, stout, densely pubescent, with the basal joint constituting rather more than one-half the mass as in Oomorphidius. Prothorax scarcely two-fifths wider than long, the sides broadly arcuate and gradually strongly convergent from the obtusely rounded basal angles to the apex, the latter not tubulate, the constriction very feeble; base transverse, the median lobe wide but very feeble; disk finely, sparsely punctate. Scutellum well-developed, elongate-oval and tumid. Elytra not at all wider than the prothorax, two-thirds longer than the latter and about as long as wide, the striæ rather fine but deep, with the edges obtuse, the intervals wide, each with a single somewhat uneven series of fine distant punctures. Anterior coxæ separated by rather less than one-third of their width, the tarsal claws small, short, very thick but free and moderately divérgent. Length 4.5 mm.; width 2.3 mm.

Florida (Lake Harney). Cab. LeÇonte. Represented, as far as known, by the unique type. The upper surface in the type is not denuded of scales as supposed by LeConte; the punctures, other than those very remote ones which bear the long isolated scales, bear each an infinitesimal seta.

II.

2 Microcholus puncticollis Lec.—Proc. Am. Phil. Soc., XV, p. 304.

Broadly oblong-oval, the elytra rapidly narrowed and sinuate at the sides behind; body and antennæ black, smooth and shining, the legs rufous; under surface, legs and elytra covered rather densely with large oval white scales, which, on the elytra, are a little closer on the third and fifth intervals toward base and behind the middle; pronotum more sparsely covered with elongate squamules, except a wide vitta at lateral sixth, which is more densely squamose. Beak glabrous but densely squamose near the base, rather stout, cylindrical and evenly, strongly arcuate throughout, distinctly punctate and nearly as long as the head and prothorax; antennæ very slender, nearly as in *striatus*, but with the first funicular joint as long as the next three. Prothorax slightly dilated, subparallel and broadly rounded at the sides, narrowed toward the apex and quite distinctly constricted but not tubulate, about four-fifths wider than long and one-half as long as the elytra, the base transverse, with the median lobe subobsolete; disk sparsely, somewhat unevenly, finely but distinctly punctate. Scutellum extremely small, flat, equilatero-triangular. Elytra at base not quite as wide as the prothorax, very slightly longer than wide, the striæ fine but abrupt, remotely and distinctly punctate, the intervals confusedly and minutely punctate. Prosternum separating the large anterior coxæ by scarcely more than one-fourth of their own width; tarsal claws small but slender, free and moderately divergent. Length 3.4–3.8 mm.; width 1.6–1.8 mm.

Florida (Baldwin). This species differs extremely from *striatus* in many important structural characters, and is the only one which has been taken in any number. The scales are rather easily abraded. The epistomal lobe is very short and narrow, occupying the median third of the width, and limited at each side by a long deep oblique and arcuate fissure, the apex broadly sinuate in the middle; in *striatus* it is more than twice as wide, not at all advanced and is transversely truncate at apex.

NICENTRUS n. gen.

The oblong-oval, sometimes almost cylindrical and convex form of the body, will readily serve to distinguish the species of this genus from those of Centrinus, where the outline is more rhomboidal. The beak is generally thick and rather short, differing but slightly in the sexes, often strongly compressed or flattened at the sides toward base, but, in *contractus*, becoming longer, cylindrical and almost impunctate, at least in the female. The antennæ are inserted at about the middle in the female or slightly beyond in the male. Mandibles rather well developed, nearly straight in external outline, with their inner edge dentellate; they are not decussate when closed, the form then being anteriorly prominent in angle or ogive.

The prosternum may be either canaliculate and feebly bicarinate along the middle or perfectly flat, sometimes flat in the female and feebly impressed in the male, but always more or less narrowly separates the coxæ, and the ante-coxal corneous processes of the male, forming so characteristic a feature of Centrinus, are completely obsolete. The scutellum, legs and abdomen are nearly as in Centrinus, and the body is similarly squamose; the mes-epimera are, however, much less frequently visible from above in the reëntrant angle between the prothorax and elytra.

Our species are not very numerous and may be recognized as follows :—

Prosternum flat or approximately so.
  Anterior coxæ separated by less than one-half of their own width; beak moderately stout and subequal throughout.
    Squamules of the pronotum abruptly and broadly dense and conspicuous at the sides, and sometimes, also, narrowly along the middle, the vestiture of the intervening regions consisting of small and more or less inconspicuous squamules.
      Punctures of the pronotum contiguous and more or less longitudinally coalescent; scales of the elytra disposed in a single even series on each interval ....1 **lineicollis**
      Punctures of the pronotum rather widely separated; elytral scales disposed in one or more series on each interval, quite broadly confused on the third and still more broadly on the fifth ....2 **ingenuus**
    Squamules of the pronotum uniform in structure throughout and but slightly uneven in distribution, usually larger and gradually a little denser toward the sides.
      Anterior coxæ very approximate, separated by about one-fourth of their own width or less.
        Prothorax about as long as wide, coarsely, rugosely but not very deeply sculptured; body narrow.........................3 **scitulus**
        Prothorax distinctly wider than long, the body more broadly oval.
                                                                  4 decipiens
      Anterior coxæ smaller and separated by nearly one-half of their own width; very small species; prosternum perfectly flat.
                                                                  5 effetus
  Anterior coxæ separated by distinctly more than one-half of their own width; beak longer, more slender and almost impunctate; body shorter and broader, the second funicular joint much longer....6 **contractus**
Prosternum with a narrow and deep but squamose longitudinal impression, limited on each side by an obtusely prominent ridge; beak very stout, especially toward base in the male...................................7 **canus**

1 **Nicentrus lineicollis** Boh.—Sch. Curc., VIII, i, p. 221 (Centrinus).

Oblong-oval, narrow, subparallel, convex, black, rather dull; vestiture whitish, the slender scales of the upper surface distinct near the sides and along a narrow median line of the pronotum, and disposed in a nearly even single line along each elytral interval; intermediate areas of the pronotum clothed with exceedingly minute setæ; scales of the under surface broadly oval and dense, except toward the sides of the prothorax, where they are fine sparse and subdenuded. Beak stout, moderately arcuate, varying in length from scarcely as long as the prothorax to as long as the head and prothorax, the antennæ inserted a little beyond the middle, the basal joint of the funicle as long as the next two, the second one-half longer than the third, the club moderate, oval, densely pubescent, with the basal joint much less than one-half the mass. Prosternum not impressed, feebly, transversely constricted toward the middle behind the apical margin, separating the anterior coxæ in the male by less than one-fifth of their own width, but in the female by a much more appreciable distance. Length 2.3–3.5 mm.; width 0.8–1.4 mm.

The series before me is from Massachusetts, District of Columbia and Texas. The beak varies considerably in length, irrespective of the usual sexual difference, which is not remarkably pronounced, and the elytral squamules are sometimes distinctly shorter and broader. I have retained the name given by LeConte to this species, although it differs from Boheman's description of the Mexican type in its piceous-black and not rufo-ferruginous legs, and the statement "antennæ apicem rostri propius insertæ," is almost irreconcilable. It is quite probable that there are several closely allied species confounded here, but my material is not sufficiently extensive to properly define them.

2 **Nicentrus ingenuus** n. sp.—Oblong-oval, black and somewhat shining throughout, the legs with a feeble rufo-piceous tinge; vestiture consisting of pale yellowish scales, broad and dense beneath, elongate and narrower on the elytra, where they are disposed in from one to two series on the intervals, the lines of the third and fifth wider and more conspicuous; on the pronotum the squamules are very small, dark in color and entirely inconspicuous, except in lateral fifth or sixth, where they become abruptly broad, denser and pale yellowish, also visible along the median line especially toward base. *Head* finely but strongly punctured, the impression very feeble, not foveate; beak moderately stout, cylindrical, deeply, densely punctate and subrugulose, not quite as long as the head and prothorax, strongly, abruptly bent at base and also strongly but more gradually arcuate toward apex; antennæ inserted just beyond the middle, the basal joint of the funicle unusually short, not longer than the next two, the second much more slender than the first and fully three-fourths as long, subequal to the next two, club about as long as the four

preceding joints combined. *Prothorax* one-third wider than long, the sides feebly convergent, broadly, evenly and feebly arcuate nearly to the apex, then gradually more strongly convergent, but not at all sinuate, to the apex, the latter truncate and one-half as wide as the base, which is straight and transverse, the lobe rather small but distinctly prominent; disk with deep and moderately large punctures, which are perforate and rather widely separated, but somewhat unevenly distributed, the impunctate line narrow but distinct, even and entire. Scutellum very densely squamose. *Elytra* slightly wider than the prothorax and about four-fifths longer, the sides quite strongly convergent throughout, the apex somewhat narrowly rounded; disk rather coarsely, deeply striate, the intervals from one-half to once wider than the grooves, closely, deeply, confusedly and somewhat coarsely punctured throughout. *Abdomen* densely squamose. Prosternum perfectly flat, separating the rather large coxæ by one-fifth of their own width. Length 3.8–4.0 mm.; width 1.7–1.8 mm.

Illinois; Iowa; Texas.

This species is not closely allied to any other, although belonging in the neighborhood of *decipiens;* it differs in its much more abbreviated basal joint of the antennal funicle and very markedly in the nature of the pronotal sculpture and vestiture. The type is a female; in the male the beak is a little shorter and thicker, with the antennæ inserted at apical two-fifths. Three specimens.

3 Nicentrus scitulus n. sp.—Elongate-oval, convex, black and shining throughout, the legs somewhat piceous; vestiture white, consisting of large dense scales beneath and narrower sparsely placed squamules above, the latter more evident toward the sides of the pronotum but not forming a definite vitta, not denser along the median line; on the elytra they form a single or partially double line on each interval. *Head* finely but deeply, rather closely punctured, not squamose, the impression entirely obsolete; beak moderately thick, rather feebly, evenly arcuate, coarsely, deeply, linearly punctate throughout at the sides and longitudinally furrowed, nearly as long as the head and prothorax, the antennæ inserted near apical two-fifths, the scape rather long but not attaining the eye, the basal joint of the funicle as long as the next three, the second one-half longer than the third, the club rather small, oval, densely pubescent, about as long as the preceding four joints combined. *Prothorax* very nearly as long as wide, the sides broadly, evenly, feebly arcuate and convergent anteriorly, becoming nearly parallel in basal two-thirds, the apical constriction completely obsolete; apex truncate, fully one-half as wide as the base, the latter transverse and straight, the median lobe one-third the total width, prominent; disk without distinct median line, the punctures coarse, not very deep and partially coalescent, forming longitudinal rugæ. Scutellum quadrate, squamose, the apical angles acute and prominent. *Elytra* a little wider than the prothorax and almost twice as long, the humeri small but decidedly prominent, the sides behind them evenly and sensibly convergent, the apex rather abruptly but not broadly rounded; disk with fine deep and abrupt striæ, the intervals flat, from two to three times as wide as the grooves, coarsely confusedly and moderately closely punctured. Prosternum not impressed, with a small transverse stria at the middle behind the apical margin, the coxæ separated by less than one-fifth of their own width. Length 3.0 mm.; width 1.15 mm.

Texas.

The sex of the single specimen before me is not determinable with certainty. It is somewhat allied to *decipiens*, but differs in its much narrower and more elongate-oval form and in the long slender scales of the elytra.

4 Nicentrus decipiens Lec.—Proc. Am. Phil. Soc., XV, p. 313 (Centrinus).

Oblong-oval, convex, moderately shining, black, the legs rufous; vestiture white, consisting of sparse slender squamules on the pronotum, which become gradually broader and denser toward the sides especially near the base; on the elytra the scales are large, elongate-oval, conspicuous and unevenly arranged in from one to two rows on each interval, very white and dense beneath. Beak moderately stout, not distinctly thicker toward base, evenly arcuate, as long as the prothorax in the male and but slightly longer and thinner in the female, densely punctured and rugulose laterally, but not as compressed as in *canus;* antennæ inserted at the middle in the female or just beyond in the male, the first funicular joint as long as the next three, still longer in the female, the second not as long as the third and fourth; club rather small. Prothorax fully one-third wider than long, the sides parallel and feebly arcuate in basal two-thirds, then broadly rounded and convergent, the apical constriction obsolete; disk not very coarsely but deeply and densely punctate, the median line almost completely obsolete but sometimes visible as a fine cariniform line. Scutellum small, densely squamose. Elytra but very slightly wider than the prothorax, nearly four-fifths longer than the latter, somewhat narrowly hemi-elliptical in form, the humeri but slightly prominent; disk with deep abrupt and somewhat coarse grooves, the intervals flat, two to three times as wide as the grooves, rather finely, confusedly, not very densely but subrugosely punctured. Prosternum feebly and broadly impressed along the middle, the coxæ separated by about one-fourth of their own width. Length 2.8–3.7 mm.; width 1.25–1.6 mm.

Florida (Cedar Keys and Haw Creek). This species bears a deceptive resemblance to *canus*, but differs greatly in its less robust

beak, non-sulcate prosternum, more narrowly squamose elytral intervals, subobsolete median line and finer punctures of the pronotum,
and in its smaller size.   Three specimens.

5 **Nicentrus effetus** n. sp.—Oblong-oval, moderately convex, black,
the legs red ; integuments rather smooth, moderately shining ; vestiture white,
consisting of slender sparse squamules on the pronotum, larger and a little closer
toward the sides and on the median line toward base ; on the elytra broader
and whiter but still narrow, disposed in a single almost even series on each
interval, sometimes partially double on the third, fifth and seventh toward
base ; scales of the under surface large but sparse on the abdomen, dense on
the met-episterna.   *Head* finely, strongly, rather closely punctate, the beak
somewhat slender, cylindrical, smooth, finely seriato-punctate, more closely
so along the sides, about as long as the head and prothorax, rather strongly
arcuate in basal half but nearly straight thence to the apex ; antennæ inserted
at the middle, the basal joint of the funicle as long as the next three, rather
stout, second but slightly elongate, club small.   *Prothorax* fully one-third
wider than long, the sides parallel or feebly divergent from the base to apical
third and nearly straight, then broadly rounded and strongly convergent to
the apex, the constriction completely obsolete ; apex truncate, rather more
than one-half as wide as the base, the latter transverse, broadly, feebly bisinuate, the median lobe small but somewhat prominent ; disk without trace of
impunctate line, the punctures small and distinctly separated.   Scutellum
small, quadrate or rounded, very densely squamose.   *Elytra* very slightly
wider than the prothorax and nearly twice as long, hemi-elliptical, the humeri
but slightly prominent ; disk deeply and abruptly striate, the intervals flat,
about twice as wide as the grooves, each with a tolerably even single series of
small deep punctures.   Prosternum flat, separating the coxæ by fully two-
fifths of their own width.   Length 2.2 mm.; width 0.85 mm.

Florida (Haw Creek).

The single specimen is a female and represents a species allied to
decipiens, but differing in its much smaller size, longer elytra with
uniseriate intervals, and in many other characters.

6 **Nicentrus contractus** n. sp.—Oblong-oval, convex, stout, black
and but feebly shining, the legs not paler ; vestiture consisting of whitish
scales, very fine, sparse and almost uniformly distributed on the pronotum,
broader, denser and widely confused on all the elytral intervals, and very
broad and dense throughout beneath.   *Head* finely but deeply, somewhat
closely punctured, the impression almost completely obsolete and with a deep
median fovea ; beak long, rather slender, cylindrical, evenly, rather strongly
arcuate, polished and almost completely impunctate except at base, where
there are also a few squamules, and where the thickness becomes somewhat
greater, fully one-half as long as the body ; antennæ inserted distinctly beyond the middle, the second funicular joint unusually elongate, more than
three-fourths as long as the first and nearly as long as the next three ; club

moderate, stout, oval, densely pubescent. *Prothorax* short, three-fourths wider than long, the sides broadly arcuate, becoming nearly parallel toward base, strongly convergent, broadly and just visibly sinuate near the apex, the latter truncate and not quite one-half as wide as the base, which is straight and transverse, the median lobe one-fourth of the total width, prominent and sinuato-truncate at apex ; disk somewhat coarsely, deeply, densely punctate, the punctures tending slightly to coalesce longitudinally, the impunctate line narrow but almost entire. Scutellum rather large, transverse, very densely and conspicuously albido-squamose. *Elytra* but little wider and about four-fifths longer than the prothorax, scarcely longer than wide, hemi-elliptical, the humeri slightly oblique to the base of the prothorax, feebly tumid and but slightly prominent ; disk deeply but not very coarsely striate, the intervals flat, from two to three times as wide as the grooves and all deeply, densely and confusedly punctate. *Abdomen* densely squamose. Prosternum flat, with a transverse nude excavation near the apical margin, the coxæ separated by three-fifths of their own width. Length 3.2 mm. ; width 1.65 mm.

Florida.

In its longer, polished and almost impunctate beak, more elongate second funicular joint and rather more widely distant anterior coxæ, as well as in its shorter and broader bodily form, this species is decidedly aberrant; but all the remaining characters seem to coincide with those of the present genus. The single specimen appears to be a female, and, in the other sex, the beak is very likely shorter and more punctate as in the group of Centrinus containing *denticornis*, to which the species of Nicentrus bear some analogy in other respects also.

7 **Nicentrus canus** Lec.—Proc. Am. Phil. Soc., XV, p. 421 (Centrinus).

Rather stout, oblong-oval, convex, moderately shining, black, the legs rufous ; vestiture whitish, consisting of long slender squamules, moderately densely and evenly distributed, a little broader and closer on the under surface. Beak in the male stout, becoming very thick toward base, moderately arcuate, scarcely longer than the prothorax, coarsely, deeply but not very densely, lineately punctate and grooved, the antennæ inserted distinctly beyond the middle, the basal joint of the funicle longer than the next two, the second three-fifths as long as the first and as long as the succeeding two, three to seven nearly equal and subquadrate; club small, rather narrowly oval. Prothorax very nearly as long as wide, the sides parallel and feebly arcuate in basal two-thirds, then broadly rounded and convergent to the apex, which is distinctly less than one-half as wide as the base, apical constriction very feeble; disk coarsely, moderately closely punctate, the punctures tending slightly to coalesce longitudinally; median impunctate line distinct except toward the apex. Elytra only just visibly wider than the prothorax, the sides feebly convergent, the apex not very narrowly rounded; disk finely but deeply striate, the intervals from two to three times as wide as the grooves, rather coarsely, moderately densely, rugosely and indistinctly punctate throughout their widths. Prosternum deeply channeled along the middle, the groove squamose and limited at each side by an elevated straight ridge, the coxæ separated by nearly one-third of their own width. Length 4.6–5.0 mm.; width 1.9–2.1 mm.

Florida (Enterprise and Haw Creek). In the female the antennæ are inserted at the middle of the beak, and the first joint of the funicle is a little longer, the second shorter; the beak however does not differ much from that of the male, being merely a little less stout, somewhat less coarsely punctate and about as long as the head and prothorax. The statements in the original description, that the beak is slender and the anterior coxæ widely separated, are greatly misleading.

CENTRINITES n. gen.

The chief characters differentiating this genus from Centrinus, are those which relate to mandibular and antennal structure, but, although in several other respects the single species representing it is somewhat peculiar, it cannot be denied that Centrinites is one of the few unsatisfactory genera necessitated by a mandibular basis of classification—unsatisfactory because there is not a sufficiently great peculiarity of habitus. I believe, however, that any other taxonomic basis for the genera in this part of the Barini, would give rise to much more pronounced and wide-spread ambiguity.

The mandibles in Centrinites are nearly as in Nicentrus, very feebly decussate and rather prominent when closed, but at the same time quite deeply notched within near the apex. The antennæ are inserted slightly beyond the middle of the beak, and the outer joints of the funicle are finely pubescent like the club, having also, however, the usual long bristling setæ or squamules; the outer joints do not merge gradually into the club, the latter being sensibly abrupt.

The prosternum is impressed along the middle, very narrowly separating the coxæ, and the prothorax is tubulate at apex. Mes-

epimera slightly visible from above. Scutellum sparsely clothed
with dark-brown squamules. Pygidium completely covered, the
fifth ventral segment not as long as the two preceding together.
Met-episterna narrow. Tarsi normal, the claws moderate, free and
divergent. In some of these characters the genus is related to
Nicentrus, but the strongly tubulate prothorax and rhomboidal
form of the body will readily distinguish them.

1 **Centrinites strigicollis** n. sp.—Rhomboid-oval, moderately stout,
convex, shining, black, the tibiæ, tarsi and antennæ more or less piceous ;
vestiture consisting of elongate slender white scales and slightly smaller piceous squamules, the former broadly along the sides and on the basal lobe of
the pronotum, and also on elytral intervals two, near the base and toward
apex, four and six broadly, and three, five and seven in single sparse lines
which are less distinct toward base and apex ; under surface rather sparsely
clothed with white scales, the met-episterna very densely so throughout.
Head finely but strongly, rather closely punctured, the transverse impression
broadly angulate but distinct ; beak somewhat stout but not much thicker
toward base, evenly, distinctly arcuate, fully as long as the head and prothorax, the flattened sides deeply densely and rugosely punctate, the dorsal
surface polished and with an even series of small punctures at each side of
the impunctate line ; antennæ inserted a little beyond the middle, the scape
extending three-fourths the distance thence to the eye, the basal joint of
the funicle fully as long as the next three, the second less than one-half
as long as the first and one-half longer than the third, outer joints finely
pubescent, and also coarsely setose, club finely, densely pubescent, moderate
in size, the basal joint forming nearly one-half the mass. *Prothorax* two-
thirds wider than long, the sides feebly convergent and nearly straight to
apical third, then strongly rounded to the well-marked constriction ; apex
tubulate and fully one-half as wide as the base, the latter transverse, sinuate at each side of the small moderately distinct median lobe ; disk
with long deep longitudinal rugæ, the median line very finely carinate.
Scutellum quadrate, emarginate behind, sparsely clothed with brown squamules. *Elytra* distinctly wider than the prothorax and more than twice as
long, the humeri rather prominent but obtuse ; sides strongly convergent, the
apex somewhat narrowly rounded ; disk moderately and not very abruptly
striate, the intervals flat, about twice as wide as the grooves, the first, third,
fifth and seventh uniseriately punctate, the others confusedly so, the punctures
moderate, deep, not very dense. Prosternum with a deep squamose parallel-
sided longitudinal impression, ending behind the anterior margin in a small
transverse nude and deeper pit, the coxæ separated by one-fourth of their own
width. Length 3.5 mm. ; width 1.7 mm.

North Carolina (Hot Springs) ; Missouri.

This species bears a deceptive resemblance to *Centrinus tortuosus*,
but is less robust and has the pale scales arranged in rows and not

sparsely sprinkled over the elytra. Its real isolation is shown not only by the characters which I have assumed to separate it generically, but by the very exceptional fact that the clytral intervals which are narrowly and uniseriately punctured and pubescent, are the third, fifth and seventh, while in the vast majority of genera these are the more conspicuously broad and pubescent intervals. The type appears to be a male.

CALANDRINUS.

LeConte—Proc. Am. Phil. Soc., XV, p. 305.

This is one of the aberrant and specialized generic types so characteristic of the centrinide group of Barini, and is entirely isolated in general form of the body, as well as in tarsal structure. The beak is rather slender and arcuate, moderate in length and cylindrical, although rather rapidly dilated and noticeably flattened toward the truncate apex, and with peculiarly small, widely distant mandibles, which can apparently do little more than mutually touch when closed; they are strongly dentate externally near the base. The antennæ possess no exceptional features, but are slender, with the club small and less densely pubescent than usual. The impression separating the beak from the head is feeble and very broad. Prothorax rather large in comparison with the elytra, subequal to the latter in width or a little narrower, subcylindrical, with broadly rounded sides, strongly constricted at some distance behind the apex, the latter conically tubulate. Scutellum very small and rather deeply seated.

The prosternum is deeply, transversely constricted at a considerable distance behind the apex, but not otherwise modified, unimpressed, the anterior coxæ rather small and remote, usually separated by fully their own width. Legs rather long and somewhat slender, the tibiæ deeply sculptured and more or less ridged and fluted, the tarsi slender, with the third joint but slightly larger than the second, emarginate, glabrous beneath, with a small setose tuft near each apical angle; claws rather long, slender, free and widely divergent.

The three species which I have been obliged to recognize may be outlined in the following manner:—

Pronotal punctures smaller, although still comparatively coarse, denser, with a broad, fusiform, polished, and sharply limited impunctate line, which attains and becomes confluent with the broad apical impunctate margin.

Elytral punctures very remote, the surface almost glabrous but squamose at the base, behind the scutellum and obliquely at the sides behind the middle ; intervals extremely unequal in width, the striæ finer and not noticeably punctate ....1 **grandicollis**
Elytral punctures closer and larger, more confused, the striæ much coarser, deep, distinctly punctate at the bottom ; vestiture more abundant, densely squamose also in a sutural line behind the middle ; intervals much less unequal in width ; size somewhat larger.............................2 **insignis**
Pronotal punctures very coarse and not dense, with merely an elongate and ill-defined median area, toward which they become still sparser ; elytra with an abbreviated post-scutellar spot which is covered with large white scales..3 **obsoletus**

Calandrinus appears to be peculiar to the somewhat isolated zoological province embracing Colorado and the northern part of New Mexico.

1 **Calandrinus grandicollis** Lec.—Proc. Am. Phil. Soc., XV, p. 305.

Oblong-oval, strongly convex, polished, piceous-black, the beak, antennæ and legs paler, rufous ; integuments sparsely and unevenly squamose, the scales yellowish-white, long, slender and sparse on the pronotum, denser and larger toward the sides, there becoming whiter and broader toward base ; on the elytra they are extremely sparse, long and very slender, becoming larger, dense and whiter toward base, behind the scutellum and in a small oblique spot behind the middle, from the third stria to the sides ; most conspicuous beneath on the prosternum, elsewhere long, fine and sparse. Beak slender, cylindrical, evenly, moderately arcuate, as long as the head and prothorax, the basal joint of the antennal funicle fully as long as the next three, the second as long as the following two; club rather small, narrowly oval, pointed. Prothorax nearly as long as wide, the sides very feebly divergent and slightly arcuate from the base nearly to apical third, then broadly rounded, the constriction large and distinct ; apex nearly three-fourths as wide as the base ; disk coarsely, deeply and closely punctate, the impunctate line wide, fusiform, abruptly limited, smooth and polished, extending to the impunctate apical margin. Scutellum very small, deeply seated. Elytra oviform, narrowly rounded at apex, quite distinctly wider and scarcely more than one-half longer than the prothorax, but distinctly longer than wide, strongly arcuate at the sides near the base, the humeral callus not evident ; striæ abrupt, deep, moderately fine, the intervals flat, extremely unequal in width, the third as wide as the first and second together, the fourth very narrow, not more than one-half wider than the grooves, each with a single series of small but deep, distant punctures, which are broadly confused on the third, and, to some extent, on the fifth. Abdomen very coarsely and deeply punctured. Prosternum flat, broadly constricted behind the apex, separating the coxæ by about their own width. Length 2.8 mm.; width 1.2 mm.

Colorado. Cab. LeConte. Represented only by the unique type from which the description is taken. This species differs from *insignis* in its smaller size, straighter and more convergent sides of the prothorax toward base, much more uneven and more sparsely punctate elytral intervals, and in many other characters.

2 **Calandrinus insignis** n. sp.—Ovulate, strongly convex, highly polished, the head alutaceous, blackish-piceous, the legs and beak rufous; vestiture consisting of long rather robust hairs, yellowish in color, sparse on the pronotum, becoming broader white denser and squamiform near the sides anteriorly and at lateral sixth toward base; on the elytra the yellowish slender squamules are moderately dense toward base, becoming denser white scales near the humeri, and also on intervals one, and four to seven, for a short distance behind the middle, the yellowish squamules elsewhere very sparse; under surface uniformly and rather sparsely clothed with elongate white scales. *Head* with a distinct, rather large frontal fovea, the impression almost completely obsolete; beak as long as the head and prothorax, arcuate, slender, finely, sparsely punctate, the punctures linearly arranged along the side of the impunctate line; antennæ nearly as in *grandicollis*. *Prothorax* very nearly as long as wide, the sides parallel, evenly, rather strongly arcuate in basal four-fifths, then rounded, convergent and broadly constricted to the apex; base feebly oblique and straight from the centre to each basal angle; disk with a wide subentire distinctly defined impunctate line, the punctures somewhat coarse, deep, very close but not quite in mutual contact. *Elytra* one-fourth longer than wide, nearly one-half longer than the prothorax, and, at basal fourth, a little wider than the disk of the latter, oval in form, the sides strongly arcuate toward base, thence convergent to the narrowly rounded apex, disk with coarse, deep, abrupt, remotely and distinctly punctate striæ, the intervals flat, from one-half wider than, to about twice as wide as the grooves, finely, sparsely and more or less confusedly punctate throughout. *Abdomen* coarsely, deeply punctate. Length 3.4 mm.; width 1.5 mm.

Colorado.

I owe the above-described type to the kindness of Mr. W. Jülich, in whose cabinet there is a series of several specimens. The species is easily distinguishable from *grandicollis* by the characters given in the table, and also by the coarser striæ and denser and more confused interstitial punctuation, although the punctures tend to form single lines on the narrower intervals. The punctuation of the prothorax is nearly the same as in *grandicollis*, but the vestiture throughout the body is much more abundant and conspicuous, and there is a sutural line of broader white scales behind the middle in this species, which is entirely wanting and replaced by the usual fine sparse squamules in *grandicollis*.

3 **Calandrinus obsoletus** n. sp.—Cylindro-oval, very convex, polished, piceous, the legs and beak bright rufous; vestiture white, consisting of elongate squamules sparsely placed on the prothorax and elytra, becoming denser and more broadly oval on the latter toward base, especially in a broad line behind the scutellum and toward the humeri, and also along intervals four to six for a short distance behind the middle. *Head* with a small frontal fovea, the beak very slender, finely, sparsely punctate. as long as the head and prothorax, strongly, evenly arcuate, the antennæ slender, inserted just behind the middle, the first funicular joint slender, as long as the next three, the second one-half as long as the first, all the joints longer than wide except the seventh, which is a little transverse, club small, as long as the preceding four joints combined, rather thin, sparsely pubescent and slightly shining, with the basal joint large. *Prothorax* very nearly as long as wide; sides parallel and broadly arcuate to apical fourth, then rounded and constricted, the apex strongly subtubulate; base broadly, evenly arcuate, the median lobe obsolete; disk very coarsely, deeply punctate, without distinct impunctate line, the punctures rather uneven in size, form and distribution, but generally separated by distinctly less than their own diameters. Scutellum minute, deeply seated. *Elytra* slightly longer than wide, very slightly wider than the prothorax and one-half longer than the latter, ovalo-conoidal, narrowly rounded behind; disk rather coarsely, deeply striate, the intervals flat, from two to three times as wide as the striæ, each with a single line of fine distant and inconspicuous punctures. Length 2.8 mm.; width 1.25 mm.

Colorado.

Readily distinguishable from *grandicollis* and *insignis* by the much coarser, sparser punctures of the pronotum, and the entire absence of a well-defined median impunctate line, the punctures simply becoming sparser at the middle; the apical margin is, however, broadly impunctate, as in the species mentioned. A single specimen.

CENTRINOGYNA n. gen.

The two species which are referred to this interesting genus, are the most remarkable of the tribe in their wonderful sexual divergencies at the apex of the abdomen. In the male, the pygidium is large, vertical, strongly convex and completely exposed, while in the female it is entirely covered, with the exception of a very small and barely distinguishable portion at the apex. In other words, assuming the division adopted by LeConte, which is still, without much doubt, the best that can be devised, the male is a normal baride, while the female is an equally pronounced centrinide. This of course destroys any idea of two perfectly isolated natural groups, and compels us to treat the genera as forming part of a single well-defined series. In fact the homogeneity of the entire tribe is proved by repeated parallelisms of structure throughout.

In Centrinogyna the body is elongate, parallel and somewhat depressed, nearly as in many species of Limnobaris. The beak is rather slender, arcuate, about as long as the prothorax, with the antennæ inserted distinctly beyond the middle, slender, moderate in length, the first funicular joint as long as the next four, the second slightly elongate but less than one-half as long as the first, the club oval, abrupt, densely pubescent and with the basal joint constituting very nearly one-half of the mass. Mandibles deeply notched within, acute, not noticeably overlapping when closed and then forming a prominent angle.

The prosternum is perfectly unimpressed, having the usual deep transverse constriction behind the apex but not otherwise modified, the anterior coxæ not very widely distant and separated by but slightly more than one-half of their own width, the prosternal process terminating midway of their length in a distinct transverse suture ; behind this, the prosternum is but slightly produced, passing for only a short distance over the edge of the mesosternum, with the apex broadly and feebly sinuate in the middle. The prothorax is strongly tubulate at apex. Scutellum very small, subquadrate or a little longer than wide. Legs normal ; tibiæ nearly smooth, the tarsal claws well developed, stout, free and divergent. Vestiture throughout consisting of very sparse slender setiform squamules, white in color and arranged in a single somewhat uneven semi-erect and bristling line on each of the elytral intervals.

This genus offers a good example of the polarity theory in the distribution of secondary sexual characters, advanced by Dr. LeConte, the beak and antennæ being quite devoid of any perceptible sexual differences, while those at the apex of the abdomen are exceptionally pronounced. The theory does not hold so well, however, in some other genera, as for example in several species of Oxytelus which I have in mind, and fails completely in Conoproctus Lac. of the present tribe, where the sexual differences in the form of the beak, point of antennal insertion and structure of the pygidium, become extreme in *C. 4-pustulatus* Fab., as before described under the genus Madarellus.

The species may be thus distinguished:—

Piceous; legs rufous; setæ long and conspicuous; pronotum strongly and longitudinally strigose..1 **strigata**

Black throughout, subglabrous, the setæ extremely sparse and short; pronotum more finely punctate, the punctures distinct, sometimes feebly coalescent longitudinally..2 **procera**

1 **Centrinogyna strigata** Lec.—Proc. Am. Phil. Soc., XV, p. 421 (Centrinus).

The original description of what LeConte designates a remarkable species from an inspection of the female alone, is well given and ample for purposes of recognition, except that the anterior coxæ are only separated by about three-fifths of their own width. The beak is rather slender, evenly, moderately arcuate and does not differ appreciably in the sexes; it is sparsely punctured and has a very even line of small punctures along each side of the median impunctate line. The prothorax is very nearly as long as wide, parallel and feebly arcuate at the sides and abruptly, broadly and strongly tubulated at apex, the base transverse, the median lobe very small and almost obsolete; disk with longitudinally, closely, unevenly and deeply plicate or rugose sculpture, the impunctate line very distinctly defined, polished and somewhat elevated. The elytral striæ are moderately coarse, deep and abrupt, impunctate, the intervals flat, nearly three times as wide as the grooves, each with a single somewhat uneven series of rather small but deep, approximate punctures. Length 3.5–4.8 mm.; width 1.2–1.7 mm.

Colorado and Wyoming. Taken in abundance by Mr. Wickham at Greeley and Laramie.

2 **Centrinogyna procera** n. sp.—Elongate, parallel, moderately convex, shining, black throughout, the vestiture consisting of very small setiform squamules, which are exceedingly sparse and inconspicuous but more evident at the sides of the pronotum and last three ventral segments, and near the apex of the met-episterna. *Head* minutely, sparsely punctured, the transverse impression strong, broadly angulate in profile; beak rather thick, subcylindrical, evenly, rather feebly arcuate, as long as the prothorax, hardly differing in the sexes, but a little thicker and more punctate in the male, the

punctures rather fine, lineate dorsally but larger denser and confused at the sides ; antennæ inserted near apical third, the scape long, first funicular joint as long as the next three, the second small, obconical, slightly longer than wide and about one-half longer than the third, outer joints transverse, club moderate, densely pubescent, the basal joint constituting more than one-half the mass and more sparsely pubescent near the base. *Prothorax* about as long as wide ; sides parallel, evenly and broadly arcuate to apical sixth, then abruptly rounded to the deep constriction ; the apex strongly tubulate, three-fourths as wide as the base, the latter transversely truncate, the median lobe small and feebly rounded ; disk with a narrow distinct and entire impunctate line, the punctures rather fine but deep, uneven, not densely crowded, well separated transversely but tending slightly to longitudinal elongation or partial coalescence. Scutellum very small, quadrate, glabrous. *Elytra* equal in width to the prothorax and fully twice as long, the sides parallel, feebly convergent in apical third, the apex rather abruptly and not narrowly rounded ; humeral callus almost obsolete ; disk with moderately deep striæ, which become finer toward apex and coarser near the base ; intervals nearly three times as wide as the grooves, each with a single series of rather small, uneven, approximate punctures, somewhat confused on the third. *Legs* short, the anterior and middle femora very robust, the posterior far less so. Length 4.0–4.7 mm. ; width 1.3–1.7 mm.

California (San Francisco). Mr. Dunn.

In this species the pygidium of the male is large, broad, vertical, convex, moderately densely punctate, and completely exposed ; in the female it is entirely covered by the elytra, with the exception of a scarcely visible fine lower margin. The prosternum is flat and the anterior coxæ separated by three-fourths of their own width. The male appears to be much less abundant than the female in both of these species. Five specimens.

LIMNOBARIS.
Bedel—Fne. Col. Bas. Seine, VI, p. 183.

The mandibles in this genus are of a completely different type from those of Centrinus, for, instead of being prominent, perfectly non-decussate and totally devoid of internal inequality, they are here short, stout, strongly arcuate, deeply notched at apex and broadly decussate when closed, the anterior outline then being broadly, feebly arcuate and not in the least prominent. With this radical difference of structure, there is also a decided peculiarity of facies, the species of Limnobaris being narrow, parallel or oval, generally distinctly depressed, with feebly developed humeral callus and more or less glabrous integuments. Of the genera with prominent mandibles, the closest ally of Limnobaris appears to be Centrinogyna, and, in this connection, it should be stated that in the former the tip of the pygidium is occasionally exposed, especially in the male.

The basal joint of the antennal funicle is generally long, the second decidedly short, becoming longer in the fifth group, and the club varies considerably, being moderately robust, with a large basal joint in the first group, but narrower and with a much shorter basal joint in the others.   There is also considerable variation in the amplitude of the prosternal process between the coxæ, the latter being generally more or less remote, but occasionally narrowly separated, again demonstrating the slight weight of prosternal characters in some parts of the centrinide series.   The prosternum is usually flat, but in some species may be flat in the female and deeply excavated in the male, and, in *longula*, is narrowly impressed along the middle in both sexes.

The beak varies in structure to a noticeable extent in the several subgeneric groups as detailed below, and in some of these sections, the prosternal processes of the male are invariably wanting, while in others they may or may not be present.   In several species, which happen to belong to all of the subgenera except the first, the beak varies perceptibly in length in different individuals, necessitating some caution in separating the species.   I have observed this variation in length in *prolixa*, *rectirostris*, *ebena*, and possibly *seminitens*, also, as before stated, in *Nicentrus lineicollis*.

The five sections, into which it is convenient to separate our species, may be outlined as follows:—

Antennal club more robust, with the basal joint large, constituting more than
   one-half of the mass and frequently more sparsely pubescent and shining
   toward base; beak generally thicker, more strongly and evenly arcuate
   and not tumid at base, the antennæ inserted distinctly beyond the middle
   in the male but more medially in the female; prosternum always widely
   separating the coxæ and never armed in the male; punctuation deeper,
   denser and more uneven as a rule, the vestiture frequently more conspicuous and always uneven; body usually more or less rufo-piceous in
   color and noticeably depressed..**I**
Antennal club generally narrower, densely pubescent throughout, the basal
   joint much shorter; body always intense black throughout, except in
   the next subdivision, occasionally somewhat depressed.
Body oblong, moderately convex, densely, confusedly punctate and densely
   but unevenly clothed throughout with oval whitish scales; beak as in
   the preceding section; antennal club strongly annulate, the basal joint

constituting scarcely more than one-third of the mass; anterior coxæ widely separated, the prosternum flat, not armed in the male ....**II**

Body more or less oblong-oval, subglabrous, the beak extremely slender, sometimes nearly straight, tumid above at base, the transverse constriction distinct; prosternum generally armed or otherwise modified before the coxæ in the male; second funicular joint short ....**III**

Body narrow and linear, subglabrous; beak very slender, not tumid at base; prosternum armed in the male, the processes sometimes extremely developed; second funicular joint short; anterior coxæ rather narrowly separated ....**IV**

Body moderately dilated, convex, subglabrous except in *longula;* beak thicker, not at all tumid at base, the transverse impression completely obsolete, represented by a frontal fovea; prosternum never armed in the male; anterior coxæ rather narrowly separated; second funicular joint long ....**V**

The species may be distinguished as follows:—

Subgenus I.

Elytral intervals each with a single series of punctures, the third not more conspicuously squamose behind the middle.

Pronotum bordered at the sides with an abruptly defined vitta of pale scales.
Vitta broad, composed of very large, broad and close-set scales; pronotal punctures coarse.
Prothorax distinctly wider than long, strongly constricted at apex; anterior coxæ separated by one-half of their own width; body stout.
1 bracata

Prothorax almost as long as wide, more feebly constricted near the apex, almost evenly but still more coarsely punctate; anterior coxæ separated by nearly their own width; body elongate-oval...**2 limbifer**

Vitta narrow but conspicuous, composed of slender, elongate but large and rather close-set scales, which are easily removable; pronotal punctures fine..**3 blandita**

Vitta broad but very faint, composed of small, narrow and remotely distant scales; body much narrower and more depressed........**4 tabida**

Pronotum without an abrupt marginal vitta, the vestiture, however, often gradually a little more distinct toward the sides.
Elytral grooves coarse, always more than one-half as wide as the intervals, the punctures of the latter coarse.
Form depressed, the pronotum parallel, nearly as long as wide, rounded and narrowed anteriorly ....**5 deplanata**

Form rather convex, the pronotum much wider than long, narrowed through apical half...**6 punctiger**

Elytral grooves generally finer, or with the intervals more finely punctate.
Pronotal punctures fine, very remote, unevenly distributed and irregular in size; body rather dark rufo-testaceous throughout.
7 denudata

Pronotal punctures much closer and more evenly distributed.
    Legs red; elytra rufo-testaceous; interstitial punctures of the elytra minute and distant, the setæ very minute.......8 **planiuscula**
    Legs black or piceous-black; entire body black, the elytra occasionally feebly picescent, at least in *nasuta.*
      Elytral intervals flat, the punctures small and rather distant; setæ somewhat long and distinct but sparse.................9 **nasuta**
      Elytral intervals somewhat concave, the punctures small and very close-set; setæ minute and scarcely observable; body narrower, more oval and less oblong-parallel........................10 **oblita**
Elytral intervals with the punctures deep, distinct and broadly confused throughout, the third more conspicuously squamose in a short line behind the middle ....11 **seclusa**

Subgenus II.

Oblong-oval, moderately convex, piceous, the elytra and legs rufous, the former blackish along the suture; apex of the pygidium exposed....12 **grisea**

Subgenus III.

Punctures of the elytra confused, at least on the broader intervals.
    Beak in both sexes shorter than the prothorax; form rather depressed; lustre dull ....13 **confusa**
    Beak in the female very much longer, but apparently somewhat variable in length; body much more convex, sparsely punctate and more shining.
                                                    14 **ebena**
Punctures of the elytra forming an even single series on each interval.
    Punctures of the intervals finer and remote.
      Elytral setæ very minute and inconspicuous.
        Male with two short, acute, ante-coxal processes and a large, rounded, extremely deep median excavation ....15 **puteifer**
        Male without ante-coxal horns, but with a broad obtuse cusp before each coxa; prosternum just visibly and broadly impressed.
                                                    16 **confinis**
        Male unarmed, the prosternum very feebly, broadly impressed and with a short obtuse ridge, extending for a short distance in advance of each coxal cavity..17 **concurrens**
      Elytral setæ long, white and conspicuous although remote; male without trace of ante-coxal processes, the prosternum flat.......18 **concinna**
    Punctures of the intervals strong, deep and close-set.
      Small species, the elytral setæ very minute and inconspicuous.
                                                    19 **fratercula**
      Larger species, more elongate; elytral setæ longer, distinct but not very conspicuous; pronotal punctures finer and sparser...20 **seminitens**

Subgenus IV.

Legs black; beak in the female generally not longer than the prothorax.
                                                        21 **prolixa**

Legs pale and bright rufous throughout, more elongate; body more polished
and with a distinct æneous lustre, the elytral striæ still finer; beak in
the female longer ....22 **nitidissima**

Subgenus V.

Anterior coxæ separated by fully three-fourths of their own width; vestiture
of the upper surface rather sparse but conspicuous, even, consisting of
long white squamules; prothorax evenly narrowed almost from base to
apex, the subapical constriction very broad and feeble.......23 **longula**
Anterior coxæ separated by not more than one-half of their own width; vestiture of the upper surface inconspicuous; prothorax rather pronouncedly
subtubulate.
Pronotal punctures rather sparse shallow and variolate...24 **rectirostris**
Pronotal punctures very deep and much denser; anterior coxæ separated
by scarcely more than one-fourth of their own width.............25 **calva**

I.

1 **Limnobaris bracata** n. sp.—Robust and rather strongly convex,
oblong-oval, shining, piceous-black, the beak and antennæ rufo-piceous; legs
paler, rufous; vestiture uneven, sparse, whitish, consisting of broad close-set
scales in a marginal pronotal vitta and at the base of the third and fifth elytral
intervals, also distinct on the scutellar lobe of the prothorax, elsewhere slender sparse and inconspicuous but mingled with a few more conspicuous scales
on the seventh interval, sparse and uneven throughout beneath. *Head*
sparsely and obsoletely punctulate, the transverse impression distinct; beak
rather slender, evenly, distinctly arcuate, cylindrical, fully as long as the
prothorax in the male, finely, sparsely, linearly punctate, more coarsely and
irregularly so at the sides toward base; antennæ inserted distinctly beyond
the middle, the basal joint of the funicle as long as the next three, second one-
half as long as the first, outer joints a little thicker, club well developed, the
basal joint forming more than one-half of the mass, shining and sparsely
pubescent. *Prothorax* one-third wider than long, the sides feebly convergent
and slightly arcuate to apical third, then rounded to the deep subapical constriction, the apex strongly, conically tubulate, one-half as wide as the base,
the latter transverse, moderately lobed in the middle; disk rather coarsely
but not densely and irregularly punctate, with two large discal spots and a
broad flat median line impunctate. Scutellum small, glabrous, trapezoidal.
Elytra but slightly wider and one-half longer than the prothorax, as wide as
long, hemi-elliptical; striæ coarse, deep, not crenulate toward base; intervals
one-half wider than the grooves, flat, uniseriately but unevenly and rather
coarsely punctate. *Abdomen* coarsely densely and somewhat rugosely punctate. Prosternum separating the rather large anterior coxæ by not more than
one-half of their own width. Length 3.1 mm.; width 1.6 mm.

Missouri (St. Louis).   Mr. Schuster.

This isolated species is readily distinguishable by its stout convex
form, the two impunctate areas of the pronotum and many other

characters. It is represented by a single male, having the abdomen unusually deeply impressed in the middle near the base, the impression hirsute with thickened suberect hairs. The apex of the pygidium is quite distinctly exposed.

2 **Limnobaris limbifer** n. sp.—Oval, moderately convex, polished, piceous-black, the antennæ hardly paler, the beak and legs rufous; vestiture very uneven, nearly white, consisting of large broad and rather dense scales in a broad marginal region of the pronotum and with scales of various sizes very remotely scattered over the remainder of the disk, especially evident on the basal lobe; on the elytra the scales are of varying sizes and scattered remotely along the intervals in nearly single lines, with a more distinct spot at the base of the third interval; on the under surface they are also of different sizes, rather sparse but dense toward the apex of the met-episterna. *Head* extremely minutely feebly and sparsely punctate, the transverse impression feeble but distinct, the beak cylindrical, rather stout, feebly flattened toward apex, polished, smooth but sparsely and sublinearly punctate at the sides toward base, evenly, rather strongly arcuate and about as long as the head and prothorax; antennæ inserted distinctly beyond the middle, slender, the first funicular joint as long as the next three, the second one-half as long as the first and one-half longer than the third, the club abrupt, small, with the basal joint composing nearly two-thirds of the mass, pubescent toward apex but gradually nearly glabrous and polished toward base. *Prothorax* very nearly as long as wide, the sides parallel and feebly arcuate to apical fourth, then rounded convergent and quite distinctly constricted to the apex, which is rather more than one-half as wide as the base, the latter transverse, the median lobe small, slightly prominent, the mes-epimera strongly visible from above; disk very coarsely punctured, the punctures deep, somewhat uneven and generally separated by nearly their own widths; impunctate line rather wide and conspicuous. Scutellum quadrate, flat, polished and glabrous. *Elytra* a little wider and about three-fourths longer than the prothorax, hemi-elliptical, acutely rounded behind, the humeri feebly tumid; disk rather coarsely, deeply striate, the intervals flat, one-half wider than the grooves, each with a singe series of rather small but deep, distinct, rather remote punctures. Under surface coarsely but not very densely punctured; prosternum flat, separating the large coxæ by not quite their own width, the subapical constriction distinct and coarse. Length 3.6 mm.; width 1.5 mm.

Florida.

The single type is apparently a female. This species belongs in the neighborhood of *punctiger*, but is not at all closely allied to it. I have before me a specimen from Colorado which is possibly conspecific; it has the interstitial punctures coarser, the squamose border narrower and the elytra rufescent.

3 **Limnobaris blandita** n. sp.—Oblong-oval, rather depressed above, strongly shining, black, the elytra and legs more or less rufous; vestiture

yellowish-white, very uneven, consisting of larger and smaller squamules which are always long and slender, only distinct on the pronotum in a narrow rather abrupt and dense marginal vitta, on the elytral intervals very remotely dispersed in single series, with a distinct spot at the base of the third; beneath, the squamules are very fine and ·sparse throughout, except on the met-episterna where they are coarser and dense, becoming sparser posteriorly. *Head* minutely but only moderately sparsely punctate, the impression feeble but distinct and broadly angulate in profile; beak cylindrical, rather slender, subequal throughout, evenly, distinctly arcuate, scarcely as long as the prothorax in the male, a little longer than the latter but not sensibly more slender in the female, finely, lineately punctate, the punctures denser and confused at the sides toward base; antennæ inserted well beyond the middle in both sexes, the first funicular joint as long as the next three, the second scarcely one-half as long as the first and one-half longer than the third, club moderate, strongly annulate in apical half, the basal joint constituting one-half the mass, obconical, densely pubescent, only just visibly less densely so very near the base. *Prothorax* scarcely one-fifth wider than long, shaped nearly as in *limbifer*, although a little less convex, the punctures fine but deep, somewhat sparsely distributed, the median line narrow but evident. Scutellum small, quadrate, glabrous and shining. *Elytra* but very slightly wider than the prothorax and barely two-thirds longer, hemi-elliptical, rather obtusely rounded behind, the humeral callus almost obsolete; disk deeply but not coarsely striate, the grooves distinctly crenulate toward base; intervals twice as wide as the grooves, each with a single series of small, rather feeble and irregular, not very close-set punctures. *Abdomen* rather finely, not densely punctate. Prosternum flat, the anterior constriction moderate, not crossing the middle parts but represented there by a series of three or four punctures; anterior coxæ rather small, remote, separated by a little more than their own width. Length 3.2 mm.; width 1.3 mm.

Texas (Austin).

Somewhat allied to *limbifer*, but differing greatly in its more depressed form and much finer sculpture, the scales at the sides of the pronotum are not broad as in the species mentioned, and form a border which is only one-half as wide. Two specimens.

4 **Limnobaris tabida** n. sp.—Oblong-oval, subparallel, narrow and rather strongly depressed, somewhat shining, piceous-black, the legs and antennæ slightly rufescent; integuments subglabrous, very sparsely clothed with long and conspicuous yellowish-white setæ, slightly more robust and distinct but still sparse in lateral fifth of the pronotum, very sparse throughout beneath. *Head* glabrous, minutely, very sparsely punctate, the transverse impression deep and distinct; beak rather stout, evenly, somewhat feebly arcuate, almost equal in diameter throughout, coarsely, densely, rugosely punctate, with some coarse bristling squamules at the base, about equal in length to the prothorax; antennæ inserted at apical third, scape long, first funicular joint as long as the next three, second one-half longer than the third,

club moderate, sparsely pubescent and shining toward base. *Prothorax* very
nearly as long as wide, the sides parallel and broadly arcuate to apical fifth,
then more strongly rounded, thence strongly convergent and distinctly sinuate
to the apex, which is about three-fifths as wide as the base, the latter transverse and very broadly, evenly and feebly bisinuate, the median lobe not
prominent ; disk rather coarsely, not very densely, unevenly punctate, the
impunctate line visible behind the middle, the punctures unequal in size, unevenly distributed and often slightly elongate. Scutellum very small, wider
than long. *Elytra* but slightly wider than the prothorax and three-fifths
longer, the sides rather strongly convergent and broadly feebly arcuate, the
apex evenly, not broadly rounded ; humeri not prominent ; striæ very coarse,
deep ; intervals just noticeably wider than the grooves, each with a single
series of coarse, deep, close-set punctures, uneven in size, often slightly elongate and frequently anastomosing. *Abdomen* strongly but not very coarsely or
densely punctate. Prosternum flat, separating the coxæ by a little more than
their own width. Length 2.8 mm. ; width 1.15 mm.

Illinois.

The single specimen appears to be a male, and the species somewhat resembles *deplanata*, differing in its distinctly narrower form,
much smaller pronotal punctures and longer, more conspicuous dorsal
vestiture, as well as the characters given in the table.

5 **Limnobaris deplanata** n. sp.—Oblong, depressed above, moderately shining, brownish-black throughout, subglabrous, the squamules small
narrow and very sparsely, almost uniformly distributed above and beneath.
Head minutely punctate anteriorly, alutaceous and impunctate in basal half,
the transverse impression strong, broadly angulate in profile ; beak with a few
bristling squamules at base, rather slender, cylindrical, evenly, somewhat
feebly arcuate, coarsely lineato-punctate, more densely so at the sides toward
base, equal in length to the prothorax, the antennæ inserted distinctly beyond
the middle, the basal joint of the funicle subequal to the next three, second
one-half as long as the first, not quite equal to the next two, club abrupt,
rather robust, scarcely as long as the preceding five joints combined, densely
pubescent, the basal joint constituting a little more than one-half the mass
and more sparsely pubescent very near the base. *Prothorax* almost as long as
wide, the sides broadly, evenly arcuate and convergent anteriorly, becoming
straight and parallel in basal half, subapical constriction feeble ; apex one-
half as wide as the base, the median lobe of the latter broadly rounded and
feeble ; disk coarsely, deeply, somewhat unevenly punctate, the punctures
slightly elongate-oval and distinctly separated ; impunctate line incomplete.
Scutellum small, glabrous, subquadrate, widest behind. *Elytra* but very
slightly wider than the prothorax and three-fourths longer, hemi-elliptical,
the apex narrowly subtruncate ; humeri not prominent ; disk rather coarsely
deeply evenly and abruptly striate, the intervals narrow, scarcely one-half
wider than the grooves, each with a single series of coarse, deep, not very close-
set punctures, the line of the series slightly impressed. *Abdomen* rather

coarsely, moderately closely punctate. Prosternum flat, evenly, feebly constricted but not foveate behind the apex, separating the coxæ by very slightly
more than their own width.   Length 3.0 mm.; width 1.25 mm.

Iowa (Keokuk).

The single specimen, apparently a male, represents a species entirely distinct from any other here described in its more depressed
form and coarse sculpture, and especially in the distinctly concave
elytral intervals.   From *tabida*, which it more closely resembles, it
may be known by the shorter, less conspicuous vestiture, more slender beak and very much coarser sculpture of the pronotum.   There
are, judging by material which has been recently sent me, apparently
a number of species in our Central States allied to *deplanata* and
tabida, and their separation will prove to be a problem of some
difficulty.

6 **Limnobaris punctiger** Lec.—Proc. Am. Phil. Soc., XV, p. 314
(Centrinus).

Oval, rather narrow, piceous, the legs, beak and antennæ paler,
rufous; vestiture beneath consisting of fine sparse squamules, almost
absent above, but each puncture of the elytral series apparently with
a long slender whitish scale.   Beak slender, equal throughout, cylindrical, evenly, moderately arcuate, nearly as long as the head and
prothorax, smooth, finely, linearly punctate at the sides toward base,
the antennæ inserted a little beyond the middle, the scape long, extending almost to the eyes, the first funicular joint as long as the
next three, the second fully one-half as long as the first and nearly
as long as the next two, the club rather small but abrupt, the basal
joint constituting a little more than one-half the mass, somewhat
obconical, sparsely pubescent and slightly shining.   Prothorax one-
third wider than long, the sides parallel and feebly arcuate to just
beyond the middle, then broadly rounded and convergent to the
apex, the latter one-half as wide as the base, the apical constriction
very small and feeble; punctures coarse, somewhat irregular in
form, not very dense; mes-epimera strongly exposed from above.
Scutellum small, quadrate.   Elytra distinctly wider than the prothorax and more than twice as long, hemi-elliptical, the apex rather
narrowly rounded, the humeri feebly tumid; striæ deep, abrupt,
remotely punctate along the bottom, the intervals flat, equal, one-
half wider than the grooves, each with a series of relatively coarse
deep rounded and somewhat remote punctures.   Prosternum flat
but with a very strong transverse subapical constriction, the coxæ

separated by their own width. Abdomen coarsely punctured, the last two sutures gradually very wide toward the middle as usual. Length 3.2 mm.; width 1.3 mm.

Texas. Cab. LeConte. Represented by the unique type, which is in a rather poor state of preservation, being much rubbed; it is apparent, however, from broken fragments, that the elytral scales are normally quite distinct, and that there are some scattered scales toward the sides of the pronotum.

7 **Limnobaris denudata** n. sp.—Oval, rather depressed, rufo-piceous throughout, the integuments shining, the vestiture consisting of very small sparse and yellowish squamules, only evident toward the sides of the pronotum and elytra, and, on the latter, especially near the apex; on the under surface they are only distinct toward the abdominal apex. *Head* minutely, very remotely punctate, the impression strong, the beak rather stout, cylindrical, evenly, distinctly arcuate, not quite as long as the prothorax, minutely, linearly punctate, more coarsely densely and rugosely so at the sides very near the base; antennæ inserted well beyond the middle, the first funicular joint as long as the next three, the second but slightly more than one-half as long as the first and about as long as the next two, outer joints gradually robust and almost continuous in outline with the club, which is very small, oval, scarcely longer than the preceding three joints together, densely pubescent throughout, and with the basal joint fully one-half the mass. *Prothorax* but slightly wider than long, the sides parallel, evenly and distinctly arcuate, gradually convergent from apical third, feebly constricted behind the apex, which is fully three-fifths as wide as the base, the latter transverse, broadly bisinuate; disk with a rather broad impunctate line, narrow or obsolete toward apex, the punctures small but uneven in size and generally very sparse, much smaller near the median line. Scutellum small, subquadrate, glabrous. *Elytra* subequal in width to the prothorax and barely three-fourths longer, the sides feebly convergent and slightly arcuate, the apex abruptly, somewhat narrowly but obtusely rounded; humeri very feebly tumid; disk rather coarsely but only moderately deeply striate, the intervals flat, nearly twice as wide as the grooves, each with a single series of punctures which vary greatly in size, but generally deep, somewhat coarse, especially toward base and moderately approximate. *Abdomen* with the first suture evident and strongly arcuate toward the middle, the first two segments moderately strongly, not densely punctured, narrowly and feebly impressed along the middle. Prosternum flat, coarsely punctate, separating the coxæ by distinctly more than their own width. Length 3.3 mm.; width 1.3 mm.

Florida.

This species is not at all closely related to any other; it is represented by a single male. The sixth funicular joint is longer than either the fifth or seventh, and the club is unusually small.

8 **Limnobaris planiuscula** n. sp.—Oval, rather strongly depressed,
polished, black, the elytra, legs and beak more or less rufous, the first somewhat clouded with piceous toward the scutellum; vestiture throughout above
and beneath consisting of very small, remote and entirely inconspicuous setæ.
Head minutely, sparsely punctate, the transverse impression strong; beak
slender, cylindrical, equal throughout, evenly, rather feebly arcuate and not
longer than the prothorax, smooth, minutely, sublineately punctured, more
coarsely and confusedly so at the sides toward base; antennæ inserted just
beyond the middle, the first funicular joint rather robust, as long as the next
three, second but slightly longer than wide, a little longer than the third and
scarcely more than one-third as long as the first, club moderate. *Prothorax*
about as long as wide; sides parallel and feebly arcuate to apical fourth, then
broadly rounded, convergent and somewhat broadly and feebly constricted to
the apex, which is rather more than one-half as wide as the base, the latter
transverse, the lobe small and feeble, rounded; disk rather coarsely, deeply,
somewhat unevenly and closely punctate, the punctures always distinctly
separated, the impunctate line narrow but evident. Scutellum small, flat,
glabrous, anteriorly parabolic, wider behind, the hind margin broadly, evenly
arcuate. *Elytra* but just visibly wider than the prothorax and three-fourths
longer, hemi-elliptical, rather acutely rounded at apex, the humeri not prominent; disk with moderately deep striæ, the intervals flat, scarcely more
than one-half wider than the grooves, each with a single series of fine but
deep, irregular and unevenly but generally remotely spaced punctures. *Abdomen* shining, the first suture entirely obliterated except near the sides, the
first two segments finely, very remotely punctured, the last three rather coarsely
and much more closely so. Prosternum flat, the coxæ remote, separated by a
little more than their own width, the subapical constriction distinct. Length
2.9 mm.; width 1.0 mm.

Texas.

The single specimen appears to be a female, the basal parts of
the abdomen being entirely unmodified, but as the male impression
is generally very slight indeed in this genus, it is not possible to be
entirely certain of the sex, especially in consideration of the short
beak.

9 **Limnobaris nasuta** Lec.—Proc. Ac. Nat. Sci., Phila., 1859, p. 79
(Baridius).

Oval, depressed above, strongly shining, black, the vestiture consisting of small and very sparse setæ. Beak slender, cylindrical,
evenly, feebly arcuate, as long as the prothorax in the male and
one-fourth longer in the female, smooth, polished, finely, sublinearly
punctate, more closely so at the sides; antennæ inserted distinctly
beyond the middle, the first funicular joint almost as long as the
next four, the second more than twice as long as wide but not quite

as long as the next two; club rather small but abrupt, densely pubescent throughout, and with the basal joint constituting a little more than one-half the mass. Prothorax about as long as wide, the sides parallel and broadly, evenly arcuate to near apical fifth, then convergent and distinctly constricted to the apex, which is scarcely more than one-half as wide as the base; disk rather finely but deeply, somewhat unevenly and not very densely punctate, the median line narrow. Scutellum small, glabrous, quadrate, the posterior angles rather prominent. Elytra slightly wider and four-fifths longer than the prothorax, hemi-elliptical, evenly, rather narrowly but not acutely rounded behind, the humeri feeble; disk with rather coarse but moderately deep striæ, the intervals nearly twice as wide as the grooves, flat, each with a single series of generally small but deep, not very close-set punctures, which vary greatly in size, more or less broadly confused toward the base of the third. Abdomen polished, rather finely, not very densely punctured. Prosternum flat, separating the coxæ by more than their own width, the punctures not conspicuously coarse. Length 3.7–4.4 mm.; width 1.35–1.75 mm.

California (San Francisco) and Texas (El Paso). Numerous specimens. The male does not differ from the female by any structural peculiarities of note.

10 **Limnobaris oblita** n. sp.—Elongate-oval, moderately convex, strongly shining, the elytra minutely granulato-reticulate and slightly alutaceous, black throughout, the legs and antennæ with a piceous tinge, subglabrous, the vestiture excessively sparse throughout, the setæ very small and inconspicuous. *Head* minutely but strongly, sparsely punctate, the impression quite distinct; beak slender, cylindrical, evenly, rather feebly arcuate, shining, finely, linearly and not very densely punctate, with two or three bristling squamules at the upper border of the eyes, about as long as the head and prothorax; antennæ inserted just beyond the middle, the basal joint of the funicle nearly as long as the next four, second barely one-half longer than the third, club oval, nearly as long as the five preceding joints combined, the basal joint composing three-fifths of the mass and sparsely pubescent toward base. *Prothorax* slightly wider than long, the sides just visibly convergent, evenly and feebly arcuate from the base to the constriction, the latter rather deep and abrupt and situated at a somewhat unusually great distance behind the apex, the latter broadly sinuate in the middle, one-half as wide as the base, which is transverse and almost perfectly straight throughout; disk not very coarsely but deeply, somewhat closely punctate, the punctures rather unevenly distributed, a median line not extending to the apex and a wide apical margin entirely impunctate. Scutellum small, flat, polished, triangular, widest and truncate behind. *Elytra* quite distinctly

wider than the prothorax and nearly twice as long, the sides parallel and very feebly arcuate in basal two-thirds, then gradually convergent, the apex rather narrowly rounded; humeral callus small and but slightly prominent; disk deeply, abruptly, moderately coarsely striate, the intervals flat or feebly concave, from one-half to once wider than the grooves, each with a single series of small, not very deep, close-set and uneven punctures. *Abdomen* strongly but not densely punctate. Prosternum flat, with a fine transverse impressed line behind the apex, the latter feebly sinuate in the middle; coxæ rather large, separated by fully three-fourths of their own width. Length 3.5 mm.; width 1.4 mm.

Wisconsin.

This species is not closely allied to any other and appears to form one of the transitions from the species with stout beaks and remote anterior coxæ, to those with very slender straight beaks and more narrowly separated coxæ. The unique specimen is a female.

11 **Limnobaris seclusa** n. sp.—Oval, moderately stout, rather feebly, evenly convex above, shining, piceous, the legs rufous; vestiture very uneven, consisting, on the pronotum, of large broad and pale scales toward the sides and before the scutellum, the scales becoming narrower and posteriorly oblique anteriorly and toward the middle, elsewhere dark in color, smaller and inconspicuous; on the elytra the large pale scales form a short line on the third interval behind the middle, and several small spots along the base, elsewhere narrow, elongate, darker and of different sizes from very minute setæ to conspicuous scales; on the under surface they are elongate and rather sparse throughout. *Head* almost completely impunctate but minutely granulato-reticulate, the impression distinct; beak cylindrical, rather stout toward base, evenly, feebly arcuate, with bristling scales just before the eyes, a little longer than the head and prothorax in the female, but not quite as long as the prothorax in the male, rather coarsely, sublinearly punctate; antennæ inserted at the middle in the female or distinctly beyond in the male, the basal joint of the funicle as long as the next three, second but slightly longer than the third, club moderate, the basal joint forming much more than one-half the mass, densely pubescent but gradually more sparsely so and slightly shining toward base. *Prothorax* nearly as long as wide, the sides parallel and scarcely arcuate to apical third, then broadly rounded and convergent to the apex, which is about one-half as wide as the base; apical constriction almost obsolete; base transverse, broadly bisinuate; disk with a wide entire and conspicuous polished impunctate line, the punctures coarse and dense. *Scutellum* small, glabrous, a little longer than wide. *Elytra* slightly wider and about one-half longer than the prothorax, evenly hemi-elliptical, the humeral callus feeble; disk with rather fine, moderately deep, finely, conspicuously and remotely punctured striæ, the intervals flat, fully twice as wide as the grooves, finely, confusedly, very deeply but not densely punctate throughout. Prosternum flat, separating the coxæ by much more than their own width. Length 2.5–3.2 mm.; width 1.1–1.4 mm.

Arizona; Southern California.

The general characters of the above description are drawn from the female; in the single very small male before me, the prothorax is quite distinctly wider than long, with the apex three-fifths as wide as the base. The great disparity in the length of the beak is, however, the only very prominent sexual difference. In certain general characters of sculpture and vestiture, *seclusa* makes an excellent transition from the normal forms of this subgenus to *grisea*.

II.

12 **Limnobaris grisea** Lec.—Proc. Am. Phil. Soc., XV, p. 312 (Centrinus).

Oblong-oval, moderately convex, piceous-black, the elytra and legs rufous; vestiture consisting of large elongate-oval yellowish-white scales, not contiguous beneath except in anterior two-thirds of the met-episterna; on the pronotum they are still more elongate, denser near the sides and finest and sparsest at lateral fourth; on the elytra they are broadly oval and unevenly disposed in strongly marked lines along the intervals, the line of the third interval being especially wide and conspicuous. Head glabrous, minutely, sparsely and feebly punctate, the impression very feeble; beak cylindrical, rather stout, evenly and rather strongly arcuate, as long as the head and prothorax in the female, but only as long as the latter in the male, the basal joint of the funicle as long as the next four together, the second as long as the next two, outer joints very short and transverse; club in the male large, densely pubescent, as long as the six preceding joints together, oval, pointed, the rings decreasing abruptly in transverse diameter, the basal joint much less than one-half the mass. Prothorax coarsely, closely punctate, two-thirds wider than long, the sides subparallel in basal two-thirds, then strongly rounded and rapidly convergent but not distinctly constricted to the apex, basal angles obtuse, the mesepimera strongly exposed from above. Scutellum rather large, quadrate, glabrous, but indented and setose at each side. Elytra a little wider than the prothorax and about twice as long, hemi-elliptical in outline, the striæ fine, the intervals strongly, confusedly punctate and from two to more than three times as wide as the grooves. Length 3.4 mm.; width 1.65 mm.

The three specimens before me are from Arizona and New Jersey; it was originally described from Texas. In the female the antennal club is notably smaller than in the male, and the funicle is longer and more slender, but aside from the shorter beak of the male I do not observe any other sexual differences.

III.

13 **Limnobaris confusa** Boh.—Sch. Curc., III, p. 740 (Centrinus).

Oblong-oval, subdepressed, alutaceous, black throughout, the antennæ slightly paler; integuments subglabrous, the vestiture consisting of very small fine white squamules, sparsely disposed above and beneath. Beak in the male rather stout, cylindrical, finely, densely punctured and squamulose toward base, straight in basal two-thirds, then bent, scarcely more than three-fourths as long as the prothorax, the antennæ inserted distinctly beyond the middle, the basal joint of the funicle robust, not as long as the next three, the second small, obconical, one-half longer than wide, the club moderately stout, oval, densely pubescent and nearly as long as the preceding five joints combined. Prothorax slightly wider than long, sides parallel and feebly arcuate, rounded convergent and constricted toward apex, the latter one-half as wide as the base; punctures fine, not very close-set, the impunctate line distinct. Elytra a little wider and three-fourths longer than the prothorax, hemielliptical, the humeral callus large but feeble; striæ fine, the intervals flat, wide, finely and more or less confusedly punctate. Prosternum separating the coxæ by two-thirds of their own width or less, with two slender slightly contorted ante-coxal spiniform processes, which are very oblique, and immediately before which there is a large deep excavation. In the female the beak is more slender, more evenly and distinctly arcuate, smooth, polished and evidently punctured only near the base, not longer than in the male, being about three-fourths as long as the prothorax; the prosternum is flat and the intercoxal process is not noticeably wider than in the male. Length 2.7–3.5 mm.; width 1.1–1.5 mm.

In the description of Boheman, the beak is said to be as long as the prothorax in the italicized diagnosis, but as long as the head and prothorax in the description which follows, the fact being, if I have correctly identified the species, that it is much shorter than the prothorax in both sexes. In the description referred to I cannot comprehend the allusion to a "pygidium."

The material before me includes series from Florida, North

Carolina, New York, Indiana, Nebraska and Colorado, some being
smaller, others larger, some with the male prosternal spines short,
others so long as to nearly attain the anterior margin. The want
of any accurate definition of the species deters me, however, from
further investigation of these forms, although from the constantly
small size and less developed ante-coxal processes of several good
series, collected in definite localities, it is possible that two or three
species or subspecies may be commingled. This species is said to
occur in California (Mann. Bull. Mosc., 1843, 2d, 293), but I have
not seen any specimens from that region.

14 **Limnobaris ebena** n. sp.—Oblong-oval, moderately convex, polished, black throughout; vestiture above and beneath consisting of small and
very sparse slender white squamules, much less conspicuous than in *concinna*,
but more so than in *confinis*, unevenly sublineate on the elytra. *Head* minutely,
scarcely visibly punctate, the constriction feeble but distinct, caused by a
slight gibbosity at the base of the beak, the latter very slender, evenly cylindrical, almost straight, much longer than the head and prothorax, shining,
moderately punctured; antennæ inserted scarcely at all beyond the middle,
slender throughout, the basal joint of the funicle as long as the next three,
the second nearly two-thirds as long as the first and equal to the next two,
the club very slender, fusiform, not abrupt, densely, coarsely pubescent and
rather longer than the preceding four joints combined, the basal joint composing nearly one-half of the whole. *Prothorax* nearly one-third wider than
long, the sides just visibly convergent from the base to the distinct apical
constriction, and broadly, evenly arcuate; apex one-half as wide as the base,
the latter transverse, the median lobe small and feeble; mes-epimera strongly
exposed from above; disk rather finely, not deeply and somewhat sparsely
punctate, the impunctate line distinct. Scutellum small, quadrate. *Elytra*
oblong, one-third longer than wide, distinctly wider than the prothorax and
fully twice as long, the sides parallel and nearly straight, slightly rounded at
base to the prothorax and very broadly rounded in apical third; disk with
deep, very even, abrupt grooves, the intervals from two to three times as wide
as the striæ, finely feebly and sparsely punctate, the punctures forming rather
even series on the second, fourth and sixth, but confused on the others.
Abdomen finely, feebly and sparsely punctate. Prosternum broadly, feebly
impressed, separating the coxæ by three-fourths of their own width, the
transverse subapical impression even, distinct, with a small impressed pit
adjoining it anteriorly. Length 3.8 mm.; width 1.65 mm.

Texas.

One female example. This species is allied to *confinis*, but is
more robust, with a longer beak in the female, more widely separated anterior coxæ and more distinct squamules.

With the type I associate a male and female from Indiana, which

differ only in being a little less robust and less polished, with the
beak in the female not longer than the head and prothorax, and, in
the male, distinctly shorter than the latter, this sex having two long
slender prosternal processes.

15 **Limnobaris puteifer** n. sp.—Oblong-oval, moderately convex,
black, rather shining and subglabrous throughout, the vestiture consisting
of very minute remote setiform squamules, more distinct beneath than above.
Head minutely, sparsely punctured, deeply inserted, the transverse constriction very feeble; beak in male rather stout, evenly cylindrical, feebly arcuate,
three-fourths as long as the prothorax, roughly, deeply punctured and sparsely
squamulose; antennæ short, inserted beyond the middle, the basal joint of
the funicle robust, not as long as the next three, the second one-half longer
than wide and one-half longer than the third, outer joints gradually transverse and coarctate, club nearly as in *confinis*. *Prothorax* about one-third
wider than long, the sides feebly convergent from the base and slightly arcuate, the apical constriction strong; apex a little more than one-half as wide
as the base, the latter transverse; median lobe very small, feeble; disk alutaceous, rather finely sparsely and not deeply punctate, the impunctate line
passing only slightly beyond the middle. Scutellum small, oblong. *Elytra*
nearly one-third wider than the prothorax and two and one-half times as long,
oblong, parallel, evenly rounded in apical third, the humeri scarcely prominent; disk rather finely, abruptly, evenly striate, the intervals flat, about
three times as wide as the grooves, each with a single series of fine remote
punctures. *Abdomen* rather closely punctured toward the sides, sparsely in
the middle, the punctures fine. Prosternum with a large oval extremely deep
excavation in the middle, and with a short straight acute and very oblique
process before each coxa, the coxæ separated by two-thirds of their own width.
Length 3.0 mm.; width 1.25 mm.

Indiana?

This species bears an extreme resemblance to *confinis*, being
identical in sculpture and vestiture, but the ante-coxal processes
are much more developed, the elytra relatively wider and longer,
the second joint of the antennal funicle more elongate, and the prosternum differs radically in having a large extremely deep median
excavation. A single male, without definite indication of locality,
but in all probability from the region indicated.

16 **Limnobaris confinis** Lec.—Proc. Am. Phil. Soc., XV, p. 317
(Centrinus).

Oblong-oval, moderately convex, black throughout, shining, subglabrous, the vestiture consisting of very small sparse and subrecumbent setæ which, on the elytra, are arranged in single inconspicuous series. Beak in the male thick, cylindrical, nearly straight,

scarcely more than three-fourths as long as the prothorax, roughly punctured, dull, sparsely squamulose, the antennæ inserted distinctly beyond the middle, short, the basal joint of the funicle robust, not as long as the next three, the second a little longer than wide and slightly longer than the third, outer joints transverse; club densely pubescent, rather robust and fully as long as the preceding five joints together. Prothorax subconical, slightly wider than long, the sides evenly, feebly arcuate, the apical constriction distinct; apex three-fourths as wide as the base; punctures rather fine, shallow and sparse, the impunctate line distinct. Elytra oblong, parallel, obtusely rounded behind, distinctly wider than the prothorax and more than twice as long; striæ fine, abrupt; intervals fully three times as wide as the grooves, each with a single series of minute, extremely distant punctures. Prosternum broadly, very feebly impressed, with a feeble elevated cusp before each coxa, and a small foveiform pit just behind the apex, the coxæ separated by three fifths of their own width. Length 2.3–2.9 mm; width 0.9–1.2 mm.

The four specimens before me are from New York, Virginia, Iowa and Texas, the latter being the only female. In this sex the beak is very slender, cylindrical, nearly straight, as long as the head and prothorax, and the antennæ are longer and with a more slender club, but, as the elytral punctures are not by any means so distinct as in the northern specimens, it may not actually belong to this species.

17 **Limnobaris concurrens** n. sp.—Oblong-oval, distinctly convex, black, moderately shining and subglabrous throughout, the minute slender setiform squamules very sparse above and beneath, forming single series on the elytra. *Head* dull, minutely, sparsely punctate, the transverse impression fine and distinct, the basal portion of the beak feebly tumid above the eyes; beak in the male rather slender, cylindrical, coarsely, densely punctured at the sides, fully as long as the prothorax, straight in basal two-thirds, slightly arcuate thence to the apex; antennæ inserted well beyond the middle, the basal joint of the funicle robust, not as long as the next three, the second scarcely one-half as long as the first and a little longer than wide, club very narrow, elongate-oval, densely pubescent, as long as the five preceding joints combined. *Prothorax* but slightly wider than long, the sides feebly convergent and nearly straight to apical third, then broadly rounded, the apical constriction distinct; apex truncate, three-fifths as wide as the base, the latter broadly, feebly bisinuate, the lobe small and feeble; disk alutaceous, finely, not strongly, sparsely punctate, the impunctate line narrow but almost entire. Scutellum very small, subquadrate, glabrous. *Elytra* about one-third wider than the prothorax and a little more than twice as long, parallel, evenly rounded in

apical two-fifths ; humeral callus not prominent ; disk polished, rather finely, abruptly, evenly striate, the intervals flat, a little more than twice as wide as the grooves, each with a single series of fine, rather distant punctures. *Abdomen* feebly, not closely punctured. Prosternum broadly, very feebly impressed along the middle, with a small feeble subtransverse fovea behind the apex, the sides of the longitudinal impression slightly prominent in the form of a low obtuse ridge for a short distance before each coxa, but without trace of ante-coxal cusp, the coxæ separated by slightly less than one-half of their own width.   Length 2.2–3.2 mm. ; width 0.85–1.4 mm.

District of Columbia. Mr. Jülich.

The above description is drawn from the male. In the female the beak is slightly more slender very feebly arcuate and as long as the head and prothorax, with the antennæ inserted at or just behind the middle. The antennæ are longer and more slender, the second funicular joint almost as long as the next two, and the prosternum is perfectly flat, separating the coxæ by fully three-fourths of their own width. *Concurrens* is allied to *confinis*, but differs in its much longer beak, especially in the male, and by its narrower antennal club. Numerous examples.

18 Limnobaris concinna Lec.—Proc. Am. Phil. Soc., XV, p. 316 (Centrinus).

Oblong-oval, decidedly convex, black throughout, moderately shining, smooth, the vestiture consisting above and beneath of long sparse narrow white but very distinct squamules, arranged in single lines on the elytral intervals. Beak not quite as long as the prothorax and slender in the female, distinctly shorter and thicker in the male, feebly arcuate, slightly gibbous at the basal constriction, which is fine but distinct, roughly punctured and dull in the male, a little smoother in the female, the antennæ very slightly ante-median in both sexes, short, stout, the first funicular joint as long as the next three, two to seven small, equal in length but increasing in width ; club relatively large, fully as long as the preceding six joints, densely, rather coarsely pubescent, the basal joint composing nearly one-half the mass. Prothorax not quite as long as wide, parallel, distinctly constricted at apex, the latter about three-fourths as wide as the base ; disk rather sparsely, strongly punctate. Scutellum very small, elongate-oval, glabrous. Elytra equal in width to the prothorax and three-fourths longer, parallel, rounded behind in apical third ; striæ very fine ; intervals minutely, uniseriately punctate and remotely transversely creased. Prosternum flat, separating the coxæ by three-fifths of their width, the anterior constriction in the form of a transverse fold of the surface, immediately before which there are two small moderately distant punctiform foveæ. Male without trace of ante-coxal spines. Length 1.8–2.5 mm.; width 0.7–1.0 mm.

Florida (Enterprise and Baldwin) and Texas, also said by LeConte to occur in New York, but I have not recognized it from this locality.

19 **Limnobaris fratercula** n. sp.—Oval, feebly convex, deep black throughout, rather strongly shining, subglabrous, the fine squamules very small and sparse above and beneath. *Head* alutaceous, very minutely, sparsely punctate, the beak tumid at base, the transverse impression distinct; beak in the male rather stout, cylindrical, just visibly shorter than the prothorax, feebly arcuate, becoming straight in basal two-thirds, punctured at the sides, especially toward base, shining; antennæ slightly ante-median, the first funicular joint stout, not longer than the next two, the second slightly longer than wide, outer joints broader, almost continuous in outline with the club, the latter densely pubescent, moderately stout, about as long as the preceding four joints together, the first one adjoining it being more pubescent than the others. *Prothorax* very nearly as long as wide, the sides feebly convergent and broadly arcuate from the base, the apical constriction almost obsolete; apex truncate, rather more than one-half as wide as the base; basal lobe small and very feeble; disk not coarsely but somewhat strongly, moderately sparsely punctured, the impunctate line distinct. Scutellum small, subquadrate. *Elytra* a little wider than the prothorax and fully twice as long, elongate-oval in form, the humeri but slightly prominent; disk rather finely striate, the striæ becoming coarser and feebly crenulate toward base; intervals flat, about twice as wide as the grooves, each with an almost even single series of rather coarse, deep and somewhat distant punctures. *Abdomen* polished, finely, not densely punctate. Prosternum flat, with a small, rather deep pit behind the apical margin; coxæ separated by barely one-half of their own width; ante-coxal processes completely obsolete, the surface even. Length 2.5 mm.; width 1.0 mm.

Florida.

The three specimens before me are males, the abdomen having a small elongate-oval and rather deep subbasal impression. The species is related to *confusa*, but differs in its small size, uniseriate elytral intervals, simple male prosternum and slightly longer beak. From *confinis* it differs in its broader, more depressed form, much coarser elytral striæ and larger, more close-set serial punctures.

20 **Limnobaris seminitens** n. sp.—Elongate-oval, feebly convex, moderately shining, minutely reticulate, the pronotum alutaceous, black, sub-

glabrous, the small fine squamules very sparse throughout. *Head* minutely, sparsely punctate, the transverse impression feeble; beak slender, feebly, evenly arcuate, evenly cylindrical, smooth, polished, finely, sparsely lineato-punctate, confusedly so near the base, equal in length to the prothorax, the antennæ inserted just behind the middle, slender, the first funicular joint fully as long as the next two, the second twice as long as wide and one-half longer than the third, club rather narrow, oval, as long as the preceding four joints combined. *Prothorax* nearly as long as wide, the sides nearly parallel and straight in basal two thirds, then gradually broadly, evenly arcuate and convergent to the apex, the subapical constriction feeble; apex truncate, distinctly more than one-half as wide ·as the base, the median lobe of the latter feebly rounded; disk finely, sparsely punctate, the impunctate line distinct. Scutellum small, subquadrate, slightly broader behind. *Elytra* but little wider than the prothorax, fully twice as long as the latter, parallel, evenly rounded in apical third; humeri scarcely at all prominent; disk with fine abrupt rather deep and even striæ, the intervals flat, fully three times as wide as the grooves, each with a single series of fine, feeble, rather distant punctures, confused toward the base of the third. *Abdomen* finely, sparsely punctured, but, as usual, densely so toward apex. Prosternum flat, with a small subapical pit, the coxæ separated by one-half of their own width. Length 3.5 mm.; width 1.4 mm.

Nebraska.

Not closely allied to any other species known to me, and represented by a single specimen which is undoubtedly the female, although the abdomen has a small feeble subbasal impression, and the fifth segment a small rounded indentation. A specimen in my cabinet from Florida also belongs apparently to this species, but is larger and with a much longer beak.

IV.

. 21 **Limnobaris prolixa** Lec.—Proc. Am. Phil. Soc., XV, p. 317 (Centrinus).

Slender, parallel, convex, shining, subglabrous, the dorsal setiform squamules very minute but longer and more visible toward the sides of the prothorax. Beak feebly, evenly arcuate, slender, cylindrical, as long as the prothorax in both sexes, a little thicker and much more densely punctate in the male, the transverse basal constriction almost obsolete; antennæ inserted at the middle in the male, or far behind this point in the female, the first funicular joint as long as the next three, second one-half longer than the third; club moderate, as long as the four preceding joints combined. Prothorax slightly but distinctly wider than long; the sides parallel,

feebly arcuate; subapical constriction small, distinct; apex nearly
three-fourths as wide as the base, the disk finely, sparsely punctate
and slightly alutaceous. Scutellum small, glabrous, quadrate.
Elytra very slightly wider than the prothorax and nearly three
times as long, parallel, obtusely rounded behind in apical fourth;
humeral callus small but rather prominent; striæ very fine but
deep; intervals wide, uniseriately, minutely and remotely punctate.
Prosternum broadly but strongly impressed along the middle in the
female; in the male it has a deep rounded pit near the middle, and,
before each coxa, a slender process which is much more developed
than in any other of our apygidiate Barini, projecting very nearly
as far beyond the apical margin of the prosternum as the distance
between the latter and the coxæ, the apices diverging horizontally
toward apex in order not to interfere with lateral movements of the
beak; coxæ separated by nearly one-third of their own width.
Length 2.3–3.4 mm.; width 0.75–1.1 mm.

Illinois and Michigan. I also associate with this species a number of specimens taken by Mr. Wickham at Greeley, Colorado,
which seem to be merely a little smaller in size; in the single male,
however, the prosternal spines are very much shorter, only projecting as far as the anterior margin. I do not notice the bronzy lustre
mentioned by LeConte.

22 **Limnobaris nitidissima** n. sp.—Very elongate, parallel, convex,
highly polished, black with a rather strong æneous lustre; legs pale, bright
rufo-testaceous; integuments subglabrous, the minute setæ very sparse above,
slightly longer and more evident toward the sides of the pronotum, only distinct beneath on the met-episterna, where they are broader, somewhat dense
and squamiform. *Head* very minutely, sparsely punctate, the impression
almost obsolete, broadly subfoveate in the middle; beak very slender, straight
in basal half, gradually feebly arcuate and rufescent thence to the apex,
smooth, cylindrical, punctate at the sides toward base and fully as long as the
head and prothorax; mandibles small, strongly arcuate, thick, deeply notched
and unevenly bidentate at apex, and with two or three strong denticles externally toward base; antennæ inserted at basal two-fifths, slender, the scape
just attaining the eye, basal joint of the funicle not quite as long as the next
three, second one-half longer than the third, club moderate. *Prothorax* about
as long as wide; sides straight and parallel fully to apical third, then broadly
rounded, convergent and sinuate to the apex, which is two-thirds as wide as
the base, the latter transverse, the median lobe extremely feeble; disk with
a feebly defined, incomplete median line, the punctures minute and very
sparse. Scutellum small, quadrate, glabrous. *Elytra* quite distinctly wider
than the prothorax and two and three-fourths times as long, parallel, the

sides feebly convergent in apical third, the apex narrow but obtusely rounded; humeri slightly prominent; disk nearly as in *prolixa*, but with the punctures still more minute and feeble. Prosternum strongly impressed along the middle, separating the coxæ by fully one-third of their own width. Length 4.1 mm.; width 1.35 mm.

Texas (Galveston).

A single female. This species may be recognized at once by its polished æneous surface and red legs; it differs greatly from *prolixa* in the latter respect, and also in its longer beak.

V.

23 Limnobaris longula Lec.—Proc. Am. Phil. Soc., XV, p. 316 (Centrinus).

Elongate-oval, convex, black, the tarsi and antennæ somewhat pale, shining, the vestiture white, consisting of long, slender, rather sparse but conspicuous squamules, almost evenly distributed above and beneath, becoming shorter and·squamiform on the sternal parapleuræ. Head finely, sparsely punctate, the constriction obsolete, the frontal fovea very small and prolonged anteriorly for a short distance; beak in the female moderately slender, slightly thicker toward base, cylindrical, smooth, polished, evenly, moderately arcuate, about as long as the head and prothorax, almost impunctate but abruptly densely so and with erect squamules before the eyes; antennæ inserted a little behind the middle, the basal joint of the funicle not as long as the next three, the second scarcely two-thirds as long as the first and as long as the next two; club moderate, densely pubescent, not very slender. Prothorax two-fifths wider than long, the sides broadly, feebly arcuate, becoming convergent and gradually broadly and just visibly sinuate to the apex, parallel toward base, the apex nearly three-fifths as wide as the base; disk rather strongly, not very densely punctate, with a narrow impunctate line. Scutellum small, glabrous. Elytra scarcely at all wider than the prothorax and about twice as long, hemi-elliptical, the striæ not very coarse, with the edges finely, feebly, unevenly, subcrenulate, the intervals finely, sparsely, unevenly, punctured and transversely, unevenly rugulose. Prosternum strongly impressed along the middle, separating the anterior coxæ by fully three-fourths of their own width. Length 4.0–4.3 mm.; width 1.65–1.8 mm.

Texas and Florida. In the original type, from which the above description is taken, the abdomen has, near the base, a narrow elongate and very feeble impression; it is however a female, as is conclusively shown by the polished, almost impunctate beak; the impression is spurious, and has very nearly misled me in several species of genera allied to this. There are but two examples known to me, and the Florida specimen in my cabinet is a male, a little larger than the Texas type, intense black throughout, the beak short, rather thick, cylindrical, densely, deeply lineato-punctate, evenly, feebly arcuate and distinctly shorter than the prothorax, the antennæ being inserted at apical two-fifths; otherwise the two specimens seem to agree very well indeed, except that the male is a little stouter and with less elongate elytra, rather the reverse of what might be expected.

24 **Limnobaris rectirostris** Lec.—Proc. Am. Phil. Soc., XV, p. 315 (Centrinus).

Elongate-oval, convex, black, polished, the pronotum slightly alutaceous, subglabrous, the vestiture consisting of minute slender white squamules, very sparse throughout. Beak in the male scarcely as long as the prothorax, thick, densely punctate, evenly cylindrical throughout, compressed and carinate above, the frontal constriction obsolete but represented by a large deep and transversely angulate fovea; antennæ inserted at the middle, the second funicular joint nearly as long as the first and as long as the next two; club moderately stout, elongate-oval, densely pubescent, as long as the four preceding joints combined, and with the basal joint constituting two-fifths of the mass. Prothorax not quite as long as wide, feebly subconical, the sides more strongly arcuate before the middle, the apex two-thirds as wide as the base; punctures rather uneven in distribution but generally not very close; median line distinct. Elytra but little wider than the prothorax and much more than twice as long, the striæ fine, abrupt; intervals wide, finely, feebly, rather sparsely and transversely punctate, the punctures confused on the third, but more or less evenly uniseriate on the others. Prosternum broadly sinuate at apex, strongly, transversely constricted behind the apex, broadly, feebly impressed along the middle, separating the coxæ by one-half their own width. Length 4.2–4.7 mm.; width 1.7–1.9 mm.

Indiana and Illinois. In the female the beak is very slender, evenly but extremely feebly arcuate and fully one-half longer than the prothorax, the prosternum flat. In three of the four males before me the beak is a little longer than the prothorax, with the frontal fovea much more feeble, the body more slender and the prosternum perfectly flat along the middle, but they are otherwise so similar to the form which I regard as typical, that I hesitate to describe them under a separate name.

25 **Limnobaris calva** Lec.—Proc. Am. Phil. Soc., XV, p. 314 (Centrinus).

Oblong, convex, moderately shining, the very small slender squamules sparse and inconspicuous above, but more distinct beneath, although still sparse. Head without trace of the feeblest transverse impression, but with a minute subobsolete median puncture, the beak in the male stout, shining but deeply, rugosely punctured, feebly compressed and subcarinate above, equal in length to the prothorax, straight, broadly bent near the middle and thence feebly flattened to the apex; antennæ inserted slightly beyond the middle, slender, the second funicular joint much longer than the next two; club slender, pointed, as long as the preceding four joints combined. Prothorax distinctly wider than long, the sides strongly, evenly rounded at apical third to the constriction, the apex tubulate and slightly wider than one-half the base; disk not very coarsely but deeply and somewhat densely punctate, the impunctate line narrow and not attaining the apex. Scutellum small, quadrate. Elytra two-fifths longer than wide, scarcely at all wider than the prothorax and barely twice as long, obtusely rounded behind; sides distinctly convergent throughout; disk finely striate, the intervals from two to three times as wide as the grooves, coarsely, confusedly, rugosely but not very densely punctured. Abdomen very closely punctured. Prosternum obsoletely impressed along the middle, separating the coxæ by barely more than one-fourth of their own width. Length 5.2 mm.; width 2.2 mm.

Pennsylvania, Georgia and Florida. The male has a small elongate-oval feeble impression near the base of the abdomen. In the original type the sides of the prothorax are parallel and almost perfectly straight nearly to apical third, but in other specimens they are slightly convergent and strongly arcuate; in the Pennsylvania male the legs are black and the interstitial punctures coarse, while in another example the legs are red and the punctures finer. The description is drawn from the type specimen.

OLIGOLOCHUS n. gen.

The single species referred to this genus, greatly resembles *Microcholus striatus* in its general features of form, sculpture and vestiture, although much smaller in point of size, and would have been referred to Microcholus were it not for the distinctly different structure of the mandibles, which are not large and prominent as in that genus, but very small, thick, strongly arcuate, notched at apex and broadly decussate when closed.

The principal generic characters have been given in the table, and those of minor importance are referred to in the description of the single species given below. Oligolochus does not resemble Zygobaris either in habitus or structure.

1 **Oligolochus convexus** Lec.—Proc. Am. Phil. Soc., XV, p. 422 (Zygobaris ?).

Oval, moderately and evenly convex, polished, black, the legs rufous; vestiture very sparse and uneven, white, consisting of large scattered scales towards the sides of the pronotum and on the median line before the scutellum, also on the elytra toward the base of the third and fifth intervals and a few widely scattered on the disk toward the sides, the latter smaller and narrower; on the under surface sparse but more evident on the sternal parapleuræ; all other punctures of the upper surface bearing extremely minute setæ. Beak moderately slender, evenly, not very strongly arcuate, coarsely, sparsely, unevenly punctate at the sides, as long as the prothorax, feebly thickened toward base and slightly flattened toward apex, the basal impression extremely feeble; antennæ inserted a little beyond the middle, the scape almost attaining the eye, the first funicular joint longer than the next three, the second small, slightly longer than the third; club moderate, abrupt, oval, densely pubescent, as long as the preceding four joints, with the basal joint one-half of the whole. Prothorax one-third wider than long, the sides very feebly convergent and distinctly arcuate from the base to the well-marked subapical constriction, the apex not tubulate, three-fifths as wide as the base, the median lobe of the latter small and feeble; impunctate line entire; punctures coarse, not dense. Scutellum very small, quadrate, impressed behind, glabrous. Elytra but slightly longer than wide, a little wider than the prothorax and three-fourths longer, hemi-elliptical, the apex narrowly subtruncate;

humeri rather prominent; striæ rather coarse, deep, abrupt, one-half
to two times wider than the grooves, each with an uneven single
series of small, not very close-set punctures, more confused on
the third. Abdomen closely, rather coarsely punctate, the fifth
segment not as long as the two preceding, the pygidium slightly
exposed at tip in the male. Length 2.3 mm.; width 1.2 mm.

Florida (Enterprise). Cab. LeConte. Represented by the unique
male type. The prosternum is flat, the subapical constriction fine,
even and continuous entirely across the surface and not obsolete at
the middle as stated by LeConte; the surface between the constriction and the apex being rather strongly reflexed over the basal part
of the head, the author quoted quite pardonably mistook the groove
for the apical margin. The anterior coxæ are separated by distinctly less than one-half of their own width. The legs are more
slender than in *Microcholus striatus*, but the tarsal claws are very
nearly similar, thick and approximate, though divergent and free at
base.

IDIOSTETHUS n. gen.

This genus, though related to Stethobaris, is conspicuously distinct in antennal and pectoral structure, as well as in the general
nature of the sculpture and vestiture. The antennæ have the
second funicular joint elongate when compared with that of Stethobaris, and the club is generally smaller than in that genus; the club
varies, however, quite remarkably in size and structure.

The prosternum is noticeably tumid, especially before the coxæ,
reminding us in this respect of Orthoris, and the narrow, deep but
not abruptly defined median canaliculation is formed in much the
same manner, as a depression between the ante-coxal prominences.
The coxæ are much more approximate than in Stethobaris, never
being separated by more, and generally by less, than one-third of
their own width. The pronotal sculpture is always in greater or
less part longitudinally rugulose, and the vestiture consists of small
sparse slender and recumbent setæ and squamules, the latter, in one
of the species, widely dispersed over the elytra; they are generally,
but not always, more distinct toward the sides of the body beneath,
occasionally becoming conspicuously dense.

In the short tubulate prothorax, structure of the beak, mandibles
and transverse frontal impression, scutellum, legs and tarsi, Idiostethus closely resembles Stethobaris, but the body is more elongate-

oval, with less prominent and especially less post-basal humeri, and
the small, slender tarsal claws are more widely divergent.

The four representatives here recognized may be easily identified
from the following characters, the species being more isolated among
themselves than in Stethobaris:—

Elytra without dispersed squamules, the antennal scape more abruptly clavate.
    Antennæ with the first funicular joint not longer than the next three to-
        gether ; club smaller, with its basal joint constituting about one-half of
        the mass ; vestiture not dense at the sides beneath.
        Sculpture coarse, the pronotum with a narrow, impunctate and generally
            subcarinate line ; interstitial punctures of the elytra coarse and deep ;
            larger species..1 **tubulatus**
        Sculpture finer, the pronotum very finely, densely rugulose and without
            median line ; interstitial punctures smaller, rather indefinite and feeble ;
            much smaller species................................2 **subcalvus**
    Antennæ with the first funicular joint as long as the next four ; club larger,
        elongate, nearly as long as the preceding six joints combined and with its
        basal joint constituting but slightly more than one-third of the mass ; vesti-
        ture extremely dense at the sides of the body beneath...3 **ellipsoideus**
Elytra with widely dispersed, longer, whiter but slender squamules ; antennal
    scape gradually clavate..4 **dispersus**

1 **Idiostethus tubulatus** Say—Curc., p. 20 ; Ed. Lec., I, p. 285
(Camptorhinus—Say, Stethobaris—Lec.).

Oval, rather robust, moderately convex, black, the antennæ, tibiæ
and tarsi piceous ; integuments polished, the vestiture very sparse,
consisting of short, slender, subrecumbent setæ, generally more
evident toward the sides of the prothorax, and in a single line
along each elytral interval. Beak slender, strongly arcuate, about
one-half longer than the prothorax, rather densely, strongly punctate ; antennæ inserted a little beyond the middle, with the scape
abruptly clavate, the second funicular joint not quite as long as the
next two, the club moderate, elongate-oval, rather abrupt, nearly as
long as the five preceding joints combined, and with the basal joint
constituting almost one-half the mass. Prothorax nearly three-
fourths wider than long, the sides rather strongly convergent and
straight to apical third, then broadly rounded and convergent to
the strongly constricted and tubulate apex ; punctures coarse, deep,
rather dense, more or less longitudinally confluent, and with a narrow subcarinate impunctate line. Scutellum small, slightly wider
than long, broadly emarginate at apex. Elytra abruptly much
wider than the prothorax and fully two and one-half times as long,

hemi-elliptical in outline, the striæ coarse, deep, remotely and distinctly punctate, but not at all crenulate, the intervals rather narrow, flat, uniseriately and more or less strongly punctate. Prosternum broadly, strongly impressed, the impression short, disappearing before the coxæ, the edges not abruptly defined; anterior coxæ rather large, very narrowly separated. Length 3.0–4.0 mm.; width 1.6–2.0 mm.

New York, Pennsylvania, Indiana, Illinois and Florida, the latter locality perhaps doubtful. Nine specimens, exhibiting considerable variation, chiefly in regard to the magnitude and density of the punctures. In some specimens the thoracic sculpture is longitudinally and strongly rugulose.

2 **Idiostethus subcalvus** Lec.—Proc. Am. Phil. Soc., XVII, p. 622 (Zygobaris).

Oval, strongly convex, shining, black throughout, the antennæ, tibiæ and tarsi more or less piceous; pubescence very short and sparse, slightly denser and nearly uniformly distributed beneath, the elytra without dispersed squamules. Head finely, distinctly punctate, the beak very densely, rugulosely so, substriate along the fine polished median subcarinate line, evenly, not very strongly arcuate, slender and about as long as the head and prothorax, the antennæ inserted at the middle, the first funicular joint robust and scarcely longer than the next two, second nearly as long as the third and fourth, slender, almost three-fourths as long as the first, outer joints stouter; club small, robust, scarcely longer than the preceding four joints together, with its basal joint constituting one-half of the mass. Prothorax rather small, conical, tubulate at apex, one-half wider than long, convex and finely, very densely, longitudinally and confusedly rugulose throughout, without median line. Scutellum small, quadrate, scarcely impressed. Elytra large, abruptly much wider than the prothorax, about two and one-half times longer than the latter, hemi-elliptical, the humeral callus small but unusually prominent; disk with fine but deep and abrupt striæ, the intervals somewhat feebly rugulose, nearly three times as wide as the grooves, each with a more or less even series of somewhat distant, moderately small, very feeble punctures, each bearing a short subrecumbent seta, often directed transversely or obliquely. Abdomen finely, extremely densely punctate and dull. Prosternum tumid, declivous anteriorly, narrowly, strongly impressed along

the middle, separating the coxæ by scarcely more than one-fourth
of their own width.   Length 1.8–2.6 mm.; width 0.8–1.25 mm.

Pennsylvania, Indiana, Kentucky and Missouri.   A sufficiently
common species, the smallest of the genus, rather more convex than
usual and with more prominent humeri, but not differing from the
others in generic structure.   The claws are perfectly free, slender
and divergent.

3 **Idiostethus ellipsoideus** n. sp.—Rather narrow, elliptical, convex, shining, black throughout, the tibiæ and tarsi piceous; vestiture whitish,
consisting above of very small recumbent setæ, slightly wider and closer
toward the sides of the pronotum and disposed in a single uneven line on
each interval, without larger dispersed squamules on the elytra, but with two
or three at each side of the middle of the pronotum near lateral fourth; under
surface sparsely squamulose, the prosternum and mes-episterna more densely
so, the met-episterna and sides of the abdomen thence to the apex covered
with an extremely dense crust of small overlapping feathery scales. *Head*
finely but deeply and distinctly, not very sparsely punctate, the beak densely,
rugulosely so and sparsely squamulose at the sides, with a feebly impressed
line of punctures on each side of the narrow subcariniform impunctate line,
slender, strongly arcuate, a little longer than the head and prothorax;
antennæ inserted beyond the middle, the scape rather long, first joint of the
funicle as long as the next four, second nearly one-half as long as the first
and almost as long as the next two; club rather large, elongate-oval, densely
pubescent, nearly as long as the preceding six joints combined, with the basal
joint constituting but slightly more than one-third of the mass. *Prothorax*
two-thirds wider than long, the sides feebly convergent and nearly straight
to apical fourth, then strongly rounded to the apical constriction; apex truncate, tubulate, one-half as wide as the base, the latter transverse, with the
median lobe small but distinct; disk not very coarsely, deeply, unevenly
sculptured, longitudinally rugulose toward the narrow abbreviated and subcarinate impunctate line. Scutellum minute, quadrate, impressed. *Elytra*
quite distinctly wider than the prothorax, and two and three-fourths times as
long, nearly one-half longer than wide, hemi-elliptical in outline, the sides
becoming parallel and nearly straight in basal half, the humeri small but
slightly prominent; disk with not very coarse but deep, abrupt striæ, the
intervals flat, about twice as wide as the grooves, each with a single wide,
feebly impressed line of coarse but feeble, close-set, somewhat confused and
uneven punctures. *Abdomen* very densely punctate. Prosternum nearly normal, tumid and strongly, anteriorly declivous. Length 2.6–3.5 mm.; width
1.1–1.7 mm.

Iowa; Missouri.

A distinct species varying considerably in size.   Four specimens.

4 **Idiostethus dispersus** n. sp.—Oval, rather stout, moderately convex, black; legs rufo-piceous; integuments polished, the vestiture sparse and

uneven, consisting, on the pronotum, of extremely minute setæ which become long slender recumbent whitish squamules in lateral fifth, and in the middle before the scutellum, also with a few widely dispersed over the intermediate regions; on the elytra there is a single series of very small setæ on each interval, with long slender squamules very widely dispersed over the entire surface; on the under surface the squamules are denser and somewhat bristling on the prosternum especially behind, and the smaller white recumbent scales are sparse throughout, but denser on the met-episterna and toward the sides of the last four ventral segments. *Head* finely, rather sparsely punctate, the beak moderately stout, densely punctate and sparsely squamulose along the sides, evenly, distinctly arcuate and equal in length to the prothorax in the male; antennæ inserted near apical two-fifths, the scape rather long and strongly, gradually clavate. *Prothorax* three-fourths wider than long, the sides feebly but distinctly convergent and nearly straight to apical fourth, then strongly rounded to the apical constriction, the apex briefly tubulate, rather more than one-half as wide as the base, the latter broadly, feebly arcuate, the median lobe very small and feeble; disk very unevenly, moderately coarsely and deeply sculptured, the impunctate line narrow but entire, well defined and somewhat elevated; sculpture longitudinally rugulose toward the middle, closely punctate toward the sides, and more finely and very sparsely punctate at lateral fourth toward base. *Scutellum* minute, quadrate, feebly impressed. *Elytra* hemi-elliptical, fully one-fifth wider than the prothorax and much more than twice as long; sides feebly sinuate toward apex, the latter narrowly rounded; humeri not distinctly prominent; disk with extremely coarse, deep, abrupt and even striæ, the intervals flat, equal, but slightly wider than the grooves, each with a single feebly impressed line of somewhat coarse close-set rounded punctures. Prosternum decidedly tumid with reference to the mesosternum, narrowly, strongly impressed along the middle, separating the coxæ by barely one-third of their width, and, behind them, declivous to the surface of the mesosternum, extending somewhat over the latter. *Abdomen* coarsely, very deeply, rather closely punctured near the base. Length 3.3 mm.; width 1.75 mm.

Alabama.

The single specimen is a male, the abdomen having a rather small but deep subbasal impression. This species is not at all closely allied to *tubulatus,* and has the anterior coxæ slightly less narrowly separated.

STETHOBARIS.
LeConte—Proc. Am. Phil. Soc., XV, p. 302.

The essential characters distinguishing this genus from others, more closely allied to it in the present section of the tribe, are the large antennal club, nearly as long as the entire funicle and resembling that of Rhoptobaris, the small, slender, free but feebly divergent claws, deeply, abruptly and broadly excavated prosternum, not very widely separating the coxæ, peculiar oval, thick and convex form of the body, with prominent humeri situated at quite a noticeable distance behind the base, and the polished black integuments, which are practically entirely glabrous, each puncture bearing an excessively minute seta, only visible under considerable amplification. Stethobaris is one of the genera connecting the more normal forms of the tribe with the aberrant Oomorphidius and Eisonyx.

The beak is separated from the head by a feeble but distinctly marked transverse impression and is strongly arcuate, moderate in length and thickness, and nearly always noticeably tapering from base to apex, with the antennal scrobes strongly oblique and broadly confluent beneath; the mandibles are short, arcuate and broadly decussate. The tibiæ are deeply and longitudinally sculptured.

The species of Stethobaris are moderately numerous, and, with one exception, more than usually homogeneous in external appearance. It is possible, however, that they may be recognized by the characters given in the following table:—

Integuments more or less finely and sparsely punctate, the interstitial punctures of the elytra very minute and sparse.

    Sides of the prothorax broadly arcuate, becoming parallel in basal half; pronotal punctures minute and very sparse, becoming larger but not at all confluent at the sides beneath......................................1 **corpulenta**

    Sides convergent from the basal angles, the prothorax smaller and more conical, less sparsely and more conspicuously punctured.

        Prothorax with a distinct but narrow subentire impunctate line; punctures of the elytra confused, at least on the wider intervals; sides of the prothorax beneath obliquely and finely rugose; last ventral segment in both sexes distinctly shorter than the two preceding together.

        Elytral grooves very coarse, strongly, remotely punctured, the edges feebly but distinctly serrato-crenulate; form stouter, the prothorax a little more transverse...................................2 **incompta**

        Elytral grooves less coarse, much more finely punctate at the bottom, the edges never serrato-crenulate, except occasionally very feebly so near the base...3 **ovata**

    Prothorax more conical and more densely punctate, never with a clearly defined entire impunctate line, the punctures beneath at the sides distinct, not forming elongate rugæ; elytral striæ very coarse and remotely but conspicuously punctured, the extremely minute interstitial punctures forming a single line on each.......................4 **congermana**

Integuments coarsely, densely punctured, the punctures of the elytra forming a single deep coarse and confluent line on each interval........5 **egregia**

1 **Stethobaris corpulenta** Lec.—Proc. Am. Phil. Soc., XV, p. 420.

Robust, oval, convex, glabrous, strongly shining and black throughout, the antennæ with the first funicular joint nearly as long as the next four, second to seventh equal in length, the former not as long as wide; club large, evenly elliptical, densely pubescent, equal in length to the six preceding joints combined and equally trisected by the first and second sutures. The prothorax is short, four-fifths wider than long, the sides very strongly, evenly arcuate, convergent anteriorly to the strong apical tubulation, and becoming gradually parallel in about basal half, the apex not quite one-half as wide as the base, the latter broadly, feebly arcuate, the median lobe small but prominent, truncate; disk sparsely, uniformly, very finely and rather feebly punctate, coarsely but not confluently so beneath, the impunctate line narrow, distinct and subentire. Scutellum a little longer than wide, impressed toward apex, quadrangular. Elytra, at a short distance behind the apex, fully one-fifth wider than the prothorax, a little more than twice as long as the latter, the humeri obtusely prominent; outline hemi-elliptical; striæ coarse, deep, with the margins remotely and finely serrato-crenulate toward base; intervals from two to three times as wide as the grooves, minutely, feebly, sparsely and confusedly punctate. Length 3.3 mm.; width 1.8 mm.

Florida (Tampa). Cab. LeConte. I have seen only the unique female type in the Museum of Comparative Zoology at Harvard University.

2 **Stethobaris incompta** n. sp.—Oval, strongly convex, somewhat robust, black, glabrous and strongly shining throughout. *Head* finely but strongly, sparsely punctate, the beak densely punctured at the sides, evenly, strongly arcuate, moderately slender, distinctly tapering from base to apex and equal in length to the head and prothorax, the antennæ inserted at basal two-fifths, nearly as in *corpulenta*, but with the first funicular joint a little shorter and the club distinctly longer, equalling the entire funicle excepting one-half of the basal joint, with its first joint a little longer than the second. *Prothorax* about four-fifths wider than long, the sides feebly but noticeably convergent and nearly straight to the middle, then gradually, broadly rounded, becoming strongly convergent to the apical tubule, which is distinctly less than one-half as wide as the very broadly, feebly arcuate base; median lobe of the latter small but distinct, truncate; disk rather finely but deeply, not very densely punctate, with a narrow impunctate median line, the punctures coarser, and forming long oblique rugæ beneath. Scutellum minute, quadrate, scarcely impressed. *Elytra*, at a little behind the base, barely one-fifth wider than the prothorax, nearly two and one-half times longer than the latter;

humeri obtusely prominent; outline behind them hemi-elliptical; striæ rather coarse, deep, remotely, distinctly serrato-crenulate, the intervals differing greatly in width, the third twice as wide as the grooves, the fourth but slightly wider than the latter, flat, minutely but deeply and distinctly punctate, the punctures confused, sparse but becoming closer toward base, forming nearly even single lines on the narrow intervals.   Length 3.1 mm.; width 1.65 mm.

Florida.

This species differs from *corpulenta* in its less obese form and larger antennal club, smaller and quite differently shaped, slightly more conical, much more coarsely, deeply and less sparsely punctate prothorax, with the punctures not isolated beneath at the sides, but forming long rugæ; also in its flatter, still more unequal and less polished elytral intervals, with the punctures less minute, deeper and becoming denser toward base; and finally, and quite remarkably, in the form of the mes-epimera, which in *corpulenta* are gradually pointed upward, but much more truncate and rounded in *incompta*.   The present species is closely allied to *ovata*, and agrees with that species in all the characters given above to distinguish it from *corpulenta*.   It is represented by a single female.

3 **Stethobaris ovata** Lec.—Proc. Acad. Nat. Sci. Phila., 1868, p. 363 (Baridius).

Ovate, polished, black and glabrous, rather strongly convex. Beak moderately slender, strongly arcuate, about as long as the head and prothorax, the antennæ inserted just behind the middle, the first funicular joint robust, about as long as the next three, second quadrate, just visibly longer than the third, two to seven small, the club very large, abrupt, elongate-oval, nearly as long as the entire funicle, densely pubescent throughout and with the basal joint composing but slightly more than one-third of the mass, the second long.   Prothorax about two-thirds wider than long, the sides feebly convergent and nearly straight to slightly beyond the middle, then broadly rounded and gradually convergent to the strong constriction; apex tubulate; base broadly arcuate, the lobe distinct, truncate; disk rather finely, sparsely and unevenly punctate, the punctures larger along the basal-margin; impunctate line narrow, entire.   Scutellum small, longer than wide, the apex emarginate and the surface impressed posteriorly.   Elytra, at a little behind the apex, quite distinctly wider than the prothorax, the humeri large, tumid; outline hemi-elliptical; striæ moderately wide, deep, remotely punctate, abrupt, not at all crenulate, the intervals wide, flat, generally rather ·more than twice as wide as the grooves, minutely sparsely and confusedly punctate. Prosternum rather widely, very deeply and abruptly excavated anteriorly, the anterior coxæ small and separated by two-thirds of their own width. Length 2.5–2.8 mm.; width 1.3–1.5 mm.

Massachusetts to Virginia; five specimens, exhibiting comparatively little variation.

4 Stethobaris congermana n. sp.—Suboval, moderately robust, rather strongly convex, black, polished and glabrous, the legs slightly piceous. *Head* finely, sparsely but distinctly punctate, the transverse impression feeble but distinct, the beak somewhat stout, evenly, moderately arcuate, as long as the prothorax in the male, about one-fourth longer in the female, densely, deeply punctured at the sides, the antennæ inserted at the middle in the female or just beyond in the male, nearly as in *ovata*, the club a little shorter than the entire funicle. *Prothorax* subconical, two-thirds wider than long, the sides rapidly convergent and very feebly arcuate from the base to the strong apical constriction, the apex tubulate and one-half as wide as the base, the latter transverse, bisinuate and somewhat trilobed, the median lobe stronger than the lateral, rounded; disk rather finely, deeply, somewhat closely punctured, the median impunctate line subobsolete. Scutellum small, quadrate, truncate behind and with a deep lunate impression in apical half. *Elytra*, just behind the basal margin, one-fifth wider than the prothorax, two and one-half times longer than the latter and distinctly longer than wide, the humeri rather prominent; sides thence distinctly convergent and broadly arcuate to the apex, which is rather suddenly and broadly subtruncate; disk coarsely, very deeply striate, the grooves conspicuously, remotely punctate, feebly crenulate toward base, the intervals flat, one-half wider than the grooves in the male, nearly twice as wide as the latter in the female, each with a single series of extremely minute feeble punctures. Prosternum broadly, extremely deeply and abruptly excavated anteriorly, the excavation polished and impunctate, short, rapidly narrowed behind and separating the coxæ by not quite two-thirds of their own width. Length 2.8–3.0 mm.; width 1.5–1.8 mm.

Massachusetts; New York; Missouri.

Easily distinguishable from *ovata* by its very coarse, strongly punctured and subcrenulate elytral striæ, with the intervals uniseriately punctate throughout, by its less widely separated anterior coxæ, less transverse, more rapidly conical and more coarsely, closely and evenly punctate pronotum, without a distinctly marked impunctate line, and by several other characters as stated in the table.

5 Stethobaris egregia n. sp.—Oblong-oval, convex, subglabrous, shining but deeply, densely sculptured, black, the elytra somewhat piceous. *Head* minutely, sparsely but distinctly punctate, the beak rather coarsely, densely so, with the punctures more or less longitudinally coalescent, strongly,

evenly arcuate, as long as the head and prothorax, the antennæ inserted behind the middle, the club very large, more robust than usual, as long as the
entire funicle excepting one-half of the basal joint, the latter as long as the
next three, second not longer than the third. *Prothorax* less transverse than
usual, one-half wider than long, the sides feebly convergent and slightly
arcuate to apical third, then rounded to the tubulate apex, which is one-half
as wide as the base, the latter transverse, arcuate at the sides, the median
lobe distinct; disk with a small, ill-defined elongate impunctate spot behind
the middle, the punctures coarse, deep, rounded, dense. Scutellum quadrate,
small, strongly impressed. *Elytra* somewhat abruptly nearly one-fourth wider
than the prothorax, more than twice as long as the latter and distinctly longer
than wide, the humeri moderately prominent, smaller and more basal than
usual; sides behind them only moderately convergent, the apex rather broadly
and abruptly rounded; disk with coarse deep very abrupt and non-crenulate
grooves, the intervals flat, subequal, but slightly wider than the grooves, each
with a single series of coarse deep confluent punctures. Length 2.8–3.1 mm.;
width 1.4–1.65 mm.

Arizona.

In one of the specimens before me the pronotal punctures are
very dense, almost in mutual contact, but in the other are separated
by one-half of their own diameters, displaying, as in many other
species, marked variation in the coarseness and density of sculpture.

ZAGLYPTUS.
LeConte—Proc. Am. Phil. Soc., XV, p. 236.

In this remarkably distinct genus, the body is minute and sparsely
covered with long stiff erect bristles, the beak moderate in length,
evenly, feebly arcuate, with the antennæ inserted just beyond the
middle, the prosternum broadly, rather feebly impressed along the
middle, separating the coxæ by much less than their own width,
and the tarsi very slender, the third joint elongate, subcylindrical
or feebly obconical and not in the least dilated. Zaglyptus was in-
advertently placed in the Cryptorhynchini by its author.

We have but two species, one of which I do not have before me
at present; they are distinguished by LeConte as follows:—

Elytra with coarsely punctured shallow striæ, the intervals rather wide.
                                                          1 **striatus**
Elytra deeply sulcate, the grooves punctured; interspaces narrow; color
    darker ....2 **sulcatus**

These species appear to be rare, or at least seldom taken; they
are probably of peculiar habits.

1 Zaglyptus striatus Lec.—Proc. Am. Phil. Soc., XV, p. 237.

Oval, convex, dark red-brown, polished, the upper surface with a few fulvous prostrate hairs in addition to the long stiff setæ, more especially noticeable on the prothorax and toward the base of the beak.   Beak quite distinctly longer than the head and prothorax, rather strongly, longitudinally sulcate, slightly punctate toward base; antennæ rather slender, the basal joint of the funicle robust, nearly as long as the next three, two to seven short, coarctate, sub-equal in length and gradually slightly thicker, club moderate.   Pro-thorax conical, one-half wider than long, the sides feebly inflated and distinctly arcuate at the middle; apex one-half as wide as the base; punctures distinct but not very dense.   Scutellum small. Elytra at base abruptly barely one-fourth wider than the prothorax, about twice as long, not longer than wide; sides broadly arcuate, becoming parallel near the base; disk with just visibly impressed series of rather coarse, deep, not very close-set punctures, the inter-vals nearly flat and fully twice as wide as the strial punctures· Length 1.4 mm.; width 0.8 mm.

Pennsylvania and District of Columbia.   The head is impunctate but minutely, densely granulato-reticulate; it is not separated from the beak by a transverse impression.   This is the most minute baride known within our faunal limits.

2 Zaglyptus sulcatus Lec.—Proc. Am. Phil. Soc., XV, p. 237.

Represented by the unique type almost similar in size to *striatus*. Alabama (Mobile).

OOMORPHIDIUS n. gen.

It is necessary to separate *Microcholus erasus* and *lævicollis* of LeConte as a very distinctly defined genus, forming a passage from Stethobaris to Eisonyx, and differing radically from Microcholus in its strongly convex body, tubulate prothorax, peculiarly modified elytral striation, impressed prosternum and stout, strongly decus-sate mandibles.   In many of its most striking characters it resem-bles Eisonyx, and in fact is so evidently allied to that genus as to prove the feeble value of ungual structure in the present section of Barini; this is shown also below in the case of Barinus and Bari-lepton, which are related in much the same way as Oomorphidius and Eisonyx.

Oomorphidius is distinguished by an oval, extremely convex and subglabrous body, rather long, moderately stout, arcuate beak, with broadly arcuate and somewhat advanced epistomal lobe, rather robust legs, with subarcuate femora, dilated third tarsal joint and very small, slender, free and divergent claws. The scutellum is minute. The two species differ subgenerically as follows :—

Subgenus I.

Apical constriction of the prothorax not extending across the dorsal surface ; prosternum narrowly and feebly sulcate, the sulcus squamose along its edges ; anterior coxæ apparently separated by less than one-third of their own width ; elytra without dispersed squamules ; scutellum nearly as wide as long ; size larger, the elytra nearly as in Eisonyx and wider than the prothorax..1 **erasus**

Subgenus II.

Apical constriction in the form of a deep abrupt groove, extending without change in character entirely across the dorsal surface ; prosternum very broadly, moderately strongly subsulcate, the sides of the impression not well defined and completely glabrous; coxæ separated by one-half of their own width ; elytra with a few widely dispersed squamules toward the sides and apex ; scutellum elongate, triangular ; size small, the prothorax much shorter and equal in width to the basal parts of the elytra.

2 lævicollis

I.

1 **Oomorphidius erasus** Lec.—Trans. Am. Ent. Soc., VIII, p. 217 (Microcholus).

Oval, very strongly convex, black, the legs slightly piceous, the antennæ rufescent ; integuments smooth, almost completely glabrous and very highly polished, the elytra slightly alutaceous. Head minutely, sparsely punctulate, the transverse impression broad and feeble ; beak rather long and somewhat stout, distinctly, evenly arcuate, sparsely, deeply punctate and fully as long as the head and prothorax ; antennæ inserted just behind the middle, the scape long, first funicular joint as long as the next three, the second one-half as long as the first and fully as long as the third and fourth combined ; club robust, moderate in size, abrupt, densely pubescent. Prothorax nearly one-half wider than long, the sides rather strongly convergent and nearly straight to apical third, then gradually rounded and convergent to the strongly tubulate apex ; base broadly, evenly arcuate throughout the width, the lobe obsolete ; disk sparsely, extremely minutely and feebly punctate throughout and glabrous. Scutellum very minute, triangular. Elytra nearly as in Eisonyx, broadest just before basal third, where the sides are broadly subangulate, one-fourth wider than the prothorax and a little more than twice as long, the sides strongly convergent behind and feebly arcuate, the apex narrowly subtruncate; disk with but feeble traces of fine impressed striæ, which are abruptly, deeply foveate just behind the basal margin, the intervals very minutely obsoletely sparsely and confusedly punctulate, entirely glabrous excepting a few long recumbent yellowish squamules at the base of the second to fourth intervals. Prosternum narrowly and feebly sulcate along the middle, the sides of the sulcus with recumbent yellowish squamules, the coxæ separated by less than one-third of their own width. Length 4.3 mm.; width 2.3 mm.

Kansas (Topeka). Cab. LeConte. Still represented by the unique type.

II.

2 **Oomorphidius lævicollis** Lec.—Proc. Am. Phil. Soc., XV, p. 304 (Microcholus).

Oval, very strongly convex, rapidly narrowed behind, dark rufo-piceous, the elytra blackish and the legs paler; body almost glabrous, rather alutaceous in lustre and minutely reticulate. Head almost impunctate, the impression very feeble; beak finely, sparsely punctate, moderately long and slender, strongly, evenly arcuate and fully as long as the head and prothorax, the antennæ inserted at apical two-fifths, slender, the scape rather long, the first funicular joint robust, clavate, not as long as the next three, the second more slender, two-thirds as long as the first and fully as long as the next two combined, club not large, robust. Prothorax very transverse, twice as wide as long, the sides broadly rounded and gradually more convergent from the base to the apical constriction, which is in the form of a narrow deep groove extending entirely across the dorsal surface, the apex strongly tubulate; base broadly, feebly arcuate; disk excessively minutely feebly and sparsely punctured. Scutellum very small, elongate, triangular. Elytra a little longer than wide, two and one-half times as long as the prothorax and equal in width to the latter, with the sides straight and parallel to basal fourth, then, to the narrowly rounded apex, strongly conical with the sides nearly straight; disk with very fine, nearly obsolete striæ, each terminating at some distance behind the basal margin in a moderately deep dilated fovea, the intervals not perceptibly punctulate, the surface glabrous, excepting three or four long slender white squamules widely dispersed laterally, and a few also at the base of the second and third intervals. Prosternum glabrous throughout, the coxæ more widely separated than in *erasus*. Length 2.2 mm.; width 1.1 mm.

Missouri (St. Louis). Cab. LeConte. This remarkable species is still represented as far as I know by the unique type.

EISONYX.
LeConte—Trans. Am. Ent. Soc., VIII, p. 216.

This is perhaps the most aberrant and specialized baride genus within our faunal limits. In general form it is totally unlike our other genera, but is satisfactorily connected in this respect by Oomorphidius. The original diagnosis of LeConte will serve for its recognition, but is greatly misleading in several important points. The middle and hind tibiæ are, for example, not in the least conical in outline, but are very thick and quite peculiar in structure, indicating perhaps a burrowing habit; they are strongly carinate externally near the base, then straight for a short distance, then feebly bent outward, becoming distinctly dilated and densely bristling with fulvous setæ. The elytral striæ are not by any means replaced by series of coarse punctures, as stated in the original description, the striæ being all but completely obsolete, but marked by series of exceedingly minute feeble and distant punctures, and terminating at base in larger deep foveæ as in Oomorphidius; the large deep circular perforate and widely distant punctures referred to by the author, are unevenly spaced along the middle of the intervals. Each of these large punctures bears a very small slender seta, but some of them, which are widely isolated and a little larger than the others, bear instead a single large white recumbent scale.

The beak is extremely thick, short, feebly arcuate and scarcely three-fourths as long as the prothorax, bristling with coarse erect setæ at the sides toward apex, and the antennæ are inserted slightly beyond the middle, the scrobes being very oblique. Scutellum minute, rather deeply seated, feebly tumid and nude.

1 Eisonyx crassipes Lec.—Trans. Am. Ent. Soc., VIII, p. 217.

Rhomboidal, widest between basal third and fourth of the elytra, black, rather dull, finely alutaceous and smooth throughout, convex, the vestiture extremely unevenly distributed, consisting of a cluster of elongate fulvous squamules among the deep coarse punctures occupying the lateral portions of the anterior thoracic constriction, also at the base before the scutellum and along the margin toward the sides, also with a few similar squamules near the base of the third and fifth elytral intervals; elsewhere on the upper surface, with the exception of the few widely scattered white scales of the elytra, the setæ are very minute. Head almost impunctate, the beak sparsely but deeply so, separated from the head by a transversely arcuate shallow but sharply defined groove. Prothorax finely, feebly and very sparsely punctate, as long as wide, convex, the sides feebly convergent from the base nearly to the apex and straight; base strongly, anteriorly oblique from the scutellum to each basal angle, the median lobe nearly obsolete. Elytra about one-half wider than the prothorax and nearly twice as long; sides about equally and strongly convergent anteriorly to the base of the prothorax, and posteriorly to the very narrow subtruncate and conjointly arcuate apex, the sutural notch completely obsolete. Length 4.8 mm.; width 2.5 mm.

Texas—Cab. LeConte. But two specimens are known, one of which is in the cabinet of Dr. Horn.

ZYGOBARIS.

LeConte—Proc. Am. Phil. Soc., XV, p. 317.

A single widely isolated subtropical species, with coarsely punctured elytral striæ and very long slender strongly arcuate beak, alone constitutes this genus as far as known. LeConte placed here, also, several other small and obscure forms; these, however, belong to widely diverse genera, and have been described under the preceding Oligolochus and Idiostethus, and Catapastus which follows.

Zygobaris may be distinguished easily by the structure of the tarsal claws, which are moderate in length and completely connate, without trace of suture, through at least one-third of their length. The mandibles are small, thick, arcuate, notched at apex and strongly decussate. Prosternum flat, separating the coxæ by about their own width, the subapical constriction feeble and only visible laterally, represented in the middle by a small, moderately deep, subtransverse fovea, limited at each side by a small longitudinal ridge. Other generic characters are mentioned below:—

1 Zygobaris nitens Lec.—Proc. Am. Phil. Soc., XV, p. 318.

Robust, rhomboidal, moderately convex, strongly shining, black, the legs slightly piceous; integuments subglabrous, the vestiture white, consisting of very minute and sparse setiform squamules, with large white scales remotely dispersed but more condensed at the base of the second elytral interval, more distinct but sparse beneath. Beak long and slender, evenly, strongly arcuate, slightly tumid at base with the constriction distinct, feebly compressed and densely punctured at the sides, especially behind the antennæ, two-fifths as long as the body in the male and two-thirds in the female, smoother and less punctate in the latter sex; antennæ inserted at basal two-fifths in the female or a little behind the middle in the male, the scape nearly attaining the eyes, the scrobes almost completely inferior, basal joint of the funicle not quite as long as the next four, the second one-half longer than the third; club moderate, elongate-oval, densely pubescent, with the basal joint composing about one-third of the mass. Prothorax conical, one-half to two-thirds wider than long, the sides feebly, evenly arcuate; constriction rather strong; disk very coarsely, deeply, moderately closely punctate, without trace of impunctate line. Scutellum small, oblong, glabrous. Elytra at base much wider than the prothorax, rather more than twice as long as the latter, parabolic in outline, the humeral callus not laterally prominent; disk with very fine striæ, which are widely and deeply impressed and coarsely, not closely punctate, the intervals convex, each with a single series of coarse deep remote punctures, about as large as those of the striæ but more than twice as distant. Length 2.6–3.7 mm.; width 1.4–2.0 mm.

Southern Florida. A distinct and easily recognizable species.

CATAPASTUS n. gen.

This genus contains some of the smallest centrinides thus far discovered, and is rather isolated. Its nearest relative is probably Zygobaris, but the divergence from even this form, which is itself a strongly specialized type, is very notable.

The beak is short, stout, broad, flattened toward apex, very densely but finely punctate throughout, squamose and without trace of basal constriction. The antennæ are inserted distinctly beyond the middle, which contrasts greatly with their position in Zygobaris, the scape nearly attaining the eye, the basal joint of the funicle long and the remaining ones small, the club relatively rather large.   The mandibles are small, stout, arcuate, notched at apex and broadly decussate.   Scutellum small, densely squamose.   Prosternum with a broad, moderately deep impression along the middle, which becomes gradually narrower, more profound and more abruptly defined toward apex.   Anterior coxæ rather approximate, separated by scarcely one-half of their own width.   Tarsal claws small, perfectly connate through about basal third.   The two species before me may be readily recognized as follows:—

Form narrowly rhomboid-oval ; prothorax but slightly wider than long ; scattered white scales of the elytra long and narrow ; legs black ; antennæ piceous, with the club abruptly pale rufo-testaceous........1 **conspersus**
Form rather broader, the prothorax much more transverse ; scattered white scales larger, broader and much more conspicuous ; legs and antennæ pale rufo-testaceous throughout...2 **diffusus**

1 **Catapastus conspersus** Lec.—Proc. Am. Phil. Soc., XV, p. 318 (Zygobaris).

Narrow, subrhomboidal, convex, black, the antennæ piceous-black with the club rufous ; vestiture dense, consisting of small narrow dark red-brown squamules, which are broader, denser and nearly white beneath, and with larger white scales remotely dispersed on the elytra and more or less dense toward the sides of the pronotum, the scutellum densely clothed with white scales.   Beak thick, feebly flattened toward apex, evenly, rather strongly arcuate, as long as the prothorax in the male and scarcely longer in the female, densely punctate and squamose, the basal constriction obsolete ; antennæ inserted distinctly beyond the middle in both sexes, basal joint of the funicle about as long as the next four, second but slightly longer than the third ; club rather large, oval, densely pubescent, with the basal joint constituting one-third of the mass and not longer than the second.   Prothorax fully one-third wider than long, conical, the sides arcuate at apical third, the constriction distinct ; apex three-fifths as wide as the base ; punctures somewhat coarse, very deep and dense, without impunctate line ; basal lobe very small.   Elytra distinctly wider than the prothorax and a little more than twice as long, narrowly parabolic in outline, the striæ rather coarse, abrupt, normal ; intervals flat, about one-half wider than the grooves, finely but strongly, confusedly and rather rugosely punctate.   Length 1.7–2.3 mm. ; width 0.8–1.1 mm.

Illinois, Michigan and Iowa ; numerous specimens.   One example is labeled '' Florida,'' but I think by mistake.

2 Catapastus diffusus n. sp.—Rhomboid-oval, rather stout, convex, black, the legs and antennæ throughout pale rufo-testaceous : vestiture as in *conspersus*, the scattered white scales of the elytra larger and broader. *Head* finely, very densely punctate, the impression obsolete ; beak and antennæ nearly similar to those of *conspersus*. *Prothorax* one-half wider than long, conical, the sides feebly, evenly arcuate ; subapical constriction distinct ; apex truncate, a little more than one-half as wide as the base, the latter transverse, the median lobe small but rather prominent ; disk coarsely, very densely punctate, with traces of a fine impunctate line. Scutellum small, rounded, very densely clothed with white scales. *Elytra* distinctly wider than, and obviously more than twice as long as, the prothorax, parabolic, the humeral callus rather prominent laterally ; disk not coarsely, deeply, abruptly striate, the intervals flat, twice as wide as the grooves, finely, closely, confusedly and subtransversely punctato-rugose. *Abdomen* nearly flat, closely punctured and moderately densely squamulose, the middle of the third and fourth segments glabrous except along the apex ; fifth segment rather longer than the two preceding. Length 2.2 mm. ; width 1.15 mm.

Florida (southern).

This species is closely allied to *conspersus*, and resembles it in structure and vestiture, but differs in its slightly more robust form, pale legs and antennæ, more transverse and more coarsely punctured prothorax, and in several other characters. It is described apparently from the female, but there is very little sexual disparity in this genus.

BARINUS.
Casey—Bull. Cal. Acad. Sci., II, 1886, p. 255.

In this genus the beak is as short, thick and arcuate as in Baris, although beyond this mere suggestion, there is nothing at all in common. As in Barilepton, to which Barinus is closely allied, the head is larger in proportion to the size of the prothorax than in any of the other genera, and the tarsi have the second and third joints dilated, very broadly so in *bivittatus*, but Barinus can always be readily distinguished by the tarsal claws, which are two in number and completely connate through at least one-half of their length.

The antennæ are inserted just beyond the middle of the beak, very near the median line of the flank, the scrobes rapidly oblique, the scape nearly attaining the eye, the club moderate and the basal joint of the funicle unusually long, although varying somewhat in length in the different species. The mandibles are small, stout, feebly arcuate externally, decussate and with a large internal notch.

Prosternum more or less deeply and narrowly impressed or sulcate, the coxæ large, prominent and narrowly separated. The metepisternum varies in width according to the species, and the abdomen is convex, becoming strongly ascending toward apex, where it is generally retracted slightly above the plane of the sutural angles of the elytra. The scutellum is small, glabrous or nearly so and the body is always unevenly and more or less densely squamose.

The species are moderately numerous; those known to me may be identified as follows:—

Body glabrous above, with two wide, abruptly limited vittæ of large pale densely placed scales, the outline evenly elongate-oval....1 **bivittatus**
Body elongate-oval, unevenly squamose above, the scales forming shorter or longer lines on the elytral intervals or, when the latter are densely squamose throughout, with the intervals two, four and six in greater or less part paler, especially toward base.
  Elytra not densely squamose throughout.
    Elytral punctures fine, the sixth interval with a broad dense line of scales, abruptly terminating at basal fourth; white scales of the second interval not extending beyond apical fifth......................2 **cribricollis**
    Elytral punctures coarse and dense, the sixth interval with the line of large white scales extending fully to the middle and thence nearly to apex, but with narrower, sparser and darker scales; second interval broadly clothed with large white scales from base to apex.
                                                 3 **squamolineatus**
  Elytra densely squamose throughout, the scales ochreous-brown in color, but white on the alternate intervals through portions of their extent and more especially toward base.
    Prothorax with the scales of the under surface large and dense throughout toward the sides; pronotal punctures rather finer and moderately close.
                                               4 **suffusus**
    Prothorax with a large quasi-denuded area involving the lateral portions of the under surface toward base, on which the scales become very fine and sparse; pronotal punctures coarse and denser.........5 **difficilis**
Body unevenly squamose above, the scales of the elytra not at all lineate in arrangement, but more or less denuded, especially on the flanks and often also at the posterior callus.
  Body more broadly oval.
    Vestiture dense, the anterior coxæ separated by about one-fourth of their own width ....6 **lutescens**
    Vestiture sparse, the scales narrower; anterior coxæ separated by nearly one-half of their own width...............................7 **curticollis**
  Body narrow and linear, almost as in the second division of Barilepton.
    Vestiture of the pronotum broadly and abruptly dense toward the sides, the median glabrous area occupying but slightly more than one-third of the total width..8 **albescens**

Vestiture of the pronotum sparse and evenly distributed throughout, although slightly sparser in a feebly defined, oblique line at each side, extending from the middle at lateral fourth to the scutellar lobe, not at all condensed toward the sides.....................................9 **linearis**

1 **Barinus bivittatus** Lec.—Proc. Am. Phil. Soc., XVII, p. 431 (Barilepton).

Elongate-oval, convex, polished, black with a faint violaceo-metallic lustre, the legs dark rufo-piceous; vestiture of the dorsal surface very minute except a broad vitta on each side, extending from the apical margin of the pronotum to the elytral apex, of large, broad, densely placed, yellowish-white scales, the meso- and meta-sternal episterna and margins of the abdomen similarly clothed with denser scales. Head excavated beneath; front with a large feebly impressed fovea but without transverse constriction, the beak stout, cylindrical, scarcely compressed, evenly, moderately arcuate, three-fourths as long as the prothorax, polished, coarsely punctured toward base, the antennæ inserted just beyond the middle, a little nearer the upper than the lower margin, the basal joint of the funicle very slender and as long as the entire remainder, the club small, elongate-oval, as long as the four preceding joints combined. Prothorax not quite as long as wide, feebly inflated at apical third, the sides thence straight to the base; subapical constriction strongly marked, the apex two-thirds as wide as the base, the latter transverse, the basal lobe obsolete; disk rather coarsely but not very densely punctate, the impunctate line narrow, irregular and entire. Scutellum small, a little wider than long and rather deeply seated. Elytra equal in width to the prothorax and twice as long, the sides evenly, gradu-ally convergent from base to apex and very feebly arcuate, the apex narrowly but obtusely rounded; humeri not prominent; striæ fine but deep and abrupt, the intervals wide, minutely, rather sparsely and confusedly punctate, the fourth very narrow toward base. Pro-sternum narrowly, moderately deeply sulcate along the middle, separating the coxæ by only one-third of their own width. Tarsi very broad, the posterior as long as the tibiæ, with the first joint small but wider than long, the second and third equal in width and both very strongly dilated, squamose above, densely pilose beneath, the third with a narrow median emargination extending to basal third; fourth joint very slender, extending only slightly beyond the lobes of the third, the claws small, parallel and completely connate through fully one-half of their length. Length 5.3 mm.; width 1.8–2 0 mm.

Georgia (St. Catharine Island). This is the most conspicuous and one of the most interesting barides within our faunal limits, remarkable not only in ornamentation, but in its extremely dilated tarsi and very elongate basal joint of the antennal funicle.

2 **Barinus cribricollis** Lec.—Proc. Am. Phil. Soc., XV, p. 422 (Barilepton).

Elongate-oval, convex, polished, black, the legs slightly piceous; vestiture very uneven, consisting of large white densely placed scales in a sublateral pronotal vitta, on the second elytral interval except near the apex, where they are gradually replaced by small narrow dark brownish squamules, on the third for a short distance behind the middle, on the fourth near the base and from basal to apical fourth, and on the sixth in the broadest and most conspicuous line of all, abruptly confined to basal fourth of the length; on the under surface the white scales are dense and conspicuous in a small spot near the anterior coxæ, on the inner half of the mes-episterna, throughout the met-episterna, and toward the sides of the abdomen, much more densely on the third and fourth segments and becoming fine, browner and sparser toward the apical angles of the second segment, which is more reflexed posteriorly at the sides than the third or fourth. Beak extremely short, thick, arcuate, not more than two-thirds as long as the prothorax, strongly punctured toward base at the sides, the basal joint of the antennal funicle as long as the entire remainder and slightly longer than the club. Prothorax very nearly as long as wide; sides parallel and straight in basal two-thirds, then gradually rounded, feebly convergent and rather strongly constricted to the apex, the latter three-fourths as wide as the base; disk coarsely punctate, the punctures circular, deep, perforate and quite distinctly separated; impunctate line evident in basal two-thirds. Elytra distinctly wider than the prothorax and fully twice as long, narrowly, obtusely rounded at apex; striæ moderately coarse; intervals flat and unequal, about twice as wide as the grooves, finely, not densely and more or less confusedly punctate. Prosternum deeply, longitudinally impressed, the coxæ very prominent, almost conical, separated by less than one-third of their own width. Length 3.6 mm.; width 1.35 mm.

Florida (Enterprise). Cab. LeConte. Represented by the unique type, which is in a perfect state of preservation. All of the punctures of the upper surface, except where densely covered with scales as described above, bear each a very small inconspicuous seta.

3 **Barinus squamolineatus** Cas.—Bull. Cal. Acad. Sci., II, p. 256.

Elongate-oval, convex, black, the legs red; elytra coarsely, very densely sculptured; upper surface in great part covered with large white closely placed scales, which are replaced toward the sides of the elytra by smaller browner squamules, becoming fine inconspicuous setæ toward the humeri, also very inconspicuous on the first interval except toward the scutellum, and in middle half of the pronotum, except along the median line; pronotum in entire lateral fourth and second elytral interval throughout clothed very densely with large scales. Length 3.1–3.7 mm.; width 1.2–1.3 mm.

Illinois; several specimens. This species is allied to *cribricollis*, but differs in its slightly longer, less robust and arcuate beak in the smaller punctures and much broader, denser lateral vitta of the pronotum, in the very much coarser, deeper and denser punctures, and more conspicuous vestiture of the elytra, paler legs and in many other characters.

In my original description, the sculpture of the elytral intervals is stated to be finely and feebly punctate; this mistake arose from the fact that in the single type specimen, the dense scales in great part covered and concealed the punctures; in some denuded examples before me, however, they are readily seen to be coarse and deep, and, in comparison with those of *cribricollis*, very large indeed. The types of both *cribricollis* and *squamolineatus* are males.

4 **Barinus suffusus** n. sp.—Elongate-oval, convex, black, with the legs red, moderately shining but extremely densely covered throughout with large brownish scales, becoming broadly white toward base of the sixth interval, also feebly whiter on the second and fourth near the base and behind the middle, also broadly white in lateral fourth of the pronotum and toward the sides of the body beneath; median half of the pronotum sparsely clothed with slender but distinct squamules, becoming broad dense scales on the median line toward base, the scutellum abruptly black and glabrous, small, triangular, widest behind and lying in a broad shallow depression between the elytra. *Head* and beak glabrous but with an abruptly dense line of large scales bordering the eye anteriorly, the former finely but strongly, not very sparsely punctate, the transverse constriction feeble but evident; beak thick, compressed, strongly arcuate and distinctly punctate toward base, straighter and feebly flattened toward apex, about four-fifths as long as the prothorax in the female;

antennæ inserted a little beyond the middle, the basal joint of the funicle not quite as long as the next six, club as long as the preceding five joints, rather elongate, oval, densely pubescent, with the basal joint constituting less than one-half of the mass. *Prothorax* perceptibly shorter than wide, the sides straight and parallel in basal two-thirds, then broadly rounded, feebly convergent and broadly constricted to the apex, which is three-fourths as wide as the base, the latter transverse, the median lobe very small, feeble ; disk rather finely and somewhat closely punctate, the punctures very distinctly separated ; impunctate line feebly defined ; apical margin polished and impunctate for a short distance throughout the width. *Elytra* distinctly wider than the prothorax and a little more than twice as long, elongate, hemi-elliptical in outline, the apex with a feeble sutural notch, the humeral callus long but not prominent ; disk moderately striate, the intervals flat, confusedly, coarsely punctate when denuded. Prosternum deeply impressed along the middle, rather narrowly separating the coxæ as usual. Fifth ventral segment with a small impressed and denuded median area, the last three segments rapidly ascending in the female type, convex, and, at the extreme apex, retracted above the plane of the elytral apices. Length 3.6 mm. ; width 1.4 mm.

Texas.

A single specimen, which appears to be a female, the abdomen being entirely devoid of median impression toward base. The species is allied to *squamolineatus*, but is easily distinguishable by the dense crust of scales, and the much finer denser punctures and conspicuous squamules of the pronotum.

5 **Barinus difficilis** n. sp.—Elongate-oval, convex, black, shining, the legs rufous ; vestiture dense, consisting of large close-set scales, pale brown in color but gradually white in basal half on the second and sixth intervals, and also on the fourth very near the base, also broadly white and dense at the sides of the pronotum and on the under surface toward the sides, but with a large subdenuded spot on the prothorax just before the mesosternal side-pieces, which is sparsely clothed with long slender squamules ; median parts of the pronotum rather sparsely clothed with very long, wider and narrower, brown scales, which are conspicuous. *Head* finely, sparsely punctate, glabrous, the eyes margined anteriorly with an abrupt line of coarse scales ; impression feeble but distinct ; beak glabrous, thick, strongly arcuate and densely punctate toward base, much shorter than the prothorax, the basal joint of the antennal funicle distinctly shorter than the remainder ; club moderate. *Prothorax* not quite as long as wide, the sides parallel and nearly straight to apical third, then broadly rounded and moderately convergent to the apex, the constriction almost completely obsolete ; disk coarsely, deeply and closely punctate, the punctures not in actual contact ; median impunctate area fusiform. Scutellum moderate, quadrate, tumid, not deep-set, glabrous but squamulose at the sides. *Elytra* slightly wider than the prothorax and a little more than twice as long, elongate hemi-elliptical, the sides becoming parallel toward base and very feebly constricted at apical fourth ; humeri

not prominent; disk rather finely striate, the intervals wide, flat, not coarsely but very densely, deeply, confusedly punctate. *Abdomen* clothed throughout with large dense scales, which are sparse in the subbasal indentation and toward the middle of the last three segments. Prosternum normal, rather narrowly separating the coxæ. Length 3.25 mm,; width 1.25 mm.

California (southern).

This species is rather closely allied to *suffusus*, but differs in its much more sparsely punctate head, in its coarser, denser punctures, narrower lateral vittæ, more uneven and more conspicuous vestiture of the median parts of the pronotum, and in the denuded area beneath, the latter being entirely wanting and clothed with large dense normal scales in *suffusus*. It also differs in having the metepisterna decidedly narrower, and the elytra covered with a dense crust of scales which entirely conceal even the striæ, the latter being indicated by wide partings of the scales in *suffusus*.

6 **Barinus lutescens** Lec.—Trans. Am. Ent. Soc., VIII, p. 218 (Barilepton).

Rather robust, oval, the upper surface only moderately convex, black, the legs piceous-black; integuments shining, densely clothed with large ochreous scales, which are rather elongate, evenly distributed on the elytra, where they become gradually semi-erect behind and denuded at the sides in more than basal half, also broadly dense at the sides of the pronotum, the median glabrous area oval in outline; under surface polished and with very minute remote setiform squamules, which are abruptly dense and broader on the met-episterna and at the sides of the abdomen behind. Beak thick, strongly arcuate and punctured at base, three-fourths as long as the prothorax, the transverse impression very broad; surface glabrous but with a few very small, scarcely visible squamules near the anterior margin of the eye; basal joint of the antennal funicle as long as the next five; club rather small, but slightly longer than the preceding four joints combined. Prothorax fully one-third wider than long, the sides parallel and nearly straight in basal two-thirds, then broadly rounded, convergent and scarcely at all constricted to the apex, the latter scarcely more than one-half as wide as the base; disk rather coarsely and sparsely punctate, the punctures becoming smaller and much denser anteriorly. Scutellum very small, tumid, quadrate, glabrous and polished. Elytra scarcely perceptibly wider than the prothorax and a little more than twice as long, parallel, parabolically rounded in apical two-fifths, the subapical sinuation very feeble and the sutural notch broad; disk rather finely striate, the intervals rather finely, moderately densely punctured. Prosternum rather deeply but very narrowly sulcate, the coxæ large, prominent, separated by scarcely more than one-fourth of their own width. Length 3.2 mm.; width 1.3 mm.

Texas (Columbus). Cab. LeConte. The unique type is the only specimen which I have seen; it is a female. This species is allied to *albescens*, in spite of the great dissimilarity in form of the body; the arrangement of the vestiture beneath is almost identical, but *lutescens* does not possess the denuded subapical spot of the elytra, is much more coarsely punctate, and differs in so many characters that there cannot, I think, be the least doubt of its distinctness.

7 Barinus curticollis n. sp.—Rather narrowly oblong-oval, somewhat convex, polished, black, the legs dark rufo-piceous; vestiture yellowish, consisting, on the pronotum, of dense elongate-oval scales in lateral third, on the elytra of nearly similar scales almost uniformly but not very densely distributed throughout, becoming finer and still sparser on the flanks, very sparse throughout beneath, except on the met-episterna, where they are much denser, also denser at the sides of the last three ventral segments. *Head* dull, finely, sparsely punctate, the impression distinct; beak short, thick, very strongly arcuate, not as long as the prothorax, coarsely but sparsely punctate, somewhat squamulose above the eyes; antennæ slender, the basal joint of the funicle not quite as long as the remainder, club moderate. *Prothorax* short, two-fifths wider than long, the sides parallel and straight to apical third, then gradually rounded convergent and nearly straight to the apex, which is three-fifths as wide as the base, the latter transverse, the median lobe broad and feeble; disk coarsely, rather sparsely punctate, the punctures round, deep, perforate and isolated, with a narrow and irregular impunctate line. Scutellum small, oval, tumid and glabrous. *Elytra* slightly wider than the prothorax and nearly two and one-half times as long, elongate hemi-elliptical, obtusely rounded at apex, the humeri not laterally prominent; disk deeply striate, the intervals flat, from two to three times as wide as the grooves, coarsely, confusedly but not very densely punctate. *Abdomen* finely, remotely punctate, the basal segment coarsely and much more closely so. Anterior coxæ separated by about one-half of their own width. Length 2.7–3.0 mm.; width 1.0–1.2 mm.

Missouri; Louisiana.

The description is drawn from the male, the abdomen having a small deep elongate-oval impression near the base. This species is allied to *lutescens*, but differs in its shorter prothorax, narrower form, more slender, much sparser scales of the elytra and more widely separated anterior coxæ.

8 **Barinus albescens** Lec.—Trans. Am. Ent. Soc., VIII, p. 218 (Barilepton).

Elongate, subparallel, somewhat wider toward posterior third of the elytra, black, the legs red, convex, polished with a very faint violaceo-metallic lustre; vestiture pale ochreous-white of different shades, very dense but uneven in distribution, consisting of large elongate scales, abruptly dense in lateral third of the pronotum and on the elytra throughout, except along the flanks and in a discal spot near the apex, these denuded areas and the median parts of the pronotum having the squamules exceedingly minute, sparse, and setiform; squamules of the sutural interval also finer and darker toward apex, and the entire vestiture in apical fourth erect and bristling, especially at the intersection of the third and ninth intervals, behind the feeble subapical callus; vestiture of the under surface very minute and sparse, but denser on the met-episterna and at the sides of the abdomen behind. Beak three-fourths as long as the prothorax, very thick and arcuate, punctured toward base, the constriction strong, the eye bordered anteriorly by a line of three or four subrecumbent scales; antennæ with the basal joint of the funicle as long as the next five, the club rather large, pale, nearly as long as the preceding six joints. Prothorax a little wider at apical third than at base, then very strongly convergent and deeply constricted to the apex, which is three-fourths as wide as the base; sides nearly straight; punctures fine and sparse. Scutellum very small, subglabrous. Elytra at base scarcely noticeably wider than the prothorax, the sides straight and extremely feebly divergent thence to apical third, then broadly rounded, constricted at apical fifth, the apex obtuse; humeri very feebly swollen; striæ fine; intervals almost impunctate in the denuded lateral area. Femora bristling beneath with long setæ. Prosternum longitudinally, narrowly sulcate, the coxæ narrowly separated. Length 2.7 mm.; width 0.9 mm.

Texas (Columbus). Cab. LeConte. Represented, as far as I know, by the unique type, taken by Mr. Schwarz. This species bears no resemblance, in any way, to *linearis*, with which it is accidentally united in the Henshaw Check-list, except in its generally narrow subparallel form.

9 **Barinus linearis** Lec.—Proc. Am. Phil. Soc., XV, p. 422 (Barilepton).

Elongate, parallel, convex, black throughout, smooth but alutaceous in lustre, the vestiture white, consisting of moderately large, broad, triangular scales, almost evenly and quite sparsely distributed throughout but more denuded and sparse along the sides of the elytra, more broadly so toward base, and also in a small discal spot near the apex; on the under surface the scales are dense on the met-episterna and toward the sides of the abdomen behind, elsewhere sparse but only absent on that part of the mesosternum bounding the middle coxal cavities externally. Head impunctate, but with a few extremely minute feeble punctures anteriorly; beak glabrous, punctate, very thick toward base, with some large scales bordering the eyes, much shorter than the prothorax; basal joint of the antennal funicle scarcely as long as the next four together; club moderate. Prothorax not quite as long as wide, the sides straight and parallel or very feebly divergent to apical two-fifths, then rounded and convergent, the constriction very broad and feeble; apex not more than three-fifths as wide as the base; disk finely, rather unevenly but not very closely punctate, the scales almost uniformly distributed and sparse throughout; impunctate line distinct, entire. Elytra just visibly wider than the prothorax and a little more than twice as long, parallel, narrowed in apical third, then obtusely rounded; striæ fine; intervals flat, rather finely, unequally, confusedly and not very closely punctate. Prosternum impressed, the coxæ large, prominent, rather narrowly separated. Length 3.7 mm.; width 1.25 mm.

Florida (Sumter Co.). Cab. LeConte. Represented by the unique type, in which the last ventral segment has a rounded glabrous polished and extremely deep median excavation.

BARILEPTON.
LeConte—Proc. Am. Phil. Soc., XV, p. 318.

The species of Barilepton are probably the most slender of the Barini. The beak is short, thick, arcuate, strongly compressed, with the flanks crossed obliquely by the antennal scrobes, the latter beginning near the upper margin and slightly beyond the middle. The under surface of the head is frequently excavated transversely as in Barinus, and the basal joint of the funicle is elongate. The prosternum is broadly impressed and very narrowly separates the coxæ. One of the most remarkable characters of the genus is the structure of the tarsi, in which however it strongly resembles Barinus; the four posterior tarsi are almost invariably longer than the tibiæ, and have the second and third joints dilated, the first being much smaller. There is but one tarsal claw, which is simple and moderately stout.

The close relationship existing between Barilepton and Barinus affords another illustration, parallel to that of Eisonyx and Oomorphidius previously mentioned, of the slight value to be attached, among some of the centrinide genera, to radical differences in the tarsal ungues, in comparison to the significance attending these modifications in the baride series.

Our four species of Barilepton may be thus defined:—

Elytra at base not wider than the base of the prothorax.
    Beak almost evenly arcuate...1 **filiforme**
    Beak strongly bent near the base; body much smaller and still more slen-
        der; pronotal vestiture decidedly sparser...................2 **famelicum**
Elytra at base wider than the contiguous base of the prothorax; form a little
    stouter, the prothorax much less elongate.
    Prothorax constricted behind the apex; antennal club robust; basal joint
        of the hind tarsi longer, the second not quite as wide as the third and
        rather longer than wide, the third a little wider than long.
                                          3 **quadricolle**
    Prothorax without trace of subapical constriction; antennal club much
        less robust; basal joint of the hind tarsi shorter and thicker, the second
        equal to the third and not longer than wide, the third scarcely as wide
        as long...4 **falciger**

1 Barilepton filiforme Lec.—Proc. Am. Phil. Soc., XV, p. 319.

Cylindrical, convex, shining but very densely clothed with large broad pale scales, sparser on the pronotum except at the sides, pale fulvous on the elytra but white along the flanks and in a feebly defined streak attaining the base at each side of the scutellum. Head and basal parts of the beak punctured and squamose, the impression obsolete but with a small inconspicuous median fovea; beak distinctly shorter than the prothorax, stout, arcuate, compressed toward base, smooth and almost impunctate, the antennæ inserted near the middle, the basal joint of the funicle as long as the next five together, the second slightly longer than the third; club moderately stout, as long as the first funicular joint, the basal joint apparently large. Prothorax about as long as wide, sometimes feebly dilated at apical third, generally parallel, broadly rounded toward apex, the constriction obsolete; apex fully three-fourths as wide as the base; punctures deep, moderately coarse and not quite in mutual contact. Elytra about as wide as the prothorax and barely two and one-half times as long, the fine striæ indicated by narrow partings of the very dense crust of scales. Prosternum feebly impressed, separating the coxæ by one-fifth or sixth of their own width. Second tarsal joint almost as wide as the third and nearly as long as wide. Length 2.5–2.9 mm.; width 0.7–0.85 mm.

Michigan and Illinois; also said by LeConte to occur in Virginia. Five specimens.

2 Barilepton famelicum n. sp.—Very slender, cylindrical, convex, black, shining, the scales moderately large and broad, sparse and slender on the median parts of the pronotum, dense throughout on the elytra, very sparse, minute and narrowly lineate throughout on the abdomen except the sides of the last three segments, which are densely squamose. *Head* finely, sparsely punctate and squamulose; beak punctured and sparsely squamose toward base, elsewhere smooth and polished, compressed, thick, scarcely more than three-fourths as long as the prothorax, very strongly arcuate near the base, nearly straight in apical two-thirds, the antennæ inserted at or slightly behind the middle, the basal joint of the funicle longer than the next four, the club robust, a little shorter than the preceding six joints together. *Prothorax* fully as long as wide, often apparently a little longer, the sides parallel, nearly straight, feebly convergent and slightly rounded near the apex, the latter fully four-fifths as wide as the base, which is transverse, the median lobe almost obsolete; subapical constriction completely wanting; disk finely, rather sparsely and unevenly punctate. Scutellum very small, quadrate, glabrous, with one or two setæ at each side. *Elytra* equal in width to the prothorax and about two and one-half times as long, parallel; sides convergent in apical third, the apex obtusely rounded; humeri not prominent; disk with very fine striæ, the intervals wide, flat, densely, confusedly squamose. *Abdomen* sparsely punctate. Prosternum transversely constricted behind the apex, broadly, distinctly impressed along the middle, separating the coxæ very narrowly. Middle and posterior tarsi longer than the tibiæ, the second joint not quite as wide as the third but much wider than the first. Length 2.1–2.65 mm.; width 0.4–0.7 mm.

Colorado (Greeley). Mr. H. F. Wickham.

This very small species is closely allied to *filiforme*, but may be distinguished by its smaller size, more slender form, sparser and more slender scales especially on the pronotum and along the median parts of each elytron, and also by the form of the beak which is more abruptly and strongly arcuate near the base. Seven specimens.

3 Barilepton quadricolle Lec.—Proc. Am. Phil. Soc., XV, p. 423.

Cylindrical, convex, black, the legs rufescent; integuments shining but densely clothed with pale scales, narrow on the pronotum, broad and denser on the elytra, moderately dense on the abdomen. Head sparsely, finely punctate, the impression obsolete; beak thick, about as long as the prothorax, compressed, smooth, polished, punctured and squamose near the base, strongly, abruptly arcuate at base but nearly straight and gradually feebly flattened thence to the apex; antennæ inserted near the middle, the basal joint of the funicle as long as the next four. Prothorax slightly wider than long, swollen at the sides anteriorly and wider at apical third than at base, the sides convergent and feebly constricted thence to the apex, the latter barely two-thirds as wide as the base; disk rather closely, strongly, unevenly punctured, with a narrow impunctate median line. Scutellum very small, quadrate, glabrous. Elytra quite distinctly wider than the base of the prothorax, feebly subinflated behind the middle, distinctly more than twice as long as wide, the humeral callus slightly prominent; striæ fine, deep and abrupt; intervals flat. Prosternum broadly, deeply impressed along the middle, the margins of the impression not abruptly defined; transverse constriction moderately distinct; anterior coxæ separated by one-fifth of their own width, the intermediate by slightly less than their width. Length 3.1–3.3 mm.; width 1.0–1.1 mm.

Nebraska. Distinct from *filiforme* in its larger size, more robust outline, elytra wider than the prothorax, longer beak and many other characters.

4 **Barilepton falciger** n. sp.—Cylindrical, convex, black throughout, shining and with a feeble violaceo-metallic lustre, densely clothed on the elytra with rather large, pale scales, which are sparse and narrower on the pronotum, also dense toward the sides of the sterna and last three ventral segments. *Head* rather finely, closely punctate, almost impunctate and broadly excavated beneath; basal constriction obsolete, the outline straight in profile; beak short, robust, sickle-shaped, very strongly bent at basal third and strongly compressed, slightly flattened toward apex, smooth, polished, punctured toward base, not quite as long as the prothorax, the antennæ inserted just beyond the middle and near the upper margin, the scrobes rapidly oblique along the flattened flanks, the basal joint of the funicle longer than the next four, obconical, the second much narrower, cylindrical, not quite as long as the next two, outer joints more robust; club moderate, nearly as long as the preceding six joints. *Prothorax* but slightly wider than long, the sides feebly divergent and nearly straight to apical third, then rounded and convergent to the apex, the constriction obsolete; apex three-fourths as wide as the base; disk not very coarsely, somewhat unevenly punctate, the punctures well separated; narrow impunctate line distinct. Scutellum very small, nearly glabrous. *Elytra* not at all wider than the disk of the prothorax, but, at base, just visibly wider than the base of the latter, distinctly more than twice as long as wide, parallel, parabolic in apical third; humeri not prominent; disk with a more prominent humeral condensation

of scales, finely striate. *Abdomen* strongly but sparsely punctate. Prosternum with a broad median impression, the coxæ narrowly separated. Length 2.75 mm.; width 0.8 mm.

California (San Bernardino).

The four hind tarsi are much longer than the tibiæ, the basal joint of the posterior obconical and distinctly shorter and narrower than the second, the latter large, as wide as long and fully as wide as the third, which is not transverse but narrowly deeply emarginate, the fourth joint is rather short and very slender. The type is a male, having a long narrow impression near the base of the abdomen.

EUNYSSOBIA n. n.

Euchætes || LeConte—Proc. Am. Phil. Soc., XV, p. 319.

This genus was proposed by LeConte, unfortunately under a name which had been employed several times before in zoology, for one of the most remarkable curculionides thus far discovered. Its aberrant nature was in fact only partially known to its author, who makes no reference whatever to the mandibles. The general habitus of the body, abdominal structure and conformation of the mes-epimera, show that it is a normal member of the Barini, but its rostral and mandibular characters indicate that it should be widely isolated, forming with Plocamus a group or subtribe.

The beak is extremely slender, cylindrical and strongly arcuate, but becomes abruptly inflated and thickened behind the antennæ, the under surface of the dilated portion having a narrow deep groove along the middle, which is gradually narrowed posteriorly and confluent at base with a deep transverse constriction, extending upward at the sides just in front of the eyes, becoming gradually attenuated and extinct and not attaining the upper surface. This longitudinal groove is but a remnant of the usual channel formed by the confluent scrobes, and is far too narrow to receive the antennal scape, the latter being free. The antennæ are completely inferior in insertion and are situated between basal third and fourth in both sexes, the scape rather thick, short and extending to the under surface of the head between the eyes, the latter being normal and widely separated beneath.

The mandibles are very short and thick, compressed, bent upward and move in a nearly vertical plane as in Balaninus, the condyles being contiguous above and received in broad deep fissures at the sides of the buccal opening beneath; the upturned apex is very coarsely and deeply notched. It can be readily seen that in this position, the condyles have the largest and most powerful muscular attachment permissible under the circumstances. The habits of this species, as well as Balaninus, necessitate a slender cylindrical boring tool, not at all enlarged at apex, and, if the condyles were horizontal in their plane of motion, they would, because of their slight lateral development, be very feeble in muscular action; they have therefore been gradually turned into a position as nearly vertical as possible, simply to allow of a broader base for the attachment of the muscles. Mandibles of this kind are of course incapable of grasping or pinching to any useful degree, and can be used only in cutting and scraping a passage for the advancing beak, and it does not follow at all that because the mandibles are similar in their action to those of Balaninus, that there is any special relationship between these genera. In point of fact the remaining structural characters of the body, including the form of the mandibles themselves, are so widely different in Balaninus and Eunyssobia, that there cannot be the least affinity between them, except in the method of using the beak as a boring instrument.

The buccal fissure is very narrow and deep, being, at the anterior extremity, not more than one-fourth as wide as the rostrum, and the mentum is long and extremely slender; the remaining organs of the mouth appear to be atrophied or very feebly developed. The prosternum is broad, strongly, transversely constricted behind the apex but not otherwise modified, and separates the rather small coxæ by nearly twice their own width. The legs are normal, the tarsi very slender, with the two basal joints elongate, feebly ob-conical and subequal, the third small, scarcely wider than the apex of the second, deeply emarginate, the fourth with its basal node, about as long as the first two together; claws rather slender, arcuate, simple and divergent. Pygidium completely concealed.

1 **Eunyssobia echidna** Lec.—Proc. Am. Phil. Soc., XV, p. 320 (*Euchætes*).

Oval, convex, very uneven, black, the antennæ brown; slender portion of the beak rufous; body extremely densely clothed throughout with a crust of large, closely adherent, scale-like plates, variegated white, brown and blackish in color and sparsely clothed with very long, stiff and erect spiniform bristles. Beak three-fourths as long as the body in the female, sensibly shorter but otherwise entirely similar in the male, very slender, cylindrical, glabrous, shining, sparsely punctured in even series, evenly and strongly arcuate from the antennæ to the apex, but abruptly, strongly inflated, thickened but straight in lateral profile, spinose and very densely covered with a rough crust of scales from that point to the base; antennæ slender, the scape short, the basal joint of the funicle subequal to the next two; club moderate, oval, densely pubescent and without distinct sutures. Prothorax much wider than long, very strongly constricted and tubulate at apex, the base twice as wide as the apex, transverse but deeply sinuate at each side of the lobe, which is abrupt, prominent and rounded, its surface with a dorsal impression receiving the scutellum; disk uneven, a large shallow impression on each side of the median line, behind the middle, especially obvious. Scutellum moderate, slightly tumid, oval, ogival behind, anteriorly prominent in the middle of the sinuation which receives the thoracic lobe and slipping partially over the surface of the latter. Elytra barely as long as wide, distinctly wider and two-thirds longer than the prothorax, the sides rapidly convergent and broadly evenly arcuate from base to apex, the latter very narrowly rounded, ogival, with a small sutural notch; striæ indicated only by very fine partings of the crust. Under surface and legs densely clothed with a squamose crust of cinereous scales and with short sparse erect and stiff setæ. Length 2.6–3.2 mm.; width 1.3–1.6 mm.

Ohio, Kentucky and Iowa, apparently not rare and said to depredate upon the hickory; its habits are probably quite similar to those of Balaninus. It should be remarked that in some species of Centrinus, such as *hospes*, the beak is strongly inflated behind the antennæ, especially in the female and probably from causes similar to those which have produced the inflation here; but in Eunyssobia it does not appear to be at all sexual in character, and, in the species of Centrinus, the antennæ are not inferior in insertion, although in *hospes* they are inserted very near the lower margin, the scrobes being broad and entirely inferior.

PLOCAMUS.

LeConte—Proc. Am. Phil. Soc., XV, p. 320.

The single small species forming the type of this genus is unmistakably allied to *Eunyssobia echidna*, but differs in several peculiarities of indubitable generic import. The principal of these are the shorter beak, which is gradually stout and conical near the base and not abruptly inflated, the channel beneath being broad, shallow, and serving as a partial shelter for the antennal scape, the absence of any trace of the transverse basal constriction, and the shorter second joint of the antennal funicle. The mandibles are entirely similar, but the trophi, and especially the maxillary palpi, seem to be larger and better developed, and the tarsi are shorter, particularly the second joint, which is but slightly longer and scarcely at all narrower than the third, the fourth being nearly as long as the first three together.

1 **Plocamus hispidulus** Lec.—Proc. Am. Phil. Soc., XV, p. 320.

Oblong-oval, moderately convex, black, the beak rufous; antennæ brown; integuments densely clothed with large contiguous squamiform plates, variegated with white, brown, and piceous, a transverse spot of the latter color just behind the middle of the elytra especially noticeable; under surface white; erect dorsal bristles very short and sparse. Beak but slightly longer than the head and prothorax, slender, arcuate, glabrous, linearly punctated and finely bicarinate beneath from the antennæ to the apex, but rapidly and conically robust thence to the base, the basal portion densely clothed with large rough concave and squamiform plates; antennæ inserted at basal fourth on the under surface, the scape short, attaining the head, the basal joint of the funicle slightly longer than the next two, second one-half longer than the third, seventh obconical, nearly as long as the fifth and sixth, club small, slender, not abrupt, oval, compressed, sparsely pubescent on the inner, densely on the outer side, devoid of sutures but with a small terminal button. Prothorax small, transverse, constricted and tubulate at apex, rather distinctly and densely punctate. Scutellum distinct, white, oval. Elytra abruptly much wider than the prothorax, more than twice as long as the latter, the sides subparallel toward base, gradually, broadly and obtusely rounded behind, with a minute and feeble sutural notch; striæ evident only as very fine partings of the crust. Prosternum large, not in the least impressed, separating the coxæ by not quite twice their own width and evenly, transversely constricted behind the apex. Length 1.9–2.2 mm.; width 0.8–1.0 mm.

Maryland. This species has been taken also by Mr. Ulke in the District of Columbia.

ADDENDA.

I.

It is to be regretted that a number of species, described by the older writers, continue to remain unknown, and that it will be forever impossible to surely identify them, because of the neglect on the part of their several authors to record structural characters, which might enable us to form an opinion concerning their proper generic positions. These species are the following :—

1 Baridius anthracinus Boh.—Sch. Curc., III, p. 727.

The depressed form may indicate a close relationship with Limnobaris, as before remarked (p. 554), but I do not know any species with decidedly transverse interstitial punctuation ; perhaps, like *crenatus*, the references to which are similar in the Munich Catalogue, it may be Mexican and not an inhabitant of the United States.

2 Baridius californicus Mots.—Bull. Mosc., 1845, II, p. 372.

May possibly be the species subsequently described by LeConte under the name *Centrinus nasutus*. At any rate it might for the present be appropriately assigned to Limnobaris.

3 Baridius californicus Boh.—Eug. Res., Ins., 1859, p. 137.

This is probably a species of Baris, allied to *rubripes*, but having the beak longer and the elytral intervals smooth, or it may possibly be *Onychobaris seriata*. It is said to have been taken near San Francisco.

4 Baridius confertus Boh.—Sch. Curc., III, p. 728.

Described from Florida. It may be assigned at present to Onychobaris, although I have never seen a representative of that genus from the Atlantic regions.

5 Centrinus dilectus Harris—Trans. Hart. Soc. Nat. Hist., 1836, p. 79.

The description enables us to assign this species to Centrinus without much doubt, and it may possibly be a large female example of one of the densely squamose variations of *Centrinus salebrosus* The locality is not recorded.

6 Centrinus pistor Germ.—Sch. Curc., III, p. 170.

I can add nothing to the remarks made by LeConte (Proc. Am. Phil. Soc., XV, p. 433), except to suggest that this also may be the female of *Centrinus salebrosus*, or of a species closely allied.

II.

Baris scolopacea Germ.—This species, introduced from Europe, may be known by its elongate-oval, convex form and dense but uneven vestiture of white and brown scales, of which a subsutural white spot at the middle of each elytron is especially conspicuous. I have seen several specimens taken near Philadelphia.

Scolopacea may be attached provisionally to Baris, but the long beak, separated from the head by a fine deep abrupt groove, and the scaly vestiture, would necessitate its removal from the genus if studied with reference to the homologies of the American series of genera.　The European species of Barini are more difficult to treat generically than our own.　Some of them, such as *schwarzenbergi, limbata, artemisiæ, atronitens, carbonaria, chlorizans,* ar:l other similar forms, seem to be consistent with our conception of Baris, but there are many aberrant types, having the beak longer or separated from the head by a deep abrupt groove, or with the third tarsal joint undilated, the body covered with a waterproof coating of scales, or the tarsal claws subconnate at base, such as *spoliata, loricata, convexicollis, picturata, sellata* and *nitens,* which cannot be retained in Baris proper, and yet the structural differences do not appear to be great.　In judging genera in this tribe, especially among the European representatives, much dependence will have to be placed upon that summation of minor characters known as "habitus", and, if with this difference of facies we can perceive some real structural peculiarity, a study of the European species in connection with our own seems to show that it will eventually have to be accepted as a generic criterion.　There is no other way in which the old and new world species can be consistently arranged in homogeneous succession from a generic standpoint.

III.

The measurements of length throughout the present paper include the entire body and head, but exclude the beak as usual.

CALANDRIDÆ.

CALANDRINÆ.

CACTOPHAGUS Lec.

This is a very well defined and somewhat isolated genus, distinguishable from Sphenophorus by the larger smoother body, cylindrical uncompressed beak and several other characters.　It will include a number of species inhabiting northern Mexico and the regions adjacent.　Our species are entirely black, but there are several before me from Mexico, in which each elytron has a subbasal and subapical crimson fascia.　The two species which are at once distinguishable among the Arizonian specimens in my cabinet, may be described as follows :—

Body densely dull and velvety-black above, not in the least shining, the pronotum not transversely grooved at base; elytral striæ but just visibly coarser near the base, very finely, remotely punctate throughout, the punctures only slightly less minute laterally. Length 22.0 mm.; width 8.7 mm..**validus** Lec.
Body less dull, alutaceous, not at all velvety, the head and beak polished; punctures throughout larger and deeper; pronotum with a deep entire transverse groove before the basal margin; elytral striæ fine but very deep, much coarser and more strongly punctate toward base, distinctly and less remotely punctate throughout, the punctures distinct by unaided vision laterally and toward base; elytra relatively less elongate. Length 18.0–19.5 mm.; width 7.0–8.0 mm. Arizona. Three specimens.

subnitens n. sp.

Subnitens is not to be confounded with the individual variation described by Dr. LeConte under the name *procerus*, the latter is dull, opaque and velvety-black like the typical forms of *validus*.

The dull lustre in this genus is caused, not by granuliform reticulations, but by a beautifully regular system of extremely minute, subcontiguous but not in the least confluent punctures, which are deep and with the edges abrupt. In *validus* these minute punctures are finer and deeper than in *subnitens;* in the latter each of the fine sparse punctures of the intervals is surrounded by a polished ring, caused by an obliteration of the minute ground-sculpture, while in *validus* these areolæ do not exist.

CALANDRA Clairv.

It is possible that this genus may have originated in the hypothetical continent, represented at present by a few islands extending from Ceylon to Madagascar; several species are, however, now endemic in the East Indies and one or two perhaps on the west coast of South America. From these regions a number of species have been distributed throughout the world in various kinds of grain. It is quite impossible, therefore, to be sure of the native country of any unfamiliar forms which may occur among us, and, perhaps because of this uncertainty, the genus as a whole has been neglected of late by systematic writers.

In arranging the numerous examples in my cabinet I find four widely distinct species and two subspecies. The true species, one of which it is impossible to identify from published descriptions, may be characterized as follows:—

Elytra with impressed and feebly punctate sulci, the intervals smooth and
　　alternately wider and more elevated especially toward base; pronotum
　　with coarse sparse and elongate punctures...............................**granaria**
Elytra with contiguous double series of coarse deep punctures, the double
　　series separated by narrow uniseriately punctate intervals.
　Pronotal punctures fine even and distinctly separated, the surface smooth
　　　and unusually convex...**linearis**
　Pronotal punctures rather coarse, deep, very dense especially toward the
　　　sides, rounded and not elongate, the surface rather depressed on the disk.
　　　　　　　　　　　　　　　　　　　　　　　　　　　　　　　oryzæ
　Pronotal sculpture extremely coarse deep and dense, consisting of long
　　　sinuous anastomosing and obscurely punctate rugæ, with a narrow but
　　　entire subcariniform median line; elytral sculpture exceedingly deep and
　　　dense..**rugicollis**

C. granaria Linn.—Syst. Nat., Ed. X, p. 378; *remotepunctata* Gyll.: Sch.
Curc., IV, p. 979.

The differences given by Gyllenhal to distinguish *remotepunctata*
are apparently not sufficient, for, color being of little or no value,
the only character given to distinguish it is the slightly greater
distinctness of the strial punctures toward the suture and of the
punctured series of the sutural interval. Length 3.3–4.0 mm.;
width 1.1–1.3 mm.

Distributed throughout the United States.

C. linearis Hbst.—Käf., VII, p. 5, t. 100, f. 1.

Described from the West Indies but occurring at times in the
Atlantic States. It may always be known by the fine even punctuation of the pronotum. Length 3.3–3.8 mm.; width 1.1–1.15 mm.

Probably a native of India, from which region a variety is noted
in the Munich Catalogue.

C. oryzæ Linn.—Amœn. Ac., VI, 1763, p. 395.

The typical form of this cosmopolitan species is perhaps the
smallest member of the genus. It somewhat resembles the two
previous species in outline, but is very densely punctured on the
pronotum, the punctures much coarser than in *linearis* and not
elongated as in *granaria*. A series of eleven specimens of what
may be regarded as the typical form, give the length 2.1–2.8 mm.
and width 0.75–1.0 mm.

Var. zea-mais Mots.—Etud. Ent., IV, 1855, p. 77.

Similar in every appreciable detail of structure to *oryzæ*, but
always larger and especially stouter. A series of eight specimens

from Texas (Austin) and Florida give the following dimensions. Length 3.2–3.4 mm.; width 1.1–1.25 mm.

Another variety is represented before me by two specimens from Guerrero, Mexico, which are of about the same size as *zea-mais*, but more coarsely and densely punctate, and more opaque, with the elytral punctures more quadrate.

C. rugicollis n. sp.—Oval, moderately stout, rather flattened above, dull, very sparsely clothed with short erect yellowish setæ, forming single series on the alternate elytral intervals. *Head* deeply but not coarsely, rather sparsely punctate, with a large deep fovea between the eyes; beak in the female slender, feebly arcuate, smooth, minutely sparsely and sub-seriately punctate, fully as long as the prothorax, abruptly and angularly dilated, duller and coarsely, seriately punctate near the base; antennæ inserted at basal sixth, slender, the second funicular joint obconical and one-half longer than the third. *Prothorax* barely as long as wide, the sides rather strongly convergent from near the base, rounded at base, deeply, tubularly constricted at apex, the latter fully one-half as wide as the base; disk deeply, rugosely punctate. Scutellum dull, impressed. *Elytra* at the humeri exactly equal in width to the disk of the prothorax, two-fifths longer, the sides strongly convergent throughout and nearly straight; apex conjointly rather narrowly rounded; disk with contiguous series of very coarse, quadrate, closely crowded punctures, alternately separated by narrow flat intervals, each of which is coarsely, uniseriately punctate, the punctures oval and almost contiguous. Pygidium and under surface coarsely deeply and densely punctate. Length 4.0 mm.; width 1.5 mm.

Florida.

A single specimen, taken by Mr. F. Kinzel in the southern part of the State and presented to me by Mr. W. Jülich. This species is undoubtedly allied to the African *rugosus* Thunb., but differs according to the description of Schönherr, in its much shorter, non-canaliculate prothorax, and its more strongly and closely punctate abdomen. *Rugicollis* is brownish-black in color, the elytra each clouded feebly with rufous along the middle. The base of the prothorax is transverse and perfectly straight. In *rugosus* the prothorax is said to be one-half longer than its basal width.

RHININÆ.

YUCCABORUS Lec.

This singular genus is unmistakably allied to Rhina, being in fact nearly identical in rostral structure, but differs in many important features, among which may be mentioned the widely separated

eyes, much more abbreviated, dilated and semi-corneous antennal
club, deflexed beak, short legs, and smaller size of the body.   The
three species before me may be easily separated as follows:—

Piceous-brown, the punctuation of the upper surface finer and more remote.
  Body narrowly cylindrical, the elytra more than twice as long as wide;
    punctures of the elytral series becoming very fine and feeble in apical
    half, the fifth and sixth series coalescent at base; humeri tumid and
    prominent..**frontalis**
  Body much more robust, the elytra not quite twice as long as wide; punc-
    tures of the elytral series deep throughout, although small in apical half
    as usual; fifth and sixth series widely separated at base; humeri not
    tumid...**sharpi**
Black, much larger, coarsely and deeply sculptured; legs and tarsi stouter.
                                                       grossus

Y. frontalis Lec.—Trans. Am. Ent. Soc., 1874, p. 70 (Rhina).

Readily distinguishable by its slender cylindrical form and castaneous color.   The prothorax is very nearly as long as wide, the
sides broadly, evenly arcuate, the apex finely and deeply constricted,
three-fourths as wide as the base, the latter broadly evenly and just
visibly arcuate.   Elytra but slightly wider than the prothorax and
much more than twice as long, strongly alutaceous especially behind, the series feebly impressed, the intervals toward base three .
to four times as wide as the strial punctures, sparsely punctured.
Length 9.8 mm.; width 3.2 mm.

Southern California.   Found under the bark of Yucca in the
Mohave Desert.

Y. sharpi n. sp.—Moderately stout, cylindrically convex, dark chestnut-
brown, polished and glabrous throughout, the elytra but faintly alutaceous
behind. *Head* convex, polished, strongly but remotely punctate; eyes very
remote above, contiguous beneath; beak in the male straight, wider than
thick, parallel, coarsely deeply and rugosely punctate, feebly dilated at the
antennæ, barely three-fourths as long as the prothorax; antennæ inserted
just beyond the middle, the scape thick, attaining the eye, second funicular
joint longer than the first and as long as the next two, club oval, compressed,
as long as the four preceding joints, the polished corneous part extending, on
the flat side, to apical third. *Prothorax* about as long as wide; sides evenly,
broadly arcuate; apex finely constricted, three-fourths as wide as the base;
punctures coarse, perforate, remote, close on the flanks. Scutellum small,
polished. *Elytra* one-third wider than the prothorax, more than twice as
long, the punctured series strongly impressed toward base; interstitial
punctures remote, confused but forming nearly even single series on the
narrower intervals.   Length 9.7 mm.; width 3.7 mm.

Mexico (Guerrero). Mr. Baron.

Allied to *frontalis* but distinguishable by its stouter form, more polished integuments, much less prominent humeri and several other characters. I take great pleasure in dedicating this species to Dr. D. Sharp.

Y. grossus n. sp.—Oblong, subcylindrical, broadly feebly convex above, deep black, polished, the elytra dull. *Head* coarsely, rather sparsely punctate ; beak in the male straight, wider than thick, coarsely, densely, rugosely punctate, feebly dilated and tumid at the antennæ, thence feebly and evenly narrowed to the apex, two-thirds as long as the prothorax; antennæ inserted distinctly beyond the middle, the scape rather long, thick, evenly and gradually claviform, attaining the eye, second funicular joint much longer than the first, equal to the next two, four to six transversely subcuneate, club nearly as long as the preceding four joints, the corneous portion extending on the flat side to apical two-fifths. *Prothorax* about as long as wide, the apex constricted, two-thirds as wide as the base ; sides broadly arcuate ; disk evenly convex, very coarsely perforato-punctate, the punctures well separated above, coalescent on the flanks. *Elytra* one-third wider than the prothorax and more than twice as long, not quite twice as long as wide ; strial punctures deep, coarse, contiguous, continuing large and distinct to the apex ; intervals toward base two to three times as wide as the striæ, coarsely, unevenly, sparsely punctate, anterior tibiæ broadly, feebly arcuate toward apex, having an internal series of small denticles. Length 11.5–14.0 mm. ; width 4.2–5.2 mm.

Texas (El Paso); Arizona. Mr. G. W. Dunn.

The largest species which I have seen and quite distinct from either *frontalis* or *sharpi*.

Cossoninæ.

METOPOTOMA n. gen.

The single species is an interesting addition to the anomalous group of genera allied to Gononotus.

Body in form and convexity nearly as in Gononotus. Head short, subglobular, smooth and polished, deeply, transversely incised throughout just behind the eyes, which are situated at the sides of the beak at base, rather large, distinctly convex and composed of very large facets, which are flat and not convex. Beak rather long, thick, parallel and arcuate, the antennal scrobes rapidly descending at first, becoming completely inferior, not coalescent. Antennæ subcylindrical, long but thick, inserted at apical two-fifths, the scape clavate, attaining the limits of the eye beneath, longer than the apparent funicle, the latter consisting of six joints, the first scarcely more robust, oval, the second obconical, subelongate. much longer than the first and one-half longer than the third, three to six subequal, wider than long, parallel-sided, not increasing much in thickness, with the articulations deep ; club large, as long as the preceding five joints, complex in structure, the basal half, composed of the modified seventh funicular joint, obconical, as long as wide, polished and sparsely setose, the apical paler, oval, obtuse, densely pubescent and indistinctly annulate. Scutellum small but distinct. Metasternum short. Anterior coxæ large, globular, extremely approximate ; intermediate very narrowly separated ; posterior rather remote. Legs somewhat long and thick : femora sinuate beneath near the apex ; tibiæ subparallel, the apical uncus well developed, the anterior also with an internal subapical tooth ; tarsi cylindrical, rather stout, the third joint scarcely visibly thicker and sparsely setose beneath, not bilobed.

From Gononotus this genus differs in its composite antennal club, undilated third tarsal joint, elongate prothorax, smooth, polished head and many other characters.

M. repens n. sp.—Elongate-ovoidal, convex, dull, black and subglabrous, each large fovea, however, with a small fulvous seta ; there are also a few clusters of such setæ on the more tumid portions of the elytral intervals. *Head* glabrous ; beak not quite as long as the prothorax, dull, with coarse shallow punctures, sublinearly arranged but becoming finer and irregular toward apex. *Prothorax* quite distinctly longer than wide, the sides parallel, broadly feebly and evenly arcuate, rather abruptly rounded and moderately deeply constricted behind the apex, the latter three-fourths as wide as the base and broadly sinuate in the middle ; base broadly feebly snd evenly arcuate ; disk evenly, feebly convex, very coarsely, remotely foveate, the foveæ shallow, rounded, and annulate just within their edges with fine cinereous tomentum ; median line finely and strongly carinate, the carina attaining neither base nor apex. *Elytra* oval, at the middle one-half wider than the prothorax, not quite twice as long as the latter ; humeri obsolete ; base broadly emarginate ; disk with series of very large deep and unevenly impressed foveæ, the intervals uneven, not wider than the series and remotely, feebly tumorose, the tumid parts setose and also finely cinereo-tomentose. Under surface coarsely, remotely foveate, the foveæ shallow. Length 5.2 mm. ; width 2.0 mm.

California (Humboldt Co.).

I took the type specimen in some loose mossy turf, covering the gravelly slopes of a shallow ravine near the town of Arcata ; its sex is not apparent. This is one of the largest cossonides in our fauna excluding the genus Cossonus.

HIMATIUM Woll.

There is some doubt concerning the actual identity of Wollaston's genus with the species assigned to it by LeConte. According to the description, however, it must be very closely allied to our representatives, to such a degree indeed that these could not be advantageously separated without inspecting the original type.

As represented by *nigritulum*, the genus has the body rather depressed above, feebly cuneiform, with the head short and almost entirely enclosed within a subtubulate extension of the prothorax, the eyes small, flat, coarsely faceted and in great part inferior, not visible from above but widely separated beneath. Beak short but slender, feebly arcuate, parallel, inserted at an angle with the surface of the front, so that it is distinctly separated from and very much narrower than the head. Antennæ inserted quite distinctly behind the middle, the scrobes nearly horizontal, not attaining but directed upon the eye; scape short, clavate; funicle slender, 7-jointed, the basal joint rather longer than the next two; second to seventh feebly increasing in thickness, equal in length, subquadrate; club as long as the preceding four joints, narrowly fusiform, polished, sparsely setose, not annulate. Scutellum distinct. Prosternum flat; anterior coxæ remote, separated by fully their own width; intermediate one-half more widely separated. Metasternum long. Legs short, slender; tibiæ without internal spur, the uncus well developed; tarsi short, the third joint feebly dilated, the fourth about as long as the preceding three combined.

The three species, which it is necessary to include at present within the genus, may be recognized as follows:—

Prothorax truncate laterally at apex, remote from the eyes.
   Body parallel, ferruginous, densely but coarsely pubescent, the pronotum coarsely, subconfluently punctate, the elytral series coarse and approximate...**errans**
   Body subcuneate, more convex, black, much less pubescent, the pronotal punctures much smaller, distinctly defined; elytral series not impressed, the intervals wide..**nigritulum**
Prothorax partially concealing the eyes at the sides; beak not distinctly separated from the head by a transverse impression...............**conicum**

H. conicum must certainly constitute a genus distinct from that including *errans*, if the characters given by LeConte are correct (Trans. Am. Ent. Soc., VIII, p. 218), and the probabilities are that each of these species will ultimately become the type of a distinct genus.

H. nigritulum n. sp.—Black, the elytra somewhat shining, legs, antennæ and apical parts of the prothorax piceous-brown, vestiture very sparse, consisting of erect setiform scales, especially visible on the beak and toward the elytral apex. *Head* smooth, vaguely sculptured, polished; beak three-fourths as long as the prothorax, opaque, finely but deeply, rugosely and very densely sculptured. *Prothorax* conical, a little longer than wide, constricted behind the apex, the apical tubulation feebly inflated, receiving the head; apex three-fourths as wide as the base; punctures moderately coarse, deep, rounded but subcontiguous, without median line. *Elytra* slightly wider behind the middle than at base, nearly two-thirds wider than the prothorax and more than twice as long; sides feebly arcuate, abruptly convergent and sinuate near the apex; humeri broadly exposed but rather obtuse; disk with unimpressed series of moderately large deep oblong and almost contiguous punctures; intervals flat, a little wider than the serial punctures, feebly rugose but shining. Under surface densely deeply and rather coarsely punctate. Length 1.75 mm.; width 0.6 mm.

Florida.

A single specimen without more precise indication of locality.

ALLOMIMUS Lec.

In this genus the beak is rather thin or but moderately stout, nearly straight, parallel, not conspicuously separated from the front, the eyes moderate in size, rather convex, not very finely faceted and situated at the sides of the head, the antennal scrobes deep, sublinear, directed feebly downward to the lower limit of the eye, the funicle 7-jointed, with the basal joint larger, the second obconical and distinctly longer than the third. Our two species differ greatly in structure and should perhaps be assigned to separate subgenera; they may be defined as follows:—

Beak thinner, a little more than one-half as long as the prothorax; anterior coxæ larger, separated by their own width; elytra deeply striate, the sulci coarsely punctate, the sutural sulcus much less distinctly so.

dubius Horn

Beak shorter and stouter, scarcely one-half as long as the prothorax; pronotal punctures smaller and closer; elytra feebly sulcate and much less coarsely punctate, the punctures of the sutural stria as distinct as the others; anterior coxæ much smaller and more remote, separated by nearly twice their own width. Head polished, almost impunctate, separated from the beak by a feeble transverse impression, the beak throughout coarsely deeply and subrugosely punctate. Prothorax about as long as wide, subconical, feebly depressed above, slightly constricted behind the apex, the latter barely two-thirds as wide as the base. Scutellum distinct. Elytra a little wider than the prothorax and about twice as long, parallel, the sides convergent and nearly straight in apical third, the apex narrowly rounded. Abdomen deeply but not very densely and somewhat unevenly punctate. Length 1.9 mm.; width 0.65 mm. Texas (Columbus and Austin)..**politus** n. sp.

Politus is slightly smaller, relatively broader and more depressed than *dubius*, and may be known at once by the shorter beak, finer, more even sculpture, paler color and smaller, much more remote anterior coxæ.

STENANCYLUS n. gen.

The principal characters may be expressed as follows:—

Body elongate, slender, convex, the scutellum distinct, the metasternum elongate and the anterior coxæ widely separated. Head rather elongate, conical; beak short, broad, parallel, not in the least constricted or transversely impressed at base. Antennæ inserted behind the middle, the scrobes deep, beginning beyond the middle, rapidly descending to the lower margin of the eye; scape moderate in length; funicle 7-jointed, the basal joint rather stout, as long as the next two; second to seventh rather short, subequal, feebly increasing in width, just visibly obconical; club moderate, oval, densely but coarsely pubescent, with the basal joint constituting about one-half of the mass. Eyes not very large, situated at the sides of the head, very convex, prominent and coarsely faceted. Legs short; tibiæ rather slender, with a small internal spur at apex, the external uncus well developed; tarsi rather stout, the third joint feebly dilated, fourth slender, arcuate, not quite as long as the three preceding together.

This genus is allied to Macrancylus, but differs in its rather stouter, more elliptic body and radically in its oblique and not horizontal scrobes, also in its more prominent and coarsely faceted eyes, and parallel beak; in Macrancylus the beak is conical in form. From Rhyncolus it may be known at once by its more widely separated coxæ and coarsely faceted eyes, as well as its more slender bodily form.

S. colomboi n. sp.—Elongate, narrowly oval, cylindrically convex, glabrous, polished and pale rufo-piceous throughout. *Head* and beak continuous, transversely convex, finely but strongly, not very densely punctate, the eyes situated at a great distance from the prothorax; beak scarcely as long as the head and two-fifths as long as the prothorax, straight. *Prothorax* a little longer than wide, broadly, very feebly constricted near the apex, the sides feebly arcuate; apex slightly arcuate, three-fourths as wide as the base; punctures rather fine but strong, uneven but separated by about their own widths without trace of median line. Scutellum small, oval. *Elytra* distinctly wider than the prothorax and more than twice as long, twice as long as wide, the sides parallel and straight to apical third, then convergent and sinuate, the apex narrowly obtuse; humeri right; striæ coarsely feebly impressed, coarsely punctate; intervals narrow, finely, uniseriately punctate. Under surface coarsely but not very densely punctate. Length 2.2–2.4 mm.; width 0.6 mm.

Florida (Biscayne Bay and Cape Jupiter).   Mr. Schwarz.

I have dedicated this species to the memory of the distinguished navigator Cristoforo Colombo.

CARPHONOTUS n. gen.

A single species, boreal in habitat and partially pubescent, possesses several peculiarities of structure which appear to prevent its assignment to any of the described genera.

Body moderately stout, somewhat depressed above, the elytra parallel, much wider than the prothorax ; scutellum distinct, flat, ogival. Head short, the beak straight, moderately short, parallel, not separated from the head by a transverse impression. Antennæ inserted a little beyond the middle, the scrobes deep, obliquely descending beneath the eye ; scape moderate ; funicle 7-jointed, the basal joint stout, as long as the next two ; second to seventh equal in length, but slightly wider than long, gradually a little thicker ; club abrupt, moderate in size, the basal joint large, polished, sparsely setose. Eyes on the sides of the head at their own length from the prothorax, not very finely faceted, somewhat convex and prominent, transversely oval. Prosternum separating the large anterior coxæ by one-half of their own width ; intermediate coxæ rather more than twice as widely separated as the anterior. Metasternum long. Legs stout ; tibiæ parallel, the external uncus well developed but without trace of internal spur at apex ; tarsi rather stout, the third joint distinctly dilated and bilobed.

This genus is somewhat allied to Stenancylus, but differs in its broader form, relatively narrower prothorax, less prominent, more finely faceted eyes situated much nearer to the anterior margin of the prothorax, shorter head, longer beak with the antennæ inserted beyond the middle, relatively less widely separated anterior coxæ, absence of internal tibial spur, and in the hairy vestiture.

C. testaceus n. sp.—Oblong-oval, feebly depressed above, pale rufo testaceous throughout, smooth and polished, the upper surface with short coarse and very sparse, subrecumbent pubescence, becoming erect toward the elytral apices and somewhat bristling on the beak. *Head* and beak minutely but strongly, not very densely punctate, the beak twice as long as the head and three-fifths as long as the prothorax, viewed anteriorly nearly twice as long as wide. *Prothorax* about as long as wide, feebly constricted near the apex ; sides subparallel and very slightly arcuate ; apex broadly, feebly arcuate and but slightly narrower than the base ; punctures rather fine but deep, perforate, somewhat sparse ; median line obsolete. *Elytra* one-half wider than the prothorax and two and one-half times as long, twice as long as wide, parallel and straight at the sides, obtusely ogival in scarcely more than apical fourth ; humeri right, blunt ; disk with entirely unimpressed series of large oblong-elongate subbilobed punctures; intervals flat, but slightly wider than the serial punctures, each with a single uneven series of minute, feeble punctures.   Under surface throughout rather finely but deeply and somewhat densely punctate.   Length 2.8 mm.; width 0.9 mm.

Minnesota.

Easily distinguishable from any species of Rhyncolus by its depressed form, narrow beak and prothorax, and pubescent surface.

APOTREPUS n. gen.

A single species again constitutes a genus which is without any close ally in our fauna.

Body stout, subcylindrical, moderately convex, the elytra wider than the prothorax, the scutellum distinct; upper surface setose.   Head short, broad, cono-globose, not conspicuously separated from the beak.   Beak rather short, robust, parallel toward base but dilated toward apex.   Eyes situated at the sides, partially on the beak, distant from the prothorax, feebly convex and rather prominent, somewhat coarsely faceted.   Antennæ inserted at the middle, the scrobes deep, linear, obliquely descending to the lower limit of the eyes; scape robust; funicle long, 7-jointed, the two basal joints equal, each longer than wide and longer than three to seven, which are subequal in length, gradually thicker, obconical, submoniliform, the articulations strongly marked; club oval, densely but coarsely pubescent, abrupt, fully as long as the preceding four joints, not annulate.   Anterior coxæ small, remote, separated by fully their own width; intermediate still more widely separated.   Metasternum long.   Legs rather long but somewhat stout, the tibiæ parallel, with a small internal spur and well-developed external uncus at apex; tarsi rather long, the basal joint nearly as long as the next two, third feebly dilated, fourth but slightly longer than the preceding two combined.

Apotrepus is related to *Caulophilus latinasus* perhaps more closely than to any other North American species, resembling it in general form of the body, but differing greatly in its shorter beak dilated near the apex, in its smaller eyes, longer second funicular joint, and in the sparse bristling and setiform vestiture.

A. densicollis n. sp.—Black, the antennæ and legs feebly rufescent, rather shining, the setæ short, stiff, erect, forming an uneven single line on each elytral interval. *Head* very short, finely, sparsely punctate, the beak nearly straight, densely, subrugosely punctate, more than twice as long as the head and separated therefrom only by a very broad transverse impression, from the anterior margin of the eyes to the apex one-half as long as the prothorax, not twice as long as wide viewed anteriorly. *Prothorax* about as long as wide, broadly, strongly constricted behind the apex, the sides feebly convergent and distinctly arcuate; apex three-fourths as wide as the base; disk rather coarsely deeply and extremely densely punctate, the punctures polygonally crowded, without median line. *Elytra* one-third to two-fifths wider than the prothorax and rather more than twice as long, two-thirds longer than wide; sides parallel and nearly straight in basal two-thirds, then gradually rounded convergent and sinuate to the apex; humeri right, narrowly rounded; striæ coarse, feebly impressed, coarsely deeply and approximately punctate, the intervals about as wide as the strial punctures, scarcely perceptibly punctate. Under surface rather coarsely, densely punctate, the abdomen more finely and sparsely so. Length 2.8–3.0 mm.; width 1.0 mm.

Arizona. Two specimens.

PSEUDOPENTARTHRUM Woll.

This genus was founded by Wollaston upon a small species from Mexico, resembling Phlœophagus, and with the anterior coxæ approximate as in that genus, but having the antennal funicle 5-jointed. It is distinguished from Pentarthrum by its much less distant anterior coxæ and more abbreviated cylindrical form. I now assign to it two other species, having the beak very short, thick but parallel, not constricted at base, though sometimes separated from the head by a broad feeble transverse impression. Eyes moderately developed, feebly convex, finely faceted, situated at the upper part of the sides and conspicuous from above; scrobes horizontal, deep, ending at quite an appreciable distance in front of the eye and there flexed abruptly downward. Antennæ inserted at basal third, thick, the basal joint of the funicle large, two to five transverse, parallel, subequal, closely coarctate, the club continuous with the funicle, and, together with joints two to five, strongly compressed. Scutellum distinct. Metasternum rather long. Anterior coxæ closely approximate. Legs short, robust, the tarsi stout with the third joint but slightly wider than the second, the fourth not as long as the remainder, arcuate and very slender.

Pseudopentarthrum differs from Pentarthrinus in its shorter, more parallel form, relatively larger prothorax, in the greater distance between the antennal scrobes and the eye, in the more compact and compressed antennæ, with the club not abrupt, and in its stouter legs. The species may be separated by the following characters:—

Beak not separated from the head by a pronounced transverse impression; larger species, the pronotum highly polished......................**robustum**

Beak separated by a broad transverse impression; head and basal parts of the beak finely, remotely punctate, the remainder of the beak densely so; pronotum dull ....**simplex**

P. robustum n. sp.—Robust, cylindrical, the elytra perfectly parallel and a little wider than the prothorax, polished, black and glabrous throughout. *Head* rather finely but deeply, not densely punctate; beak thick, finely punctate, not separated from the head by a transverse impression, two-fifths as long as the prothorax; scrobes not extending to the eye, rectangular; antennæ inserted at basal third, first funicular joint large, wider than long, rather longer than the next two, second concealed partly within the apex of the first, apparently shorter than the third, two to five coarctate, forming a thick compressed mass, the club scarcely at all wider or thicker and forming nearly a prolongation of the funicle. *Prothorax* about as long as wide, broadly rounded on the sides, constricted behind the apex, the latter three-fourths as wide as the base; punctures coarse, deep, perforate, separated by about one-half of their own diameters, with a polished impunctate central spot. Scutellum rounded, slightly tumid. *Elytra* one-half longer than wide; striæ deeply impressed, coarsely deeply and closely punctate; intervals two to three times as wide as the strial punctures, convex. Under surface coarsely, closely punctate, the abdomen more sparsely so, and more finely, except at base. Length 3.7 mm.; width 1.3 mm.

Texas (Austin).

The single specimen is of undetermined sex.

P. simplex n. sp.—Cylindrical, moderately stout, black, glabrous, the pronotum subalutaceous. *Head* very finely, sparsely punctate; beak finely, closely punctate except toward base, separated from the head by a rather deep wide transverse impression, which is very sparsely punctate and minutely, obsoletely foveolate, thick, parallel, as long as the head, not one-half as long as the prothorax; scrobes deep, rectangular, not attaining the eye by a very noticeable distance; antennæ inserted near basal third, nearly as in *robustum*, but with the joints much less transverse. *Prothorax* nearly as long as wide, feebly constricted behind the apex, the latter broadly arcuate and nearly four-fifths as wide as the base; sides feebly arcuate; punctures coarse, deep, separated by much less than their own widths, without median impunctate area. *Elytra* parallel, barely three-fifths longer than wide, nearly twice as long as the prothorax and slightly wider; striæ deeply impressed, coarsely, deeply but not very closely punctate; intervals convex, finely, sparsely, subseriately punctate, twice as wide as the strial punctures. Under surface not coarsely but strongly, rather sparsely punctate throughout. Length 2.5 mm.; width 0.95 mm.

Nebraska.

Allied to *robustum* but differing in its smaller size, dull and not polished pronotum, relatively longer elytra with narrower intervals, different structure and sculpture of the beak and antennæ, and in many other features.

PENTARTHRINUS n. gen.

I refer to this genus several species which have been previously assigned to Amaurorhinus Fairm. Amaurorhinus, according to Wollaston, has the scutellum obsolete, the eyes rudimentary or obsolete, the elytra oval or fusiform, the antennæ inserted far beyond the middle of the beak, and the metasternum short, all of which characters are at variance with the species under consideration. As represented by the four species in my cabinet, Pentarthrinus may be known by the following characters:—

Body feebly subcuneiform, moderately convex, polished and glabrous, with the scutellum distinct, metasternum elongate, anterior coxæ approximate, and the intermediate separated by much less than their own width. Beak very short, thick, parallel, longitudinally convex, separated from the head by a very broad transverse impression. Eyes well developed, moderately convex, at the sides of the head, distant from the prothorax and finely faceted. Antennæ inserted at basal third, in deep wide scrobes which are horizontal nearly to the margin of the eye, then dilated or flexed downward; scape short, thick; funicle 5-jointed, the basal joint large, the others subequal in length, obconical, wider than long, the articulations distinct; club abrupt. Legs short and slender, the tarsi slender with the third joint but slightly dilated.

Pentarthrinus is quite closely related to Pentarthrum and Pseudopentarthrum, but differs from the former in the more approximate anterior coxæ, and from the latter in the abrupt antennal club. The species may be separated as follows:—

Anterior coxæ extremely approximate but not in actual contact; beak not impressed in basal half.
 Pronotum rather coarsely deeply and conspicuously punctate, with the interspaces highly polished.
  Elytral intervals twice as wide as the striæ, flat, minutely, very sparsely and somewhat confusedly punctate in single series ....**nitens**
  Elytral intervals narrow, not wider than the striæ, each with a single series of fine but distinct punctures, more or less confused on the sutural interval; prothorax small ....**parvicollis**
 Pronotum slightly alutaceous, sparsely, less deeply and much more finely punctate; elytral intervals narrow, polished, strongly convex, with the punctures of the single series remote, excessively minute and scarcely discernable ....**piceus**
Anterior coxæ narrowly though quite perceptibly separated; beak narrowly impressed along the median line in basal half or more......**atrolucens**

P. nitens Horn—Proc. Am. Phil. Soc., XIII, 1873, p. 434 (Amaurorhinus?).

Subcylindrical or feebly cuneate, moderately convex, just visibly wider behind the middle of the elytra, polished, black and glabrous throughout. Head finely, sparsely, the beak equally finely but more densely, punctate, the latter separated from the head by a broad, shallow transverse impression which is rather deeply foveate in the middle; scrobes deep; antennæ inserted at basal third, the first funicular joint large, the club rather large, compressed, much wider than the outer joints of the funicle, sparsely pubescent. Prothorax scarcely as long as wide, feebly constricted and very briefly sub-tubulate at base; sides feebly convergent and broadly arcuate from near the base, still more convergent but scarcely constricted near the apex, the latter three-fifths as wide as the base; punctures strong, sparse, without distinct median line. Elytra one-fourth wider than the prothorax and two and one-half times as long, constricted near the apex, the striæ feebly impressed, rather coarsely and approximately punctate; intervals wide, flat, fully twice as wide as the striæ, very minutely punctate. Metasternum rather finely but deeply punctate, closely and more coarsely so anteriorly, the abdomen finely and sparsely punctate. Length 3.3 mm.; width 1.2 mm.

Florida. Readily distinguishable from either *parvicollis* or *atrolucens* by the much broader elytral intervals and the well-marked frontal fovea. The single specimen in my cabinet is considerably larger than the original type as measured by the author.

P. parvicollis n. sp.—Rather short and robust, subcuneate, convex, glabrous, polished and black, the legs and antennæ rufous. *Head* minutely, extremely sparsely punctate, the beak throughout more coarsely deeply and closely so, the punctures somewhat uneven; front not in the least foveate; eyes well developed, situated midway between the apex of the prothorax and end of the beak, the latter robust, very short, less than one-half as long as the prothorax, the antennæ inserted at basal third. *Prothorax* small, oval, strongly convex, about as long as wide, the sides evenly and strongly arcuate, a little more convergent anteriorly but not in the least constricted; apex three-fourths as wide as the base; punctures coarse, deep but not dense, somewhat uneven in distribution but generally separated by rather more than their own widths; median line obsolete. *Elytra* two-thirds wider than the prothorax and nearly three times as long, rather short, not twice as long as wide, very slightly wider behind than at base, obtusely ogival but not constricted in apical fourth or more; sides just visibly arcuate; humeri broadly exposed but rounded; striæ feebly impressed, very coarsely but not approximately punctate, the intervals narrow. *Abdomen* finely, sparsely punctate, the metasternum coarsely and more closely so. Length 2.1–2.5 mm.; width 0.8–0.9 mm.

Pennsylvania; Virginia.

This species is easily distinguishable by its rather shorter, broader elytra, small, oval prothorax and very coarse punctuation. My specimens were labeled *Phlœophagus apionides*, but the latter is evidently a widely different species, with the "lateral striæ entire;" in *P. parvicollis*, the ninth and tenth striæ are united behind the humeri, as in all the species of this genus.[1]

P. piceus n. sp.—Cylindro-cuneate, strongly convex, glabrous, piceous, the elytra polished; pronotum feebly alutaceous and minutely reticulate. *Head* and beak minutely and sparsely punctate, the latter parallel, convex, one-half as long as the prothorax, separated from the head by a broad, transverse impression, which is foveate in the middle; scrobes deep, widening behind; antennæ inserted behind the middle, the basal joint of the funicle large, two to five transversely obconical, subequal in length, the second partially concealed within the apex of the first as usual; club rather large, oval, fully as long as the four preceding joints combined. *Prothorax* fully as long as wide, the sides subparallel, broadly arcuate, convergent and very feebly sinuate toward apex, more abruptly rounded convergent and constricted at base, the apex broadly, feebly arcuate, nearly four-fifths as wide as the base; punctures small, sparse, separated by twice their own diameters; median line obsolete. *Elytra* distinctly wider than the prothorax and more than twice as long, gradually slightly wider behind, the sides straight; humeri feebly prominent, narrowly rounded; striæ deeply impressed, rather coarsely but not very closely punctate; intervals narrow, strongly convex, twice as wide as the strial punctures, each with a single series of scarcely perceptible, remote punctures. Under surface finely, sparsely punctate. Length 2.6 mm.; width 0.9 mm.

Florida.

One specimen, apparently a female. The head is not much more sparsely punctate than the beak, but is almost impunctate toward base and has a small, feebly impressed frontal fovea. This species may be known at once by its fine punctuation and piceous-brown color.

P. atrolucens n. sp.—Narrow, feebly cuneate, strongly convex, polished, black and glabrous throughout, the legs slightly piceous, the apical margin of the prothorax feebly rufescent. *Head* and basal half of the beak finely and very sparsely punctate; beak longitudinally, convex, very short, two fifths as long as the prothorax, narrowly impressed along the middle in basal half, more closely punctate in apical half; antennæ inserted just beyond basal third; eyes rather nearer the prothorax than the tip of the beak. *Prothorax* as long as wide, the sides subparallel and almost straight from before the base nearly to apical third, then more convergent and quite distinctly constricted to the apex, the latter rather narrow, three-fourths as wide as the

---

[1] It is probable that *Phlœophagus apionides* Horn, should constitute a new genus, but I cannot distinguish *P. minor* from the true Rhyncolus.

basal margin, the latter much narrower than the disk, which is convex, coarsely, deeply but not densely punctate, with a smooth apical margin; median line obsolete. *Elytra* a little wider behind, nearly one-third wider than the prothorax and more than twice as long, three-fourths longer than wide; sides nearly straight, rounded, convergent and feebly constricted in apical third, the apex narrowly subtruncate; striæ coarse, feebly impressed, the punctures coarse, rounded but not very close-set; intervals nearly flat, feebly elevated, but slightly wider than the strial punctures, each with a single series of fine but distinct punctures. Metasternum coarsely and closely punctured, the abdomen more finely and sparsely so. Length 2.3–2.6 mm.; width 0.7–0.9 mm.

Florida (Biscayne Bay).

This species differs from *nitens* in its smaller size, narrower form, coarser striæ, larger punctures, sculpture of the beak, and rather more widely separated anterior coxæ; from *piceus* it may be known at once by its color, more polished surface, and very much more coarsely punctured pronotum. Three specimens.

NYSSONOTUS n. gen.

The principal characters distinguishing this pentarthride genus may be stated as follows:—

Body cylindrically convex, deeply and closely sculptured, setose. Beak thick, short, parallel, arcuate toward apex, not separated from the head by a transverse impression. Antennæ inserted a little behind the middle, the scrobes deep, beginning beyond the middle, thence straight and feebly descending nearly to the lower limit of the eye, thence abruptly transverse beneath; scape short, as long as the first three joints of the funicle, the latter 5-jointed, the basal joint large, two to five feebly obconical, subequal, a little wider than long; club abrupt, compressed, oval, with the basal joint large. Eyes moderate, rather finely faceted, subdepressed, at the sides of the head and very remotely separated. Scutellum distinct. Metasternum long. Anterior coxæ extremely approximate, the intermediate rather widely separated. Legs nearly normal, external tibial uncus well developed, the anterior also with a short internal terminal spur; tarsi short, thick, the third joint slightly dilated, deeply emarginate, the fourth slender, fully as long as the preceding three together.

Nyssonotus is closely allied to Pseudopentarthrum, but differs in the obliquely descending and not horizontal antennal scrobes, in the longer beak, still more widely separated and lateral eyes, and in the stiff erect and bristling setæ.

N. seriatus n. sp.—Cylindrical, feebly shining, black, the upper surface throughout with very short erect stiff setæ, sparsely placed but forming a single close-set series on each elytral interval. *Head* and beak strongly, rather closely punctate, convex, without frontal fovea; antennæ feebly rufescent, sparsely setose. *Prothorax* not quite as long as wide, the sides broadly, feebly arcuate, gradually slightly convergent and not constricted to the apex, strongly arcuate near the base, the latter slightly wider than the subtruncate apex; punctures coarse, deep, extremely dense, without median line. *Elytra* parallel and straight at the sides, three-fifths longer than wide, distinctly wider than the prothorax and more than twice as long; humeri right, not prominent, narrowly rounded; apex broadly, evenly parabolic, the sides not constricted; disk with feebly impressed series of coarse, rounded, approximate punctures, the intervals flat, equal in width to the strial punctures, each with a single series of much smaller but strong and conspicuous setiferous punctures. *Abdomen* coarsely, closely and subrugosely punctate, the metasternum more finely but rather densely so. Length 3.0–3.3 mm.; width 1.1 mm.

Texas (El Paso). Mr. G. W. Dunn.

This species somewhat resembles a rather stout Rhyncolus, and may be easily identified otherwise by the coarse, dense sculpture, and erect setæ. Three specimens.

RHAMPHOCOLUS n. gen.

Body narrowly cylindrical, glabrous, shining. Head very short, merging gradually into the beak, the latter short, gradually wider from apex to base, not separated from the head by a transverse impression. Eyes almost flat, but well developed, oval, rather finely faceted, situated at the lower part of the sides of the head, not very distant from the prothorax and but slightly visible from above. Antennæ inserted at basal third, the scrobes narrow, straight, gradually descending and directed upon the middle point of the eye; scape slender, feebly clavate; funicle 7-jointed, the basal joint stouter, as long as the next three, two to seven wider than long, subequal in length, gradually wider, the articulations distinct; club abrupt, moderate in size, oval, annulate toward apex. Anterior coxæ narrowly separated, the intermediate separated by much less than their own width. Metasternum rather long. Legs somewhat short, the femora stout; tibiæ slender, very minutely uncinate within at apex, the external uncus distinct; tarsi slender, the third joint completely undilated, not at all wider than the second. Scutellum distinct.

The form of the beak and several other structural characters show that Rhamphocolus must be associated with Rhyncolus, but it differs notably from that genus in its much less convex and more inferior eyes, with the antennal scrobes directed upon them and not below them, in its more slender tarsi and still more approximate anterior coxæ.

R. tenuis n. sp.—Narrowly cylindrical, convex, black, the legs and antennæ dark brown; integuments polished and glabrous. *Head* and beak finely, rather sparsely punctate, the latter feebly conical, three-fifths as long as the prothorax, one-half longer than wide. *Prothorax* very nearly as long as wide, broadly, just visibly impressed behind the apex; sides feebly convergent and nearly straight from before the base to the apex, the latter broadly arcuate, subequal in width to the basal margin; punctures coarse, deep, rather close-set and uneven, without median line. *Elytra* but very slightly wider than the prothorax and scarcely more than twice as long, twice as long as wide, the sides parallel and straight nearly to apical fourth, then convergent and nearly straight to the narrowly rounded apex; humeri angulate and somewhat anteriorly prominent; disk with feebly impressed series of coarse deep rounded and close-set punctures, the intervals flat, barely as wide as the striæ, each with a single series of fine but distinct, rather remote punctures. Under surface rather coarsely but feebly and not densely punctate. Length 2.1–2.3 mm.; width 0.6–0.7 mm.

Texas (Austin).

Readily recognizable by its resemblance to an unusually slender Rhyncolus.

RHYNCOLUS Germ.

The species of this genus vary greatly among themselves, especially in the structure of the antennæ and the degree of separation of the anterior coxæ. The following descriptions will indicate some of these discordances.

R. pallens n. sp.—Cylindrically convex, shining, pale flavo-ferruginous throughout, the head, beak and apical parts of the prothorax piceous-black. *Head* and beak minutely, the latter rather closely, punctate, impressed along the middle, conical, extremely short, much wider than long and shorter than the head; eyes small, rounded, prominent; antennæ moderate, the scape nearly as long as the funicle, with one or two stiff erect setæ on the under surface, the funicle slender with the second joint obconical, as long as wide and longer than the third, club abrupt, oval, densely pubescent and about as long as the five preceding joints combined. *Prothorax* a little wider than long, feebly constricted behind the apex, the latter as wide as the base; sides feebly convergent from before the base to the apex and nearly straight; disk very fiuely closely punctate, without entire median line. *Elytra* but slightly wider than the prothorax and more than twice as long, twice as long as wide; sides straight; apex obtusely rounded; disk with almost entirely unimpressed series of fine, rounded, approximate punctures, the series impressed on the apical declivity and the fifth also toward base; intervals flat, minutely punctate in single uneven series, about twice as wide as the serial punctures. Under surface very finely, densely punctate, the abdomen evenly but less densely so, the first suture deep throughout, broadly angulate in the middle. Anterior

coxæ separated by nearly one-half of their own width.   Length 2.4–3.0 mm. ;
width 0.75–0.9 mm.

California (San Francisco).

This is the commonest species of the middle coast regions, and is
not closely allied to any other.   It is represented by a large series.

R. spretus n. sp.—Cylindrical, shining, dark rufo-piceous, the occiput,
legs and antennal club paler, rufous.   *Head* almost impunctate toward base;
beak finely but strongly, densely punctate, very short, wider than long,
scarcely as long as the head, conical, narrowly impressed along the middle;
eyes well developed, moderately prominent; antennæ inserted just before the
eyes, the scape not quite as long as the funicle, swollen and setose near the
middle beneath as in *pallens*, funicle moderately slender, the second joint a
little wider than long and but slightly longer than the third, club abrupt,
oval, nearly as long as the preceding five joints.   *Prothorax* slightly wider than
long, the sides very feebly convergent and straight from before the base to the
subapical constriction, which is pronounced but not abrupt ; apex scarcely as
wide as the base; disk very finely, closely punctate, without impunctate line.
Elytra not distinctly wider than the prothorax and about twice as long, three-
fourths longer than wide, parallel and straight at the sides, obtusely rounded
at apex, the disk with scarcely at all impressed series of large, shallow,
rounded and well separated punctures, the intervals nearly flat, not wider than
the strial punctures, each with a single series of minute remote punctures.
Prosternum finely, densely punctate, the metasternum and abdomen toward
base finely but more sparsely so ; fifth segment finely, extremely densely punctate and dull.   Anterior coxæ separated by barely one-fourth of their own
width.   Length 2.3 mm. ; width 0.8 mm.

California.

Related to *angularis* Lec., but with shorter prothorax and elytra,
the serial punctures of the latter being larger, more distant and less
deeply impressed, the pronotum is much more finely and closely
punctate, and the beak is impressed in the middle.   The first abdominal suture is deeply impressed and nearly straight.   A single
specimen.

R. dilatatus n. sp.—Cylindrical, robust, polished, dark rufo-piceous,
the legs and antennal club paler.   *Head* sparsely but strongly, the beak more
finely but rather densely, punctate, the latter nearly as long as wide, conical,
a little longer than the head, feebly impressed or flattened and less densely
punctate along the middle ; eyes small, rather feebly convex, situated much
nearer the prothorax than the tip of the beak ; antennæ inserted just behind
the middle, the scape long but not quite as long as the funicle, gradually,
strongly clavate, funicle cylindrical, the basal joint rather more robust and
as long as the next two, second distinctly wider than long and barely longer
than the third, club rather abrupt but not longer than the four preceding

joints, oval. *Prothorax* about as long as wide, the sides very feebly convergent and straight from before the base to apical third, then gradually a little more convergent to the apex, which is four-fifths as wide as the base; constriction fine and feeble; disk rather coarsely, very deeply and somewhat unevenly punctate, the punctures separated by about their own diameters, without impunctate line. *Elytra* short, just visibly wider and barely two-thirds longer than the prothorax, one-half longer than wide; sides parallel and straight, the apex semi-circularly rounded; disk with coarse, rather deep, coarsely and profoundly punctate striæ, the intervals narrow but nearly flat, scarcely more than one-half as wide as the striæ, each with a single series of fine remote punctures. Under surface densely punctate, the abdomen more sparsely so, the fifth segment closely. Anterior coxæ large, separated by rather less than one-third of their own width. Length 3.0 mm.; width 1.05 mm.

California.

The type to which this isolated species is referable, differs from that of *pallens* and *spretus* very greatly in the antennal scrobes, which, in those species, are basal and nearly transverse; in *dilatatus* they begin near the apex of the somewhat longer beak, descending thence obliquely beneath the eye; the scape, also, is gradually and evenly clavate in *dilatatus*, and not swollen in the middle beneath, and the head is shorter with the eyes less remote from the prothorax. The first ventral suture is deep and straight, the next two extremely coarsely excavated but straight. One specimen.

R. relictus n. sp.—Ovo-cylindrical, dark piceous-brown, the tarsi and antennal club paler. *Head* very minutely, sparsely, the beak more strongly, rather densely, punctate, the latter as long as the head, nearly as long as wide, parallel and straight at the sides and distinctly impressed along the middle; eyes situated nearly midway between the prothorax and tip of the beak; antennæ moderately long, the scrobes narrow, obliquely descending, scape gradually thick and clavate, inserted at basal third, distinctly shorter than the funicle, the latter rather slender, the second joint longer than the third, outer joints thicker, club distinctly wider, oval. *Prothorax* one-third longer than the head and beak, fully as long as wide, widest at basal third where the sides are broadly arcuate, thence feebly convergent and nearly straight to the apex, which is just visibly narrower than the basal margin; constriction feeble; disk finely, not very deeply, somewhat unevenly and not densely punctate, generally with a feebly defined median impunctate spot. *Elytra* one-fifth wider than the prothorax and fully twice as long, not quite twice as long as wide; sides straight and parallel, convergent and constricted in apical third, the apex somewhat produced and narrowly, almost semi-circularly rounded; disk with impressed series of rather large, very deep, well-separated punctures, the intervals feebly convex, barely one-half wider than the striæ, each with an uneven series of extremely minute distant punctures. Under surface not very coarsely but deeply and densely punctate, the abdomen more sparsely so except on the fifth segment; first suture very fine, broadly curved throughout and just traceable, the other three very coarse and deep anterior coxæ separated by barely one-third of their own width. Length 2.8–3.4 mm.; width 0.8–1.1 mm.

New Mexico.

This species shares to some extent the characters distinguishing both the *pallens* and *oregonensis* types of the genus, having the somewhat longer uncontractile second funicular joint and the oval and wider club of the former, and the fine and feeble first abdominal suture of the latter. In *oregonensis* the club is but very slightly wider than the tip of the funicle, and the eyes are larger, more circular and decidedly nearer the apex of the prothorax. The beak in *relictus* is somewhat aberrant in being parallel and not conical.

R. nimius n. sp.—Cylindrical, moderately stout, polished, black throughout, the tarsi and antennal club paler. *Head* very minutely and sparsely punctate, the beak more coarsely deeply and rather densely so, just visibly and unevenly subimpressed along the middle, conical, about as long as the head and nearly as long as wide; eyes rather large, very convex, finely faceted as usual, situated at a little more than their own length from the prothorax; antennæ short and very thick, aberrant, inserted at basal third, scrobes deep and coarse, beginning at apical third and rapidly obliquely descending, scape short, thick, the funicle very thick, cylindrical and equal in diameter from the second joint to the widest part of the club, the basal joint a little thicker, wider than long, with its apex excavated, the second joint deeply received in the cup-like excavation and having only a very short apical margin exposed beyond it; joints two to seven short, extremely transverse but somewhat compactly perfoliate, each joint being deeply concave at apex; club not in the least wider, scarcely longer than the three preceding joints combined. *Prothorax* a little longer than wide, the sides broadly, almost evenly arcuate, gradually convergent anteriorly, the constriction distinct; apex broadly arcuate and a little narrower than the base; disk coarsely, deeply but rather sparsely punctate. *Elytra* not wider than the prothorax and scarcely more than three-fourths longer, not quite twice as long as wide; sides straight, apex broadly, obtusely rounded throughout, not at all constricted; disk coarsely, deeply subsulcate, the grooves coarsely, deeply punctate; intervals about as wide as the sulci, each with a single series of fine remote punctures. Metasternum rather finely but closely punctate, the abdomen but slightly more sparsely so. Anterior coxæ large, separated by scarcely one-fifth of their own width. First ventral suture broadly arcuate, very fine, not impressed. Length 4.7 mm.; width 1.3 mm.

New Mexico (Las Vegas).

The single specimen is probably a male, the abdomen having near the base, an elongate-oval, feeble impression, which is finely, extremely densely punctate and coarsely pubescent. This is one of the largest species of the genus.

R. discors n. sp.—Narrowly cylindrical, black and polished; legs and antennæ paler, dark rufo-testaceous. *Head* minutely, remotely punctate toward base, rather longer than the beak, which is feebly conical, densely punctate, not impressed and wider than long; eyes rather small but strongly convex and prominent; antennæ moderately thick, the basal joint of the funicle more robust, excavated at apex and enclosing the second, with the exception of a short apical margin, two to six subequal, strongly transverse, compactly perfoliate, the seventh rather longer and wider, obconical; club wider than any joint of the funicle but not abrupt, oval, with its basal joint composing one-half the mass, polished and sparsely setose, the remainder densely pubescent. *Prothorax* fully as long as wide, the sides very slightly convergent and nearly straight from just before the base to the apex, the constriction fine and very feeble; apex broadly arcuate and about as wide as the base; disk coarsely, deeply, moderately closely punctate, with a wide impunctate spot in basal two-thirds. *Elytra* not distinctly wider than the prothorax and not quite twice as long, scarcely twice as long as wide, the sides straight; apex evenly obtusely and semi-circularly rounded; disk very coarsely, deeply sulcate, the grooves strongly punctate; intervals not quite as wide as the sulci, each with a single series of small, very remote punctures. Under surface rather coarsely deeply and densely punctate, the abdomen scarcely more sparsely so; first suture straight, very fine, not impressed. Anterior coxæ not large, separated by one-fifth of their own width. Length 2.8–3.0 mm.; width 0.8 mm.

Florida.

Allied in antennal structure to *nimius*, but differing greatly in its small size and more slender form; the antennal club is relatively thicker than in *nimius* and the funicle gradually thicker toward apex. If the antennal funicle of these two species were not examined with great care, it would surely be pronounced 6-jointed, so thoroughly is the second joint hidden within the apex of the first.

APPENDIX.

I.

The following remarkable genus was received too late for insertion in its proper place among the tribes discussed in the present paper :—

SCHIZONOTUS n. gen. (Erirhinini).

Body narrow, suboval, elongate and moderately convex above, the prothorax flexed downward. Head deflexed, deeply inserted, not visible from above. Eyes completely wanting. Beak nearly straight, bent slightly at apex and separated from the head by a distinct transverse impression. Antennæ inserted at apical third, the scrobes inferior, bounded along their upper margin by an acutely elevated carina ; scape robust, gradually claviform, attaining the under surface of the head ; funicle 7-jointed, joints two to five gradually decreasing in length, the second rather elongate but not quite as long or thick as the first, outer joints but slightly thicker ; club well developed, abrupt, elongate, ovo-conoidal, gradually pointed, densely pubescent, the distinct sutures marked by dense recumbent laciniæ. Prothorax oval, very oblique laterally at apex, transversely truncate at base, broadly, feebly constricted near the apex. Scutellum exceedingly minute. Elytra apparently connate, broadly, evenly emarginate at base, the latter not receiving the base of the prothorax. Prosternum rather long, sinuate at apex, broadly, deeply excavated along the middle, the sides of the sulcus acutely elevated. Meso- and metasterna extremely short. Abdomen very long, flat, the first two segments long, separated by a very fine arcuate suture ; third segment short, the second and third sutures coarse and deeply impressed ; fourth segment a little longer than the third, separated from the fifth by a very fine straight and almost obsolete suture ; fifth segment much longer than the two preceding combined. Legs short but extremely robust, the femora stout, almost straight along the lower margin ; tibiæ very broadly triangular, strongly compressed, partially fimbriate at apex ; tarsi attached at the inner angle of the tibiæ, short, flattened, the subbasal joints transverse, the third but feebly dilated, fourth very short, scarcely one-half longer than wide, received for about one-half its length in the apical emargination of the third joint ; claws rather long, slender, free, divergent and simple.

This genus is closely related to the European Raymondionymus Woll.—which appears to constitute a subgenus of Alaocyba,—so closely indeed, that if Wollaston (Trans. Ent. Soc. Lond., 1873) did not repeatedly state that the antennal funicle in that genus is 6-jointed, I should be inclined to regard them as identical.

Besides the entire lack of eyes, thick fossorial legs, deeply excavated and bicarinate prosternum, excessively short sterna of the hind body and very elongate abdomen, with the fourth suture fine and almost obsolete, Schizonotus is remarkable in having the deflexed prothorax non-conformable with the elytra at base, the base of the former being truncate or even apparently somewhat sinuate, while that of the latter is deeply emarginate, the two bases being always widely separated and exposing a large part of the mesonotum.

It is not altogether surprising that Wollaston made the mistake of assigning these genera to the Cossoniæ; they certainly have a cossonide facies in some respects. The rostral, antennal, and prosternal characters, however, prove them to be aberrant members of the bagoide series.

S. cæcus n. sp.—Rather dark red-brown throughout, polished, sparsely covered with short pale bristling setæ, which form single series on the elytral intervals. *Head* finely, the beak more coarsely, sparsely punctate throughout, the beak not quite as long as the prothorax, inflexed in direction, making an acute angle with the plane of the elytra. *Prothorax* rather longer than wide, the sides broadly arcuate, constricted at the sides just before the basal margin, the apex broadly arcuate and scarcely three-fifths as wide as the base; disk perfectly even, feebly convex above, finely but deeply, very sparsely punctate, without median line. *Elytra* elongate-oval, more than twice as long as wide and two and one-half times as long as the prothorax, in the middle nearly one-half wider than the latter; sides parallel and nearly straight in the middle, convergent and rounded toward base, convergent and straight or feebly sinuate in apical third, the apex narrowly rounded; basal margin acute laterally; disk with unimpressed series of rather small but deep, somewhat distant punctures, becoming coarse and deep on the inflexed flanks; punctures of the intervals toward the suture nearly as large as those of the series, the latter becoming almost obsolete toward apex. *Abdomen* very sparsely punctate but strongly so toward base. Length 2.0–2.1 mm.; width 0.7–0.75 mm.

California.

A most interesting species, apparently the only completely blind curculionide thus far recorded from North America; as might have been anticipated it has revealed itself in the subasiatic fauna characterizing our Pacific Coast.

The two specimens in my cabinet were kindly communicated by Mr. Chas. Fuchs, who discovered them while sifting mouldy earth among the red-woods north of San Francisco.

II.

CYCLOSATTUS n. gen. (Tenebrionidæ).

The species which I described under the name *Eusattus websteri* (Col. Not., III, p. 56) has the outline and general habitus of certain forms of Eusattus, but was placed in that genus without due examination of its generic characters; these I find to be very different, and, in order that the species may be understood, it is necessary to refer it to a new genus far removed from the Coniontini. It forms the second of the only two known North American generic types of the tribe Opatrumini (Col. Not., II, p. 391), the other one being Ephalus Lec. The principal characters may be given as follows:—

Body very broadly, evenly oval, rather strongly convex, the margins of the pronotum broadly, and of the elytra narrowly, reflexed. Head prominent at the sides before the eyes, transversely truncate at apex. Eyes transverse, emarginate at the middle. Anterior, intermediate and posterior coxæ equally and not very widely separated, the abdominal process narrow and obtusely angulate at apex. Legs not very long but slender, the anterior tibiæ with an externally produced apical process, the internal spur very minute ; intermediate and posterior with two small slender terminal spurs. Tarsi slender, short, slightly compressed, coarsely pubescent beneath, the basal joint of the posterior not quite as long as the remaining three combined. Elytra widely embracing the body, the epipleuræ very wide, especially toward base. Third and fourth abdominal sutures fine, vertical and coriaceous.

On examination of the under surface the epipleuræ appear at first to attain the elytral apices, but this is not so in reality, the portion attaining the sutural angles being the narrow reflexed margin of the elytra, the plane of the under surface of which makes a strongly marked angle with that of the epipleuræ proper, throughout the entire extent.

Mr. F. Blanchard of Lowell, to whom I am indebted for calling my attention to the fact that *websteri* could not be retained in Eusattus, tells me that Dr. Levette found this specimen at Pueblo, Colorado, but whether collected there or otherwise ·obtained he is unable to state. I see no reasonable grounds for doubting its

North American origin, however, as it is no more out of harmony
with the general tenebrionide fauna which surrounds it than the
monotypic Epbalus of the Atlantic States.

III.

LIPAROCEPHALUS Mäkl.

It is somewhat singular that the true affinities of this genus
should have so long escaped observation, especially as its entire
lack of harmony with all other types of Pæderini is so strikingly
evident.   Liparocephalus is a typical but highly specialized member
of the tribe Aleocharini, belonging near Phytosus, and having the
tarsal joints 4–4–5 in number.

IV.

SYNONYMICAL NOTES.

In the Revision of the Stenini of America North of Mexico
(Philadelphia 1884), I have created a considerable number of
synonyms, these becoming evident from time to time as more
extended series were compared with the somewhat meagre material which served as the basis of that memoir.   A small part of the
synonymy has already been given by M. Fauvel, and I now take
pleasure in bringing forward as much as I have been able to observe from recent studies.

S. rugifer Cas. = *anastomozans* Cas.   This is another interesting example
showing the correspondence between the arctic fauna of the summit of Mt.
Washington and that of the Rocky Mts.
S. vexatus Cas. = *insularis* Cas.
S. placidus Cas. = *tumicollis* Cas.
S. villosus Cas. = *jejunus* Cas.
S. milleporus Cas. = *sectilifer* Cas.
S. difficilis Cas. = *tenuis* Cas.
S. nanus St. = *nanulus* Cas.   The eastern *pusio* Cas. is an allied but appa-
rently distinct species, of narrower form and much larger head.
S. humilis Er. = *mammops* Cas.
S. rigidus Cas. = *ageus* Cas.   The European *argus* is somewhat allied, but is
much narrower, more parallel and less fusiform, with the abdominal segments
decreasing less rapidly in width.
S. brumalis Cas. (♀) = *pauperculus* Cas. (♂)
S. gratiosus Cas. = *hirsutus* Cas.

The species in the neighborhood of *morio* Grav. are very much confused, and, in my efforts to view a typical specimen from Europe, I have received four distinct species, in one or two cases differing radically in male sexual characters. The following synonymy is however sufficiently evident :—

S. morio Grav. = *indistinctus* and *haplus* Cas.

The type of *subgriseus* represents a species quite different from *morio*, in the abruptly very narrow sixth ventral segment and other characters.

S. umbratilis Cas. = *fraternus* Cas.

S. pollens Cas. = *patens* Cas.

S. reconditus Cas. = *propinquus* Cas. This species is stouter than the European *tarsalis*, and has the punctuation stronger and coarser; it also differs in male sexual characters. The differences become quite evident with the large series of both these species which I have before me. *Cunadensis* is closely allied but has much shorter elytra.

S. callosus Er. = *varipes* Cas.

S. punctatus Er. = *dilutus* and *obsoletus* Cas.

S. hubbardi Cas. = *simiolus* Cas.

S. lucidus Cas. = *leviceps* and *politulus* Cas.